Edna Lyall

Donovan - A Modern Englishman

A Novel

Edna Lyall

Donovan - A Modern Englishman
A Novel

ISBN/EAN: 9783337032920

Printed in Europe, USA, Canada, Australia, Japan

Cover: Foto ©Andreas Hilbeck / pixelio.de

More available books at **www.hansebooks.com**

DONOVAN:

A MODERN ENGLISHMAN.

A NOVEL.

BY

EDNA LYALL,

AUTHOR OF

'WE TWO,' 'IN THE GOLDEN DAYS,' 'WON BY WAITING
'KNIGHT-ERRANT,' ETC., ETC.

> And I smiled to think God's greatness flowed around
> our incompleteness,—
> Round our restlessness, His rest.'
> E. B. BROWNING.

Twelfth Edition.

IN ONE VOLUME.

LONDON:

HURST AND BLACKETT, LIMITED,

13, GREAT MARLBOROUGH STREET.

1888.

TO ONE

WHOSE LOVING HELP

I LOVINGLY ACKNOWLEDGE.

CONTENTS.

DONOVAN.

CHAPTER I.

EXPELLED.

Oh, yet we trust that somehow good
   Will be the final goal of ill,
   To pangs of nature, sins of will,
Defects of doubt, and taints of blood.

That nothing walks with aimless feet ;
   That not one life shall be destroyed,
   Or cast as rubbish to the void,
When God hath made the pile complete.
                       In Memoriam.

'So Farrant is really to be expelled? Tell me about it, for I've heard next to nothing these last few days up in the infirmary.'

The speaker was a boy of about seventeen, who was walking arm-in-arm with a companion of his own age in the quietest part of a large playground.

'Well, on the whole, I think you were well out of it. There was no end of a row on Saturday evening when it all came to light. Little Harrison turned rusty, and told the Doctor that some of the sixth had taken to gambling, and then there was a solemn convention, and we were all called upon to reveal anything we knew, and, before I could have thanked my stars for ten seconds that I knew nothing, up sprang Donovan Farrant to confess that he had been the first to introduce card-playing. I fancy the Doctor thought him rather too brazen-faced about it, for he was awfully severe; but Farrant, you know, is one of those fellows who look stony when they feel most, and he stood there, with his head thrown back, looking as if he'd like to knock us all down.'

'I can just fancy him. He's certainly a touch of the Roman in him; but what in the world did he do it for ?'

B

'Don't know. He's a queer fellow. Such crazy ideas of honour too! Enough to make him spring up in that way to answer to a general accusation, and yet so little that he could go on for weeks as the ringleader in this affair.'

'But what's all this row about Harrison?'

'Why, Harrison—who's his fag, you know—says Farrant forced him against his will to give his pocket-money for the gaming, whereupon you can fancy the Doctor was furious, exaggerated things, and told Farrant he was found guilty of disobedience, stealing, and bullying, though everyone knows he's no more a bully than you are.'

'Bully! I should think not! Why, the little weakly chaps make a regular hero of him, and he was always hanging about after poor little Somerton, who died last term. That Harrison is a rascally young cub. I don't believe Farrant took his money.'

'Asked him to lend it, I daresay, and gave the young beggar a look from those extraordinary eyes of his.'

'Poor fellow, there he is!' said the first speaker. 'Why didn't they send him off by the early train? He must have had enough of this sort of thing yesterday.'

'Yes, in all conscience! He won't soon forget that Sunday. By Jove! it was a slashing sermon the Doctor gave us, preached straight at Farrant—hurled at his head. But there must be some reason for keeping him here. I say, I wish you'd go and speak to him, Reynolds.'

After some little discussion, Reynolds gave a reluctant consent, and, crossing the playground, made his way to the place where the culprit was standing.

Donovan Farrant looked somewhat unapproachable, it must be confessed. He was a tall slight fellow of nearly eighteen, with dark hair and complexion, a curiously-formed forehead, bespeaking rare mathematical talent, a faultless profile, a firm but bitter-looking mouth, and strange eyes—black in some lights, hazel in others, but always curiously contradictory to the hard resoluteness that characterised the rest of the face, for they were hungry-looking and unsatisfied.

He was leaning against the wall, but there was no rest in his attitude. With an expression of cold scorn, he was watching the boys in the playground. His face softened a little as a friendly greeting attracted his notice.

'I am very sorry you are going, Farrant,' said Reynolds, who had been racking his brain for words which would be at once kind and yet bear no reference to his disgrace. This was the best he could think of.

The strange eyes met his unflinchingly, Reynolds felt they were not the eyes of a thief or a bully; yet there was something defiantly hard and scornful in the tone of the answer.

'Why should you be sorry? Why make yourself the exception to prove the contrary rule? Among all those'—he made an impetuous gesture towards the other boys—'not one cared a rush for me—not one would speak a word, though they knew that, except what I confessed, the charges were false.'

Reynolds was about to reply when someone approached Donovan with a message—Colonel Farrant had arrived, and was waiting for him. A sort of spasm passed over the cold face, but, recovering his self-control in an instant, Donovan replied, icily—

'Tell him I will come.' Then, as the messenger turned away, he folded his arms and leant this time really for support against the wall. A glow of shame had mounted to his forehead; Reynolds could see that he was in terrible distress.

'Did you not know that your father was coming?' he ventured to ask, after a few minutes.

Donovan signed a negative.

'He was only to come back from India on Saturday, and—and *this* is what he is met with!'

There was something in the tone of this sentence which made Reynolds feel that here the real Donovan Farrant was showing himself, the sudden boyish shame and grief were so perfectly natural, so strangely contrasted with the tone of bitter scorn which he had at first assumed. But the words called up a sad enough picture even to the schoolboy's mind, and his throat felt choked, and he was shy of offering any consolation.

'You will begin over again in some new place,' he said at last. 'You have been left to yourself so much, surely your father will understand and be lenient.'

'Do you think I care for his anger?—it's not that!—but to have brought this disgrace to him, to have——' he broke off abruptly, with a stifled sob.

Reynolds was amazed, for no one credited Donovan Farrant with over-much feeling. But even as he wondered his companion regained his composure, and wrapped himself once more in that impenetrable mantle of cold scorn.

'Well, I must go; there is nothing to wait for,' he said, glancing round at the place he was leaving for ever—leaving under a cloud.

A look of pain came into his eyes, but a satirical smile played about his lips. The smile faded, however, when he remembered the message which had just been brought to him, and his hand was icy cold as he abruptly took leave of Reynolds, then walked steadily on towards the school-house.

All this time Colonel Farrant waited within the house. He had seen the head-master, had heard the particulars of his son's disgrace, and now he was waiting alone at his own request, trying to face this sorrow, trying to endure this terrible new shame. He was a middle-aged man, tall and soldierly; his features were almost exactly similar to those of his son, but his expression was so much more gentle that at first sight the likeness did not seem at all striking. Grief and disappointment were expressed in his very attitude as he sat waiting wearily with his head resting on his hand; and the disappointment had not been caused by Donovan only. He had returned from India only two days before to re-join the wife and children whom he had not seen for years, and somehow the home was not quite what he had expected, and the long separation seemed either to have altered his wife or to have raised a sort of barrier between them. He had been absorbed in his work, had been leading a singularly self-denying active life; she had been absorbed in herself, and had allowed circumstances to drift her along unresistingly. No wonder that Colonel Farrant had already found how few interests he and his wife had in common, no wonder that, even in the brief time since his return, he had realised that his two children were growing up in a home which could not possibly influence them for good. Bitterly did he now regret that love of his work and dislike of the quiet life of a country gentleman had kept him so long in India. Mrs. Farrant's reception of the news of Donovan's disgrace had perhaps more than anything revealed the true state of matters to her husband. What to him was a terrible grief was to her merely 'very tiresome;' she hoped people would not hear about it, lamented the inconvenience of having the boy home just as they were going up to town for the season, spoke in soft languid tones of his wilfulness, but evidently was quite incapable of feeling keenly about anything so far removed from her own personal concerns.

Donovan must not come home to that, the Colonel felt that it would be the very worst thing for him. He must go himself to the school, find out the whole truth, learn something of his son's real character, and, if possible, win his love before taking him back to the doubtful influence of that strangely disappointing home.

Waiting now in the quiet room, with the slow monotonous ticking of the clock, with the May sunshine streaming in upon him, the Colonel tried to recall Donovan as he was at their last parting years and years ago at Malta. How well he remembered the little bright-eyed merry child of three years old! what a wrench it had been to leave him when his regiment had been ordered out to India, and the little boy—their only child then—had been sent back alone to England. And this was the same boy whom he came to-day to find disgraced and expelled! How was it possible that his little high-spirited, loving child should have become a thief, a bully, a breaker of rules? He could not believe it. And yet the head-master told him that Donovan had with his own lips confessed that he was guilty!

A sound of footsteps without, some one speaking in a tone of remonstrance, roused him, and then another voice, indignant and vehement, made him start to his feet.

'Leave me alone! I will see him now, at once, as I am!'

And the door was thrown open, and the vision of the merry three-year-old child faded suddenly, and in its place stood the son of to-day, pale, haggard, miserable, only upheld by a desperate resolve to face the worst.

Donovan looked at once straight into his father's eyes to read there what he had to prepare himself for, and the very first expression he read was neither anger, nor shame, nor disappointment, but only love and pity. His father's hand was on his shoulder, his right hand clasped his, and, when he spoke, there was not the slightest sound of upbraiding in his tone.

'Dono—my poor boy!'

That was too much even for Donovan's hardihood. He had braced himself to endure anger or reproach, or cold displeasure—but to be met in this way! For the first time an agony of remorse surged up in his heart. If only he could live his school days over again how different they should be!

Presently the father and son left the school, and, as they made their way to the station, Colonel Farrant spoke of the plan he had made. He had some business to transact at Plymouth; he thought they would go down there together, and perhaps spend a week in South Devon or Cornwall before going back to Oakdene. Donovan evidently liked this idea, but in another minute his face suddenly changed.

'I had forgotten Dot. What a brute I am!' he exclaimed. 'She will be expecting me, I mustn't disappoint her.'

Somehow that sentence cheered Colonel Farrant wonderfully.

Dot, his little invalid girl, had in a measure comforted him the day before by her evident devotion to Donovan. He had hardly dared to hope, however, that the love was mutual, or that, in his disgrace and sorrow, Donovan would yet have a thought to spare for his sister.

'Dot will not expect us,' he said in reply. 'I told her that we should not come home for a few days. She sent you this.'

They were in the train now. Donovan took the little three-cornered note from his father. It was written faintly in pencil, but in spite of the straggling letters and wild spelling it brought the tears to his eyes.

'DARLING DON,' it began, 'I am *so* sory. Papa has told me all abowt it, and he has been verry kind. I don't think he bileves all the horid things they say off you, and I never, *never* will, Don dear.

'Your loving
'DOT.'

The long, strange journey ended at last, but by that time Donovan's physical weariness was so intense that it overpowered everything else. As he threw himself on his bed that night, he could feel nothing but relief that at length this longest and most painful day of his life was over. The future was a yawning blackness, the past a horrid confusion, but he would face neither past nor future, the present was all he needed; in utter exhaustion of both mind and body he fell asleep.

CHAPTER II.

A RETROSPECT.

The canker galls the infants of the spring,
Too oft before their buttons be disclosed,
And in the morn and liquid dew of youth
Contagious blastments are most imminent.
Hamlet.

God's possible is taught by His world's loving,
And the children doubt of each.
E. B. BROWNING.

How was it that his son was so different from what he had expected? That was the question which continually recurred to Colonel Farrant, as, with all the chilliness of an old Indian, he sat beside the fire that May evening in one of the private sitting-rooms of the Royal Hotel. How was it that the child, whom he remembered as high-spirited, loving, and demonstrative, had become proud, and cold, and repressed? It could not all be owing to the sense of his present disgrace, though that no doubt accounted for it in part; but there was a restless unsatisfied expression, for which the disgrace did not account, and which appeared to be habitual to him. Perhaps, had Colonel Farrant known all the details of his boy's life during the years in which he had been separated from him, he might not have felt so much perplexed.

Donovan had a wonderfully good memory, and, though he had only been three years old when he parted with his father and mother at Malta, he carried away a certain kind of remembrance of them—a dim vision of a mother who always wore pretty dresses, and of a father who was always ready to play with him, and could roar like a bear. With these recollections he set sail for England, and was handed over by the acquaintance who had taken care of him during the voyage to the charge of an elderly woman in black, who was waiting for him when he landed at Southampton. The elderly woman's name was Mrs. Doery, and, as they made their way to the station, she informed Donovan that she was his grandfather's housekeeper, and that he must always do what she told him. Upon this, Donovan looked up at once to scrutinize her face, that he might judge what sort of things she was likely to tell him to do, and, child though he was, he could see that Mrs. Doery would be no easy mistress. Her long hooked nose and prominent chin were of the nut-cracker order, the corners of her mouth were turned down, her eyes were clear but disagreeably piercing, and her whole aspect, though irreproachably respectable, was, to say the least of it, forbidding. Donovan tried to find some reason for her name, but she was singularly unlike the soft-eyed doe in the animal picture-book; in time, however, he discovered that there was another kind of dough, and thought he quite understood the reason of Mrs. Doery's name then, for her face was exactly of that whitish yellow colour, and, in spite of all remonstrances, he would call her nothing else from that day forth but 'Doughy.'

Mrs. Doery asserted her authority at once; it was a hot summer's day, and Donovan, as he walked down the platform, complained of thirst, and begged for something to drink. He had caught a glimpse of some of his little acquaintance on board ship standing within the refreshment-room with tumblers of delicious-looking milk in their hands, and this made him feel an uncomfortable craving for some. But Mrs. Docry gave a decided negative—they would be home at his grandfather's in good time for tea; if he was hot, that was the very reason why he should not drink; she was not going to allow bits and snacks between meals, and he had better put such fancies out of his head directly.

Old Mr. Farrant had two houses—Oakdene Manor, a country house which he had built for himself in one of the western counties, and an old family house standing in the main street of a little country town at no great distance from London. It was to the latter place that Mrs. Docry conducted her little charge on the day of his arrival, for her master had lately had a paralytic stroke, and had given up all thoughts of re-visiting his newly-built house, which, after standing empty for some time, was eventually let to strangers. It was in the old red-brick house, with its narrow windows, and dark rooms, and stately solid furniture, that Donovan's childhood was to be passed.

And somehow his childhood was not a happy one. He was very lonely, to begin with; there were no children of his own age whom Mrs. Docry thought fit to associate with him; his grandfather, though very fond of him, was too ill and helpless to be his companion; there was no father at hand to play at 'bear' with him, and Mrs. Docry, though she was often excessively cross, could not in any other respect imitate that favourite animal of the nursery. Then he had so little to do. Mrs. Docry had at first instructed him daily in the three R's, and he proved very slow with the reading, only tolerable with the writing, but alarmingly quick with the arithmetic. He took to the multiplication table, as Mrs. Docry expressed it, 'like ducks to water;' he answered the questions in the book of mental arithmetic with a lightning speed which fairly baffled the housekeeper, and before he was five years old the longest sum in any of the first four rules would not keep him quiet for more than two minutes. But then certainly by this time he had taken to working problems in his sleep, and would awaken Mrs. Docry in the middle of the night by proclaiming in excited tones that if sheep were 39s. each, a flock of forty-five sheep would be worth £87, 15s., or some equally abstruse calculation. Mrs. Docry naturally liked to have her nights undisturbed; moreover, she had sense enough to be rather alarmed at this precocity, so she asked the doctor to look at Master Donovan, and the doctor, seeing at once that he was a clever, delicate, excitable child, strongly recommended that all lessons should be stopped till he was seven years old. Mrs. Docry obeyed this injunction strictly, and a time of woe to poor Donovan ensued; 'don't do that' seemed to follow everything he attempted. He was not allowed to run about in the nursery, because Mrs. Docry 'couldn't abide a noise,' or in old Mr. Farrant's room, because 'it was unfeeling to his poor grandfather;' if he ventured to make such a thing as a figure everything in the shape of a pencil was at once confiscated, and when he rebelled he was whipped.

For a little while he amused himself by turning the letters in his picture-book into figures and calculating with them, but Mrs. Docry soon found that he was up to no good, and forbade him to open a book without her leave. He was naturally bright and energetic, but he fell now into listless lounging habits, his high spirits breaking forth now and then, and carrying him into all kinds of mischief. He was very self-willed, and his battles, with the housekeeper were numerous; but, though his will was quite as strong as hers, he was generally forced into a sort of grudging, resentful submission, for Mrs. Docry had what seemed to him a very unfair advantage in the shape of a stinging lithe cane, and though, when Donovan kicked or struck her, he felt miserable the next moment, she never seemed to feel the least compunction in hurting *him*, but on the contrary appeared to find a grim satisfaction in his chastisement.

It was all very puzzling, Donovan could not understand it, but then there were so few things he could understand, except the problems about the sheep and such like. Mrs. Docry found him difficult to manage, and therefore told him that he was the worst boy she had ever known, and the more she impressed his badness upon him, the more he felt that for such a bad boy nothing mattered, and the less pains did he take to obey her.

And so the years passed slowly by, and at last in the spring, before Donovan's seventh birthday, old Mr. Farrant had another paralytic stroke and died. Donovan cried a good deal, for though his grandfather had never been able to speak to him, yet he had always looked kindly at him and had seemed pleased that he should come into his room, and the little lonely boy had been thankful for that silent love, and was the truest—perhaps the only true mourner at his grandfather's funeral.

The old house seemed in a sort of dreary excitement all through the week preceding the funeral, and Donovan saw several people whom he had never seen before, among others his father's cousin, Mr. Ellis Farrant, a dark handsome man of eight-and-twenty, who patronised the little boy considerably, and held his hand while the Burial Service was being read, an indignity which Donovan resented keenly, trying hard to wriggle away from him. In the evening, however, he began to like his new cousin better; the doctor and most of the other guests left early in the afternoon, but Cousin Ellis and the lawyer from London were to stay the night, as they had to look over old Mr. Farrant's papers. The work did not seem to occupy them very long, for when Donovan went shyly into the library with a message from Mrs. Docry, to know when it would be convenient to them to dine, Ellis Farrant declared that they had looked through everything and would have dinner at once, and then, with the bland, patronising smile which Donovan disliked so much, added that the little boy must certainly stay and dine with them too.

Patronage was unpleasant, but then late dinner downstairs presented great attractions to seven-year-old Donovan, and quite turned the scale in Cousin Ellis's favour. He sat bolt upright in one of the great, slippery leather chairs, so as to make the most of his height, and, though his grief was perfectly sincere, he nevertheless felt a certain melancholy pride in his new black suit, and a delightful sense of dignity and importance in dining with the two gentlemen. The conversation did not interest him at all, excepting once, when he heard his father's name mentioned, and then he listened attentively.

'Captain Farrant appointed you one of his trustees, I believe,' said the lawyer.

'Yes, in the will he made at the time of his marriage, which was the most terse will ever heard of; very little more than "All to my wife!"'

'Well, well,' said the lawyer, laughing, 'though it's against my own interests to say so, it's the concise wills which answer best; and no doubt this little man will be no real loser for receiving his property through his mother.'

Donovan grew very sleepy at dessert, and found it difficult to maintain his upright position. The gentlemen sat long over their wine, and he was beginning to wonder drowsily why people eat and drink so much more in the dining-room than in the nursery, when he was roused by hearing his own name.

'Look here, little man'—it was Cousin Ellis who was speaking—'are there any cards in the house?'

'Cards? Oh! yes, lots,' said Donovan, rubbing his eyes. 'They came after grandpapa's last stroke, with "kind inquiries" on them, Mrs. Docry said.'

Cousin Ellis and the lawyer laughed heartily.

'Not those cards, but playing-cards, Dono. Didn't I see a card-table in the library?'

But Donovan only looked puzzled, and his surprise was great when, on adjourning to the next room, Ellis Farrant cleared one of the tables of the books and papers which had accumulated on it, and, with the slightest push, turned the top, disclosing in its centre two or three packs of cards. In another minute the whole thing was transformed into a square of green baize, and Cousin Ellis and the lawyer were shuffling the cards for their game. Donovan was not at all sleepy now. He felt all a child's delighted curiosity in something which was new and mysterious, and then, too, what splendid things these would be to calculate with; he wished he had found their hiding-place before.

'Do tell me their names. Do let me watch you,' he begged.

And Ellis Farrant, who was in good humour at having found something to while away his dull evening, took the little boy on his knee, and while he played taught him his cards.

To hear once was to remember with Donovan. He not only learnt the names of the cards, but began to understand the principles of the game, and pleaded hard to be allowed to play too. But neither Cousin Ellis nor the lawyer would believe in his capabilities for *écarté*. The lawyer was good-natured, however, and, seeing the grievous disappointment in the little boy's face, suggested that they should let him have a game of *vingt-et-un*, and Cousin Ellis complied, limiting the stakes to threepence, and supplying the penniless Donovan from his own pocket.

Here was excitement indeed! calculation, judgment, memory, all called into action at once! And the little pile of coins before him was growing with magic speed, and *vingt-et-un* fell to him twice running, and the gentlemen told him laughingly that he was certainly born to win. It ended long before he wished, and Cousin Ellis changed his winnings for him into great bright half-crowns, and he went off to bed proud, and excited, and victorious, to play *vingt-et-un* in his dreams, only being disturbed now and then by a nightmare of a gigantic queen of spades sitting on his chest and stifling him. And so ended Donovan's first introduction to the '*tapis vert*.'

The next morning Cousin Ellis and the lawyer left for London, and the child was once more alone. The terrible flatness and depression which he felt that day might have been a lesson to him in after-life, and he did never forget it, although his experience had to be bought more dearly. He wandered drearily over the deserted house, and stole half timidly into the library, and looked again at the magical table, and felt the half-crowns in his pocket. But the fascination and excitement of the previous evening were gone, and, now that the sensation of triumph and victory had died away, he did not greatly care for the money: His head ached, too; the dreary emptiness of the house oppressed him; he began

to feel that his grandfather's absence made a great difference to
him, and that there was something very forlorn in the idea of
being left alone with Mrs. Doery.

As time passed, however, he began to grow accustomed to
things, and slipped back into much the same routine as before;
meals, walks, and pretty frequent fights with Mrs. Doery, solitary
games, fits of wild mischief, whippings, imprisonments, and vague
wonder at the perplexities of life. His greatest enjoyment was
to steal down into the library, softly to draw aside one of the
shutters, and, when quite secure that Mrs. Doery was not likely
to interrupt him, to take those wonderful cards from their hiding-
place. Then, with a dummy adversary, he would play the two
games of which he had mastered the rules, and various others of
his own invention, always playing his adversary's cards with the
strictest impartiality.

Another occupation there was too which helped to relieve the
tedium of the long days, and this was carpentering. He was
very clever with his fingers, and, luckily, the housekeeper did
not object much to this pursuit, so long, as she expressed it, ' he
didn't hurt the carpets or himself.' And Donovan obediently
cleared up all his shavings and chips, and bravely endured his
cuts and mishaps in silence. He became very expert, and one
unfortunate day, when Mrs. Doery had gone out to see a friend,
his ambition rose to such a height that he resolved to take the
nursery clock to pieces in order to see how it was made, intending,
after he had thoroughly mastered the details, to put it together
again. So to work he went as soon as the housekeeper was well
out of sight, and, with the aid of pincers, screw-drivers, and his
dexterous little fingers, succeeded in dissecting the clock. It
was wonderfully interesting work, so interesting that, although
he was studying the anatomy of the recorder of time, he forgot
that there was such a thing as time at all, and that, although
the hands of the clock were detached from its face, and the pen-
dulum was lying motionless in his tool-box, the inexorable old
gentleman with the scythe was travelling at his usual pace, and
bringing tea-time and Mrs. Doery in his train. He had just
settled everything entirely to his own mind, and arranged which
wheels to re-adjust first, when the door opened; he looked up—
and there stood Mrs. Doery with a face of mingled astonishment
and wrath which baffles description. It was in vain that Donovan
pleaded to be allowed to set it right, and showed how neatly he
had arranged the pieces; Mrs. Doery would not listen to a word,
but taking the culprit to his room, gave him the severest whipping
he had ever had, and Donovan cried piteously, not at all on

account of the pain, for he bore that like a little Trojan, but because he was quite sure he could put the clock together again if 'Doughy' would only let him.

It was not only by fits of mischief and wilfulness that Donovan gave the housekeeper trouble. Soon after his grandfather's death, he began, as she said, 'to plague the very life out of her with questions.' What was this? and why was that? and what was the reason of the other? pursued poor Mrs. Doery from morning till night. Taking the doctor's general directions into every detail, she had brought up her little charge in utter ignorance; he knew no more of religion than the veriest little heathen, and though Mrs. Doery had taught him a short doggrel prayer to say as he went to sleep, he was much too matter of fact and logical to care to say a charm addressed, as far as he knew, to no one in particular, and for which he could not understand the reason. It did not make him any happier to say

> 'Three in One, and One in Three,
> One in Three, save me.'

It only puzzled him completely, so he left off saying it.

But the service at his grandfather's funeral had awakened his curiosity; he could not understand it, and he could not bear not being able to understand. Mrs. Doery found herself obliged to give an answer now and then in order to quiet him, and Donovan learnt that people knelt down to 'ask God for things,' that 'God was a Being who loved good people and hated bad people,' and that 'grandpapa had gone to heaven.'

'Why, that's what you always say when you're surprised!' he exclaimed, when this last piece of information had been received. '"Good heaven!" you know. Is heaven a great surprise? What is heaven?'

'It's a nice place where good folk go,' said Mrs. Doery, as if she grudged the admission.

'Is it in India?'

'Dear heart! The ignorance of the child! No, it's up in the sky.'

'What do they do up there?'

'Sit and sing hymns and say prayers.'

'What, like they did at the funeral?'

'Bless the child, I don't know; but you needn't trouble so about it, for it's only good boys as goes there.'

'I don't want to go, I'm sure,' said Donovan, defiantly. 'I hate sitting still.'

But his mind was not satisfied, and Mrs. Doery was questioned still further.

'Doughy, what did they mean when they said grandpapa would never be ill again?'

'Why, folks never are ill in heaven.'

'What, never? Oh! that is another reason, then, why I don't want to go there, for the nicest time I ever had was when I'd the measles; you never were so little cross in your life, Doughy.' Mrs. Doery made no comment on this, and the little boy continued, rather anxiously, 'I suppose, Doughy, *you* are very good, aren't you?'

'Well, Master Donovan, I try to do my duty by the house, and by you,' said Doery, gloomily.

'That's a good thing!' said Donovan, relieved, 'for you see, Doughy, I don't think we'd better go to the same place, we should be happier away from each other.'

Mrs. Doery was wonderfully uncommunicative, but still the little boy occasionally plied her with fresh questions. One day he came to her with a perplexity which had long been troubling him.

'Doughy, who gives us homes?'

'Your papa, of course, Master Donovan.'

'And who gave papa his home?'

'Why, your poor grandpapa.'

'But who gave the first papa that ever was his home?'

'Bless the child! how should I know? I don't suppose Adam had no home, so to speak.'

'Why are some people's homes so much happier than other people's? It's very unfair.'

'The good little boys are happy,' said Mrs. Doery, 'and the bad ones aren't.'

'Then, if I was never naughty, should I have a nice home like little Tom Harris, with a mother to take me out with her?'

'That's impossible to say,' replied Mrs. Doery, gravely; 'let alone the unlikeliness that you ever would be good, you see there's all them past times you was naughty; so you've not much of a chance.'

Poor Donovan went away sadly, and yet with a great sense of injustice in his childish mind. That was almost the last question he troubled Mrs. Doery with.

But, though he was represented as so incurably bad, he would not entirely bow to Mrs. Doery's opinion. In his heart of hearts he cherished an ideal mother, who was to come back from India, make him good, and fill his life with happiness; she was to be

just like Mrs. Harris, the grocer's wife, who took her little boy
out walking, only her dresses were to be prettier, for the one
thing he remembered about his mother was that she always wore
pretty clothes. The events of his life were the arrival of the
Indian letters, in which 'papa and mamma sent their love to
Dono;' but these were few and far between, for, although Mrs.
Doery wrote each mail to give an account of Master Donovan's
well-being, neither Colonel Farrant nor his wife understood the
importance of keeping their memory green in the remembrance
of the child by writing to him. The Colonel was absorbed in his
work, Mrs. Farrant was absorbed in herself. Donovan had his
ideal mother, nevertheless, and would rehearse her return, and
talk to her by the hour; and when Mrs. Doery took him for his
walk he would put his hand a little out on the side away from
the housekeeper, making believe that his mother held it, and
would turn his face up, as if he were talking to her, just as he
had seen little Tom Harris do.

At last one never-to-be-forgotten day Donovan heard that he
had a little baby sister, and before the novelty and delight of this
news had had time to fade came a second letter with yet more
wonderful tidings, a large letter for Mrs. Doery, and a little one
enclosed for Donovan from his father—'Mamma and baby were
coming to England to live with Dono, and he must take great
care of them, and try to make them happy.'

Never had the little boy known such happiness, his dream
was actually coming true, mother was coming, mother who would
not mind answering his questions, who would make him good,
who would rescue him from Mrs. Doery's whippings. He could
watch the grocer's little boy now when he passed by without the
least shade of envy, for in a few weeks would not he too be walking out with his mother?

He watched the preparations which were being made in the
house with a sense of exultant happiness, his grave step changed
to the bounding skipping pace of a merry child, and he was so
good that even Mrs. Doery had no complaint to make of him.
Then at length came the real day of arrival, and Donovan's
feverish impatience was at length rewarded; a carriage stopped
at the door, Mrs. Doery, smoothing her black apron, bustled out
into the hall, and Donovan rushed headlong down the white steps
to throw his arms round his mother's neck. But a sudden chill
of disappointment fell on his heart, it was so different from
everything he had planned. The tall pretty-looking lady stooped
to kiss him, indeed, and her voice was soft and refined, if somewhat languid, as she exclaimed, 'Dear me! what a great boy you

have grown!' but it was not his ideal at all, not the mother to whom he could tell everything, or who would care to know. All this Donovan read in almost the first glance, as clearly as he had read Mrs. Doery's character on Southampton Pier.

He followed everyone else into the house and shut the door. Mrs. Farrant was already on the way to her room, and did not notice him any further, and he was too bewildered and disappointed to care to bestow more than a glance on the ayah and the little baby in long clothes.

By-and-by, he saw his mother again, but by this time he had grown shy, and only made the briefest responses to her questions, and before long she had disposed herself on the drawing-room sofa with a book, and he was left standing at a little distance with a Calcutta costume doll which she had just given him, and a very heavy heart. The doll only added to his disappointment. Surely the ideal mother would have understood how little he, a boy of eight years old, would care for a doll? He did not want presents at all, he wanted the dream-mother back again, and the conviction that she never could come back again was terrible indeed. It got worse and worse as the evening advanced, and at last he could bear it no longer, but, wishing his mother good-night, crept upstairs though it was not yet his bed time, and shutting himself into the cupboard among Mrs. Doery's dresses gave vent to his misery. He did not often cry, even at the severest whipping, but that night he sobbed as though his heart would break; life had seemed hard and perplexing already, and now his ideal was gone!

But the loving hand which was guiding Donovan, though he so little knew it, was not going to leave him desolate. The perfectly loving sympathetic mother had indeed been denied him, but another treasure had been provided for him, which though it could not fill entirely the place of the dethroned ideal—the place which was to be always empty, always longing to be filled—was yet to call out his best and strongest feelings.

When at last he checked his sobs and crept out of the cupboard once more, the first thing his eyes rested on was the new baby sister lying asleep in her cradle. He was so miserable that he would even have thrown himself on Mrs. Doery's mercy if she had been there, and in another minute his tears broke forth again, as he pressed his face close to the baby's and told her all his trouble. Of course she woke directly, but he still sobbed out his story.

'Oh! baby, I'm so miserable—so miserable—mother isn't a bit what I expected.'

The baby began to cry feebly, and Donovan, penitent at having disturbed her, took her with great care and difficulty from her cradle, and began to rock her in his arms, and as she slept once more, and as her weight became more and more difficult to bear, a new sense of love and protecting care sprang up in the little boy's heart, and he was comforted. Before long Mrs. Docry's step was heard without, and Donovan knew that if he were found he would certainly be whipped, but to try to put the baby back in the cradle would be sure to wake her, and she was worth suffering for.

Mrs. Docry was of course wrathful, and poor Donovan went to bed supperless and sore both inwardly and outwardly; but, as his wistful eyes closed on that day of disappointment, he clung to his one comforting thought, the little sister, his new possession.

As time passed on, the bond beyond these two grew stronger and stronger. Donovan centred all the love of his heart on the frail little life of the baby. The element of protection was his most pronounced characteristic; he was strong, and liked above all things to have something to take care of. And Dot, as they called the tiny delicate little girl, needed any amount of attention. From the very first everything seemed against her; her Indian birth, the trying voyage; the want of any real care from her mother, the miserable mismanagement of an incompetent doctor, all told grievously on the delicate little child. She had only just learnt to walk, or rather to trust herself to be piloted along by Donovan, when she began to pine and dwindle, and before long the hesitating footsteps were hushed for ever, and Dot lay down upon the couch on which her little life-drama was to be acted. A fall from her ayah's arms had, it was supposed, been the cause of the hip-disease which now declared itself. For a time every-one was sorry and disturbed, but soon they became resigned, and talked about 'the dispensations of Providence.' Only Donovan nursed his sorrow and indignation apart, conscious, in spite of his youth, that it was human carelessness, human misunderstand-ing, which had ruined the only life he cared for.

In the meantime, the lease of Oakdene Manor came to an end, and Mrs. Farrant and her children left the house where Dono-van's childhood had been passed, to make their home in that place which old Mr. Farrant had planned so carefully, but had never seen.

The change was in some respects good for Donovan; he was just old enough to take an interest in the property which would, he supposed, be his own some day, and he liked the free country life. But in that comfortable English home, the apparent mode

C

of refinement and propriety, he grew up somehow into a very unsatisfactory mortal, unsatisfactory to himself as well as to others. He was scarcely to be blamed perhaps, for, with the exception of little Dot, there was not one good influence in the Manor household.

His mother's selfishness was perfectly apparent to him; he accepted it now with a sort of cold indifference when it only affected himself. It was so, and there was an end of the matter; he just put up with it. But, when Mrs. Farrant's absorption in self affected Dot, Donovan's indignation was always roused; there was an almost fierce gleam in his eyes when he found Dot suffering from the unmotherliness which had chilled and cramped his own life.

What, however, told most fatally on him was his mother's conventional religion. Mrs. Farrant went to church because it was proper, and insisted on her son's accompanying her. He obeyed, but went with a sort of stubborn disgust, hating to share in this act of hypocrisy. He was naturally acute, and at a very early age he found out that the lives of the professing Christians around him were diametrically opposed to the principles of Christianity. It was all a hideous mockery, a hollow profession; he came to a child's sweeping conclusion, 'They are all shams, these Christian people,' and naturally went on to the resolution, 'I at least will profess nothing.'

His views received a sort of amused encouragement from his tutor, a man whom Mrs. Farrant had been delighted to secure for her son, because he was 'so highly connected, such a very gentlemanly man.' Mr. Alleyne was, however, in spite of his high connections, unfit to be the tutor of a boy like Donovan. He was clever, but shallow, and he had dabbled in science, and rather prided himself on being able to appreciate the difficulties which great minds found in reconciling the new discoveries of science and the old faiths. He quoted Tyndall and Huxley with great aptness, and, though on occasion he was quite capable of appearing to be exceedingly orthodox, yet he was rather fond of styling himself an Agnostic when quite sure of his audience. He was not a sincere man; he liked talking of his 'intellectual difficulties,' and regarded scepticism as 'not bad form now-a-days.' When Mr. Alleyne found that his pupil was, as he termed it, 'a thorough-going young atheist,' he was a little amused and a good deal interested. He was not at all unwilling to forsake the more ordinary routine, and, throwing aside the classics, he allowed Donovan to devote most of his time to scientific subjects, which were far more interesting to both teacher and pupil.

Donovan had no respect for his tutor, but he was a good deal influenced by him. When by his father's desire he was sent at last to a public school, he was just in the state to derive all the evil and none of the good from school life. He had grown up in isolation, and he was naturally reserved, so that he did not easily make friends, and he was too wilful and incomprehensible to be a favourite with the masters. In mathematics, indeed, he could beat every opponent with ease, and carried off several prizes, but his success was merely that of natural talent, and never of industry, so that even to himself it brought little satisfaction.

And all the time slowly strengthening and developing was the intense love of play which had shown itself in his earliest childhood. Ellis Farrant had crossed his path several times since their first meeting, and Donovan, though he did not like his cousin, always enjoyed his visits, for then his passion could be gratified, and his monotonous and already unsatisfying life could be broken by the most delicious of all excitements.

Later on came the temptation at school; the suggestion made by a weaker and more timid boy was carried out unscrupulously by Donovan, his conscience completely overmastered by the thirst for self-gratification. Then followed exposure, disgrace, some injustice, and a most bitter humiliation.

His school-days were abruptly ended. What was now to become of him?

CHAPTER III.

THE TREMAINS OF PORTHKERRAN.

'But faith beyond our sight may go,'
He said; 'the gracious Fatherhood
Can only know above, below,
Eternal purposes of good.
From our free heritage of will
The bitter springs of pain and ill
Flow only in all worlds. The perfect day
Of God is shadowless, and love is love alway.

WHITTIER.

GOLDEN sunshine, clear blue sky, the fresh green of spring, and a light delicious sea breeze—all this outward beauty and gladness there was on the morning after Colonel Farrant and his son had

arrived at Plymouth. And yet surely never had heart felt more
heavy, never had existence felt more unbearable, than Donovan's
as he walked slowly and dejectedly on the Hoe. Colonel Farrant
had left the hotel early in order to get his business settled, and
Donovan, with a restless craving for something to divert his
mind from his disgrace, had wandered out alone. He was not
very successful in his search for peace, for the more he struggled
to find interest or diversion in all around, the more he felt the
bitter pangs of remorse and angry resentment. Groups of happy
noisy children were playing on the grass, and he thought of his
own lonely repressed childhood, and felt that the lots of men
were unjustly and unequally arranged.

He stood on the highest point of the Hoe, and looked at the
exquisite view before him—the stately ships at anchor in the
Sound, Drake's Island, with its miniature citadel, Mount Edg-
cumbe, with its beautifully wooded banks, and its foliage fringing
the water, the clear sharply-defined line of the breakwater, and,
far out over the sparkling dancing waves, the distant Eddystone.
And yet, though he could not be altogether insensible to the
beauty of the scene, the brightness and rejoicing, even the
industry and success which he saw, made him more angry and
resentful, more hopeless and despairing. Was not he disgraced,
humiliated? and at the same time, had not his faults been
unjustly exaggerated, his punishment unjustly given? Life
seemed one long perplexity, and now he felt both hopeless and
purposeless, for success and pleasure had been his chief objects
hitherto, and now he felt that he had failed shamefully, and that
the failure was so great that all pleasure in life was over.

Yet, in spite of his remorse and misery, he was neither
repentant nor humble, for Mrs. Doery's early training had ruined
him in this respect. The soft, pliable years of his childhood had
been left in ignorance, and when his powers of reason and calculation had been well roused and brought into action, he was
presented with the image of a God always watchful to detect sin,
always in readiness to punish, a hard, stern, inexorable Judge,
who admitted fortunate people to heaven, and dismissed unfortunate people to hell, with strict impartiality and entire absence
of feeling. No wonder that an angry sense of injustice grew up
in Donovan's heart, no wonder that he turned from the cruelly
false representation which was offered him, and steadily refused
to believe in it. And when, in course of time, he heard other
and truer views than these, his heart had grown hard, and he had
become so accustomed to rely on himself and his natural strength
of will that he felt no need of higher help. Moreover, religion

required that he should own himself to be weak and God all-powerful, and he would own neither the one nor the other. Even now, with his sense of failure and misery, he would not yield; fate had been against him, he was sorry to have brought disgrace on his father, he was angry and indignant with the world, and dissatisfied with himself, but that was all.

Two vessels in the Sound had just weighed anchor. He watched them with a listless interest, wondering whither they were bound, and what would become of them; whether they would safely reach their destination, or whether a cruel fate would cast them on rocks or quicksands, to be hopelessly, irretrievably wrecked. A fate to be struggled against! It was his notion of life; and, as the stately ships left the harbour and sailed out into the immeasurable expanse beyond, he turned away with a firmer, more decided step, and a less dejected heart; fate had been against him all his life, but he would not despair. He would conquer fate by the power of his will, he would live yet to be an honour to his father!

Colonel Farrant's business did not detain him very long, and, as soon as lunch was over, he suggested that they might as well at least begin their tour that afternoon. Donovan was relieved at the proposal, and assisted in the choice of a horse and dog-cart with resolute if somewhat forced cheerfulness. His father was further than ever from understanding him now, and began to doubt whether the driving tour would be a success; but, with all his perplexing contradictions, Donovan was very loveable, and his eager questions as to the Colonel's Indian life could not but be gratifying to the father's heart. He, for his part, however, was a much less successful questioner, and could elicit very little as to his son's past life, for Donovan was reserved by nature, and had been made still more so by his education. He drew an impenetrable veil over his childhood, and answered all allusions to his mother with quick abrupt monosyllables; for he was far too proud to be a grumbler, and indeed his grievances were too deep to bear speaking of. Little Dot was the only subject upon which he talked naturally and unreservedly, and Colonel Farrant was glad to make the most of this.

Before long the weather claimed their attention; the sky, which had been bright and clear when they left Plymouth, was now black and threatening, while the light breeze of the morning was growing stronger and keener. Everything betokened a storm, and before long the rain descended in torrents, drenching the occupants of the dog-cart to the skin, while the western wind blew so strongly and gustily that to hold an umbrella was out of the question. For himself Donovan rather enjoyed it. There was a sort of pleasure in being buffeted by wind and rain, but he was anxious for his father, as he knew he was subject to severe attacks of rheumatism, consequent on rheumatic fever. They resolved to stop at the first place they came to, and at last, to their relief, they reached a quaint little fishing town, which boasted a very fair inn.

But in spite of warm rooms, a good dinner, and a change of clothes, Donovan's fears were realized. The next day his father was entirely incapacitated by rheumatism, and to proceed was an impossibility; the rain, too, continued without intermission, and everything seemed to augur some little stay at Porthkerran. The day passed slowly and wearily. Donovan wrote letters at his father's dictation, read the *Western Morning News* from beginning to end, and finally set out, notwithstanding the rain, to reconnoitre the place. On coming in again, he found his father so much worse, and suffering such pain from his heart, that he tried hard to get leave to go for the doctor, but Colonel Farrant did not take to the idea.

'There is nothing to be done. I've had these attacks dozens of times,' he replied, reassuringly. 'Besides, ten to one we should only find a quack in this outlandish place.'

'The landlord says there's a first-rate doctor named Tremain; do let me send a line to him,' said Donovan, anxiously.

'Well, well, perhaps if I'm not better to-morrow we'll have him. I'm sorry to keep you in this dull place, my boy ; but to-morrow, if it's fine, we will try to push on.'

Colonel Farrant spoke cheerfully, and as if he really hoped to be well again before long ; and yet Donovan could not shake off an uneasy dissatisfied feeling, which returned to him more and more strongly after each visit to his father's room. They had a great deal of talk that evening, and Donovan began to feel that home would be very different now that his father had returned, more like the ideal home he used to fancy. Colonel Farrant, too, was immensely relieved and cheered, for his sickness and helplessness had brought to light many of Donovan's best qualities—his strength, his tenderness, and his ready observance ; while his evident anxiety seemed to speak well for his awakening love.

It would be hard to say which was the more disappointed when, on the Thursday morning, Colonel Farrant proved to be rather worse than better. He was suffering so much when Donovan went into his room in the early morning, that he could no longer say anything against the plan for calling Dr. Tremain, and Donovan dispatched a messenger at once with a note to the doctor, and before half-an-hour had passed was called down into the little sitting-room to receive him

Dr. Tremain was standing by the window when he entered, and Donovan, glancing at him rather curiously, was at once prepossessed in his favour. He was a middle-aged man, but looked younger than he really was, in spite of evident signs of ill-health : his brown eyes were clear and shining, and there was a kindly light in them which was very attractive; his forehead was high and very finely developed, his features were regular and good, while a long light brown beard concealed the one defect of the face, a slightly receding chin.

Donovan was a rather good judge of character; his first sensation was one of relief that he had found a man whom he could trust, and who would probably understand his father's case ; his next was one of surprise that any one so refined, and evidently so clever, should remain buried in a Cornish village. He led the way at once to Colonel Farrant's room, and then waited anxiously below for the report. The doctor's visit was a long one, and when at length he came downstairs Donovan was alarmed to find that he spoke very seriously of Colonel Farrant's illness. The rheumatic fever had left his heart weak, of that Donovan was aware, but Dr. Tremain spoke of really grave symptoms of further mischief, aggravated, no doubt, by the fatigue of his return from India, and by the chill which he had taken during the drive to Porthkerran.

'And any mental shock, any trouble, would that be likely to affect him ?' asked Donovan, speaking calmly though his heart began to beat very uncomfortably.

'It might, yes, it probably would,' replied the doctor, ' but he told me of nothing of the sort.'

'No, I didn't think he would,' said Donovan, controlling his voice with difficulty, ' but he has had great and unexpected trouble ; I have given him trouble.'

The confession, coming from one evidently so reserved, had a strange pathos ; Dr. Tremain held out his hand warmly

'That must make the anxiety doubly trying to you ; but do not be despondent, this afternoon I may be able to give a better account ; in the meantime only see that your father is kept perfectly quiet.'

Donovan had been miserable enough before, but this news added tenfold to his misery. At Colonel Farrant's request, he wrote at once to his mother, giving her full particulars of his father's state, and describing the kind of accommodation which was to be had at Porthkerran, if she thought of coming down to nurse him. He added these details because his father told him to do so, but he himself did not think for a moment that she would come, she always shrank from witnessing pain, and even disliked being in little Dot's room for any length of time.

As Donovan wrote, Colonel Farrant lay perfectly still, thinking deeply, and when in the afternoon Dr. Tremain made his second visit, and could still give no more favourable report, the subject of his anxiety was revealed.

' Doctor, have you any lawyer in the place who would draw up a will for me ? '

' There is one ordinarily,' said Dr. Tremain. ' But Mr. Turner is away now ; I am afraid there is no one nearer than Plymouth.'

' I have been thinking things over,' said the Colonel. ' It is many years since my former will was made, and, owing to many changes, I feel that it will be better to make an alteration. I feel fidgety and anxious to get things settled, it is provoking that there is no lawyer here.'

' I do not know that you need feel any immediate anxiety,' said the doctor ; ' what I have told you need not necessarily affect your life for many years.'

' No, but it *may* affect it at any moment,' said the Colonel, gravely. ' I want to be prepared, I want to have everything in order for my boy.'

Dr. Tremain, aware that worry or anxiety was very bad for his patient, thought of the best means of re-assuring his mind, and, after a moment's consideration, suggested that he should write both briefly and clearly his own wishes until a formal will could be drawn up. Colonel Farrant was much relieved by the idea, and directed the doctor to ask Donovan for a sheet of paper, upon which Dr. Tremain wrote at his dictation a clear and properly worded form, expressing his desire to devise and bequeath the bulk of his property to his son, Donovan Farrant, and providing an ample allowance for his widow during her life. Then one of the servants and the doctor himself witnessed the will, and the Colonel lay back again relieved and satisfied.

They were still talking on the subject when Donovan's voice was heard without ; it was just post time, and he knew his father had a letter to send.

' I do not wish my son to see this, I wish him to know nothing of the transaction,' said the Colonel, quickly.

Dr. Tremain had, however, already given the word of admittance, and Colonel Farrant, starting up hurriedly, took the will from the table and put it into the doctor's hand.

'Take it, take it, and not a word.'

There was a sudden pause; Donovan came towards the bed just in time to see his father fall forward, and to hear a slight sound in his throat, of which he did not know the meaning. Dr. Tremain gave an inarticulate exclamation, raised the inanimate form and bent down close to it; then he glanced to the other side of the bed, to that other form almost as still and inanimate, to that other face, white, rigid, and agonized and saw there was no need of words; Donovan understood that his father was dead.

All that a good unselfish man can do at such a time Dr. Tremain did. He felt the most intense pity for Donovan left thus utterly alone, with a burden of remorse on his conscience, and this overwhelming grief at his heart; but it was difficult to be of much use to one so completely stunned and paralysed, and the doctor could only persuade him to leave the room.

Donovan moved away mechanically, and went down below to the little sitting-room. He felt scarcely anything but a dim, vague, undefined horror, a consciousness of a sudden blank in his life. The shock had been so great that, for the time, all his faculties were numbed, and he scarcely heard the doctor's words; he stood by the mantelpiece silent and motionless, with his eyes fixed on the centre ornament—a little tawdry shell house mounted on a board strewn with dried seaweeds. How many times he had dreamily calculated the number of Cornish cowries which would be needed to adorn fifty houses he did not know, but he was roused at length by the doctor's hand on his shoulder.

'If I can be of any use in sending off any telegrams for you, or helping you in any other way, pray tell me.'

The words seemed to rouse Donovan, the rigid stillness of his face changed suddenly, the look of suffering deepened.

'My mother, I must let her know.'

He sat down by the table and hid his face in his hands, battling with his emotion. The doctor had brought paper and pen; he offered to write the telegram, but at the proposal Donovan raised his head once more, and, controlling himself, took the pen in his hand and wrote, without a moment's pause or hesitation, the brief words which were to convey the news of Colonel Farrant's death to the rector of the church near Oakdene. He was the only person fit to break the news to Mrs. Farrant, the only person Donovan could think of at all, except Mrs. Doery or Ellis Farrant, and from them he instinctively shrank.

Dr. Tremain promised to see that the message was sent, and then very reluctantly took leave, trying, as he walked along the wet muddy road, to think of any means by which he could help

the poor boy who seemed left in such a miserable friendless
state. But it was a difficult question, and the doctor had arrived
at no satisfactory solution by the time he had passed through the
village and reached the gabled ivy-covered house where he lived.

Trenant was a delightfully comfortable house, prettily fur-
nished, exquisitely neat, and in every way well ordered. Some
one was singing on the staircase as Dr. Tremain opened the front
door, and as he took off his wet coat there was a sound of hurrying footsteps, and a pretty bright-looking girl of about sixteen
ran to meet him.

'Papa, how long you have been out, and how shockingly wet
you are!'

'Yes, it is raining heavily,' said the doctor, taking one of the
soft little hands in his as he crossed the hall. 'Is your mother
in, Gladys?'

'Yes, she's with the children in the drawing-room, and we've
kept some tea for you. I'll go and see to it,' and she ran off,
finishing the song which had been interrupted, while her father
went into the drawing-room.

Gladys was the eldest daughter of the house, and when her
parents had chosen her name—a name which they considered as
emblematic of happiness, in spite of certain questionings which
had arisen among name fanciers on the subject—it would seem
that some unseen fairy godmother had really bestowed that best
of all gifts on their child, for Gladys was the happiest, most contented, sunshiny little person imaginable. Everything about her
looked happy, her sunny golden-brown hair, her bright, well-
opened, grey eyes, her laughing mouth, her little unformed nose,
her dimpled chin, and fresh glowing complexion. She had, of course,
her ups and downs like most people, but she was too unselfish to
be depressed for any length of time, and too easy and accommodating to make much of such troubles and difficulties as she had.

In a few minutes the tea was ready, and Gladys, with a
dainty little hand-tray filled with a plate of crisp home-made
biscuits and the cup and saucer, crossed the hall once more,
passed the little conservatory where two canaries were singing
with all their might, and entered the drawing-room, in which she
found her father and mother talking together.

'They are strangers. The father had just returned from
India,' Dr. Tremain was saying. 'And they were taking a
driving tour in Cornwall; it's the saddest thing I've heard for
a long time. Without the slightest preparation the poor fellow
is left in this way, without a friend near him.'

'He is quite alone then at the inn?' asked Mrs. Tremain.

'Quite alone, and I don't see how we are to help him. I thought of asking him here, but I feel sure he wouldn't come.'

'Poor boy! how old is he?'

'About eighteen, I believe; but he's decidedly old for his age, he is a man compared with Dick.'

'Oh! Dick never will grow old,' said the mother, with a little sigh, as she remembered how far away was the sailor son. 'But we cannot leave this poor Mr. Farrant without any sympathy. Would it be any use if I went to see him?'

'It would be the very best thing possible,' said the doctor, 'if you do not shrink from it too much. I am afraid you will find it very difficult to make any way with him, but I can't think of any other plan for helping him.'

'I will try to see him, then, after dinner,' said Mrs. Tremain.

'Is Mr. Farrant's father dead?' asked Gladys, as her father left the room.

'Yes, dear, quite suddenly. The shock must have been terrible to the poor boy.'

'Oh! mother, how will you comfort him? How dreadful it must be to have such sorrow all alone!'

'Yes, terrible indeed,' said Mrs. Tremain. 'I am afraid we cannot do very much to comfort him, dear Gladys, but God can comfort him, and perhaps He may use us as His messengers of comfort; at any rate we can all pray for him.'

'Yes, we can do that. But, mother,'—and a shade crossed Gladys' bright face—' it does seem so strange that some people should have so much more trouble than others. Dick and I, for instance, we have had scarcely anything but happiness all our lives. Of course, Dick's going away is always sad, but I mean we've had no great sorrows. Doesn't it seem almost unfair, unjust, that lives should be so unequal?'

'It must seem so, until we can realize that we are all the children of a loving Father, who gives to everyone just what is best for them. If we remember that God's will is to draw us all nearer Him, to fit us for the greatest happiness of all, we shall surely trust Him to choose our joys and sorrows, and those of everyone else too.'

'And yet, mother, it seems very often as if the troubles were just the very worst things for us, the things that made us go wrong. Think of poor Ben Trevethan at the forge; his wife died, and directly afterwards his son grew so wild, and took to drinking, and then just when Ben hoped to steady him again he was laid up for months and months, and the son grew worse, and at last ran away; it seems as if it would have been so much better if all those troubles hadn't happened together, as if the son would have had so much more chance of getting right.'

Yes, it seems so to us, dear,' said Mrs. Tremain ; 'but you must remember that we cannot see the pattern which our lives are weaving, we can only go on bit by bit, remembering that there *is* a pattern, and that one day we shall understand why the dark shades, and the long plain pieces, and the bright glad colours were sent us. Ben Trevethan's life, and his son's too, will not be wasted, you may be sure ; they will help to influence, to guide, or to warn other lives, all the time that they are weaving their pattern.'

'Our pattern is very bright just now,' said Gladys, raising her happy contented face for a kiss. And baby Nesta is the very brightest sunniest part of it all !' and she sprang up to receive from the nurse the little white-robed baby, the new delight and treasure of the whole house.

Her song was taken up once more as she walked to and fro with her little charge, and the voices of the other children at their play came from the further end of the room, while Mrs. Tremain's thoughts reverted to the sad story she had heard, and to the work which lay before her that evening.

Her task was no easy one ; she trembled a little when she was actually standing in the passage of the inn, having sent a messenger to ask if Mr. Farrant would see her. Dr. Tremain had been called out, and she had been obliged to come alone ; this made the interview seem all the more formidable, but she was too unselfish to shrink from the difficulty. The messenger returned quickly, and she was ushered into the little sitting-room, speedily forgetting all thought of herself as she saw the misery written on Donovan's face. He came forward to meet her, and bowed gravely ; then, as she held out her hand with a few words of explanation and sympathy, he took it in his, answered briefly but courteously, and drew a chair towards the fire for her. She sat down, and he fell back into his former position, with his elbows resting on the mantel-piece and his face half hidden, as if he had done all that courtesy required of him, and intended to return to his own thoughts.

Mrs. Tremain's voice roused him ; it was a very low gentle voice, and fell pleasantly on his ear.

'I cannot bear to think of your being all alone here,' she began. 'This inn seems so forlorn and comfortless for you   I wish we could persuade you to come to our house, you should be perfectly quiet and undisturbed.'

She hardly thought that he would consent to this plan, but it made an opening for conversation, and it roused Donovan at once; his tone, as he replied, was more than merely courteous, and his sad eyes met hers fully.

'You are very kind and good to think of it, but I don't think I can come, thank you; to-morrow my mother will be here, and to-night I can't leave—I would rather——' he broke off hastily, unable to control his distress.

'You must do just what you like best,' said Mrs. Tremain; 'I can quite understand your feeling.'

'It would be of no use,' continued Donovan, recovering himself, but speaking in a low constrained voice. 'Can I escape from my thoughts at your house any more than here? Nothing can make misery and remorse bearable.'

'I suppose we all see the full beauty and goodness of those we love only when we lose them,' said Mrs. Tremain, not quite understanding him, 'and then we wish we had often acted differently to them; those bitter regrets are very hard to bear.'

'Ah! you don't know, you can't understand what reason for remorse I have!' cried Donovan; and then he looked steadily at Mrs. Tremain for a minute, to decide whether he should tell her of his disgrace or not.

He saw a sweet, gentle, motherly face, a calm serene forehead, smooth bands of dark hair beginning to turn grey, delicately-arched and pencilled eyebrows, and dark grey eyes, which seemed to shine right into his, eyes which were clear, and unswerving, and truthful, yet full of tender sympathy.

His voice trembled a little, but yet it was a relief to him when he said, with lowered eyelids, and a burning flush on his cheek, 'I have disgraced my father.'

Before long Mrs. Tremain had heard all the particulars of his trouble at school, and had listened sadly to his account of the journey, and of his father's illness. She was sure that it was good for him to talk; if she had known that he had never in his life had such a disburdening, she might have encouraged him still more. She gave him all her sympathy, and when at length he relapsed into silence, it was with a look of less hopeless misery on his face. Mrs. Tremain glanced round the room then, and saw that the meal prepared on the table was untouched.

'I have been keeping you from dinner!' she exclaimed, regretfully.

'No, indeed. I want nothing. I could not eat,' said Donovan, decidedly.

Mrs. Tremain hardly felt surprised as she looked at the tough steak and greasy gravy, now perfectly cold.

'You must eat something,' she said, assuming a gentle authority over him, which he was not at all inclined to resist. 'Give me *carte blanche* with the landlady, and you shall have something you can eat directly. This must have been waiting.'

'Yes, it has been up an hour or two,' said Donovan, wearily, and he threw himself back in an arm-chair, while Mrs. Tremain left the room, returning before long with some hot coffee and a far more appetizing repast. She sat down with him, taking some coffee herself, and inducing him both to eat and to talk; and when at last she was obliged to go, he was really cheered and refreshed.

'Mrs. Farrant will be here to-morrow,' she said, at parting. 'That will be a comfort to you.'

Donovan did not answer. He would not show what his real feeling on the subject was, but only hardened his face, and, thanking Mrs. Tremain for her kindness, wished her good-bye.

CHAPTER IV.

'MY ONLY SON, DONOVAN.'

So drives self-love through just, and through unjust,
To one man's pow'r, ambition, lucre, lust.

POPE.

ON the following evening the little inn-parlour witnessed a very different scene. Donovan, who had known what was coming, had, after a night and day of misery, settled down into a stony speechless sorrow, largely mingled now with bitterness, for the meeting with his mother had been most painful.

The trouble had sharpened Mrs. Farrant, and in the selfishness of her grief she made not the slightest allowance for the feelings of other people. Without intentional cruelty, without indeed thinking at all, she was absolutely merciless. Donovan had tried hard to meet her affectionately. Even his stiff reserve had melted in the greatness and honesty of his desire to comfort her. Anyone not absorbed in self, must have seen and accepted such very real sympathy, but Mrs. Farrant saw nothing, thought of nothing, but wearied with her journey, unnerved by the sudden shock, vented her petulant grief on the only victim at hand.

It was a very grievous scene. On the sofa lay the widow, a

beautiful and still young-looking woman, her face distorted now, however, by passionate sorrow, and wet with tears—that violent stormy grief which is soon spent, and which even already was mixed with angry reproaches. Standing by the window, in an attitude expressing rigid endurance, was the son, his face very still and quiet in contrast to his mother's, but with an indescribable bitterness about it which almost overpowered the sadness. He had learnt quickly that his presence was irritating instead of comforting to his mother. In a sort of proud hopelessness he moved away from her, and stood looking out across the dreary street to the grey sea beyond, while, as if in a sort of dream, he heard all that was going on : the ceaseless drip of the rain, the distant breaking of the waves upon the shore, the weary reiteration of sobs and reproaches from within. Harder and harder grew his face as he listened, just because his heart was anything but hard, and ached and smarted under that 'continual dropping.' How long it went on he had not the faintest idea, but it seemed to him that he had heard many times of his 'disgrace,' had often winced at the mention of his father's name, had silently listened to many unjust accusations, had long felt the grating incongruity of this stormy passion with the silent room of death above. It was a relief when at length, exhausted with her sorrow, Mrs. Farrant fell asleep. He drew nearer then, and stood silently watching her, looked at her soft brown hair, her faultless features, her singularly delicate complexion. It seemed incredible that one so beautiful and gentle-looking could have uttered such cruel reproaches, but it was by no means surprising to Donovan. He had been quite prepared for it, had learnt many years ago that his mother was a mother only in name, that the outgoing love of true motherhood was not in her, that the most he could ever expect for himself or Dot was a ghastly shadow in place of a reality. He had been a fool to think of comforting her! He would waste no more hopes on anything so hopeless. He flung back to the window, yet returned to spread a shawl over her feet.

The wretched evening wore on, Mrs. Farrant awoke, and with scarcely a word went upstairs to bed. Once more the room was lonely and still—infinitely more lonely even than it had been on the previous evening, for now Donovan's whole being was crying out at the injustice of its loneliness. Why, when he would willingly have shown tenderness and love, was he coldly repulsed ? Why was he cut off from all sympathy ? What was the meaning of the pain which had relentlessly pursued him from his very childhood ? To these questions what answer could he make ?—all seemed to him hopeless confusion and injustice. If for a moment his mind did revert to the thought of a Providence ruling over all, it was only to be as quickly repelled by the vision of the God presented to him in his childhood, for it was always to this teaching that he recurred when he allowed the subject to enter his thoughts at all. Mrs. Doery's misrepresentation had left its impress on his mind, while in later years the truths he had heard had always been so resolutely and speedily rejected that they had failed to leave their mark.

The room began to grow intolerable to him ; he rushed out into the open air, and breathed more freely as the cold night wind blew upon him. The rain was still falling fast, but he scarcely noticed it, as he strode on recklessly. The mere mechanical exercise was in itself soothing, and he might have trudged along the muddy road for an indefinite time, had not his attention been attracted by a distant sound of music. Drawing nearer, he found that the house from which it proceeded was Dr. Tremain's, and, hardly knowing what he did, he approached one of the windows, and looked through the half-opened Venetian blind at the scene within.

Not a detail of that picture escaped him. A soft light falling through the opal lamp globe illumined the room, the pale French grey walls, the running oak-leaf patterned carpet, the deep crimson curtains, all harmonized to perfection. Seated at the piano was Gladys Tremain, her bright hair gathered back from her face, and her complexion, which was at times almost too highly coloured, looking most beautiful in the mellow lamp-light. She wore a very simple white dress, and her small soft hands seemed to touch the keys almost caressingly.

Donovan forgot his sorrow for a moment, and felt vexed when, as she stopped playing, the spell which had bound him was for the time broken by a voice which came from within the room.

'Sing something, Gladys ; I'm tired of those old "songs without words,"' and the speaker crossed the room, and came close to the piano, so that Donovan could see he was a boy of about his own age, of slight build and fair complexion, but not sufficiently like Gladys to be any relation, he fancied.

'You dare to grow tired of Mendelssohn!' says Gladys, with a fine show of indignation. 'You boys have no taste whatever; one might as well play to—to——' She paused for a comparison.

'To the heathen Chinee,' suggested her companion. '"What a lot of chop-sticks, bombs, and gongs!"—you remember the song, of course. That's Chinese art, you know.'

Gladys laughed, and there was a merry little squabble carried on, as the two tried to play the air of the old nursery rhyme.

'Well, now, will you sing after all?' said the boy at last; 'we will allow, if you like, that it's a case of pearls before swine.'

'Don't, Stephen,' and Gladys really looked vexed.

'Why, isn't even that allowable? I didn't know you were such a little Puritan.'

'You know I can't bear that kind of thing; it is such a pity to use——'

'A fellow can't be always picking his words—I'm sure it's as good as a proverb now,' interrupted Stephen. 'If you only knew what it was to have such a strait-laced mother as I have, you——'

'Find me a song,' said Gladys, handing him a portfolio, and, though she spoke sweetly, there was a certain grave dignity in her tone.

The choice was soon made, but Donovan was so absorbed in watching Gladys that he scarcely noticed the first verse of the song, until a mournful refrain of 'Strangers yet' recalled him painfully to himself. With strained attention he listened to the remaining verses :—

'After childhood's winning ways,
After care and blame and praise,
Counsel asked and wisdom given
After mutual prayers to heaven,
Child and parent scarce regret
When they part are strangers yet.

'Will it evermore be thus,
Spirit still impervious?
Shall we never fairly stand
Soul to soul and hand to hand?
Are the bonds eternal set
To retain us strangers yet?'

'Absurdly impossible,' was Stephen's comment at the end. 'I had no idea it meant that kind of strangers—very dull too.'

'The song or the parents?' asked Gladys, laughing. 'In either case your answer will be equally rude. Here is papa,' she continued, as Dr. Tremain came into the room. 'I shall tell him what a teaze you are, Stephen; you're really getting worse than Dick.'

'What is that doleful song?' asked the doctor, putting his hand on her shoulder, as he bent down to look at the piece of music. '"Strangers yet!" Who were the strangers?'

'A parent and child, papa, and Stephen declares that it's absurdly impossible.'

'Of course it is!' said Stephen, hotly. 'Why, do you think

D

when my father returns from his voyages that he feels a stranger
to me, or that my mother doesn't know everything about me—
rather too much, perhaps, sometimes.'

The doctor could not help smiling at the rueful tone of the last
sentence.

'Well, Stephen, I think in your case it would be "absurdly
impossible,"' he said, laughingly. 'But I am afraid perfect comprehension between parents and children is not so universal as it
ought to be, or as you seem to think it. Here comes the mother
to give her opinion. But how is this?' for Mrs. Tremain had
in her arms a clinging four-year-old boy in the tiniest of white
night-shirts.

'Jackie had a very bad dream, and the only thing that would
set him right was just to come downstairs and see all the world
again,' she explained, smiling at the general exclamation.

In a moment the suffering Jackie became the hero of the
evening, and was allowed to confide all his terrors to 'papa,' how
a great tiger from the 'Shosical Dardens' had come close to his
bed to eat him up, till just at the supreme moment 'mother'
had heard his screams and had rescued him. A little re-assuring
talk on the safety of tigers' cages, and a laughing affirmative to
the question 'And 'oo is very strong, isn't 'oo?' soon set Jackie's
mind at rest, his sleepy eyelids began to close, and having kissed
everyone with drowsy solemnity, he cuddled up again to his
mother and was carried off to bed.

'There is no doubt that those two understand each other,'
said the doctor, smiling thoughtfully.

'No, indeed!' said Gladys and Stephen, emphatically.

'No, indeed!' echoed Donovan, under his breath, and he
turned quickly away with burning tears in his eyes, unable to
bear the sight of the little home drama any longer.

Mr. Ellis Farrant happened to be in town when the news
of his cousin's death reached him. It was the time of year
when he found that it answered best to be in town, a time when he
was sure of plenty of amusement, and could reckon on getting
most of his dinners out. He was a man without any settled profession, of moderate income, but expensive habits, and, in order
to reconcile these conflicting elements, he found it necessary to
live as much as possible on his friends. It was not until late on
Saturday afternoon that, on returning from his usual saunter in
the park, he found Donovan's letter, with its brief formal intima-
tion of his father's death. Ellis Farrant was startled, awed; he
did not like being confronted with anything so gloomy yet so
inevitable as death, it was a subject he invariably dismissed from

his mind as quickly as possible, and now his cousin had died with an awful suddenness, and Ellis, whether he would or not, found his thoughts turning to his own death, that dismal goal which awaited him in the future. Where should he die, and how, and —and *when*?

His hand trembled a little as he again took up Donovan's letter, and strove to banish the uneasy reflections which were troubling him by a fresh perusal of the startling news; he found himself, however, gazing vacantly at the handwriting, rather than reading the sense conveyed by the firm, clear, somewhat cramped letters. Then his mind wandered off to Donovan himself, perhaps something in the writing reminded him of the clever, strong-willed, self-reliant boy who had so often been his companion. He had been expelled from school, the letter stated, the very absence of further comment or explanation showing how deeply the disgrace had galled the proud nature. Well, he would pass from disgrace to ease and pleasure, for was not he his father's heir? Ellis Farrant reflected for a few minutes on his good luck. Then with a sudden and vehement exclamation, he started to his feet. No, it was not so—he recollected now his cousin's simple will at the time of his marriage,—Donovan was not his father's heir, everything had been left to Mrs. Farrant. It had been little more than ' All to my wife.' He had laughed over the story of the shortest will long ago, he could not recall where or with whom, but he remembered clearly that Colonel Farrant's will had been to that effect, and the remembrance seemed to excite him strangely.

'In another year I shall be forty,' he mused to himself, ' what the world will call a middle-aged man. I hate that term middle-aged; but anyhow, I shall not look it, and I am tolerably—yes, really decidedly handsome.'

He rested his elbows on the mantel-piece and surveyed himself critically in the mirror. In colouring and general outline of face he was sufficiently like Colonel Farrant and Donovan to show near relationship, but his features and expression were entirely different. The eyes of very dark steel-grey lacked the peculiar admixture of brown in the iris, which was so noticeable in Donovan's; they were hard, bold-looking eyes, unpleasant to meet. The firm well-shaped chin was contradicted by a weak mouth, which was only partially concealed by a bristling black moustache. But, in spite of these defects, he was, as he had said, a handsome man, or, at any rate, he was possessed of a certain brilliancy which generally passed for good looks.

Satisfied apparently with his own reflection, he turned at

length from the mirror, and, sitting down to the table, dispatched first a telegram to Donovan announcing his intention of coming to Porthkerran the following day, and, secondly, the advertisement of Colonel Farrant's death to the *Times*, with an elaborately-worded eulogy and feeling description of the grief of the family. After that he relapsed into a profound reverie, from which he only roused himself to calculate what was the probable value of the Oakdene estate.

Donovan's Sunday at Porthkerran was almost as trying a day as the previous one at school had been. Possibly his grief and wretchedness might have induced him to enter the church, had not his recollections of the last Sunday deterred him. Never could he forget the slow torture to which he had then been subjected! The intolerable length of the day, the two services, the sermons with their direct reference to the sin which he had promoted, their unsparing condemnation of the ringleader, the sudden turning of all eyes to his place, the struggle between his sense of shame and his pride, the angry resentment of the injustice and exaggeration. He lived it all over again as he walked gloomily along the Porthkerran cliffs, and the silent repressed indignation did him no good.

It was with his very worst expression that he went to meet Ellis Farrant; his face was dark and proud and cold, yet even then the contrast between the cousins was very marked. Donovan's, though the more hopeless face of the two, had a certain nobility nowhere traceable in Ellis's bold, self-satisfied mien; the one face expressed a restless craving for something beyond self, restrained only by a powerful will, the other expressed little but self-satisfaction, and a sort of defiance and bravado.

Yet the sympathy which Ellis expressed so readily and fluently both to Donovan and to his mother was not altogether artificial; he was by no means heartless, although undoubtedly he was a selfish scheming man, bent upon furthering his own interests. In the pursuance of his own aims, however, he occasionally felt kindly disposed towards others, and he admired, even liked, Donovan.

But on the Monday all was changed. The simple and beautiful Burial Service had fallen with little effect on the ears of the two chief mourners. Colonel Farrant's body had been laid in the little churchyard of Porthkerran. The two cousins and the doctor had returned in silence to the inn, and then, as soon as Donovan was out of earshot, Dr. Tremain took Ellis Farrant aside.

'There is but one more duty, Mr. Farrant, which I have to

discharge, and that is to put you in possession of the will which Colonel Farrant executed just before his death. I should have given it you earlier in the day, only there has been no opportunity.'

'A will—a codicil, I suppose,' said Ellis Farrant, hurriedly taking the sheet of paper from Dr. Tremain, and unfolding it. Though he was weak and impulsive, he was too thorough a man of the world not to have his facial expression in very fair command; he betrayed little but surprise as he read his cousin's most unwelcome change of purpose, and his voice was cool and steady as he again folded the paper and turned to Dr. Tremain. 'I am named as my cousin's sole executor, I see; this must be referred to his lawyer in London. Many thanks to you, doctor, for your considerate help.'

Dr. Tremain rose to take leave, and Ellis, accompanying him to the door, found Donovan in the passage outside, and left him to see the last of the guest.

'We leave early to-morrow,' he began hurriedly, 'so I must wish you good-bye now, Dr. Tremain—thank you for your kindness.'

'I hope we may meet again,' said the doctor, shaking his hand warmly, and looking with grave compassion at the miserably hopeless face before him.

'Will you thank Mrs. Tremain for her kindness to me,' continued Donovan, still with the air of one wearily discharging a duty of courtesy, 'and for the flowers she kindly sent this morning?'

'Certainly, I will give her your message, and when next you come westward I hope we shall see you at Porthkerran. Goodbye!' and the doctor turned away rather sadly, and set out homewards.

Before he had gone far, however, he heard hurrying steps behind, and his late companion once more stood beside him.

'Forgive me,' he said, hoarsely, 'I was cold and ungrateful. I shall not forget your kindness, only now I'm too wretched to feel it. Don't think too hardly of me.' And before Dr. Tremain could do more than show his answer by look and gesture, Donovan was half-way back again to the inn.

During this time Ellis Farrant had been giving vent to his rage and disappointment within the house. That all his schemes should be frustrated by a paltry piece of note-paper, witnessed by a doctor and a servant, was inexpressibly galling. Had the will been elaborately drawn up, and duly besprinkled with meaningless legal phrases, it would not have caused him half the annoy-

ance. It was the absurd littleness, the perfect simplicity of the
thing which chafed him so. Was there no flaw to be detected?
—no, not the very slightest even to his longing eye. Would it
be possible to call his cousin's sanity into question? No, quite
impossible, there could be no doubt of that. There was a moment's
pause in Ellis Farrant's thoughts, a pause in which he fully
realized the defeat of his purpose; he heard Donovan return to
the inn, and at the sound of his footsteps he hastily shuffled the
will into his pocket, but the precaution was needless, for the
footsteps passed by, and presently the door of Donovan's room
was closed and locked. Again Ellis drew out the will and looked
at it fixedly; it was a little crumpled now, he noticed the impression of his Indian-grass cigar-case upon it; what a frail,
trumpery, perishable thing it was—he began to dwell on this
thought with satisfaction instead of bitterness. Then he looked
again at the signatures of the witnesses: 'Thomas Tremain,
Surgeon, Trenant, Porthkerran.' 'Mary Pengelly, Servant, Penruddock Arms Inn, Porthkerran.'

A maid-servant and a doctor living in an obscure Cornish
village, what had he to fear from them? And the boy upstairs?
Why, he knew nothing, and never need know—never *should*
know, and with sudden resolution Ellis tore the sheet of paper in
half, and then in half again. Then a great horror seized upon
him, he turned very cold, and fell back in his chair, shuddering
violently. It was done, and there was no retrieving the deed!
He mechanically fingered and counted the six fragments, looking
at each with a vacant terror. By and by the terror began to
take definite shape. What if the boy were to come down? He
must destroy all remains of this detestable will, of this little heap
of paper which *had been* the will. He was very cold, he would
order a fire, and he crossed the room with unsteady steps to ring
the bell, but paused with the caution of guilt when his hand was
on the bell-rope. Supposing Mary Pengelly should come, supposing she caught sight of these fragments! he felt as if she
would instantly perceive them in the securest hiding-place. No,
he must light the fire himself, and with nervous haste he drew a
box of fusees from his pocket, and with considerable difficulty
succeeded in kindling the damp wood into a blaze. Then he
carefully placed the little heap of paper in the very centre of the
grate, and watched anxiously while gradually the edges curled
upwards, the whiteness was scorched to brown, then to black,
fringed with sparks of red, finally to a swift yellow blaze, while
the last black shreds of Colonel Farrant's will were borne up the
chimney by the sudden draught. Not quite the last, however,

for one fragment had fallen to the side of the fireplace, and floated down on to the fender just as Ellis thought all was over. He snatched it up and would once more have thrown it to the flames had not something forced him to look at it, scorched and half charred as were its edges, he could plainly read the words—'My only son, Donovan.' A swift pang of regret thrilled him for a moment; then a sound in the passage outside renewed his guilty terror, and, stooping down, he held the fragment to the blaze with his own fingers, scarcely feeling the near approach of the hot flames, in his relief that the last vestige of the will was finally disposed of.

CHAPTER V.

REPULSED AND ATTRACTED.

DUCHESS OF YORK.
   'Tetchy and wayward was thy infancy,
   Thy school-days frightful, desperate, wild and furious.

  .   .   .   .   .   .
   What comfortable hour caus't thou name
   That ever graced me in thy company?'
KING RICHARD.
   'If I be so disgracious in your eyes
   Let me march on, and not offend you, madam.'
                    King Richard III.—Act iv. Sc. 4.

In this country the power of the man in and out of society is all but supreme. Wherever he is he overpowers and rules, and shadowy crowds yield to his spell. At his beck they join a crusade, or forswear their own existence. As he dictates they are protoplasms and sporules, or divinities. They throb with his affections, they pant with his desires, and rise to his aspirations. They see as he sees, hear as he hears, and believe as he believes. This is the power for evil or for good.
            The Times. Christmas Day, 1880.

OAKDENE MANOR was a comfortable though somewhat prosaic modern house, built by Colonel Farrant's father on the site of the old Manor House Farm, which had belonged to the Farrants from time immemorial. It stood on the very verge of a beautifully-wooded hill overlooking one of the simple yet lovely valleys which abound in Mountshire, with distant glimpses of blue-grey downs, a view of which it was impossible to tire. The shrubs, which had been planted nearly eighteen years, were now in their full perfection; a long approach, bordered on each side by pines and laurels, led to the pretty creeper-laden porch, while beyond and to the front of the house lay a curiously-planned garden, formed into four terraces cut one below the other on the side of the hill. At the foot of the lowest terrace there was a rather overgrown pond, and beyond this a thick wild wood, sloping down to the valley.

It was a late season, and, though the first week in June was nearly over, the trees were only just beginning to look really green. It seemed a wonderfully slow process this reclothing of Nature, at least to little Dot Farrant it seemed so; but she lay watching the trees so continuously from day to day that, although Mrs. Doery affirmed that she must see them grow, the long expectancy of spring was really more protracted to her than to those who watched the growth and progress less carefully.

Her couch was, as usual, drawn close up to the window on a showery afternoon of early June, and she had contrived to while away the time very pleasantly by watching the sudden changes of storm and sun on the wood below, for Dot had something of an artist's eye, and was quick to mark the effects of light and shade. Happy little observations of this kind were indeed but too often all she was fit for; grievously fragile and delicate, she was, as Mrs. Doery expressed it in broad terms, ' diseased through and through.' And yet it was on the whole a happy and singularly child-like face. Her complexion was pale but very fair, the delicate contour of her features was still so far unharmed by suffering as to show her childish years; her hair was strained back from the forehead and just fell to the shoulder in soft, dark-brown masses, and her eyes were almost exactly like Donovan's, dark hazel, full of pathos, but expressing less painfully the sad unsatisfied craving so noticeable in his.

This was perhaps to be accounted for; to Dot everything she needed, so it seemed to her, was summed up in her brother. Donovan was her friend, her comforter, her teacher, her playfellow; when he was with her, her days were almost uniformly happy. She would bear her pain in patient silence for the sake of pleasing and sparing him; and when he was absent the thought of what he would have liked, and the remembrance of his own patience and control, nerved her still to endure and to copy her ideal. Her love really amounted to worship.

But, deeply as he loved her, Dot could not at all fill this position to Donovan. She was indeed to him both friend and comforter, and, in a sense, also teacher and playfellow, but he was of course the strong one, she leant on him utterly, and he—he had nothing to lean on but himself, or rather would accept nothing.

The strong craving was there, only his pride of will held it in iron fetters.

> 'If the ash before the oak,
> Then you may expect a soak;
> If the oak before the ash,
> Then 'twill only be a splash,'

quoted Dot, merrily, as she lay watching the dripping trees glistening in the sunlight. 'Docry, do you hear? We are going to have a fine summer, for the oaks are twice as forward as the other trees.'

Mrs. Docry was sitting before a large work-basket, darning stockings; by the gloom and sourness expressed on her features, it might have been supposed that she was the constant sufferer, and bright-faced Dot the able-bodied person.

'Well, Miss Dot,' she answered in a depressed voice, 'I'm not much of a believer in such signs as them. The weather is as contrairy as most other things and folks; reckon that it'll do one thing, it's sure to go and do another.'

'I suppose things do go rather contrairily,' said Dot, coining a word upon Mrs. Docry's model. 'Certainly, just now everything seems gone wrong,' and she thought with a sigh of the loss of the father whom she had never learnt to know, and of Donovan's school disgrace.

'I've lived sixty-eight years come Michaelmas,' replied Mrs. Docry, 'and I never knew it otherwise; folks generally get just what they don't want, and when they don't want. There was your poor grandpapa, just as he'd built this house, he was laid up with paralysis, and never so much as saw it finished. There was me myself' (Mrs. Docry was very fond of dilating on her past life), 'just as I'd got used to doing for my poor master, comes Master Donovan to plague the life out of me; and then, as if I hadn't had enough of trouble and worriting, you, who I thought would have been a good baby, turns out sickly and invalidated.' (Mrs. Docry rather confused long words at times.) 'This last month, too, has been a regular chapter of misfortunes; I counted on it that at least Mr. Donovan would have done us some credit at school, seeing that all the folk say he's so clever— too clever, Dr. Simpkins used to say when he was little; and now here he is home again, with nothing but disgrace to bring us.'

'Docry, how can you!' interrupted Dot, with burning cheeks. 'You know how sorry he is—how dreadfully unhappy.'

'Miss Dot,' said Docry, a little severely, 'I've known Mr. Donovan a sight longer than you, and, mark my words, he's no more sorry—than—than you are,' she ended, not very conclusively. 'It always was the way; the more I punished him for his faults, the less sorrow he'd show; he'd only get angry, and that's what he is now. I know well enough that look on his face, and it's never sorrow that brought it there. If you think he's a-grieving over his fault, you're mistaken, Miss Dot.'

Doery had a good deal of shrewd common-sense, and she was not far wrong here; the only pity was that her penetration did not go a little further, and convince her how very much at fault her early system of training had been.

'Oh! but, Doery, they were so hard and unjust,' pleaded Dot, with tears in her eyes. 'How can you wonder that he felt angry? Oh! I can't think how anyone could have thought such things of my dear, dear Dono!'

'Those who do wrong suffer for it,' said Mrs. Doery. 'Mr. Donovan had done harm to the school, and the school was bound to show what it felt. Not but what I'm sorry enough that they've expelled him, for now he can never go into the army, and he's a fine handsome lad, no one can't deny,' and for a moment the old woman's face was softened, for she was not without a certain pride in her troublesome, ill-starred ne'er-do-weel.

'Will people always remember about it, do you think?' questioned Dot, anxiously.

'Always,' said Mrs. Doery, with a sigh; 'he'll be marked by that disgrace like Cain, to his dying day.'

'Who is Cain?' asked Dot, whose bringing up equalled Donovan's in ignorance.

'Cain was a bad man who murdered his brother, and had a mark put on his forehead,' said Mrs. Doery.

'How horrid!' shuddered Dot. 'But I thought you said the other day that it wasn't proper for little girls to hear about murders, when I wanted to hear what cook had shown you about one in the newspaper.'

'There are murders and murders,' said Mrs. Doery, sagely. 'Cain is different from the ones now-a-days; he's—he's—instructive as well as destructive.'

Dot smiled a little, but did not ask for the story; her thoughts had wandered back to Donovan.

'I am sorry, you know, Doery, that people will always remember that Dono was expelled. I did so want them to forget very soon.'

'You won't find that folks will forget, Miss Dot, so don't expect it; a bad beginning is a bad beginning, nobody can't deny, and I've always found that, if people once get a bad name, they keep it. I can't say, either, that I see any signs of Mr. Donovan's turning over a new leaf; he's as obstinate and as headstrong as ever. I've told him many a time since he wasn't higher than that table how "Don't care" came to the gallows, but he was always one for tossing back his head in that haughty way, minding no one in the world but himself. He'll come to no good.'

'Don't say such dreadful things, Doery,' said Dot, between laughing and crying. 'Dono will be "contrairy," as you say the weather is. He will turn out exactly the opposite to what you fancy he will, I am sure. People can't help loving him, and then, you know, he will get happy again. Oh! I am so glad he comes back from London to-day. How long it seems since Cousin Ellis took him away! What is the time, Doery? Do look before you begin that new row. He was to be at the station at four o'clock.'

Mrs. Doery's respectable silver time-keeper pronounced it to be four already, and, though the station was three miles off, Dot insisted on having her couch wheeled to the window facing the carriage drive, that she might watch for him.

In the drawing-room below, Mrs. Farrant was roused by the sound to a remembrance that her son was returning that afternoon.

'Doery really should oil the wheels of Dot's couch,' she reflected, drowsily, with the discomforted feeling of one disturbed in the middle of a siesta. But somehow she could not compose herself to sleep again, though she still lay comfortably on the sofa, allowing her thoughts to roam idly where they pleased.

It was now three weeks since Colonel Farrant's funeral. His widow had returned to Oakdene, and had resumed her former habits of life, not exactly with the courageous 're-beginning' of submission—for it was no very great effort to her—but rather with the acquiescence of an inert mind. The passionate vehemence of her grief had exhausted itself at Porthkerran. It had been an unusual effort to her, for she was not by nature passionate. Her reproachful anger with Donovan, and her long fits of weeping, had worn her out; all bodily exertion was distasteful to her, and this excessive agitation, so very foreign to her nature, had told greatly on her physical health. It was therefore perhaps well for all parties that her inactive mind and dormant affections allowed her so soon to return to her ordinary life, though Donovan, with what seemed like inconsistency, maintained that he would rather have gone through endless repetitions of the stormy scenes at Porthkerran than have witnessed this calm, placid forgetfulness. To his strong and positive nature his mother's character was a complete enigma. The bitter anger was something he could comprehend, though it had wounded him to the quick, but the speedy return to quiet indifference could not possibly be understood by him, or sympathised with, and for that reason it wounded him still more.

And yet it would be hard to blame poor Mrs. Farrant altogether, for her natural temperament and her circumstances had a great deal to do with her failings. The only daughter of a widowed cavalry officer, she had never known anything of home-life. She had married Colonel Farrant almost as soon as she left school, and had passed at once into all the cares and responsibilities of a household, and the pleasures and trials of a military life abroad. At Malta she had been the gayest of the gay, and, though feeling some natural pride in her child, had very little time to notice him at all. In India her health had suffered, and, naturally indolent, she had fallen into the luxurious, semi-invalid ways so hard to break loose from. Then came the return to England, which had been agreed upon on account of her health, and for the last ten years she had led a quiet, indulgent, easy life, enjoying the society to be had near Oakdene in a subdued lazy way of her own, and making one yearly effort, namely, the removal to the London house for the months of May and June. So far as circumstances and natural character can be put forward as an excuse, Mrs. Farrant might reasonably claim a lenient judgment, but no one need be the 'slave of circumstance,' and no nature can be so hopelessly inert, or weak, or bad, that rightly directed and resolute efforts will not reform it. But Mrs. Farrant had never made a resolute effort of this kind. She was one of those people who let themselves drift along the stream of life. She never tried to row, never hoisted a sail, never even touched a steering rope. She had had a sharp, sudden shock; for a moment her quiet course had been interrupted, but now she had resumed it, and allowed herself to drift along placidly as before.

This was the head of the Oakdene household, the influence for good or for evil of the inmates of the Manor; a woman who could best be described by negatives—not good, and yet not exactly bad, not evil intentioned, and yet without a single good motive, not unkind to her children, yet never loving, not in the world's opinion irreligious, yet never penetrating beyond the outer shell of religion. There was only one thing in which she was positive—love of herself. Her dreamy, unregulated thoughts generally hovered round this point of interest; her health, her comfort or discomfort, her dress, her employments, her amusements, and curiously, *one* exception outside herself, her lap-dog. Upon a handsome, bad-tempered, snowy Pomeranian named Fido, she lavished the time and caresses which her children had failed to obtain from her.

On the afternoon in question she lay calmly meditating on the sofa in her usual fashion, meandering on from subject to subject.

'Doery should really oil those wheels. I wonder what nerve is affected so strangely by any sound like that? Perhaps it is the sympathetic nerve. If so, my sympathetic nerve must be very susceptible—very. But all my nerves are susceptible; as Dr. Maclean used to say at Calcutta, "You are all nerves, my dear madam." He was a handsome man, Dr. Maclean, only a little too grey. How pleasant those years in Calcutta were; if it hadn't been for the heat and for my health suffering so, I could really wish to go back there. Charming society it used to be, only one paid for the exertion of going out; the balls were delightful, but I was a martyr to headaches the next day.' An interlude of vacancy terminated by a series of sharp barks from Fido. 'Down, Fido, down! What is it, poor little dog? Ah! he heard wheels. Good little Fido, quite right, little doggie, bark away, only not too near my ears, please! It cannot be a visitor, for I've not sent out my "return thanks." It must be Donovan. I do hope he has come back in better spirits, it is so wearing to me to see him with a gloomy face. Is my cap straight, I wonder?' and she glanced at her reflection in the looking-glass. 'This new cap really suits me very well, only the lappets are so in the way on a sofa. What a quick, sharp step Donovan has, quite a military tread like his poor father's. Ah! he has gone upstairs to Dot's room, so I may as well have my afternoon tea before seeing him.' Another thoughtless interval, this time broken by the entrance of the servant with a little *solitaire* tea-service, and a plate of broken biscuit for Fido. Mrs. Farrant roused herself.

'I forgot to tell Charlotte this morning that Mr. Donovan was expected. Just tell her to get his room ready.'

The page received the message, and retired noiselessly, while Mrs. Farrant stirred her tea, and sighed over the cares and troubles of housekeeping.

In the room above, the 'quick, sharp step' had been listened to with very different feelings. Dot wriggled about on her couch impatiently.

'Oh! Doery, do open the door,' she cried. 'I'm so afraid he will go into the drawing-room. I want so to hear. Yes—no— he is coming upstairs!' and she half raised herself in her excitement.

' Lie still, Miss Dot, and be patient,' said Doery, scrutinizing
the heel of a fresh stocking. 'Dear me ! one would think you
were expecting the Prince of Wales and all the royal family !'

'Here he is ! here he is !' cried Dot, ecstatically. ' Oh !
Dono !' and her little weak arms were round his neck in a minute,
with all the clinging warmth of a childish, half worshipping love.

' Well, little woman,' he exclaimed, after she had released
him, ' how have you been getting on ? You have actually a little
colour in your cheeks for once.'

' Oh ! it is so beautiful to have you back again,' said Dot,
happily. ' It has seemed such a long fortnight ; and how tall
and old you look, Dono. And oh ! you are letting your moustache
grow again. Look at him, Doery.'

Thus reminded of Mrs. Doery's presence, Donovan turned
round hastily to greet his old enemy.

' How are you, Doery ? And how do you think Miss
Dot is ? '

' Thank you, Mr. Donovan, my health is very well,' answered
Doery, precisely, ' And as to Miss Dot, her face is flushed just
from excitement, and nobody can't deny that she's been very
poorly this last week.'

He listened with the wistfulness of one obliged to obtain the
news nearest his heart from a detailer not greatly interested in
the matter. A shade of disappointment and anxiety stole over
his face as he turned to look at Dot, but she soon made him
smile again.

' I am as well as possible now you are come. Last week it
got hot so quickly. Was it hot in London ? And what did you
and Cousin Ellis do ? '

Donovan gave as bright a description as he could of what had
been in reality an unhappy and unsatisfactory time, but he was
not sorry to be interrupted before long by a sound of scratching at
the door.

' It cannot be Fido, because he always barks so at you,' said
Dot, wonderingly.

' No, I think it is my present for you, who has had the impu-
dence to run upstairs before he was called.'

' Your present ! Oh, Dono ! and a live one !'

Donovan opened the door, and admitted a fox-terrier puppy,
whose whines of delight at finding his friend were drowned in
Dot's delighted exclamations.

' Is he for my very own ? Oh ! Dono, what a dear old boy
you are ! What made you think of it ? '

' The fellow tacked himself on to me one day in the Strand,

and refused to go. That's ten days ago now, and, as he's not been advertised for, I thought I'd bring him home to you. Come here, old fellow, and see your new mistress.'

The dog pattered up obediently, and Donovan lifted him on to the couch that Dot might stroke him.

'He's a darling,' said the little girl, rapturously; 'such nice eyes he has, and half his face black and half white, and a white and yellow coat.'

'White and tan,' corrected Donovan. 'He'll be a capital dog when he's full-grown; he's quite young now. What shall we call him? Harlequin?'

'No, that's too long, and it must mean something that's lost and all alone,' said Dot, meditatively. 'Rover would do, only it's so common.'

'Vagabond, Tramp, Waif, or Stray,' suggested Donovan.

'Oh! Waif—that's beautiful, and so nice to say. Does that mean something that's all alone, with nobody to take care of it?'

'Yes, a thing tossed up by chance; it'll just suit the beggar. We must teach him——' he broke off hastily as the door opened, and rose to meet his mother; but their greeting was brief, for a sudden barking, yelling, and howling filled the room, and caused both mother and son to turn hastily.

There stood the handsome Pomeranian in a perfect fury, his tail bristling with wrath, and there, from his vantage-ground on the couch, stood the plucky little Waif, barking vigorously in self-defence. Before Donovan could re-cross the room, Fido had sprang on to the couch and had seized the smaller dog by the ear, while poor little Dot shrank back in terror, adding her cries to the general hubbub. Donovan's first care was to put one of his arms between her and the combatants, and then seizing his opportunity to sweep both dogs on to the floor with the other.

'Fido, Fido! my poor dog! Save him, Donovan; take him from that savage creature,' cried Mrs. Farrant, fairly roused and frightened.

'He's twice the size of the other,' said Donovan; 'he'll maul Dot's poor little puppy to pieces. Leave off, you brute!' and, with a well-directed blow, he drew Fido's attention from the fox-terrier's ear to his own hand, and, after a sharp tussle with the angry animal, succeeded in turning him out of the room.

'Where did this dreadful new dog come from?' asked Mrs. Farrant. 'I never saw a more hideous creature. You surely don't intend to keep it in the house?'

'He shall not be in your way, and Fido will not attack him

again, I should think. He certainly isn't a beauty, but he's of a very good breed,' and Donovan called the dog to him, and began to examine his ear.

'It is all bleeding,' said Dot, piteously; 'and oh! Dono, look at your hand.'

'A souvenir of Fido's teeth,' said Donovan, smiling rather bitterly; for, though as a rule he was exceedingly fond of animals, he had a strange dislike to the Pomeranian—perhaps because it usurped so much of his mother's time and thoughts, perhaps because of the dog's marked aversion to himself.

'Dear me! I hope it won't bring on hydrophobia; I have such a horror of hydrophobia,' said Mrs. Farrant, nervously contemplating the wound from a distance.

'I'll put a hot iron to it, if it will relieve you,' said Donovan, half scornfully, adding, with a touch of malice, 'And, if Fido is mad, a bullet will soon settle him.'

It was an uncalled-for and foolish speech; it touched Mrs. Farrant in her most sensitive part, and widened the gulf between her and her son. He felt it the next minute, and was vexed to have put himself in the wrong.

'You are very inconsiderate,' said Mrs. Farrant, plaintively. 'You know what a companion Fido is to me, and yet you can speak so unfeelingly about his death. And the poor dog may be hurt and suffering now. I must find him at once.'

Donovan opened the door for her, just pausing to see Fido run to meet her safe and unharmed; then he turned again into Dot's room, muttering under his breath, 'Managed to put my foot into it, as usual!'

Mrs. Doery offered to bind up his hand, while Dot, with all the colour flown from her cheeks, watched sympathetically, observing at last, after a long silence,

'It is very odd, Dono, but you and mamma never do like the same things.'

It had been an unfortunate meeting, there was no doubt of that, the feud between the dogs seemed likely to destroy what little peace there ordinarily was in the household. Everything was as usual against him, so Donovan bitterly complained, he never got a fair start in anything. It was with a very clouded brow that he went down to dinner—the *tête-à-tête* dinner with Mrs. Farrant. It was not that he had expected great things, he knew the return would be painful; but half unconsciously when away from his mother she always slipped back into a sort of faint resemblance to his childish ideal; with him it was the very reverse of the proverb—'*Les absens ont toujours tort.*' Absence toned down his mother's failings, magnified her good points. Thus at every fresh meeting the sense of loss was borne in upon him with new force, and he was invariably sore-hearted, restless, and ill at ease. This evening, too, he was vexed with himself, and, with the perverseness of a proud nature, he showed his vexation not by trying to make amends for his unguarded speech by extra courtesy, but by becoming silent, and grave, and constrained. Perhaps it was scarcely to be wondered at that, on returning to the drawing-room after this singularly dull and spiritless meal, Mrs. Farrant should at once sink into an easy-chair and become engrossed in a new novel. Donovan stayed only a few minutes, his mother never looked up, Fido growled at him; he resolved to go up at once to Dot. But even this was denied him. Mrs. Doery met him at the head of the stairs like a dragon—he could not see Miss Dot, it was impossible; she had been very much upset indeed with all the excitement and noise, and Mrs. Doery had just managed to get her to sleep.

Donovan slowly walked downstairs again. Alone, with nothing to fall back upon, with a miserable sense of present injustice, and a past from which he was always trying to escape, the quietness of the house seemed unbearable to him. He must go somewhere, do something to drown these miserable thoughts, to fill this wretched emptiness. The servant was in the dining-room clearing the table; he suddenly made up his mind.

' Tell Jones to saddle the cob at once.'

The order was given briefly and decidedly; he turned on his heel, hesitated one moment, then crossed the hall to the drawing-room.

' I am going to ride over to Greyshot, mother—can I do anything for you ? '

' Nothing, thank you,' said Mrs. Farrant, drowsily ; then, half rousing herself, ' You'll not be late, Donovan, because the servants don't like sitting up.'

' I shall not be late,' he repeated, mechanically, as he glanced round the prettily-furnished room, comparing it with that other brightly-lighted room which he had looked into not very long before. Such contrasts were dangerous in his present state of mind ; he closed the door, and paced up and down the hall, fiercely flicking at his boots with the end of his whip. Then his horse was brought round, and, mounting hastily, he rode off in the direction of the neighbouring town.

The cool evening air and the peaceful summer twilight were in themselves soothing. Donovan was neither artistic nor imaginative, but yet such things had a certain influence over

E

him, and the beauty, perhaps still more the peacefulness of the
scene, quieted for a time the bitter inward cry. But it could be
only for a time; his restless misery was far too great to be subdued by any outward agency; he soon fell back into his habitual
reverie of gloomy dissatisfaction. How perplexing and useless
life seemed to him!—the past how full of pain and failure, the
present how unjustly empty of all that could be called happiness,
the future how dreary and hopeless! He put his horse into a
hand-gallop, and tried to stifle his thoughts—tried to think of
anything in the world but his own wretchedness, but without
success, his mind was self-centred, his thoughts naturally turned
to that centre. He could force himself for a time to think of
other things, but there was always an under-current of morbid
discontent colouring his views of everything.

It was in this state of unavailing mental struggle that he
reached Greyshot. It was now between eight and nine in the
evening, and the traffic of the day was nearly over, the shops
were closed, or in the act of closing, and the pavements were
crowded with people belonging to the poorer classes, tired hard-
worked men and women, either returning from their employment,
or lounging about in the cool of the evening for the sake of
change and refreshment.

Greyshot was rather a gay place, and, though the season fell
later in the year, the streets had been fairly full that afternoon,
when Donovan had passed through them on his way from the
station to Oakdene. He was struck with the contrast between
the afternoon and evening crowd. Fashionable, well-dressed,
smiling idlers at the one time; tired, hard-featured, shabby toilers
at the other. Here was fresh injustice, he said, with his usual
hasty judgment and strong conviction. He almost hated himself
for riding at ease through the throng of tired pedestrians; could
only reconcile himself to it by remembering his many grievances,
and surmising that the poorer street passengers were better off
than he in many ways. He did not bring the same argument to
bear on the question of the afternoon promenaders, or remember
that the evening throng at least had the satisfaction of using
their life, while the idlers—perhaps he himself—were simply
abusing it.

Still brooding over this injustice in the different lots of men,
he reached the town-hall, and reined in his horse for a minute
that he might look at the various placards. He saw with relief
that something unusual must be going on that night, for the hall
was lighted, and a pretty continuous stream of people, chiefly
men, were passing up the broad flight of steps. 'Grand Con-

cert on Wednesday Evening !' no, that was the Wednesday in
the following week; a 'Rose Show !' the next day ; ah ! here
it was. 'This evening, at 8.30, Mr. Raeburn will deliver a
Lecture, in the Town Hall, on "The Existence of a God—
Science *versus* Superstition."' Donovan looked at his watch ; it
was exactly the half-hour. He hastily rode on to the nearest
inn, put up his horse, and, returning, passed swiftly up the steps
and into the hall.

The place was crowded with men, chiefly artisans and
mechanics, though with a sprinkling of the more highly educated. Donovan glanced first at the eager, listening throng, and
then instinctively his eyes followed theirs to the platform at the
further end of the room, and were riveted as by a magic attraction on the speaker. The fascination was instantaneous and
complete. He saw before him a tall, powerful-looking man,
with masses of tawny hair overshadowing a very striking face—
a face which, in spite of its rather austere lines, still allowed
play to a variety of expressions : to burning zeal, to infinite sadness, occasionally to withering sarcasm.

Luke Raeburn was, before all things, a strong man, and in
looking at him specialities sank away into insignificance. His
deep-set earnest eyes, his firm uncompromising mouth attracted
little notice, because the whole man was pervaded by a marvellous force, a concentration of energy which carried all before it.
His voice was at once deep and powerful, aided by no theatrical
gestures, but made particularly winning by its mellowness, its
perfect modulations, its thrill of intense earnestness. All these
were powerful accessories to the lecture itself. They influenced
Donovan undoubtedly, but it was not the voice or the 'presence'
of the man which stirred his soul so strangely. The very first
sentence which fell on his ear forced him to listen as though his
whole life depended on it. 'I can find, and you can give me, no
proof of God's existence.' The words caused an electric thrill of
sympathy in his heart. He stood motionless, quite unconscious
of all around, his whole being absorbed in the argument of the
lecturer—this man, who, through the firmness of his convictions,
was spending his life in trying to overthrow what he termed the
'mischievous delusion of popular Christianity.'

To Donovan, with his miserable sense of injustice, every word
seemed a relief, although it was only a more vigorous repetition
of his own cry. But in this lay the secret of its influence. The
lecturer was putting into words, and clothing with marvellously
able arguments, all his own thoughts and opinions. To some of
the listeners the force and fascination of the lecture lay in the

E 2

novelty of the ideas it conveyed, but with Donovan it was otherwise. The lecturer's beliefs exactly coincided with all his own ready-formed notions, and perhaps no idea is more powerfully attractive than that which, being at the same time higher and more subtly argued than your own crude previously-formed judgment, yet in the main corresponds with it. A speedy sympathy is established; the pride of the less gifted mind is gratified; the great powerful intellect agrees with it, has experienced its doubts, has felt its miseries. Donovan felt himself one with the speaker, and he was so very, very rarely agreed with anyone that the sudden consciousness of unity and sympathy was almost intoxicating in its novel delight. He listened breathlessly to the clear, satisfying arguments, and when, at the end of an hour, the lecturer brought his address to a close, and invited answers and objections to what he had said, Donovan felt giddy and exhausted, half inclined to leave the hall, and yet unable to go while the man who had fascinated him so strangely remained. During the brief pause that ensued a middle-aged mechanic, who was seated at the end of one of the benches not far from the place where Donovan stood, rose to go. Donovan moved forward to take his place, and for a minute, owing to a fresh influx of people, the two were kept facing each other. A shade of pity crossed the rough features of the mechanic as he looked at the flushed, excited face of the boy, so young and yet so full of unrest.

'My lad,' he said, in a low tone, 'I see you're sore moved, but take my advice and come away. Yonder man speaks grand words, but it's not the truth.'

Donovan was too much of a Republican to be the least offended by this speech, but he was little accustomed to receive good advice, still less accustomed to put it in practice. He hardly gave it an instant's consideration, so firmly was his mind set upon hearing Raeburn speak once more.

'One doesn't get this chance every day,' he answered. 'I must hear the end of it.'

And so the warning friend passed by, and Donovan, having rejected the guidance sent, took the vacant seat, and waited with some impatience for the reply of the first objector.

The speeches of the opponents were limited to ten minutes, too ample an allowance, Donovan thought, for the first speaker was insufferably dull and wordy. After the clear, terse, powerful sentences of the lecturer, anything so verbose was at once irritating and bewildering, and the minds of the audience, which had been strained to the very highest tension during Raeburn's address, now began to wander. Donovan again found his gaze riveted on

the lecturer's face, and gave a sigh of relief when the ten minutes'
bell was struck in the middle of one of the meandering sentences,
before the speaker had made a single point. After another brief
pause, a tall, nervous-looking clergyman mounted the platform,
and with evident reluctance, conquered only by a sense of duty,
began to speak. His voice was weak, but he was very much in
earnest, almost painfully so, and real earnestness felt and expressed cannot fail to arouse interest. He prospered well at first,
yet his argument was not in the least conclusive to Donovan's
mind, and he was not surprised when, at the close of the ten
minutes, Luke Raeburn drew attention to an illogical statement
which had escaped the speaker. An earnest parting protest and
attempted explanation were not of much use, for Raeburn re-
sponded with perfect courtesy but crushing logic, and the clergyman went back to his place with a terribly grieved look. Donovan
saw it all, was sorry for the man, and half won over by his
humility, his evident sorrow, and by sympathy with his sense of
failure. For a moment he wavered, or rather allowed the arguments of the other side to recur to him, but it was only for a
moment. The third speaker mounted the platform with no diffidence; he was a large, solid, self-satisfied man, with a voice which
made the hall echo again. Evidently he thought noise would
make up for want of matter, for he scarcely tried any steady line
of argument. He was vehement, positive, illogical, and, after a
violent tirade against the wickedness of atheism, finally turned
round upon the lecturer, and hurled the most insolent questions
at him. Donovan was disgusted alike at his vulgarity and the
worthlessness of his speech. Raeburn was at once invested with
the dignity of a martyr, or, at any rate, of an unjustly-used man,
and his sharp and powerful retort delighted Donovan as much as
it irritated the vehement objector. The contest ended grievously,
for—the chairman refusing to give him any more time—the
speaker hopelessly lost his temper, became violent and abusive,
and quitted the platform and the hall in a towering rage. It was
a sad display for one who professed to be an ardent supporter of
Christianity. Luke Raeburn felt that nothing could have weakened
the cause more successfully, and naturally he did not hesitate to
use the argument in favour of his own views.

There was a prolonged pause after the exit of the angry man;
no other objectors cared to come forward, however, and at length
Raeburn stood up for his final speech. The clear, quiet, impres-
sive tones fell like rain after a thunder-storm upon the rapt
listening men. Donovan scarcely breathed; he had never in
his whole life heard anything so attractive. The cool penetrating

words, the sarcastic yet dignified allusions to the last speech, the wonderfully able arguments, were irresistible to him.   This man was in earnest, terribly in earnest, and he had the grave calmness of perfect conviction.

What was he upholding, too ?   Self-restraint, self-sacrifice, temperance, truth at whatever cost.   There was, indeed, much that was noble and elevating in his speech—only the one great blank, which to Donovan was no blank at all.

It was over at last, the assembly broke up, and Donovan groped his way down the street, and, mounting his horse, rode back to Oakdene in the starlight.   He felt wonderfully stimulated by what he had heard, roused to enthusiasm for the man, for the views he held, for the life of toil for the general good which he not only recommended, but himself lived.   Luke Raeburn had influenced him greatly, but it was the speech of the self-satisfied opponent which sent him home that night a confirmed atheist, a bitter-hearted despiser of Christianity.

CHAPTER VI.

AUTUMN MANŒUVRES.

> Love seeketh not itself to please,
> Nor for itself hath any care,
> But for another gives its ease,
> And builds a heaven in hell's despair.
>
> WILLIAM BLAKE.
>
> Give a dog a bad name, and hang him.
>
> *Proverb.*

ELLIS FARRANT had taken Donovan up to town on the pretext of arranging various matters of business, but he had been careful to leave many things unattended to, as he was anxious to have an excuse for a speedy visit to Oakdene.   His guardianship was likely to prove a very convenient aid in the furtherance of his scheme, for what could be more natural than that he should frequently go down to inspect his young wards, and what could offer more convenient opportunities for winning his way with Mrs. Farrant than such visits ?   A little time, however, must be allowed to pass first.   Ellis made arrangements for staying in town till the middle of July, and resolved to go down to Oakdene then for as long a visit as seemed advisable.

His arrival really pleased and roused Mrs. Farrant, for it must be owned that Oakdene had not been the liveliest of homes during the summer. Visitors of course had not been received, Donovan had been unusually taciturn and moody, and though the favourite Fido, and the unfailing succession of new books, and the comfortable sofa by the open window, rendered life bearable, any interruption to such quiet monotony was a relief even to one so indolent as Mrs. Farrant.

To Donovan the arrival of his cousin brought a strange mixture of annoyance and satisfaction. He too was glad of an interruption to the dreary quiet of the house, but nevertheless Ellis managed to irritate him not a little. The nominal business matters which had formed the excuse for the visit were put forward from time to time, but neither mother nor son was businesslike, and Ellis used to let the conversation float on quietly into other channels, so that very little was really arrived at. He was a clever, shrewd man, and his visit was a long series of manœuvres. He never lost sight of his two great aims, the first was to win the regard and confidence of Mrs. Farrant, and to secure this he studied most carefully her character and tastes; the second was to induce Donovan to lead as inexpensive a life as might be during the time of his guardianship. What became of him after he was of age he neither cared nor thought of, for before that time he hoped to have won Mrs. Farrant's hand.

It was about two or three days from the beginning of his visit that he first began to question Donovan cautiously as to the future. They were out riding when he resolved to risk the attempt.

'Beautiful country about here,' he remarked, carelessly.

'Yes,' replied Donovan, laconically; he did not care to show any interest in such a remark from one who evidently cared nothing in reality for scenery.

'Much hunting in the neighbourhood?'

'No; it's not a hunting county.'

'But you have good shooting, I hear.'

'Oh! yes, we can have any amount of that. Won't you come down for it this autumn?'

'Thanks. If I have time I should like nothing better. You will be here, of course?'

'Yes, I suppose so,' said Donovan, rather hesitatingly.

Ellis Farrant felt a little uneasy. Had the boy made up his mind to go to the university? Would he want to enter any expensive profession? He must find out, and, if so, try to put some reasonable obstacle in the way.

'You have found these months a little dull, I expect, but

next year you'll be up in town for the season—it'll be very different.'

'Life's disgusting everywhere,' said Donovan, gloomily.

'No, no,' replied the man of the world, lightly. 'There's plenty of enjoyment if you look out for it. Cheer up, my boy, you let yourself brood over things too much. "Let bygones be bygones," and face the future, and let your guardian know plainly what you want.'

The speech sounded frank and kindly. Donovan involuntarily came a little out of his shell.

'I don't know that there's anything I want,' he said slowly, 'and yet I want everything. Did you ever feel as if nothing in the whole world were worth a fig, as if nothing could ever satisfy you?'

A perplexing question! Why did the perverse fellow begin to moralize on abstract subjects, just when he wanted to arrive at plain facts?

'I know quite well what you mean,' he replied, glibly. 'You will soon live it down. I think you should mix more with companions of your own age.'

He felt that this was a hazardous suggestion, but ventured it with his customary boldness.

'I hate fellows of my own age,' said Donovan, shortly.

'You are a misanthrope, I'm afraid,' said Ellis, breathing more freely. 'You would not like to go to Oxford or Cambridge, I suppose?'

'No, certainly not.'

'And you are not exactly—not passionately—fond of work?' Donovan smiled a little.

'Well, no, I can't say I am.'

'You would not like to be a barrister or a—parson?'

'I?' cried Donovan, in amaze. 'In all conscience—no!'

'There is no need, not the slightest,' said Ellis. 'In fact, I don't think you're in the least suited for any profession. You can live on here very comfortably. No doubt your mother will make you a handsome allowance when you're of age; for, though you are not exactly your father's heir, it will come to much the same thing in the end.'

'Yes, I suppose so,' said the unconscious Donovan.

'I should rather like you to do a little reading, however,' continued Ellis. 'I must not forget that you are my ward, you know. What do you say to going in to some tutor at Greyshot two or three times a week?'

'I don't mind. I will do so, if you wish it. How would a

travelling tutor be? I must say I should like to spend a few months abroad.'

An inconvenient and expensive project! If Donovan were away, he could not come down to Oakdene so easily. But Ellis was too far-sighted to give a definite refusal to the request.

'Well, we will think of it,' he said, quite in his pleasantest manner. 'I'm glad you told me what was in your mind. We can talk it over with your mother.'

The two relapsed into silence after this, Ellis trying to think of reasonable objections to this new idea, Donovan sketching out in his mind the plan of his tour on the continent. He longed inexpressibly for change of scene, and travelling offered very strong attractions to his restless mind.

But a sudden revulsion of feeling came before long. As they rode down the long, shady drive, and dismounted at the door of the Manor, he heard a childish voice calling him, and, looking up, he saw Dot's little pale face eagerly watching him from her window.

He mounted the stairs very slowly, struggling hard with himself. Dot would certainly miss him very much, would be much happier if he did not go, and yet the craving within him for change was almost irresistible. Oakdene began to feel like a prison to him. Selfishness, or, as he called it, common-sense, whispered that it was mere folly to think he could always be tied down to one place. It would be narrowing, cramping, bad for his health. The absurdity of thinking of this, however, struck him with sudden force as he entered Dot's room. How could he think of himself so much, when she lay on the same weary couch day after day, and yet contrived to be so patient!

'I'm so glad you've come back, Dono,' she exclaimed. 'Doery's been down in the housekeeper's room for hours, and Waif and I have been so dull.'

The loneliness rose up before him vividly—months and months of it. At the same time a glorious vision of life abroad —Italy, Switzerland, mountains, freedom! He was quite silent, but Dot was accustomed to his taciturn moods, and chattered on contentedly.

'And poor Waif, you forgot to take him with you, and he was so miserable when he heard you ride off, he scratched at the door and whined dreadfully, and I couldn't of course get up to let him out, so at last he came back very sadly with his tail between his legs, and cuddled up to me for comfort. Do you know, Dono, I believe he begins to love you as I do, almost.'

'And you don't cry when I go out riding,' said Donovan, smiling.

'No, only when you go quite away; when you used to go back to school, and when Cousin Ellis took you away last time.

'What a silly little Dot! What makes you cry?'

'Why, because I love you so,' said Dot, wistfully. 'And everything seems so horrid when you're away. Will you have to go away again, do you think? Will Cousin Ellis and the lawyers want you any more?'

'Oh! no, I shall not be going away again,' he said, in rather a forced voice. Then, after a pause: 'I say, Dot, this room is stifling. Shall I open the other window?'

She assented, and he crossed the room quickly, threw up the sash, gulped down a mouthful of fresh air, and registered a silent vow that he would never leave her.

'I wonder what makes your forehead look so battered to-day, resumed Dot, as he sat down beside her again. 'It always reminds me of a bent penny I had for a long time. And some days the bend in the middle seems to show more. I think it's on the days when you don't talk much.'

Donovan laughed heartily, shook off his taciturnity, and did his best according to Dot's principles to straighten his brow.

'A phrenologist once told me that my forehead meant all sorts of things: mathematical ability, reasoning, and music, but he was sadly out, poor man, in that last, for I haven't a grain of music in me.'

'I wish you had,' said Dot, 'because I like it so much, and the hand-organs so very seldom come.'

'Shall I get one, and grind away in the passage?'

'That would be always the same one. We should get so tired of the tunes.'

'Yes,' said Donovan, laughing again. 'Don't you remember the story of the organ-grinder who somehow came in to some money, and the first thing he did was to rush frantically at his organ with, "Bother! *you* shall never go round again," and smash it to pieces.'

Dot laughed long and merrily.

'I wish you could play the piano as Cousin Adela used to. It sounded so nice coming up from the drawing-room.'

'Would you really like it?' said Donovan. 'I will try to learn then. We'll have a piano over from Greyshot, and it can be put up here.'

'Oh! Dono, how delightful! But won't it be dull for you, as you don't like music? And do you think you'll be able to learn?'

'We'll have no end of fun over it,' he replied, cheerfully.

'And as to being able—I believe we're able to do anything we've a will for.'

That evening, after Mrs. Farrant had left the dinner-table, Donovan relieved his guardian's mind by one of his quick abrupt speeches.

'On thinking it over, I find I had better not go abroad.'

'Oh! just as you like, my dear fellow,' said Ellis, trying to conceal his satisfaction. 'Most happy to advance you the necessary funds, you know. I should think though that, as you say, it would be better to stay here. Your mother will be glad to have you.'

Donovan bit his lip, and did not reply, and Ellis, well aware that he had touched on a sore subject, changed the conversation. His ward's decision was convenient. For once he must be careful to please and humour him a little. So he renounced for a time the pleasure of irritating his victim, and they spent a very amicable evening over the billiard-table.

It is an undisputed fact that one piece of villany invariably leads to others. When Ellis Farrant, in a moment of anger and disappointment, had destroyed his cousin's will, he never once thought of all it would lead to, but little by little he began to realise that a good deal of plotting and scheming would be necessary, and perhaps a few trifling deceptions and injustices, before he could profit by his crime. He was relieved to find that the coldness between the mother and son still existed, for it was, of course, all in his favour. He had rather dreaded the effects of those months of quiet intercourse; but all had gone as he wished. Mrs. Farrant did not in the least understand Donovan, he was not in any sense a comfort to her, therefore there was all the more hope that she might be led to confide in Ellis, that he might become a necessary part of her existence. During this visit he was obliged to be kind and conciliatory to his ward, and was too prudent to show any marked attentions to Mrs. Farrant, but he succeeded in enlivening the house wonderfully, and received a pressing invitation to come down in the autumn, bringing his sister Adela with him. He remained till the 12th of August, and then went up to the North for grouse-shooting, well satisfied with his success at Oakdene.

The Manor was not a little dull after he left. Mrs. Farrant, to relieve the monotony, sent out her cards, and found some slight occupation in receiving the visits of her neighbours and acquaintance. Donovan rode in to Greyshot three times a week to his tutor's, studied 'Mill's Logic,' and worked hard at his music. Strangely, although he was really no lover of the art, he found a peculiar satisfaction in working even at the mechanical exercises; his master scarcely knew what to make of a pupil who, with very little actual talent, surmounted difficulties so quickly, and showed such untiring perseverance. Indolent as he seemed, he could yet show the most indefatigable zeal when he had a sufficient motive, and, with a view to pleasing Dot, he bent his whole will to the work.

With the exception of this satisfactory effort, the autumn was a very painful one to him. As soon as his mother began to receive visitors again, he could not fail to become aware of the marked coldness with which almost everyone treated him. He had never had any special friends in the neighbourhood, but now he noticed that old acquaintances who had formerly been civil and friendly looked askance at him; he was under a cloud, he had lost his good name. It was not much to be wondered at, perhaps, and yet it seemed cruelly hard that he should be thus cut off from all intercourse with those better than himself. The cautious world said, with its usual prudence, that it would never do not to show marked disapproval of disgrace and wrong-doing. Donovan Farrant had been expelled from school for most dishonourable behaviour (his crimes were by this time absurdly exaggerated by report), it was quite impossible that he could be allowed to mix with the immaculate sons of the neighbouring homes. Intercourse must be as much as possible discouraged; the acquaintance was most undesirable. A young man who never went to church, who had been seen at one of Racburn's lectures, who was dangerously handsome, and unmitigatedly bad, could not be visited. The neighbours all tried to ignore his existence ; he was either entirely cut, or treated with the coldest and most distant civility.

Misanthrope as he was, Donovan felt this treatment keenly, and resented it. It was hard, and cruel, and unjust ; he used it, as he used everything else at that time, as an argument against Christianity. Nor did his mother make matters pleasanter to him. She, too, found out the coldness with which he was treated, and it vexed her; one or two of the more kind-hearted neighbours referred delicately to the subject, and, though Mrs. Farrant paid little attention to her son's doings as a rule, this roused her to remonstrate with him.

'Donovan,' she said, in her complaining tone one evening, 'I really wish you would be more careful how you go on. Mrs. Ward was here to-day, and she said she was extremely sorry to hear that you had attended some shocking infidel lecture at Greyshot. Is it true that you went?'

'Perfectly, barring the adjectives,' replied Donovan, crossing the room, and resting his elbow on the mantel-piece.

'But really you should not do such things,' said Mrs. Farrant, plaintively. 'What made you think of going?'

'I wished to hear Luke Raeburn's views,' said Donovan, still keeping his face steadily turned towards her.

'It is absurd for a boy of your age to think of such things. What can you understand about his views?'

'More than I can of any other views. But I'm no Secularist —I don't care enough for the human race.'

Mrs. Farrant wandered off to another grievance.

'Well, I really wish you wouldn't get yourself so talked about; it's very unpleasant for me. Why won't you come to church on Sunday, and be like other young men?'

'Because, whatever I am, I'll not be a hypocrite,' said Donovan, with some sharpness.

There was silence for a few minutes after this. Mrs. Farrant fanned herself, and Donovan tormented the feathers of an Indian hand-screen. At last, with a rather softened expression, he continued—

'I'm sorry, mother, if I spoke rudely, but that is a thing I cannot do to please anyone. If you dislike my going to hear Raeburn so much, I will not do it again.'

'I only wish you not to make yourself a byword to the neighbourhood,' said Mrs. Farrant, peevishly. 'I do not care what you do as long as you behave respectably.'

'No, you care for nothing, I see, as long as people hold their tongues,' said Donovan, with one of his rare and curiously sudden bursts of passion. 'Is it wonderful that I should be going to the dogs, when this is all you give me? What else can you expect?'

She did not in the least understand him, but his vehemence terrified her; she burst into tears.

'It is very unkind of you to speak so angrily; you know how anything of this sort upsets me,' she sobbed. 'I did think that the only son of a widow was expected to show some feeling for his mother, and you—you are only a grief and a disgrace to me.'

He was softened in an instant, tried to take her hand in his, and spoke as gently and tenderly as he would have spoken to Dot.

'Forgive me, mother—I was to blame. But indeed, if you would let me, I would try to be more to you."

He would have said more, but words never came easily to him, and he felt half choked now with emotion.

'You are so inconsiderate,' said Mrs. Farrant, drying her

eyes. 'I'm sure I wish your guardian were here; he at least would have some sympathy with me. I wish you would try to copy him a little more.'

The reference to one whom Donovan so little liked or respected was very trying; he drew back.

'It is just as I told you at Porthkerran,' continued Mrs. Farrant. 'You never think of anyone but yourself; you are always bringing trouble and sorrow to others.' Then, looking up, and seeing that Donovan in his agitation was breaking the feathers of the hand-screen, she sharpened her voice, 'Cannot you even help destroying the things your poor father brought back?'

He did not attempt to answer. What was the use of speaking? What was the use of trying to bridge over the hopeless gulf between them? It was more in despair than in passion that he flung down the screen and strode out of the room.

After this there was peace for some little time, if such dreary aimless existence could be called peace. There was, at any rate, no open disagreement. Mrs. Farrant was too inert and Donovan too self-restrained to admit of frequent quarrels between them; they lived on in quiet coldness, meeting at meal times, talking on indifferent subjects, then parting again, each to resume his or her separate life. There were faults, perhaps, on both sides; a resolute and continuous effort from either must have broken down such an unnatural state of things. But neither of them made such an effort. Mrs. Farrant, even had she thought of it, would have been too indolent to persevere; Donovan had tried twice and thrown up the attempt, at once too proud and too hopeless to resume it.

In October Ellis Farrant came according to his promise, bringing his sister Adela with him. She was some years his junior, and as she had the same class of good looks and general brilliancy as her brother, and dressed fashionably, she still passed for a 'young' lady, although she was considerably over thirty. Ellis had not introduced her to Oakdene without a special reason. She of course knew nothing of the depth of his schemes, but he trusted her with enough to make her a valuable ally.

'Now, this is how matters stand,' he had said to her, as they were driving from Greyshot to Oakdene. 'Mrs. Farrant is as dull as she well can be in this hole of a place, and I want to have plenty of opportunities for letting her feel that I can enliven it. Do you understand me, or must I speak more plainly?'

His sister laughed and shrugged her shoulders.

'Do not trouble yourself, I understand well enough. You

wish to be beforehand with the army of suitors who are sure to attend upon a pretty, rich widow, by no means past her youth.'

'Exactly,' said Ellis, rubbing his hands with satisfaction 'Last time I was here I could do but little, it was too early days, for one thing, and then there was the boy to be looked after; but now I want you to engross him a little, and set me at liberty—do you see?"

Adela Farrant laughed again.

'You cunning Ellis! You have entrapped me into a dull country-house just to further your own ends, and then you set me down to amuse a schoolboy.'

'Pardon me, but he is by no means a boy,' said Ellis. 'He is, or considers himself, all sorts of things, a philosopher, a radical, an atheist, and, joking apart, he really is old for his years. You may find him a little stiff and haughty at first, but you'll soon get to know him, and he'll give you some amusement; besides, he's handsome—very—an Apollo—an Adonis.'

'And in his nineteenth year!' concluded Adela, with a gesture of contempt. 'However, I'll try to amuse him, out of regard for you. Why, here we are at the Manor, and there *is* your Apollo of the clustering curls at the door. What a grave saturnine face! but you're quite right, he's very good-looking. Roman, not Greek, though. Augustus Cæsar come to life again.'

The first evening was, according to Ellis Farrant's views, a perfect success. He had free scope for conversation with Mrs. Farrant, and she grew quite merry and talkative under the combined influence of his attentions and his sister's animation and gaiety.

'It is so pleasant to hear fresh voices,' she said at dinner time. 'I grow very tired of *tête-à-tête* dinners with Donovan.'

This was exactly what Ellis wished, it was quite an effort to conceal his satisfaction. He looked at the young host at the head of the table, and wondered how he would enjoy being ousted from his position.

Adela's work was not quite so easy. She found Donovan very grave, almost repellent, not at all inclined to be more than coldly courteous. She persevered, however, and, being clever and really good-natured, she gradually won her way. Nor was she so dull as she had fancied would be the case. The haughty *nil-admirari* spirit of her special charge rather attracted her. She found herself really anxious to win his good opinion, and set herself to find out his likes and dislikes. And Donovan really liked her in a manner, was grateful for her kindness, and felt a sort of relief in having a bright, talkative, pleasant woman in the house.

When Ellis did not care to go out shooting, Adela generally proposed a ride, and so managed to engross her young cousin for two or three hours; in the evening, too, she would keep him turning over the leaves of her music in the back drawing-room, leaving her brother to amuse Mrs. Farrant, and her light, meaningless talk generally sufficed to prevent one chance of their being interrupted by Donovan.

Sometimes, however, her conversation jarred on his mind. One afternoon when Adela in her light fawn-coloured dress was sauntering round the garden, gathering a few late roses, with her usual cavalier in attendance, their talk turned upon rather graver matters than was ordinarily the case.

'What a pretty view that is of the church tower,' she exclaimed. 'I should like to sketch it, such a tiny grey little place it is! but really I was quite surprised last Sunday to find it a regular resort of fashion, the toilettes were amazing, quite a study; your mother says that the people come to it from Greyshot, that they are attracted by the surpliced choir and the chanting. It seems so odd to think of things of that sort being novelties; you are dreadfully behind the world here in Mountshire.'

'No great loss perhaps in those matters,' said Donovan.

'What a prosaic mind you have!' said his cousin, lightly. 'And, by-the-by, that reminds me, I meant to take you to task before. Last Sunday I looked round expecting to find you ready to carry my prayer-book, and behold! you were nowhere to be seen. Your mother says you never do go to church. How is that? it is really very shocking, you know.'

'One can't profess what one does not believe,' said Donovan, gravely.

Adela passed on into the greenhouse and cut the last rose there before replying; then, joining him again, she said, in her light half laughing tone,

'You men are really dreadful now-a-days, the whole race seems to have grown sceptical. Now, why don't you come to church, and be good and orthodox?'

As she spoke she handed him the rose to put into the basket. It was an exquisite blush rose, and he held it in his hand abstractedly, not exactly seeing its beauty, and yet feeling some subtle influence from its purity and fragrance. He did not answer, and Adela continued:

'Don't think I shall be hard on you, there never was a more lenient person—besides, scepticism is always interesting. Not, you know, that I am not all that is proper and orthodox, you mustn't think that for a moment. I like to be *comme il faut* in everything—that is not quite a right expression, is it? more suited to matters of etiquette than religion,—however, it does not signify, turn it into Latin in your mind. I am very orthodox, but I can quite sympathise with sceptics—is that sense? Now do tell me why you don't believe the things that I believe; they say it is always well to hear all sides of a question, and on this subject I have scarcely heard anything.'

She had rattled on in her usual fashion without looking up; had she noticed the change in Donovan's face, her womanly tact would have warned her to be more careful, for he looked as nearly contemptuous as good manners would allow. His voice was grave and displeased as he replied, and had a strange ring of pain in it.

'It is not a subject I care to discuss, thank you.'

They walked on in silence, Donovan trying uneasily to understand his own feelings. *Why* did he not care to discuss this subject? Was it that his cousin's lightness jarred on him? was there some latent sense of reverence in him—some yet slumbering faith faintly touched by her flippant tones? Or was it—could it be—that he, Donovan Farrant, was ashamed of the views he held? ashamed of not being like the rest of the world?

Adela knew, from the tone of the answer which her question received, that she had made a mistake; flippant, conventional, semi-religious talk evidently grated somehow on her cousin's mind; she made haste to recover her place in his estimation by referring to the subject nearest his heart.

'Shall we take these flowers to Dot? She likes flowers in her room, doesn't she?'

His brow cleared instantly.

'Yes, let us go. Dot is very fond of you, Cousin Adela, you have cheered her up wonderfully.'

Adela smiled; her kindness to little Dot was the one fair bright spot in her life just then; it was pleasant to dwell on one thing in which her motive was really good, and she was too really kind to like to remember that she was acting as a sort of decoy towards Donovan.

Dot held out her hands eagerly for the flowers.

'What beauties!' she cried. 'I was afraid they were all over.'

Donovan took the blush rose and arranged it in her dress, where its soft colours helped to relieve the blackness.

'You and Cousin Adela have had such a long talk,' said Dot, watching with interest while the flowers were arranged in her

F

vase. 'I saw you from my window. What were you talking about?'

'Oh,' said Adela, with a little pause, as she adjusted a leaf, 'we were talking about the church.'

'There's many changes there, miss,' said Mrs. Doery, looking up from her work. 'Seems to be the way with these new-fangled ministers. Still, they say the boys in their whites is very attractive, and nobody can't deny that the church is fuller then it used to be.'

'I have been telling Mr. Donovan that Mountshire is very much behind the world,' said Adela. 'In our parts we should be quite surprised not to find a choir.'

'Well, miss, I suppose it's very right and proper, but for myself I liked the old days when we had just the parson and the clerk. Now they sing-song all the things so, and I can't seem to pick myself up.'

Adela tried not to laugh, and asked the name of the clergy-man.

'Mr. Golding, he's the white-haired one. You'd have thought he was too old to like such new ways, but I make no doubt he's led on by the curate, who is but young; and as to him, miss, he gets through the service so quick you wouldn't believe, but I never can hear a word when he reads off the old fowl's back.'

Adela and Donovan burst out laughing, and no sense of the respect due to Mrs. Doery could stop them. Dot, not understanding, looked perplexed till Adela explained.

'The reading-desk in church, dear, the lectern, is like an eagle. Oh! Mrs. Doery, you mustn't mind our laughing, but really that is worthy of *Punch*.'

Doery was, luckily, not at all offended. She could not pretend to learn all the new names they gave the things, and probably she thought of the lectern as the 'old fowl' till the day of her death.

After a certain fashion Adela's visit really did Donovan some good. It roused him from his moody silence, made a change in his monotonous life, and shielded him to some extent from Ellis Farrant's annoyances. For, during this visit, Ellis was not all careful to keep himself in the boy's good graces, and, in the brief time that they were necessarily thrown together, managed to annoy him considerably. Donovan had always the ruffled, uncomfortable consciousness that his guardian was making a good thing out of his office. He was naturally very careless about money matters, scarcely giving them a thought; but even easy and generous natures are often roused by feeling that they are being traded upon. The length and frequency of his cousin's visits might be overlooked perhaps, but when, in the course of the month, he went with Donovan to some races at a neighbouring town, and coolly put down all the expenses to Mrs. Farrant, his ward was naturally indignant; and this happened not once only, but several times. The loss of the money was nothing, but the injustice was very irritating. Injustice was Donovan's watchword, and this slight but aggravating specimen of it was a constant thorn in his side.

Another vexing thing was Ellis Farrant's behaviour to his mother. He used to perform all kinds of little services for her; waiting on her sedulously on every possible occasion, with a marked ostentation which seemed always trying to indicate to Donovan, 'This is what *you* ought to do.' Even had such attentions been possible to him, he would have been far too proud to take such a broad hint, and Ellis was probably aware of this, or he would not have risked giving the advice; it was everything to him that Mrs. Farrant should feel the great difference between his conduct and her son's. On the whole, there was some reason in Donovan's complaint that autumn—life had always seemed to him hard and perplexing, and it grew more so.

CHAPTER VII.

THE BLACK SHEEP OF OAKDENE.

O, ye wha are sae guid yoursel',
  Sae pious, and sae holy,
Ye've nought to do but mark and tell
  Your neebour's faults and folly.
Ye see your state wi' theirs compar'd,
  And shudder at the niffer,
But cast a moment's fair regard
  What maks the mighty differ?

  . . . .

Wi' wind and tide fair i' your tail,
  Right on ye scud your sea-way,
But in the teeth o' baith to sail,
  It makes au unco lee way.
Address to the Unco Guid, or Rigidly Righteous. BURNS.

'I MAY be wrong, Mr. Ward. I can't pretend to much wisdom. I'm an old, unlettered man, but it seems to me that folks are rather hard on the poor boy; but I may be wrong, I quite allow I may be wrong.'

The speaker was a grey-haired, elderly man, with a thin, worn face, kind eyes, and rather bent shoulders. His companion, Mr. Ward, was the Squire of Oakdene, a short, broad, grey-whiskered country gentleman, somewhat bluff, but still good-natured enough in his way. The two were returning from a meeting of the church-wardens on an afternoon in January, and happening to see Donovan Farrant sauntering along the road in front of them, with his dog at his heels, they had begun to talk of him.

'I'm sure I wish to be hard on no one,' said the squire, swinging his stick rather vigorously. 'But you know, Hayes, the fellow has a very bad reputation. No one has a good word to say for him.'

'Poor boy,' said old Mr. Hayes, compassionately. 'I suppose it's all true; but you know one must remember that he's never had a father to look after him.'

'Yes, I know that,' said the squire, reflectively; he had sons of his own, and had very strong ideas about paternal influence. 'That's quite true, and may excuse him to a certain extent. But then it's impossible to take up with him. I couldn't have him mixing with Harry and Ned. It isn't that I wish to be uncivil to the fellow, but really it would be most unwise. I don't know what Mrs. Ward would say if I proposed it. Now you, Hayes, it's different with you; you're a bachelor, and could easily be a little friendly with him.'

'Yes,' hesitated Mr. Hayes; 'but you know I'm afraid he'd find me a very dull companion. I'm only a stupid old man, and he is young, and very clever, they say.'

'Bosh!' said the squire, contemptuously—'he ought to be proud to shake hands with you. You're a great deal too humble-minded, Hayes. I've no idea of being so deferential to the young generation. There's a great deal too little of the Fifth Commandment now-a-days; it wasn't so when I was a boy.'

'I felt very sorry for them this Christmas,' resumed Mr. Hayes, gently; 'the Manor must have been a sad house; but it's very hard to know how to help people when you can't send them blankets, or coals, or Christmas dinners.'

'And young Farrant is a precious deal too proud to be helped in any way,' said Mr. Ward, with a laugh. 'But, after all, I am sorry for the boy; it's a sad start in life to have lost one's good name. What's he after now, stooping down in the snow? We shall catch him up, and, if so, I must speak to him.'

A miserable-looking cat, drenched with water, and with a

tin pot tied to its tail, had been lying half dead by the roadside. Donovan, who was a great lover of animals, had of course hastened to the rescue ; he had just released the poor terrified creature from its instrument of torture, and was holding it in his arms, rubbing its wet draggled fur, when, hearing steps, he glanced round, and found himself face to face with Mr. Ward and Mr. Hayes. The colour rushed to his cheeks ; he had not time to assume the look of cold haughty indifference with which he usually confronted his neighbours. He looked so handsome and boyish, and so unlike a reprobate, that Mr. Ward felt his compassion rising and his scruples diminishing ; besides, the conversation had rather softened him, and he held out his hand cordially.

'Well, Farrant, how are you ? Mrs. Farrant quite well, I hope ? You know Mr. Hayes, don't you ? Why, what's that ? —a drowned cat ? '

'Some brute of a boy has nearly killed it,' said Donovan, indignation making him speak naturally. 'I think it will come round, though, as soon as I can get it to a fire.'

That an atheist should bestow his attention on a stray cat was very surprising to the squire. He began to like the fellow. After all, there was some good in him.

'Had any skating yet ? ' he asked, in his kindly voice.

'No ; our pond is half overgrown with marestail ; besides, it's too small so be worth anything.'

'Oh ! you must come over to our place,' said the squire, with good-humour, which astonished Mr. Hayes. 'Our young people have been on the small lake to-day, and I dare say the large one will bear to-morrow. You used to be rather a swell at skating, if I remember right.'

'I am very fond of it,' said Donovan, and his eyes danced.

'Then come over to-morrow, and whenever you like ; it isn't often we get a frost like this.'

'Thank you—I will be sure to come,' said Donovan ; and as they parted he lifted his eyes to the squire's with a long searching look, at once wistful and surprised ; then, whistling to Waif, he walked away with the cat under his arm.

'Now, what on earth did I do that for ?' said the squire, as he and Mr. Hayes turned down the lane leading to the Hall gates. 'I don't know what my wife will say, but really, Hayes, I don't dislike the boy ; and how his face lighted up at the thought of the skating ! He's not a bad fellow, after all.'

Mr. Ward was quite right in surmising that his wife would be vexed when she heard of the invitation he had given ; he tried hard to mention it casually when he got home, but there was an undisguisable anxiety in his voice as he observed,

. ' Oh! by-the-by, my dear, I met young Farrant just now, and asked him to come over for skating to-morrow.'

Mrs. Ward looked up with as much annoyance as it was possible for a good, kind-hearted woman to show.

' You asked Donovan Farrant to come *here?* '

' Not to the house, my dear, only to skate on the lake. I really don't see how I could avoid it; he is a first-rate skater, and this is the only ice for miles round.'

' But only the other day, Edward, you said you wouldn't have him about with the boys on any account. I really think you might be more careful. It will be beginning an intimacy, and then, with such near neighbours, we shall find it impossible to break it off. It is just the most dangerous time, too, with Harry back from Oxford, ready to make friends with anyone, and Ned fresh from school.'

' My dear, surely they needn't become friends because they skate on the same lake; besides, I assure you young Farrant is not so bad as people make out.'

' Well, Edward, he is not at all the kind of companion I like for the boys, and I've heard you say the same thing yourself. No one visits him, he reads with that Mr. Alleyne at Greyshot, a most unprincipled man, and you yourself heard that he attended Racburn's lectures.'

' I heard that he had been seen at one,' said the squire, rather testily.

' And that is quite enough, I am sure, to prove him an unfit companion for our children,' replied Mrs. Ward. ' Only the other day, too, I met him at the library and heard him asking for books on Positivism ; besides, no one invented the account of his school life, I suppose.'

' Well, he's not likely to talk either of Racburn or of Positivism on the ice, I should think,' said Mr. Ward, with a smile.

' Come, my dear, it is not like you to be inhospitable ; let the poor fellow be here just this once.'

' Of course he must come now you have asked him,' said Mrs. Ward, with a sigh. ' But I am vexed about it. I do think one should be careful with boys like Harry and Ned, and with three girls only just out. Donovan Farrant is so good-looking.'

She sighed again. The squire laughed heartily.

' Now, about the boys I don't feel so positive, I own, but you may set your mind quite at rest about the girls, for this dangerous young fellow whom you dread so much is a professed woman-hater. And you know, my dear, even the author of evil is not so black as he's painted.'

Mrs. Ward sighed, but she said no more, only secretly in her heart she hoped the frost would not continue.

Donovan was on the ice before anyone else the next morning, and for some time had the lake to himself. By-and-by two or three carriages drove up with people from the neighbourhood whom he knew slightly, and towards the middle of the day the squire and his two sons came down, but, beyond an ordinary greeting, very little passed between them. The squire was too good-natured a man not to feel glad that, in spite of his wife's scruples, he had invited the objectionable neighbour to come; his keen enjoyment and his first-rate skating were pleasant to watch, too. Mr. Ward really felt sorry when, early in the afternoon, he saw him taking off his skates.

'You are leaving very soon,' he said, kindly. 'I hope it is not on account of luncheon.' Won't you come up to the house and have something?'

The invitation slipped out naturally, the squire found it hard not to be hospitable. But luckily Donovan declined. He never left Dot now for a whole day, and giving the ordinary excuse of 'an engagement,' he left the lake, the squire of course inviting him to come again the next day, and as long as the frost lasted.

Mrs. Ward was much relieved when, on coming down from the house with her daughters and her niece, she found that the object of her alarms was really gone. Everyone was singing his praises—that was a little annoying, certainly—but she learnt from her husband that he had been far too much taken up with his figure-cutting to trouble the boys with his company, and with that she was satisfied, and dismissed the subject from her thoughts.

The next day, however, was not nearly so propitious. To begin with, the girls would go on the ice in the morning, and, though Mrs. Ward hurried over her housekeeping, and followed them as quickly as possible, she found that already the intimacy which she so much dreaded had begun. The first sight that met her eyes as she emerged from the shrubbery was a little knot of people gathered together on the bank. Her husband leaning on his stick and talking jocosely, her younger daughter and her niece, Maggie White, just preparing for their first start, and Donovan Farrant kneeling in the snow, putting on her elder daughter's skates. It was very provoking! Why had not the girls been more careful? Why had she not sent down the ser-

vant to help them?   Why did her husband stand there so carelessly, laughing and talking?   Her greeting to Donovan was
stiff and chill, but he was much too happy to care; the day was
gloriously fine, the frosty air invigorating, Mr. Ward and his
daughters had been kind and friendly, Maggie White was be-
witching, for once in his life Donovan was perfectly and healthily
happy.   He had been on the ice for some time, his usually pale,
dark face was all aglow with the exercise, and his eyes were
sparkling with excitement, he certainly looked most provokingly
handsome, and perhaps there was some cause for Mrs. Ward's
anxiety.

'How could you let him help the girls like that?' she said
reproachfully, as the skaters glided swiftly away.   'I thought,
Edward, you told me he was a regular misanthrope.'

'Well, I don't see that he has done much harm, my dear,'
said the squire.   'Common courtesy would require him to help
the ladies, and I'm glad to see him lose that cold proud look; he
was more of a boy to-day.'

'I have warned the girls to be careful, but there's no knowing
what Maggie will do.   She's a dreadful little flirt!' and Mrs.
Ward looked anxiously across the lake to the place where Donovan was giving her niece a lesson in the figure eight.

'Well,' said the squire, consolingly, 'Maggie's a very nice
girl at any rate, and if she is, as you say, a flirt, then you may
be pretty sure that she won't get her heart broken.   Ah! here
come the Fortescues.   We have quite a nice number here to-
day;' and the hospitable old gentleman hastened forward to
receive his friends.

'You are the only good skater here,' said Maggie, looking up
admiringly at her instructor.   'Where did you learn?   And how
can you manage to do all those wonderful figures?'

'They are only learnt by practice,' said Donovan.   'I learnt
at school, and at my old home near London.   You can do anything well, if you give your whole will to it.'

'Can you?' said Maggie.   'I can't.   I expect I've had as
many weeks of skating as you have had days.   I come from
Canada, you know; but I shall never be able to do these figures
as you do.'

It was pleasant to be made much of and flattered; an
entirely new experience to Donovan.   He thought Maggie
White the prettiest and pleasantest girl he had ever seen.   They
talked on naturally and easily, and it was not surprising perhaps
that Donovan was in no hurry to part with his new companion,
or that he enjoyed skating rapidly up and down the lake hand in

hand with her more than cutting figures by himself. Nor did it
occur to Maggie that she was guilty of any great enormity in
enjoying herself too. Once she said, in her pretty way,

'I am keeping you from doing what you like, please go away
and leave me. I am taking up all your time, and spoiling your
skating.'

And Donovan, though he was no 'lady's man,' could answer
very truthfully,

' You are making me enjoy it perfectly.'

Then they began to talk again of Canada, and she described
all its delights to him.

' Such fun we used to have in the skating season. Sometimes
we had regular balls on the ice. It was so delightful! Oh!
Mr. Farrant '—as a sudden thought struck her—' could we dance
now? I'm sure you, who skate so beautifully, would waltz to
perfection.'

It was very innocently proposed. In a minute Maggie had
proclaimed the news to her cousins as they passed.

' We are going to dance. Why don't you?' And then in a
minute the deed was done, and Mrs. Ward saw with dismay
that Donovan Farrant and her niece were actually dancing
together.

Ice-waltzing was a novelty at Oakdene, and everyone turned
to watch the graceful movements of the little Canadian girl and
her partner. Twice they made the circuit of the lake, then, as
they passed near the bank where Mrs. Ward and one of her
daughters were standing, Donovan overheard the words:

' I must stop this. With Donovan Farrant, too—the last
person in the world——'

Maggie felt a quick movement in the arm that was round her
waist, and suddenly her partner stopped, saying, in an odd
changed voice,

' I think Mrs. Ward wishes to speak to you.'

' To me? All right, auntie, I'm coming. I won't be a minute,
Mr. Farrant.'

She skated swiftly to the bank, and listened, with downcast
eyes, to her aunt's words.

' My dear, I don't quite approve of this. I'm sorry to interrupt your pleasure, but you must allow me to judge in. this
instance.' Then, as Donovan drew near, she turned to him, trying to convey her meaning as civilly as she could. ' I have been
telling my niece that I think perhaps ice-dancing is a little out
of place here. You will understand, I am sure, Mr. Farrant.'

Yes, he understood perfectly. The face which had so lately

been boyishly happy and bright was suddenly overcast, the eyes saddened, the mouth re-assumed its bitter look, and, without a single word, Donovan raised his hat, turned away, and skated rapidly to the other end of the lake.

The brightness of the day was gone for him after that. He went on skating, but with no animation. Once young Ned Ward came up and asked him to do the figure of double eight, with which he had been astonishing the quiet Oakdene skaters early in the morning, but he complied so moodily that the boy soon left him to seek more genial companions. Then Donovan resolved to go home. He had been repulsed, and, just as it was in his home life, so too, in this instance, one repulse was enough. He had neither enough love nor enough humility to lay himself open again to the chance of a fresh rebuff. After the first, he invariably shrank into himself, becoming a little harder, and colder, and more severe in manner.

He skated to a deserted corner of the lake, climbed the bank, and took off his skates; then involuntarily he looked back on the animated scene with a sore-hearted regret. The sun was already getting low, though it was not three o'clock; its level rays cast a red glow over the wide white expanse, dotted here and there by the dark gliding figures of the skaters. The shore was fringed with tall trees, their black stems serving as a relief to the general whiteness, and their branches drooping gracefully under the heavy yet feathery-looking rime. There was an intense stillness in the sharp frosty air, the voices of the merry crowd rang out clearly; once Donovan felt sure he heard Maggie White's girlish laugh, and it grated on him. But in another minute all his morbid and selfish thoughts were suddenly scattered to the winds, for while he was still looking across the lake he saw the ice in the centre bend, then, with one vast booming crack, it parted asunder. In an instant all was confusion. Donovan sprang from the bank, and ran at full speed to the scene of the disaster, all petty and personal feelings driven out by the absorbing general interest and alarm. Several people were in the water, struggling, sinking, rising, vainly clutching at the slippery edges of the broken ice. Those who were safe bent forward helplessly on their skates, trying to reach a hand to their friends in distress, or calling loudly for help, for ropes, for every sort of aid which was not at hand. Two ladies were submerged; Donovan coolly selected one of them while he drew off his coat, then, without an instant's hesitation, he plunged into the icy water. His example was speedily followed by Harry Ward, ropes were hastily brought on to the ice, the rescue began to seem hopeful. Donovan was an expert swimmer ; a few strokes brought him up to the sinking girl, who, dragged down by the weight of her clothes, was being drawn in under the ice. From this he freed her without much difficulty, but she was insensible, and he found that to get her out of the water was quite another matter ; he tried several times, but without success ; each time the edges of the ice broke away with the weight, and all he could do was to keep her head above water, while with increasing difficulty he struck out with his free arm. The others had been rescued, or were being helped, and at length a rope was brought to his aid, a noose was thrown round him and his burden, and after a short fierce struggle, he found himself safely on the ice.

With a masculine dislike of being helped, he sprang quickly to his feet, left his insensible burden to the care of other hands, and looked round for his coat. Perhaps those who had seen him helped out with the rope did not know he was a rescuer—perhaps in the excitement and hurry of the moment, he was overlooked ; at any rate, no one spoke to him, and all at once his sore morose feeling returned with double force. The people were beginning to leave the ice quickly, the girl whom Donovan had rescued began to revive and was carried up to the house ; he turned away in the opposite direction, picked up his skates from the bank where he had left them, and strode fiercely away in the direction of the Manor. He had done his best ; one word of praise, or even of recognition, would have sent him home happy, but by some odd chance, even when he deserved commendation, he failed to get it. Probably he would have disliked being thanked above all things, and yet the absence of gratitude irritated him ; it was unjust, no one ever gave him his due, the world was full of injustice. Over and over in his mind went the weary, bitter, discontented cry ; perhaps his outward condition affected him a little, adding fuel to the flame, for, although he considered himself too philosophic to be troubled by mere bodily inconveniences, the truth was that he felt them more than most men, though he had great powers of endurance. The icy cold bath which he had just had, and the discomfort of his cold, clinging, dripping clothes, at any rate served to remind him continually of his grievance. He had scarcely passed the Hall gates, when he was roused from his dismal thoughts by an unexpected greeting.

'Nice bright afternoon,' said old Mr. Hayes, shaking his hand. 'Have you been on the ice ? Ah, yes, I see you have your skates.'

'Yes ; there's been an accident,' said Donovan, 'so I am going home. The ice on the large lake gave way.'

'Bless me!—no one hurt, I hope? Did anyone go in? Why, now I notice you are all wet. Dear, dear! what a terrible thing! How many people fell in?'

'I should think about half-a-dozen,' replied Donovan, swinging his skates and trying to look unconcerned.

'And all were rescued? that's a comfort. And you were helped out quickly, I hope?'

'Oh! yes,' said Donovan, too proud to explain, 'I was hauled out.'

'Poor fellow! but what a shock it must have been! You'll be taking a chill. You must come in with me and have something hot, yes, indeed you must, I'll take no denial. Here we are, you see, at my door. Come in quickly and have something, and then walk home briskly and change. Now what shall it be, whisky-punch or negus? I'm an abstemious man generally, but this is the real time for such things, wet to the skin and chilled to the bone, dear, dear! Now come in, come in.'

Mr. Hayes had not been disabused of the old ideas about alcohol, but, whether he was right or wrong, Donovan's brow gradually relaxed under the influence of the old man's kindness and hospitality; he followed him obediently into the little villa, which, though only inhabited by the bachelor Mr. Hayes, was as scrupulously clean as any old-maid's dwelling.

Mr. Hayes rang the bell in the parlour, all the time making much of his guest. Could he not accommodate him with a change of clothes? Should he send up to the Manor?

A grave, staid housekeeper appeared to answer the bell, and Mr. Hayes perhaps thought it would be well to quicken her movements by telling her the news of the village.

'Some hot water and a lemon and some sugar, please, Mrs. Brown. There has been an accident on the ice in the Hall grounds, and this gentleman has been in the water and is very wet.'

Then the old man went to the cellaret, and, the housekeeper having returned with the other ingredients, he began with infinite pleasure and fussiness to make the punch. He would not let Donovan stay for long, but as soon as he had done justice to the steaming beverage, started him on his walk home, with paternal injunctions not to stay about in his wet things, and to be sure to come in again soon and cheer up a solitary old bachelor.

Donovan smiled to himself at the last speech. Was it not rather the 'solitary old bachelor' who had cheered him! The kindness and hospitality drove away for the time his gloomy thoughts, but they returned to him as he entered his own home and threw down his skates.

'Good-bye to you, at any rate,' he murmured. 'I shall never go there again.'

Dot, with her quick all-observing eyes, saw at once that something was wrong when Donovan came into her room. Yesterday he had returned in the highest spirits, that very morning he had started with the look of bright expectation on his face which the little sister liked to see, but now he was grave and with the expression which he always wore when any allusion was made to his school disgrace—the expression which Dot never cared to put into words—a hard bad look.

'You are back earlier than you said,' she began. 'Have you not had good skating?'

'Yes—no,' he moved away from her to the fireplace, and kicked the coals in the grate with his heel.

'He never stirs the fire with his foot except when something is wrong,' soliloquized Dot; then aloud,

'Have you seen mamma, Dono?'

'No.'

It could not be any quarrel then in that quarter. What could have happened? He was so disinclined to talk, however, that she did not venture to ask any more questions, and in a minute or two he walked across the room, opened the piano, and began to practise. He had chosen something of Sebastian Bach's, and laboured away at it, first mechanically and doggedly enough, but by degrees with immense satisfaction and relief to himself. A stately, measured, dignified strain it was, with one little fidgety, fugue-like passage; he played five bars of it over and over till the disappointment, and anger, and moodiness gradually died out of his heart, and poor Dot began to beg for mercy.

'You must have played it a thousand times,' she said, laughing, and Donovan laughed too, left the piano, and came to sit beside her.

'Bach is as good as a tonic,' he said, cheerfully. 'That old fellow always sets me right.'

She saw now that she might talk to him, and began to question him about his day. He always told her his troubles, but this afternoon he tried to make light of them.

'We had a glorious time in the morning, the ice was perfect. About the middle of the time the Miss Wards came down, and their cousin, Miss White, a very pretty girl from Canada. She skated nicely, was much more up to things than anyone else, and for a little while we danced together. Mrs. Ward did not approve

of that, though. I overheard her say something not too complimentary, and then she managed somehow to stop it, at which,
you know, Dot, I was just a little cross. But, just as I was
coming away, guess what happened.'

'An accident! Oh! was it an accident?' cried Dot, excitedly.
'And you were brave and helped the others, and Mrs. Ward was
obliged to like you very much?'

He laughed a little, but rather sadly.

'No, Dot. You are running on too fast. I was born under
an unlucky star, and shall never be able to win honour or
respect.'

He gave her a detailed account of the whole affair, and was
rewarded by her delighted pride in his attempted rescue.

'Dono dear, you ought to have a medal for it, a medal, you
know, from the Society for Promoting—what is it?'

'Cruelty to animals,' suggested Donovan, wickedly.

'No, no, you bad boy Something about being "*humane*," and
they give medals to people who save people's lives. Just fancy,
Dono, you could wear it on your watch-chain. It would be *so*
nice.'

'Too nice for the like of me,' he said, lightly, but with a
stifled sigh. 'They keep things of that sort for the good boys.'

'And no one even thanked you? That was a shame,' said
the little sister, indignantly. 'Never mind, Dono, you are my
hero, my very own, and you're the dearest old boy in the world.'

Perhaps it was as well that the frost only lasted three days
longer. The skaters grumbled sadly, but two people at Oakdene
were considerably relieved. The one was Mrs. Ward, who
rejoiced that 'that dangerous young man' could not again im-
peril her children, the other was the 'dangerous young man'
himself. But if Donovan did not easily forget injustice, neither
did he forget even the most trifling piece of kindness. After his
next day's shooting, he left a brace of pheasants at old Mr.
Hayes' door, and this made an opening for a further acquaintance.
Mr. Hayes wrote to ask him to dinner, and, as such invitations were
rare, Donovan was pleased enough to go. It was a *tête-à-tête* dinner.
Old Mr. Hayes was past sixty, and Donovan not yet nineteen,
but, in spite of this disparity in age, the evening was a very
pleasant one, and did him good. It was a fresh interest, an insight into a new home, and also into a life whose simplicity,
kindliness, and content could not fail to strike the most casual
observer.

Mr. Hayes lived very frugally as a rule. The game was an
unwonted luxury, and his evident appreciation of it was very

pleasant to Donovan. He himself had a hearty but philosophic appetite, to which nothing came amiss, dainty discrimination was not at all in his line, but he enjoyed watching old Mr. Hayes discuss his present, glad that what had been pleasure to him in the shooting should be real pleasure to some one else in the eating.

'You are like Squire Thornhill in "The Vicar of Wakefield,"' said Mr. Hayes, when the housekeeper had removed the game, 'who brought his own venison with him when he dined at the vicarage. What! You don't know the book? Is it possible? Well, I suppose it's old and behind the times now; but, my word! how I have laughed over it, and cried, too, for the matter of that. "Moses at the Fair," and then "Olivia!" Ah! he was a grand fellow, old Goldsmith. There are no such writers now-a-days.'

Then by-and-by some question of Donovan's drew out an account of Mr. Hayes' former life, the rough discipline of the old boarding-schools, the early drudgery in a merchant's office, his gradual advance till he had become a partner in the firm, the losses they had had in the time of the Crimean War, finally his ill-health, and his retirement, with a modest income, to the little country villa. A life of toil, and care, and hardship, with what seemed to Donovan a very slight reward, but which the old man himself evidently considered quite sufficient.

'And now, you see,' he concluded, 'when my health is uncertain, and I can't do what I once could, why, here I have a cosy little berth to myself, with no cares or anxieties. It was always my castle in the air, this, a little house in a country village, with a bit of garden, and a place to keep fowls in. The thought of this helped me through years of care and labour. Always remember to have your castle in the air. That's my advice to you.'

'What is the use, sir, if it never comes to anything? Except at cards, the luck is against me always. And is there not a proverb, "Blessed is he that expecteth nothing"?'

'Well, well,' said Mr. Hayes, 'perhaps you're the wiser and more rational. I don't know exactly about *expecting*—you must expect very patiently, at any rate. But a "castle" is a great blessing; I should miss mine sadly.'

'You have a new one, then?' said Donovan, amused.

'Oh, yes; Switzerland will be my next move. I've been saving up for it this long time, and I've mapped out my route, and chosen what hotels to go to, and calculated just what it will cost; and then, you know, when I meet with travellers, I get hints from them, and put them down in my note-book. Now this is what I intend to do, starting, you know, from Newhaven to Dieppe,' &c., &c.

The whole tour was detailed with enthusiastic delight, and Donovan listened, unable to help admiring the child-like, contented old man.

'And when do you think your "castle" will come off, sir?' he asked, when the whole plan had been related.

'Oh! that I can't tell at all,' said Mr. Hayes, rubbing his hands. 'I have not saved enough yet; but won't it be a *grand* tour! Come, own that it's a "castle" worth having?'

CHAPTER VIII.

'TIED TO HIS MOTHER'S APRON-STRINGS.'

Now a boy is, of all wild beasts, the most difficult to manage.
PLATO.

'You see, dear Mrs. Tremain, one must be so careful with boys; there are so many temptations into which they are likely to fall, and, humanly speaking, there is no such careful and saving influence as a mother's.'

The speaker, Mrs. Causton, was a middle-aged lady, with no-coloured hair brought low on each side of her brow, and a rather careworn face, which expressed kindly intentions, but yet at the same time seemed a little formal. An old friend of Dr. Tremain's, and the wife of a naval officer, she had lately settled down at Porthkerran in order to be with her son Stephen, a boy of nineteen, who was to spend a year in Dr. Tremain's surgery before going up to London to 'walk the hospitals.' Mrs. Causton was such a near neighbour that she was an almost daily visitor at the doctor's house, and her easy informal comings and goings never interfered with anything that was going on. The two ladies were sitting by the open window of the breakfast-room one warm summer morning, when Mrs. Causton made the remark about 'a mother's influence;' Mrs. Tremain, with the daintiest and most exquisitely neat workbox before her, was busy with some folds of blue cambric, out of which her skilful and therefore graceful-looking hands were devising one of little

Nesta's frocks; and Gladys, at the far end of the room, was giving Jackie a reading-lesson.

'And yet,' began Mrs. Tremain, in answer, 'I can't help thinking that a certain amount of independence is almost necessary; a boy must learn sooner or later to stand alone.'

'Yes, yes, sooner or later, of course. Stephen must be alone in London next year. I wish it could be otherwise; but you know I never could be in London, unfortunately; the air is like poison to me. He must be alone then, but I can't help dreading it very much; he has scarcely ever been away from me, not for more than a few days at a time in his whole life. I could never make up my mind to send him to school; there are *so* many temptations in school life; I always dreaded it for Stephen.'

'One wants a great deal of faith with children,' said Mrs. Tremain; and as she spoke, though the words were by no means lightly meant, there was a little smile of amusement about her lips, for she knew she was poaching on Mrs. Causton's manor.

'Ah! dear Mrs. Tremain, no one knows that better than I do; it is faith from the beginning to the end, how else could one bear the anxieties, the—— Well, Jackie dear,' as the sturdy little four-year-old boy, released from his lessons, sprang towards her with the affectionate rough demonstration of arms and legs common to most children of his age.

'Aunt Margaret,' said Gladys, for, though Mrs. Causton was no real relation, the children had known her all their lives, and had christened her 'auntie,' in American fashion—'Aunt Margaret, what would you have done if Stephen had had to go to sea like Dick?'

'My dear, I could never have allowed it,' said Mrs. Causton, quickly. 'Of course, naturally enough, at one time Stephen did wish to go with his father, but it could never have been allowed. From the very first I determined that he should be a clergyman or a doctor, the only thoroughly good and Christian professions, to my mind.'

'Oh! but, auntie, think of the number of good men there are in other professions,' said Gladys, with girlish vehemence, provoked by the narrowness of the remark.

'I like a consistent calling,' said Mrs. Causton, 'and you know, Gladys, humanly speaking, it is often difficult to lead a consistent life in a more secular profession.'

Gladys was silenced but not satisfied. When Mrs. Causton had gone she returned to the subject.

'Mother, Aunt Margaret seems to think that very few people

G

are Christians. She talks as if all the world, except just a few people like herself, were wicked.'

'Your aunt has very strong opinions. I do not agree with her always,' said Mrs. Tremain. 'Nor need you, Gladys.'

'But, mother, it's so tiresome to have to hear people say things like that, it's so—so narrow! What would she do if there were only two professions in the world, if every man was a clergyman or a doctor? And if the other things must be done and seen to, why, it must be right for some one to do them.'

'Do you know,' said Mrs. Tremain, smiling, 'that you are a very hot little arguer, Gladys? I fancy, like most women, that you have just a little personal feeling mixed with your views. Were you not thinking of Dick when the other professions were being decried?'

'You always know everything,' said Gladys, resting her arm on Mrs. Tremain's knee, and shading her brow with her hand. 'Yes, I was thinking of Dick. I believe he's the best middy in all the navy. You know, mother, what Captain Smith said about him. I'm sure he is worth ten Stephens!'

'We are getting rather little and personal,' said Mrs. Tremain. 'Don't let us take to crying up our own belongings, and comparing them with other people's. Of course you are proud of Dick, dear, and so am I, but he is not a paragon of virtue.'

'Oh, no! I can't bear paragons,' said Gladys, laughing, 'they are always prigs. Dick is a regular boy still, that's why he's so nice. I wonder whether Aunt Margaret thinks it very risky for him to be left to himself so much. I believe Stephen wants to be let alone a little, he always looks so bored when auntie begins to talk at him. You know, mother, she really does talk rather much, she always tries to drag in religion, and sometimes it does come in so oddly. And then she is always saying "humanly speaking." I can't bear those little phrases. I think auntie must be descended from some of the old Puritans. I'm sure she'd have liked those funny, made-up names. She chose Stephen's name because it was in the Bible, and she thinks Gladys sounds so like a heathen. She wonders you and papa chose it for me.'

Mrs. Tremain laughed.

'Well, Gladys dear, live up to the best meaning of your name, and I shall be quite satisfied. Now let us have our reading together. The weather looks promising for our picnic this afternoon, does it not?'

Later in the day the whole family, including Stephen and Mrs. Causton, were to meet for an out-of-doors tea-drinking. It was a half-holiday, and the two younger boys, intervening between

Dick and little Jackie, were to come over from their school at
Plymouth. The doctor had promised to get his rounds done
quickly, and Stephen was released from his duties for an hour or
two. To children, and to child-like minds, it is seldom that a
great expedition or an expensive picnic gives the pleasure which
a more simple and homely one does. It is not the great, formal,
country excursion, with its grand toilettes and champagne lunch,
which dwells in the memory, and is looked back upon with
pleasure, it is rather the simple 'day in the country,' when there
were no liveried servants to carry the provisions, when our own
arms ached with the burden, when, with a sense of delicious
novelty, we ourselves spread the cloth on the turf, or boiled the
kettle over a gipsy-like fire of sticks, or roamed in delightful
freedom in what seemed a paradise of rest and greenness, away
from the 'haunts of men.'

About two miles west of Porthkerran the cliffs were broken
into a sort of cleft or narrow valley, and here a beautiful wood
had sprung up, which in spring was carpeted with primroses and
anemones, and where in summer forget-me-nots were to be found
by the side of the little stream which trickled through the wood
to the sea. It was in this space that the Tremains were to spend
their afternoon.

'It was very good of you to spare Stephen,' said Mrs. Causton
to the doctor, as he helped her out of the little pony-carriage, in
which the elder ladies and the two younger children had come.
'I sometimes fancy that he does not get out enough. I hope he
deserves his holiday?'

'Yes, a little country air will freshen him up,' said the doctor,
without replying directly to the question.

The mother's instinct was quick to note this.

'I hope you are really satisfied with Stephen?' she said,
anxiously. 'I hope he isn't idle?'

'Oh,' said the doctor, re-assuringly, 'I don't think he's more
idle than many boys of his age. I daresay he told you that I was
down upon him rather sharply yesterday. He forgot an important
message, and I was obliged to lecture him a little.'

'He never told me,' said Mrs. Causton, with some vexation
in her tone. 'I would always so much rather know things of
that kind. I cannot get him to be open with me.'

'You can hardly expect that he will tell you of every
trifling scrape he gets into,' said Dr. Tremain. 'That was all
very well while he was in petticoats, and the more spontaneous
telling there is still the better, but perhaps one can hardly look
for it in such a matter as that.'

'I like *perfect* confidence between a mother and son,' said Mrs. Causton. 'Who should help him and advise him, if I do not?'

'Quite so. It is everything to have strong sympathy and understanding, but forced confidence is worthless, and a boy of nineteen is generally rather a tough customer to deal with.'

'You think so?' questioned Mrs. Causton.

'Yes, I think undoubtedly that from eighteen to one-and-twenty is one of the most difficult periods of life. Boys, and in many instances girls too, begin then to have a good deal of liberty. The old discipline is cast off, they have to rule their own actions to a great extent, they have to face the problems of life, and forming their own opinion strongly on every point, whether it is beyond their comprehension or not, they battle along not unfrequently a misery to themselves and to their friends, till, after dearly-bought experience, they at last settle down, more or less contentedly, with some of their conceit knocked out of them.'

'Stephen is not conceited,' broke in Mrs. Causton. 'I don't think anyone could call him conceited; and as to his opinions, why he holds everything that I do. He has never been any trouble to me in that way, and in these days, when young men so often hold such dreadfully unorthodox views, that is saying a great deal.'

'I don't think Stephen is in any danger of being unorthodox,' said the doctor, rather drily. Then after a little pause he added, 'I meant that I don't think he ever thinks enough to have any difficulties. But in one way, Mrs. Causton, I do think he might be in danger, he is far too easily led.'

'He is naturally gentle and pliable,' said Mrs. Causton. She would not say 'weak.'

'And there is, I think, his danger,' said the doctor. 'Old John Bunyan showed a wonderful knowledge of life when he made Pliable the one to go half-way into the Slough of Despond, and never win through it. I don't want to make you anxious about Stephen, but of course, since the lad's been with me, he's been in my mind a good deal, and I can't help thinking that he wants more of a backbone; he has not enough steadiness; he is too loose in his management of himself. I do not think he knows how to steer his own course.'

'But I am still with him; he cannot go wrong now very well,' said Mrs. Causton.

'But you cannot always be with him,' replied the doctor. 'Depend upon it, the best thing you can do is to teach him *self-management*. There is an old saying, which of course you know, about the child who is "tied to his mother's apron-strings;" perhaps it seems cruel of me to quote such a rough simile to you, but, you see, there *is* danger in it—it makes a boy weak and helpless, instead of bracing him for his part in life, as I know you and all good mothers would wish to do.'

'Well, what shall I tell him?—what is his chief fault in his work?' said Mrs. Causton, with the rather fretted manner of one taking uncongenial advice.

'Don't bother him—let him alone a little,' said the doctor, cheerfully. 'Some day I mean to give him a good blowing up; he must learn to keep the surgery more tidy.'

Mrs. Causton was a little annoyed at this sudden descent to what seemed to her such a trifling and mundane matter, but Dr. Tremain's next sentence cleared her brow once more.

'You must not mind my talking so plainly to you about the boy; you see, I've been his father's friend ever since we were lads together, and so I can't help taking a special interest in Stephen. But don't let us spoil our afternoon's pleasuring with educational bothers. Where will you and the mother sit? Here is a nice tree ready felled—what do you say to that? I shall leave you to gossip while I go mothing.'

So the doctor, taking his butterfly-net, walked off into the wood, tapping the tree-trunks every now and then in search of spoil, and closely followed by Jackie, who promised to be as keen a naturalist as his father.

Mrs. Tremain took out her knitting, and, while talking with her companion, kept an eye on little Nesta, who was now more than a year old, and just beginning to run alone. From their place the two ladies could catch glimpses of the deep blue of the Porthkerran Bay through the overhanging trees, while occasionally merry voices in the distance told of the presence of the children. The quiet country stillness was very refreshing, but Mrs. Causton could not quite free herself from the uncomfortable impression which the doctor's words had left on her mind; had she been able to see into her son's heart at that moment, her anxiety would have been still greater.

'How jolly this is!' said Stephen, as, leaving the dusty highway, they entered the cool green shade of the wood. 'I used to think it must be so dull down here at Porthkerran; it seemed like the ends of the earth when we were living in Sussex.'

'Cornwall is the best place in the world,' said Gladys, with pride. 'I can't think how people can live in places where they have to wear gloves always, and walk about in their best clothes.'

'I thought girls always liked dress,' said Stephen.

'Oh! yes, of course, in a way; it is nice to have pretty things, but not to be always bothered with them,' said Gladys, stooping down to gather some forget-me-nots.

The younger boys had wandered on in front. Stephen was not sorry to be left behind, for he was rapidly gliding into love with Gladys. He gave to her now the confidence which his mother had so much wished for.

'Sometimes I think, Gladys, that I shall be obliged to go away from here,' he began—'before my year is over, I mean.'

'Oh, will you?' said Gladys.

'Would you—would you be sorry if I went?' questioned Stephen, anxiously.

'Of course,' said Gladys, with almost more frankness than he desired—'dreadfully sorry. We should all miss you; and besides, Aunt Margaret has taken the house now.'

It was too general and prosaic a view to please Stephen; however, he continued—

'I fancy your father is not pleased with me; he was awfully vexed yesterday.'

'Was he? Why was that?' asked Gladys, looking up with innocent sympathy.

'Why, they sent up word from the inn that Mary Pengelly was much worse, and I forgot to tell him.'

'Oh, Stephen! and did it matter much?'

'I don't know. I don't think it could have made much difference. She died this morning.'

There was a little silence after this, then Gladys said,

'I've often noticed that papa is more vexed by carelessness than by great big faults, and you see, Stephen, this might have been so dreadful, if he could have saved her by going earlier.'

'Oh, I don't think he could. She's been supposed to be dying for a week. Don't look so awfully grave, Gladys, I shall be very careful, of course, after this. I mean to turn over a new leaf. You don't know how I should hate to leave this place. You don't know how I care for—for you all.'

The colour had risen to the roots of his hair, and Gladys for the first time caught his meaning. Half pleased, half frightened, her strongest impulse was to run away, to put a stop somehow to the tête-à-tête; for the first time she felt that there was a difference between walking alone with Dick and walking alone with Stephen, and, with a sudden shyness which she had never known before, she looked about for some way of escape.

A brilliant butterfly fluttered past her, and, with relief in her voice, she said quickly,

'Oh! I do believe there is that rare "blue" which Jackie wanted. I must catch him.'

And, while Stephen wished all the rare 'blues' at the other side of the world, Gladys sprang across the little brook, running in swift pursuit of her victim. Stephen sauntered on rather discontentedly, but taking care not to lose sight of the brown holland and blue ribbons, which flashed rapidly hither and thither in the chase, threading the woody labyrinth. When at last he came up with her, the butterfly was secured, and the rest of the party were in sight.

Then came the merry preparations for tea; the boys gathered sticks and nursed the flickering blaze, Gladys began to spread bread and honey, like the queen in the nursery rhyme, and Dr. Tremain, returning with his prey in a dozen little boxes, devoted himself to making jokes for Mrs. Causton's benefit, and good-naturedly entered into all the children's arrangements, though, like most middle-aged men, he hated the discomforts of an out-door meal. The most noteworthy incident in the day to Stephen was that afterwards as they were still resting in the shade, from time to time singing rounds and catches, Gladys began to make her forget-me-nots into tiny nosegays. There was one for everybody, but the greater number of them were destined to 'bloom their hour and fade,' only one was carefully preserved among Stephen's untidy haunts. There was this much of good in him, that he was capable of recognizing Gladys' beauty and goodness, but unfortunately she did not greatly influence him.

CHAPTER IX.

DOT VERSUS THE WORLD.

> She was sent forth
> To bring that light which never wintry blast
> Blows out, nor rain nor snow extinguishes—
> The light that shines with loving eyes upon
> Eyes that love back, till they can see no more.
> LANDON.

> **A little child shall lead them.**
> *Book of the Prophet Isaiah.*

IT is an old saying, and perhaps a truism, that self-sacrifice always brings its reward; not exactly the substantial reward promised in a certain moral song which is put into the lips of children, in which a charitable loaf-giver is represented as receiving 'As much and ten times more,' but a reward in some form perhaps hardly understood now, but no less real because we cannot grasp or fathom it. In one sense great gain is consistent with loss, perhaps follows upon it almost as closely as joy follows upon pain.

It was not a tangible reward which Donovan's self-sacrifice met with. Our highest and best gifts are never tangible, but it was a reward which was one of the best and most lasting influences of his life. When he resolved to devote himself to Dot, instinctively his thoughts grew less morbid and selfish. His life, which seemed so purposeless and useless, twined itself round her life, and found the object it needed. His creed indeed remained unaltered; the angry sense of injustice still lurked in his heart, but everything was now subservient to the one ruling interest, and, through all the bad influences which were besetting him continually during the two years which elapsed after his father's death, the unconscious loving influence of the little child kept its hold upon him.

His was a nature formed either for great good or for great evil. Whatever he did he did thoroughly; whether it was the reading of a fairy tale to Dot, or the mastery of some difficult passage of music, or his nightly card-playing at the Greyshot Club, he bent his whole will to the work, intent upon making whatever he was engaged upon a masterpiece of its kind. In spite, then, of all the evil at work within him and without, Donovan had really improved. At twenty, he was far more manly, more tender and considerate, and, though his self-reliance was still unshaken, he was no longer the self-absorbed, gloomy, taciturn fellow he had been. To make himself companionable to Dot, he had been forced to rouse himself; abstract speculations, long, dismal reveries, were incompatible with the line of life which he had marked out for himself. What might have done very well among the Alps, must be avoided in the little invalid's room, and he exerted himself with such firmness of purpose that in spite of his natural tendency to melancholy, and the bitter spirit which his early education had produced, he became bright and cheerful, sometimes even merry. This was, of course, when he was with her; at other times he was often sadly moody, and the coldness with his mother increased rather than diminished; indeed, he saw very little of her, for, when Dot did not need him, he could always find amusement at Greyshot, though his passion for cards did not lead him among the very best companions.

And all the time Mrs. Farrant allowed herself to drift down

the stream of life placidly. The world seemed to her a little dull, but no doubt other people found it so. She had many comforts ; she would not complain. In what she considered peaceful and virtuous content, she stroked Fido, received visitors, drove out in her victoria, and read light literature. Twice a day she visited Dot's room; a sort of duty call, which both mother and child took as a matter of course, but did not in the least care for ; and occasionally Donovan occupied her thoughts for a few minutes. She would feel a sort of pride and pleasure as she noticed what a fine-looking fellow he was, or would be vexed and annoyed that the neighbours shunned him, but it never occurred to her that she was at all responsible for him, that it was through her neglect and unmotherliness that he was driven away from home to spend his evenings at a disreputable club.

In the second spring after Colonel Farrant's death, it was arranged that the Oakdene family should go up to town for the season. Mrs. Farrant had left off her weeds. Ellis and Adela urged them to come up for at least a few weeks, and as the house in Connaught Square, which had been let for the last two years, was now at liberty, there seemed no reason against it. Donovan was glad enough to go. He had begun to crave for a change of scene, and, though he was too unsociable and silent to care for the sort of gaieties which his mother enjoyed, London offered many other attractions to him.

Dot's room was in the front of the house, that she might have the benefit of the square garden, and, when she had recovered from the fatigue of the journey, she was able thoroughly to enjoy the change. Donovan had not noticed how very thin and weak she had grown lately. He was never away from her, and so did not see the change as a fresh comer would have done. It was a chance word of Adela Farrant's which first drew his attention to the fact.

'Why, my poor little Dot,' she exclaimed, coming into the room a few days after their arrival, 'how thin and white you have grown ; you're just like a little shadow. What have you been doing to her, Donovan ?'

The light tones and the smiling face of the speaker were a strange contrast to the startled abrupt interrogative which escaped Donovan, and the look of pain which came over his face.

'You think her changed ?'

'Yes, very much ; I believe, dear, they've kept you mewed up in the country a great deal too long. You wanted a little change and amusement. You wanted me to look after you, now didn't you ?'

Conscious that she had made rather an unfortunate remark, Adela talked on good-naturedly to the little girl, and once or twice tried to draw Donovan into the conversation; he did not seem to hear her, but stood leaning against the wall at the foot of Dot's couch, looking at her with a sad, anxious, pained scrutiny. Adela's words had sent a cold chill to his heart? Was it true? Was Dot really changed? Was she more fragile and delicate-looking than usual? He tried to look at her as if he were a stranger, tried to find the bare undisguised truth.

Dot was now twelve years old, though her little helpless form was so tiny that she looked more like a child of eight; he seemed never to have really *looked* at her before, and, though he knew every line of her face by heart, its beauty had never before struck him. She had always been to him just Dot herself, it had never entered his head to think whether she was pretty or not. She wore a loose white dress, and over her feet was spread a many-coloured Indian shawl, the same shawl which he remembered seeing in the ayah's arms on that day of wretchedness and disappointment in his childhood. The window was open, and the summer wind played with her soft brown hair as it lay on the pillow; he noticed a strange waxen look about the little childish face, and the beauty of the rounded serene forehead, with its too apparent network of blue veins, the soft grey-brown eyes, the tender little smiling mouth, struck him as it had never struck him before. It could never be, oh! surely it could never be, that she would be taken from him! Fate had been so cruel to him, it would surely leave him the one thing he cared for still! The mere thought caused him such agony that he could hardly contain himself; it was only from his habitual self-control, and from his love to Dot, that he could force a smile to his lips as she looked up at him appealingly.

'Dono, do you hear what we are saying? We are saying you must go out more while you are here. Cousin Adela says you are very unsociable.'

'Yes, you are a regular bear,' said Adela. 'I'm quite ashamed of you, sir, you've no excuse whatever. With your advantages you might turn the heads of half the girls in town.'

'A desirable employment,' said Donovan, veiling far deeper feelings with a sarcastic smile.

'There, I told you he was a bear! See how he speaks to me!' said Adela, with mock anger.

'I beg your pardon,' he said, laughing. 'But if that is the " whole duty of man," it's beyond me; I can't turn neat compliments to pretty women, it's not in me. Some fellows are born to it, it comes as naturally to them as card-playing comes to me. One can't go against nature.'

'You ought to do your duty,' said Adela, with playful severity.

'And if I were to ask, like Froude's cat, "What *is* my duty?" you would answer, I suppose, like the sagacious animals in the parable, "Get your own dinner," and add, perhaps, "at some grand house belonging to one of the 'upper ten.'" That is my duty, I suppose.'

'He is talking riddles to me, Dot,' said Adela, smiling. 'What cat does he mean?'

'Oh! the cat in "Short Studies on Great Subjects,"' said Dot, readily. 'Such a jolly story it is! The cat wanted to know what was the good of life, and everyone gave her such funny answers. The owl said, "Meditate, oh! cat," and so she tried to think which could have come first, the fowl or the egg. Dono laughed over that story more than I ever saw him laugh before.'

'But to return to the charge,' said Adela, 'why were you not at Lady Temple's last night?'

'Because I've forsworn such vanities,' said Donovan, contentedly. 'The night before I dutifully attended my mother to three fashionable crowds—"perpendiculars" is the best name for them, for there is seldom more than standing room—and, as we elbowed our way through the third set of rooms, I made up my mind that society wasn't in my line.'

'People never know when they're well off,' said Adela. 'Many men would be thankful enough to be in your shoes, and to be introduced to such a good circle, and, instead of making the most of your advantages, you think of nothing but those wicked cards.'

'Of course it is very wicked indeed to think of such things as whist, or loo, or euchre; instead of that my cousin would wish me to spend my evenings in the virtuous employment of talking nonsense in aristocratic drawing-rooms, or flirting in ball-rooms,' said Donovan, with a satirical smile.

'Your cousin would wish you to be a great deal more polite,' said Adela, laughing, 'and she does not like to be snapped up in that way, for all the world as if you were a machine for cutting people's words up—a chaff-cutter!'

'At any rate, I was not chaffing,' said Donovan, relapsing into good humour.

'Did you ever know anything like him?' said Adela, with another laugh. 'He can make as many bad puns as ordinary men when he tries, but let him be in society, and he's a bear—a gloomy Spanish don—more morose and formal and stupid than anyone I have met in my whole life.'

'You mustn't scold him,' said Dot, not quite understanding the banter, and hurt that anyone should think Donovan otherwise than perfect; 'you don't know a bit how good he is if you say that. When I was so ill six months ago, he was with me almost always, and often he used to sit up all night with me.'

'I didn't know you had been ill—worse, at least,' said Adela.

'Yes; it was in the autumn, when Cousin Ellis had come down for the shooting, and Dono missed ever so many days because he wouldn't leave me. Dono is the best nurse in the world; his hands are so clever, they never hurt like Doery's, and, do you know, once our old doctor wondered how it was he was so quick and clever and steady-handed, and Dono told him it was because he played billiards so much.'

'Some advantages, you see, Cousin Adela, in being a born gamester,' said Donovan, with rather a sad smile, as he looked down at Dot's little weak fingers wreathing themselves in and out of his.

'Well, I'm glad you can turn into a sick-nurse,' said Adela. 'You have brought out a new side of his character, Dot, and deserve a vote of thanks.'

'Oh! and Waif brought it out too,' said Dot, eagerly. 'Waif had the distemper dreadfully last year—he nearly died. The vetchi—what do you call the animal-doctor?—said that he would have died if Dono hadn't taken such care of him; he sat up with him two nights, and that saved his life. Isn't Waif a dear dog, cousin?'

'Well, I don't think he's a beauty,' said Adela, looking down at the fox-terrier, who was licking his master's hand.

'He can do lots of tricks, though,' said Dot; 'he's wonderfully clever, and he loves Dono so!'

'Have you seen Ellis's new dog?' asked Adela, who rather wanted to bring the conversation round to her brother. 'He has a new retriever. I suppose you have seen Ellis himself, have you not?'

'Well, yes, seeing that he's been in here every day,' said Donovan, not in his pleasantest tone.

'Oh! but, you're such an unsociable fellow,' said Adela. 'One might be in the house for hours and not see you. Ellis said something about meeting me here at five o'clock. I think I had better go downstairs and see if he has come.'

'Oh! stay with Dot a little longer,' said Donovan. 'I daresay he has not come yet; I'll go and see.'

Adela consented to stay on, and Donovan, with Waif at his heels, went downstairs. Opening the drawing-room door unconcernedly, and hastily glancing round to see if his cousin were there, he was suddenly confronted by a sight so unexpected, so disagreeably startling, that for a moment he stood rooted to the spot, unable to speak or move. His mother, half smiling, half tearful, had both her hands clasped in Ellis Farrant's : he was kneeling beside her in such a theatrical attitude that, if Donovan had not been altogether dismayed and astounded, he must have been amused.

Mrs. Farrant, looking up, saw her son, and, with a sudden blush, began nervously, ' Oh, Donovan ! ' then, turning to Ellis, faltered, ' You must tell him.'

It was not a pleasant task, but Ellis, in the triumph of his victory, could afford to meet a trifling annoyance of this sort. With much real trepidation carefully hidden beneath his most jaunty manner, he crossed the room to the mute statue-like form, which would not move a hair's-breadth to meet him.

' Well, my boy, I see there is little need to tell you ; I'm the happiest man in London, Donovan. Your mother has consented to be my wife. You must not be angry with me ; come, now, I am not going to steal her away from you—of course we shall all live on at Oakdene together. It is not every fellow of your age whom I should look forward to having as a son ; but you, Donovan, it is very different with you ; we have always been friends, have we not? I remember him,' he continued, turning to Mrs. Farrant, ' when he was quite a little fellow, and as sharp as a needle, though he couldn't have been more than seven.'

All this time Donovan's face had only grown more hard and flint-like. Ellis, with his usual tact, saw that his best policy would be to retreat at once, ignoring his ward's anger, and taking his congratulations for granted. He pressed Mrs. Farrant's hand in his.

' I must leave you now, dearest. You must talk this over with your son.' Then turning to Donovan, ' Stay, and hear all from your mother. No, leave me to let myself out. Adela said I should meet her in Dot's room. I'll just run up.'

Already he seemed to behave as if the house were his own. He held out his hand cordially, but Donovan would not see it ; still in perfect silence he turned hastily to open the door for his cousin, moving for the first time during the interview. Ellis went out smilingly, pretending not to notice the absence of all response, but as the door closed, and he went slowly upstairs alone, his brow clouded even in this his moment of victory, and between his teeth he hissed out the words, ' Young viper ! I'll

teach him to find his tongue! We'll have a rather different
interview, my friend, when you come of age!'

Donovan had been half paralysed while Ellis remained in the
room, but no sooner had he left it than, with sudden reaction, the
frozen blood seemed to boil in his veins. The stony look on his
face changed to passionate earnestness, and crossing the room in
hurried strides, he stood close to Mrs. Farrant.

'*Mother!*' he gasped. Only that one word, but there was
such intensity, such pleading, such misery in the tone, that the
most eloquent entreaties could not have been so stirring.

'Don't agitate me, Donovan. I have been so excited already,'
cried Mrs. Farrant, shrinking from him, really alarmed by his
looks. 'Don't, pray don't look so wild. I am very sorry if you
have been taken by surprise. I thought, of course, you saw last
autumn how it was.'

'Last autumn!' said Donovan. 'Last autumn I could think
of nothing but Dot. I was blind—hoodwinked by his devices.
Oh! mother, do not, do not let it be. I see now how it has all
been—one long piece of manœuvering from the very first. He
has been trading on us. He brought his sister down to dazzle
me, to draw off my attention. Mother, do not trust him, he is
false, and treacherous, and mean. He will make you miserable!'

'It is not your place to speak like this,' said Mrs. Farrant,
with some resentment in her tone. 'You forget that Mr. Farrant is my future husband; you forget that you are speaking to
your mother.'

'I do not forget,' cried Donovan, vehemently. 'It is because
I cannot forget you are my mother that I must speak. I am
your son, and you must and shall hear me. I know Ellis Farrant
better than you do. You only see the sleek, bland, polite side
of him; but I have seen him with other men. He is false, and
grasping, and selfish. If it had not been for him I might not
have been what I am now. Mother, do not throw yourself away
on such a man as that. It will bring nothing but wretchedness
on us all. For Dot's sake, for your own sake, do not let this be!'

'I wish you wouldn't talk so wildly,' said Mrs. Farrant half
crying. 'I don't know what you mean by saying such dreadful
things about your—your guardian. It is very hard that directly
some one else begins to love me you should suddenly wake up
from your usual indifference. You never loved me yourself, and
you will not let anyone else love me.'

'It is not true,' said Donovan, greatly agitated. 'I could
have loved you dearly, mother, if you would only have let me. I
do love you—far, far more than that other man, who only wants

your money. Send him away; do not listen to him. Let us be what nature meant us to be to each other!'

'You are mad! You frighten me. You make my head ache,' said Mrs. Farrant, petulantly. 'You have never shown me any particular attention. I scarcely see you, except at meal-times. It is unreasonable of you to be vexed because I accept an offer of marriage.'

'Have I driven you to it?' cried poor Donovan. 'Would I not willingly have been more to you! Did I not tell you so long ago? And you turned from me. You told me to be more like that knave!'

'If I told you so before, I certainly repeat it now,' said Mrs. Farrant. 'Your guardian is a gentleman. He would never speak in such a way to a defenceless woman. When my only son can attack me so fiercely, I think it is time I accepted a husband to protect me.'

'Fiercely! Protect you!' echoed Donovan, in a voice which, though less vehement, was full of pain. Could she have thought his passion of re-awakening love, his eager longing to save her certain misery, was fierceness? Bitterly wounded, he turned away with one despairing sentence. 'We shall *never* understand each other.'

'Perhaps not,' she replied, 'but, at any rate, we must not again discuss this subject. It would not be right for me to listen to you, or for you to say such things again. Do you understand?'

'Yes,' he murmured, 'I have said my say.' Then looking down at her again, he added, in a repressed voice, 'When will it be?'

'I do not know,' she faltered. 'Perhaps—perhaps at the end of the season.'

There was a moment's pause, then in silence Donovan crossed the room, and would have gone out, but, by some sudden unknown impulse, Mrs. Farrant stopped him.

'Dono!' it was the old childish name, and it checked him at once. 'Dono, come back, come back and kiss me.'

For years and years the formal salute had passed between them every day, now for the first time it was spontaneous, or rather Mrs. Farrant felt for the first time a mother's natural craving for affection, and Donovan was allowed to give expression to the love which had never really been quenched, only shut down and restrained.

The unwonted piece of demonstration helped in part to take the sting from the unwelcome news. Donovan's face as he returned to Dot's room was sad indeed, but no longer bitter.

'Oh! Dono,' she cried, eagerly, 'have you heard? Has Cousin Ellis told you?'

'Yes, I have heard all,' said Donovan, much more quietly than she had expected.

'And you do not mind so very much. I was so afraid you would be vexed, because last time Cousin Ellis was with us you kept on wishing he would go.'

'I shall wish it pretty often again,' said Donovan, with a slight smile, 'but there is no good in crying out now, the deed is done, and we must make the best of it. I have said all I can say, and it is no good.'

'You have been with mamma?'

'Yes, we had a strange talk and a strange ending to it; we must not forget she is our mother, Dot.'

'Oh! but what shall I say when she comes?' said Dot, anxiously. 'I can't say I'm glad. What am I to do?'

'Show her that you love her,' said Donovan.

Dot looked doubtful and troubled, but, as Donovan sat down to the piano, and began to play one of her favourite airs by Mozart, she reasoned with herself till her resolution was made.

'It is far worse for him than for me, he will have to give up all sorts of things when Cousin Ellis marries mamma, and I know that he does not like him at all. Doery said last autumn that Cousin Ellis spoke shamefully to him sometimes, and Doery doesn't often make excuses for Dono. I am very selfish to mind about it myself, when I don't even know why I mind. I'll try to be nice when mamma comes up.'

While the mournful sweetness of 'Vedrai Carino' was still filling the room, Mrs. Farrant entered. Donovan went on playing, knowing that Dot would be less shy if her words were sheltered by the music; but there were no words at all, Dot only looked her love and put both arms round her mother's neck.

Donovan had not known his father sufficiently well to feel his death very acutely. The shock at the time had been great, and his grief then had been very real, but he had soon recovered from the blow, and now regarded it rather as a loss which was to be deplored than as a life-long sorrow. But with the prospect of his mother's second marriage his thoughts naturally reverted to his father; he lived over again the sad meeting after his school disgrace, the day at Plymouth, the brief time at Porthkerran, and lastly the awful scene, when in an instant, without a farewell word or look, his father had been snatched from him. Slowly and carefully he retraced the past, recalled all the conversations between them, remembered his father's courtesy, his sympathy, his gentle yet deeply-pained allusion to the 'breach of honour.' What a contrast he was to Ellis Farrant! The one refined, dignified, upright; the other ostentatious, false, and grasping! Donovan could not judge people by the highest standard, but he had a standard of his own, and Ellis fell immeasurably below it. His mother had once accused him of being self-satisfied, but his self-reliance was not self-satisfaction, he was in reality often bitterly out of heart with himself, only the sweeping condemnation of all his acquaintances forced him to assert himself. They considered him a black sheep, and yet he felt he was not all that they represented him. Still there had been truth and sadness in his words to his mother, when he said that Ellis had made him what he was; even with his scanty light he knew that his life was not what it ought to have been; goodness and honour were to be respected, and he struggled on in a blind endeavour to reach his own standard. The remembrance of his father helped him to a certain extent, but it could not exercise a really strong influence over him, for it was merely the remembrance of what had once existed, and had now passed away for ever.

When not occupied with Dot, or engrossed with his favourite pastime, life seemed to him very hollow and unsatisfactory. When Mrs. Farrant desired it, he went out with her; when Adela particularly asked him, he would consent to escort the two ladies to whatever place of amusement they wished to go to, but it was all very uncongenial to him. At concerts, not being really musical, he soon grew weary and bored; at the theatre he laughed bitterly at what seemed to him a mere travesty of life, in which virtue was rewarded and vice punished in an ideal way, very unlike the injustice of real existence. At balls, or at fashionable receptions, he saw merely the falseness of society, the low motives, the heartless frivolity, the absurd vanity of the individuals composing it. He was certainly free from the annoyances he met with at Oakdene; no one looked askance at him here, no one had time to think of such trifles; but, after the first novelty had worn off, the change ceased to satisfy or relieve him. He was really unhappy, too, about his mother's second marriage. Little by little, as he felt sure of his ground, Ellis Farrant had withdrawn the mask of friendliness, and had allowed Donovan to see what he really was; it had at present been done only in part, and with great judgment and tact, but it was just sufficient to rouse his dislike, and to make him inclined in arguments with his mother to speak against his guardian, while Mrs. Farrant was of course stimulated to defend him.

Matters were thus with the son; with the accepted lover—

the successful schemer—they were not much more happy. A
great writer of the present day has said that, if we do injustice
to any fellow-creature, we come in time to hate him. It was thus
with Ellis Farrant; he had gone down to Porthkerran at the
time of his cousin's death, feeling a sort of admiration and fond-
ness for Donovan; the boy had always been pleasant and companionable; he liked him as well as he liked anyone outside
himself. But then followed the sudden act of glaring injustice,
and as time passed he began to dislike his unconscious victim
more and more. The sight of him was a continual reproach; he
was uneasy and restless in his presence, even at times afraid of
him. In the moment of his triumph and success, his hatred increased tenfold, and though, when he went up to Dot's room after
his interview with Mrs. Farrant and Donovan, his manner was
bland and smiling, Adela knew him too well not to detect the
latent irritation. Anxious to know all the particulars which
could not be mentioned before the little girl, she took leave
rather hastily, tripped lightly down the stairs, and, as soon as
the hall door had closed behind them, turned round eagerly to
her brother.

'I congratulate you, Ellis!'

Ellis had overheard Donovan's eager tones of expostulation
as he passed the drawing-room door, and the scowl on his face
did not at all befit an accepted lover.

'Where do you want to go to?' he said, crossly, not attending to her words.

'Back to Eaton Place,' said Adela, who was staying with
some friends. 'What is the matter with you? I thought all
had gone so well.'

'So it has in the main, only that young cub came in and spoilt
it all. He's really insufferable.'

'Now don't speak against my Augustus Cæsar,' said Adela;
'he's not a bad boy at all. What did he do?'

'Do!' said Ellis, smiling a little—'he did nothing; he stood
and looked at me with a stony face, very much like an old Roman,
as you are always saying.'

'I can just fancy it,' said Adela, laughing, 'and my noble
brother didn't quite enjoy the lofty scorn. What did he say to it
all?—was he not surprised? He went down so casually and
unsuspectingly to see if you had come that I had hardly the
heart not to give him warning. However, I kept my promise to you, didn't I? It was well past five when I let him go
down.'

'You managed very well, and I'm much obliged to you,' said

Ellis, recovering his good humour; 'he came in the very nick of time, and saw it all at a glance.'

'Poor fellow!—what did he say?'

'Nothing; he looked thunderstruck, and never said a single word—was as mum as a dummy, in fact.'

'Or as dumb as a mummy,' said Adela, with a light laugh. 'And you, I suppose, talked glibly, and promised to be a devoted step-father?'

'Something of the sort,' said Ellis, smiling.

'Well, I don't wonder he doesn't like it,' said Adela. 'Of course, he is practically master at Oakdene; he won't enjoy making way for you.'

'I don't suppose he will,' replied Ellis, thinking of far more serious matters than his sister. 'But, you know, my dear, we can't all win in the game.'

'The winner can afford to moralise,' said Adela, rather contemptuously; 'but I must not scold you, for you have managed your work very neatly, and of course I'm glad of your success. When is it to be?'

'The wedding? I don't know. Perhaps the end of July. Anyhow, I'm afraid I shall miss the grouse this year.'

'You horrid, matter-of-fact creature, to think of it even,' said Adela. 'Middle-aged lovers are no fun. They have lost the romance of their youth.'

'We will leave that kind of thing for you and your Cæsar,' said Ellis, laughingly, as they took leave of each other.

'A thousand thanks,' said Adela, with a mocking bow, 'but I have done with my "beardless youth," now that your affairs are settled. It was the dullest flirtation I ever had; for, quite between ourselves, that sort of thing is not in Cæsar's line.'

'I daresay not. Mum as a dummy, you know!' and Ellis turned away with a laugh in which there was much spite and little merriment.

CHAPTER X.

LOOKING TWO WAYS.

Accuse me not, beseech thee, that I wear,
  Too calm and sad a face in front of thine ;
  For we two look two ways, and cannot shine
With the same sunlight on our brow and hair.
On me thou lookest with no doubting care,

    •   •   •   •   •   •   •

. . . But I look on thee—on thee—
  Beholding, besides love, the end of love,
Hearing oblivion beyond memory ;
  As one who sits and gazes from above,
Over the rivers to the bitter sea.'

E. B. BROWNING.

'On the 29th inst., at St. George's, Hanover Square, Ellis Farrant, only son of the late J. E. Farrant, Esq., and nephew of the late Thomas Farrant, Esq., of Oakdene Manor, Mountshire, and Rippingham, Surrey, to Honora, widow of Colonel Ralph Farrant, R.A., and daughter of the late General Patrick Donovan. No cards.'

Two old maiden ladies, who were spending their summer holiday at a watering-place in the south of England, and were partaking of a rather late breakfast in the coffee-room of the best hotel, wondered what there could be in the first sheet of the *Times* to cause such a sudden change in the face of their neighbour at the next table. The kind old souls had made a little romance about the handsome, grave-looking young fellow, who had come to the hotel a few days before, and used to sit down to his solitary table in the coffee-room, never seeming to care to talk with anyone. Miss Brown the elder had made up her mind that he was an Italian. He was dark and melancholy-looking; Italians were dark and melancholy-looking, therefore the young man was doubtless Italian. Possibly he was an exile, and probably he was married. the Italians, she believed, did marry young, and no doubt his wife was a heartless, worldly person, and caused her husband endless trouble. Miss Brown the younger was inclined to think the young man a Spaniard, there was something very Spanish in his grave, dignified deportment. (N.B.—Miss Brown had never seen a Spaniard in her life.) She had met him on the stairs one day as he was going out, and he had taken off his hat as he passed her. Very few

Englishmen would have done that; he was certainly a foreigner
of some sort. She, however, scouted the idea that he was married,
and made up her mind that he was crossed in love.

'There is the young foreigner,' Miss Brown had said to her
sister as Donovan came into the coffee-room that morning. They
had agreed to call him the *foreigner*, as a sort of general term
which suited the opinions of each.

'He is coming to this side of the room,' said Miss Marianne,
looking up from her egg, but hastily and decorously turning to
the window, and making a vague remark about the weather when
she found the dark, flashing eyes of the stranger glancing across
at her from the other table.

'He looks rather happier this morning,' said Miss Brown in a
low tone.

Miss Marianne of course wished him to look gloomy, and
tried to see something melancholy in the way in which he sipped
his coffee, stroked his moustache, and cut his roll in half, gently
insinuating to her sister that men in good spirits would have
broken a roll; that to be so methodical in trifles was, she thought,
rather a sign of—in fact quite supported *her* theory. Both ladies
were a little startled when the hero of their romance called a
waiter, and without the slightest foreign accent asked if the
morning papers had come.

'Strange that he should care to see English papers,' said Miss
Brown, musingly.

'I believe I have heard that Spaniards are very good linguists,' said Miss Marianne, timidly.

'Not half so good as Italians, my dear,' said the elder sister.
'Think of Dante, and—and Garibaldi.'

Miss Marianne was rather overwhelmed by the mention of
these great men, and did not for a moment question that they
had been renowned linguists; she did indeed try to think of
some Spanish celebrity of equal renown, and racked her brains
for the name of the author of 'Don Quixote,' but it had escaped
her memory, and before she could recall it the waiter returned
with the newspapers. The 'foreigner' took the *Times* and glanced
rapidly down the first column; Miss Brown would have liked to
think that he looked at the agony column, but his eye travelled
too far down the page for that, he would have passed the space
allotted to sentimental messages, and have reached the uninteresting notices of lost and found dogs, &c.; Miss Marianne had the
best of it now—he was evidently looking at the marriages. The
two sisters almost gave a sympathetic start when suddenly their
neighbour's forehead was sharply contracted, and a quick flush

rose to his cheek.   What could it be?   The marriage of the girl
whom he loved?   There was real and undoubted romance here,
not a question of it.   How interesting hotel life was, it must be
something like watching a play, though Miss Brown had never
been to the play—she would have thought it exceedingly wrong.
Poor boy! how impatiently he throws down the paper, it falls on
to the floor, and Miss Marianne leaning back in her chair and
trying to see below the cloth of the adjoining table, maintains
that he has put his foot on it, actually 'crushed it under foot,'
that is very romantic!   Then he hastily drains his coffee cup,
and when he puts it down, the flush has died away from his face,
and has left it very pale, and cold, and still.   The arrival of the
paper seems to have taken away his appetite, for he abruptly
pushes back his chair, leaves his half-finished breakfast, and stalks
out of the room.

The sisters were much excited.   As they walked on the beach
that morning they agreed that East Codrington was a charming
place.   Some people called it dull, but for their part they thought
it a most amusing little town.   It was very pleasant to meet
fresh faces, very interesting to watch other people's lives.   Miss
Brown said that the sea air or *something* made her feel quite
young again.   Scarcely were the words out of her mouth when
Miss Marianne suddenly caught her arm, exclaiming,

'Sister, look, there is the " foreigner " again!'

Miss Brown looked along the esplanade for the solitary figure
with the grave dark face, but could not see it.

'There! there! not nearly so far off,' said Miss Marianne.
'Don't you see him reading to that little girl in the invalid
chair?'

'Impossible!' said Miss Brown, quickly.   'He is far too
young to have a child of that age; but it is the " foreigner," I
see, she must be his sister.   Suppose, Marianne, we sit down a
little.'

Miss Marianne owned that she was tired, and the two ladies
established themselves on the beach, about a stone's throw from
Dot and Donovan, taking care to choose a side posture, so that
on one hand they could watch the sea, and on the other the hero
of their romance.   Every now and then the breeze wafted a
sentence of the reading to the two sisters.   They exchanged
glances with each other, and Miss Marianne whispered ' English!'
Then something in the book made both the reader and the
listener laugh heartily, and the name of ' Ali Baba ' was caught
by Miss Brown, who nodded to her sister, and whispered, ' The
Arabian Nights.'   Then came a fresh mystery, the reader's face

suddenly became dark and overcast, and there was quite a
different tone in his voice as he read the words, 'You plainly see
that Cogia Houssain only sought your acquaintance in order to
insure success in his diabolical treachery.'

Now why should Cogia Houssain bring such a strange bitter
look into anyone's face? Presently the story of the 'Forty
Thieves' was finished, and the hero's face was good-tempered
again, he moved the little invalid's chair quite to the edge of the
esplanade, as near as possible to the shingle, so that without
wilful listening the two old ladies could hear all that passed;
whatever their hero was when alone, there could be no doubt
that he was merry enough now.

There was a laughing discussion about the dog's swimming
powers.

'You only tried him once in the Serpentine, you know,' said
the little invalid. 'I don't believe you dare try him here.'

'See if I don't!' said Donovan, laughing, and whistling to the
fox-terrier. 'I'll throw him a stone.'

'No, no, that's no test,' said Dot. 'Throw him your new
stick. Ah! I believe you're afraid to! You don't think he'll
get it back!'

'You dare me to?' asked Donovan. 'Come along, Waif, and
show your mistress how clever you are.'

The dog followed his master obediently across the shingle to
the water's edge, and plunged in valiantly as soon as the stick
was thrown. Donovan had sent it far out, and the receding tide
was bearing it further still, but Waif swam on indefatigably, and,
after some minutes, clenched it successfully in his teeth, and
turned back again. Dot waved her handkerchief from the
esplanade in congratulation, and both dog and master hurried
up the beach towards her; on the way, however, Waif paused to
shake the water from his coat, and, unluckily, the two old ladies
were within the radius of the drops, and received a sort of shower
bath. Donovan hastened up to apologise.

'I am afraid my dog has been troubling you. I hope he has
done no damage?'

'Oh! none, thank you,' said the sisters, smiling. 'Salt
water never gives cold. We were much amused by watching him
in the sea.'

'He's a capital swimmer. My little sister wouldn't believe
he was a water-dog,' and then, raising his hat, Donovan passed
on with a triumphant greeting to the little invalid.

'Well, Dot! own now that you're beaten.'

'Quite beaten. He was splendid,' said Dot, enthusiastically.

Presently, as the old ladies rose to move on, and passed close to the brother and sister, Dot looked up in her sweet shy way, and said,

'I hope Waif did not hurt your dress just now?'

Miss Marianne, with a beaming face, hastened to re-assure her.

'Not in the least, my dear, thank you,' and then, touched by the fragile little face, the old lady began to search in a Mentone basket that she carried for some of the beach treasures which she had been picking up. 'Would you like some shells, my dear? We have found some rather pretty ones this morning.'

Dot's shy gratitude was very charming, and Donovan, always pleased by any attention shown to her, began to talk to the old ladies, quite forgetting his usual haughty reserve.

The Miss Browns' romance certainly died out in the light of truth, but they were much interested in the brother and sister, though their hero had proved to be neither a Spaniard nor an Italian. Donovan, however, was rather a puzzle to them. In a few days' time, Miss Marianne learnt to her regret, from some other people at the hotel, that her hero, though so devoted to his little invalid sister, was the most noted billiard-player in the place, and the gentle old ladies regretted it, for, as Miss Brown the elder said, 'it was a dangerous taste for such a young man, particularly as he seemed to be his own master.' They talked the matter over together, but agreed that they could not presume to offer advice; however, an occasion soon came when their consciences would not allow them to keep silence.

It was Sunday morning; Miss Marianne timidly suggested that, if it would not be wrong, she would very much like a little turn on the esplanade before going to church. Her sister was rather puritanical; however, she thought there could be no harm in 'taking the air,' so, armed with their large church-services and hymn-books, the two old ladies set out. The day was intensely hot and sultry, the sea was as calm as a mill-pond, the tiny waves lazily lapping the shore as if they, too, felt the heat, and could not dance briskly as usual. There was a quiet Sunday feeling all around; no stir of business or traffic; the church bells ringing for service, and the passers-by walking quietly, with none of the hurry and bustle of the ordinary every-day passengers. The old ladies enjoyed their walk, but just as they had turned for the last time before going in the direction of the bells they caught sight of their friends in the distance; there was the invalid chair, with the little pale-faced child, and on a bench beside her was Donovan, in a most unsabbatical light-brown shooting-jacket and cloth travelling-hat; to add to it all, he was smoking, and to the Miss Browns the sight of a cigar was always a sight to be deplored, but on Sunday smoking seemed to them little better than sacrilege. Miss Marianne was almost disarmed by the courtesy of the greeting, but her sister would not allow her face to soften; good looks and pleasant manners were all very well, but 'Sabbath breaking' was a sin which could not be passed by, so she tried not to see the fascinating dark eyes, and said gravely,

'Are you not coming to church to-day, Mr. Farrant ?,'

'No, Miss Brown,' replied Donovan, not at all offended by the question, to which indeed he was pretty well accustomed, 'Dot and I mean to sit here and enjoy the view. A beautiful day, is it not?'

'It is very pleasant to see you so attentive to your sister,' said Miss Brown, severely, 'but religion ought to stand first, young man. The soul ought to be considered before the body.'

'There is a very good preacher at St. Oswald's,' suggested Miss Marianne, timidly.

Donovan looked at her half sadly and half amusedly, but shook his head, and the two ladies passed on.

He resumed his cigar, but with rather a clouded brow, wishing that people would leave him unmolested. Dot was the first to break the silence.

'What does "soul" really mean, Dono?' she began, in her childish voice. 'Doery calls old Betty, the charwoman, "poor soul," but I fancy that is because her husband drinks. Are we all poor souls?'

'Most of us,' said Donovan, shortly.

'But what is a soul?' persisted Dot.

'A name given by some people to the mind,' he replied. 'Though I daresay those old ladies would not agree to that, and would tell you it was quite a different part of you.'

Now Dot had lived on contentedly for many years in entire ignorance, but she was just beginning to be roused, and the words of the two old ladies had perplexed her.

'What part of us is it?' she questioned.

He hesitated for a moment.

'The part you love me with, I suppose.'

'Then do you think it would be really good for the part you love me with to go to church?'

'No, you sweet little arguer, I don't,' he replied, smiling; 'and, if it would, I shouldn't go and leave you in your pain, but don't trouble your head about the matter, darling. If religion makes sour, selfish soul-preservers like that, it stands to reason

it's false. I'll have none of it! Fancy listening to a sermon
with the idea that it was virtuous, and leaving you to Doery's
tender mercies, or all alone with the sun blazing in your eyes!'

He held the umbrella more protectingly over her as he spoke,
and was rather vexed to see that her usually smooth serene forehead was knitted in anxious thought.

'What is the matter?' he asked, jealous of anything which
she kept back from him.

'I am so puzzled,' said Dot, wearily. 'I don't know what
people mean by religion; my head aches so. Do you think I
ought to make myself think what it is?'

'Of course not, you dear little goose,' he said, stroking back
the hair from her hot face. 'Who put such morbid ideas into
your head?'

'No one,' said Dot, wistfully, 'only it seems as if we ought
to find out which is right, you or the other people.'

'It will not make much difference, perhaps,' said Donovan,
throwing away the end of his cigar. 'We shall all come to an
end, I suppose—be smoked out and thrown away, so to speak.'

Dot looked troubled, and he hastily bent down and kissed her.

'We are talking of things we know nothing about, dear. You
and I must love each other, that is all I know. Don't let us talk
of this any more, it only worries you.'

'But, Dono, just one thing more. When it is all done, when
we die, shall I have to leave off loving you?'

A black shadow passed over his face, but he did not answer.
Dot understood what he meant, and clasped her tiny fingers round
his tightly.

'Oh, Dono,' she said, mournfully, 'I couldn't bear to stop
loving you—I had never thought about that. Oh, I hope I shall
live to be very, very old, even if I'm always ill. Why is your
face so white and stiff, Dono? Are you thinking what you would
do if I didn't live to be old?'

'*Don't!*' he cried, passionately, and there was such anguish in
his tone that Dot looked half frightened, and faltered,

'I didn't mean—I'm very sorry.'

His kissed her, and she noticed that his lips were very cold,
and his voice, though quieter when he next spoke, sounded odd
and unnatural.

'It is all right, darling—I didn't mean to frighten you—it is
nothing. I must be alone—I must think.'

He moved her chair into the shade, and then walked along the
shore battling with the terrible thoughts which filled his mind.
What if Dot should be taken away from him? It was the same

agonizing idea which Adela's words had suggested to him not long before. Now he was alone and could allow himself to face it, could relax for the time the control which in her presence he was obliged to keep up. Throwing himself down on the shingle, he allowed the shadowy foes one after another to throng up into his mind, wrestling with each in a vain, hopeless endeavour to crush them. Sooner or later the end must come, he knew it perfectly well, and yet, like a hunted creature, he tried for some possible means of escape, or at any rate of delay. Could he force himself, for the sake of peace, to believe what popular religion taught? No, he told himself that it would be as impossible as to believe in the old Norse legends of the happy hunting fields. There was no escape for him, the separation must be faced.

He lay stretched out on the pebbles with his face turned from the light, more wretched and forlorn than the poorest beggar in East Codrington. His miserable struggle and dumb despair were at last broken in upon by the sound of a voice in the distance, a high-pitched man's voice, which beat uncomfortably on his ear, and sounded melancholy and depressing, as open-air speaking generally does sound. He started up impatiently, and saw that a street-preacher had gathered together a little knot of men and women on the beach, at no great distance from him. He disliked the interruption, and yet, with a sort of curiosity, sauntered towards the little group, and listened for a few minutes; but unfortunately the preacher happened at the minute to be denouncing 'modern ritualism' with much bitterness, and he soon turned away contemptuously. Did not these professing Christians 'bite and devour' one another? Did they not unsparingly condemn all with whom they did not agree? And, holding the views they did about the future state, did they not still live easy, quiet, indulgent lives, though they believed that more than half mankind would finally be 'lost'?

By-and-by there was singing; with great gusto the preacher started the hymn 'There is a fountain.' Donovan's misery had been keen enough before, this just made it complete. The old melody—powerful though it is when sung by a great multitude—has something extremely aggravating about it.

'I *will* believe—I *do* believe!'

Over and over again with emphatic untunefulness the motley crowd roared and shouted the refrain.

Donovan's dark face grew darker, he set his teeth, listened for a time, then walked away with a look of intense scorn, resolving in his own mind that, miserable though he was, he would at least be honest, no cupboard faith for him!

Dot did not allude to the conversation again. She could not bear to risk recalling the look of pain to Donovan's face, and if she puzzled over the difference of opinion which had attracted her notice, she kept her difficulties to herself; but she fancied she understood why it was that, not long after that Sunday, Donovan made arrangements with an artist staying in the hotel to paint a miniature of her. A sweet, wistful, and yet childlike face it was, but the artist idealised it, and gave to the beautiful eyes more fulness of satisfaction than just at that time they really expressed, leaving it to the lips to show whatever latent sadness or desire there remained.

In September the visit to Codrington was ended ; Mrs. Doery was obliged to be at Oakdene to superintend the preparations for the return of her master and mistress, and Donovan wished to be at home when his mother arrived, chiefly from a dislike to coming back when his step-father was actually installed in his new position as head of the household. He chose to be there beforehand, and awaited the return in a sort of proud silence, never even to Dot breathing a single word which could tell how much he dreaded it.

On the whole the event proved to be not half so disagreeable as he had expected. Ellis was kind and conciliatory at first, and, though his patronage was hard to bear, Donovan had sense enough to be thankful for whatever would avert an open quarrel. He felt instinctively that sooner or later there would be disagreement between them, and for Dot's sake he was glad to keep the peace.

What he really suffered from chiefly that autumn was an utterly different thing. Under the new *régime*, Doery had been constituted housekeeper ; Ellis was hospitable, and constantly had the Manor full of his friends, so that Mrs. Farrant did not care for the burden and anxiety of household management ; it was quite another thing to the quiet routine which she had been able to superintend with little trouble before her second marriage. Mrs. Doery therefore ascended in the domestic scale from nurse to housekeeper, and a new attendant waited on Dot in her place. It seemed a very trifling change in the house, only a new servant, only one insignificant addition, hardly worth thinking of, but to Dot the change meant the opening of a new life. Now, at last, she began to understand the meaning of things. Phœbe, who had been blessed with better teaching than poor old Mrs. Doery, and was more loving and kind-hearted, opened an entirely new world to her little helpless charge, and Dot, in her simple, childlike happiness ir the new revelation, wondered why people

had not told her before, but never thought of blaming them for
the ignorance in which they had let her grow up.

Her simple, unquestioning acceptance of the most incomprehensible doctrines was a marvel to Donovan; he could not the
least understand it. Dot once or twice spoke with him on the
subject, but he always silenced her gently, for, though he could
not understand or sympathise with her new happiness, he was
unwilling to interfere with it, or to trouble the child's mind with
his own views. He thought it all a delusion, and it pained him
that she should believe it; but, seeing how much it must soften
both life and death to her, he was willing that she should believe
in the delusion. Still the trial to himself was very hard to bear,
for though to Dot the change seemed only to intensify her love,
and in no way to interfere with Donovan's place in her heart, he
necessarily felt that there was a barrier between them; what to
him did not exist was everything to her; till lately she had
depended entirely on him, now he was superseded—dearly loved
still, but yet superseded. This was a greater trouble than all
the annoyance of his mother's second marriage. Donovan loved
Dot so blindly and solely that the idea of not reigning alone in
her heart was terrible to him. Ever since his childhood he had
been her protector; to yield her to any other love in which he
believed would have been very hard, but to allow his place to be
usurped by that which he could not comprehend or believe to be,
was bitter beyond all thought. It was, perhaps, the most severe
test of his love that there could have been; he passed through
it without faltering, tried to find comfort in the sight of her
serene happiness, and bore his pain in silence; the fact that it
was a strange, unnatural, morbid pain did not make it any easier
to endure, but quite the contrary.

Ellis Farrant, not having too tender a conscience, managed
to enjoy his new position for the first few months. He was in
many ways a good-natured man, and it was very pleasant to
him, after his bachelor life and small income, to find himself at
the head of a comfortable and even luxurious home. His wife
was pretty and placid, his means were ample, he was able to ask
his friends down to Oakdene for the shooting, and altogether he
appreciated his change of fortune. For a little while he even
felt kindly disposed to Donovan, for, as he said to himself, the
poor wretch would have a hard enough life next year, when he
came of age, and might as well enjoy the present. He even at
times began to regret the part he had set himself to play, wavered
a little, and half contemplated starting his ward in some profession fairly and honourably. If Donovan had behaved sensibly,

this really might have come about, but he was not sensible. In a very short time he began to grow weary of making polite responses to his step-father's patronage; he never openly disputed his authority or actually quarrelled with him, but he allowed his dislike to show itself, and took no pains to be pleasant and companionable. Ellis was not a man to be trifled with; his kindness was a mere impulse, and directly he found that Donovan did not respond to it he took offence, and disliked him a great deal more than he had previously done.

It was a most unsatisfactory household. An outsider, looking into the luxurious dining-room of the Manor, might not have discovered anything amiss, certainly; Mrs. Farrant, at the head of the table, looked young and pretty and languid; Ellis, at the opposite end, seemed hospitable and good-natured; Donovan had apparently everything that could be wished in circumstances, health, and personal advantages. But beneath all this outward appearance was a miserable reality of injustice, jealousy, and hatred.

One evening in December, after Mrs. Farrant had left the dinner-table, the storm broke at last. Donovan had been more than usually gloomy and depressed. Dot had just had one of her bad attacks; he was worn out with attending to her; he was morbidly unhappy at the change in her views, and her supposed change toward himself, and his manner towards his step-father had been so short and sullen that the elder man's patience at length gave way.

As the door closed behind Mrs. Farrant, her husband refilled his glass, drained it, and then suddenly confronted his step-son with the fierceness of a weak, impulsive man who is thoroughly exasperated.

'I tell you what, Donovan, if you go on any longer in this way, you can't expect me to be civil to you. Do you think I shall stand having a mute morose idiot of a fellow always at my table, a skeleton at the feast? If you don't mend your manners pretty quickly, you won't find this house comfortable.'

Donovan did not reply, but cracked three walnuts in succession without even looking up. The absence of retort only made Ellis more angry, however.

'Do you not hear me, sir?' he continued, still more vehemently.

'Yes,' said Donovan, looking up at last, and speaking in a singularly controlled voice, which contrasted strangely with his step-father's violence.

Ellis raged on, doubly irritated by the monosyllable.

'Do you think it is pleasant to me to have your gloomy face

always haunting me? I tell you I'd rather sit opposite a skull and cross-bones! I'm not going to have my new home spoilt by an insufferable cub of your age.'

Now, with all his faults, Donovan had one good quality which often stood him in good stead. Old Mrs. Doery had at least taught him one useful lesson in his childhood. She had taught him to restrain himself, a lesson which, in these days of universal license to the young, is too often neglected. Many people would have fired up at once, if they had been spoken to in such a way. It would have been hard under any circumstances, but when the words were addressed to him in the house which had been his own father's, and by the man who had ousted him from his proper place, it must be owned that they were most intolerable. He flushed deeply and bit his lip.

'I am glad to see you have the grace to be ashamed,' said Ellis, provokingly, impatient of this continued silence.

By this time Donovan had himself well in hand. His face was calm and rigid, and he could trust himself to reply without losing his temper, though his cold pride was not likely to choose wise words.

'I am sorry to have annoyed you, but naturally " as you have brewed so you will drink." I have not changed particularly in the last few months, and I suppose last summer you foresaw that there would be two incumbrances in your new home.'

Of course this only angered Ellis still more.

'You young puppy,' he exclaimed, angrily, 'do you remember whom you are speaking to? Do you know that I can turn you out of the house, if I like? Do you recollect who I am?'

'Yes,' said Donovan, ironically, 'I remember that you are my father's executor and my guardian.'

Ellis suddenly changed colour, pushed back his chair, and began to pace up and down the room. His step-son's words had stung him far more deeply than the speaker intended. 'His father's executor!' yes, and what an executor! The name itself was a reproach and a mockery! He felt afraid of Donovan, ashamed to look at him; his recent anger and hatred suddenly died away into a trembling shrinking dread. This boy, whom he had cheated and robbed and fatally injured, was able at times to influence him greatly. He felt that he must be pacified and kept at bay during the few months which remained of his minority.

On the whole, Ellis did not look very much like a happy bridegroom and head of the household as he came back to the table. He was ashy pale, and his hand shook as he poured out

his next glass of wine. Donovan, as he waited with his cold
impassive face expecting a fresh burst of anger, was surprised,
when his step-father next broke the silence, to find that the
storm had been as brief as it had been severe: There was an
almost pitiable struggle for really frank reconciliation in Ellis's
tone as he said,

'Come, old fellow, don't let us quarrel; we have always been
friends. I spoke hastily just now, but, you know, you really
cut your own throat by looking so glum. Everyone would
like you twice as well if you had a little more go in you.
Probyn was saying only the other night what a clever fellow you
were. He said he hadn't met a better whist-player for years.
You think everyone's against you, and so you are morose
and reserved, but I don't know a fellow who has more advantages
than you, if only you'd condescend to use them a little more.
There! you see I'm giving you quite a paternal lecture. Put
that in your pipe and smoke it. What do you say to some crib-
bage now?'

'I'll come down at ten,' said Donovan, allowing his face to
relax; then, sweeping up a handful of walnut shells, he left the
table, and spent the rest of the evening with Dot, making a
miniature fleet of boats, to her great content.

CHAPTER XI.

'LET NOTHING YOU DISMAY.'

Heart's brother, hast thou ever known
  What meaneth that No more?
Hast thou the bitterness outdrawn,
  Close hidden at its core?

Oh! no—draw from it worlds of pain,
  And thou shalt surely find,
That in that word there doth remain
  A bitterer drop behind.
                    ARCHBISHOP TRENCH.

'PHŒBE says she doesn't think I shall be really frightened when
the time comes, and there isn't anything to be afraid of, you
know—it is so different now; when we talked about it at Codrington it all seemed so dark and dreadful I couldn't bear ever

to let it come up to be thought over. How long one can put away things when they are not nice to think about ! '

' Then why do you talk like this, what good does it do ? ' questioned Donovan. It was a December afternoon, and they were talking in the twilight.

' I'm sorry, I had forgotten. It was very selfish,' said Dot, penitently. It was so hard for her to remember that Donovan did not share in her new sense of relief, that she more than once made little allusions of this sort; had she been less simple and childish, his want of participation would have made her unhappy; as it was, however, she was content to leave it, sure that in time it would come to him.

Donovan was very irritable that day, not, of course, with Dot, he was always gentle with her even when in his worst moods, but he was in one of his querulous, carping humours, and quarrelled with everything he read. The oft-quoted line of Pope's,

> One truth is clear, whatever is is right,

was quite sufficient to call forth an angry tirade.

It was a lie, it could not possibly be proved ! Were murder, and fraud, and oppression, and injustice *right?* People had no business to make great, false, sweeping assertions of that kind. The anger soon came down to more personal matters.

' Was it right, do you think, that you and I should have been left to old Doery, and bullied and tormented as we were ? Was it right that you should be mismanaged and half killed by an owl of a country doctor ? Is it right that you should be suffering as you are now ? '

' Some things do seem hard,' said Dot, ' but we have not got to understand why everything is, and I think it's best to be still and take what comes. Do you know, Dono, sometimes when I'm very cross with the pain for coming back so often, I think of what we saw at Codrington. Do you remember the little bay where the rocks were, and how we used to watch the waves dashing so angrily against the very tall upright rock, and passing so quietly over the little ones? I think if we are patient, and don't set ourselves up to fight against the pain and grumble at it, it is not half so hard to bear.'

Now Donovan had always felt a sort of sympathy with the tall solitary rock, with its hard jagged outline, braving in its own strength the power of the waves. Dot's idea did not please him ; patience, lowliness, and submission were virtues far beyond his comprehension, and he felt very strongly that painful sense of separation which had sprung up so strangely between them

I

during the last few months. He felt far away from Dot, and he hated the feeling and quickly changed the subject.

'Shall I read something else to you?' he asked.

'I should like some music,' said Dot, knowing that this would lead to no discussion which could displease Donovan, and then ensued what some people would have thought a rather incongruous selection, ranging from Sebastian Bach to the latest popular song, and from 'Vedrai Carino' to 'The Green Hill far away.' There was no distinction in music to Donovan, he played all Dot's favourites one after the other. In the middle of the last hymn Mrs. Farrant came in. It was the time of her second daily visit.

'Pray stop that tune, Donovan,' she said, plaintively. 'We are always having it in church, and I am so tired of it, the boys sing it frightfully out of time, and always get flat in the last line. How do you feel this afternoon, Dot?'

'Better, thank you, mamma,' said Dot, looking wistfully across the room at Donovan, as he tossed aside the hymn-book impatiently.

'Really better?' questioned Mrs. Farrant, with anxiety, for Dot had been suffering so much more lately, that even her calm phlegmatic nature had been stirred to uneasiness and apprehension.

'Yes, I think so,' said the little girl. 'Dono and I have been settling our Christmas presents, and what do you think he is going to give me, mamma? A clock—a dear little clock of my very own.'

She had gained the end she wanted; Donovan, who had been at the other side of the room, turned round, met her eyes, and came to her.

'Dono spoils you, I think,' said Mrs. Farrant, smiling; and somehow the words, trifling as they were, drew the three together. Donovan recovered his temper, and for once talked naturally before his mother, teased Dot merrily, and quite surprised Mrs. Farrant by his high spirits. 'I never saw you so talkative before,' she remarked, as the dressing-bell rang, and she rose to go.

'It is Dot who teaches us how to laugh,' said Donovan. 'You are a little witch, and sweep away bad humours instead of cobwebs.'

Christmas to Donovan only meant a full house, an incomprehensible gaiety and good humour, a conventional old-fashioned dinner, which he did not like, and a certain amount of holly and ivy. In his different way he was quite as far from understanding it as

poor old Scrooge in the 'Christmas Carol.' The year before old
Mr. Hayes had dined with them, but he was now far away, for,
not many weeks before, his 'castle in the air' had become a
reality. An old friend of his had returned from the United
States, having made his fortune ; he had come to Oakdene to see
Mr. Hayes, had discovered the great wish of his old school-
fellow, and had suggested a six months' tour on the Continent,
in which he was to bear the greater part of the expense. So the
old man in childlike glee had let his cottage and started for
Italy, taking a cordial farewell of Donovan, and recommending
him to follow his plan, which was now coming to such a successful issue.

The guests, therefore, this year only consisted of Adela and
two of Ellis's friends, nor was the misanthropical Donovan very
sorry that such should be the case. There was something almost
ghastly to him in the merriment which everyone seemed to think
it right to force up. The real happiness of the season was of
course unknown to him, and he had not even any recollections of
the 'merry Christmas' of childhood to fall back upon.

Adela tried to tease him into a little conversation as she sat
beside him at dinner, but it was hard work.

'Do you know, Donovan, I was staying at a country-house in
Sussex last September, and the first night I got there I saw some
one who reminded me so much of you.'

'Indeed !' replied her taciturn companion.

'He was not so much like you in face as in manner ; I
thought to myself, no one but my cousin Donovan sits through
an evening in such complete silence, and afterwards—what do
you think ?—I found out that your double was dumb.'

Donovan laughed a little.

'I can't make small talk,' he said—'I told you so long ago.'

'Oh! of course your great intellect can't stoop to frivolities,'
said Adela, with pretended sarcasm in her tone, but laughter in
her bright eyes. 'Perhaps you would kindly give me a little
instruction, though, on some of the weighty subjects that fill
your brain.'

He laughed again, but then, thinking of his misery at Codrington, added, quite gravely,

'My brain is anxious just now to forget certain weighty subjects, not to rake them up. Dot came out with one of her quaint
remarks the other day, which mix in so strangely with her
childishness ; she noticed how wonderful it was that you can put
any subject out of your head, when it is not pleasant to think of
it, for an almost unlimited time.'

'My dear cousin,' said Adela, 'do you mean you always keep skeletons in your cupboard?'

'The world is full of grim things—I try to forget them,' said Donovan.

'You're the most extraordinary person,' said Adela. 'You actually never mean to face these things?'

'Not till I'm obliged to,' said Donovan.

'Perhaps that accounts for your stupidity,' said Adela, with a daring flash of her dark eyes. 'A thousand pardons—I mean the brevity of your remarks.'

'There you have the worst of it, cousin, for "Brevity is the soul of wit,"' said Donovan.

'Ah! well, I think you are improved; you shall not be scolded,' replied Adela, good-humouredly; then, resuming her playful maliciousness, she continued—'It was such a pity you weren't at church this morning; the decorations were beautiful, really quite worth seeing—a cross and two triangles of white azaleas sent by the Wards, any amount of wreathing round the pillars, and some charming devices in Epsom salts on a red background.'

Donovan naturally scoffed at this.

'I can't think how you can like that sort of thing—if you despise and condemn pagans, why do you borrow their customs?'

'You hard, matter-of-fact creature! Why, of course we must have a little beauty. Can't you understand what a help it is?'

'No, I can't,' said Donovan, shortly. Then, as the blazing Christmas pudding was brought in, he continued his grumble. 'This, too, is an absurd, senseless old custom. What good does it do us all to sit round the table and watch blue flames, and then eat a horrible, black, burnt compound, like hot wedding-cake?'

'You are a wretch,' said Adela. 'You would like to sweep away all the dear old manners and customs, and start us in a new order of things, where men would be machines, and everything would be done by rule and measure. You would like us all to be as rational and comprehensible as vulgar fractions, now would you not?'

'It would simplify life,' said Donovan, smiling.

'I knew you'd say so,' said Adela, triumphantly. 'It's really quite dreadful to talk to such a flint. Have you no associations with the dear old things? Were you never young?'

'No, I don't think I ever was,' said Donovan, with a touch of sadness in his voice.

The conversation somehow paused here, until an uncontrolled yawn on Donovan's part stimulated Adela to a fresh effort.

'You are horribly uninteresting,' she said.

'Yes, I'm most abominably sleepy. I was up last night.'

'Ah! so Dot told me,' replied Adela. 'You tell her stories, she says, just like the wonderful story-teller in the "Arabian Nights," one after the other.'

'It amuses her,' said Donovan, 'and sometimes I have sent her to sleep in that way, but we couldn't manage it last night. She is dreadfully worn out to-day after all the pain.'

'These attacks seem much more frequent than they used to be,' said Adela.

'Yes,' he replied, and there was something in his voice which made Adela suddenly grave, but in a minute he recovered himself, and with his ordinary manner asked if he should peel an orange for her.

Just then some carol-singers began a hymn outside, but the rest of the party were not quite in the humour for hymns.

'Oh, those boys sing so badly,' said Mrs. Farrant. 'Do send them away, Ellis.'

'Yes, I think we had about enough of them this morning at church,' said Ellis, and he would have sent word to them to go had not Donovan risen.

'I'll take them round to the other side of the house,' he said, 'Dot likes music.'

'What!' exclaimed Adela, 'you mean to countenance a heathenish old custom, after all you have said?'

'Dot will like it,' he replied, as if this were a sufficient reason for countenancing anything.

The little invalid's room seemed very quiet and dim after the merry voices and bright lights down below, and yet it was an unspeakable relief to Donovan to be there with her once more, away from the hollow merriment of his step-father and the other guests, away from Adela's good-humoured banter. Dot was in bed, and there was about her that terrible stillness of utter exhaustion which makes illness, and especially a child's illness, so very sad to see. She was quite worn out with sleeplessness, and, though the pain was less severe than it had been, her face still bore marks of suffering. She did not move as Donovan entered, but welcomed him with her eyes.

'You have done dinner quickly to-night,' she said. 'You have not been hurrying to get back to me?'

'No; but some carol-singers have come,' said Donovan, 'and I thought you would like to hear them.'

'Oh, I am so glad!' she said, with child-like pleasure. 'I did so want to hear the carols that Phœbe has been telling me about. Please draw up the blind, Phœbe, so that they may know we are listening. Oh! there is my clock striking. Hark!'

Donovan's present, an exquisite little travelling clock, stood on the mantel-piece, and as Dot spoke it chimed the hour, then struck eight o'clock in sweet, low, muffled tones, like the sound of a distant cathedral bell.

'It *is* so beautiful,' she said, happily. 'It will make the night go so much more quickly. Now put your arm round me, Don dear.'

Then the choir-boys outside began their carol, the voices sounding sweet and subdued as they floated up into the silence of the sick-room. At first the words seemed almost incongruous, the dear old Christmas hymn had surely not been meant for such sadness, and suffering, and anxiety? But the shrill fearless trebles went on, and Donovan and Dot listened.

'God rest you, merry gentlemen,
Let nothing you dismay,
Remember Christ our Saviour
Was born on Christmas Day;
To save us all from Satan's power,
When we were gone astray;
O tidings of comfort and joy,
        Comfort and joy,
O tidings of comfort and joy!'

Dot caught the refrain which came at the end of every verse, and was delighted with it. By-and-by the singers went away, and Dot asked to have some reading. Some one had sent her a leaflet hymn; it was a description of the 'City with streets of gold,' and Donovan read it through patiently, though it seemed to him sensational and unsatisfying, and he was grieved to think that she could care for such material delights as were described. It was a positive relief to him that she did not like it. To sing and rest in a luxurious city could not be her ideal of a future life.

'And besides,' she said, in her quaint way, 'there isn't time to think about the houses, and the streets, and the gardens, they don't make the home; it is something like the home here, I think; you know, though Oakdene is so pretty, it is only because you are here that I love it, it is you that I think of, not the house.'

There was a pause in which the candle flared for a moment in its socket, and then died out, leaving the room in darkness. The maid had gone away. Donovan would have rung, but Dot stopped him.

'We won't have another,' she said. 'I like to be in the dark when you hold me near you; and, look, we can see the stars, there is dear old Orion, he's my very favourite of all, I always look for him. And, Dono dear, while we are all alone like this I want to tell you something; you won't like it now, but some day I am sure you will. When Phœbe first told me everything it was only through you that I could at all understand. I had to think first what love was, and what giving up was, and then I thought of you, and how you loved me and gave up all your life to me; no, I know you will say you didn't give up anything, but you have, Don, you have given up pleasure, and rest, and change, and all sorts of things.'

'But do you think I could have been happy, do you think life would have been tolerable if I had gone away to enjoy myself and left you alone?' said Donovan, hoarsely.

'No, Don,' she replied, nestling closer to him, 'I was quite sure you never could, and then you see I could believe how the greatest love of all could not leave us.'

He gave a mental ejaculation of thankfulness that Doery had never grieved the tender little soul with her cold-blooded Calvinism. Dear little girl! she was happy enough in her new convictions, he would not for the world have disturbed her; in the dark he even smiled a little to think that he had actually helped towards establishing the 'delusion' in her mind, had helped to set up his rival.

The next few days passed hopefully, Dot seemed to grow a little stronger again, and, as she had rallied from so many attacks, they all began to feel relieved, and to fancy that anxiety was over for the present. There was to be a dance at the Manor on the 31st, and when, at Christmas, Dot had been so seriously ill, Mrs. Farrant had almost decided to postpone it; however, she seemed to recover quickly, so the arrangement was not altered, and the house was soon in that state of excitement and turmoil which invariably precedes any unusual event of the kind. Adela Farrant was quite in her element, and even succeeded in stirring up Donovan to such an extent that he came down from what she called his 'high horse,' and condescended to show some interest in the arrangements. She was therefore doubly astonished when, about eight o'clock on the evening of the dance, she met him on the stairs, to find that all his interest had suddenly abated.

'Try to get this affair over as quickly as you can,' he said, as they passed each other.

'What do you mean?' said Adela, standing still. 'You are coming down, are you not?'

'No, I can't, it's quite impossible. Dot is so restless and poorly, I am afraid she is in for another of her bad attacks; I want you to get the people away as soon as may be, the noise is sure to worry her.'

'Oh! she'll be asleep before it begins,' said Adela. 'No one will be here till nine o'clock, I should think.'

'Well, I hope it will be so. It's an abominable nuisance, though, that the house should be all upset to-night.'

As he spoke, he opened the door of the little invalid's room, and shut himself in, while Adela passed down the stairs to the drawing-room, a little annoyed at what she called 'Cæsar's desertion,' and vaguely uneasy at his account of Dot. One of the guests was, however, greatly relieved at his absence; Mrs. Ward really began to enjoy the evening when she found that the 'dangerous young man' did not appear; she was quite content that her daughters should dance with Major Mackinnon and Mr. Probyn, two friends of Ellis Farrant's who were staying at the Manor. They were quite distinguished-looking men; Mrs. Ward was glad that her girls should have such nice partners, and remained in happy ignorance that they were in reality characters beside whom the poor black sheep of Oakdene would have become almost white in contrast.

Meanwhile, in the room above, Dot was in that state of strange restless misery which always preceded her attacks—a sort of anticipation of the pain. This was the time when her courage was most apt to fail; she could not bear the thought of the suffering beforehand, though, when it actually came, she was always brave and patient. In vain did Donovan try every possible means of sending her to sleep. Every preventive which the doctors had ordered to be tried at such times had of course been brought to bear upon the poor little girl, but to-night nothing seemed to have any effect. Donovan read to her, played to her, told her story after story, but she grew rapidly worse, and they at length realised that some fresh form of illness must have set in; much as she had suffered, she had never been in such terrible pain before. Old Mrs. Doery, who had nursed her through so many illnesses, was summoned at once, and the younger nurse went downstairs to find a messenger who could be sent for the doctor. The house, however, was all in confusion, and in a few minutes Phœbe returned in despair; the other servants were too busy to go; she could not even persuade any of the servants of the guests to ride over to Greyshot with the message.

'This miserable dance!' exclaimed Donovan, angrily. 'Well,

I must go myself, then; I shall be quicker than any of those lazy knaves.'

But Dot clung to him.

'It is so hard to bear without you. I will be good if it's really best, but—but——'

It cost him a hard struggle to decide, but, knowing that an unwilling messenger would be slow, he felt that the only sure way was to go himself; there was no time to be lost. He bent down to kiss the poor little quivering lips, and said very gently and firmly,

'It *is* best, darling. Be brave; I shall not be long.'

She tried to smile, and he hurried away, sick at heart. Rushing headlong downstairs, snatching up his hat from the stand, brushing past some astonished visitors, he ran at full speed to the stables, saddled the cob with his own hands, and in five minutes was on the road to Greyshot. He had dashed out from the heated room just as he was; the night was piercingly cold, the snow was falling fast, and the north wind blew the flakes into his eyes, so that he was almost blinded by them; he shivered from head to foot, but did not know that he shivered—all that he felt was an overwhelming anxiety and dread. What if he should never see Dot again? The extraordinary severity and suddenness of this illness had alarmed them all—what if she sank under it? And he had refused her last entreaty! Oh, bitter agony! what if he reached home too late! 'Too late! too late!' The very sound of the horse's hoofs echoed his fears, the muffled footfall as they galloped on over the snowy road. And yet it was the only sure way of getting the doctor; he knew he had been right to come; it might—it was just possible that it might save Dot some minutes of pain—it might save her life. But again his heart sank down like lead under the oppression of the one horrible fear. That ride was ever after a sort of nightmare recollection to him.

At last he thought it was ended; he sprang down at the door of the doctor's house and rang furiously. The footman appeared in answer.

'Dr. L—— was dining at Monklands.'

Monklands was about two miles on the other side of Greyshot.

Poor Donovan rode on almost despairingly, cursing his cruel fate. It was half-past ten by the time he reached the house; then, to his relief, he saw that Dr. L——'s carriage was standing at the door. He would not dismount; the doctor came out to him at once, and, on hearing his account of Dot, prepared to come to her directly, left a hurried message of farewell to his host, and, springing into his carriage, drove home, promising to come on to the Manor as quickly as possible.

Donovan had neither whip nor spurs, but he had what is far more efficacious—the power of communicating his thoughts to animals ; the cob seemed to gather from the feeling of his hand on her neck, from his occasional ejaculations, all the anxiety of this ride.   In spite of the deep snow, he galloped on bravely ; on through the open country, through the silent Greyshot streets, along the white, deserted road, till at length the lights of the Manor shone out through the branches of the ghostly-looking oak-trees, the bright lights in the lower windows, and the dim light in the upper room.   Donovan's heart gave a great bound when he heard in the distance the music of the string quartette and the sound of dancing.   It was well with Dot then !   In common decency the house would have been in silence if his fears had been realised.   Forgetful of everything but the one absorbing interest, he dashed into the house, through the hall and up the broad staircase; Miss Ward and her partner, who were pacing up and down in the cool, stared at the sudden apparition with its snowy garments and strained expectant face ; he never even saw them, but, hurrying on, threw aside his wet clothes, and in five minutes had reached Dot's room.   As he opened the door two sounds mingled for an instant in his ear.   From below came the sound of the ' grand chain ' in the ' Lancers,' and from the sick-bed came a low sobbing moan.   Phœbe was saying something to the little girl; he caught the words of one of her favourite hymns—

> ' We may not know, we cannot tell,
>   What pains He had to bear.'

Dot saw him in a minute and gave a relieved exclamation.

'Oh, Dono ! I'm so glad you are back; I've wanted you so dreadfully.   Let me hold your hands.'

His face, which had been rigid during the time of his anxiety, was changed now to the look of tenderness, and even cheerfulness, which he had learnt to wear when with the little girl.

' Dr. L—— will be here almost directly, and then he will make you more comfortable,' he said, taking his place at the bedside.

' Oh, Dono !' she gasped, ' sometimes I think I shall never be comfortable any more.'

' You thought so last time you were ill,' said Donovan, soothingly, ' and then after all you had some quiet days.'

'Yes, but this is worse. Oh, Dono, Dono!' and again she broke into that wail of pain which pierced the hearts of the watchers. Donovan was the only one who never lost his control; he was always ready with quiet, tender words; sometimes when the pain was lulled for a few minutes he would even make the little girl smile.

At last the doctor came, and Donovan waited in fearful suspense for his opinion; he waited outside the room in the gallery, pacing up and down miserably, feeling chafed and annoyed by the laughter and noise which reached his ears from below. After some time Dr. L—— came out, with a face which only too fully confirmed his fears.

'Cannot this noise be stopped?' he asked, a little impatiently.

'It *shall* be,' said Donovan, with bitter earnestness. 'She is in danger, as I thought?'

'Yes,' said Dr. L——. 'Mrs. Farrant ought to be told at once.'

'You mean that—that the end is near?' questioned Donovan, startled, in spite of his forebodings.

'It is an acute attack of inflammation; I am afraid she must sink under it,' replied the doctor, gravely.

Without a word Donovan went slowly down the stairs to the room where the dancing was going on. A Highland reel had just begun; the tune 'Tullochgorum' rang in his head for weeks after. The greater number of the guests were looking on at the dancers. Donovan saw that his mother was quite at the other end of the room, and, as he was arranging how best to reach her, Ellis caught sight of him and hurried towards the place where he was standing.

'How now, Donovan, come to dance after all, and in that old shooting-coat?'

'You must stop this; Dot is ill,' said Donovan, in a hollow voice.

'My dear fellow, you ask impossibilities; one can't turn away seventy guests at a moment's notice.'

'She is dying,' said Donovan, and the words sounded strangely out of place in the midst of all the gaiety and merriment.

'*Dying!*' echoed Ellis, startled and shocked. At an ordinary time he would have enjoyed the opportunity of thwarting and annoying his step-son; only a moment ago and something of this sort had been in his intentions. But that one word scattered all mean and unkind thoughts; before the angel of death even this selfish and dishonest man became softened and awed.

'I will arrange it. The music shall of course be stopped,' he said, in really kind tones.

Donovan thanked him, and asked him to tell Mrs. Farrant, and Ellis at once complied, crossing the room to the place where his wife was talking with the squire, and telling her that she must speak to Donovan for a moment outside.

She was so completely overcome by the unexpected news that Donovan was almost in despair. To be kept away from Dot was terrible, and yet he could not leave his mother in her distress. Speaking with the gentleness and control which seemed specially given to him that night, he at last persuaded her to come and see the little girl, overruling the sobbing, shrinking appeal, 'that it was so terrible, so sad—and she couldn't bear to go in that dress.'

But a very few minutes beside the poor little child's bed proved too much for Mrs. Farrant's powers of endurance. The sight of her suffering was indeed terribly painful, and with a mother's instinctive love awakening in her heart, but without a mother's long training and self-denial and devotion, Mrs. Farrant naturally could not control herself in the least; she burst into tears, agitated Dot, and had at last to be taken from the room.

'I love her so,' she said, piteously, to Donovan, as he half carried her along the gallery, and helped her on to her sofa.

He bent down and kissed her.

'You will come in again when you can?' he said. 'We will tell you when there is any change.'

Adela came in while he was speaking, and he left her with Mrs. Farrant, and hastily returned to the sick-room. Dot was now growing delirious with the pain, but, though she could not bear anyone else even to touch the bed-clothes, she liked him to hold her hand, and her unconscious words were always spoken to him. The solemn midnight was undisturbed by music or merriment; instead of dancing the old year out and the new year in, the guests were driving sadly from the Manor. Dot was moaning in the last sharp struggle of her little life, and Donovan was watching beside her in anguish which could only have been suppressed by the purest and truest love.

There was not the smallest hope now. The long night hours dragged slowly on, the death-agony grew more and more intense, and the doctor could do absolutely nothing to lessen the pain. Poor old Mrs. Docry quite broke down, and sat rocking herself to and fro with her face buried in her apron. Phœbe, with a white face, stood ready to do whatever she was told. Donovan, never once faltering, bore up with what the doctor described afterwards as 'really extraordinary fortitude, almost as if the poor little girl's death would not be such a dreadful blow to him.' In reality, he was so absorbed in her that he had not a thought to spare for the future, and while he was near her it was neces-sary that he should be quiet and controlled.

Once, for a few minutes, however, the doctor asked him to leave the room, and then his strong will gave way. Ellis had left Adela with his wife, and, unable to go to bed, had stretched himself on a sofa which, in the general disarrangement of the house, had been placed at the end of the gallery ; he was begin-ning to get drowsy when the opening of a door roused him. Was it all over, he wondered ! He sat up and listened. A terrible cry of anguish in a wailing, child's voice told him that Dot still lived. Then for the first time he noticed that, in the dim light, a few paces from him stood Donovan. He, too, must have been listening, for he made a half-choked exclamation as the sound reached him, and staggering forward, not noticing his step-father, sat down on a chair near him, and with his arms stretched across the table, and his head buried, gave way to an overwhelming burst of grief. Ellis was really touched, and almost infected too. Instinctively he tried to show his sympathy.

'Donovan, my poor fellow, don't give way. While there's life there's hope, you know.'

'I wish she were dead,' he groaned ; 'out of the pain.'

'But she may get better,' suggested Ellis.

'No,' he answered, with a great sob which shook his whole frame, 'it's only a question of hours—hours of torture ! '

Then springing up in a sort of frenzy, and dashing the tears from his eyes, he seized hold of Ellis's arm.

'Here ! you who believe in a God—get down on your knees and pray for her—pray that she may die ! '

Without waiting for an answer from the astonished Ellis, he turned to the window, tore back the curtain, threw open the casement, and leant out into the black night. Somewhere, some-where in that yawning space there surely must be a Power who could help him in his fearful need ! His whole heart went out in a passionate cry to the vast unknown.

'God ! God ! Exist ! Be ! Stop this agony ! Let her die ! What good can it possibly do ? Let her die ! '

It was the first prayer he had ever prayed.

There was a touch upon his arm, he turned and saw Phœbe standing beside him.

'Miss Dot is asking for you, sir, but won't you take some-thing before you go back ? '

He shook his head, but, as he passed Ellis, asked him to give Phœbe and Mrs. Doery some wine. Then he went back to the sick-room, composed his face with an effort, and resumed his place beside Dot.

'Dono, talk to me,' was the very first request, and he did talk bravely and soothingly, in the continuous way which Dot always liked. Taciturn and unimaginative as he really was, he had long ago learnt to overcome all his natural difficulties, and utterly to disregard his own tastes and inclinations when Dot was in any way concerned.

At last the pain grew less severe, the poor exhausted little life began to ebb away fast. When the longed-for relief came, Donovan knew that the end was very near. He breathed more freely.

'The pain is all gone,' whispered Dot, after a long quiet interval; 'will it never come again? Is it gone for always, Dono?'

'Yes, darling, I think quite gone,' he replied; his dreary creed did not allow him to say more.

'It is so comfortable,' she murmured, drowsily.

Before long Mrs. Farrant and Adela were summoned, and Ellis too came in, and kissed the little worn face, and poor Waif crept after them all, Donovan lifting him up that Dot's hand might stroke his head for the last time.

By-and-by the room was quiet again, only Donovan, the two nurses, and the doctor stayed to watch the end. The perfect silence was at last interrupted, a sudden shiver passed through the little wasted form.

'I am so cold, Dono,' she murmured, moving her hands nervously about the coverlet, 'put your arm round me again; oh! it is getting so dark, hold me, Dono, hold me! Is it wrong to be so frightened?'

'I am holding you, darling,' he replied, 'there is nothing to fear.'

But the words died from his cold lips as he uttered them, he felt that he could not comfort her, that she was beyond his help; and her next words seemed to pierce his heart.

'I can't feel your arms, Dono, I can't see you.'

A stifled moan escaped him, he bent low over her, and again and again kissed her cold damp brow.

'I didn't mean to vex you, darling,' she gasped, 'it will be better soon, perhaps. Say me the hymn about the light.'

He repeated Newman's 'Lead, kindly Light,' which, for some unknown reason, had always been a great favourite with Dot, he knew it well, and would, of course, have said anything to please her ; nor did he feel what a hideous mockery the words were to him, he was too completely absorbed in thinking of her. After he had finished the hymn, there was a long pause during which her breathing became more and more difficult. Donovan's whole being seemed to live with each effort, he too drew each breath slowly and painfully. But there came a respite before long, the light did shine through the gloom, and a look of almost baby-like peace stole over Dot's troubled face. She did not speak a word, it never had been her way to say very much, but by-and-by Donovan overheard faint half-dreamy whispers, and knew that she was speaking with a little child's confidence to God.

'You will comfort Dono, won't you ? and we will be all quite happy together.'

The words died away into indistinct murmurs, she sank into a painless, half-unconscious state.

It was not till this time that one thought of himself came to trouble Donovan, but as he knelt by the bedside, with Dot's head resting on his arm, as he listened to—almost counted—the sighing breaths, his desolation broke upon him. In a few minutes all that to him made life worth living would have passed away for ever ! Death, to him truly the king of terrors, was here at the bedside, and he was powerless, helpless, he could only wait for the grim unknown to snatch little Dot away—away into a forever of nothingness ! His brain reeled at the thought, he could not control the shuddering agony which made his limbs almost powerless and brought to his strong firm face a pallor almost as deathly as that of the little dying child.

'You had better rest a minute,' said the doctor. 'It is too much for you.'

But the thought of losing even one of those precious last minutes—of resigning his place to another—seemed intolerable. He signed a negative with some impatience, raised Dot a little higher, smoothed back the hair from her cold forehead, and waited, trying to control the trembling which might disturb her, to regulate the half-choked gasping breaths which would agitate his whole frame.

Then came an unconquerable longing for one more word from her, one more recognizing look. The struggle between this desire and his unwillingness to break in upon the comparative peace of her last moments grew to anguish ; passionate entreaties rose to his lips, and were only checked by the fiercest effort of will, wild impossible longings surged up in his heart, and above all was a fearful realisation that the time was short, that minutes, perhaps seconds, were all that was left to him.

But the spiritual current of sympathy which had united the two in life was as strong as ever, they had been all-in-all to each other, and even now, in the very moment of death, little Dot felt instinctively that Donovan wanted her.

Half rousing herself from the state of dreamy peace she had fallen into, she felt for his face, drew it nearer to hers, and, with long pauses between the words, whispered,

'I've asked to be quite near you still. I think God will let me. He is so very good, you know—you will know.'

That perfect confidence of hers made death a happy thing. In her untroubled child-like faith she had no manner of doubt that the Father who loved them both so dearly would one day teach Donovan what His love was.

A minute after came a scarcely audible request.

'Kiss me, Dono.'

He folded his arms round her, and pressed his cold lips to hers; in another moment a shudder passing through the little frame told him that he was alone in the world.

CHAPTER XII.

DESOLATE.

Then black despair,
The shadow of a starless night was thrown
Over the world in which I moved alone.
SHELLEY.

Truth's golden o'er us although we refuse it.
R. BROWNING.

GREAT sorrows affect people so differently that it is often hard to know how to sympathise with those in trouble, the spoken words of comfort which may soothe one person may torture another, the reverential silence congenial to some seems cruelly cold to others. Grief, too, falls in so many different ways; to some it comes like a heavy physical blow, the bitterness of the pain, the shock to the whole system, is so great that for a time the senses fail, and a merciful unconsciousness and a faint, gradual return to life lessen to some extent the first anguish of suffering. To some sorrow comes piercingly, their imagination —all their faculties—seem for the time quickened by the pain, memories of the past crowd around them, visions of a barren future stretch out before their aching eyes, and this in the very first moments of their sorrow; grief is to them a sharp-edged sword, laying bare in an instant the very fibres of their being.

But there are others to whom sorrow comes in a more awful form, the blow falls on them, but no momentary unconsciousness comes to their relief, they do not sink under their load of pain, but stagger on in dull hopelessness; they may be spared the sharp realisation of the grief which pierces the heart, but their case seems more pitiable; for, instead of struggling from the depths of woe to calmness and peace, they labour on with a terrible weight on their hearts, a weight which numbs the faculties, and crushes the bearer into 'dull despair.' And then, as nature re-asserts herself, and the perceptions regain their vividness, a fearful reaction sets in, the despair deepens, the weight of woe becomes each day heavier to bear; this is the stony sorrow which human sympathy seems utterly powerless to reach, and which finds no outlet.

And yet the ' All ye that labour and are heavy laden ' has for hundreds of years brought to the world's Consoler those who are most borne down—most crushed by their grief.

Donovan knew the invitation well enough, but these things were to him as 'idle tales;' to his suffering there was no relief because he would not stretch out his hand to take; he was as much alone as it is possible for any of us to be alone. A child may refuse obedience to its father, may reject all love, in its ignorance may even refuse to believe in the love. Strong in its rebellion, it may shut itself away, bolting and barring the door upon the love that would seek it out; but, though it may refuse to remove the barrier, the father is still the father, and though the child cannot see how true and real his love is, because of the obstacle it has with its own hand raised between them, the strong love will surely never rest until it has conquered the child, and shown it its mistake ; nor is it ever really alone—the barrier is only a barrier.

Donovan had thus shut himself into himself; with the dead calm of a worn-out body and a despairing heart, he closed the door of Dot's room behind him, and with slow, dull, spiritless steps walked along the gallery. Ellis was standing in the doorway of his dressing-room ; he came forward as his step-son passed, but the question he would have put died on his lips as he looked at Donovan's rigid face. He shuddered as the hollow, unnatural voice uttered the words he had expected, but had not dared to ask for—' She is dead ! '

Ellis had not very often visited his little step-daughter's room ;

K

every now and then he had bought some trifling present for her, or had sent her a message by Donovan, and occasionally he had spent a few minutes beside her sofa, partly because he was anxious to keep up appearances, and wished the household to think him a worthy successor to Colonel Farrant, partly because of the real good-nature which still to some extent guided his actions. His sorrow at her death was more genuine than might have been expected, and he had enough sympathy with Donovan not to torment him with commonplace condolences, but to let him pass by in silence, feeling rightly enough that he was the last person who could venture to approach his grief. He waited until the door of his step-son's room had closed behind him, spoke a few words to the doctor, and then with rather hesitating steps went to Adela's room to tell her the news. At his knock she came to the door; she was wrapped in her dressing-gown, and her hair was loose and disordered. Ellis thought she had never looked so old before; her greyness and wrinkles, which he had never noticed, showed plainly enough now that she was *en déshabillé;* she looked what in truth she was, a middle-aged woman, and Ellis, who could not bear to face the fact that both he and his sister were no longer young, shivered a little. Did not each advancing year bring them nearer to the dreariness of old age, and, what was worse, nearer to the terrors of death! Death was an awful thing, and death was in the house at that very moment.

'What is it?' asked Adela—'is it all over?'

'Yes, it is over,' he replied, gravely. 'I must tell poor Honora. Come with me, Adela; she is so exhausted, I am half afraid how she will bear it.'

'Other people may be exhausted too,' said Adela, rather sharply. 'What has become of Donovan? He has been in there all night.'

'He has gone to his room. I was afraid to speak to him, he looked—I can't tell you how he looked. Yes, go to him, if you like, but you won't do him any good, poor fellow. It must have been an awful night.'

Adela was thoroughly kind-hearted; she hurried at once towards Donovan's room, not allowing her natural shrinking from the sight of pain to hinder her an instant. It was certainly a relief, when she had received the word of admittance, to find that no spectacle of overpowering grief was to meet her gaze. The room was very cold and almost dark; a faint glimmer of light from the window, and the outline of a figure with the head drooped low, showed her where her cousin was. She groped her way towards him, her misgivings returning when he still did not speak nor stir.

'Donovan,' she said, with quick anxiety in her tone, 'is anything the matter with you? Are you faint?'

Her words surprised him; he mused over them half-curiously before replying. How strange it was to be asked if *anything* were the matter when he was simply crushed! And yet perhaps, in a sense, nothing was the matter—nothing mattered at all now that Dot was dead. And Dot *was* dead, she had passed away for ever.

'Donovan,' pleaded Adela, 'do speak to me—do break this dreadful silence!'

'She is dead,' he replied, slowly, and then again his head drooped, and there was another long pause.

The window was wide open. The icy night-air made Adela shiver; she looked from the faint grey sky to the snowy earth, and then in despair she looked back to her cousin's face, which, though indistinctly seen in the dim light, was evidently as cold and still as marble. The tears rose to her eyes and overflowed as she felt her powerlessness to relieve that stony sorrow. A half-stifled shivering sob roused Donovan at last.

'You are cold,' he said, still in the same terribly hollow voice, and then he moved forward and shut the window.

She was now so thoroughly frightened by the strangeness of his manner that she lost all control over herself, and it was, after all, Donovan who had to quiet her grief.

'Why do you cry?' he said. 'The pain is over for her, all is over; after all, it is only ourselves who suffer. One can endure a great deal, and sooner or later we too shall die; think of the peace of that nothingness.'

'Oh, don't say such terrible things!' said Adela, shuddering and sobbing still more violently.

'It is my one comfort,' he said, 'but you, with the belief you profess, can need no comfort from such as I—your beautiful legend should comfort you.'

'Yes, yes,' she answered, 'only it is so hard to be resigned. But, Donovan, I did not mean to be so weak; I wanted to be of use to you, indeed I did, and I have worried instead of comforted you.'

'You have been very kind,' he said, in a more natural tone; 'but there is only one comfort, and I have told you what that is.' Then, as she started with a sudden new terror, he put his cold hand on hers and added, 'No, you need not be afraid; death is the comfort, but I shall not seek death in the way you fear. You need not think I shall try that way to rest.'

'But is there nothing I can do for you?' asked Adela, awed and quieted by his strange manner.

'I should like you to go to my mother,' he replied, without any hesitation.

Adela looked again at the white, stony face, but it was quite resolute, and she had no choice but to obey. With a heavy heart she went to see the other mourner, and tried to soothe the passionate weeping and bitter remorse of the mother.

The interview with his cousin had in some degree roused Donovan; he could not sink back to the state of lethargy in which she had found him. His power of realisation had to some extent returned, and the dead calm gave place to restlessness. He paced up and down the room with unsteady steps, then, chafed by the narrowness of the space, he opened his door and wandered along the gallery, down the stairs, and through the deserted rooms below. Everything had a most desolate look; the faint morning light revealed the drooping wreaths and decorations, the remains of the candles, which had guttered down into shapeless masses of wax, looked grotesquely forlorn, while the supper-room, with its disordered table and its profusion of fruit and flowers, was perhaps the most dreary-looking of all. The effect of the whole to Donovan seemed ghastly; 'The Reel of Tullochgorum' rang in his ears, recalling all its miserable adjuncts, the noise of the gay crowd, the scraping and twanging of the instruments, above all Dot's cries of anguish—those heart-piercing cries which were to haunt him for months.

By-and-by, as the daylight increased, the household began to stir; a maid-servant came into the drawing-room and re-arranged and dusted the furniture, from time to time casting half timid half compassionate glances at the restless figure pacing to and fro; doors were opened and shut, a general sound of sweeping and moving furniture made itself heard, a clatter of cups and saucers; bells were rung, footsteps hurried to and fro; Major Mackinnon's voice was heard asking for his boots. There was something awful in this business-like re-beginning of life. Dot was dead, yet for him life must go on in the old grooves,

> Evening must usher night, night urge the morrow,
> Month follow month with woe, and year wake year to sorrow.

The commonplace bustle, the vision which had crossed his mind of the long barren years, became at last intolerable. He hastened up the stairs once more, and from the force of long habit found himself on the way to Dot's room. The blinds were down; the cool green light quieted his restless impatient movements.

He closed the door, and stole with hushed steps to the bedside. Then the forlornness of his grief broke upon him fully. No eager welcome from the soft, childish voice, no loving look from the dark eyes, no arms stretched out to cling round his neck, but only a motionless silent outline beneath the white sheet. He could not look at the veiled face, he turned away and threw himself on the ground in a terrible, silent agony.

After a time, the quietness of the room began to influence him. Only a few hours before it had been the scene of such weary suffering that the peacefulness of the present could not but seem doubly striking. The peace of non-existence! He hugged the thought to his heart, and in thinking of it forgot for the time his own pain. Then he slowly dragged himself up, and kneeling by the bed drew aside the sheet. Nothing could have softened his suffering so completely as the sight which met his gaze. The beautiful little face seemed only a degree more pale and waxen than in life; the forehead, no longer contracted with pain, gleamed white and serene and starlike; the brown hair lay lightly on the pillow, the pale still lips smiled, the tiny thin hands were folded in solemn repose. How long he knelt silently beside her he never knew. He was roused at last by old Mrs. Doery. She came in, wiping her eyes with her apron, and for a minute stood at the foot of the bed, watching the two children whom she had brought up—the dead and the living. Perhaps the sight of the living one touched her heart the more keenly, for there was an unwonted tenderness in her manner as she addressed him.

'I was looking for you, Mr. Donovan,' she said, putting her hand on his shoulder. 'It's time you took some rest. You must be worn out.'

Worn out! Ah, no! How he wished he had been! But he did not resist her when she urged him to go to his room. The quiet, passive, painless state he was in led him to acquiesce in anything. Later on, Ellis came to him, offering to see to all the necessary arrangements; he thanked him quietly, and consented. Then Adela came and begged him to see his mother, and he went for a little while to his mother's room, and described everything which had happened on the previous night, tranquilly, almost coldly. So the day passed on, and night came. The household was still once more, all were sleeping quietly; only Donovan lay with wide-open eyes, staring out at the black night, counting the hours mechanically as they passed, wondering now and then if he still lived, if this strange, numb passiveness were life at all.

The next two days went on in much the same way. The

funeral was to be on the Saturday; on the Friday morning Donovan's unnatural calm began to give way. He had now been four nights without sleep, and the dull weight, the numbness of stifled pain, was beginning to tell on him. When, on that day, he went as usual to Dot's room to gaze on the one sight which had served to comfort him, he received a sudden shock. The first great beauty of death had faded gradually, but, as that morning he gazed down on the tranquil face, he saw for the first time the faint evidences of mortality. The sight seemed to pierce his heart; he rushed away wildly, as though to escape from his grief; he paced with desperate steps up and down his room, trying in vain to forget what he had seen, trying to assure himself that it would not, could not be. 'Dust thou art, and unto dust shalt thou return.' The bitterness of the verdict was almost unbearable, for to him the perishable body was all that was left; unspeakably dear as it must be to all, it had to him a tenfold preciousness. His grief bordered so nearly on madness that everyone began to shrink from him in terror, and all that terrible day he was alone, now battling with his anguish, trying in vain to govern himself—now allowing his crazy sorrow to drive him as it pleased. At length, when night was come—the last night before Dot was to be borne away from him to the churchyard— he went once more to the death-chamber. The little white coffin was closed—he did not regret it; he would not look on her again, only his frantic pacings to and fro seemed more bearable in that room than in his own. Dot's little clock chimed the hours softly in muffled tones, and each stroke seemed to fall with knife-like sharpness on his heart. Time had ceased for her, but for him it went on, wearily, ceaselessly. That was the only distinct thought which continually surged in upon him. 'My days go on. My days go on.'

At last with a feverish craving for air he threw open the window, and leaned out into the cold still winter night. A winding sheet of snow on the earth, purple black heavens, and stars shining out gloriously in the frosty atmosphere met his gaze. All was grand and peaceful, all contrasted strangely with his mad, fevered agony. He grew more quiet. Orion gleamed down on him pityingly, a child's voice whispered from the past, 'He is my very favourite of all.' Were the soft dark eyes watching him perhaps in his anguish? was the happy free spirit near him? Would all—every comfort be denied him because in his ignorance and self-reliance he refused to believe?

He shut the window once more, stood quietly for a minute beside the coffin, then stretched himself out on the hearthrug, and, before the little clock chimed again, was sleeping profoundly. The only comfort he was capable of receiving was given him—a night of unbroken rest, a short lull from his despair.

That sleep saved him; the terrible strain of his attendance on Dot, his hopeless sorrow and long wakeful nights, had brought him to the very verge of serious illness; when he awoke late on the following morning, his mind had recovered its balance, he was sufficiently strengthened to take up his heavy load of sorrow and bear it manfully. Ellis and Adela were unspeakably relieved, when they met him, to find how great a change the night had wrought, the stony want of realisation, the frenzy of overpowering grief, had given place to a more natural sorrow, he looked indeed very much as usual only that all his former characteristics seemed deepened, the mouth looked a little more bitter, the eyes more despairing and contradictory to the rest of the face, the curious brow had more of what Dot had called its ' battered ' look, the whole expression was sterner and older.

For the first time he came down to breakfast and took his usual place at the table, perhaps anxious to face the rest of the party before the funeral, or with a sort of desire to go through with everything properly. They were all very kind to him, there is enough of good in most people to make them compassionate to great grief—for a time. As they left the breakfast-room a servant met them carrying some beautiful hot-house flowers.

' From Mrs. Ward, sir,' she said, putting into Donovan's hand a card with, ' kind enquiries and sympathy.'

He looked at it for a moment, then threw it aside with bitterness which astonished Adela, and said in his most chilling tone,

' It is too late now.'

' No, I think there will be room,' said Adela, misunderstanding him, ' we have a great number of wreaths, but I think I can arrange these flowers.'

' The world's sympathy !' he replied, bitterly, clenching and unclenching his hands rapidly, as was his habit when strongly agitated, ' never to come near her in all those years of suffering, but to send a showy wreath for her coffin.'

' Would you rather they were not used ?' asked Adela, doubtfully.

' Oh! let us take what we can get from the sympathising world,' he answered, ' rate it at what it's worth, only don't ask me to be grateful.' And then with a fierce sigh he turned away.

The day was clear, bright, and frosty, the little churchyard at Oakdene was crowded with people, for poor little Dot's death had awakened sympathy which her life had failed to win ; rumours had got about that the funeral was to be a choral one, and all the acquaintances of the Farrants who had been at the interrupted dance drove to the little country church to ' show their respect ' to the dead and the living, while many of the Greyshot townspeople walked over either from curiosity, or from that love of a pathetic sight which is latent in not a few hearts.

The sun shone brightly down on the snow-covered graves, on the throng of spectators, on the clergyman and the choristers, the rays fell too on the white pall laden with wreaths, on the black dresses of the mourners, and on Donovan's stern hopeless face. He would willingly have dispensed with the service, which was to him only a mockery, but the arrangement of all had helped to cheer Mrs. Farrant, and as long as he could see the last of the little coffin he was willing that the others should gratify their taste, and gather round Dot's grave with prayers and hymns and flowers. Gravely he followed the choir into the church, gravely sat in the pew while the last strains of the hymn were sung ; the other mourners knelt for a minute, he was too honest to do that, but the consistency of an atheist rarely receives anything but hard words, and all the spectators were inexpressibly shocked.

He was far too miserable to notice the looks of shrinking aversion or righteous indignation which some of the congregation turned on him as the procession passed out to the grave, but just outside the porch, in a momentary pause, one whispered sentence fell on his ear.

' Oh, no, atheists are always hard and unfeeling !'

He could not help knowing that the words bore reference to him : their injustice stung him a little, and he became conscious that the eyes turned on him were hostile and unsympathising—became indeed aware for the first time that the churchyard was crowded. Well, it would soon be over. He heard nothing more till the sound of the earth falling on the coffin roused him from his own thoughts ; then with a sudden pang and shudder he caught the words—' Earth to earth, ashes to ashes, dust to dust '—and he was one of the ' men without hope.'

The people bowed their heads as the clergyman read the closing prayers, but Donovan, with a wild look in his eyes, stood erect and motionless ; his one longing was for solitude, and when, after the benediction, another hymn was given out, he felt that he could bear up no longer. Turning rapidly away he strode through the staring crowd. What did it matter if his action were misinterpreted ? What did he care if the general sense of decorum was offended ? It mattered little, for whatever he did

was sure to be considered the wrong thing! 'Dust to dust.'
How the words haunted him! Oh, to get away somewhere from
his anguish—away from the cruel world with its harsh judg-
ments—to lose himself in darkness! He rushed on wildly
through the churchyard, past the long line of carriages, along
the snowy road to the Manor. He was mad enough and miserable enough for any desperate deed, but whatever his intentions
had been they were frustrated, for his physical strength gave
way; he sank down exhausted on the floor of a little arbour in
the Manor grounds.

He was roused at length by a soft stir in the place; then
came a low whine, and, looking up, he saw Waif beside him, his
round brown eyes full of tears.

'Ah! you understand, do you, old fellow?' he exclaimed,
faintly.

He allowed the dog to lick his face and hands for a minute
or two, then, as the carriages were heard in the drive, he started
up; he knew that Dr. L—— and one or two other visitors would
return to lunch, and, though he shrank painfully from seeing
them, he felt that he ought to go in. Waif's loving devotion had
soothed him. Ashamed of the longing to end his life which had
almost overmastered him, he struggled to his feet, patted the
dog, and made his way to the drawing-room, there to do what
he felt to be his duty in the way of talking to the visitors. Well
for the world that it is not all made up of logically consistent
men and women, well at any rate for the Donovans of the world
that there are children and dumb animals who love and sympathise without question, without reservation.

Blessed little Waif! You have done a better day's work
than all the throng of people in the church and churchyard;
you have been the saving of your master. There is indeed
One

Who by low creatures leads to heights of love.

So, Waif, take courage and keep your eyes open, this is your
day; men have for the present little to say to Donovan, they
shrink from him; it is clearly intended that you should see to
him, and in doing so you will be following in the steps of those
other dogs who tended the deserted beggar as he lay at the rich
man's gate.

CHAPTER XIII.

WISHES AND CHESTNUT ROASTING.

The possible stands by us ever fresh,
Fairer than aught which any life hath owned.

. . . .

A healthful hunger for the great idea,
The beauty and the blessedness of life.
          Gladys and her Island.   J. INGELOW

THE school-room at Trenant was quite the favourite room in the whole house. In summer time its two French windows, opening on to the lawn, gave a cool out-of-door feeling, and, if you are obliged to spend a lovely June morning in the house, it is some consolation to have nature brought as near to you as possible; in winter its coziness was admitted by all, its fireplace was large and burnt better than any other, its half high brass fender made an enchanting footstool, its old-fashioned sofa was exactly the shape which tempts you to curl yourself up with a story-book and forget the cold, and its bookshelves contained such a hetero-geneous assortment of volumes that almost everyone could find something to his or her special taste. But the time most favour-able of all to the school-room was the time known as 'blind man's holiday' in the winter; it had long been the favourite family gathering place, and on the afternoon of New Year's day —the same New Year which had brought sorrow and bereave-ment to Oakdene Manor—a very merry party had congregated round the hearth. In the centre of the group knelt Gladys with one arm round Jackie to ward off all danger of fire accidents, and with the other spare hand distributing smooth, brown, hard-skinned chestnuts from a bag; the school-boys, home for their Christmas holidays, sat on the fender punching holes in the nuts before they were put down to roast, and Stephen Causton stood, poker in hand, ready to rake out the lowest bar of the grate at the last moment. It was what Gladys called a 'toasty' fire, not a blazing one, but a deep still red one which sent out as much heat as could possibly be desired, and cast a rich glow over wall and ceiling, making the holly wreaths on the picture frames shine out in bold contrast to the blackness of the shadows, and adding such lustre to the old green curtains and furniture that their faded shabbiness was no longer noticeable. The faces, too, of the little group were ruddy in the firelight, and the golden threads in Gladys' brown hair shone out brightly as she bent down over the wriggling struggling Jackie, whose patience was sorely tried by the slowness with which the chestnuts roasted.

'We must take some to mother and Aunt Margaret in the drawing-room,' said Gladys; 'how soon will they be ready, Stephen?'

'Not yet; besides, I'm certain my mother wouldn't touch one, said Stephen, a little sulkily, 'she doesn't understand that sort of thing.'

'My stars! What, not like chestnuts!' ejaculated Bertie, with raised eyebrows.

Gladys and Stephen laughed a little, it was not exactly the want of appreciation of chestnuts which had given the sullen tone to the assertion; Mrs. Causton's contempt for the things of this world was not a little trying to her son, and Gladys understood that it was this in general to which he referred. Certainly it did seem a pity, she thought, that Aunt Margaret should speak so very unreservedly, and often so very inopportunely, about religious details, and it seemed strange that she did not notice how it repelled and annoyed her son.

Stephen had left Porthkerran in the previous October, and was now 'walking the hospitals.' The few months of London life seemed already to have altered him a good deal, he was older, more decided and opinionated, even—Gladys fancied—a little less refined than when he left. But the change which she noticed chiefly in him was an increased dislike to Mrs. Causton's peculiar little phrases and her untimely allusions. His mother worried him, and he allowed this to appear far too plainly.

'Let us wish over them,' said Jackie, meditatively, 'cos you know it's quite the first time this year we've eaten them.'

'I know what the Jackal would wish for,' said Bertie, teazingly, 'he'd wish for jam at tea; wishing's awful bosh, Jackie, you mustn't be such a baby.'

The corners of Jackie's mouth were turned down ominously, and nothing but Gladys' promptitude averted a storm.

'Nonsense, Bert, he wouldn't do anything of the kind; we shall all wish over them, and Jackie shall have the first that's done, because he's the youngest; now, Jack, a very wise wish; what is it to be?'

Jackie thought for the space of thirty seconds, while he tore open the hot chestnut. Then with the conscious importance of one who looks far into the dim future, he announced,

'I wish to be a tiger-hunter in Aflica, I shall not go now, I shall wait till I'm sixteen, then I shall be a man, and I shall

shoot all the animals, except a few which I shall catch with nets,
and bring home to keep in the nursery.'

This wish excited a good deal of laughter, for the heroic
tiger-hunter of the future had been known to run away from a
good-sized dog, and the unkind brothers were sceptical as to the
bravery his sixteen years would bring him; but Jackie gnawed
his chestnut contentedly, and joined in the laughter.

Nor did the wishes of the other boys rival his in enterprise.
Bertie wished to be a sailor like Dick, with a 'jolly lot' of
climbing to do.   Harold aspired to an archbishopric, because it
would be 'such a lark to be cock of the walk, and to have a big
palace to live in.'   Stephen expressed a modest wish to discover
something like the 'circulation of the blood,' as Harvey had done,
and make himself a name to be remembered.

Last of all came Gladys' wish, and all eyes turned upon her
as she tossed a chestnut to and fro in her hands, and thought.   At
last raising her face, she said,

'I wish to be like the people in "Real Folks," who got a lot of
little children together on Saturday afternoons, in some great, bad
town, and gave them a "good time."'

'Dirty little children—ugh!' exclaimed Bertie, in disgust.

'Beastly!' said the archbishop of the future, laconically.

'Oh! if you want dirty children,' said Stephen, 'come to
Lambeth.   You'll see a goodish few there.'

As he spoke the door was opened by Mrs. Tremain.

'All in the gloaming,' she said brightly.   'I told Aunt Margaret we should most likely find you here; what a delicious smell
of roasting!'

'It's chestnuts, mammy,' shouted Jackie, at the top of his
voice, as he dragged his mother to a chair, and took up the
position on her knee to which, in Nesta's absence, his right
was indisputable.   'Mammy, do eat this one, it's such a
beauty.'

'Aunt Margaret, do you like this low chair?' said Gladys, as
Mrs. Causton joined the group gathered round the fireplace.

'Thank you, my dear, no, I think I will sit at a little distance;
as I must face the cold outside in a minute, it is well not to enjoy
too much of the warmth.   You have a very large fire.'

This last sentence had something of reproach in it, and it
stimulated Stephen to a quick rejoinder.

'Prime, isn't it?'

'Still,' continued Mrs. Causton, 'in such a severe winter it
seems almost incumbent on one not to be too lavish in the coals,
which are so much needed by the poor.'

'It doesn't make the poor people any warmer for us to be cold,' said Stephen, with a suppressed growl.

'Nurse always makes up big fires,' said Gladys. 'She says it's more economical than always feeding a little one. Won't you have a chestnut, auntie?'

'No, thank you, my dear. It is not more than two hours till dinner time, and I do not think it well to eat between meals.'

The chestnut eaters, conscious of a wicked enjoyment, munched on in silence, the idea of a possible abolition of all promiscuous and informal 'feedings' between meal times was not to be tolerated for an instant.

Mrs. Tremain changed the subject.

'And you really go back to London to-morrow, Stephen? You have had a very short holiday.'

'Yes; still a few days is better than nothing,' he answered, tilting his chair backwards and forwards.

'I only hope, Stephen, that you'll work well,' said his mother, anxiously. 'These long winter evenings are excellent for reading.'

Stephen yawned.

'Do you like your lodgings?' asked Mrs. Tremain.

'Oh! they're awfully dull,' said Stephen. 'Still they're near the hospital, and that's a great thing.

'And your landlady seems a thoroughly nice woman,' said Mrs. Causton, who had taken the rooms herself, and had been favourably impressed by the four large family Bibles placed as ornaments on the conventional lodging-house drawing-room table, as well as by the conversation of the landlady,

'She's well enough,' said Stephen, 'when she's sober.'

Mrs. Causton lamented the deceitfulness of appearances, and said she would look out a tract which Stephen could give to the poor woman. The younger boys, wearying of this talk, began to grow noisy, and it was a relief to everyone, including Stephen, when Mrs. Causton said it was time for them to go home.

When Gladys came back to the school-room, after seeing the last of the two visitors, she found her mother alone; the children had dispersed to play, and Mrs. Tremain sat silently by the fire, which had now sunk rather low.

'A few more coals, I think, dear,' she said, as Gladys closed the door, 'and then, as the room is quiet, I want to have a little talk with you.'

Gladys put on the coals quickly; her mother's tone had made her feel anxious, for though their 'talks' together were many, they were not generally spoken of beforehand in this way. Was there

some new arrangement to be made, some difficulty to be discussed?
Could there be bad news from Dick? Gladys tormented herself
with a variety of suppositions, and lifted up such an anxious face
to her mother that Mrs. Tremain could not help smiling.

'Did my voice sound so very serious,' she said, 'that you con-
jure up all sorts of evils in a minute?'

'Oh! mother, how did you know I had?'

Mrs. Tremain smoothed the anxious, questioning forehead by
way of reply, then she began, without further delay, to relieve
he child's mind.

'Nothing is wrong at all, dear; but your Aunt Margaret has
been talking this afternoon to your father and me. You know
that she has taken a little villa at Richmond for the next six
months; she wants to be nearer Stephen, and, though she cannot
live in London, she thinks that, if she were there, Stephen could
spend his Sundays with her. But she dreads the loneliness very
much, and cannot bear the thought of settling down by herself
in a strange place. She is very anxious, dear, that you should
go with her for a time.'

Poor Gladys' heart sank; that indefinite expression 'a time,'
rang unpleasantly in her ears, and the thought of being weeks,
or perhaps months, away from home, was terrible to her. Then,
too, though she was fond of Mrs. Causton, she was often a good
deal annoyed by her peculiarities; and if these were noticeable
in the sort of intercourse which they had had at Porthkerran,
what would they not be in the close intercourse of daily companionship? It was in rather a choked voice that she asked,
after a pause,

'*Must* I go, mother?'

'It is, of course, dear, for you to decide,' said Mrs. Tremain
'If you feel very strongly against it, we should not think of
sending you.'

'But you wish me to go,' said Gladys, a little resentfully,
feeling, too, that the very fact of having the matter left in her
own hands hardly gave her the choice of doing as she wished;
she could not deliberately choose for herself the easy, comfortable,
home-keeping path which she longed to take.

'That is hardly a fair way of putting it,' said Mrs. Tremain.
'For ourselves, darling, of course we want to keep you; for Mrs.
Causton's sake and your own, I should like you to go.'

'For my own!' exclaimed Gladys, greatly surprised.

'Yes, quite for your own, dear; you have scarcely ever been
away from home, and it is time that you should se a little more
of life; the change will be good for you in every way. I think
it will help to widen you.'

'You think me narrow-minded?' said Gladys, pouting.

'Yes, dear, I do—a little,' said Mrs. Tremain, laughing. 'I don't think you have much sympathy with people you don't agree with, and the best cure for that will be to get out of the old grooves for a little time.'

'But you surely don't want me to learn to think differently, and to come home again not agreeing with you and papa?' questioned Gladys.

''That sounds like only shifting your narrowness in a new direction.'

'But Aunt Margaret is the narrowest person imaginable,' said Gladys, perversely. 'I shall grow like her.'

'I think not,' said Mrs. Tremain; 'you would more likely be driven to the opposite extreme. But that is not exactly what I want to happen. I want you to learn to see her real goodness, and to sympathise with that, trying to pass over the little things which annoy you. Besides, you will see other people; the world of Richmond is larger than the world of Porthkerran.'

Gladys was not convinced all at once, but before many days had passed her decision was made. Home was to be renounced for six long months, and a new phase—not the least arduous— of her education was to be begun under Mrs. Causton's guidance.

Her stay at Richmond was certainly productive of some good results. Stephen found his home visits attractive, and never failed to appear on Saturday afternoons. Mrs. Causton enjoyed her bright cheerful companion, and Gladys herself, in spite of unconquerable home-sickness, found much that was pleasant in her new life, and for many reasons never in after-years regretted the decision she had made.

She saw then, with the strange thrill of joy and wonder which such realisations bring, that on this decision and on this visit to London hinged almost all that was most dear to her in the future, and that, unconsciously, she had then taken the first step towards the attainment of her wish over the chestnut-roasting.

CHAPTER XIV.

CAST ADRIFT.

Ruin's wheel has driven o'er us,
Not a hope that dare attend,
The wide world is all before us,
But a world without a friend.
                                        BURNS.

Two dry sticks will set on fire one green.
He that takes the raven for a guide shall light upon carrion.
                                        Eastern Proverbs.

How long were things to go on in their present state? That
was the question which, as the spring advanced, Ellis Farrant
continually asked himself. One afternoon, towards the end of
May, the thought pressed itself upon him more pertinaciously
than ever. He was in the smoking-room, leaning back meditatively in his chair, from time to time reading a few lines in the
Sporting News, but more often looking discontentedly and per-
plexedly at his step-son, who had drawn up his chair to the other
side of the hearth, and whose fine profile was clearly marked out
against the light as he bent over his newspaper. Two days ago
Donovan had come of age, yet Ellis had not carried out his pre-
conceived plan of revenge; in the past he had always intended
to have the final breach with his step-son on the very day that
his guardianship ended, but when the time actually came his
heart failed him—no fitting opportunity presented itself. Instead
of quarrelling with him, he drank his health at dinner, played
billiards with him most of the evening, and was as good-natured
and friendly as possible. But, although the few months which
had elapsed since Dot's death had been singularly peaceable ones
at the Manor, Ellis had not lost his strong dislike to Donovan.
He had at first felt sorry for him, and had left him unmolested;
but it is one thing to sympathise with a person in the first
poignancy of his grief, and quite another to understand or feel
for his prolonged sorrow.

As the months passed on, and Donovan's grave stern face
still remained unaltered, Ellis began to feel aggravated; he saw
little enough of his step-son, but what he did see was quite sufficient to annoy him. Donovan would perhaps come down to
breakfast, then he would disappear for the rest of the day, for
long solitary rides or walks seemed to be his only relief; at
dinner he would be in his place again, but would rarely utter a

single word, and in the evening, though he was decidedly Ellis's superior at every game, he was too gloomy and taciturn to be a pleasant companion. The elder man's dislike and impatience began to grow uncontrollable; he found himself looking out eagerly for an opportunity of picking a quarrel.

As he sat looking thoughtfully across the room at his companion, his doubts were suddenly resolved by an unexpected turn of affairs. Donovan threw down his paper, and, turning round to his step-father, asked abruptly—

'When do you go up to town?'

'Next week, I believe,' said Ellis, knocking the ashes out of his pipe and refilling it.

There was a pause. Then Donovan continued—

'I have been thinking over things for the last few days, and I've made up my mind that this sort of life won't do for me any longer. I must begin to work at something.'

'A most commendable decision,' said Ellis. 'And that's the longest sentence I've heard from you for many a month.'

Donovan knew from the tone of this speech that his step-father was in a quarrelsome humour. He frowned, but continued, with some additional constraint in his manner,

'Since we are agreed, then, perhaps it would be as well if we arranged matters before leaving Oakdene. I am thinking of going into chambers and studying for the Bar; if you and my mother will settle my allowance, there is nothing that need keep me here longer.'

'Gently, my good fellow,' said Ellis, getting up from his chair with the feeling that he could carry things through with a high hand if he were standing above his step-son. 'You are in rather too great a hurry; you rattle off in a few words what involves a great deal. I too have been thinking matters over, not only for the last two or three days, but for some time; by all means set to work if you like, only do not expect me to support you any longer. Live in chambers, if you will, and be a law student for as many years as you please, only don't think that I shall keep you during the interval or pay your premium.'

Donovan started to his feet.

'I don't understand you,' he said, with repressed indignation. 'What do you mean by this?'

'Simply what I say,' said Ellis, provokingly.

'You mean me to understand that I am not to have any proper allowance made me?'

'Exactly so, though I don't admit the adjective.'

The two men stood facing each other. For a few minutes

L

neither spoke; Donovan's eyes dilated, and his face glowed with indignation. Ellis met his look with a cold, bold effrontery.

At length the silence was broken by Donovan's voice.

'And *this* is what you have waited and plotted for! this is the part of the honourable English gentleman, to steal into a house, and win your way craftily, and mislead wilfully and shamefully those who never suspected your wickedness! Yes, you have fulfilled your duties as a guardian nobly, and now you would oust the "insufferable cub," whom you longed to kick out months ago, only you couldn't; instead, you hoodwinked him, flattered, lured him on with false hopes. You *scoundrel!*'

'The step-son waxes hot,' said Ellis, with a sneer, 'as, naturally, we par' this day, I will allow a few last shots.'

'Do you dare to turn me out of my father's house?—you an interloper, a defrauder!'

'I have tolerated your presence in the house for ten months,' said Ellis; 'I knew that the time remaining was short, I let you stay on in peace; you have aggravated me at times beyond bearing, and now, with the greatest pleasure in life, I show you the door. You surmise quite truly, I have often longed to "kick you out," as you express it; take care that you do not force me to interpret the words literally.'

'Do you think,' said Donovan, angrily, 'that my mother is so utterly unnatural that she will allow me to be treated in this way? I tell you you are mistaken, sir.'

'You forget that your mother is my wife,' said Ellis, watching his victim's writhing lip with a sort of enjoyment. 'But, come now, I'll overlook what you said, and we will part amicably; do not cut your own throat by refusing the pardon I offer.'

'*Pardon!* and from you!' cried Donovan, passionately. 'Am I to accept forgiveness for words which are a hundred times too mild for your conduct? I'll let the world know of the injustice, I'll publish your scandalous behaviour everywhere in the neighbourhood!'

'The only drawback to that scheme of revenge is the unfortunate character you yourself bear in the place,' said Ellis, maliciously. 'The neighbourhood will not very readily sympathise with any stories which the far-famed Donovan Farrant, the professed atheist, thinks fit to fabricate.'

The statement was so true that Donovan could not deny it, but the consciousness of his isolation and the sense of injustice drove him almost to madness.

'That may be true!' he stormed, 'anything may be true in

a cruel, self-seeking, unjust world, but though everyone is against me, though I've not a creature on earth to hold out a hand to me, I will at least speak my mind to you. You are a traitor, sir, and a villain ! '

' Take care,' said Ellis, his colour mounting, ' I give you fair warning that those words are actionable ; use them again at your peril.'

' You dare me to use them ! ' said Donovan, furiously. ' I will repeat them a thousand times—you are a treacherous, despicable villain ! Were a hundred witnesses present, a hundred actions possible, I would repeat it ! What ! am I to submit to be ruined without a word ?—am I to sink down meekly into beggary because a plotting, scheming traitor like you dares to condemn me ? '

Ellis was trembling with mingled fear and rage.

' You had better go while I can keep my hands off you,' he said fiercely. ' Stay longer and I'll have you sent to Bedlam.'

Donovan's brain seemed to reel. It was almost impossible to believe that he was actually being turned out of his father's house.

' I will see my mother,' he said, with angry resolution in his voice. ' She will not suffer it, she cannot.'

He strode out of the room fiercely, and hurried across the hall to the dining-room. Waif, hearing his step, sprang up from the door-mat and pattered after him, Ellis, following quickly, blocked the doorway before the door closed. Donovan turned back wildly.

' I tell you I *insist* on seeing my mother alone,' he said, with a look so full of anger and hatred that Ellis shrank beneath it, but still he was able to answer with cold decision.

' And I tell you that I refuse to leave my wife with a maniac.'

' Be it so,' cried Donovan, ' but though you deny me everything, you cannot alter the instincts of nature. Mother, you will not—you cannot agree to this wickedness ? You will not turn me away from this house penniless ? You will not listen to what he says ? '

Mrs. Farrant had been lying on the sofa ; she started up from a doze to find the room in an uproar—Donovan and her husband storming at each other in a fashion without parallel. They had often before disagreed, even quarrelled in her presence, but in a quiet gentlemanly way, to which she did not object. This angry vociferation terrified her beyond measure. Donovan's rare and almost tropical outbursts of passion had always alarmed her. She turned now from his wild looks and impetuous words to her husband, who stood by in cold silence.

'What is the matter? What has happened, Ellis?' she asked, helplessly. 'Pray stop this terrible noise. It is quite impossible for me to understand anything, Donovan, if you agitate me so.'

'I will be quiet,' he gasped, softening his voice with an effort. 'I will not worry you for a moment. Only trust me, mother; listen to me fairly, and promise that you will not side against me. He—your husband insults me, drives me out of the house—this house which never ought to have been his—he turns me away penniless—say, only say that it is against your wish!'

Mrs. Farrant's tears began to flow, and she turned to her husband imploringly.

'Oh! Ellis, what has he done? Do not be hard upon him. He is the only child I have left. What has he done?'

Even in that moment of tumult, Donovan felt a thrill of joy at his mother's words. Was it possible that at last they might understand each other—that Nature would assert herself above the thick clouds of selfishness and uncongeniality which had so long divided them?

'Honora,' said Ellis, in his coldest voice, 'you must be content to trust me with this. I cannot allow Donovan's presence in my house any longer. For your sake I will let him go without calling him to account for the disgraceful language he has used to me, but go he must. He has been supported in idleness quite long enough: let him win his way in the world now as he can.'

Donovan stood with his back against the window frame, and with arms folded, listening in silence to his step-father's words, listening, too, with painful intensity for his mother's answer. Would she again plead for him, or would she be overruled by Ellis's cold speech?

'There has been nothing but trouble about him,' sobbed Mrs. Farrant. 'There seems to be a fate against me; nothing goes well. I have trouble after trouble. Oh, Donovan! why did you bring about this quarrel? For my sake you might have respected your step-father.'

'At least believe that it was not my doing,' cried Donovan, bitterly disappointed by her tone. 'If you would only have believed what I told you last summer, we could not have been in this position; but who can stand against the coils of a serpent!'

'Go, sir,' said Ellis, angrily, 'go at once, and do not try my patience by upbraiding me before my wife.'

'Did I not tell you that he would bring nothing but wretchedness to us?' said Donovan, desperately. 'The time may come when you will see it more clearly. I can only hope that one victim may satisfy him and that you may never suffer.'

Mrs. Farrant sobbed convulsively, Donovan stooped down and kissed her, but as he felt her tears wet on his check, he thought bitterly how one brave decided word from her would have been worth all this passionate sorrow.

With a dazzled bewildered feeling he crossed the hall and went up to his room; in a few minutes his bell was rung and a message sent down to the housekeeper's room for Mrs. Doery to come upstairs. She came to him at once, looking so unchanged, with her nut-cracker features, sharp eyes, and respectable black dress and apron, that he felt almost as if time had been standing still with her, while it had brought such changes to him.

'Well, Mr. Donovan, what do you please to require?' she asked, severely.

He roused himself, and said in his natural voice—a rich mellow voice, but with a great ring of sadness in it—

'I am going away, Doery. Mr. Farrant has, in fact, turned me out of the house. I want you to put up my things for me.'

Then, with that strange contradictoriness whereby the very last persons in the world whom we suppose to love us, suddenly reveal depths of unsuspected tenderness under the stress of some unusual event, Mrs. Doery broke into indignant sobs. She had never heard the like in her life! Turn her lad out of the house when he ought to have been made his father's heir! It was impossible, intolerable, she never would believe the law of England would allow it!

Her indignation rather softened Donovan, it was such a relief to feel that anyone, even this cross-grained old woman, would take his part! It seemed a strange reversal of the old order of things— Doery, stimulated by the cruelty of others, to allow some merit in him, or at least to bestow her pity on her ne'er-do-weel. He left her with a substantial souvenir, both for herself and for Dot's maid, Phœbe, generosity which in the precarious state of his finances was more natural than wise. Then he took a last look at Dot's room, put her little carriage clock with his own hands into his portmanteau, and leaving directions with Doery for his things to be sent to the Greyshot Station in time for an evening train, he went downstairs. Ellis was in the hall, waiting half nervously for the full accomplishment of his plans, for the crowning moment of his triumph. Donovan passed by him without speaking, deliberately took down his stick and riding-whip from the rack, and then, facing round upon his step-father, said with a depth of concentrated contempt and hatred—

'We part here, then. Remember always that you have goaded me on to ruin!'

Then the door was closed behind him, and Donovan left the house which should have been his, and walked away alone.

It was a beautiful spring afternoon, the dark fir-trees and the early crimson of the copper beech stood out against the blue of the sky, the oaks were beginning to show their green leaves, the pink and white thorns were in full bloom. The beauty of the place seemed never to have been so great before, and though very often Donovan had thought the Manor dull and prison-like, yet now that he was exiled from it he found how large a place it had in his heart. And he was to leave it for ever! his home was to remain in the hands of his greatest enemy! At the first bend in the carriage drive he involuntarily turned back for a last look at the house. It stood there in the afternoon sunshine, with just the same air of sleepy luxurious comfort which it had always worn; there, above the creeper-laden porch, was the window of his old room, and close by it Dot's window. He remembered the day when he had decided to give up his foreign tour for the sake of being with her, and heard in fancy the childish voice which could never again call him. How strange now seemed the struggle of the past to give up his longing for a change of scene! how he grudged every hour that he had spent away from Dot! It was hard, very hard, to turn away from the place so full of her memory; no thought of future difficulties had as yet forced itself upon him, indignation and bitter sorrow drove out everything else—everything but a vague feeling of more complete desolation, more utter loneliness. He had thought that he had drained the full bitterness of the cup of life in the agony of bereavement, but here was a fresh draught which in its humiliating injustice was gall and wormwood to him.

All this time he was not, however, so friendless as he imagined; Waif followed him closely. His devotion to his master, which had always been very great, had become more marked since Dot's death. In Donovan's lonely rides and long walks Waif had always accompanied him, he had learnt to understand his master's moods and knew quite well when to keep to heel in silent unobtrusiveness, and when to frisk and gambol about him; he had watched the stormy scene in the drawing-room, had followed Donovan noiselessly up and down stairs, now he trotted demurely behind him, well aware that this was not the right time to draw attention to his presence.

The gates were passed at length, and Donovan stood without in the white dusty road; he did not pause or hesitate or look back now, but strode along with fierce rapid steps, down the hill, through the little village, past old Mr. Hayes' deserted house, to the tiny grey church in the valley. Everything looked cruelly peaceful, on the hillside some cows were browsing, a column of blue smoke curled up from the chimney of a little farmhouse close by, a country woman passed him singing to the brown-eyed baby in her arms. Contrasted with all this were Ellis's cruel words ringing in his ears, and the recollection of the hateful look of vindictive triumph which he had seen in his step-father's face. The frenzied passionate indignation surged up in his heart with redoubled force, he threw open the churchyard gate, and hurried up the flagged path, pausing, however, beside the little porch to look at a notice which had met his eye, as trifling things do sometimes force themselves upon us in moments of great agitation. He read with growing bitterness the words :—

'NEW ORGAN FUND.—Ellis Farrant, Esq., of Oakdene Manor, having generously promised £200 to the above fund, it is earnestly hoped that the additional £100 still required may be obtained. A special collection will be made, &c., &c.' Charity, church-organs, generosity to win a good name with the world! behind the outward show, injustice, tyranny, and hatred!

Donovan turned aside past the great yew tree to the place where little Dot had been laid. The stone had just been put up, a recumbent cross, the sharp outlines of the white marble standing out clearly against the green grass; he threw himself down upon it in one of his terrible paroxysms of grief, in pain so unalleviated that it seemed like strong physical torture added to the mental suffering. How long he lay there with his face pressed down to the cold marble, and his hands grasping strainedly at the turf, he never knew; it must have been for a long long time, for when he staggered to his feet again the sun was setting, and he found that only by walking briskly could he reach Greyshot in time for the evening train to London. With a still white cold face, which seemed to have absorbed something of the hard rigidity of the marble cross, he looked his last at the little grave, then hastily recrossed the churchyard. Waif, who had been watching him all the time with considerable anxiety, trotted on in front of him, but at the gate turned back to meet him and began to draw attention to himself by a series of whines and barks and bounds in the air. He could not have chosen a better moment for making his presence known, Donovan felt at once the relieved reaction from hard bitter despair to a half-amused gratitude ; this dumb creature loved him, there could be no doubt of that, and there are times in the lives of most of us when the love even of dumb things wins a tenfold preciousness because of its unquestioning faithfulness, its fearless devotion, its contrast to the changeful doubting unreliable affection of men, who can judge and speak their judgment. He stooped down and let the dog spring up to his knee, while he patted the sagacious white and tan head; then, remembering that his time was short, he started up again with a sudden return of energy.

'Come along, old fellow,' he said, in his usual voice, 'you and I will go through the world together.'

Waif wagged his tail, pricked up his black ear, drooped the white one, and bounded along as if he enjoyed the thought of the companionship.

It was growing dusk when the dog and his master reached Greyshot; the station lamps were lighted; somehow Donovan's choking indignation began to diminish under the influence of the excitement. He had been unjustly used, certainly, but the world was before him, and the world began to seem more attractive than he had thought; the cool evening wind blew through the station, the platform was rather crowded, for the first time a boyish sense of the pleasure of freedom stole across him. Here he was accountable to no one, free to do exactly as he pleased, with his portmanteau and his dog he could roam where he liked. He took a ticket for himself and Waif to Paddington without any very distinct idea why he chose London as his first resort, turning to it perhaps only as the sort of natural home which the great city seems to most Englishmen. Then he sauntered up and down, waiting for the train, looked at the brightly lighted book-stall, scanned the faces of the crowd, while all the time his thoughts were running pretty much in this way :

'I must make the best of life; hateful and worthless as it is, I may as well enjoy myself as much as I can. The world is full of injustice, I will pay it back in its own coin.'

Presently the train was heard in the distance, in another minute his golden-eyed destiny flashed into sight, there was haste and confusion on the platform. Waif, with his ticket tied to his collar, kept close to his master's heels, till Donovan, opening the door of a carriage, prepared to lift him in. The occupants, however, objected, a nervous middle-aged lady started up from her corner, she could not endure dogs, she really must beg that he did not get into that carriage. Donovan retreated, and hurried on to the next vacant place, taking care this time to put the question,

'Do you mind the dog?'

'Oh, dear no,' said a pleasant bland voice, and he sprang in just as the train started.

When he had put up his bag and walking-stick, he threw himself back in a corner seat, and began to scrutinize his fellow-passengers. They were three in number, and they were beguiling the time with a game of euchre. The individual with the pleasant voice, who had consented to Waif's admittance, sat next to Donovan, so that he could only see his profile; he seemed to be a short, heavily-made man between fifty and sixty, with an unnaturally red face, thick neck, and scanty red hair sprinkled with grey; he was singularly ugly, but his expression was more weak than unpleasant, especially when he turned round with some trifling remark to Donovan, and showed his little twinkling watery eyes, good-natured mouth, and round face. His two companions were much younger men, the one furthest from Donovan was faring badly in the game, he was a sleek-looking, bearded man, dressed rather extravagantly, and wearing a heavy watch-chain and bunch of charms; there was an air of vulgar prosperity about him, and Donovan surmised that he was some wealthy manufacturer or tradesman. The remaining traveller was a much more perplexing study. After watching him for some time, Donovan had not in the least arrived at any decision about him, he might have been a sporting gentleman, or a superior commercial traveller, or a newspaper correspondent, or possibly a card-sharper. Donovan tried to fit every one of these 'callings' upon him; each succeeded for a time, and then fell to the ground. He was, however, peculiarly attractive. His companions were very soon forgotten altogether in the absorbing interest of watching this man's exceedingly clever play and curious face. He had a square massive forehead, black hair receding from the temples, and just beginning to turn grey, a dark oily complexion, very small black eyes, with a dissatisfied look in them, and heavy dark eyebrows, level towards the bridge of the nose, but arched at the other end, and raised still higher when he became interested.

Before very long the manufacturer was beaten, and the dark-browed man turned to Donovan, shuffling the cards as he spoke.

'Will you make a fourth at whist?'

The question was asked so casually, as if the speaker cared little whether he complied or not, that Donovan, who had rather inclined to the opinion that he *was* a professional gambler, was completely deceived by it. He only hesitated a moment, then the red-haired elder man turned round with his good-humoured smile, and said, in his pleasant voice,

'We should be delighted, if you would join us. One needs something of the sort on a long journey, to while away the time.'

Without further preamble the game began. The stakes were high; Donovan grew excited, and forgot for the time his anger and the bitter treatment to which he had been subjected. He was partner with the rich manufacturer; the strange-looking, dark-browed man was playing with the elder with the red hair. He was a daring opponent, and Donovan, who was accustomed to carry everything before him, was roused and interested to a most unwonted degree. It was a close and exciting game eventually won by the two strangers, but Donovan's skilful play had evidently surprised his dark-looking opponent, who scrutinized him curiously, while the red-haired traveller began to compliment him.

Presently they stopped at Swindon, and Donovan, beginning to be conscious that he had eaten nothing for many hours, hurried away with the others towards the refreshment-room. As he waited for an instant among the crowd of passengers, he heard a sharp voice, low, and yet singularly distinct, not far from him.

'Now mind, your work's not done yet, so be careful.'

Glancing round, Donovan saw that the speaker was his late opponent; the good-humoured face of his red-haired companion clouded a little, and there was something of the expression of a spoilt child about his mouth as he replied,

'Plague upon it! You never can let a fellow enjoy himself, Noir. I'm sure I've been as temperate as old Oliver himself——'

The rest of the sentence died away in the distance, but apparently Noir enforced his advice, for, some minutes before Donovan left the refreshment-room, his two fellow-travellers repassed him on their way to the carriage.

Waif sat guarding his master's property. The two men did not notice him; the younger one, who had been addressed as Noir, flung himself back in his place, the elder fidgeted about restlessly, talking in his hearty voice the while.

'What do you think of our two friends?'

'The manufacturer is a fool,' said Noir, decidedly. 'The young one's as sharp as a needle.'

'Ha! I thought as much. He'd have beaten us hollow, wouldn't he, if it hadn't been for certain——'

'Be quiet!' said the younger man sharply. 'You'll undo us some day by your want of caution.'

'Shall you try any more this evening?'

'I don't know. I think not. I wish I could get that young fellow for a second instead of you. He'd be the making of us.'

'A cut above our sort of thing, isn't he?'

'Can't say, but he looks discontented enough. We'll sound him, get the manufacturer to draw him out.'

Then, as the other traveller returned, Noir suddenly changed his tone, and very skilfully drew the conversation round to the desired subject. They had just been talking of his partner. He seemed a clever fellow. They were wondering what he was. For his part, he would bet ten to one that he was in the Army. The manufacturer thought he was an undergraduate. There was some laughter over the dispute. It was agreed that, by hook or by crook, they would find out which was in the right by the end of the journey. Then the bell sounded. There was hurrying to and fro on the platform, and at the very last moment Donovan stalked back to his place, perfectly unconscious of the small plot which his companions had been making.

He had brought back a biscuit for Waif, and the dog made a good opening for conversation. Then the manufacturer mentioned by chance that he came from Bristol, and Donovan, to the satisfaction of the three conspirators, began to ask questions as to the likelihood of finding any suitable employment there.

'Oh, with capital, you can always get on,' said the rich man, easily. 'Nothing can be done in this world without money, but there are plenty of openings there for any young men wanting employment.'

'Provided they are capitalists,' said Donovan, with bitterness, which did not escape Noir's keen observance.

'Well, of course you might meet with a clerkship,' said the manufacturer, 'but it's a difficulty to get them very often, there's such a run on them; and besides, that would hardly be in your line, would it?'

'No,' said Donovan, haughtily; then, with a touch of humour, he added, 'Though, to be sure, I've not much right to talk of "my line."'

The talk drifted on by degrees to the recent strikes in Lancashire, and the manufacturer and Donovan had a hot argument on the subject of wages, in which the latter's keen sense of injustice and oppression was fully brought to light. He talked so fiercely of the tyranny of the rich, the grinding down of the poor, the dishonest grasping of the capitalists, that Noir felt sure there was some personal feeling involved in the dispute, certain that in some way this young fellow's life had been embittered by the tyranny and injustice which he inveighed against. The dark brows were raised higher and higher as the argument went on; evidently Donovan's words had touched some kindred feeling in the man's heart. At last he could contain himself no longer, but

joined in the dispute, linking his vehement words with Donovan's,
till between them they fairly overwhelmed the rich Bristol man.
Then at once there was established between them that strange
sympathy which comes like a lightning flash, when two minds
are entirely one upon a subject not usually agreed upon. They
had been united in argument, and in an argument very nearly
touching their own lives; instinctively Donovan held out his
hand when they parted at Paddington, and the dark-browed man
grasped it with a warmth and heartiness curiously contradictory
to his disposition. He was in reality a hardened cheat, but his
one vulnerable spot had been touched, and he at once conceived
a strong liking for his young ally.

Perhaps few places are so dependent on the frame of mind one
is in as London. No place seems so pleasant to a sociable person in
a happy humour, no place so cold and uncongenial to anyone in
trouble. Then with what heartless indifference the busy crowd
passes by, how the careless talk, the hearty laugh, the cool stares
of one's kind wound and sting; with what envy does one look at
the smiling faces, and how (foolishly and morbidly, of course)
one compares them with the priest and the Levite in the parable;
though how they can help 'passing by on the other side,' when one
is only stripped and wounded and robbed by the unseen foes of
life which prey on the inner man, a troubled mind is generally
too illogical to consider. The forlornness of his position did
not come upon Donovan all at once. During the months which
had passed since little Dot's death, in his sorrow 'without
hope,' worthier and more manly thoughts had grown up in his
heart; he had made up his mind to work at something, and,
though his chief object had been merely to divert his thoughts
by the work, the resolve was still in the right direction. The
rude repulse which he had met with from Ellis when he suggested
his new idea, and the hardness of his expulsion from Oakdene,
crushed down for the time all these better thoughts; but in a
little while, from sheer necessity, they sprang up again. It was
evidently impossible that he could live for any length of time on
the remains of his last allowance; he must gain his living in
some way, and now, for the first time, he felt fully how fatal to
his interests Ellis's guardianship had been. Had he been forced
to enter some profession, or had he even received a better education after his school career was ended, he would not now have
been so helpless: yet, after all, he would scarcely have consented to leave Dot, even had he known beforehand of Ellis's
malignant intention; only now it added bitterness to his indignation to think how coolly and systematically his step-father had

planned his ruin. Why was it?—what had he done to earn such hatred? He asked himself those questions over and over again, knowing nothing of the first great wrong which Ellis had done him—the wrong which was at the root of all the subsequent evil.

The morning after his arrival he hurried off at once to Bedford Row to consult his father's solicitor, the same who had come down to his grandfather's funeral, and had initiated him into the mysteries of *vingt-et-un.* He was by this time an elderly man; but though he listened to Donovan kindly, and refused to take any fee for the consultation, he showed him at once that he had no legal claim whatever on Ellis Farrant or his mother now that he was of age. His case was no doubt a very hard one; he should think that by continued applications he might reasonably expect to extort some allowance, if only a small one, from his step-father. As to his mother she had no power at all apart from her husband; he could take counsel's opinion if he liked, but it would be simply throwing away his two guineas—it was a matter quite out of the province of law, a family matter which must be arranged by family feeling and natural affection. As to employment, he should advise him to apply to any influential men he knew in town; it was possible he might get some post in one of the Government offices. The lawyer hoped that Mr. Farrant would dine with him some evening—he had just moved to a new house at Brompton; if he could ever be of any service to Mr. Farrant, he should be most happy.

Donovan went away several degrees more depressed than before. His prospects did indeed seem dreary; 'continued applications' to Ellis Farrant, or, in plain English, 'begging letters,' could not for a moment be thought of, and the lawyer's kindness failed to impress him. It was easy enough to ask a fellow to dinner, and to hold out vague offers of service; but Donovan had seen too hollow a corner of the world to put any faith in this sort of friendship. He resolved, however, to call on two or three great men whom in the old times he and his mother had visited; his name at least would be known to them. He would follow the lawyer's advice, and try for work. But each effort was doomed to fail. The first of the old acquaintance was kind indeed, but not encouraging; he knew of nothing in the least suitable, regretted extremely his inability to help his young friend. The second flattered him, assured him that with such advantages he could not fail to get on in the world, and promised that if ever he heard of any appointment likely to suit him he would let him know at once. The third, an overwrought man, always oppressed by twice as much work as he could properly manage, received him with scant courtesy, listened to his story coldly, and dismissed him with a curt refusal; it was no use coming to him, he had a thousand applications of the kind—they were, in fact, the bane of his existence. He could offer no help at all—he wished Mr. Farrant good-day.

It was not till the close of this third interview that Donovan altogether realised his position. With hot cheeks, for he was still young enough to flush easily at any discourtesy, he turned his back on the chambers of the harassed and churlish man of the world, made his way along the crowded pavements of Parliament Street, and without any distinct purpose bent his steps towards the river. It was a hot afternoon in early June, but what little air there was reached him as he leant on the parapet of Westminster Bridge, his face propped between both hands, his eyes bent down on the sparkling sunlit water. What was the use of his life? he asked himself dejectedly. How indeed was he to live? His acquaintances one and all refused or were not able to help him, his home ties were all broken, there was not a single being in the world who would help him or care for him. Under such circumstances would it not be well to seek that 'refuge in the cavern of cold death' which he had taught himself to consider as the goal, the end of all things? What harm could it do to anyone? There was no one to miss him except Waif, and not to be would be ineffable peace! No more craving for Dot's presence, no more gnawing disappointment and weariness of life, no more suffering from injustice, no more misery of loneliness. And yet—— What would his father have said? And then, too, was there not some natural physical shrinking from such an end? After all, he was very young, and the boy-life within him began to assert itself above the morbid overgrowth. Life, as it was, was certainly not worth having, but surely there must be some brightness in store for him! The sun shone down in golden splendour on the river, the pleasure-steamers and the smaller boats were borne past him rapidly, the mere animal joy of existence overcame for the time his darker thoughts.

Yet what was he to do? He did not know the Bible well, but he had of course heard it read in his school days and before he gave up church-going; now from some odd recess of memory there floated back the words—'Make to yourselves friends of the mammon of unrighteousness that when ye fail they may receive you into everlasting habitations.' He smiled a little to himself as he thought of the solution of this perplexing passage which his life was bringing to light. He had certainly taken no

pains in the old days to make friends; where he could have
wished friendship there had always been a shrinking back on the
other side; his bad name had kept back good companions; his
natural nobility had guarded him from making real friends of bad
people, although he had been in the way of evil companionship
very often. But a real friend he had never known. Certainly
his circumstances were sufficiently dreary to have brought to
despair a far better regulated mind than his; the misery and
hopelessness surged in upon him afresh, the healthy pleasure in
existence died away, the brightness of the summer day only increased his sick longing for something to fill the emptiness of
his life.

Just as he had slowly raised himself and was about to move
on from the place where he had been leaning, he heard himself
addressed in a voice which, though not exactly familiar to him,
he yet seemed to have heard somewhere.

'Good-day, I think we've had the pleasure of meeting before.'

Turning round hastily, he at once recognized the dark-
browed man with whom he had travelled up from Greyshot, his
antagonist in the game, his ally in the argument.

'I've been watching you for some minutes,' said the stranger,
'only you seemed so deep in meditation that I wouldn't disturb
you. I've often thought of you since that day we met on the
Great Western.'

'Have you?' said Donovan, brightening a little, for the
man's manner had a certain attractiveness in it; then, after a
moment's pause, he added, 'Why, I wonder?'

'Why?' repeated the stranger, 'because I like you, and it is
so seldom I do like anyone that naturally, from the very oddity
of the thing, I thought of you.'

They had moved on while talking, and now, leaving the
bridge, walked along the embankment. Donovan liked the man,
and yet was too reserved and too prudent to care to make any
advances to him. The stranger began to see that he must take
the initiative.

'Have you found the work you were looking out for?' he
asked, turning his dark restless eyes on his companion.

Donovan shook his head, all his despondency returning at
this allusion.

'I thought as much from your look,' said the stranger.
'You haven't found it such an easy matter as you expected. If
you are hard up though, it is just possible that I may know of
employment which would suit you.'

'You! Do you indeed?' cried Donovan, eagerly. 'But

perhaps I shan't be up to it; I don't mind telling you that, up to a very little time ago, I never dreamed that I should have to work for my living; now, through a great injustice, I am on my own hook, with only a five-pound note between me and beggary.'

'So bad as that,' said the stranger, thoughtfully, 'then perhaps you will not be too scrupulous for the work I was thinking of; you are certainly well cut out for it. Look! If I treat you with entire confidence and openness, may I take it for granted that you will not abuse my trust?'

'Of course,' said Donovan, growing interested.

'If you will come with me, then, to my rooms, I will explain the sort of work which I mean, you will not of course be bound to accept it if you don't like it. My name is Frewin. The old man you met with me the other night is my father—we are generally called *Rouge et Noir*.'

Donovan smiled at the singular appropriateness of the nick-name. The stranger continued,

'That you may believe me, I will tell you that it is not all from disinterested motives that I seek you out and try to help you, no one in the world goes upon such motives, self-interest is the great ruling principle. You are admirably suited to help me in my work, that is my first reason. I like you and am sorry for you, that is my second. Now I have made a clean breast of it all, will you come?'

'Of course I will,' said Donovan, without an instant's hesitation. He committed himself to nothing by this, why should he not go? And besides, these were the first helpful friendly words which he had heard for so long.

CHAPTER XV.

ROUGE ET NOIR.

The fall thou darest to despise—
May be the angel's slackened hand
Has suffered it that he may rise
And take a firmer, surer stand ;
Or, trusting less to earthly things,
May henceforth learn to use his wings.

And judge none lost, but wait and see
With hopeful pity, not disdain,
The depth of the abyss may be
The measure of the height of pain,
And love and glory that may raise
This soul to God in after-days.

A. A. Procter.

Noir Frewin took his companion up one of the narrow streets leading from the river, along the Strand as far as St. Mary's Church, and through the dingy foot-passage opening into Drury Lane.

'This is not what you have been accustomed to, I expect,' he said, taking a quick glance at Donovan's face. ' I suppose you've been putting up at some tip-top hotel by way of economising.'

Donovan coloured a little, for the surmise was true enough, but there was nothing impertinent in the man's tone, and he added,

'You'll learn differently as you see more of life. I've lived in Drury Lane on and off now for five years, and am in no hurry to leave the old place, dirty as it is. Here we are!' and he stopped at the private door of a dingy picture-dealer's shop, admitted himself and Donovan, and led the way up a dark staircase to the first floor.

Expecting a room of corresponding dinginess and dirtiness, Donovan was not a little surprised to find himself in a snug neatly-arranged room, where an odd combination of a variety of the brightest colours lent an almost Eastern look to the whole. Curious shells and corals were ranged on shelves along the walls, maps and nautical charts hung in conspicuous places, a case of gorgeous foreign birds occupied the entire length of the room, and a live parrot, in a brass cage, hung in one of the windows, looking at the new-comers with his shrewd, questioning, round eyes. Leaning back in a smoking-chair, absorbed in a newspaper, and with a long clay pipe between his lips, was old Rouge

Frewin, no longer in the irreproachable suit which Donovan had first seen him in, but wearing a rough blue serge jacket and red-tasselled cap. He hurried forward at a word from Noir with more than his former heartiness and good humour.

'Delighted to see you, sir. How has the world gone with you since we parted? I must introduce myself to you as Captain Frewin, unless, perhaps, my son has already done so, Captain Frewin, formerly of the steamer *Astick*, Bright Star Line, carrying between Liverpool and New York, latterly of the *Metora*—first-rate little steamer she was, too—carrying between Southampton and West Africa.'

Donovan could hardly keep his countenance, the whole scene was so irresistibly comic, the funny old sea-captain, in his red smoking-cap, gesticulating with his long clay pipe, the odd room, and the sudden burst of confidence which had revealed the history of its owner. But his face clouded again as Rouge asked him the same question as to his success in finding work which Noir had put to him on the embankment.

He had only just begun his dispirited answer, however, when he was interrupted by a loud nasal voice, which screamed out, 'Keep up your pecker! keep up your pecker!' and glancing round he met the goggle eyes of the parrot. It was too much for the gravity even of depressed, ruined, ill-used Donovan, he burst out laughing, a natural, hearty, boyish laugh, such as he had not enjoyed for many months.

'You see Sweepstakes encourages you,' said Noir, tormenting the bird by thrusting a piece of string through the wires of its cage.

'What's its name?' asked Donovan, still laughing.

'Sweepstakes we call him,' said old Rouge, coming to the rescue of his pet. 'I've had him for seven years, we're great friends, aren't we, Sweepstakes?'

'Poor Sweepstakes!' said the bird, with its head on one side. 'Poor Sweepstakes! 'Weep, 'weep, 'weep,' and he broke off into an exact imitation of the street cry.

'We have a little business to talk over,' said Noir, when the parrot subsided at last. 'Suppose,' turning to Rouge, 'you were to go to Olliver's and order dinner for three in half-an-hour, and we'll meet you there. You won't refuse to dine with us, I hope,' he added, glancing at Donovan.

'Oh, no,' said Rouge, heartily. 'You mustn't do that. Besides, I've not half shown you round our little cabin. I'm very proud of my curiosities, I can assure you. The bird has evidently taken to you already. You must make yourself quite at home.'

As soon as the door had closed behind the old man, Noir Frewin drew up a chair for his guest, and seating himself opposite, with his elbows planted on the table, and his chin between his hands, said,

'And now, if you've the patience to listen, I will tell you a story. I shall trouble you with some account of my own life, because only by that can I show you why it is I take an interest in you. I hate most of the world. I should hate you, if you weren't unfortunate, but I see you are in some way the victim of injustice, and, as I told you before, I like you. Bear with me a little. This will all help to explain the work I propose for you.

'My father, as he told you, was once the captain of a mail-steamer. He was, of course, absent most of the year. I lived with my mother, and as soon as I left school got a clerkship in a bank at a town—no matter in what county. Things went very smoothly with us for a long time, and at last my father, who is a very warm-hearted man and hated being away from his home, thought he had saved enough to retire and settle down in England. He resigned his ship, and for a few months we lived on happily enough. I was as contented a fellow then as you'd often meet with. I liked my work, and received a good salary; moreover, I was engaged to be married, and the future looked—well, no matter! I lived in the usual fool's paradise of a lover.' He paused a moment, as if reviewing from the distance the old happiness, then, with a bitter sneer, he continued: 'Of course I paid dearly for all this foolishness. I don't think I was a bad fellow in those days; goodness knows I'd no excuse for being so, for my mother was the best woman in the world. However, though I did well enough then, I couldn't stand the hard times that followed. There was a grand row one day at the bank, for it was found that by some forgery a cheque for one hundred pounds had been unlawfully abstracted. Suspicion fell on all those connected with the bank, and it narrowed down, as such things do, till it was clearly proved that either I myself or the son of the manager had done the deed. Of course I had not done it—the truth came to light later on—but at the time everything seemed against me, and since the manager was not a second Brutus he was naturally inclined to believe his son in the right. I don't care to go into all the misery of that time. There was, of course, a mockery of a trial. I was found guilty, and the real perpetrator of the forgery sat in court, and heard me condemned. I saw him turn pale when he heard me sentenced to seven years' penal servitude—perhaps, though, he was only thinking of the danger he had escaped.'

'But did he make no effort to save you?' questioned Donovan.

'I shouldn't have thought a man could have been such an utter brute.'

'You have yet to learn the world then,' said Noir, with a fierce laugh. 'Oh, yes, of course he was kind enough to do all in his power to get me recommended to mercy. I think he hoped for a lighter sentence. However, what difference did it make to me? I was sent to Pentonville, and there I ate my heart for a year. Then I was sent to Dartmoor, and I think the change just saved me from madness. That year my mother died. We had been everything to each other. She couldn't stand the disgrace which had come to us, or the separation. I was young, and had to stand it, but I think from that day I wasn't the same fellow. The next thing which happened made me ten degrees worse. In one of my father's letters—letters are very few and far between in convict life—I learnt that the girl I had been engaged to was married to another. I told you I paid dearly for my fool's paradise. After that I didn't care what happened. Of course I had lost my character, and I knew that it would be next to impossible for me to get any situation when my term was over. I made a friend at Dartmoor, a fellow of the name of Legge, a clever man, too, and good-natured. We came out at the same time, and he helped me on a little. But things were worse even than I had fancied. My father, in his trouble and loneliness, had fallen into bad ways. I found that in my seven-years' absence he had become a confirmed drunkard. You can fancy what a return that was! I could get no employment, and at last, with Legge's help, I began to practise my present profession.'

'You mean the profession you practised in the train the other night?' said Donovan.

'Precisely,' rejoined Noir, 'and I've made it answer. People may say what they like, but the world's one great cheat, and I delight in taking it in unexpectedly. It has ruined me, why may not I get a little out of it in return! I told you though that the truth would come to light, and my innocence came to light in time, though I didn't care a straw about it then. A year after I was released from Dartmoor I was traced out with some difficulty by the manager of the bank, his son had just died and had confessed to the forgery. The manager tried to express his great shame and sorrow, hoped he could make some reparation for the injury, offered me money—think of that! Money to make up for the ruin of a whole life! I told him there could be no reparation —that if he would bring back my mother from the grave, if he would reclaim my father, if he would restore me my betrothed, if he would give me back those wasted seven years, and give me

again the faith in God and man which had been beaten out of
me by the maddening injustice, then, and only then, could he
repair the injury.'

'I'm glad you've told me all,' said Donovan, when the narrator
paused. 'Yours is a hard story—bitterly hard. How long is it
since you were released?'

'Five years,' said Noir, relapsing into his ordinary tone, a
quiet cold tone, very different from the one in which he had
recounted his wrongs. 'I have lived here with my father chiefly,
trying to keep him in order, but it's a hopeless task. Where the
taste is once acquired it's almost impossible for a weak-minded
person to cure himself. I have lived on, making money in the
way I told you, and the other day, when you got in at the Greyshot Station, there was something in the look of you that attracted me. Then you played uncommonly well, and for the first
time in my life I felt sorry that I was cheating a fellow. Afterwards when you talked to that capitalist, I took to you still more ;
my father had so often been more of a hindrance than a help, and
I couldn't help thinking what a capital second you would make.
That is the work I propose for you. You should of course have
a certain percentage of the profits, and if you live with us all the
better. There's a room at the back which you could have, and
though I suppose it's a very different life from what you've been
used to, still you might do worse, and I can promise you what I
couldn't promise to another fellow in the world—real honest
liking. Perhaps you will say the friendship of a professional
gambler isn't worth having ; however, such as it is I offer it to
you, sometimes anything is better than nothing. No, don't give
me an answer yet. We'll have dinner now, and you can think
things over for a day or two, and let me know.'

Had Donovan given his answer then, it would probably have
been a refusal, but he went to the Frewins' club, listened to the
captain's long yarns, grew doubly interested in Noir, and had a
series of brilliant successes at the card-table. Then he went
home—that is, to his hotel—to think over the offer that had been
made to him. All that night he struggled with his perplexities.
On the one hand were his rich acquaintances coolly, if civilly,
refusing to help him, on the other was the open hospitality and
friendliness of the Frewins ; midway between the two his conscience put in a plea for a further search after honest work. In
his heart of course he disapproved of the proposed scheme, but
his principles of right and wrong were somewhat elastic, and just
now, in his anger and misery, the good within him was at a very
low ebb. Moreover, it was true enough that these Frewins were

the only people who had shown him kindness, and naturally
caught at the sympathy and liking of even a bad man, when it
was the only thing to be had.   It was like the old familiar saying
of a drowning man catching at a straw, he may know well enough
that the straw is frail and hollow, but it is something to lay hold of,
if only for a moment, and in the absence of a better support it
seems worth clinging to.

To say that he made the choice while he was unconscious of
its evil would not be true.   Some people are so ready to admit
excuses, there are always so many extenuating circumstances, or
states of mind or body which account for the fall, that very few
sins are put under the head of 'Wilful.'   But in after-years
Donovan never allowed that he had taken the step unconsciously.
Of course sin, taken in its usual sense, did not now exist for him,
but he was perfectly aware that he was entering upon a wrong
and immoral course ; he made the false step desperately perhaps,
but deliberately.   The very last words he had had with Noir
Frewin were sufficient to prove this.

'I may ask your name now ?' the man had said as they
parted.   And Donovan, for the first time in his life, had shrunk
from giving it.   How could he let his father's name become the
name of a—but there he checked even his thoughts, and hastily
gave only his Christian name.

For a little while he thought things over, as Noir had
suggested.   It was true there were ways and means of raising
money, but, even if he had had good security to offer, he would
not have cared to put himself into the hands of a money-lender.
Or there was another alternative ; he had heard Mr. Probyn,
Ellis Farrant's friend, relate proudly the length of time he had
lived 'on tick,' as he called it—this was most likely the course
which would have been chosen by nine persons out of ten, had
they been placed in his predicament.   But there was nothing to
commend this expedient to him, living in debt was simply robbing
tradespeople, there could be no doubt of that ; if he must live by
chicanery, he might as well do so in a more amusing way than
by a skilful eluding of duns, and it was better to cheat fools who
chose to risk their money in a game than honest shopkeepers.
Thus he argued with himself, what his school-fellows had called
'his crazy ideas of honour' coming out strongly ; but he held
fast to his theory, and never had a single debt.   The true and
honest course never once entered into his head.   If he had had
sufficient humility to visit his father's solicitor again and beg his
assistance, in all probability he would have been helped, for in
such an extreme case people are often kind-hearted enough.   But

to throw himself on anyone's mercy was impossible to Donovan—
he was at once too proud and too distrustful of human nature.

The consideration ended, as might have been expected, in
an acceptance of the Frewins' offer. In a few days Donovan was
established in Drury Lane, and with all the natural force of his
character, and the retaliatory spirit produced by Ellis's injustice,
and fostered by Noir's sympathy, had plunged into the lowest
and most painful phase of his life.

Poor old Rouge Frewin was the only gainer by the new
arrangement. He had always disliked the part his son had
made him play, and to be left at home in peace with his parrot
and his pipe, and as much cognac as he could manage to get
hold of, seemed to him all that heart could wish. He took the
most vehement liking to Donovan, and, in his odd way, was very
kind to him. The secret of his affection probably lay in this—
the new-comer treated him with respect, and the poor old captain
was now so little used to such treatment, that it was doubly
delightful to him.

'I am a better fellow since you came,' he would often say,
looking up with real affection in his little watery eyes at the
dark handsome face of his boy friend—the face which seemed to
grow harder, yet more hopelessly sad, every day.

It was a world of nicknames into which Donovan had fallen.
In the club to which he and the Frewins belonged—a club which
was a gaming-house in everything but the prohibited name—
every member had been dubbed with some *sobriquet*, often of
singular appropriateness. Noir's Dartmoor friend, for instance,
was familiarly known as Darky Legge. The two Frewins had
received their names of Rouge et Noir, and before very long
Donovan, whether he liked it or not, was invariably addressed as
'Milord.' The parrot was the first to draw attention to it, but
certainly old Rouge must have taught him, for whenever Donovan came into the room, or attracted the bird's notice in any way,
Sweepstakes would scream out 'Well, milord! Well, milord!'
in his harsh voice, often adding remarks which were quite the
reverse of complimentary.

One morning, while Donovan was sitting in the little parlour
with a cigar and a newspaper, circumstances combined together
in such a way as to make him for the first time ashamed of himself. They had been out very late on the previous night, or
rather that morning, and Noir was lying half-asleep on the sofa ;
as the clock struck twelve, however, he roused himself, and with
many yawns and stretches prepared to go out.

'Look here, milord,' he said, turning at the door, 'I've an appointment in the City, and must be off. You'll remember that we've arranged to go down to Manchester by the evening express. Be in the way about that time, and I'll join you here on the way to Euston.'

'All right,' said Donovan, not looking up.

'Yes, but be sure you remember, for I've reason to believe we shall make a good thing of it. Do you hear?'

'Yes,' replied Donovan, shortly.

'What on earth makes you such a sulky brute to-day? One would have thought the luck had been against you instead of all on your side last night,' said Noir, glancing at him rather curiously. His question met with no reply, however, and with a shrug of the shoulders he turned away.

When the door had closed behind him, Donovan threw down his paper, and sat silently thinking over the words which had stirred long dormant feelings in his heart. How he disliked this arranging and scheming!—what paltry work he was engaged in!—how low and base and despicable it all was! There was much to dislike, too, in Noir Frewin; in spite of his misfortunes, and the consequent sympathy which had arisen between them, there was necessarily a great deal in him which was most repulsive to Donovan. Old Rouge, moreover, had managed to escape his son's vigilance, and had made a disgraceful scene on the previous evening. Altogether, Donovan felt disappointed with his companions and disgusted with his work—not yet, unfortunately, with himself.

He could not help feeling sorry, however, for Rouge when the old man came slowly and wearily into the room. Remembering how his intemperance had begun, and what a good-hearted old fellow he was, his contempt and disgust, which had been strongly roused the previous night, died away into pity.

'Good-morning, captain,' he said, in his usual voice, and using the title which he knew the old man liked better than anything.

'Eh, Donovan, my lad, it's anything but a good morning,' sighed poor Rouge, stretching himself out on the sofa. 'How one does pay for a little extra enjoyment!' Then, catching a look of contempt on his companion's face, he added, piteously, 'Don't you turn against me, lad; I know I am not what I should be, but don't you give me up too. Everyone despises me now, everyone looks down on me, and thinks anything good enough for such a poor old fool. Don't you take to it too, lad, for you've been good to the old captain till now.'

'I don't wish to change,' said Donovan, 'but I hope you won't repeat last night's amusement. How can you expect anyone to respect you, when—well, after all, it's no business of mine.'

Rouge sighed heavily.

'Such is life!' screamed the parrot, mimicking the sigh.

Then there was silence in the room for a few minutes, till the old man broke forth again, this time with the tears running down his cheeks.

'I'm a miserable old sinner, there's no doubt of that, but I was driven to it. It's easy for other people to talk who don't know what temptation is, but I tell you, lad, I was driven to it. I was lonely and miserable, and there was more money than I knew what to do with—how could I help it?'

Donovan did not answer; he crossed the room, and leant with his back against the mantel-piece, thinking—thinking more worthy thoughts than usual, too, for his face had something of the old bright look upon it, which nothing had been able to awake since Dot's death. He liked this poor old man genuinely; he liked very few people in the world, but where his love was once given it was very true and sterling—no mere idle pretence, not a selfish taking of what can be got, but a real outgoing from self. Given an object to spend his love upon, he was capable of immense self-sacrifice; it was his bitter misanthropy, and his resolute shutting out of the source of love, which had so cramped and narrowed his life. In spite of all his shortcomings, there was much that was noble in his character; his face was full of eager desire as he turned to the old man—the lofty, almost passionate desire which must come at times to those who have, if it be but one spark of the Divine fire, the longing to turn from evil those who are overwhelmed by it, to save the weak from temptation.

'Captain,' he began, dropping the severe, yet half contemptuous tone which he had at first adopted towards the poor old drunkard—'Captain, I know you had hard times, and have a great deal of excuse. But things are different now, and it's your turn to drive back along the road you were driven. Look, we'll have a try together! You give up the drink, for a time at any rate, and so will I.'

'Bless my heart!' exclaimed the old captain, starting up. 'Why, my dear fellow, I should be dead in a month. Do you think, after all these years, I could give it up in a moment? Why, it's meat and drink to me! I couldn't live without it, I tell you.'

'More die by drinking than by abstaining,' said Donovan.
'I dare say you'd miss it at first, but you'd soon get over it.
You couldn't be more miserable than you are this morning after
your last night's carouse.'

'But to turn teetotaler!' exclaimed Rouge.   'Why, milord,
you'd never hear the last of it at the club!   We should be the
laughing-stock of the place.'

'And do you think that you were not their laughing-stock
last night?' said Donovan. 'Better be laughed at as a teetotaler
than as a drunkard.   Plain speaking, you will say, captain, but
you and I don't generally mince matters.   Come, agree to my
bargain, and my respect for you will rise ten degrees.'

'You don't think it would kill me, then?' hesitated Rouge.

'Stuff! more likely to add ten years to your life,' said Donovan. 'Come, now, we'll each sign an agreement to give it up
for—say three months.'

'So long,' groaned poor Rouge. 'Think of the dulness!
Why, what will life be worth?'

'Not much, indeed,' said Donovan, 'but more than your present life, at any rate.'

And then, after a little more discussion and hesitation, the
papers were signed.

By-and-by the old captain fell asleep on the sofa, and Donovan went out to get his lunch, and to test the desirability of
water-drinking.   In the afternoon he for the first time made his
way to the park, with a sort of desire to see the side of the world
from which he had been ejected, the gay fashionable world in
which only a year before he had moved.   Lighting a cigar, he
sat down on one of the benches, and scanned the faces of the passing crowd, wondering whether he should see any of his old
acquaintances, longing, though he would hardly admit it to himself, for a sight of his mother.   Before he had been seated many
minutes, a rather prim-looking lady and a bright-faced girl passed
by, hesitated a moment, and then took the vacant places on the
bench beside him.

'We have still half-an-hour before the appointment, do let
us sit here—it is such fun to watch the people.'   It was a clear
girlish voice which said this, and Donovan involuntarily looked
round at the speaker, a little curious to see who it was who could
find pleasure in what to him was so full of bitterness.

A fair, rounded face, sunny hair, and well-opened blue-grey
eyes.   Where had he seen her before?   Somewhere, surely, for
he remembered the face distinctly now.   It was one he had
watched and admired—and he admired very few women.   He

must have heard her speak too, for he recognised her rather unusual voice—a voice in every way suited to the face, mellow and full of tone, with a great gaiety and happiness ringing in it, softening off tenderly now and then into earnestness. He had met dozens of girls last season, but somehow she did not seem like a London girl, she was too fresh and simple. Where could he have seen her.

He listened with a good deal of interest to all she said, though it was nothing in the least remarkable, merely comments on the passers-by, and a laughing defence of fashionable people, when her companion complained of the frivolity and uselessness of their lives.

'Now, auntie, I shall think it is because you and I are on foot and the grand people are driving that you find fault with them! Don't you remember the French proverb about the pedestrians commenting on the carriage people?'

'My dear, I should be very sorry to change places with them,' answered the prim-looking lady.

'Yes, auntie, you would, I daresay, but really some people just complain of rich people because they envy them, I'm quite sure they do.'

This was rather a home-thrust to Donovan, he threw away his cigar, and listened more attentively, but the conversation drifted away to other things, home matters evidently, details and allusions which came very strangely to him in his semi-vagrant life—the last letters there had been from Dick—Nesta's quickness in reading—how father and mother meant to come up to town before they left. He listened to it half sadly, half amusedly, it was a glimpse of such a different life from his own, such a simple, innocent, pure life, with such strangely different interests! An unaffected girl, sweet, and bright, and pure-minded, how black his life seemed in contrast with hers! Musing on this he lost the thread of their conversation, and as they rose to go he only caught the words, 'Yes, I know, he doesn't profess much, but he's such a good man, the sort of man one can trust.'

A man one can *trust!* how she leant on that last word! and with what a sharp thrill it pierced Donovan's ear. What would she have said of him had she known the sort of work he was engaged upon? He was quite glad she had moved away, for he did not feel fit to be near her. He had disliked Noir Frewin's plan in the morning, now he shrank from it doubly; in the brief revelation of purity, something of his own true character had been brought to the light, he began to see very faintly indeed, but still to see in some degree his own falseness and blackness.

He would not go with Noir that evening ; it would involve some trouble, no doubt, if he did not keep his appointment, Noir would be exceedingly vexed, there would inevitably be a quarrel when he returned from Manchester, and of course he would lose the opportunity of enriching himself, but he would not go, with the light of those clear grey eyes fresh in his memory he felt tha⁺ he really could not.

Scarcely had he made this resolution when he caught sight of his mother's victoria. There was Ellis Farrant looking just as usual, and beside him was Mrs. Farrant. She was leaning back in the carriage so that Donovan only saw her face for an instant, but he fancied that she looked a little paler than usual, a little sad and worried. The sight moved him, he felt a great longing to see her again, and in the evening, not caring to return to Drury Lane, or to go to the club he was in the habit of frequenting, for fear of meeting the Frewins, he turned instead in the direction of Connaught Square. There was the house he knew so well, the house which ought to have been his, with its balconies gay with flowers, and a brougham standing before the door. His mother was probably going out, he would wait and see her as she came down the steps, but he would not himself be seen, that would be too humiliating, he would wait a little way off, and crossing the road, he leant with his back against the square railings. It was a strange watch. Bitter feelings mingled with the returning family love as he stood there in the summer twilight ; it *was* hard, even his most stern condemner would have been forced to allow that ! He was standing alone in the street, cast off by those who should have helped him, watching their comfort and luxury from his state of misery and conscious sin. Instinctively he took up poor Rouge's cry, ' He has driven me to it—how can I help going to the dogs—it is his fault ! '

And then the house door opened, and one of the footmen came out to the carriage. Donovan watched eagerly, and his breath came fast and hard. There was his mother, quite placid and happy-looking now, with a white Chuddah over her shoulders, and a diamond star in her hair, and there was Ellis, with his opera hat, and his false smiling face, and his shallow politeness.

Certainly, judging by the outward appearance, there could have been no question which was the more to be pitied, the rich man stepping into his carriage, or the unjustly used outcast who looked on in bitterness of soul. But in reality Donovan's misery was as nothing compared with his step-father's. Years of plotting and scheming, years of growing deterioration, harassing anxiety, and patient waiting, all this had Ellis gone through, and for what? For a rich wife, a town house, and a country house, accompanied by an ever-present remorse, a nameless terror of discovery, a wretched sense of shame, and a haunting dread of his victim Donovan. The good was striving within him, it would not abandon him, would not for a moment let him enjoy his unjust gains; he fought against it with all his strength, and tried to be careless and comfortable, but he fought in vain.

They went to the opera that evening and heard 'Faust.' It stung him as no sermon would have done. How like his part had been to that of Mephistopheles! How deliberately he had planned his step-son's harm! And above the voices of singers and chorus, above the grand orchestral accompaniment, there rang in his ears one sharp despairing sentence, 'Remember how you have goaded me on to ruin!'

Faust and Margherita were nothing to him. He hardly noticed the beautiful little *prima donna.* It was the grim basso, with his red livery, his stealthy yet rapid movements, his satanic look of triumphant cunning, who preached to him that night, as no clergyman in surplice and stole, or gown and Geneva bands, had ever preached to him. In the 'serenata,' where Mephistopheles sings his mocking song of triumph to the guitar, and augurs further successes for himself, Ellis sat actually shuddering at the horrible sense of likeness. The song was encored. He could bear it no longer, but shrank back into the very furthest corner of the box, trying not to see or hear. By-and-by it was all over, and Ellis, with a grey face, forced up a smile, and tried to talk in his ordinary way, as he led his wife to the carriage. But the effort was intolerable; he was, in truth, a miserable man that night, but happier had he known it for that very misery. It was the sign of that other Presence within him which will not leave us to an unequal struggle with evil.

Donovan, seeing only the prosperous outward show, knowing nothing of all the real remorse, watched the carriage drive off with feelings which in their vehemence are quite indescribable. He was almost terrified himself at the storm of hatred, and anger, and wild longing for revenge that took possession of his heart, as well he might be, owning nothing to quell it but the power of his own will. He stood quite still, his face pale and rigid with that terrible white-hot passion, the over-mastering passion in which great crimes are often committed. In his wrath nothing was too dark for him to contemplate, no revenge too sharp to be resolved upon. He had grasped hold of the iron railing of the garden, involuntarily turning away his face from the houses. A voice close to his ear made him start. If the good still strove with

Ellis Farrant, still more did it lead Donovan, who was more sinned against than sinning, and to him no fiend like Mephistopheles came to scare and terrify, but a little child was sent to lead him.

'Do you want to come in?   I thought I saw you tugging so at the gate, and I came to ask you.'

A little girl of nine or ten was addressing him, looking shyly through the iron bars of the gate.   No child had spoken to him since Dot had died.   This seemed to him like a voice from the grave, and instinctively, even at the remembrance of the love which he deemed all a thing of the past, lost to him for ever, the evil thoughts and the revengeful anger died out of his heart.

'I should like to come in,' he said, in reply to the question, 'but I have no key.'

'I will ask the Fräulein to open the gate,' said the little girl, and she ran across the garden, returning in a few minutes with a German lady, who looked up from her knitting rather curiously to see this gentleman who was waiting for admittance   It was easily explained.   He had not a key, but he pointed to his mother's house in the square.   The Fräulein, without any demur, unlocked the gate and admitted him.

He had not often been into the garden before, but two or three times he had brought Dot there in her invalid chair, and the place was therefore sacred to him.   He went at once to her favourite seat, and there, in the cool of the summer evening, better thoughts returned to him.   It had been a hot day.   The children were all enjoying the change; they had the garden almost to themselves, and, as they played, their laughter and chatter floated to him.   It was what he wanted—something innocent, and pure, and merry.   A faint, very faint return of little Dot's influence came back to him, and when he left the garden again he was a better man.

Drury Lane had never seemed to him so dingy as when he returned to it that evening.   A street-organ was playing a popular air in one part, and a crowd of wretched-looking bare-headed girls were dancing on the pavement.   Every now and then he passed one of those appalling courts or alleys which open into the lane, and, pausing once or twice, he caught a glimpse of the seething human crowd, the filth and misery which they lived in; then on again past the shabby gaslit shops, the disreputable-looking passengers, until he almost fell over a little child who ought to have been in bed long before, but who was sitting on the curb-stone, grubbing with both hands in a heap of mud in the gutter. Donovan was very tender over little children.   He stooped down at once to see whether he had hurt the small elf. A pair of dancing blue eyes looked up at him from a dirty little face, and something very unsavoury was held towards him, while, with the confidence of a great discoverer, the elf shouted, gleefully,

'See what I've got! A real old duck's foot! A real old duck's foot!'

It was a very pitiful sight, but it touched Donovan. He dropped a penny into the hand which was not occupied with the new treasure and went away moralizing, till, reaching the print-shop, he drew out his key and went up the stairs to the deserted rooms, for even Rouge was gone, and, for the next three days, Donovan was left to the tender mercies of Waif and Sweepstakes.

He lit the gas and took up a book, but the bird awaking caught sight of him, and instantly began in his most scolding tones,

'*Well*, milord, *ain't* you a fool! Oh, lor, *ain't* you a fool!'

Evidently the Frewins had not made any complimentary remarks upon his absence, and doubtless poor Rouge had hardly been fit for the journey. But he could not help it. If he had not seen that bright-faced girl, and been so shamed by her unconscious words, it would have been different. What a strange glimpse of another kind of life she had given him!

Sweepstakes sat with his shrewd grey head on one side, and his crimson tail feathers drooped. Before long, with a wicked look in his round eyes, he began to say plaintively,

'Be yit t'ever so wumble,
There's no place li k'ome.'

'Be quiet,' said Donovan, sharply, for the words did not at all suit his present frame of mind.

But Sweepstakes only reiterated,

'Be yit t'ever so wumble,
There's no place like—'

Donovan made a dash at the cage with a cloth and interrupted the song, a proceeding which enraged the parrot.

'You go to Tophet!' he screamed, angrily, and then, being out of temper, he swore for five minutes on end, till, for the sake of peace, Donovan had to make up the quarrel.

But there was a good deal of obstinacy about Sweepstakes, and, though he allowed his anger to be appeased by a Brazil nut, he treated Donovan for the rest of the evening to a mild muttered refrain of 'Be yit ever so wumble, umble, umble——' *ad infinitum.*

For the first time since he had been in London, Donovan that night went to his room early. He had got into the habit of turning

night into day, but he was dull that evening and tired, and it was
not much after half-past eleven when he left Sweepstakes for the
night and turned into his own shabby little room at the back. A
dreary lodging-house bed-room it was, with a strip or two of
carpet thrown down over the dirty unscrubbed floor, a moulder-
ing green wall-paper, and over the fireplace one solitary picture
in a gilt frame black with age, a dingy sea-piece in oils, a ship
being dashed to pieces on rocks. A room is said to show in a
certain fashion the character of its occupant; there were only four
things here which could in any way bear traces of Donovan's individuality. On the mantel-piece was Dot's clock, in one corner
a great bath, on the chest of drawers one or two anti-theological
books by Luke Raeburn, and at the foot of the bed a woolly rug
for Waif.

The window was open; it looked out on to that fearful network of byeways and alleys which Donovan had seen as he came
home. He had often seen them before, but one can see many
times and yet never observe. He had generally gone to his
room between three and four in the morning when all was quiet
enough; this evening it was just after closing time, the public-
houses had let loose their wretched throng, and the cry of the
city went up to heaven. People talk of the noise of London, and
think generally of the street traffic, the crowded pavements, and
the ceaseless wheels, but let them once hear the appalling noise
of human life in a poor quarter, and they will not complain of
anything else. Wild, drunken singing, fierce quarrels, blows,
cursing, a Babel of tongues, a wailing of children, angry disputes
between men and women, in which too often the woman's voice
in its awful harshness seems unlike that of a human creature.
These are the sounds one may hear, the fearful realities which
make up the dark side of the world's metropolis.

Donovan stood beside the open window and let all this tide
of human wretchedness beat upon his ear. He was shocked and
awed, struck with a great pity and indignation, for he was not
hard-hearted, only narrow-hearted, and though this crampedness
kept him from action it did not prevent the great suffering of
humanity from touching him with a sense of pity. The incomprehensible suffering! what a mystery it was! it made him
wretched and pitiful, and yet angry, though where the fault
of all lay he could not have said. Christianity, or rather the
horribly false notions of Christianity which he had received,
would have said that all these drunkards and degraded beings
were forging the chains which should bind them for ever and
ever in hell. According to Mrs. Doery's ideas the West-End

must have seemed the region of the elect, and Drury Lane the
abode of that other numerous band who were foredoomed to
everlasting torture.   Perhaps almost naturally Donovan had a
fellow-feeling for sinners, for in his very young days, when he
had for a short time believed in what he was taught, he had fully
made up his mind that Docry was one of the elect, and that he
had better go to the other place.   Now from his atheism, with
which he persuaded himself he was quite contented, he looked
back with amusement on the picture of his sturdy defiant childhood, which preferred even the awfully described fiery furnaces
to companionship with Docry in an unjust and partial favour.

He turned away from the window at last, but not till he had
closed it and drawn down the blind.   He shut out the misery of
his fellows as he shut out many other things, for at present he
was one of those who, as Coleridge puts it—

> Sigh for wretchedness, yet shun the wretched.

It was not to be expected that the passing words of a stranger
would be sufficient to alter the whole current of Donovan's life,
nor did Gladys Tremain exercise such an unheard-of influence.
The Frewins returned, and after sundry upbraidings from Rouge
and a sharp quarrel with Noir, things fell back to their former
state.

Once, quite unexpectedly, he met the grey-eyed stranger
again, two or three weeks after their encounter in the park.   It
was a July evening, the Frewins, Legge, Donovan, and two or
three other men were travelling up together from Goodwood.
The train was crowded; Mrs. Causton and Gladys, who had been
spending the day with some friends, were waiting on the platform
of a station not far from Chichester, but they found it almost impossible to get places.

'Such a dreadful crowd, and such disagreeable-looking
people,' said poor Mrs. Causton, nervously, 'what is the reason
of it?'

'Goodwood races, mum,' said the porter, wondering at her
ignorance, 'there's room for one in here, and one next door;
come, miss, the train's just starting.'

'My dear! you can't go alone in there,' said Mrs. Causton,
distractedly, looking at the not too reputable travellers.   But
the next carriage was every bit as bad, the train began to move,
there was really no help for it; whether she liked it or not,
Gladys was shut in alone among this strange-looking crew.   She
knew there was nothing to fear, but at the same time it was a
very uncomfortable predicament, a fast girl would have been

N

amused by such a novel adventure, but Gladys was not fast, she
was a pure womanly woman, and though she could not have
explained why, she had a peculiar shrinking from these people.
The little conversation at the door too had attracted the notice of
a coarse-looking man who was sitting next her. He turned round
upon her with a cool inquisitive stare, then made some remark to
his neighbour on the other side which caused a general laugh, and
Gladys, though she would not have understood a word even had
she heard, felt the colour flame up in her cheeks.

'Why can't you behave decently?' said a voice from the
other side of the carriage.

'Rouge, it's your deal.'

Then Gladys, who had instinctively lowered her eyes, looked
up, for the attention of the passengers was diverted from her.
With an overcoat spread over their knees, by way of a table,
they were soon absorbed in a game of 'Nap.' She looked round
at their faces with a sort of longing to find one from which she
need not shrink. All seemed bad, or coarse, or in some way
repulsive. Exactly opposite her was an elderly man fast asleep,
next to him was the one who had called his companions to order.
Gladys looked at his face half hopefully, the voice had at least
been refined, and the words—well, the best she had heard in this
company. The face too was not otherwise than refined, the
features were strikingly handsome, there were no tokens of excess
about the clear dark complexion, but oh, what a hard bitter
saturnine look there was about the whole! He was evidently
much younger than any of his companions, yet not one of them
looked so reckless and hardened, still she felt that he was
a gentleman, and was at once less uncomfortable and forlorn.
Apparently he took not the slightest notice of her, and that was
pleasant after the uncomfortable rude staring and comments.

It was a very strange and very sad revelation to her—a side
of life which she had heard of indeed, but had never in the least
realised. She had felt impatient when Mrs. Causton had lamented
the temptations of London life for Stephen. Yet the danger was
not imaginary; for here was one who could not be older than
Stephen or Dick surrounded by evil companions, gambling with
a recklessness and *sang-froid* which bespoke long habit. There
was a sort of horrible fascination in it all, she could not help
watching the eager faces; on all of them was written the strong
desire of gain; on all, except that one dark saturnine face opposite
her, which, though apparently caring for little else but the game,
never seemed to unbend, in spite of repeated successes. Gladys
watched him as he pocketed his winnings, watched pityingly his

unmoved face, and once he looked up and their eyes met. It was not a look from which she need shrink—the eyes were not bad eyes—they were very strange, hungry-looking, sad ones. She understood then why he was so different from his companions— evidently in his heart he disliked the life he was leading. By- and-by a dispute arose, a fierce, loud altercation between her disagreeable neighbour and one of the other men. Language such as she had never heard was shouted across the carriage, and the lookers-on laughed. Poor Gladys glanced across in despair to the one passenger in whom she had any faith. He was leaning back with a look of ineffable disgust and weariness on his hand- some face, but, as the angry Babel grew louder, he turned to Gladys; she hardly knew whether she were relieved or only more frightened when he bent forward to speak to her.

'This must be very unpleasant for you,' he said, and she knew at once from his manner that she had found a protector. 'We shall be at a station in a minute or two, and then, if you like, I will offer to change places with the lady you are with.'

'Oh, thank you so much,' said Gladys, her frightened eyes brightening with gratitude and relief. 'My aunt is in the next carriage, if you really wouldn't mind——'

'Not in the least. I wish I had thought of it before, that you might have been saved this unpleasantness.'

Then, without another word, he returned to his former position, but with a less hard and contemptuous expression than before. The others appealed to him for his opinion in the matter of the dispute, and he spoke coldly and quietly, but evidently what he said was to the point; the disputants quieted down, and agreed to some sort of compromise. At last, to Gladys' intense relief, they reached the station. Donovan got up and let down the window, then, looking back, said carelessly,

'You can leave me out in the next deal; I'm going to change carriages.'

The announcement caused a chorus of inquiry.

'What's up with milord now?' asked Gladys' neighbour.

'Oh! some craze, I suppose,' said a dark-browed man on the other side of the carriage; 'he took a moral fit the other night, and rushed away no one knew where. There's no reckoning on him—"a wilful man must have his"—— Why, what's this?' as Donovan returned to help Mrs. Causton in. 'We didn't reckon on this, at any rate. Donovan, what *are* you thinking of?'

'A cigar in peace next door,' he replied readily. And then he retreated, leaving Gladys greatly relieved and the card-players not a little embarrassed by the large bundle of tracts which Mrs.

Causton began to distribute among them. At London Bridge they saw him again for a minute, and Mrs. Causton pressed two tracts into his hand and thanked him for his courtesy. Gladys looked up at him shyly and gratefully, but did not speak again, except, as he raised his hat and turned away, to utter one earnest-toned 'good-bye.' He heard it, and treasured it up in his heart —a wish, he knew it was, no mere formal parting, but the wish of a pure-minded woman that good might be with him.

Gladys watched sadly as Noir Frewin rejoined her protector. He was thoroughly out of temper, as she had seen on the journey, and greeted his companion with a torrent of angry reproaches. Gladys caught only a word or two here and there—'Confouded folly!—playing fast and loose with the agreement!'—and one bitter taunt—'A pretty knight-errant to help distressed ladies! Such as *you*, a professional——'

But the word gambler did not reach Gladys. She did not then learn what a life Donovan was leading, but she had seen and heard quite enough to know that he was in great need of help, and from that night he always had a place in her prayers. Without that how could she have borne the revelation of evil and wretchedness, the contrast between the shielded life of those she knew and the life of constant temptation of these her fellow-creatures? Painful as the evening's experience had been, she could not altogether regret it. In after-life she thanked God for that brief journey, upon which had hinged so much.

CHAPTER XVI.

'THE RAVEN FOR A GUIDE.'

> What thou wouldst highly
> That wouldst thou holily; wouldst not play false,
> And yet wouldst wrongly win.
> > *Macbeth.*

> Till life is coming back, our death we do not feel,
> Light must be entering in, our darkness to reveal.
> > ARCHBISHOP TRENCH.

As the autumn wore on, both the dog and his master began to show traces of the life they were living. Poor Waif pined for the country. He had always been his master's companion in his

long rides and walks, and town life was of course a great and
very undesirable change for him. Donovan, too, lost his strength
considerably. It was an unhealthy life he was leading, full of
the worst kind of excitement; at times idle and unoccupied, at
times full of fatigue. Naturally, too, his state of mind told on
his physical strength. The year, beginning with the terrible
strain of little Dot's death, had brought him overwhelming grief;
the long spring months had been spent in a fierce inward struggle,
a vain search for peace ; then had followed his quarrel with Ellis
and his expulsion from Oakdene, and ever since that he had been
in the poisoned atmosphere of the society into which Noir Frewin
had led him. No wonder that as the winter advanced he began
to fail. Even the Frewins, who were not more observant of such
trivial matters than selfish people usually are, noticed at last that
something was wrong.

'There's no getting a rise out of the boy now,' observed
Rouge, one December afternoon. 'I don't know what's come to
him, unless, as I expect, it's this absurd fad he's taken into his
head about water-drinking. I told him it was enough to kill a
fellow to give it up all at once like that. I should have died that
very week, if I'd kept my agreement.'

Noir gave a contemptuous sneer.

'No fear of your dying in that way, at any rate. I wonder
Donovan was ever such a fool as to think you'd give it up. He
is an odd fish. There's no making him out.'

Rouge glanced at the subject of all this talk, who was lying
asleep on the sofa, and then for the first time he noticed how
worn and thin he was. All the boyishness had gone from his
face now.

'I say, Noir, he looks to me uncommonly queer,' said the old
captain. 'I've seen one or two fellows look like that before now.
There was one, I remember, on the *Metora*.'

'Pooh! I daresay many of them looked badly enough before
they found their sea-legs,' said Noir, coolly.

'Well, the fellow I mean died,' said the captain, impressively.
'And I must say milord does look to me awfully out of health.'

'Oh! nonsense. He's only seedy—a cold, or something of
that sort. We got drenched the other night coming from
Legge's place. It's time we were starting. Just wake him up.'

Rouge complied, and Donovan started up at once, and looked
sleepily at his watch.

'Time to go? Oh! I'd forgotten. It's this Brighton
scheme.'

He looked wretchedly ill and tired, not at all fit to turn out of the warm room into the cold drizzle of the December twilight, but he was not one to shirk an engagement for the sake of mere bodily disinclination, and there was no one to tell him what madness it was to trifle with such a severe chill as he had taken. He drew on his great-coat, and without a word stood waiting for Noir, who was sorting his cards on a side-table.

'Take my advice,' said Rouge, paternally, 'and have something just to hearten you up before you go. With such a cold you want something to warm the cockles of your heart.'

For the moment Donovan was strongly tempted. He did feel very much in need of some such comfort, but his hesitation was but momentary. He knew that his only hope of influencing the old captain lay in the steadiest adherence to his plan of abstinence. The three months of the agreement were over, but, though Rouge had long ago broken his pledge, his companion's example had often kept him from excess, and Donovan knew well enough that even for his own sake the safe-guard was a very good thing.

'Oh! as to the cockles of one's heart,' he said laughing, 'that's all bosh, one only takes cold the easier, as any doctor would tell you. Present loss, future gain, is our motto to-day! we ought to bag a good many head of game to make up for turning out in this wet mist. Good-bye, captain. Look after Waif.'

And then Noir and his young accomplice set out on their expedition. As they passed the window of the print-shop, Donovan involuntarily paused.

'Why, there's your very double,' he said, laughing, and, in spite of the rain, Noir stopped to see what he meant.

It was an old print of Brunel the engineer. The curious forehead and eyebrows, and the general cast of countenance, certainly bore a strong resemblance to Noir, though the expression was very different. Underneath, in copper-plate, was written the couplet—

> Whose public works will best attest his fame,
> Whilst private worth adds value to his name.

It was rather a curious contrast to Noir Frewin's life, and the words stung him.

'Well, well!' he said, with his bitter laugh, 'my "public works" are not of the first water, perhaps. You needn't give me that epitaph.'

The Brighton expedition proved a great success. Noir and Donovan returned in two or three days' time well content. They had chosen an evening train to come back by. Noir went on as

usual to select a favourable carriage ; Donovan followed him
more leisurely, for it answered their purpose best not to appear
to be companions. Donovan's part was usually that of a decoy,
a well-to-do, gentlemanly-looking fellow who consented to play,
and thus induced others to try their hand. They had this evening chosen a most auspicious-looking carriage full of young men
returning to town, for it was the week after Christmas, and, the
brief holiday being over, many had chosen this late train to take
them back to the busy London life again. Scarcely had they left
the station, however, when Noir's countenance suddenly fell.
Two or three of the passengers were commenting on a placard
which, printed in large letters, was put up on the side of the carriage.
He was vexed and disconcerted, for it effectually put an end to his
schemes for the journey. With a slight warning pressure on his
companion's foot, he drew his attention to the placard which was
above his head. Not in the least knowing what to expect,
Donovan took off his hat and put it in the netting, thus getting
an opportunity of turning round, and there, staring at him in
large type, were words which he never forgot, words which
seemed to burn themselves in upon his brain at the very first
reading. 'Caution. Passengers are earnestly recommended to
beware of pickpockets and card-sharpers dressed as gentlemen,'
&c., &c. He could read no further, he fell back into his place
like one stunned, then the hot colour rushed to his cheeks,
mounted higher and higher till his whole face seemed to burn
and tingle. Had he actually come to this ? Was he, Donovan
Farrant, a cheat against whom the public must be warned,
classed with pickpockets ? He, his father's only son, had sunk
so low, then, that this description would apply to him—a 'card-
sharper dressed as a gentleman !' That moment's sharp realisation was terrible. Noir, anxious to veil his sudden confusion,
held out a newspaper to him, but he only shook his head, and
the elder man, who was merely annoyed by the occurrence, began
to feel alarmed at the strange effect the caution had had on his
accomplice. Such misery, such shame, were written on his face
that Noir began to fear he should lose his able assistance.

They got out at London Bridge, and he linked his arm
within Donovan's with an anxious attempt at raillery.

'Why, milord, what made you play such a false card just
now, colouring up like a girl at a mere piece of paper ? I gave
you credit for more self-control.'

Donovan bit his lip ; the last words vexed him. and changed
the current of his thoughts, for he rather prided himself on his
powers of self-control, which were indeed considerable.

'It startled me,' he confessed after a brief silence. Then again, with a slight hesitation, 'Noir, do you consider yourself a card-sharper?'

The question was asked with a kind of innocence which made Noir shudder; he forced up a mocking laugh, however.

'Ask a thief if he considers himself a thief, and he will tell you " no," but a professional adept, with a gift for acquiring other people's property.'

Donovan winced.

'If that's the definition of a thief, you and I belong pretty much to the same class.'

Noir wrenched away his arm.

'And what do I care if we do?' he cried, angrily; 'I don't know what makes you so cantankerous to-night. Have you forgotten your favourite maxim, that the world is a mass of injustice, and that a little more or less evil makes no difference? You stand by that, and I'll undertake to stand by you, for the world *is* unjust, and I delight in cheating it when I've the opportunity. If you're going to turn moral, milord, we'll dissolve partnership at once, and you can go back to those fine friends you know, who were so ready to help you before you came to us.'

Donovan did not reply to this taunt, he only shivered and drew his comforter over his mouth. He felt worn out and giddy, his steps began to falter, and Noir, who in his strange rough fashion loved him, forgot his anger, and, taking his arm again, half dragged him home.

'The fact is, you're seedy and down in the mouth, Donovan,' he said, as they reached their rooms, 'you'll see things very differently to-morrow.'

Donovan did not answer, he stumbled up the dark staircase after Noir, and followed him into the parlour. There, with the gas flaring, a huge fire blazing up the chimney, and supper waiting on the table, was the old captain; his hearty welcome was generally pleasant enough, but this evening Donovan felt he could not stand it. He was half perished with cold, and involuntarily made for the fire, but it was only for a minute, the warm comfortable room was not in keeping with his doubt and misery.

'Double, double,
Toil and trouble,'

sang Sweepstakes, following the tall dark figure with his shrewd eye, 'Double—double—dou-ble——dou—ble.'

'First-rate luck all three days,' Noir was saying. 'To-night our little game was stopped, and milord's down in the depths.

Here, Donovan, come to supper, we didn't get much of a feed at Brighton.'

But Donovan shook his head.

'Good-night, captain,' he said, and, disregarding Rouge's remonstrances, left the room. He opened his own door, and Waif, with whines of delight, sprang to greet him.

'Waif—poor old fellow!' he exclaimed, stooping for a minute over the dog, but hastily raising himself again. 'No, no, down, get down, I say, I'm not fit to touch you.'

Poor Waif was utterly bewildered, his master had never spoken to him in that way before, something must be wrong, very much wrong. It was dark, but the faintest glimmer of light from the uncurtained window served to show him that his master had thrown himself on the ground, it was a sure sign that he was in trouble, Waif knew that well, and did not just at first dare to interrupt him. Presently he began to walk disconsolately round and round him, stopping every minute or two to sniff at him, listen, whine in a subdued way.

Donovan was beyond dog help just then, in the depth of his self-abasement he could not sink low enough; in his abject self-loathing to be touched by a being whom he loved would have been unbearable. He had known well enough that he was doing wrong before. Something of his blackness had been borne in upon him when Gladys Tremain had spoken those words in the park, but now it was all before him, in hideous array, the very vision of sin itself. How could he have delighted in anything so ghastly? it was not even a great revenge he had taken on the unjust world, but the pettiest, meanest, most despicable revenge. What had he not fallen to in these months? why, these hands of his—the hands that had waited on Dot—had stooped to pick up paltry half-crowns won by cheating foolish wretches in a railway carriage. And then came the remembrance of his father. 'You are hardly in a position, Dono, to speak of breaches of honour.' Not even then! oh! what would his father have said to him now! Yet little as he had known of him, that little was enough to tell him that his father would always think more of the future than of the past. There was a future for him even now, he must no longer wage war upon the unjust world, he must—he *would* alter his way of living if only for the sake of redeeming his father's name. But for the first time in his life he felt a want in himself, that agony of remorse, despair, utter self-abhorrence had done its work, he was no longer blindly confident in his own strength.

Presently from sheer exhaustion he fell asleep. Waif was

happier when he heard the deep regular breaths; a strange process of thinking began in the dog mind. He went back to his woolly rug and lay down, but in a minute jumped up again, ran to his master, licked his hand, and then returned to his rug. Still he could not settle himself to sleep, a second and a third time he got up, making an uneasy circuit round the prostrate figure on the ground. At last, as if unable to lie on his rug while Donovan was on the floor, he curled himself up at his feet, and there slept peacefully.

In the adjoining room Noir, having made a hearty meal, drew up his chair to the fire and lighted his evening pipe. The old captain was evidently uneasy. Noir was uneasy, too, in reality, but he kept it to himself.

'He's a very queer customer that lad,' said Rouge, meditatively. 'You think it really is this piece of paper which frightened him?'

'Yes, he's young,' said Noir, in an excusing tone. 'It gave him a turn; I daresay it will soon pass off. If not, we must get a little change somehow. It wouldn't be a bad plan to go abroad for a month or two, plenty to be done there, and he'd be sure to like it. After all, of course we do run some risk here. A month or two of absence wouldn't be a bad notion.'

'"He who prigs what isn't his'n,"' quoted Rouge. 'Well, don't carry it too far, and don't drive the boy away, whatever you do.'

'No, no, I'd sacrifice a good deal to keep him,' said Noir, 'but he's upset to-night about it.'

Presently the old captain lighted his candle and went up to bed, but Noir sat on long after his pipe was finished, long after the fire had sunk down in the grate to a handful of dying embers. He was thinking, brooding painfully over the comparative innocence of his boy accomplice, and his own villainy. How despairing and wild the fellow had looked, too, as he left the room. He quite started when the door opened, and Rouge, with his night-cap on, appeared again upon the scene.

'I say, Noir, I don't feel happy about that lad. It was very strange of him to go off like that with no supper.'

'Pooh!' said Noir, contemptuously, though his father was speaking his own thoughts. 'He's ashamed of himself and vexed about that caution.'

'Yes, but to go off, ill as he is, cold and supperless. If he was a Catholic he might do it as penance, but he's nothing, you know.'

It did not strike them that in very deep **inward** trouble it is

at times impossible to enjoy or permit bodily ease. Indeed, if the
poor old captain had been guilty of the most heinous crime, he
would probably have eaten his supper after its committal,
and found a solace in the eating to his pangs of remorse. He
could not understand anything which went deeper than this, and
his good heart had been stirred with pity as he lay down warmed
and satisfied in his comfortable feather-bed.

Noir's thoughts went at once to darker suspicions. He had
seen something of that same despairing look on Donovan's face
when, on that bright June afternoon, he had watched him unknown on Westminster Bridge. He had read his intentions then,
was it possible that misery and shame had driven him again to
the same longing?

'We'll just give him a look on our way up,' he said carelessly. And then he turned the door-handle noiselessly, and with
well-disguised anxiety stole in. The room was very quiet, the
bed empty. Noir's heart stood still, and, with an exclamation of
dismay, he hurried to the dark form which was stretched out on
the floor.

'Bring the candle quick,' he said to his father, and Rouge,
trembling with fear, held the light nearer, while Waif growled a
little at the unusual disturbance.

Noir bent down for a moment close to the half-hidden face,
then he started up again with an expression of relief, which came
rather oddly from his lips—

'Thank God!'

'Well, it did give me a turn,' said the old captain, stooping to
pat the dog.

'Hush!' said Noir, 'you'll wake him.'

And then for a minute the shabby little room witnessed a
strange scene. Donovan stirred uneasily, half turned round, but
sank again into profound sleep, and the two Frewins bent over
him, why, they could scarcely have said, but in their relief it
seemed almost a necessity. They watched the face of the sleeper
—flushed as if even now the shame were making itself felt—the
sad face which seemed all the more despairing because of its
stillness, the fixedness of its misery. And Noir's heart smote
him, his conscience cried out loudly, 'You have brought him to
this, you have dragged this boy down into shame and dis-
honesty.'

Rouge thought only of the discomforts of a night on the floor.

'Wake him up,' he urged. 'It's frightfully cold, he oughtn't
to be there.'

But Noir would not wake him, he knew that it would be

cruel to bring him back to his anguish of remorse. Rouge could never understand anything higher than bodily comfort, it was what he lived for. His son, though a far worse man, had nevertheless a capability of entering into greater things, he had himself sinned and suffered, and though it was years since he had known real remorse, he had once known it, and to a certain extent he understood Donovan's feelings.

'Better leave him,' he said. But, with the words upon his lips, he nevertheless turned to the bed, and, dragging off a railway-rug which covered it, threw it over the prostrate form on the floor. Strangely indeed in life do the lights and shades intermix, faint flickerings of the light divine stealing in, in spite of the vast black shades of sin.

The next day—the last of the year—was a dreary one in the Frewins' rooms. Noir kept out of the way, not caring to face his accomplice; old Rouge, in great depression, dusted his curiosities as usual, and put things tidy and ship-shape; and Donovan sat coughing and shivering over the fire, with an expression of such despondency, often of such terrible suffering, that the old captain scarcely dared to speak to him. The sharpness of his remorse had for the time died away, it was swallowed up in the misery of his recollections, for this was the anniversary of Dot's last day of life, and remembrances strange, tender, pitiful, but always full of pain, thronged up in his mind. Brooding over it all, his brain excited with the events of the past night, his body worn out with pain, it was no wonder that the overtaxed nature at last gave way.

His mood seemed to change. Rouge, who had not been able to extract a word from him all day, was astounded as the evening drew on to find him suddenly in the wildest spirits.

'Come,' he said, 'we'll go to Olliver's, it's time we had dinner. Come along, captain.'

And poor old Rouge found himself dragged off, in spite of his remonstrances.

'You'd better not go out, milord; you're really not fit.'

'Not fit!' said Donovan, with a wild laugh, cut short by a cough. 'I'm fit for anything. Come along, old fellow; we'll drown care, stifle it, kill it, what you like!'

Rouge, really frightened, panted along after his companion, with difficulty keeping pace with his fevered steps; and then ensued an evening of mad merriment. A year ago, only a year ago, and Donovan had been watching Dot's last agony; with the strong manly tenderness of great love he had held the little quivering hands in his. Now in a crowded billiard-room he grasped the cue instead, and betted wildly, losing, winning, winning again considerably, then with the Frewins, and Legge, and two or three other companions returning to Drury Lane and gambling the old year out and the new year in.

'I back the winner, I back the winner!' screamed Sweepstakes from his cage.

And above the sounds of dispute, and merriment, and eager play, the clock of St. Mary's Church struck twelve, and in the distance Big Ben's deep notes echoed over the city, and, just because an agony of remembrance rushed back into Donovan's mind, he staked higher and higher. The room rang with his wild laughter.

Noir broke up the gathering much earlier than usual, and with flushed cheeks and wild glittering eyes Donovan staggered to his feet. But he could hardly stand, his head seemed weighted, his limbs powerless.

'I've done for myself now,' he said, catching at Noir to keep himself up. Noir did not answer. With his father's assistance he helped him into the next room, and with some pangs of conscience kept guard over him through the night of feverish excitement and misery which followed.

The next morning the bright New Year broke over the great city, there were *fêtes*, and rejoicings, and merry family parties, but in the lodging-house in Drury Lane all was silent. Even at night no gamblers' wild revelry broke the stillness, for Donovan was prostrated by an attack of congestion of the lungs in its acutest form.

CHAPTER XVII.

STRUGGLING ON.

Men are led by strange ways. One should have tolerance for a man, ope of him ; leave him to try yet what he will do.

On Heroes and Hero-worship.

May we not again say, that in the huge mass of evil, as it rolls and swells, there is ever some good working imprisoned; working toward deliverance and triumph?

French Revolution. CARLYLE.

HE had known for a long time that he was out of health, and at times the dread of being ill had haunted him painfully, as it will at times haunt those who are practically homeless. For it is

indeed very terrible to face the thought of illness with no mother
at hand to nurse you, no sister to whom the duties of tending
will be a pleasure rather than a tiresome duty, no house in which
you have a right to be ill, where you need not feel burdened
with the sense of the trouble you are causing. To Donovan,
with his utter want of belief in human nature, or in the very
existence of anything above human nature, the sense of helplessness came with double power; only, fortunately for him, things
were not really as he believed. Close beside him, though unknown, the love of the All-Father watched and shielded from
evil the son who, by such wretched wanderings, was being led
on. And the pity which springs up very readily in most of our
hearts, when we are brought face to face with pain, brought
human help and comfort to his sick-bed. The landlady, careworn
and harassed with many children and a good-for-nothing husband, yet found time to do the few absolutely necessary things
in the sick-room ; she could not help being sorry for her apparently friendless lodger. Once or twice she pained him terribly
by asking,

'Haven't you no mother who could come and see to you?'

And Donovan would sign a negative, and, when she had left
him to himself, would feel the loneliness and suffering with double
keenness.

Noir Frewin would come in two or three times a day and ask
how he was; the old captain would hang about the room with
anxiety written on his kind old face, but he missed his companion's vigilance and example, the drinking mania seized him
strongly, and he was seldom quite sober. There was one
other amateur nurse, the poor little over-driven servant. She
used to shuffle into the room every now and then, and with infinite
care and clumsiness would drag the pillow from under his head,
shake it up violently and turn it, or hold a glass to his burning
lips and spill half its contents down his night-shirt. But he
learnt to be grateful even for such rough attentions, for there is
nothing like weakness and suffering for teaching patience. The
loneliness was so terrible, too, that he would detain anyone who
came to him as long as possible. Old Rouge, with his unsteady
gait and half incoherent talk, was better than no one, and even
the little slipshod servant, with her rough head and dirty hands,
was worth the exertion of talking, just for the sake of having a
human creature within reach.

'I allays liked you, sir,' she said to him once. 'You ain't
allays a-calling for your boots, like Mr. Frewin, or in drink, like
the captain, and you never shouted out "slavey" down the stairs

for me, as though I was one of the poor blacks. I allays liked you, Mr. Donovan.'

Donovan was amused, and in spite of his burning head and aching misery, threw out some question or response to detain her.

'And I've done things for you as I've not done for no other lodger,' the girl continued. 'I've blacked your boots a sight better than any of the others, and though you did want such a terrible lot of bath water hevery day, I allays brought it up reg'lar. If the lodgers h'is civil and kind-spoken, I do my best for 'em, but most of 'em—why, they treat us poor girls like dogs, that they do. And talkin' of dogs, I've done that un of yours many a good turn ; times and times I've stolen bits o' meat and things for 'im.'

'Oh ! but you shouldn't do that,' said Donovan, quickly. 'Don't do it again. It's wrong to steal, you know.'

But then he paused. What was he saying ? How trivial were this poor ignorant girl's dishonesties compared with his own !

Bitter were the regrets which thronged up into his mind as he lay wearily on his bed of pain. He could not escape from his secret foes now ; he could not banish thought by violent bodily exercise, or by wild excitement. All his anguish of last year returned with terrible force, all the agony of self-loathing weighed upon him with cruel ceaselessness. This, combined with the want of good nursing, aggravated his illness. The doctor began to look grave, and one day Anne, the little servant, fairly burst into tears when she came up to tidy his room.

'What's the matter ?' asked Donovan, feebly. 'Have they been scolding you ?'

'No, no, it ain't that,' said the girl, holding her apron to her eyes. 'But missus she says you'll die, sure as a gun ; she did say so, I heared her, sir, not a minute since.'

Donovan did not speak for some time. He lay thinking silently over the girl's words, 'You'll die, sure as a gun.' He smiled a little, thinking that few had been told of their danger in a more open and undisguised way, but it ought to have been good news to him, and for a time he tried to think he was glad. And yet ? He did not go straight to the root of the matter, and own that the ' peace of nothingness ' looked less attractive when viewed nearly ; he said instead what a wretched life he had had, how little enjoyment, how much suffering, and now he was to die forlorn and unattended in a miserable London lodging. Then come a great longing to see his mother.

He called the girl to him, made her find writing materials, and, raising himself on his elbow, wrote with great difficulty a few pencil words.

'I am very ill. My death will perhaps ease more consciences than one. Will you not come to me, mother?—it may be our last meeting.'

He was growing faint; the effort had been very great, but, still exerting all his strength of will, he controlled his weakness sufficiently to scrawl the address on the envelope. Then he sank back again exhausted.

'You'll have to see the clergyman if you get worse,' said Anne, sympathetically. 'There's one as come next door to an old chap as was dying last summer, and they say he do make the folks quake and sweat.'

Donovan was past smiling.

After that he did not remember much. There was only an ever-present consciousness of endless pain, the raging, burning, aching misery of fever. Till then the hours had dragged on with the terrible slowness of which only those who have been alone in illness can form any idea. But now he lost all thought of time, and was only dimly aware of the visitors who came to him. Now and then he had a sort of vision of Rouge's round red face anxiously peering down at him. Once he fancied himself chained down in one of Doery's red-hot furnaces, where Dives-like he had cried for water, and then he had looked up, and Noir was beside him with the cooling draught he had thirsted for, and he had fallen back again refreshed, wondering greatly that his request had been granted. The Christian's God was, after all then, merciful! Wild thoughts they were which haunted him in his delirium, and yet Noir Frewin, as he watched beside him, was struck by the tone of his fevered utterances. He was prepared for ravings against injustice, but, instead, Donovan's most vehement words were of self-reproach. At times he would take a theological turn, and would argue for and against every conceivable doctrine, and then again he would fancy himself back among his late companions, gambling or indulging in wild revelry; but throughout there was never one impure word, and Noir marvelled at it. A strange wild life was revealed, with an undercurrent of anxious questioning, one predominant vice, but behind it much that was noble, a familiarity with every kind of evil, but, in spite of it, a strange retaining of purity.

One name, too, was constantly on his lips—a name which Noir had never heard him mention before. He wondered much to whom it referred, what gave rise to the agonised longing for this one presence.

Perhaps in this was Donovan's keenest suffering. He dreamt continually of Dot; she was beside him, no longer ill and help-less, but happy, and strong, and bright. As yet, remembrance was such terrible pain to him—it was so entirely his object not to remember the past—that the vision which kept recurring to him was almost more than he could bear, and the extraordinary reality of it deluded him at times. It must be real, she had come back to him, and he would stretch out his arms to keep her; then, coming to himself, would find that it was only a dream. One night the dream was more vivid than ever. He fancied himself on a wide-open down; he was ill and faint, and the sun was beating down upon him pitilessly. He closed his eyes to shut out the intolerable brightness, and then suddenly became aware of a shade between him and the sun, and, looking up, saw Dot standing beside him. Such a rapturous meeting it was! Her face seemed changed, and yet the same, and her bright eyes shone down upon him with just the old loving light. He could feel her fingers ruffling up his hair as she used to do in the old times, and her voice, merry and child-like as ever, seemed to give him new strength. 'It is my turn to nurse you now,' she said. And then, just as he was feeling the full bliss of her presence, a thick white mist rose from the ground and rolled between them. He stretched out his hands, tried to struggle up, helplessly beat-ing against the cold white wall. Dot was there just beyond. He must reach her! this sudden meeting, only to part, was too cruel! But the more he dashed himself against the impenetrable barrier, the harder it became, and, maddened by hearing her voice in the distance, he grew more and more reckless, till at last his own cry of despair woke him. Trembling, exhausted, panting for breath, he stared round the little room. The scene was changed. Fight as he would, there was no chance of his seeing Dot again; even the white barrier was gone. The gas was turned low, and close beside it sat Noir, nodding over his newspaper. The blank of realisation was so terrible that he felt he *must* call on some one or something outside himself, and his companion was roused by a call so wild, so despairing, that he started up at once and hurried to the bedside.

'What is it?' he asked anxiously. But Donovan could not answer, his breath would only come in gasps, his whole frame was convulsed. By the strange freemasonry of suffering, Noir Frewin understood him. He did not say a word, but just took the two burning hands in his, and Donovan, with a sense of relief, tightened his hold till the grip was absolutely painful. Anything human would have served to support him; he clung to the hands of this hardened cheat with helpless gratitude.

And Noir, as he looked down at the struggling agony, understood it all far better than many would have done. A well-regulated mind accustomed to view things quietly, or a Christian who has never known what it is to be anything else, would probably not have known so exactly what to do; they would have offered words to a state beyond the comprehension of speech, or would have advised self-control when the very fact of the convulsed frame and sealed lips showed that no control was needed. But Noir had been through just the same fierce conflicts in his cell at Dartmoor; he knew that no words would avail, no thought comfort, that what nature cried out for was a *presence* stronger than self—something or some one who would not preach, but would understand. He gave, poor fellow, all he could give—himself, and after a time Donovan's convulsed limbs relaxed, the hands loosened their hold, the face settled into its usual stern sad expression.

'Thanks, old fellow,' he said, faintly.

Noir, with an odd choking in his throat, turned away and made ready some gruel which had been heating. By the time he had brought it, Donovan had recovered a little more, and there was a sort of smile on his worn face.

'I can't get over you turning nurse, Noir,' he said, in rather trembling tones; 'you've been—awfully good to me.'

'Only make haste and get well,' said Noir, roughly, but kindly.

'Am I not doing my best by swallowing this abomination?' said Donovan, trying to form his lips into a smile, but failing piteously.

'You'd better be quiet, or you won't get off to sleep again,' said Noir, peremptorily, the fact being that he could not stand the effort at cheerfulness which his patient was making, for there are few things more painful than to see a thin veil of assumed cheerfulness drawn over great suffering. But the effort was a brave one, he could not help knowing it, and as he returned to his place beneath the gas, instead of taking up his newspaper, he mused over the hidden trouble which had been half revealed to him, from time to time casting a glance towards the bed. Nothing, however, was to be seen there except a mass of rough brown hair; Donovan had turned his face away from the light, and Noir only knew that he was not asleep by the absolute stillness of his form, and by the long-drawn but half-restrained sighs which reached him every few minutes.

The next morning the old captain, with his feather-brush,

was as usual dusting his shells and corals, when he was interrupted by the little maid-of-all-work.

'If you please, sir,' she said, with unusual animation, ''ere's a lady as will 'ave it that Mr. Farrant lives 'ere, and I can't get 'er away no 'ow.'

Rouge, removing his smoking-cap, hurried forward, and found himself face to face with an elderly woman with a thin severe face.

'There must be some mistake, madame,' he said in his pleasant voice. 'No one of the name of Farrant lives here. We are the only lodgers, except one poor fellow named Donovan, who is very ill.'

'There!' exclaimed Mrs. Doery, with relief. 'Now why didn't you tell me that before, though I was certain he must be here somewhere, he'd never make a fault in the address. Take me to him at once, please, sir—I've come to nurse him.'

'Bless me!' exclaimed the old captain, 'now that's really a wonderful piece of luck, for he's in need of better nursing than we can give him. You are a relation of his?'

'Relation, indeed!' said Mrs. Doery, with virtuous indignation—'relation, sir! A pretty pass he must have come to if you take me for a relation. I am the housekeeper.'

'Your pardon, madame,' said the captain. 'May I not offer you some refreshment after your journey?' and he put his hand on the inevitable black bottle which was always within convenient reach.

'I'll thank you, sir, to take me to Mr. Donovan,' said Doery, severely, 'and not go offering a respectable party spirits at this time of day.'

Rouge, feeling snubbed, hastily led the way to the sick-room, muttering under his breath, 'A very dragon!' But nevertheless he rather enjoyed the new arrival, and there was a ring of amusement in his hearty voice as he went up to the disordered uncomfortable looking bed where Donovan lay.

'Well, milord, I've brought you a new nurse.'

If anyone had told Donovan in his childhood that he would ever welcome the sight of his grim tyrant he would not have believed it, but nevertheless there was an unspeakable comfort and relief in the advent of poor old Doery.

'Oh! Mr. Donovan, what have they been a-doin' to you?' she exclaimed, horror-struck at his looks, for he was evidently quite clear-headed, but utterly weak and helpless, and with a face so thin and worn that she hardly recognised it.

'Did my mother send you?' he asked, as soon as the captain had left the room.

'No, sir, master sent me, with orders to say nothing about it to mistress. It was the only way he'd let me come, Mr. Donovan, so you mustn't mind. Mistress is to be told I'm gone to nurse my sister. I promised I wouldn't say a word to her, otherwise master wouldn't have told me where you was.'

'He opened the letter, then?' asked Donovan.

'He had your letter, sir. I made no doubt it was sent to him, for the mistress hadn't seen it.'

Evidently, then, it would be quite useless to attempt writing to his mother; after the lapse of all these months of silence, Ellis still kept guard over her correspondence. A sort of dim idea which had crossed his mind of appealing to his mother for money to start him in some honest calling, died away. He must continue to support himself by his precarious winnings, only—and here all his strength of will asserted itself—he would *never* be a party to Noir's deceptions again. It was not a very cheering prospect, he saw that it must involve an entire break with the Frewins, and they had been so good to him that he shrank very much from the thought. After all, as he often said to himself, his death would solve many difficulties.

But he was not to die—that was evident. Thanks to Mrs. Doery's good nursing he began to recover steadily, and, as his strength returned, a certain enjoyment of life returned to him, too, at times. He began to wish very much to be out and about again, even though so many difficulties would have then to be faced.

His intercourse with old Mrs. Doery was a good deal hampered by various causes. He never mentioned Dot's name, he never mentioned his present way of life, so that their range of conversation was rather limited. He asked a thousand questions, indeed, about his mother, and the whole Manor household, but except with regard to this subject he was very silent and utterly uncommunicative. From day to day he would lie with a sort of rigid patience, abstractedly watching Doery as she sat mending his linen, or with his eyes fixed on the hateful little oil-painting of the 'Shipwreck,' which stared down at him from the dingy green wall paper with black spots. It used to remind him a good deal of his own life, that forlorn-looking vessel with broken mast and battered hull.

One night when he was almost recovered he was roused from his first sleep by noisy merriment in the adjoining room, and found poor Mrs. Doery fairly frightened out of her wits.

'Such a calling and a shouting and a quarrelling as she'd never heard in her life!'

'They are only enjoying themselves,' said Donovan, with weary sarcasm.

'Well, Mr. Donovan, it's more like animals than like men, that I will say,' replied Doery, with her customary shrewd severity.

'May be,' said Donovan, turning from side to side with the restless discomfort of one disturbed.

'And nobody can't deny that it's a dreadful place that you're in,' continued the housekeeper. 'Such a shocking goings on in them courts out at the back, and then all this noise in the very next room when honest folks ought to be a-bed and asleep. It's a dreadful place, I call it.'

'London isn't made up of Connaught Squares,' said Donovan, bitterly; and then he drew the bed-clothes over his face, and would not say another word.

The next day was Sunday, and by dint of many assurances of his perfect recovery, Mrs. Doery was at length persuaded to leave him for a little while and go to church, Donovan having over-ruled her dread of losing her way by assuring her that the old captain went every now and then to salve his conscience, and would be delighted to escort her. When she had left him he lay for a few minutes listening to the church bells, but his thoughts were very troublesome that day, and just to stifle them he reached out his hand and took Mrs. Doery's Bible from the table. It was nearly four years since he had opened one, and then it had only been under compulsion at school, and though he had read many books written against it, he had never had the slightest inclina-tion to study the book itself. Beyond a few chapters which he had been made to learn in his childhood as a punishment, he remembered little but a sort of general outline of the history, and a few of the more striking parables.

He took it up now rather curiously, opened at St. Matthew's Gospel, and, skipping the Table of Genealogy, began to read in a careless, cursory way. By-and-by, however, in spite of himself, he grew interested. From the few isolated chapters which he had heard occasionally in church and during his school life, he had never gained any idea of the character of Christ. Now reading straight on, with a great craving after some fresh interest, he was naturally very much struck. A life of poverty, and suffer-ing, and self-denial, a career of apparent failure, surroundings low and incapable of understanding, a trial of glaring injustice, and an unmerited death of the deepest pain! It was a story which could not fail to touch him; a character which filled him with great admiration. There were two things which especially

appealed to his sympathy—the injustice suffered, and the strong
endurance manifested. He put down the book reluctantly when
he was too tired to hold it any longer, not even thinking of any
possible change in his fixed beliefs, but simply very much struck
by a noble life, which, it seemed probable, had been lived many
years ago—with something of the same sort of interest which
he had felt for one or two of the old Romans, and for a few of
Shakespere's characters. Modern Christianity—or the so-called
Christianity which had been brought under his notice—offered
no attractions to him. The whole system seemed to him hollow
and false, a great profession, and a niggardly performance, a
mixture of selfishness, hypocrisy, and superstition. But the life
of Christ was grand! Such an unexampled career of noble self-
devotion filled him with wonder and reverence. However much
the misguided followers had fallen off, there could be no doubt
that the mind of Christ had been—he naturally used the past
tense—one of dazzling purity and beauty.

In the enforced stillness of convalescence the story haunted
him strangely, and undoubtedly he was influenced by it—his
admiration of a noble mind ennobled him. At present that was
all; but it was much.

As soon as he was about again, he took an early opportunity
of telling Noir the decision which he had made before his illness.
Noir, who had already shrewdly surmised that he should lose
his young accomplice, made no attempt to turn him from his
purpose.

'Turned good, I suppose, as most fellows do when they have
been within an ace of dying,' he remarked, sneeringly.

'Glad to hear you think so,' said Donovan, with coolness. 'I
own you've a proverb to fall back on. "The Devil he fell sick;
the Devil a monk would be." However, I've no monkish ten-
dencies, only I don't mean to be your decoy any longer.'

'Well,' said Noir, good-humouredly, 'I myself shan't be sorry
to leave the old trade for a bit. We've been talking of going
abroad. Come with us. It would set you up in no time. What
do you say to Monaco? A try at the red and black?'

'Anything for a change,' said Donovan; but there was relief
in his tone, for the break with the Frewins, which he had dreaded
a good deal, would be no longer necessary. 'Honest' gambling
of course he had not renounced, in fact by means of it he must
live, and this proposal to go to Monaco exactly fell in with his
present frame of mind. His spirits began to rise.

The old captain coming into the room was surprised at the
change in his look and voice.

'Well, captain!' he exclaimed. 'Has Noir told you? It's all settled, we leave this hole next week, and go to try our luck at Monte Carlo.'

'So I hear,' said Rouge. 'It'll be first-rate for you; for myself I like Old England best. None of your froggy Frenchmen for me. I'm going out, milord, d'you want anything? papers? books?'

A change came over Donovan's face.

'Oh! yes, that reminds me. Here!'—he threw down eighteen pence on the table, scrawled something on a piece of paper and handed it to Rouge,—'Just get me that if you're passing a bookshop.'

The captain looked at the paper, lifted his eyebrows, but did not venture any comment. On it was written, 'Renan's "Life of Jesus."'

CHAPTER XVIII.

MONACO.

I heard a thousand blended notes
As in a grove I sat reclined,
In that sweet mood when pleasant thoughts
Bring sad thoughts to the mind.

To her fair works did Nature link
The human soul that through me ran;
And much it grieved my heart to think
What man had made of man.

WORDSWORTH.

Spots of blackness in creation to make its colours felt.
Modern Painters.

'Now this is first rate,' said the old captain, as he stepped off the pier at Folkestone on to the steamer. 'Ah, Donovan, my lad, if we were going for a good cruise it would do you all the good in the world, better than a dozen Monacos, eh? Not so profitable, you say? Well, perhaps not, but I wish I was captain of the *Metora* again, a prime little steamer, she was, you wouldn't think much of such a tub as this if you'd been aboard the *Metora*.'

Donovan with the delicious sense of returning strength, rolled himself up in his railway-rug, and with his elbow resting on the deck railing looked out seawards. The captain was in great spirits, the breath of sea air seemed to awake his better self, and he was besides very happy in having his favourite companion with him again.

'Now that you're about again, milord, I shall be a different man,' he said, cheerily. 'I've been dreadfully down in the mouth since you were ill, and there was Noir as grim as death, and even Sweepstakes as cross as could be. You wouldn't believe what a bother we had with that bird, milord. Just after you were laid up, he caught, somehow or other, one of his old couplets which always enrages Noir. I suppose I'd said it, and he'd remembered it, for day and night that creature said nothing but

"He who prigs what isn't his'n;"

you know the old rhyme!'

'There's something uncanny about Sweepstakes,' said Donovan, laughing, 'he has a good deal of the wizard about him. It's to be hoped he'll be quiet on the journey, or Noir will threaten to wring his neck.'

'Yes, he doesn't approve of our menagerie,' said Rouge, adjusting the covering of the parrot's cage, 'though I will say that the dog is a marvel of obedience.'

'I back the winner!' screamed Sweepstakes, as the bell sounded and the steamer began to move. 'Now be gentle, be gentle.'

'Hollo! the creature is beginning to talk,' said Donovan, 'you'll have a crowd round him.'

And true enough before long they found themselves the centre of an amused group to whom the parrot held forth in his choicest language. But presently Noir came up, and directly the bird caught sight of him he put his head on one side and began with his most sanctimonious manner to say,

'He who prigs what isn't his'n
When he's cotched shall go to pris'n.'

'You must keep the parrot quiet,' said Noir, crossly, 'he's disturbing the whole deck.'

The passengers at once disclaimed this, and expressed their admiration of the bird's cleverness, but Noir was not to be baffled, he drew the black covering over the cage, and Donovan saw by the frown on his brow that he was vexed by this particular sentence of the malicious parrot. He sat down on the other side of the cage, ready to check any further talking, but he could not prevent the mild refrain which Sweepstakes invariably resorted to when he was snubbed, and all through the crossing he gently murmured to himself, ' When he's cotched—cotch—cotch—cotched ! '

It was a grey day at the end of February, and the English shore was enveloped in mist, but there was, nevertheless, a strong breeze blowing. ' East-nor'-east,' Rouge declared it to be, ' and a heavy swell which would prove fatal to the land-lubbers.'

Donovan, though making no pretensions as to his sailing powers, enjoyed the change and novelty most thoroughly, and, indeed, after seven or eight weeks of the unwholesome atmosphere of Drury Lane, the fresh sea-breeze was almost intoxicating. In spite of adverse circumstances and a naturally melancholy temperament, the young life within him sprang up to greet the novelty of all around, his eyes brightened, his taciturnity disappeared and he and the old captain sat talking together as happily as two school-boys.

Then came the landing at the sunny little French town, with the chatter of bad English and broken French, the hurry and bustle of the passengers, Rouge's anxiety over his precious parrot, and Donovan's difficulty in steering him safely past the door of the *buffet*, with all its temptations. After a few minutes' delay they were off once more, fairly started now on their route to the south, and Donovan, in the first exuberance of his new strength, really thought he had found something to satisfy his restlessness, and to fill the emptiness of his life. Fair France, with her sunny plains and genial atmosphere, looked very tempting, Monaco offered plenty of excitement—why should he not be happy now ?

They were to travel straight on to Nice, a rash project for a semi-invalid, but naturally the Frewins consulted their own wishes, and Donovan, though tired enough when they reached Paris, preferred going on with them to staying for the night alone, for he was still not at all fit to be left quite to himself; old Mrs. Doery had only resigned her post a few days before, and he shrank from entire self-dependence. So the night journey was undertaken, and he sat back in his corner watching his sleeping companions, sometimes dozing himself for a few minutes, but oftener wide awake, and fully conscious of his weary misery, bearing it with a sort of philosophic endurance, and thinking a good deal of the life he had left behind him, of his parting conversation with Mrs. Doery, of the interview which by this time she had probably had with his step-father, of the luck which he had had at the club a few nights ago, which had enabled him to pay his doctor's bill and start comfortably on his foreign trip, and of sundry passages which had impressed him in Renan's book. An odd medley, truly, in an unregulated but well-disposed mind—well-disposed, that is, as far as it was capable of seeing the light.

At last the long night wore away; as they passed Lyons, with its gleaming lights and its broad river, the first faint grey of dawn was quivering on the horizon, and gradually the pale morning twilight began to steal into the railway carriage, falling with a most ghastly effect on the faces of the sleepers—Noir, with his hard, grim features, Rouge serenely comfortable and animal-like, a priest with a heavy face, which nevertheless looked quite spiritual compared with the old captain's, and four average Frenchmen in every variety of night *déshabillé* and posture. Donovan glanced at them curiously, then, with that shivering misery which invariably accompanies the dawn, he once more looked out over the grey landscape. His cough began to be troublesome, nor did his discomfort end till the sun had risen. In the early morning, when they stopped for a minute at Orange, he dashed out of the carriage, held face and hands under the pump on the platform, and, somewhat refreshed by the cold water, got in again, to endure as well as he could the long day of travelling.

A night's rest at Nice set him up again, however, and he was as eager as either of his companions to go on to Monaco the next morning. The day, too, was so gloriously bright, and the air so exhilarating, that he fancied himself stronger than he really was. Nor was the exquisite scenery altogether wasted on him; it is to be doubted whether it has any effect on the *habitués* of Monte Carlo who daily pass through it, but Donovan was a stranger, not yet seized with the gaming mania, which seems to destroy all the nobler faculties.

Leaving Nice behind them, with its green hills and clustering white villas, they sped on through a paradise of beauty. To the right lay the Mediterranean, with its wonderfully deep blue, broken here and there by the tiniest foam-wreathed breakers, gleaming whiter than snow; to the left rose the Maritime Alps with their softly mantling olive groves, while in the distance every now and then a snowy peak stood out clearly against the blue sky.

The three Englishmen certainly took their own fashion of enjoying it all, there was no studying of Murray or Bædeker, not a single exclamation of wonder or admiration. Rouge looked sleepily at the sea, and thought of his voyages in the *Metora*; Noir, who for the last day or two had been engrossed with his 'system,' and had done nothing but cover sheets of paper with dots, barely looked up from his employment; Donovan looked at all the beauty silently, with no lack of admiration, but with a certain sadness, his one definite thought being how much Dot would have enjoyed it. In a very short time they reached their destination; old Monaco on its rocky promontory, new Monaco, with its gay white houses and red-tiled roofs, Monte Carlo, with its gorgeous casino—all lay as it were in a nutshell. Strange little Principality! one of the most ancient in Europe, originally a sort of garden of Eden, but now a perfect hot-bed of vice! Noir, who knew the place well, had his own reasons for avoiding the fashionable Condamine. He took his companions to an out-of-the-way hotel in old Monaco, where at the expense of a stiff climb they would be free from some of the objections of the more frequented quarter.

Before long they had set off for an afternoon at Monte Carlo, all three in good spirits; Noir with implicit faith in the system of play which he was about to try; Donovan exulting in the sense of novelty and excitement; Rouge ready to be amused by anything, and eager to try his luck so far as the restricted allowance which his son made him would permit. Driving up the long hill they were set down at last at the entrance to the casino. This, then, was the goal they had been making for, this the place where fortunes were won—or lost, this the refuge for all who craved excitement, for all who would fain banish thought! It felt half dream-like to Donovan, a palace of the genii, transported straight from one of the 'Arabian Nights.' Passing into the beautiful vestibule with its great marble columns, gorgeously decorated roof and walls, and handsome mosaic floor, the impression grew upon him, but was speedily dashed into the world of cold realities by a word from Noir.

'Come, we won't waste time. You'll have to give your name at the *bureau*, and get your ticket. Of course, by-the-way, you're twenty-one? Else they won't admit you.'

'All right,' replied Donovan. 'I was of age last spring,' and therewith came memories which brought a look of hard resentment to his face.

Having given the name which he used, he picked up his pink admission-card, and followed his companions through the double swing-doors into the *Salle de Jeu*. After all, even in this enchanted palace, thoughts would intrude themselves. Would this journey to Monte Carlo prove less satisfactory than he had expected?

It is a strange sight that *Salle de Jeu*. Its richly decorated walls, its heavy square pillars, coloured and begilt in the Alhambra style, form the setting to a dark picture. How many wretched faces, pale with despair, are reflected each day in those mirrors!

how many victims pace restlessly up and down the slippery par-
quet floor, never satisfied with gain, half crazed with loss.   And
yet with what persistency all throng round the tables, a curiously
mixed multitude, when one pauses to study them—people of all
ranks and ages: florid-looking Germans, sharp-faced Frenchmen, dark, vindictive Italians, handsome Russians, hard-featured
Englishmen; women, too, in almost as large a proportion as men,
and staking with quite as much *sang-froid*.   Round every table
sit the favoured few who have secured chairs, behind these stand
the eager crowd absorbed in watching the whirling roulette-
wheel, or the dealing of the cards, and on the outskirts of all
linger the mere lookers-on; Americans 'doing Europe,' and
including Monte Carlo in their list of things to be seen, pale-
faced invalids from Mentone, English tourists of every description, who come to see this sight which happily is not to be met
with in many places.   A questionable proceeding though in some
ways is this looking on, and yet to those who really study the
gamblers the sight can hardly fail to teach a very grave lesson.
Only, to anyone who expects pleasure in the mere sight the disappointment would be great.   Monte Carlo merely heard of is
one thing, Monte Carlo seen is a revelation of sin, of infatuation,
of all that is most sad and pitiable—a black spot in creation
which does indeed make the on-looker thankful for all existing
purity and goodness, but which, at the same time, cannot fail to
sober and sadden.

The three companions quickly separated, Rouge remaining at
one of the roulette-tables in the outer room, Noir steadily settling
himself at the first trente-et-quarante table, and in course of
time securing a chair, Donovan wandering restlessly from place to
place.   He had no faith in any system, though Noir had tried
hard to convert him to his, but, although he was usually as
successful by luck in games of chance as he was by cleverness
in games of skill, his customary good fortune seemed now
to have deserted him.   Before long he had not only lost a
great deal more than was at all convenient, but had conceived a strong dislike to the whole thing.   Dispirited by his
unbroken losses, he felt at once that there was nothing here to
satisfy him, nothing to call out his faculties; for he was more
than a mere gambler, he was a first-rate card-player, and to him
half the pleasure of gaming lay in the sense of power, the exulta-
tion in his own skill.   In spite of all the talk about 'systems,' he
saw that the ruling goddess at Monte Carlo was blind chance.
She had not dealt kindly with him, he would waste no more time
or money in her gorgeous shrine.

But now that all the excitement was over he began to feel unbearably weary, he threw himself down on the crimson velvet ottoman in the middle of the gaming-room, idly scanning the passers by, men old and young ; croupiers just relieved from their wearisome duties, and leaving the room with tired faces from which all other expression had died ; the servants of the casino in their blue and red livery; the ever-shifting throng of gamblers; the extravagantly-dressed women. Realising at length that his peace was in danger of molestation, he rose to go, and found his way across the vestibule to the beautiful music-hall, where the finest orchestra in Europe is made a bait to draw great crowds to the casino. Wearily he lent back in one of the luxurious arm-chairs and listened to the closing strains of a grand symphony. The concert was nearly over ; he was so weary that he almost fell asleep, but in the last piece suddenly came to himself with a thrill of pain. With exquisite expression, with unrivalled delicacy of light and shade, the orchestra was playing a selection from 'Don Gio-vanni,' and now through the great hall there rang Dot's favourite air, ' Vedrai Carino.'

It did him good in spite of the pain. When the audience dispersed, and he strolled out into the gardens, a child's pure gentle face haunted him. There among the palms, and aloes, and flowering cactus two visions of the past were with him, Dot's radiant beauty, and the quiet maidenly grace of a stranger whom he had involuntarily taken as his standard of what a woman should be. From what evil these two guardian angels shielded him who can say ?

Before long he wisely went in search of the old captain, whom he found in low spirits, having lost every five-franc piece in his possession.

' We've both had enough of this,' said Donovan, not sorry to have the old man's arm to lean on. ' I'm about cleared out too, and, what's worse, I feel awfully seedy.'

' Humph ! ' ejaculated the captain. ' In for a second go of inflammation, I'll be bound.'

' Well, Rouge, if I am,' said Donovan, slowly, ' you'll just have to bolt and bar the door and nurse me yourself. Do you understand ?'

The captain nodded assent, and little more was said as they made their way back to the hotel.

The surmise proved true, however, and that night Donovan was again tossing to and fro in weary misery, haunted by whirling roulette wheels and stony-faced croupiers, raving about the end-

less losses and the tantalizing gains which always eluded his grasp.
The relapse was the natural consequence of all the fatigue he
had gone through, and had it not been for the old captain's devoted though rough nursing, and for the care of an exceedingly
clever French doctor, he would most likely have sunk under it.

However, he struggled through, and woke one morning, after
a long sleep, to realise for the first time his position. There he
was lying as weak as any baby, surrounded by mosquito net
curtains, in an odd-looking foreign room; there was poor Waif
lying at the foot of the bed, keeping anxious guard over him;
there was Rouge sitting by the open window smoking. Where
was he? What was this new place? Not Drury Lane, for the
dingy green paper was changed to a gorgeous blue one, and the
ceiling was decorated, or defaced, with bluewash studded with
glaring white stars, in the middle of which grew by some strange
anomaly a great clump of red and yellow roses. Donovan, though
not artistic, was strangely irritated by looking at the horrid daub.
He called the old captain to him.

'So I've been ill again?' he said, interrogatively.

'Very,' replied Rouge. 'In fact, milord, we as good as gave
you up at one time; you wouldn't believe what an anxious time
I've had of it, with Noir all day long up at that casino, and no
one here who could speak a word of English.'

'You have been nursing me?'

'Well, of course, what else could I do?' said Rouge.

'Thank you, captain,' said Donovan, adding resolutely, after
a minute's pause, 'I shall get well now.'

He was as good as his word, and from that day recovered
rapidly. Not that he cared much to get well, but he was anxious
to free himself from the state of dependence he was now in, for
dependence was uncongenial to his nature, and to submit to
rough and ready attendance is never pleasant. Before many
days had passed he was up and dressed, just able to drag himself
across the room, and to relieve the monotony of the long hours
by such amusement as he could find at either of the windows.
One of these faced the Place du Palais. There just opposite to
him he could see the Prince's Palace, could count the slow
minutes by the clock in the tower, speculate when the cannon
and the great pile of cannon-balls would be used, study the two
sentries who, in their red and blue uniforms, kept guard over the
entrance gate, and watch the few passers-by. From the other
window a much wider view was obtained. Here he could see the
whole of the beautiful bay, and the exquisite loveliness of the
place made him long to quit his room.

And so the days dragged on, and little by little he regained his strength, would crawl out to the almost deserted Promenade St. Barbe, and sit on one of the green benches under the plane-trees, or, passing through the curious old archway which leads by a footpath from old to new Monaco, he would stretch himself out on the low stone wall, and rest among a sort of jungle of flowering cactus and pink geranium. Before him stretched a glorious panorama—the beautiful blue of the Mediterranean, Manaco with its gay-looking houses, the mountains skirting the water, here clothed with olive groves, there craggy, bare, and brown, or glistening pearly grey in the sunlight. Then just facing him, half way up the mountain side, the pretty little town of Roccabruna, till—the slope of the mountain hiding Mentone and its bay—the chain gradually lessened, and ended in the long low promontory of Bordighera. Only one conspicuous object stood out always as a blot on the fair landscape—the casino, with its gilded roof and its two minarets.

Donovan had wisely resolved to keep clear of modern Monaco, but he began rather to weary of the narrow bounds of the old town. True he had, as usual, made friends among the children. His favourite resting-place on the wall happened to be on the way to the school, and troops of little brown-eyed, bare-headed girls and boys passed him every day, and soon learnt to crowd round the strange English gentleman and his wonderful dog, and to bring him presents of flowers or unripe nespoli. But, as he grew stronger, he began to hate the feeling of imprisonment, until, happening one morning to notice a little boat on the sea with its white lateen sail, he conceived the happy idea of taking a daily cruise. The old captain was always ready to accompany him, and the hours which they spent in the *Ste. Dévote*, as their boat was named, did each of them untold good.

Meanwhile each evening Noir, returning about eleven o'clock, when the casino closed, would bring in one or two acquaintances who, not satisfied with the day's gambling, were anxious for play. In this manner Donovan made an easy living.

Noir tried in vain to induce him to go once more to Monte Carlo. He himself had been remarkably lucky, and he rarely let a day pass without remonstrating with Donovan on what he alternately called his 'cowardice,' his 'laziness,' and his 'puritanical fanaticism.'

This last accusation was so novel that it called forth one of Donovan's rare laughs.

'Come, this is quite a new line,' he said, when Noir's tirade was ended. 'You are the first person in the world who ever gave

me such an honourable name. Zealous folks have addressed me as
"proud infidel," and "blind atheist," and "miserable agnostic,"
but "fanatic Puritan" is a title to which I never dreamt of aspi-
ring! In the strength of it you must allow me to gang my ain
gait!'

'Please yourself,' said Noir, crossly. 'Do you know Berrogain's last name for you—for the young man who is too virtuous to be ensnared? You are the young Bayard, the—'

'He's welcome to call me what he pleases,' interrupted Donovan, sharply. 'All I know or care for is that he loses hundreds
of francs to me every evening we play. It's not the least good
talking. You'll never see me in that *Salle de Jeu* again. You
with your system, and Berrogain with his luck, may do very well.
Fortune wasn't so kind to me, and I'd rather depend on my own
brains.'

Sweepstakes ended the discussion by reiterated injunctions to
'be gentle,' and the words, coming in after a hot dispute, amused
both speakers, and really did put a stop to the quarrel.

Noir finished his lunch, and set off for his afternoon at Monte
Carlo, leaving his father and Donovan to such amusement as
they could find in a long sail in the *Ste. Dévote.* Strangely
enough, however, it so happened that the infallible 'system'
failed dismally on that very afternoon. Noir was singularly unfortunate, lost almost all that he had previously won, and
returned to the hotel at night crestfallen and dispirited. He had
burnt his fingers, and for the time lost all desire to risk a fresh
effort.

Rather sulkily he consented the next morning to go for a
walk with Donovan, and, *déjeuner* over, the two set out towards
the quaint little town of Roccabruna. As they passed through
old Monaco and down the sunny road, a furious rattling attracted
their notice. All the small boys of the place had armed themselves with impromptu policemen's rattles made of odd bits of wood
and iron, and were swinging them round with frightful energy.

'What is all this infernal row about?' grumbled Noir.

Donovan, rather amused by the comical effect of the energetic
gamins and their clumsy rattles, accosted a brown-eyed boy, and
asked him the meaning of it all.

'It is the Holy Thursday, monsieur,' was the answer. 'We
crush the bones of the wicked Judas, the betrayer. This evening, in the church, it will be very beautiful. The priests will
wash our feet, the lights will be extinguished, and all the people
will crush the bones of Judas. A great noise it will be, monsieur.
It will resemble the thunder!'

Donovan rejoined Noir with a bitter smile on his face. This then was Christianity! They walked on in perfect silence.

The day was gloriously fine and bright, the April air soft and balmy, the atmosphere in that state of almost intoxicating clearness only to be met with in the South. Certainly the two men were a strange contrast to their surroundings—the elder grim, clouded, dissatisfied, the younger worn with suffering, weary with the weariness of a life-long unrest, and bearing on his handsome features that peculiar expression of constant inward struggle which often gives pathos to the hardest face.

Around them were the thick olive groves, above the clear deep blue of the cloudless sky. It was a paradise of peace and loveliness that these two were treading together. How far it influenced them it would be hard to say, but probably both owed more to it than they knew. Roccabruna, with its cavernous houses and quaint archways, did not greatly interest them. They had come for exercise rather than for lionising, and, contented with a very brief survey of the little antique place, they struck off to the left, along a rough and rugged mule-path, and walked on silently in the direction of Mentone. Each bend brought them to a fresh loveliness, to glimpses of new rocky heights, to little silvery impetuous waterfalls, to different views of the exquisite coast and of the Mediterranean, which at its very bluest spread out before them in calm beauty. At last Donovan spoke.

'Have you had enough of Monaco yet? Shall we go?'

'Certainly, I'll go to morrow, if you'll come back on the old footing to London,' said Noir, with a quick glance at his companion.

'To that you've had your answer already,' he replied, coldly. 'I shall never go back to the old life. I told you so.'

'Saint!' said Noir, with his most disagreeable sneer.

'Saint or devil, I'm not going to do it,' said Donovan, his voice rising. 'Call me what names you like, but understand once for all that when I say a thing I mean it.'

Noir knew that this was true enough; knew, as he looked at the firm resolute face, that he might more easily move the rocks at Monaco than turn this fellow from his purpose.

'A month at Paris might not be amiss,' he suggested, after a pause. 'Berrogain is going back next week; he's made his fortune now—broke the bank yesterday.'

'I am ready to go then,' said Donovan. 'The sooner we're out of this place the better.'

'Paris would not be bad,' mused Noir, half to himself; 'we shall come in for the meeting at Chantilly—perhaps induce

Darky Legge to come over. Yes, that'll do. Are you agreed?'

'Agreed? Oh, yes,' replied Donovan, shortly. And then, as they passed a little wayside chapel in the midst of an olive grove, he said, with an abrupt change of tone, 'Let us rest here. One doesn't often get shade like this.'

And throwing himself down under one of the gnarled old trees, with arms crossed pillow-wise beneath his head, he lay watching the glimpses of blue through the graceful network of branches above him, and the still bluer depth of sea down below, against which the dark outlines of an iron cross stood out distinctly. Noir filled his pipe, and sat with his back against the trunk of the olive, not caring to attempt any further conversation.

'Life,' thought the elder man, depressed by his losses, 'was particularly worthless and uninteresting just at that time.' 'Life,' thought the younger, perplexed by his increasing difficulties, troubled within and without, 'life was more than a man could well stand! it was weary, and profitless, and utterly hateful.'

Thus they mused, each following his natural bent, each calling that 'life' which was in reality death, each wondering that they found it so barren and worthless. Neither could understand that the very sense of insatiety which came to them in their selfish lives was the token of those higher affinities within them, those faint needings and longings for the Omnipresent Fire Divine, which He can—nay, surely *does*, everywhere kindle.

By-and-by, the one with a shrug, the other with a sigh, the reveries were ended, the burden of the so-called 'life' was taken up once more, the two walked on slowly, past the beautiful villas and the fragrant orange groves, to Mentone.

CHAPTER XIX.

LOSING SELF TO FIND.

Man-like is it to fall into sin,
Fiend-like is it to dwell therein,
Christ-like is it for sin to grieve,
God-like is it all sin to leave.
            From the German. LONGFELLOW.

ELEVEN o'clock on a May morning, the bright sunshine peeping in obliquely through the *persiennes*, and lighting up the conventional French bed-room, with its wardrobe, mirror, writing-table, and gilt clock, also a well-worn, brown portmanteau, and a white and tan fox-terrier stretched at full length on the hearth-rug. Down below in the street there was the rumbling of wheels, the busy morning traffic, occasionally the cheerful voices of gay Parisians as they passed by, occupied, no doubt, but not pressed and hurried as Londoners are.

These were the sights and sounds which first greeted Dono-van on a day which he was never to forget, a day every detail of which was burnt in upon his brain with the ineffaceable brand of suffering. He woke late, rang the bell for his coffee, and then lay musing. He was a rich man! The sensation was strange. A year ago he had been cast adrift, friendless, almost penniless; he had started with hardly any possession in the world, except the brown portmanteau and the fox-terrier which met his gaze from the other side of the room. Now he was rich, a well-to-do man, for not many hours ago, when the faint dawn was just beginning to break, he had won a fortune at baccarat. In spite of Ellis's wickedness, in spite of life-long injustice, he had done well for himself.

And yet, after all, did it make so very much difference? Was this great success, this unparalleled good fortune, really worth having? His heart did not feel any lighter, life did not look more inviting when he got up that day. At the actual time of his triumph his bliss had been complete, his one passion rode rampant over everything. A splendid game, a fortune at stake, a fortune which he by his marvellous play had won! Everything else was forgotten, care for the time cast aside, weariness lost, emptiness filled, the hollow unsatisfactory world became a temporary paradise!

But now it had passed, and the dull weight of existence pressed on him once more. Was he so much better off than poor M. Berrogain even, the man by whose losses he had been enriched? Was the loser many degrees more depressed than the winner?

He was just about to leave his room when, with a hasty knock, Noir Frewin entered.

'Milord,' he said quickly, 'you're wanted in the next room; there's no end of a scene going on—Berrogain's wife in floods of tears. Her husband has made off no one knows where, and, from a few written words he left, seems to intend suicide.'

Donovan gave a dismayed start, made a gesture of horror.

'What!' he gasped, in a voice which contrasted oddly with Noir's off-hand manner.

'Only what I say,' said Noir. 'Don't look as if you'd

already seen his ghost. Of course it's a bad business, but come in
and see the wife, and don't put her down as a widow till we've
found all the facts.'

With an impatient movement, Donovan pushed past the
speaker, and in a dazed, bewildered way found himself in the
room where the old captain was trying to say something cheering
to a little dark-eyed woman, whose piquant face was wet with
tears and pale with anxiety.

'Here is M. Donovan,' said Rouge, paternally. 'He has a
good heart, madame—he will help you.'

'Ah! monsieur,' she cried, turning to him with streaming
eyes, 'listen, at least listen, to my trouble. In the night my
husband returns, he tells me he is ruined—he, the fortunate, has
been ruined—all the fortune he made at Monaco lost—gone. I
ask him how, and he tells me it is the young Englishman, the
M. Donovan, of whom so much was said at the club—he it is
who has caused the ruin. Oh! monsieur,' and here the poor
little woman's voice was broken with sobs, 'you who are so
good, so prudent, you whom they call the young Bayard, *sans
peur et sans reproche*—oh! monsieur, is it possible that you did it?
They said you were too good for Monaco, but oh! monsieur, it is
worse to ruin others than to ruin yourself. Think, monsieur—
think what it means! You have driven my husband away in
despair—he may even now be no more. Oh! *mon Dieu! mon
Dieu!* Think if the Seine be flowing over him! Monsieur,
speak to me, help me! It is you who have brought us this evil
—speak, monsieur!'

Throughout the impassioned address Donovan had stood
rigidly still. He felt sick with horror, the strength went out of
his arms, for the time he really was paralysed by the appalling
consciousness of the responsibility resting on him. He had,
perhaps—nay, probably—driven a man to suicide, ruined and
widowed the poor woman before him. Was he much better than
a murderer?

'Speak, monsieur!' reiterated Madame Berrogain through
her tears.

He turned at last to Rouge appealingly

'I can't speak to her; you must——'

'M. Donovan is much moved,' said the old captain; 'he tells
me to speak for him. Be assured, madame, that he will do all in
his power. He is good and——'

'*Do!*' interrupted Donovan, with a sudden return of strength
and vehemence—'is there anything to do? Only tell me of any
hope that all this is not true, that your fears are groundless——'

'Alas! monsieur, but who can say?' sobbed Madame Berrogain. 'He is gone—gone—see his last words!' and she held out to him a sheet of paper, on which was written in French:

*'My wife,—I cannot bear this intolerable misery. I must fly from all most dear, and seek a refuge in darkness. Life is ended for me. Farewell! Thy unhappy one,—*BERROGAIN.'

To Donovan the words conveyed little hope. Still he clung to the idea that there might possibly be time to hinder this rash act, and with the hope all the man within him re-asserted itself.

'Madame,' he said, earnestly, 'all that can be done I will do. We will advertise in all the papers. I will seek your husband in every place in Paris where we know of any chance of finding him. I will find him if I die in doing it.'

In spite of his bad French, and limited means of expression, in spite too of his grave stern face, Madame Berrogain understood the depth of the promise, and knew that the man who had ruined her husband was yet a man to be trusted.

'And you think there is hope?' she cried. 'Oh! monsieur, you think there is really hope?'

He struggled hard to speak, and, with his habitual control, forced himself at last to say,

'Be comforted, madame, I will do everything that is possible. Hope for the best, and to-night we will bring you word. You shall know all that has been done.'

'Monsieur is good,' said the poor wife, wiping her eyes. 'He will work, and I—I will pray to our Lady.'

In a few minutes more she rose to leave, and, with her *bonne* beside her, went back to her desolate rooms.

Donovan, as soon as she had left, drew paper and ink to him, and sitting down began to write rapidly. Rouge watched the forcible characters, as they were traced, with a sort of vague wonder and wilderment. A few moments before his companion had seemed utterly unnerved, now his iron face and the swift precision of his movements made him seem like a machine.

'What are you doing?' asked the captain, curiously.

'Advertisements,' was the laconic reply, spoken in the voice which more than anything tells of a mind strained to the highest tension, half sharp, half weary.

Five minutes of writing, and then Donovan rose, snatched up his hat and opened the door. The captain stopped him.

'Let me come with you, lad,' he said, in his good-humoured voice.

'Yes, come,' said Donovan, with a shade of relief in his tone; and then the two hurried down the stairs and out into the sunny street. Just outside the door they found Noir sauntering up and down with his pipe. He stopped them to ask their errand, gave his advice as to putting the matter into the hands of the police, and then turned away with his usual cool nonchalance, under which was, nevertheless, hidden more sympathy than might have been expected.

'Milord is the very worst person for such a thing to come to,' he mused; 'a man without a conscience wouldn't have troubled himself to think twice of the matter. Now Donovan's as likely as not to go raving mad if this Berrogain isn't found.'

At present there were no signs of the anticipated 'madness;' Donovan was quiet and clear-headed, he walked on swiftly with Rouge beside him, setting about his disagreeable work in the most business-like way. In spite of his English pronunciation, too, there was that about him which obliged the various officials to receive his orders with civility and obedience.

Not to think—that was his one great effort, but the horror of the overhanging dread would obtrude itself,—or if by his strong will he banished it for a time, it was only to be conscious, through the hard matter-of-fact absence of feeling which he forced himself into, of the dull nameless weight at his heart.

It was about four in the afternoon when they reached the Pont d'Arcole, and the old captain was beginning to feel both hungry and tired. He looked at his companion then questioningly, and saw a little additional sternness about his face. Groups of men were leaning over the parapet watching the river. Donovan too paused for a moment and looked down at the spark ling water; Rouge fancied he saw him shudder, but he did not speak, and walked on again more rapidly than before.

'Where next?' asked the captain, anxiously.

'To the Morgue,' said Donovan, in a firm but very low voice.

They went on in silence, and before long found themselves in the little crowd which was continually passing up and down the steps and through the doors of the small insignificant building which is dedicated to so painful a purpose.

'I will wait here for you,' said Rouge, for he rather shrank from going inside, and Donovan, without a word, left him and pushed his way in with the eager crowd.

The waiting seemed long to the old captain; he began to wonder whether his companion had found poor Monsieur Berrogain in that dread room within, and anxiously scanned the faces of those who came out. Soldiers in shabby uniforms, women in their snowy white caps, men of all ranks and ages, sometimes even little children in arms.

At length, in this motley but cheerful and unconcerned crowd, came the face which Rouge was waiting for, a curious contrast to every other, stern, and sad, and white to the very lips.

The captain was startled.

'Good heavens! milord,' he cried, 'you have not found him, have you?'

Donovan shook his head, and clutched at his companion's arm to steady himself.

'Why, you're ill,' said the captain. 'Within an ace of fainting.'

'Nonsense, nothing of the kind,' panted Donovan. 'Only let us get away from this place,' and with Rouge's assistance he crossed the road, but there, finding his strength failing, was obliged to lean up against the railings, even to cling to them for support. The horrible sight, the dread of what he might possibly find, had completely unnerved him; for one dreadful moment, too, he had fancied that he recognized M. Berrogain, and, in spite of the subsequent relief at his mistake, he could not recover from the shock.

'Only don't let's have a scene,' was his answer to all Rouge's suggestions, and at last, with the old captain's help, he managed to get as far as the entrance to the garden east of Notre Dame, and to rest on a bench under the trees.

Everything there was bright and peaceful, the grey old church with its pinnacles and flying buttresses, the fresh green of the spring leaves, the sunshine streaming down with that gaiety and brightness which seem specially to characterise Paris, and here and there a little child at play with its *bonne* in attendance. Once a tiny fairy-like little thing, whose white dress showed that she was 'dedicated to the Virgin,' stole up to Donovan—she had watched him with a sort of fascination ever since he had thrown himself down on the bench. Was it merely compassion for one who seemed ill, or was it that peculiar attraction which Donovan possessed for children? The tiny maid, prompted by some unknown influence, at any rate resolved to do her best for him, and, with her little quick fingers, began gathering *marguerites*, then, grasping the bunch with her two fat little hands, she toddled up to the silent figure, and, with a premonitory pat to arouse him, laid her offering on his knees.

'See then, monsieur, the pretty flowers, they are all for you.'

He put his hand for a moment on the dimpled one of his tiny

friend, and, as well as he could, thanked her, but the daring little mite was soon pursued by an indignant nurse.

'Mademoiselle Gabrielle, come away this moment. Ah! little wicked one! I dare not take my eyes off thee for a single instant!'

So Mademoiselle Gabrielle was led away in disgrace, but looked round nevertheless to kiss her hand, and to nod her pretty little head in farewell, and Donovan followed her with his eyes, with a great pain at his heart. The little child's gift touched him strangely; it had come in such a moment of tumult and horror, when self was feeling so hateful, the weight of dread responsibility so heavy. And this fairy-like creature had pitied him—liked him. He was grateful with the almost passionate gratitude of humility.

For it was a very terrible thing this that had come to him, this woe that he had unthinkingly brought about. He was very young still, only just two-and-twenty, and in spite of his wretched roving life, in spite of the bitter misanthropy he professed, there was still in him the chivalry of all strong natures, the nobleness which must protect what is weak. Little children and women he looked upon with a sort of devotion; from his very childhood it had been so: the ideal of motherhood, the devoted love for Dot, had been the ruling motives of his life. The ideal of the wife was still unformed, he had never loved, or even fancied that he loved, any woman. Only when the thought of home-life came to him, as now and then it would, when he saw the outer side of the lives of others, the vision of the grey-eyed stranger whom he had met in Hyde Park would rise up before him, the tender, bright, womanly woman, whose purity and sweetness had had such a powerful influence over him—had even helped to keep him straight when he had been exposed to the countless snares of Monaco.

Because of this strong reverence for women, the scene of the morning had been specially painful to him. The poor wife's misery, which must have haunted anyone with a heart, haunted him with a pain and shame almost intolerable. But fortunately he was—notwithstanding all his failings—brave and manly, he struggled now with his weakness, and began to make his plans for further searching—that 'doing' which was such a relief to his burdened mind.

'We will come to one of Duval's places and have some dinner,' was his first voluntary remark to the old captain, about as sensible and matter-of-fact a proposal as could have been made.

So they went to the nearest of the restaurants, and Rouge's devoted attendance was rewarded by the privilege of ordering whatever he liked, while Donovan gulped down enough food to support him in his work, conquering his disinclination till he had satisfied his conscience, and then calling Waif to devour the plentiful leavings.

After that came another deliberate plunge into the crowded streets, another long-continued but vain search for the lost man. Ceaseless inquiries, endless hurryings to and fro, once or twice a supposed clue to M. Berrogain's whereabouts, to be followed by temporary hope and bitter disappointment.

Once, as the evening wore on, Donovan stopped at a *café* on one of the boulevards and made the old captain have a cup of *café noir*, even permitted the *petit verre* without a remonstrance. But this time he was too sick at heart to force himself to take anything, hope had almost died out since his last disappointment, and the numbing paralysing horror was beginning to overwhelm him again.

Rouge, as he sipped his coffee contentedly, happened to look across the little marble table at his silent companion, and then for the first time realised that the day's anxiety had been something far severer than he could comprehend. For Donovan's face was worn and haggard, grey with that strange ghastliness which only comes on such young faces in times of great exhaustion ; the firm mouth betrayed suffering, the eyes, though feverishly alive to all that was passing, had a painfully despairing look in them.

'Donovan, lad,' said Rouge, anxiously, 'you will come home now, won't you ?'

'You go home, captain,' he answered, 'you've had a long day. I ? no, I can't come yet. I must see whether the police have found anything, and I must see *her*—Madame Berrogain.'

'Milord, you'll only be ill again,' remonstrated the old man, 'you'll do for yourself one of these days.'

'That means I shall do the best thing that could be done,' said Donovan, with an odd sudden smile, followed by a quick sigh. 'But you see, captain, this coil of flesh is terribly tough. Good night! go home and rest.'

He pushed back his chair suddenly, threw down a franc beside the captain's cup, and before his companion could remonstrate had walked away rapidly alone.

At length, wearily and quite hopelessly, he went to see if any of the agencies he had set to work had been successful in tracing M. Berrogain. He had some minutes to wait in the *bureau* of the chief official, but at last a small sharp-faced man appeared with a paper in his hand, and an all-pervading odour of garlic, which was quite beneath the dignity of his position.

'You are come to inquire for Théodore Berrogain, disappeared mysteriously since the hour of 4 A.M. Good! I think we have traced him.'

Donovan did not speak, only breathed more quickly and clenched and unclenched his hands, his usual sign of strong feeling.

'Inquiries have been made, and this is the result,—at the *Gare d'Orléans* the *chef* states that a man answering to your description, much above the usual height, pale, with thick light hair and moustaches, and a cast in one eye, was seen early this morning at the station. The official at the ticket-office also remembers him, and will undertake to swear that he issued a ticket to him for Bordeaux, third class. Acting upon this, monsieur, we have telegraphed to the officials at Bordeaux; the train by which it is supposed M. Berrogain left Paris reaches Bordeaux this evening at 10.30, it will be met by our agents there, and they will telegraph to us the movements of your friend.'

Doubtless the man thought the 'friendship' was a remarkable one—one must love a companion much to be so particularly anxious about him, and Donovan's intense relief, though undemonstrative, was nevertheless apparent even to the sleepy official. He arranged to call early the next morning for further tidings, and then hurried away to relieve poor Madame Berrogain's anxiety.

Anyone who knows the sensation of a sudden respite, the removal of an intolerable load, the relief from oppressing fear, will understand with what feelings Donovan hastened along the gas-lit streets. He was treading on air; new life was coursing through his veins; the very consciousness of free unburdened existence was in itself exquisite. And then came the satisfaction of imparting his hopeful news to the poor wife, amid a torrent of fervent thanks, tears, incoherent blessings, and exclamations of relief.

He tried to cut the scene short, and it was not till he was standing at the open door that he placed in Madame Berrogain's hands a small piece of paper.

'I give this to you, madame, because I think it is better so. To-morrow I shall go to your husband, and I will tell him what you hold for him.'

He would have moved to the staircase, but Madame Berrogain laid her hand on his arm. She had glanced rapidly at the paper, and now the tears were streaming down her cheeks.

'No, no, monsieur, this is too good! This must not be! Take it back, monsieur, I implore.'

'Madame asks what is impossible,' he replied, with his rare and beautiful smile. 'One day's possession is sufficient for me. Only, if I might be allowed one suggestion, I would say that it were better used for madame's own needs, not risked again at baccarat.'

'Ah! God bless you! God guard you!' exclaimed the little wife, clasping her hands together. 'Monsieur, I shall remember you always. On my knees I shall remember you—believe it. Ah! heaven! if all were but like you!'

He submitted to having his hand pressed in both hers for a moment, then, bowing low, he hastened away.

After that, naturally enough came the reaction. He was dreadfully worn out, and, apart from his relief, everything that faced him in the future was most painful. For this great shock had shown him what a hateful life he was leading, and he knew that it must be forsaken.

He found the old captain in his room smoking, told him of Monsieur Berrogain's probable whereabouts, and then, with a sigh of great weariness, stretched himself at full length on the hearthrug. Before very long Noir came in, and, having heard the news in his cool uninterested way, remarked, carelessly,

'Well, I'm glad for your sake that the fellow's in the land of the living still. I suppose he's off to America?'

'He will be watched and arrested, if he attempts it,' said Donovan. 'To-morrow morning I shall start for Bordeaux. It is the only sure way of making all right to see him myself.'

'Folly!' said Noir, crossly. 'Why, the best thing he can do is to leave the country.'

'Madame Berrogain might not agree with you.'

'But the fellow's ruined. You know he can't live here.'

'You are mistaken,' said Donovan, quietly. 'He is not ruined.'

'What!' cried Noir, in a startled voice. 'You mean that you have let him off? that you've been such an utter fool as to let those thousands slip through your fingers again?'

'Exactly—yes—such an utter fool,' said Donovan, with a touch of satire.

'Well, milord, you're a softer fellow then than I thought. A woman's tears and an absurd scare lest a weak-minded wretch should have drowned himself, and you melt directly, become the generous hero of the piece, fling *largesse* to right and left, and walk off amid cheers and applause. I'd no idea you were so weak-minded! Besides, you know well enough you'll repent your bargain in a few days. As your favourite Monsieur Renan says, "Most beautiful actions are done in a state of fever." You'll recover and repent it.'

'Do I seem feverishly excited?' asked Donovan, quietly. 'And do I generally fail in deliberation?'

'Don't bother him now,' interposed the old captain. 'We've had an awful day of it.'

'What in the world you did it for I can't conceive,' said Noir, unheeding. 'You who profess to rail at the injustice of life! you who call yourself a misanthrope! What induced you to spend your time on such a search? What does it matter to you if all the world is ruined?'

'I suppose, after all, I didn't hate the whole world,' said Donovan, slowly, 'or else the hatred was all needed in another direction.'

Noir caught his meaning, and, because he could just recognize its humility and sad honesty, it roused all the evil in him; he knew that his companion was slipping away from him.

'And how does your moral highness propose to live if you refund the money you won?' The question was put with a contemptuous sneer.

'How I shall live, Noir,' answered Donovan, gravely, 'I cannot tell, but by gambling I shall not live.'

'We shall see,' said Noir, 'when you recover from this state of fever. Why, do you think that in a moment like this you can end the strongest incentive of your life? You know perfectly well that you don't care a rush for anything except the cards.'

'You've about hit it,' said Donovan, 'but,' with a firmness which seemed to give treble force to each separate word, '*I will not play again.*'

For a minute both the Frewins were silent; both involuntarily looked at their companion as he lay, his thin skilful hands clasped over his dark hair, his face resolute and full of noble purpose. He was quietly renouncing all he had as yet cared for in life, all by which he could win admiration, success, pleasure, and these two men knew it. Rouge was the first to speak.

'Well, lad, we will do the best we can for you; you will stay on with us.'

Then the look of struggle came back to Donovan's face. He rose hurriedly, and began to pace up and down the room, scarcely hearing what his companions said to him.

At last he stopped abruptly in his walk, and said, hoarsely,

'No, I can't stay, captain.'

'Can't!—nonsense!' said Noir. 'We don't part after a whole year together in this way.'

'I must go,' he repeated. 'I dare not stay.'

'Dare not!—what, we are so bad that we shall corrupt your moral highness? Oh! go then, by all means, and may you find friends more faithful and better suited to your lofty standard!'

'Frewin,' said Donovan, very sadly, 'you know well enough that it is myself I dare not trust. If you think that I could stay with you and all our own set, and yet keep to my word, well and good. But I could not do it. It will be hard any way; impossible like that.'

'A few months ago you would have scorned to say anything was impossible.'

'Well, I've been taken down a few pegs since then, and now I do say it and mean it. Good-night, Noir.'

'When do you leave?'

'To-morrow by the 9.20. Good-night and good-bye.'

Noir took his hand for a moment, looked full in his face, as though to read what was written there, then, with an impatient gesture, he turned away.

'Good-bye. I see we have done with each other.'

Sweepstakes, waking up, screamed out his habitual greetings.

'Such a talkin', such a talkin', what a parcel of fools! Ain't you a fool!—ain't you a fool, milord!'

The old captain, with maudlin tears coursing down his cheeks, hurried after the retreating figure, and it was long before Donovan could quiet the piteous entreaties that he would change his mind, would stay at least a few days longer, or would promise to come back when he had seen M. Berrogain. Parting with his companions was a greater wrench than he had feared even; they had been very good to him, had nursed him through his illness with rough but very real care, and they were the only friends he had in the whole world. And yet he knew that he must leave them; they were inseparably bound up with the evil he was trying to free himself from—both must be renounced.

He took leave of Rouge that night, and early next day started on his solitary journey—solitary with the exception of Waif. The address he needed had been telegraphed to the official when he went to inquire on his way to the station, and it was a substantial relief to his anxiety to be able to repeat to himself the assurance of M. Berrogain's safety—'Hôtel Montré, Rue Montesquieu, Bordeaux.' There was, however, just a little flatness and depression now that all was ended; he took his ticket, and then went into the *salle-d'attente*, the 'durance vile' which generally gives an Englishman a chafed caged feeling. As he passed up and down, too, there was a touch of far-off dread in his face—the dread of the unknown future, which of all expressions is one of the most painful to see.

Noir Frewin, suddenly entering the room in search of his late companion, caught the look and understood it. Unprincipled as he was he could not help respecting a resolution which could so steadily persevere in direct opposition to personal wishes, and there was none of the malice of the previous night in his tone when he spoke.

Donovan turned hastily at the sound of his own name, he was ill-prepared just then for a repetition of the scornful upbraidings which he had borne silently a few hours ago. Noir saw that his arrival was not very welcome.

'I'm only come to see you off,' he explained. 'You're quite right, milord, after all; go and save yourself while you can.'

'Saving is not the question,' said Donovan, 'even if I believed in such a thing. But at any rate one needn't do others harm.'

'A change in your views, lad, since we first went into partnership,' said Noir. 'Your anger with whoever it was who had ruined you has cooled with time.'

'His offence looks small now that I am the bigger brute,' replied Donovan. Then, as the doors were thrown open, he put his arm within Noir's once more, and they went out together to the train.

'Good-bye, old fellow,' he said, rather hoarsely, just before the final start. 'Let us hope my lungs won't give out again, or I shall be crying out for you.'

'Till then we are best away from each other,' said Noir, giving his hand a farewell grip. 'Good-bye, Farrant. We part as we met, you see, in a railway-carriage.'

The train moved off; Frewin, with a fierce sigh, turned away, and Donovan was whirled through the vast plains of central France, marvelling not a little how his companion had learnt his real name, the name which he had taken such pains to conceal.

Thirteen hours later and he was standing in the crowded *salle* at the Bordeaux Station. He was very tired, a trifle desolate too, alone among foreigners, alone with such a 'howling wilderness' of a future as he fancied before him, the future of restraint which he had chosen. Waiting rather impatiently till the doors of the luggage-room should be opened, he scanned the faces of the crowd, the usual busy cheerful crowd of a French railway-station; a group of men whiling away the waiting-time with

laughter and occasional snatches of song, two lovers sitting on a
bench in the corner, whispering contentedly together, regardless
of their surroundings, a fat rough-featured priest, with his shovel
hat and starched bands, a respectable *bourgeois* and his wife, followed by a toddling bare-headed child.

Instinctively Donovan watched the little one. The mother
turned round, saying playfully, '*Adieu! Adieu!*' pretending to
leave it; the child let them walk on a few steps, and then, with
sudden dread of being left, ran at full speed after them with an
eager '*Non, non, non*,' and grasped its mother's skirt. Then both
father and mother laughed, each took one of the tiny hands, and
the three walked away together.

Home dramas all around him, love in all its forms and degrees
—the friend's, the lover's, the mother's, the wife's! He sighed,
and stooped down to pat Waif. Then followed the general rush
into the adjoining room, he went to claim his portmanteau, and
in a few minutes was out in the starlight, on his way to M.
Berrogain.

His desolateness made him think of Dot, of the times when
he too had had some one to love and protect. They were sad,
but on the whole peaceful, thoughts which came to him as he
crossed the bridge, pausing for a moment to look at the long
chain of lights marking out the crescent-shaped quays. She, the
holy child of his memory, was at peace, it was perhaps well that
she had passed away from him, he had not been fit to be near
such purity and loveliness, and as she had grown older it was
possible that he might have pained her—pained her by his unworthiness. That thought was intolerable. And so, unconsciously, he repeated to himself Noir Frewin's words—'We were
better parted.' Neither of them knew that the unselfishness
and humility prompting the thought was drawing them to the
Source of all love.

The walk was a long one, through broad well-built streets,
past the theatre, on again into narrower and darker thoroughfares, till Donovan began to wonder whether the porter whom he
had hired to carry his portmanteau were not perhaps taking him
by some roundabout way in the hope of extorting a larger *pour-
boire* At last, turning to the left, they passed through a circular
market-place, and down a narrow street with high dingy-looking
houses.

'There, monsieur,' said the porter, with a wave of the hand,
'that is the Hôtel Montré.'

Donovan saw at the corner the inevitable *Café Billard*, and
upon the upper storeys the name of the hotel inscribed. The

porter went on to the entrance, and Donovan, following, found himself in a paved courtyard with two mouldy-looking orange trees growing in tubs, and a dim light proceeding from the room of the *concierge*. He inquired at once for M. Berrogain, and was relieved to find that he was known still by his real name. He was within too, had taken his key not five minutes before, would monsieur see him at once or be shown to his own room?

Donovan desired to see M. Berrogain at once, and, having dismissed his guide, was ushered by a pretty, little, white-capped servant up a dirty stone staircase, along a labyrinth of passages, then up again and through a corresponding labyrinth darker and dirtier than that below.

'Perhaps monsieur sleeps,' suggested the little servant, glancing round as she paused at a door to the right. 'It is very late,' and she pretended to yawn.

'Knock and see,' said Donovan, impatient of the delay.

A quick *entrez!* relieved his fears, and, taking the candle from his conductress, he opened the door and found himself in a fairly comfortable room, where, extended on a shabby green velvet sofa, lay M. Berrogain, the *Figaro* in his hand, the *Gironde* lying at his feet. For a moment the thought would come, 'He is unconcerned and comfortable enough, you need not have troubled about him.' But while Donovan paused, the unconscious Frenchman glanced round. He had been absorbed in his paper, and had half forgotten that someone had knocked and been admitted; now, catching sight so unexpectedly of the man who had ruined him, he sprang to his feet with a cry half of fear, half of passion.

'Ah! evil one, why do you pursue me?' he said, in trembling tones. 'Would you remember a petty debt of two hundred francs when you have won a fortune from me? Stony-hearted wretch! would you pelt a fallen man? You have tracked me—you, the rich, the successful, will hunt down the unfortunate for a miserable trifle such as that!'

'I am not rich,' said Donovan, 'nor are you unfortunate.'

'Miserable Englishman!' cried out M. Berrogain. 'Why do you mock me? You are come to drive me to despair, to death! Why could you not let me leave the country in peace? Why do you come with your grasping avarice to——'

'Listen, Berrogain,' interrupted Donovan, in his firm sad voice. 'I could not let you leave the country, because there is no need for you to go. I am not mocking you. Be quiet and listen. To-morrow morning you can go back to your wife at Paris; she holds the fortune which you lost at baccarat.'

They were standing by the draped mantel-piece. Donovan turned away as he spoke, and putting aside the muslin curtains looked down into the dimly-lighted street. He was not sorry to feel the fresh air upon his face.

There was a moment's silence, then M. Berrogain came forward and took his hand.

'My friend,' he said, falteringly, 'forgive what I have said. I was in despair. But this generosity—no—no, it cannot be, it cannot be.'

'It *must* be,' said Donovan, quietly.

'No, no! leave me enough to go on upon, or allow me six months' respite, I should be more than content with that.'

'But I should not,' said Donovan, decidedly. 'No, Berrogain, everything is settled, so do not let us waste words on the subject.'

'But it is unheard of!' said M. Berrogain. 'It is noble, generous, kind, but, my good friend, before you commit yourself, think how will you get on in the world if you act in such a way?'

'That,' said Donovan, with a half smile, 'is a question yet to be solved, but I do not mean to live by other men's losses. Enough has been said though about it all. Can one get anything to eat in this place? I'm furiously hungry!'

'Ah! but you are an Englishman!' said M. Berrogain, amused by the request. 'There is a restaurant just opposite, let me come with you.'

'To watch the voracious islander!' said Donovan, laughing. 'To-night I shall keep up the national character. I could eat half a roast beef if there was a chance of getting it!'

'Ah! is it possible?' said the Frenchman. 'And at this time of night, too!'

He did not think that the anxiety which he had caused could possibly have affected his companion's appetite on the previous day, and sat amusedly at the table, watching the absolute demolition of the largest piece of *Ros-bif-roti* which the restaurant could produce.

Then somewhere in the small hours Donovan found his way to the dingy wainscoted room which had been allotted him, and, in spite of the noisy orgies being carried on in the room below, was soon sleeping profoundly.

M. Berrogain left for Paris the next day, and Donovan went to the station with him, submitted to his demonstrative gratitude, and then turned away rather disconsolately to make the best of his new life. He wandered about the place for some little time,

Q

found his way into the beautiful Church of St. Michel, looked
wonderingly and half pityingly at the groups of worshippers,
then sauntered out again, along the quays, among the tramways
and trucks, the coils of rope and the chains, idly scrutinizing the
closely-moored vessels and the busy work of lading or unlading,
or coaling, which was going on. Everywhere work and business.
And he too must work, he had been leading a wretched self-
indulgent life, he would work now, indeed he must work to live.
The question was what should he do, and where should he go?

He had rather a hankering after America, but that idea had
to be given up, for he had not enough to pay his passage. It
seemed to be a choice of trying for some situation in Bordeaux
itself, or of going back to England, the chances of finding immediate employment being about equally small in either case.
He decided at last to let fate choose his destination, and tossed
up a *petit sou*—heads he was to go to England, and thus it fell.

With a half sigh he pocketed the coin, looked at his watch,
and then hurried away to find out when the next steamer left for
Liverpool. There was one that evening to his relief, and he
hastened back to the Hôtel Montré, glad that his hours in its
dingy rooms were numbered. The passage was being swept by the
little white-capped maid-servant as he passed down it, and as he
put his things together the refrain of the song she was singing
floated in to him :

> Oui, malgré ta philosophie
> L'amour seul peut charmer la vie.

Over and over it went, a tuneless little chant, and with strange
persistency it rang in his ears long after, 'L'amour seul!—l'amour
seul!' Was it indeed that which could alone make life support-
able? He was not quite the misanthrope he had considered himself, but had he any love for his kind? Many times he asked
himself that question, as he stood on the deck of the steamer
while it ploughed its way through the Bay of Biscay, or lay with
Waif at his feet, like a recumbent crusader, looking up at the
starry skies. Did he only not hate?—was there anything more
active than that in his feeling towards the rest of the world?

All this time he had scarcely realised the hardness of the task
he had set himself. He had willed never to play again, and was
quite at rest now that the resolution was made, for never in his
whole life had he failed to do a thing which he had deliberately
undertaken. His confidence in his own strength was boundless,
and though he had reasonably enough seen the impossibility of
still living with the Frewins, now that he had once broken with

the old set he did not give a thought to other possible temptations.

And thus, satisfied with the strength of his will, and full of his new and good purposes, he was set down at Liverpool. Then followed a time of bitter disappointment; though he had just renounced a fortune, the world gave him the cold shoulder again, and his money began to evaporate, to disappear with the horrid rapidity which becomes so noticeable when we are counting by units instead of tens. And very soon came the temptation. He had been out all day in the weary useless search after work, the evening set in wet and chilly, as he passed down the gas-lit streets to his cheerless lodging a familiar sound made him pause, he was passing a billiard room—the sharp click of the balls, the eager voices, how natural it all sounded! He had taken no resolution against playing billiards. Why should he not relieve this intolerable dulness by an hour or two of amusement? A momentary struggle followed, then he pushed open the door and went in. How long he was there he could never clearly remember, but it was not until a substantial token of his wonted success lay before him that he realised the failure of his will. He, the strong, and self-reliant, had yielded to the very first temptation, had failed most miserably. He dropped the cue, pushed away the money, and amid a chorus of surprise and inquiry strode out of the room.

Too completely dismayed and bewildered to find any relief in his usual custom of rapid walking, he went back to his wretched lodging, and there sat motionless in the summer twilight in blank silent despair. Everything was lost—friends, money, pleasure, worst of all, his confidence in himself. What was there left? Nothing, he said, but a wretched life that was far better ended, a despicable ' I,' that must struggle to find itself bread, because— only because of a dim, inexplicable idea that self-destruction was wrong. What possible good was there in his life to himself or to anyone else? He did not think then of his influence with the Frewins, he could only feel that he had cheated himself, failed in his purpose, sunk irrevocably in his own opinion. What guarantee was there, too, that his will would not fail again?

Two paws on his knee and a soft warm tongue licking his hand roused him at length.

'Oh, Waif!' he exclaimed, with a great sigh, 'if only I'd a tenth of your goodness, old dog!'

By-and-by he lit the gas, dragged out the tin of dog biscuits, and gave Waif his supper, glancing in between the mouthfuls at the advertisement columns of an open newspaper which lay on the table. Once the dog was kept begging for quite a minute, for his master had become absorbed in what he was reading.

'Wanted, as secretary to the —— Institute, a young man of good abilities. Knowledge of book-keeping and a clear handwriting indispensable. Salary £100. Apply in person, on the 15th or 16th, the President, —— Institute, Exeter.'

Secretary!—surely he was well fitted for the post. Possibly, too, there would be less competition down in the quiet west-country. Here in Liverpool his chance of success seemed infinitesimally small.

'Well, my dog,' he said, almost cheerfully, as he threw down the next mouthful, 'shall we set off together and try our luck? £100 a year would keep you in biscuits, so there's some reason in it, after all.'

The necessary inquiry, however, into his resources showed him only too plainly that he had not enough money for the journey. After his present expenses had been paid, his worldly possessions would have dwindled down to a sum below the price of a third-class ticket to Exeter. His watch and chain had been in pawn ever since the day after his arrival; he had no other valuables, nothing by which he could raise money, nothing except—— His eye fell on Dot's little travelling-clock, and he started painfully. The idea of selling that had never occurred to him before. In all his wanderings it had been with him—it was almost the only thing he still had which had belonged to her —to part with it seemed unbearable, and especially so in this particular way. To take it deliberately with his own hands and bargain about it, to leave it—the very thing which she had touched, and fondled, and admired—in a pawnbroker's shop, to let the silvery cathedral chime which she had loved fall on the ears of strangers, it seemed like desecration! And only an hour ago the money he had so much needed had been his: If he had but taken it, all this difficulty would have been avoided. But then his better self made its voice heard.

'No, my little Dot, no,' he said aloud. 'Better a thousand times that this should go than that I should have been doubly false to myself.'

He did then what he very seldom ventured to do—drew his little miniature of Dot from its place and looked at it steadfastly.

Sweet, child-like little face, clear, satisfied eyes, can you not speak to him, and tell him that love cannot die, that he is compassed about with a cloud of witnesses, that his struggles to live honestly, his despair at the revelation of his weakness, even his present sacrifice to a shadowy instinct rather than to a principle—all is helping to draw him towards you ?

No, comfort cannot be his yet. He cannot see that the pain and loss are necessary to the great gain; he can only go on bravely and painfully in the darkness, holding to the track of right and duty which he begins faintly to perceive.

Presently the little clock was standing on a shelf among other clocks, large and small, in a Liverpool pawnbroker's shop, and Donovan was walking back to his room through the driving rain, with head bent low, and thirty shillings in his pocket.

CHAPTER XX.

'O'ER MOOR AND FEN.'

Self-reverence, self-knowledge, self-control,
These three alone lead life to sovereign power,
Yet not for power (power of herself
Would come uncall'd for), but to live by law,
Acting the law we live by without fear;
And, because right is right, to follow right
Were wisdom in the scorn of consequence.

TENNYSON.

AND, after all, the struggle seemed utterly useless, for the Exeter —— Institute would not accept him as secretary. He was in every way suited for their purpose, and by far the most promising of the candidates, but in a close cross-examination the insuperable barrier was brought to light.

'And your religious views, sir?' asked the president. 'As this is a charitable institution, we always make a point of knowing the views of our staff. It is well to be united. Do you belong to the High or Low party ? '

'To neither,' said Donovan, stiffly. ' I am an atheist.'

And in those four words lay his doom; *because* the institute was a *charitable* one it could not help such a hardened sinner, could not let its accounts and letters be contaminated by his touch.

'I have come from a great distance in the hope of getting this post,' said Donovan, swallowing his pride. ' I am very much in need of work. Surely in the mechanical work of a secretary such a matter as one's private creed might be passed over. What difference can it make to anyone else?'

'My dear sir,' said the head of the charitable institution, 'I can only refer you to the Bible, where you will find the injunction: "Be not unequally yoked together with unbelievers," and "What part hath he that believeth with an infidel?"'

> Alas! for the rarity
> Of Christian charity
> Under the sun.

With the indifference of his kind, however, the frigid adherence to the letter, and the disregard of the spirit, a sort of bitter resolution awoke in Donovan's heart. He would *not* be doomed by a 'charitable' institution, he would *not* sink down quietly into starvation. Life in itself was not worth a straw, but just from opposition, from a manly love of breasting 'the blows of circumstance,' he would struggle on, fight down all obstacles, live to be of use too, in spite of the president's specimen of Christian generosity and brotherliness. Fiercely through his teeth he quoted Shylock's passionate words, 'Hath not a Jew eyes? . . . fed with the same food . . . warmed and cooled by the same winter and summer as a Christian is?'

He had been two days at Exeter; now, returning to his lodgings, he sat down and resolutely went over all possible plans for his future. Should he go back to Greyshot? Mr. Alleyne, the man with whom he used to read, might possibly put him in the way of employment. It was not very likely, though, and there were many objections to a return to the old neighbourhood. Should he write to old Mr. Hayes? He might be at home again by this time, though in the winter Doery had said he was still abroad. But Mr. Hayes was poor, and would unquestionably think only of monetary help. No, that would not do. Should he go home and throw himself on his mother's mercy? But that thought was too wildly impracticable as well as too painful to be allowed for a moment. What connections had he in this part of the world? What had his father's business in Plymouth been, when four years ago they had gone there together? Searching back in his memory he at length recalled the name of his father's acquaintance, and remembered that he had described him as a pleasant elderly man. He was a banker—there would be no difficulty in finding his address.

He began a letter to him at once, a brief, business-like, stiff letter, not at all like that of a starving man asking for help. But then he had no intention of starving. He was young and strong-willed, undaunted still, notwithstanding his repulses.

Having despatched the letter, he made up his mind to follow it; there was no hope of finding work in this quiet old city; at Plymouth he would have more chance. He might just as well spend his time in getting there as in loafing about the Exeter streets. Getting there meant walking, for the proceeds of the clock were nearly exhausted, and would barely suffice to get him some sort of food and shelter, but he rather enjoyed the thought of the exercise, and even the prospect of 'roughing it' a little.

So the next morning, with his few belongings stowed away in a small bag,—the portmanteau had been discarded in Liverpool,—he set out on his walk The natural energy of his character shone out strangely every now and then, in spite of the disastrous education which had so cramped it. No one meeting him that day, as he walked briskly along the Devonshire lanes, would have imagined that he was as poor as the veriest tramp, and had infinitely fewer resources than most beggars. His stern face was lighted up with resolute perseverance, there was a sparkle, not exactly of enjoyment, but of keen determination, in his eye, he held his head just as proudly as in the days when he had been Donovan Farrant, Esq., of Oakdene Manor.

It was a lovely July day, a little hot for walking certainly, especially in the deep lanes where every breath of air seemed to be shut out; but there was something satisfactory about the whole excursion, and Donovan walked on steadily. The high hedges were in their full beauty—beautiful as only Devonshire hedges can be, with their broad green fringes of harts-tongues, their drooping lady ferns and sturdy bracken, their glorious wild roses and bramble bushes, with here and there a bit of mossy grey stone cropping out, or a miniature waterfall thrusting its silvery white head through the grasses, and tumbling with splash and splutter into the tiny wayside brook below. The smell of the new-mown hay gave a country fragrance to the air, and in most of the fields the men and women were hard at work, while wisps of sun-dried grass caught here and there on each side of the road proved that loaded waggons had already passed that way, leaving their trophies on the hedges.

Donovan had made up his mind to sleep at Chagford, and it was already late when he crossed Fingle Bridge. The view there was so exquisite, however, that he was obliged to stop for a few minutes. Resting on the grey stone parapet, he looked down at the transparently clear river, along the green meadows and wooded valleys to the hills which, encircling all, stood out clearly defined against the soft evening sky. All was quiet and peaceful; in this country stillness and exquisite beauty, it seemed possible almost to realise that once all the world had been pronounced 'very good.' Donovan thought only, however, of the contrast of this peace with the world of competition, the overcrowded market of labourers in which he was trying to push his way. It was with a sigh that he turned away and walked on to the little grey town of Chagford, where the lights were beginning to shine out from the cottage windows, and the square tower of the church stood darkly above the lower roofs, a grim silent guardian.

Very early the next day he was on his way again, exulting in the fresh morning air, and greatly looking forward to the crossing of the moor. Waif scampered on in front, enjoying the exercise as much as his master, and Donovan found himself whistling as he walked. At length, leaving the cultivated region behind him, he struck across the wild waste of Dartmoor, and then the full delights of his walk came to him. The freshest, purest, strongest air in England was blowing in his face, his feet were treading a springy elastic soil, and all around him was a scene of the wildest beauty. The heather was not yet out, but the gorse blossoms still lingered, and made a golden glow over the great undulating expanse, while all round the tors raised their rugged, granite heads, now in full sunshine silvery white, now with a passing cloud shadow darkest purple—grotesque, fancifully shaped, irregular, and yet exactly harmonizing with the barren waste surrounding them.

On sped the dog and his master, now through marshy ground, springing from one tuft of heather to another, now up across the scattered granite blocks of a tor, and down again into a fresh-featured waste on the other side, now startling a troop of the wild Dartmoor ponies which galloped away, their manes flying in the wind, and Waif barking at their heels, now stepping across one of the old British encampments with their imperishable 'hut circles.'

It was not till about five in the afternoon that he reached Prince Town, and then for the time his pleasure was clouded, for the first sight that greeted him was the great grey block of buildings where poor Noir Frewin had been unjustly immured. Passing some wretched little black cottages which are familiarly known as New London, he went down the hill to the town itself, on the way encountering a gang of convicts dragging a cart, and guarded by two warders, rifle in hand. The sight was a painful one ; the men, half patient, half sullen, looked at him curiously and envyingly ; the warders urged them on.

Donovan had half thought of sleeping at Prince Town. He

had been walking since seven o'clock that morning, and was rather tired, but the gloom of the place so oppressed him that he could not endure the thought of staying in it. He selected instead the cheapest looking public-house from the large number which the little place offered, had his dinner, and after a short rest prepared to go on again. The people of the house in vain tried to induce him to stay. He was not to be turned from his purpose, however, and having learnt that he could put up for the night at the 'Dousland Barn Inn,' if he went by the road, or at Sheepstor, if he went by the moor, he resolved to take the latter course.

By this time it was between six and seven in the evening, but he calculated that in even ordinary walking he should reach his destination before dusk, and with the bold outline of Sheepstor before him as a landmark, he steered his way across the waste. There was something awe-inspiring in the entire loneliness as he passed on further from Prince Town. Far and near not a creature, not a house was to be seen. Beauty, grandeur, even a faint shadow of the Infinite, who can fail to trace these in that glorious moor, unique in its wildness and expanse?

Involuntarily Donovan fell into a deep reverie. The purer, nobler view of the world forced itself upon him; he had seen hitherto so little but the evil. And then naturally his thoughts went back to Dot, as they invariably did in his best moments, and he comforted himself in that terribly insufficient and yet pathetic way which Byron has expressed in one of his saddest poems.

> The better days of life are ours;
> The worst can be but mine:
> The sun that cheers, the storm that lowers
> Shall never more be thine.

He had been walking on abstractedly; looking up at last, he was dismayed to find that a sudden mist had arisen, completely veiling the surrounding tors, and, what was worse, evidently spreading every minute. Here was a hindrance which he had never for a moment contemplated. The evening had seemed quite fine when he started; he had no compass, and had trusted implicitly to his eye in choosing the most direct route to Sheepstor. Now all traces of the tors were obliterated.

It was not a very pleasant prospect. All manner of stories he had heard of travellers lost in the mist recurred to his memory, dismal tales of people who had wandered round and round in a circle for hours, never many yards distant from their starting-point, or of unfortunate pedestrians overcome by fatigue and cold. He stood still for a minute or two, called Waif to heel, and steadily faced the facts of the case. The mist was rolling nearer and nearer, hemming him in on every side; even now he could hardly see a yard in front of him! Although it was a July evening, the cold was enough to make him shiver, the mist pressed down on him impenetrably, every breath he drew brought him into closer contact with the heavy damp chill fog. Standing still was out of the question; he resolved to go on. Sheepstor lay, he thought, rather to his left, and, as he had heard that the natural instinct in walking was to tend towards the right, he took a very decided course in the opposite direction.

On and on he went, ceaselessly but almost hopelessly on. He was growing very tired, too, the mist hung heavily upon him, he could not see an inch before his feet. Fearing that Waif might possibly stray, he had taken him up under his arm, and was plodding heavily along when he came to marshy ground. For three or four steps he floundered on, trying to regain the firm land, but what might have been done with sight was impossible in the blinding mist. Another step and he felt himself sinking deeper—a fierce struggle to free himself, and in a moment he was up to his knees in one of the treacherous Dartmoor bogs.

He uttered no invectives, but, when convinced of the hopelessness of struggling out, he drew Waif's head up so that he could look into the clear brown eyes.

'Waif, old boy,' he said, 'mother earth means to settle the question for us. Do you feel inclined to have done with your master, your bones, and biscuits, and wanderings?'

The dog, evidently understanding the danger, set up a howl so wildly piteous that Donovan's heart was touched.

'Poor old fellow, you'd rather go on, would you?'

And for a minute they looked full into each other's eyes with the strange comprehension that comes between some dogs and some men. Then Waif licked his master's face, and Donovan, all the time feeling that he was gradually sinking deeper, patted the white and tan head.

'Very well, Waif, as you say, we'll have a try. Take my hat, old boy,' and he put his soft cloth hat into the dog's mouth, 'scrunch it up, never mind! a hundred to one I shall never want it again! find a man if you can and bring him back here, do you understand? now go. There!' and with some effort he threw the dog as far from him as possible, and Waif, alighting where his trifling weight might be borne, tore off like the wind with the hat between his teeth.

In throwing the dog Donovan felt the soft ground beneath him sink considerably, an irresistible force sucked him down lower and lower, very soon he was up to his waist in the cold wet mud. Then he spread out both his arms and waited quietly for the end—whichever end it was to be.

He felt strangely indifferent. If death did come to him, why, then it would be well; if he was rescued, there would be the satisfaction of not being conquered by the affection of good mother earth, who, having dealt rather coldly with him all the days of his life, now seemed determined to hold him in a clinging embrace.

His jacket was not fastened, he could see three buttons of his waistcoat. With a sort of grim sense of the ludicrous he resolved to use them as a measuring gauge, by which he could judge how fast he was sinking. It was bitterly cold down in this wet slush; on the whole, he rather looked forward to the end. What was that odd recollection that came to him? He was a little child again, and Doery's prim face rose before him.

'Asleep in church, Master Donovan! oh! for shame! I wonder you wasn't afraid you'd never open your eyes in this world again.'

And in spite of his strange position, even now he could not help laughing as he recalled his childish sense of discomfort, and how for several Sundays after that he had not been able to let his eyelids drop in peace.

The first button disappeared.

Then he wandered on to recollections of his life with the Frewins. How they would wonder what had become of him! He was back in Drury Lane with Sweepstakes abusing him. He was in a railway carriage, and Noir was waving the cards before his eyes in the three-card trick. He was sitting in the park and a bright-faced girl near him was talking of home, the sort of home which he had never been able to realise.

The second button disappeared.

Then he felt a strange impression of having been through this scene before, of having felt the cold wall of mist hemming him in, and after a time he remembered it had been in his nightmare about Dot. And over and over the words rang in his ears;

The better days of life were ours
The worst can be but mine.

'You are safe, Dot, my darling. "'Tis nothing that I loved so well." I would not have you back even to the days that were ours. And the worst may be over for me, Dot, ended here out on Dartmoor!'

The third button disappeared.

'I wish I had not gone to that billiard-room,' he mused, 'I wish I could have died satisfied at least that my will was as strong as I used to think it. To fail! how hateful it is to fail! If I thought that I could get on, and not come to grief again so weakly, I should almost wish to get out of this bog and have another try.'

The mist had now rolled away, but it was almost dark and the stars were shining above him. The night wind blew through his hair, waved the cotton grass growing around him, sighed and moaned over the desolate country. Nature sang him her dreariest death-song. Ah, well! death could not be more dreary than his life had been!

By this time he was up to his shoulders, and was obliged to raise his arms, the grass and rushes blew against his face. It was exceedingly unlikely that Waif would find help. In a very short time he must inevitably die. What a strange ending to his stormy life! strange and yet perhaps not inappropriate, to die here alone in the darkness, as he had lived, the grandeur and beauty and majesty of the great moor close to him, all around, but shrouded in the black night, faint imperfect images of the beautiful tors presented to him now and then, but never a true idea of their form.

By-and-by came a light, flickering wavering far in the distance. Was it a Will o' the wisp? Could he hold out any longer? Could he keep rigidly motionless till this possible help should reach him? A sort of dogged endurance and hatred of yielding came to renew his failing powers, his voice clear and strong rang out into the night. Yet why did he call? why did he not yield, and sink down quietly into nothingness? For an instant life and death, the chances of each, hung in a perfectly even balance, and his indifference turned to a decided wish for the end of the struggle. Should he call again? he thought not. But just as he was making his final resolution to keep the silence which would inevitably lead to death, he heard Waif's sharp anxious bark from afar.

'My dog, I won't be such a selfish brute,' he exclaimed, realising Waif's faithful devotion, and thinking of his despair if the search should be of no use. 'Ho! here! help!' and then, with his usual whistle, he tried to attract the dog's notice.

In a few minutes Waif was close to him, whining with delight, snorting with impatience, and tearing madly backwards and forwards between the approaching lantern and his submerged master. Then the bearer of the lantern came into view, a sturdy

Devonshire farmer, and his almost equally sturdy son. Donovan hailed them eagerly.

'Veth!' exclaimed the farmer, 'stogg'd in Foxtor Mire that ye are!'

'Set fast here for hours,' said Donovan.

'No tanny bye! (*don't tell me!*)' exclaimed the good man, much shocked. 'But we'd best talk when the deed's dune. The missus she says to me, "Maister, you take the laistest bit o' rope with ye, likely it's a bog accident." So lay ye hold, my man, fast hold o' the end, and veth! we'll sune have ye safe and dry. Hold on, my man, and sure as my name's John Peek we'll have ye safe.'

Then, with a tremendous effort, the sturdy Devonshire men pulled at the rope till Donovan's shoulders were free once more. After that they hastily threw a noose round him, and with infinite difficulty succeeded at length in dragging him from his slimy grave.

In a few minutes Donovan, encrusted in black mud, and so stiff and weary that he could hardly drag himself along, was safely on terra firma once more, and Waif, proud and happy, was springing about his feet.

Partly from physical causes, and partly from his sudden removal from the near contemplation of death, he fell into a half dreamy state, was not sure whether the sturdy farmer and his son were not after all shadows, even doubted whether Waif was not an illusion, while every weary step he took seemed to add to his strange indifference as to what was to become of him. If left to himself he would have plodded on and on till he dropped.

But John Peek was at his elbow—he was too muddy to be touched—piloting him across the moor in the direction of the farm, talking in his half unintelligible Devonshire dialect, and at length leading him through the yard gate, across the roughly-paved granite road to the little white farm-house where he lived. At the sound of their footsteps the wife hastened out, a comely Devonshire woman, her short skirt, crossed neckerchief, smooth hair, and healthy-looking face, all as fresh and neat as could be. The husband explained matters, and Donovan was hurried into the kitchen, where, what with the warmth of the peat fire, the contrast between his horrible state of filth and the exquisite cleanliness of the place, added to the extreme difficulty of understanding the dialect of the farmer and his wife, he gradually came to himself, realised that he was actually alive, that his surroundings were no shadowy phantoms of the imagination, that he was still Donovan Farrant, possessed of little but a dog and a will which had failed, and with a blank future beyond, in which his primary object must be—not to starve.

In the immediate present, however, his only wish was to be clean once more, and with some difficulty he made himself understood. Evidently the farmer's wife thought cleanliness next to godliness, and fully sympathised with the desire.

'Zich a jakes (*such a mess*) as never was seen, fit to make my flesh crip, ess fay it is! Come ye up, zur, come ye up over the stairs,' and the good woman led the way up the spotless staircase to a room above, where, with much ado, she brought a huge wooden washing tub, hot water, an enormous piece of soap, even a scrubbing-brush, crowning all her favours by fetching him an entire set of her husband's clothes!

Cincinnatus handled the plough, and doubtless wore the equivalent for fustian. History does not relate how he looked in rustic guise, but Donovan, with his ' Roman' face and unmistakeable air of refinement, presented a very comical appearance in Farmer Peek's marketing costume. But the comfort of being dry and clean again was great, and he joined the farmer and his family in the kitchen, feeling able to speak the thanks for his rescue which till now had remained unsaid.

'And now zet down, zur, zet down, for ye luke mortal vagg'd,' said the farmer, drawing up one of the Windsor chairs to the hearth. ' Likely ye had a gude walk before ye got stogg'd i' the mire ? '

'Yes, from Chagford,' said Donovan, stretching his feet out to the smouldering peats.

'No tanny bye! on the trat the whole blessed day!' exclaimed the wife, ' and ye luke crewel tender.'

He laughed and disclaimed any 'tenderness.'

'Zich walks isn't for the likes of ye,' said the farmer, with a shrewd look at the wearer of his market-day suit; ' ye should lave it to us pewer folk—it's not for gintry and passons.'

Donovan could not help smiling at finding himself classed with parsons.

'I am poor,' he said—' a tramp.'

'Aw!' exclaimed the farmer, shaking his head with a knowing smile, ' ye won't make us belave that, zur—no, no, us knows the gintry when we zee 'em.'

'In spite of which, I am poor and a tramp,' said Donovan, ' and what few things I had left went down into Foxtor Mire!'

'Ah, gude heaven!' exclaimed the wife, 'it was a mercy ye didn't go yurself; but what will ye plase to take for zupper, zur ? there's cream i' the dairy, and——'

'Whatever you would have for yourselves, nothing else,' said Donovan.

The woman hesitated; he spoke as if he meant to be obeyed, but her hospitable soul longed to set the best things in the house before the hero of the evening.

'Veth, zur, it's not fitty for zich as ye,' she began, but Donovan interrupted her.

'Nothing else, thank you,' and his tone, more than the actual words, convinced the good woman that nothing but the usual supper must be prepared.

So Donovan sat down with the farmer and his wife to broth and 'kettle-bread,' and then, at his own request, was allowed to establish himself for the night before the fire, for, in spite of the summer evening, he had been so thoroughly chilled that he was glad of the warmth.

Before long all was quiet in the house; Donovan, with Waif at his feet, lay very still but very much awake in the little kitchen. By this time all might have been over for him—how strange was the thought; He might have entered on the 'peace of nothingness'—life might have been over, perplexities solved by the great silence, no trace of him left even, to carry sorrow to his mother, or remorse to Ellis. And, instead of this, he was still in the world, lying on his back moralising by the light of a peat fire !

It was a curious accident which had brought him like this under a hospitable roof; he had been in many odd places, but never in quite such a homely place as this. Half dreamily he let his eyes wander round the white-washed walls. Opposite him was the tall eight-day clock, and a large copper warming-pan reflecting the dull red glow of the fire—above the high mantel-shelf two rather ancient-looking guns, and a great array of tin pots and platters—below, a spotless white dimity frill hanging over the wide hearth—overhead, in the black rafters, hung sundry hams.

His own clothes were hanging up to dry as near the peat as the farmer's wife would allow, and glancing from them to the borrowed garments he wore, and for the first time realising that Farmer Peek was at least six inches shorter and immeasurably stouter than himself, that the fustian clothes hung about him in folds and that his whole appearance was most grotesque, he burst out laughing—laughed till the wooden rafters rang, till Waif started up and began to wag his tail sympathetically, till inevitably he would have roused the farmer and his wife, had they not slept as soundly as the Seven Sleepers. Certainly the personal danger he had been in had not awed him as a moralist might have desired. He went to sleep with nothing more sober in his thoughts than a verse out of Dot's 'Nonsense Book'—

There was an old man of the West
Who wore a pale plum-coloured vest;
When they asked—does it fit?
He replied, not a bit,
That funny old man of the West.

The next morning came the humiliating necessity of explaining to the farmer his inability to reward him for his rescue and his hospitality. He was received, however, with all the delightful warm-heartedness and real courtesy so general in the west country.

'Aw! zur, ye didn't think a wanted money! It's treu us a given ye the laistest bit of a help, but God bless ye, zur, us has been plased to du it.'

'When I get on in the world, I shall not forget you, Mr. Peek,' said Donovan, with firm confidence in the 'when.' 'All I can do now is to thank you very much for your hospitality.'

'Veth, zur, you're welcome. Us wull be plased to zee ye again, and I wish ye weel in zaking zarvice.'

'Seeking service!' Donovan smiled, but the expression was true enough. He wished his worthy host good-bye, managed to leave his last coin—half-a-crown—in the market-day coat, and set off briskly on his fourteen-mile walk to Plymouth.

Skirting round the foot of Sheepstor, he was soon on the road, with the bold outlines of Sharpitor and Leathertor on one hand, and far in the distance a line of silvery brightness where the sunlight fell on the sea. Life felt good. On the whole, he felt really glad that the blue vault was above him, not the black mud of the bog. Towards the afternoon, however, when he had been walking some hours, his spirits sank. The heat tried him a good deal; he began to feel very stiff and tired, as well he might after his adventure of the previous evening. And with the physical exhaustion came a degree less of confidence in the future. What if his father's acquaintance, Mr. X——, refused to help him? What if he could find no employment now? He walked on heavily, but still with resolution—come ill or well, he was ready to face it manfully, but his cheerfulness disappeared, and it was a stern-faced and very oddly-dressed candidate who presented himself at the door of the bank, and asked to see Mr. X——, the manager.

The bank was closed, but one of the clerks appeared in answer to his ring, and directed him to the manager's private house. He went there, and, with the bearing of a proud man forced to ask a favour, was shown into Mr. X——'s library.

A handsome keen-faced man of about five-and-thirty was sitting at the table writing. He glanced up as Donovan was announced, scanned him from head to foot without rising, then bowed stiffly. This was Donovan's view.

Mr. X——, on the other hand, saw before him a tall, gaunt, handsome fellow, apparently about five-and-twenty, in clothes which were stained and shrunk to such a degree that a tramp would scarcely have said 'thank you' for them, holding a ragged cloth hat in his hand, and, in spite of his beggarly array, carrying his head very high. Such a shabby-looking fellow as this could hardly be asked to sit down on one of Mr. X——'s new red-morocco chairs. The good farmer's wife had carefully dusted the Windsor chair for him the night before, the banker was not so courteous or so well-bred. Throughout the interview Donovan stood.

The banker briefly asked his business. It appeared that the elder Mr. X—— had died two years before; the present one had never heard of Colonel Farrant. And then, after a few mutual explanations, Mr. X——'s rather quick peremptory manner became a little more suave as he said,

'You must, I think, see, Mr. Farrant, that your claims upon me are of the very slightest. Our respective fathers knew each other—at least, you tell me so. Even should I take you at your word without seeking to prove this to be the fact, however, it is hardly sufficient ground for—in short, you understand me, I am sure. I need not explain myself further.'

'I quite understand,' said Donovan, coldly. 'You think I am come to beg. I am aware that I look like a beggar, thanks to one of your Devonshire bogs; but nothing is further from my thoughts. You were the only person I knew in the neighbourhood. I want work, and thought you might be able to advise me where to try for it.'

'I am afraid, Mr. Farrant, you are a novice in these matters,' said the banker. 'One cannot at a moment's notice cause situations to spring up ready to hand. Besides, in the letter I received from you from Exeter you gave me no particulars and no references.'

'I have none to give,' said Donovan, shortly.

'You can at least tell me what your previous employment has been.'

'I have only just returned from the Continent.'

The banker looked at him a little curiously.

R

'And before that?'

Donovan coloured slightly, but answered, firmly,

'Before that I was a card-sharper.'

The banker started.

'Bless me! and after this you expect me to patronise you, Mr. Farrant?'

'On the contrary,' said Donovan, quietly, 'I see plainly that that is the last thing you will do.'

There was irony in the tone; the banker smiled a little, looked again at his strange visitor, and saw that, in spite of the beggarly array, he was evidently a clever fellow. He liked clever fellows, and his next remark sounded much more cordial, but Donovan's sensitive pride at once recoiled from the slight touch of vulgarity.

'I see you're sharp enough, Mr. Farrant; no lack of brains. But even if I knew of any situation likely to suit you, what guarantee should I have that you might not prove a little *too* sharp again?'

'No guarantee,' said Donovan, wincing. 'But I should hardly have answered your question with such perfect openness if I had been the knave you take me for. I can give you no guarantee but my honour.'

'And in business that would hardly answer,' said Mr. X——, with a sharp-edged smile; 'besides, the honour of an ex——'

'Good afternoon,' said Donovan, moving to the door.

'Stay, stay,' said the banker, 'that was rather hard lines. I can't help you to a situation, Mr. Farrant, but you seem in a very bad way, and as I see you're a clever fellow I will break through my ordinary rule. Day and Martin made their fortunes by giving away a stray sovereign, and, though I can hardly hope to do that, I have still great pleasure in giving you some small assistance.'

He fumbled in his pocket, produced a gold coin, and pressed it into his visitor's hand.

There are some deeds of so-called 'charity' which wound more deeply than actual unkindness, some favours which are more hard to endure than blows, some ways of giving so intolerable to the recipient that even in need they must be rejected.

Donovan was actually penniless, he felt stiff, weary, ill, and already very hungry, but no power on earth could have brought him to accept the banker's tactless, ill-bred offer. He put down the sovereign, bowed, and hurried out of the house.

For a time indignation and those heart-stirrings which follow

after an insult has been received kept him up. He tramped up
and down the Hoe physically strong again because of the inward
tumult of feeling. Then he wandered into the town, lounged
wearily about the streets,

Homeless near a thousand homes,

and worse than homeless, destitute in every way, sick at heart,
ashamed of his past, miserable in the present, and hopeless as to
the future.

When St. Andrew's clock struck nine, he was standing at the
corner of the churchyard idly watching the passers-by, wishing
that night would come that he might hide himself in the darkness
and forget his weariness in sleep. But as time passed he grew
more and more uneasy, and the dread of illness began to haunt
him painfully. He had certainly eaten nothing since early morning, but that was not sufficient to account for the growing faintness which was stealing over him. He had had a dim idea of
enlisting, but that faded away now, he was too wretched to wish
for anything but shelter for the night, precisely the thing he had
not.

There were only three alternatives, either he must break his
resolution again and trust to his customary skill and good fortune,
or he must try to sell Waif, or he must adopt the beggar's shelter
—an arch or a doorway.

A sharp struggle was needed to dismiss the first idea, the merest
glance at the dog to prove the second impossible; then in pain
and great weariness he wandered on once more. Only a month or
two before he had had more money than he knew what to do with—
it was strange to look back to the old life, with its excitement and
success and self-indulgence—and now, through his own doing,
he was cut off from it all. But he knew that it was well, and in
a larger sense than before the words which had haunted him on
Dartmoor came to him now,

The worst can be but mine.

Failure, pain, ruin, starvation, all these were apparently his
destiny; he felt that they were endurable because they involved
no harm to others; it had been a choice of life and pleasure at
the expense of his honour and his fellow-men, and death and
suffering affecting himself alone. His contact with the world
had changed his views greatly; a year ago he had been a misanthrope, now he saw the position of self and others inverted.

More than four years had gone by since the grave-looking Indian colonel and his son had passed up the steps of the Royal Hotel. Donovan, fresh from his school disgrace, full of hurt pride and bitter resentment, had spent no very comfortable night there. Unlikely as it may seem, he slept a great deal better beneath the porch of one of the neighbouring houses than he had done before in the luxurious room. With Waif crouched up as near him as possible for the sake of warmth, with the cold night wind blowing on him, he slept well. In the old times he had been his own slave, now he was 'lord of himself.' Disheartened, humbled, with widened sympathies and self thrust low, he was now, in spite of the verdict of the president, a truer follower of Christ than some professing Christians, the only difference being that he followed bravely and painfully in the darkness, not even knowing his goal, while many of them in their full light follow sleepily and lazily, attaining to little of the broad-hearted love and self-abnegation to which they have pledged themselves.

Donovan did not dream, he was too completely worn out. His sleep was heavy and unbroken; but he woke early the next morning with a name in his mind—Porthkerran. What brought it there he could not tell. In thinking over his acquaintance in the West at Exeter, he had naturally remembered the Tremains, but it seemed improbable that a doctor in a remote Cornish village would be able to help him to work, and he had never thought even of applying to him. But now, in the freshness of the July day, as he dragged himself up from his resting-place, and felt the impossibility of seeking work in his present state, the thought of Porthkerran, of the kindly doctor, of Mrs. Tremain, came to him as a light in his darkness. He was at that stage of illness when pride—even the pride of independence—is brought low, and, though he had rejected the banker's sovereign but a few hours before, the idea of going to the Tremains and asking their help did not seem hard to him.

The only question was, should he ever get there? To loiter about in Plymouth in search of work would be both useless and impossible, but with an actual goal, a definite thing to be done, it was different. He made up his mind to go, and set off on the long walk patiently and deliberately, though anyone with a degree less of courage and resolution would have succumbed at once.

When he had walked about five or six miles the full difficulties of his undertaking came to him. On first waking he had felt ill indeed, but the sleep had to some extent refreshed him, and it was not till later in the morning that the unknown pains of hunger beset him. Still he toiled on, always on, with aching head and failing limbs, while above the summer sun blazed down on him in fullest power. What if the Tremains were no longer at Porthkerran? What if they turned him away because of his previous life, or his religious views? These were his only thoughts as he struggled on. By-and-by came faintness, and he was obliged to stagger to the side of the road and lie down on the grass, and then he lost count of time, and was very dimly aware that the intolerable heat and glare changed to cloudy coolness. It was not till a heavy shower of rain began that he came fully to himself, staggered to his feet once more, and resumed his walk.

For more than an hour the rain fell ceaselessly; when it stopped, he was soaked to the skin and very cold. Even when the sun came out once more he was shivering from head to foot. How much further could he manage? A sign-post, with ' Porthkerran three miles,' rather comforted him; he must and would get there, and once more he forced himself to go forward.

The road lay now along the cliffs overlooking the deep blue sea. Donovan scarcely noticed anything, however, and it was not till the ringing clang of metal fell upon his ear that he looked up. By the side of the road was a blacksmith's forge; the blazing fire looked tempting; he entered the shed, and asked leave to warm himself.

The smith, a fine-looking man, with thick black hair tinged with grey, and eyes of deep blue like the Cornish seas, turned round quickly on hearing himself addressed.

' Come in, friend, and welcome.'

The voice was a hearty one, but the smith was busy, and turned to his hammer and anvil once more, while Donovan drew near to the fire, and felt a little temporary relief from the warmth.

Presently wheels were heard, and a carriage stopped at the door; the smith put down his hammer and stepped briskly forward.

' Well, doctor—gude day to you—cast his shue, has he?'

Donovan heard the words distinctly, but they conveyed no meaning to his mind. He stared down vacantly into the glowing furnace, not even turning his head to see either the horse or the driver. A man's voice was explaining.

' Half-a-mile back, Trevethan. How long will you take to put him on a fresh one? I'm in a hurry to be at Mr. Penruddock's.'

' Slow and sure, doctor—not less nor a quarter hour, and maybe more.'

'Why don't you walk to the Penruddocks', papa? I can hold Star, and Ajax is so quiet there'll be no fear of his doing any harm.'

It was a girl's mellow voice speaking—a voice in which there lurked laughter, tenderness, and yet a quaint sort of dignity. Donovan recognized it in a moment, and with a sudden return of strength and energy hurried to the door.

CHAPTER XXL

ONE AND ALL.

Deal meekly, gently, with the hopes that guide
The lowliest brother straying from thy side;
If right, they bid thee tremble for thine own,
If wrong, the verdict is for God alone.

. . . .

Strive with the wanderer from the better path,
Bearing thy message meekly, not in wrath:
Weep for the frail that err, the weak that fall,
Have thine own faith, but hope and pray for all.
OLIVER WENDELL HOLMES.

ONE glance at the little group without told him everything. There was the smith scrutinizing Star's shoeless foot; standing beside the other pony was Dr. Tremain himself, a little greyer than he had been four years ago, but not much altered; and in the pony-carriage sat Donovan's ideal, whom he knew now to be Miss Tremain—Gladys Tremain—for the unusual name recurred to his memory with the thought of the evening when he had first seen her in her own home, had heard her singing words which had moved him strangely.

With this sudden revelation, all thought of his present state of need passed from his mind; he only felt that he must do something for her, and with a word to the smith he went to Star's head.

'Ah! that'll du, doctor, now ye can go up to Squire Penruddock's. Here's a chap as'll hold the pony steady.'

Instinctively Donovan kept his face turned from Dr. Tremain, he could not bear to risk being recognized just then. The doctor saw only a tall figure in very shabby clothes—some friend of Trevethan's, he supposed; he merely glanced at him, told Gladys to drive on to meet him when the pony was shod, and walked away in the direction from which Donovan had just come.

The wind had risen, a west wind, and it blew strongly, though not coldly. Donovan could see the ribbons on Gladys' hat fluttering, though, after the first, he did not directly look at her, but kept his face half hidden. He could hear her talking to Trevethan, and once or twice some antic of Star's made her laugh. She was evidently a favourite with the blacksmith. Donovan could see how the man's blue eyes lit up when she spoke to him.

Gladys, meanwhile, looked curiously at the motionless figure at Star's head. She had seen him as he came out of the shed, but for such a moment that she had only caught a sort of vision of a very pale, worn face. Who could he be? Some one whom Trevethan knew, or merely a tramp? Yet his attire was scarcely like a tramp's; shrunk, and stained, and dirty as it was, it had a look of better days about it. Who was he? She wished he had not been quite so near, for it was impossible to ask the blacksmith any questions about him. Ought she to give him something for holding the pony? Looking at him again, she was sure that he was visibly shivering, and that decided her. She opened her purse, and took out a sixpence. He looked ill, and cold, and very poor. He had been very good in holding Star, assuredly he ought to have something.

All this time she had only seen his back. When the shoeing was finished, and Trevethan had been paid, she drew up the reins, and rather shyly said, 'Thank you for your help,' holding out the coin to him as she spoke.

Oddly, though she had been rather curious to see his face, in putting the sixpence into his hand she looked at that; then, startled to find a smooth white palm instead of a hand roughened by hard work, she looked up quickly and saw a face which seemed partly familiar to her, a face with chiselled features, and dark cavernous eyes with a look of pain in them. But even as she first glanced at him his lips smiled slightly, he raised his hat.

'Oh, I beg your pardon! I did not see,' she stammered, looking at the slender fingers which had closed over her sixpence, and colouring crimson.

'Thank you,' he replied, in a tone which she could not mistake for sarcasm. 'I am very much obliged to you.'

Then he raised his hat again, and turned away, and Gladys drove off with hot cheeks. Where *had* she seen him before?

Donovan went back to the forge, partly for the sake of warming himself, partly in the hope of learning something about the

Tremains. The blacksmith was busy, however, and he could only elicit the information that 'that was their doctor up to Porthkerran, and a rale gude one he was;' that 'Miss Gladys did gude to everyone she spoke to, and was like a bit of God's sunshine, and no mistake,' with a few other most patent and obvious facts. Then, all the time swinging his great hammer, Trevethan began singing one of Wesley's hymns, and, before he had come to the end, the pony-carriage passed the door once more.

'Will the doctor be going home now?' asked Donovan, as soon as he could make himself heard.

'Yes, belike,' said the blacksmith, pausing in his work, and looking at his companion. 'You'd du weel, friend, to go and see him, for you look mortal vagg'd. If you're passin' this way again, come and take your tae with me. You shall have a gude welcome.'

'Thank you,' said Donovan, touched by the off-hand yet real hospitality.

Then, Trevethan having directed him to the doctor's house, which he already knew well enough, he set off once more.

Before he had gone far, a turn in the road brought him in sight of the Tremains' pony-carriage. It was standing still. Drawing nearer, he saw Gladys standing, bare-headed, on the verge of the cliff, her sunny hair blowing about in the wind. She seemed to be searching for something. Dr. Tremain, holding the reins at arm's length, was also peering down.

'Better give it up, my dear,' Donovan heard him say. 'We couldn't reach it, even if we could see it.'

'Can I be of any use?' asked Donovan, coming towards the two. 'Is anything lost?'

'My hat,' said Gladys, turning round, but colouring as she saw who the speaker was.

Donovan's quick eyes were soon scanning every nook and cranny of the rugged cliff, and, after a minute's steady progress up and down, he detected far below a tiny moving speck, which he pronounced to be an end of ribbon.

'Will you allow me to fetch it for you?' he asked, forgetting his weakness and weariness in his desire to serve her.

'Oh, no, it is so far down,' she said quickly. 'It is not the least worth while.'

But Donovan was not to be deterred from the errand by its difficulty, and, disregarding Dr. Tremain's remonstrances, he began to clamber down the cliff in a way which showed that he was either well used to the Cornish coast or else an expert gymnast.

'He held Star just now at the forge, said Gladys to her father. 'And I am sure I have seen him before, papa. Who can he be?'

The doctor was too intent on watching the descent, however, to answer, and when he did speak it was only to exclaim,

'Well done! he's got it.' And then to criticise his way of setting about the ascent. 'Quite right, he means to keep to the left, and skirt round that great boulder. Bravo! that was cleverly managed. Come, Gladys, after this you'll have to make a speech. It's really very good of this young fellow. Hullo! though—he's slipped.'

For Donovan had trusted to an insecure foothold, and had slipped down about six feet. Gladys gave a little cry, but happily a projecting boulder prevented any danger of a serious fall, and the two watchers saw that at least their helper was in no immediate peril. He was quite still, though; that began to frighten them.

'Are you hurt?' shouted the doctor.

But no answer came, and the figure still remained crouched up in the same position. Dr. Tremain felt very uneasy, but in two or three minutes Gladys gave a relieved exclamation.

'See, papa, he moves, he is getting up again.' They could see the tall figure struggling up, indeed, but the doctor saw at once that something was wrong.

'Are you hurt?' he shouted once more.

'Yes,' came back the answer, 'but I'll manage it in a minute.'

He had fallen with his ankle twisted under him, and had given it a sprain. It was indeed a very awkward situation, for the cliff was steep and hard to climb, and now, with the acute pain he was suffering, it seemed almost impossible; he looked at the little white hat hanging on his arm, and he looked up the grey cliff to Gladys. After all, it only needed patience and a resolute disregard of the pain—he would try it. But it was infinitely harder than he had supposed; over and over again he turned dizzy, and was obliged to pause, and at last each step became a battle. He could not attempt to answer the questions which reached him from above, every power was trained to its utmost in the physical struggle, in the conflict between the resolutely persevering 'I will,' and the overwhelming pain and weakness and difficulty.

At length, with an almost superhuman effort, he dragged himself up to the top, grasped the doctor's outstretched hands, crawled on to the smooth grassy plateau bordering the cliff, and,

without a word, sank down prone, while Waif, with low whines,
walked round and round him in great distress. Large drops of
perspiration stood on his forehead, yet his face expressed little
but hard fixed resoluteness, the iron will leaving its tokens even
in semi-consciousness. The doctor looked at him intently for a
moment, then he raised him so that his head rested on Gladys'
knee, and prepared to examine his ankle. The merest touch
caused a sharp thrill of pain, and Donovan opened his eyes.

'Oh, I am so very, very sorry,' said poor Gladys. 'I am
afraid you have hurt yourself dreadfully.'

'Only a sprain, I think,' he answered, faintly, and then his
eyes closed again.

'We must get him home as soon as possible,' said the doctor.
'I will bring up the pony-carriage as near as may be, and I
think, Gladys, you had better run back to the forge and ask
Trevethan to come and help. We shall be less likely to pain
him if there are two of us to lift him in.'

The doctor went to see to the pony-chaise, and Gladys was
just going to obey him, when she was startled by a peremptory
'No, don't go,' from the prostrate figure she was supporting.
Then, to her dismay, he slowly raised himself and staggered towards the carriage.

'You should not have tried it,' remonstrated the doctor,
helping him in, and making him put up his foot at once on the
opposite seat. 'Now, Gladys, jump in quickly and drive us
home. I shall sit here,' and he established himself beside the
injured ankle, holding it in a way which lessened the jar of the
wheels.

The last exertion had proved too much even for Donovan's
strength, however; he was only dimly conscious now, just
realizing from the pain that he was being driven somewhere,
where he neither knew nor cared, or whether this half dream of
incessant motion and incessant pain went on for ever and ever.
All seemed a matter of supreme indifference. When the carriage
at last stopped he felt no curiosity as to what was to follow, and,
after a few minutes' pause, submitted without a word to being
lifted out and borne *somewhere*, never once raising his eyelids
to see what they were doing with him. Presently he became
aware that his boot was being cut, and then came an instant's
sharp pain, and he fainted.

Everyone who has experienced it knows the extreme discomfort of a return to consciousness. Donovan came to quickly, however, partly aided by an odd association. The very first thing he
distinguished was the smell of brandy, then he felt a glass held

to his lips. From sheer annoyance he gained strength to push
it away, and, in weak but decidedly cross tones, said quickly,
'Get away with your abomination, Rouge! I tell you I
won't touch it!'

'Don't trouble him, he's coming to,' said the doctor, and
then Donovan, fully roused by the words, half raised himself and
looked round.

'I beg your pardon,' he said to the doctor, 'I thought I was
with someone else.'

'I am afraid I hurt you a good deal just now; I ought to
have seen you were getting faint and given you a restorative
first,' said Dr. Tremain.

'Faint!' cried Donovan, with all a man's dislike of making a
scene. 'You don't mean that I fainted.'

'Certainly, the moment I touched your foot,' said the doctor,
smiling; 'and, what is more, you will be fainting again before
long if you don't take something. Try this,' and he poured some
milk into a tumbler and held it to his lips.

Donovan drank it and revived a little.

'It was not the pain,' he said abruptly, 'I was half starved.'
Then glancing round the room, he continued in an odd, forced
voice, 'You shouldn't have brought me to your house. Is there
no workhouse or hospital at Porthkerran?'

'You shall consider this your hospital; I can promise you at
least one resident doctor and several nurses,' said Dr. Tremain,
smiling.

'Don't laugh,' said Donovan, 'it's no laughing matter. I
haven't a farthing in the world, I'm worse off than most beggars.
Couldn't you have seen by these that I wasn't fit for you to take
in?' and he touched his clothes.

'My dear fellow, do you think that makes any difference, or
that we show our hospitality in Cornwall by shipping off our
helpers to the workhouse? Come, don't talk nonsense, but tell
me when you had your last meal.'

'Yesterday morning between eight and nine.'

'Whew!' the doctor gave a slight whistle, felt his patient's
pulse again, and, turning to the servant, gave orders for some
gruel to be made at once. When that had been administered,
Donovan sank into a sort of doze. Presently, he knew that a
fresh voice was speaking, a low pleasant voice. He came to
that borderland of sleep when words begin to convey some
meaning, the quiet, mist-wreathed entrance to full consciousness.

'Has he got everything he wants?'

'Everything just now; he is simply worn out. Gladys has told you how we met him, I suppose.'

'Yes, everything. I wish I had been at home when you came back. Is it a very bad sprain?'

'I daresay it wasn't at first, but imagine climbing up the cliff near the forge after he'd done it! There's good in that fellow, depend upon it! It was a spirited thing to do, especially in the state he was in. He owned he was half starved.'

'Poor boy! I wonder how he happened to be in such straits.'

Donovan began to show signs of waking. The voices ceased, but he felt a soft hand putting back the hair from his forehead; it reminded him of the feel of little Dot's tiny fingers, and then, with a rush of shame, he felt how unfit he was for such tenderness.

Suddenly opening his eyes, and half sitting up, he said, quickly,

'Look, you must get me moved in some way, I'm not fit to stay here.'

Mrs. Tremain thought him feverish, but the doctor partly understood him.

'He is afraid of giving trouble; you must tell him there is nothing you like better than nursing.'

'No,' interrupted Donovan, 'that is not it; listen to me, and then, if you will—turn me out. You won't be the first who has done so. I was once a card-sharper. I haven't a penny in the world. I am an atheist. Was I wrong in saying you would be wiser if you turned me out of doors?'

'Quite wrong,' said the doctor, in an odd, quiet voice.

Then there was silence for a few minutes, and Donovan felt the soft woman's hand on his hair once more. For a moment he breathed hard, and there was a quiver in his voice when he said at last,

'I had given up expecting to be tolerated after that confession. I don't know why you are so different from other people. I might have guessed, though, that you would be. Mrs. Tremain,' he looked steadily up at her, 'do you remember me?'

She gazed at him in perplexity, half remembering the face, and yet unable to say where she had seen it. But after a minute or two a vision of the past flashed into her mind.

'Mr. Farrant!' she exclaimed.

'Donovan Farrant—yes.'

The doctor stood with an expression of surprise and great uneasiness on his face. If this were Donovan Farrant, how came

it that he was a penniless adventurer? How came it that little
more than a year after reaching his majority he had come to Porthkerran in a state of semi-starvation? There must have been foul
play somewhere. That will he had witnessed could not have been
properly executed, or such a state of things could not have been.
This evening, though, he must ask no questions, his patient was
not fit for it. So he put away the uncomfortable thoughts as well
as he could, and, coming forward, took Donovan's hand in his.

'I remember you very well now. I wonder I did not at first;
but you are a good deal changed. We have often thought of
you, and wondered whether you would ever come down to see
Porthkerran again. I was glad to have you before I knew your
name, and, knowing it, I am doubly glad. But now, as your
doctor, I must forbid any more talking. Some more food first,
and then you'd better settle in for the night.'

'One thing more,' said Donovan, 'do you realize that there
are two of us?' and he pointed to Waif. 'He's all I have in the
world. I can't part with him.'

'Not even last night when you were starving?'

Donovan shook his head.

'Perhaps, though, I ought not to ask you to take him in;
beggars can't be choosers.'

'My dear fellow,' said the doctor, laughing, and patting the
dog's head, 'will you never learn to believe that we are not utter
brutes? Of course, the dog is welcome to spend the rest of his
life here. I must quote the Cornish motto to you—"One and
all."'

With these words echoing in his ears, Donovan lay watching
the busy preparations for the night which were being made by
Mrs. Tremain and the servant. The room he had been carried to
was on the ground floor, a school-room, he fancied, but now busy
hands were converting it into a bed-room, and busy feet without
were hurrying up and down the stairs, and along the passages,
fetching and carrying. 'One and all'—they were certainly
carrying out their motto! And Donovan, who would have been
sorely chafed by having to submit to a grudging service,
watched his present nurses almost with pleasure. The comfort,
too, of being in a home-like room again was very great. He ran
through in his mind all the wretched places he had slept in, from
the room in Drury Lane to his last night's shelter under a porch.
Philosophically as he had endured them, it was, nevertheless, an
unspeakable comfort to be again where all was fresh and clean, a
relief, too, to be not in a mere living place, but a home. He
read the titles of the books in the bookshelf, then glanced round

the walls, half fearing to see once more his old enemy, the dingy oil-painting of the shipwreck. Instead, however, he found Wilkie's 'Blind Man's Buff,' next to that an elaborate chart of the kings of England, with illuminated shields and devices, which, no doubt, had been painted by Gladys; then a print of a 'Holy Family,' by Raphael, and, lastly, just opposite him, Ary Scheffer's 'Christ the Consoler.'

He looked at this long and earnestly, struck by the great beauty of the idea it embodied, and, through the wakeful feverish night which followed, the vision of the face of Christ and the thought of the Cornish motto haunted him incessantly.

The next day, the doctor not being at all satisfied with his patient's state, and being besides anxious to learn the reasons of his poverty, induced him to speak of his past life.

'You are not nearly so strong-looking as when I saw you last,' he began, drawing a chair up to the bedside. 'Tell me what you have been doing with yourself, and then, perhaps, I shall understand your case better.'

'It was four years ago that I saw you,' replied Donovan. 'It's likely enough I should be changed since then. Do you want the whole story?'

'As much as you feel inclined to tell,' said Dr. Tremain. 'Both as your friend and as your doctor I shall be glad to hear. After you left Porthkerran, you went to your home in Mount-shire, I believe?'

'Yes,' said Donovan, twisting a corner of the sheet as he spoke. 'We went back to Oakdene, and after about two years my mother married again—she married the man who was my guardian, Ellis Farrant. He came to my father's funeral. I daresay you remember him.'

Dr. Tremain tried not to show his dismay at this piece of news, and Donovan continued: 'He had always hated me, and there were constant quarrels between us; the final one would have come sooner if it had not been for my little sister. Partly for her sake I tried to behave decently to him. She died the winter before last. For a little while my step-father left me in peace, but directly I proposed entering some profession he told me I must expect nothing from him. That of course led to a quarrel, and in the end I was turned out upon the world to get on as best I could.'

'But your father's will?' questioned Dr. Tremain, trying to speak quietly.

'He left all to my mother, unconditionally, and of course she could do nothing for me, even if she wished to do so.'

The doctor sighed deeply, and there was a troubled look on his face as he glanced at his patient.

'Poor fellow! you have been hardly used. Where did you go to?'

'To London; but not one of our old friends would have a word to say to me, and I could get nothing to do. At last I fell in with a man named—well, never mind his name! he has been a good friend to me, even though he is a professional gambler. I went into partnership with him. It was impossible to live honestly, and I thought the other way would be bearable enough, for I was crazy at the injustice I had suffered, and hated everyone. But it didn't do. I found after a time I couldn't stand it. And then I went in for congestion of the lungs; that was last January. As soon as might be, I went abroad, but at Monaco had a relapse, which kept me back for another month. A little later, I found that I must break with my old friends and give up the sort of life I'd been living. I came back to England and tried hard to find work, and, by living cheaply, managed to spin out my money for a little while. I very nearly got a place as secretary at Exeter, but the man asked me point-blank what religious views I held, and that settled the question. I'd scarcely anything left then, but I made up my mind to come to Plymouth, and walked across Dartmoor. There I almost came to grief in a bog—it's a thousand pities I didn't quite—but Waif and a good Devonshire man hauled me out. The next day I came on to Plymouth, without a farthing, as I told you, and yesterday morning, being ill, either from the hours I spent in the bog, or from the unusual bed of stones, I felt only fit to crawl on to Porthkerran, hoping that you might help me.'

It was evidently a relief to him when he had finished his story, and the doctor, who had been pleased with his brief straightforward confession on the previous night, was glad that he still kept to the mere outline of his life. He never alluded to those personal thoughts and details which go to make up the interest of any life-story, never attempted to excuse himself in any way, but, with some effort, just stated the main facts.

Dr. Tremain sat in silence for a few minutes. That Donovan had been cruelly wronged, he knew, and the mere fact of that would have given him a special claim upon his love and sympathy. But the thought of his life, his rebuffs, his temptations, his fall, his efforts to do right, appealed even more strongly to the doctor's heart. 'I found I must give up the life I'd been living.' What struggles, what absolute sacrifice, lay within that one sentence!

While he was musing over what he had heard, Donovan

watched him silently. Already the very deepest love for this
man had sprung up in his heart—a strange, dependent love, which
he had never before known—the love which, latent in all hearts,
is usually awakened by the first true thought of God. A God-
like deed, and the love shining in a man, had now touched into
life this natural instinct, and Donovan, in his pain and humiliation, was yet all aglow with the strange new joy of devotion,
enthusiasm, reverent admiration, the echo of the love first given.

The prolonged silence would have been hard to bear, if he
had not had the most entire yet inexplicable faith in his new
friend, but as it was he waited in perfect content. Presently the
doctor looked up with great gladness in his face.

'Do you know I'm very glad you told me you were coming
to us?'

'Why?' asked Donovan, a little surprised that this should
be the only comment on his story.

'Because it shows that you've pluck enough to do what I
fancy was very disagreeable to your pride.'

'I don't know,' said Donovan. 'I suppose it was partly
being so done up, but I didn't think about minding the asking a
favour. I only felt need of you, and dread that I should never
be able to get to Porthkerran.'

'I can't imagine how you ever did get here,' said the doctor,
who knew that the walk would have been impossible to most
people under the same circumstances. 'I'm afraid you've been
very rash in your self-management for some time past, and that
is the reason you are suffering so much from your exposure.
After two such illnesses as you described to me, a man needs
some care for the next few months at least. Did you take any
care of yourself, or—mind, I only ask as a doctor—did you stay
on at Monaco, ruining your health by excitement at the casino?'

'I only went to Monte Carlo once,' replied Donovan, 'and
that before the relapse. Don't think it was any self-denial on
my part, it was simply because I lost the first time, and because
I hated the other evils of a gambling place. For the rest I was
quiet enough. Since I came to England, of course, I have lost
ground.'

'You have taken no care of yourself,' said the doctor.

'Life isn't worth much extra fuss,' said Donovan; 'and,
besides, I was too poor. Short commons, no work, and intolerable dulness do pull a fellow down.'

'Ah, yes, you must have felt dull when you gave up gaming,'
said the doctor, rather wishing to draw him out.

'Very,' was the laconic answer. Then, as if remembering that he had no ordinary listener, he added—'It's only since then that I've had the least idea how weak one's will is. It certainly is humbling to find that after you've resolved to do a thing it needs a constant struggle not to give in after all.'

'What made you first think of giving it up?' asked the doctor.

And Donovan then gave him an account of the miserable day in Paris, when M. Berrogain disappeared, and gradually Dr. Tremain realized how matters stood with his guest.

He came out of Donovan's room understanding him far better, yet feeling much more than he had yet done the great anxiety of his own position. This comparative stranger had peculiar claims upon him—he had been aware of that directly he had heard his name—but now, having heard the story of his life, he could not but feel what care and tenderness and wisdom were needed in dealing with such a character. Undoubtedly this great self-renunciation was a turning-point in Donovan's life, this awakening thought for others a sure sign of growth. What if by any ill-judged word or deed of his he should be thrown back or discouraged? The doctor was the most humble of men; greatly as he longed to help his guest, he trembled at the immense responsibility and difficulty, and grieved over his own unfitness for the task. For what was not required of him? Donovan was friendless—he must be his friend; cheated of his inheritance—he must, if possible, right him; burning with the sense of injustice—he must try to influence and soften him; and —most terrible thought of all—he believed in no God; some one must—— The doctor paused—nay, what? teach him— impossible! Argue with him?—probably useless. Love him, pray, agonize for him—that he must and would do. The rest?

He was standing by the open door which led from the house into the garden; he saw the grand old cedar at the end of the lawn, standing up darkly against the clear sky, the acacia and the beech-trees waving in the wind, the standard roses laden and flowers, the glorious sunshine flooding all with warmth with brightness. He heard the singing of birds, the low hum of insects, the soft breathing of the summer wind among the branches. A sense of breadth and fulness stole over him, it was a healthful morning, and gradually Dr. Tremain felt its real influence, it drew him away from the thought of weakness and soul-disease to the true Health-giver. Could he doubt that through all the changes and chances of Donovan's life He had been leading him? Then that strange and sudden impulse to walk to Porthkerran must have been part of the leading. The

doctor accepted the responsibility gladly now, as a care doubtless, but as an honour and a joy. And as the free air and light
and warmth influenced him from without, feeling that he lacked
wisdom, he turned to Him who 'giveth to all men liberally.'

While he still stood in the doorway Gladys came to him, her
usually bright face a little clouded.

'Oh! I thought you had started on your rounds, papa,' she
exclaimed, brightening at once as she slipped her hand within
his arm. 'I've come to you in a very bad temper, for Aunt
Margaret is here, and she is so much surprised at your taking in
Mr. Farrant.'

'Why is she surprised?' asked the doctor.

'Because you know so little of him. She thinks it most
quixotic of you. I came away at last, she made me so cross.'

'You and I believe in something better than chance, don't
we, Gladys?' said the doctor. 'And if Donovan Farrant was
sent to us, as I do not doubt he was, our duty is to take care
that we are fit to keep him with us.'

'Fit?' asked Gladys, looking puzzled.

'Gentle and patient and considerate enough to draw him
quite in amongst us, to make him part of the home. I will tell
you a little about him, and then you'll understand me better.
He has had a very sad life, he doesn't believe in God, partly, I
can't help thinking, because he has never come across real Christianity. He has had great temptations, and no friends to help
him, only companions whom at last he felt obliged to leave, that
he might try to keep out of evil, and now he is here, ill and poor
and I'm afraid very miserable. I know quite well that people
will say, as Mrs. Causton has just been saying, that it is rash
and quixotic to take him into one's own home, but, Gladys, I
trust all of you too well not to look upon you as helps instead of
hindrances.'

'Do you know, papa, I have seen Mr. Farrant before,' said
Gladys, when her father paused. 'I was sure I knew his face,
and last night I remembered it was when I was staying with
Aunt Margaret a year ago. Don't you recollect that journey
which auntie is always talking about, when we were in a carriage with some men playing cards?'

'I remember. There was only room for you, and one of them
got out and gave his place to Mrs. Causton.'

'Yes, that was Mr. Farrant.'

The doctor mused. In his worst times, then, Donovan had
kept a touch of chivalry, he had left his favourite pastime to save
a stranger from a slight annoyance.

'We knew directly he was a gentleman,' continued Gladys. 'You can't think how different he looked from the men he was with. I couldn't think why he belonged to them, and one of them spoke so horridly to him at London Bridge, when we all got out, I fancy because he had helped us. Why was he ever with such people, papa?'

'Because no one else would have anything to do with him, and because he was a great card-player; he has given it all up now.'

'Oh! I am so glad!' exclaimed Gladys, 'for it was dreadful to watch him playing that day, he looked so wonderfully taken up with it, as if it were the only thing he cared for. It must have been very hard to him to give it up, though.'

'Harder, most likely, than you or I have any idea of,' said the doctor, musingly. Then, rousing himself, 'And all this time we are leaving the mother to Mrs. Causton's tender mercies. I must go, little girl. Good-bye. That story has smoothed your temper, I hope.'

Gladys laughed, and ran away to give Jackie his morning lessons, while Dr. Tremain made his way to the breakfast-room.

He was not sorry to find Mrs. Causton on the point of leaving, but unfortunately his appearance on the scene caused a repetition of all her arguments.

'And do you really think it wise to take him in and let him mix with your own children—a perfect stranger, a man of whom you know nothing but evil?'

'On the contrary,' replied the doctor, half inclined to lose his temper, 'I know a great deal of good about him.'

'But it seems so unnecessary,' urged Mrs. Causton. 'No one in his circumstances could object to being taken to a hospital, and, when he comes out, there are plenty of societies which would gladly take him in hand. There are so many societies for young men, you know.'

'My dear Mrs. Causton'—the doctor spoke almost fiercely— 'what the poor fellow wants is a *home*, not a society; he wants to be treated as a son, not as a case. I don't mean that societies are not useful enough sometimes, but I do think we are too ready to shunt on to them all that is not easy, self-indulgent, conventional charity. Look at the good Samaritan now—himself, by the way, an infidel and outcast—*he* did things all round; no passing on to committees and societies there, no holding at arm's length lest the poor fellow should stain his garments. He put himself to some inconvenience—perhaps to some risk, and gave the wounded man his own beast.'

'Of course no one disputes that the parable is a great example,' said Mrs. Causton, 'an example that we should all copy: but still in this case——'

'You would have me enact the priest and Levite,' interposed the doctor, ' or pass on to some blundering committee for probing and examining and questioning a man who can scarcely bear to be touched. I know quite well that you would have most of the world on your side, for the good Samaritan style of giving is out of fashion now ; we like to ride on in state and fling subscriptions here and there. We don't like the trouble or the risk of actually dismounting and walking on foot—it isn't political economy.'

'You may be right,' said Mrs. Causton, half convinced. 'And yet, for the sake of Gladys specially, is it wise and prudent? I don't want to seem intrusive, but one cannot help seeing that there are very grave objections to such an intimacy for her.'

No one spoke for some minutes. This view of the matter had certainly not occurred to Dr. Tremain, and he was bound to own that there was some truth in it. Was he putting his child into a wrong position? And yet could he, for the sake of a distant and merely possible contingency, give up his guest? His perplexity did not last long; he was not worldly-wise, he was not prudent, and, in defiance of the possible ill, he held closely to the present good, trusting to God, and feeling perfect confidence in Gladys. He had, moreover, with the strange insight of humility, learnt enough of Donovan's real self to trust in him too. The banker had exclaimed at the honour of an ex-card-sharper, the doctor felt inexplicable yet entire confidence in the truth of his patient.

'Some risk and trouble and difficulty I owned to in the Samaritan's giving,' he said at last. 'I do not think it a risk which one ought to shrink from. Were you ever in the Cluny Museum, Mrs. Causton ? '

'Never.'

'I remember two very striking representations there of Prudence with her hands tied, and Charity with open arms.'

Mrs. Causton, not caring to discuss the question any more, soon took leave. The doctor was glad to be alone with his wife.

'You have not changed your mind ?' he asked. 'You are willing to be the open-armed Charity ?'

'Yes,' she replied, quietly, ' I am willing.' But there was some effort in her voice, for she thought of the possible sorrow which this charity might bring to Gladys.

'Then, having made up our minds, let us live in the present, and put away from us this idea, which I am half sorry has been suggested at all,' said the doctor. 'No one will put any non-sense into Gladys' head, and the friendship of a good sensible girl will be a capital thing for Donovan.'

Mrs. Tremain looked up at her husband and smiled.

'How soon you have taken that poor fellow into your heart of hearts! Oh, Tom, how far I am behind you! A dozen selfish considerations have come into my head in the last five minutes. I'm afraid I've little but pity for him.'

'Then, dear, go and spend an hour in his room, and I'll under-take to say that he will stand second only to Dick and Jackie in your heart when you come out again.'

CHAPTER XXII.

IN A HOME.

It is human *character* or developed humanity . . . that conducts us to our notion of the Character Divine. . . . In proportion as the mysteries of man's goodness unfold themselves to us, in that proportion do we obtain an insight into God's.

Essay on Blanco White. J. D. MOZLEY.

But the love slid into my soul like light.
Olrig Grange. WALTER C. SMITH.

DONOVAN looked up with a smile of welcome as Mrs. Tremain came into the room. He had been in too much pain to notice her when she had visited him earlier in the morning, but now he was comparatively at ease, and was lying in listless quiet with Waif on the bed beside him licking his hand.

Mrs. Tremain was not fond of dogs; she was even a little afraid of them, and she had a very natural feminine dislike to seeing a fox terrier lying on a clean counterpane. Donovan divined this at once.

'He oughtn't to be up here, I know,' he began, deprecatingly, 'but I can't keep him down, poor fellow! he's always miserable when I'm ill, and the worst of it is he won't obey orders, but thinks it his turn to be master.'

'Poor dog!' said Mrs. Tremain, softening towards the

offender and venturing to pat him.   'He does seem very unhappy about you; it's really wonderful the amount of expression which a dog can put into his face.'

'Yes, Waif and I can talk together quite easily.   I don't know what I should have done without him, specially when I was laid up; he was often the only nurse I had.'

Then a question of Mrs. Tremain's led to an account of his wretched winter, to a discussion of illness in general, to an amusing, though to Mrs. Tremain a somewhat sad description of his various nurses, including poor old Mrs. Doery, both in her character of guardian of the sick and instructor of youth.

'I have not been used to your kind of nursing,' he added, after a pause; 'you must remember that, and not let me take up your time; I am afraid this dependence will unfit me for the tussle with the world which I must go back to as soon as my ankle is all right.'

'You can hardly help being dependent when you can't move,' said Mrs. Tremain, smiling.

'No, but it's a training in patience to be helpless and to submit to being muddled, whereas to lie still and be spoilt, humoured, waited on, and amused must surely be demoralising, too pleasant and unusual to fit one for another plunge into the prickles of life.'

'Only that life, however hard, can't be all prickles,' said Mrs. Tremain.   'Don't you think a little spoiling, as you call it, is everyone's due at one time or another?   From your own account you have had to "rough it" a good deal, and this perhaps is your time for trying dependence without all the discomforts you now associate with it.   Besides, I daresay you have had your share of waiting on other people, and know that it is the pleasantest work in the world.'

Donovan's face changed, and for some minutes he did not speak.   Mrs. Tremain saw that her words must have called up some painful remembrance, and Waif too understood quite well, for he sprang up with his peculiar low whine and began to lick his master's face.   What could it be?   What painful chord had she unknowingly touched?

A violent start from Donovan caused Waif to jump down from the pillow, and Mrs. Tremain to return from her musing.

'What is it?' she asked.

'I fancied I heard a little child's voice,' he said, rather faintly.

'I expect it is Nesta, she is playing in the garden,' said Mrs. Tremain.

He did not answer for some minutes, but lay with closed eyes and a strangely rigid face, the only movement being in the hand Waif was licking, which was clenched and unclenched convulsively. At last, shifting his position a little, he looked up again and said, hurriedly,

'Will you let me see her? I am very fond of children.'

His voice more than anything told of the severe struggle he had passed through, but, though Mrs. Tremain doubted whether he were fit for it, she did not like to refuse his request. She went to the French window and called the little girl from the lawn.

Four-year-old Nesta came trotting in gleefully, her little rosy face shaded by a white sun hat, her pinafore full of daisies.

'This is your youngest nurse,' said Mrs. Tremain, leading her up to the bed.

Nesta looked half timidly at the invalid visitor whom she had heard of; but the moment she caught sight of Waif, all her shyness vanished, and she fairly clapped her hands.

'Oh! mother, mother, what a dear little dog! Is he doin' to stay?'

'Yes, he has come for a long visit,' said Mrs. Tremain, lifting her up to the pillow beside Donovan at his special request. Waif allowed himself to be patted and caressed, and played at 'trust and paid for' obediently, but he was too low-spirited about his master to show himself off well, and soon crept away from the little girl to the other side of the bed, where he lay with his sad brown eyes fixed on the invalid.

Then Nesta turned her attention to the new visitor, her shyness speedily passing off.

'How brave you look!' she exclaimed, after scrutinizing his face for a minute or two.

Mrs. Tremain and Donovan both laughed, and then the daisies tumbled out of the pinafore, and Nesta, being reminded by the sight of them of daisy-chains which were to have been made, set to work busily, chattering in her quaint unrestrained way meanwhile.

Donovan had won her heart—as he always did win the hearts of little children—and the daisy-chain which was to have been for the favourite doll was now destined for him.

'It will look very pretty, you know, on your white night-down,' she said, with her irresistible baby laugh.

Presently, with a puzzled face, came one of her abrupt questions.

'What's 'ou name?'

But Donovan did not hear, for he was looking abstractedly at her bright eyes, trying to see in them some likeness to Dot. And they were a little like, for, although grey, they were in a transition state, and there was a peculiar shade of brown in the iris which somehow made them like Dot's clear hazel. Moreover, they had in them the same innocence, and even in a slight degree the same look of heaven-taught love.

She repeated her question imperatively.

' What's 'ou name ? '

He came back to the present with an effort, and answered, gravely, but gently,

' You must call me Dono.'

Nesta softly repeated the unusual name, lingering over it half doubtfully.

' Don—o, Mr. Dono.'

It was the first time he had heard his child-name since little Dot's death. He caught Nesta in his arms and kissed her passionately.

' Oh ! oh ! oh ! ' shrieked Nesta, thinking it the beginning of a game. ' The drate bear's dot me ; he's doin' to eat me.'

' Not too noisy, my little girl,' said Mrs. Tremain, lifting her away. Then, noticing the deathly paleness of Donovan's face, she hastened to add, ' I think Mr. Dono has had enough of you to-day. Mother will take you into the garden.'

' Dood-bye, Mr. Dono, dood-bye,' said Nesta, as she was carried off ; but he did not answer.

Mrs. Tremain was a few minutes out of the room ; when she came back she found Waif in great distress, for what had come to his master he did not know. Donovan had buried his face in the pillow, and, almost for the first time in his life, was crying like a child.

Four years ago Mrs. Tremain had had all her sympathy called out for the reserved undemonstrative stranger whom she had visited in his bereavement ; love and tact had given her power then, they gave her power now. She listened as only a mother could have listened to the story of little Dot, gently drawing Donovan on by her perfect sympathy, until there was little that she did not know of those past times. How it all began, how it was possible for her to win him to speak the name that for months had not passed his lips, cannot be written or explained here. But those who have known a real mother will understand at once, and those who deem it impossible must be ' Donovans ' themselves, to whom sooner or later like sympathy will be given if it is needed.

And yet, in spite of Mrs. Tremain's present feelings, she had at first not been without a certain shrinking from Donovan—from close knowledge of a professed atheist. Away from him this shrinking had increased. It was not until she was brought face to face with his individuality, till he was essentially Donovan to her, not merely a strange visitor, that it was possible for love to take its right place. But her husband's prophecy was true, and before the day was over she had quite taken the invalid guest into her mother's heart, and only loved him better for his poverty of soul and body.

Class judgment, sweeping condemnation, are for the world,—its ways of dealing with its outcasts; and though the ways are neither good for condemners nor condemned, they will probably last though this age. But there are a few people who are bold enough to defy the world's opinion and to set at naught the world's ways, because they have the way of Christ ever before them, because they love the ignorant and sinning first, and by reason of that love hate only the ignorance and sin that have led them astray.

Even gentle and loving Mrs. Tremain had hitherto gone with the world in thinking of atheists as a class to be shunned and avoided, rather than as so many members of the great human brotherhood who had fallen into a grievous mistake, and to whom all possible justice, and love, and brotherliness must be shown. Mrs. Causton, good as she was, still failed to see the need of this.

'If a man voluntarily cuts himself off from religion, how is it possible to treat him as a brother?' she argued.

Mrs. Tremain, being but newly persuaded herself of the possibility, did not answer, but looked to her husband.

And the doctor answered in his quiet way:

'I never could see the difficulty of that; for the Fatherhood of God seems to me to answer it all. Universal fatherhood causes universal brotherhood, and the one is as really unalterable as the other. That we do not see it to be so is surely our own fault. As a rule, though, it is only those who believe that God "gives up" souls, who treat men as outcasts. They are quite logical in doing so. But, once believe that "lost" means "not found yet," that the Good Shepherd seeks the sheep "*until* He finds it," that the Fatherhood is for ever and ever—and then the fact that your brother is mistaken will only make you love him, and try to show your love to him, the more.'

Mrs. Causton was silent, for Dr. Tremain had touched on a subject upon which they had long ago agreed to differ. She

knew she was one of the 'logical' people, and yet, in her heart,
she half inclined to the doctor's loving breadth. She also began
to revolve in her mind schemes for 'converting' the stranger.

Meanwhile, apart from all discussions, and shielded from Mrs.
Causton's well-meaning but mistaken schemes by his continued
imprisonment, Donovan spent the most peaceful week of his life.
There was something indescribably restful in the atmosphere of
Trenant, a refinement about the daily small-talk, an entire
absence of that perpetual sitting in judgment on neighbours and
acquaintances which goes far to make the conversation in many
families, a peculiar quickness and readiness to perceive humour,
and a perfect understanding of that delicious family teazing
which is certainly the salt of home life. Though prevented by
his invalidism from coming into the very centre of all this, Donovan yet felt much of it in his sick-room. Of Gladys he saw
little, but Mrs. Tremain was constantly with him. Jackie and
Nesta were always ready to enliven him when he grew dull, and
the doctor gave him all his spare time, bringing his microscope,
or his fossils for arranging and sorting, or any of his hundred
and one naturalist hobbies, and turning the sick-room into something between a museum and an untidy workshop.

Donovan's love deepened day by day, he could have lain in
contented silence for hours, just watching the doctor at his work,
and though they generally had plenty of animated talk together,
it was no necessity to him. The delight of knowing any man
whom he could unreservedly trust was in itself absorbing, and there
was much besides. Mrs. Tremain, whom he admired and loved
scarcely less, and to whom he talked more, influenced him in a
way quite as much as her husband. Having once spoken to her
of Dot, he now continually returned to the subject, for he felt
there was not the danger in thinking of the past that there had
once been, and, daring to let it all come back to him, he was able
to realize that memory is indeed a priceless possession. Then,
too, in this week there came to him, almost for the first time, a
flickering shadow of doubt with regard to one of his most positive convictions. He had looked on Christianity as a creed
which could not be connected with any practical kindliness of
life; it had seemed to him merely a sort of *sauve qui peut*. Now
at Trenant there was none of the conventional religion to which
he was only too well accustomed, but he found himself constantly
reminded, in the small concerns of daily life, of that historical
Christ, for whose character he had conceived the greatest admiration. Little or nothing was *said*, but Donovan felt that he was
in a perfectly new atmosphere. Whether these Tremains were

living under a delusion, of course he could not say; he did not wish even to think just now.

Strange, dreamy, delicious days! often afterwards in the heat and struggle of life he looked back to them, and always associated with them in his mind were snatches of 'In Memoriam,' which, in spite of his assurances that he had an unpoetical temperament, Mrs. Tremain read to him. He had spoken quite truly, there were very few poems which could touch him, but the 'living poem' of childhood, and this one great song of immortality, took possession of his very being. The thin green volume was always near his bed—he soon knew most of it by heart.

Meanwhile, Dr. Tremain, seeing that his patient grew stronger in body and evidently happier in mind, began to dread more and more the broaching of that distasteful subject which was constantly in his thoughts. He was of course, however, too wise and too true a friend to put it off long; and at the end of the week, when his patient was well enough to be moved to a sofa and be wheeled into the breakfast-room, he made an opportunity for the private talk which must reveal to Donovan all his step-father's treachery.

The sofa had been placed by the open window, and Donovan was enjoying, as only an invalid can enjoy, the delights of a thorough change. His face was particularly bright and contented when Dr. Tremain came in from his afternoon visits in Porthkerran, with his mind made up to his disagreeable task; it was therefore all the harder to speak, but the doctor knew he had no right to delay any longer, and sitting down near his guest he began with but little preamble.

'Are you up to a business talk this afternoon? If so, I want to speak to you about a matter which has been troubling me very much for the last week—since the night you came, in fact.'

'A talk about your business, I suppose,' said Donovan, 'for I, as I told you, am penniless, so my affairs don't admit of much discussion.'

'You are mistaken,' said the doctor. 'You ought not to be penniless, and it is solely with regard to your affairs that I have been so troubled. I should have spoken to you before, but I waited till you were stronger.'

Donovan looked perplexed; the doctor continued,

'You told me the other day that your father's will left everything, unconditionally, to your mother, did you not?'

'Certainly, or else I could not be in my present straits.'

'And you ought not to be,' said the doctor, unable to speak as quietly as he wished. 'Donovan, before Colonel Farrant's

death he made and I witnessed another will, by which the property was left to you, your mother of course being——'

His sentence was never finished, for Donovan started up, his
face white and set, but with a sort of fierce light about it.

'What!' he gasped, 'that villain destroyed it then! Tell
me more—quickly—who witnessed it? when was it made?—I
recollect nothing. Are you sure—*sure?*'

'That it was legally correct, I am certain,' said the doctor;
'but do try to quiet yourself or I shall never be able to explain
it to you.'

'I am quiet,' said Donovan, lying back again with a marble
face. 'Go on, please; only let me hear all—and I'll not
interrupt.'

'The afternoon your father died,' resumed the doctor, 'I came,
as you know, about three o'clock to visit him. He was very much
worried, for Mr. Turner, the lawyer, whom he specially wished to
see, was away, and he told me that knowing his danger, that he
might really die at any minute, he was anxious to make his will
at once, so that all might be left straight for you. He explained
to me that his former will had been made just after his marriage,
and that he thought it wiser to make a fresh one. Of course
worry was the very worst thing for him, and, in order that he
might be at rest about it, I suggested that he should make his
own will temporarily, till a lawyer was at hand, and that seemed
to relieve him at once. Do you remember that I came to the
head of the stairs and called you?'

'Perfectly,' replied Donovan, speaking with difficulty. 'You
asked for a sheet of writing-paper. I brought it to you.'

'Yes, and on that paper, at Colonel Farrant's direction, I wrote
words to the effect that he desired to bequeath all his property
to you, that an ample allowance—I cannot recall the exact
amount—was to be made to Mrs. Farrant, and that Mr. Ellis Farrant was to be the sole executor. I remember he hesitated some
time about that, and tried to think of some one else who could
also be executor; he said that the second named in his former
will had lately died. Thinking it, however, only a temporary
thing, he left Mr. Ellis Farrant's name alone.'

'The witnesses?' asked Donovan.

'Myself and a servant, Mary Pengelly, who is dead.'

'Dead!' he exclaimed, a dark shade passing over his face.
'Then it's all up with me; the will can't be proved.'

'That is what I at first thought,' said the doctor. 'But I
find.that destruction of a will is felony, and that one witness is
sufficient. Directly I learnt your name and saw what must have

happened I wrote to a solicitor I know in town, and gave him all the circumstances—of course, without names. He said that a case might be made for you. But you see it would be a sort of contest of character, and I think I understand you that Mr. Farrant is much respected in his neighbourhood, while neither you nor I can show a stainless past. Then, too, the cost of an action would be enormous, and the result, of course, doubtful. I blame myself very much now for not having taken steps to see that the will was proved. A year or two afterwards, when we were in town, I did half think of it when I happened to pass Somerset House; but some chance meeting prevented me. If I had only had more insight! But I never dreamt of suspecting treachery in Mr. Farrant.'

'No, he is too bland, too clever, too consummate a hypocrite!' replied Donovan, bitterly. 'No one suspects him. He took the will from you, I suppose, and showed all proper feeling, and none of his blackguardism.'

'I gave him the will directly after your father's funeral. He took it quite unconcernedly; I noticed nothing the least remarkably in his manner. If only some one else had been present! If only I'd had the sense to be more cautious!'

'Don't blame yourself,' said Donovan, his face softening at once. 'That would be just the one thing I couldn't bear. It was no manner of fault of yours; if it had been, it would be easy to put up with—I could endure anything from you. But that traitor, that villain, who all the time is looking as smug and proper as can be, who gives *my* money to charities, who makes merry in *my* house, who goes to church and calls himself a "miserable sinner," and asks for mercy that he may go on comfortably! How can you expect me to think religion anything but a miserable sham, the veriest farce?'

There was a minute's silence when he paused, and, before the doctor had ventured any answer to this very natural outburst, the door opened, and Gladys came in, her hands full of blush-roses and seringa.

'I have brought you some flowers,' she said, crossing the room to the sofa. 'You must not be cheated of your daily nosegay because you are getting better.'

Nothing could have quieted Donovan so effectually as this interruption; he watched in silence while Gladys arranged the flowers. Very pure and fresh and flower-like she looked herself.

When she left the room again he was the first to speak.

'Forgive me for what I said just now,' he began, looking at the doctor with the light of indignation in his eyes softened down to sadness. 'I was very wrong to mock at the religion you believe in. This last week you have almost made me think there may, after all, be such a thing as Christianity, I believe for you, at any rate, there is such a thing. But the thought of Ellis Farrant made me mad! You must remember it is only *that* kind of religion I have met with till now—that injustice and loathing and discourtesy are, with scarcely an exception, all that I've received from religious people.'

'God forgive them!' exclaimed the doctor. Then, after a pause, 'But what I can't understand is the systematic way in which Mr. Farrant must have managed everything. A sudden act of passion I can understand, but deliberately to plan and calculate another's ruin——'

Donovan's face suddenly crimsoned.

'Stop!' he cried. 'Don't say you can't have pity on such meanness. Remember what I used to be!'

'Your circumstances go far to excuse you,' were the words which trembled on the doctor's lips, but he wisely kept them back and did not break in upon the perfectly natural and right shame by any speech. Instead, he just put his strong, firm hand on Donovan's.

After a long silence Donovan looked up once more. He seemed to have mastered the situation now, all indignation and agitation of manner had left him, and Dr. Tremain was struck by the sense and coolness with which he spoke.

'The next thing to be thought of is, what can we do? Under the circumstances, an action seems doubtfully wise, but I don't think that for that reason I need sit still and do nothing to right myself. Shall I send a letter to Ellis Farrant, and just tell him that I have learnt all from you?'

'I think, if you don't object,' said the doctor, 'it would be much better for me to go to Oakdene Manor and see Mr. Farrant. A letter can be ignored, but if I can once see him I shall at least get some definite answer from him. Will you consent to that?'

'It would of course be the best chance for me,' said Donovan. 'Only I can't endure that you should have the trouble and annoyance.'

'You think it is all like a game of "neighbour, I'm come to torment you,"' replied the doctor, laughing. 'You having come to me, and I being on my way to Mr. Ellis Farrant!'

'Well, I've given you nothing but trouble yet,' said Donovan. 'And this horrid business will hinder you and take you away from home.'

'My dear Donovan,' said the doctor, still laughing, ' you are so exceedingly unlikely ever to be a busybody that I'll venture to give you this maxim, "Thy business is mine, and mine thine, if there's the ghost of a chance that we can either of us help the other." Besides, have I not told you that we don't allow units in Cornwall? We're a joint-stock company, and as long as you are here you must put up with all the seeming eccentricities of the "one and all" system.'

The doctor being pretty free that week, it was arranged that he should go to Greyshot the following day, in the hope of getting an interview with Ellis Farrant. As soon as all was settled, he left the room to speak to his wife, and to make arrangements for his absence, while Donovan lay in what seemed almost strange calmness.

He had learnt that the Manor was his by right, that there was but a small chance of his getting it; he had also learnt that his step-father's injustice had been far greater than he had hitherto imagined. But then the repentance for his own past was growing more real and strong each day, and his belief in goodness and purity and love was struggling into life—his patience was perhaps, after all, not so strange!

In the midst of this home, with its love, and peace, and breadth of sympathy, his frozen heart was expanding. That very afternoon he had taken the first step towards forgiveness, he had placed himself on a level with his step-father, had not shrunk from admitting that he too had offended in much the same way. And strong in his possession of love—this new strange family love—he waited for what the future should bring, while in the present all went on quietly, the very sounds of life seeming full of peace. The gardener mowing the lawn, the birds singing in the shrubbery, the children laughing at their play, and in the next room Gladys' voice singing as she worked; he did not know her song, but the refrain reached him through the open window ·

'And truth thee shall deliver,
It is no drede!'

CHAPTER XXIII.

OAKDENE MANOR.

Oh, righteous doom, that they who make
　Pleasure their only end,
Ordering the whole life for its sake,
　Miss that whereto they tend.

While they who bid stern duty lead,
　Content to follow they,
Of duty only taking heed,
　Find pleasure by the way.
　　　　　　ARCHBISHOP TRENCH.

FOR more than a year Ellis Farrant had reigned supreme at
Oakdene Manor, but, in spite of every effort to enjoy himself and
stifle his conscience, he had been exceedingly miserable. In the
winter after Mrs. Doery's return from nursing Donovan, he
worked himself up into such a state of nervous terror that, had
he possessed a trifle more resolution, he would probably have
confessed his crime and sought Donovan out at Monaco. But he
was weak, deplorably weak, and so he lived on at the Manor, a
misery to himself and to everyone else. He interrogated the
housekeeper closely as to his step-son's means of living, asked
her endless questions about him, and received somewhat curt
answers, for Doery felt bound to take the part of her ne'er-do-
weel. Moreover, she brought him back all the money which he
had given her to use for the invalid, with an assurance that Mr.
Donovan would not touch it, had been very angry with her for
trying to persuade him to pay the doctor's bill with it, and
had said that Mr. Farrant must salve his conscience in some
other way.

Poor Ellis! it really had relieved him a little to send those
two ten-pound notes to his victim, and to have them thrown back
in his face seemed hard; they made him feel uncomfortable for
days. At last he put them in the church plate and was at ease
again.

But his remorse having only reached the stage of desiring the
personal comfort of restitution, it was scarcely wonderful that
when a chance of honest confession was given him he rejected it.
He cared nothing for Donovan, he only wanted to enjoy the sense
of innocence again, to escape from the horrible dread of future
punishment which perpetually haunted his poor, selfish soul.
Naturally enough, remorse on such a basis was like the house

built upon the sand, and when, one afternoon in July, a card was brought into the smoking-room bearing the words—' Dr. Tremain, Trenant, Porthkerran,' Ellis, half crazy with terror, was driven to take refuge in cunning.

The doctor meanwhile waited in the drawing-room, involuntarily taking stock of this place which by right belonged to his patient, and struggling to keep his indignation within bounds, that he might be cool enough for the coming interview. But he was not at all prepared for the manner of his reception.

The door opened, the master of the house came forward with outstretched hand, an easy-mannered country gentleman, full of genial hospitality; this was the character which Ellis desired to assume, and he acted his part splendidly.

'I think I have had the pleasure of meeting you before, Dr. Tremain,' he said, in a hearty voice. 'Delighted to see you, sir; I assure you we have none of us forgotten your courtesy at the time of my poor cousin's death. Are you staying in the neighbourhood?'

'I came solely for the purpose of seeing you,' said the doctor, gravely. 'Mr. Farrant, you seem to have some remembrance of our meeting at Porthkerran, after Colonel Farrant's death. Excuse the seeming impertinence, but have you no remembrance of the Colonel's will which I then placed in your hands?'

There was not a trace, not the smallest sign of guilt in Ellis's face. He raised his eyebrows, and for a moment stared blankly at the doctor.

'My good sir, I am quite ready to excuse all seeming impertinence, but I am utterly at a loss to understand your meaning.'

'Your memory must be capricious,' said the doctor. 'Do you recollect your cousin's funeral?'

'Certainly,' replied Ellis, with all due dignity.

'Do you recollect that, after the funeral, we returned to the inn, and that I then gave you a sheet of paper, on which Colonel Farrant had made his will, under circumstances which I described to you?'

A light as of dawning perception began to steal over Ellis's face.

'Ah! now I know to what you refer!' he exclaimed. 'Forgive my apparent forgetfulness. I assure you it was not forgetfulness of your services, but merely of the business transaction. Yes, I remember perfectly now. It was a codicil, which, I believe, you yourself witnessed, and in which my cousin left a legacy to a comrade of his out in India.'

'Mr. Farrant, seeing that I wrote the will from the Colonel's

T

dictation, you must at once see that it is useless to evade the truth in this way,' said Dr. Tremain, controlling his temper with difficulty. 'The will directed that this property should be bequeathed to Donovan Farrant, the Colonel's only son; and I am here to-day to demand of you why he is not in possession of it.'

'My dear sir, you are labouring under a most extraordinary delusion,' said Ellis, with a smile. 'You are most entirely mistaken. But, putting that aside, I really may have the right to ask why you intrude into my personal concerns. You are almost a stranger to me, and though I shall be delighted to show you any hospitality in my power, yet, sir, I think you must allow that to establish an inquisition with regard to my private affairs is, to say the least of it, unusual. As the proverb has it, you know, "An Englishman's house is his castle," and though——'

'If it *were* your house,' interrupted the doctor, 'I should not have intruded myself upon you, but I come now as the representative of the right owner, who lies ill at my own home.'

'Oh! the mystery begins to explain itself, then,' said Ellis. 'I am exceedingly sorry for you, Dr. Tremain, but I see now that you have been imposed upon by that miserable step-son of mine. I suppose Donovan has been fabricating this tale? He is a very clever fellow, and no doubt his story was plausible enough.'

'You know quite well, Mr. Farrant, that Donovan was ignorant of the true facts of the case, and that it was he who learnt them from me, not I from him. Since, however, you so wilfully refuse to acknowledge what you must be aware I know perfectly well, may I ask you to produce this codicil which you speak of, or to prove to me that this legacy was ever paid?'

'It never was paid,' said Ellis, coolly. 'I was, as you remember, named as sole executor, and of course put myself at once in communication with this Indian friend. I can't even recall the fellow's name now. Perhaps you can, having written the codicil. But, poor man, he died of cholera a week before the Colonel's death. The codicil was of course worthless then, and was, I believe, destroyed. So you see I cannot offer you more proof. Now, if you will excuse me, where is the proof of *your* assertion? Where is your second witness?'

'The second witness of Colonel Farrant's will—Mary Pengelly —is dead,' said the doctor.

Ellis, immensely relieved, burst out laughing.

''Pon my word, Dr. Tremain, this really is a most ridiculous affair. You, with no manner of proof, expect me to believe your assertion, and I am in the unfortunate dilemma of having nothing to convince you of my assertion. We might go on arguing till Doomsday, and be no nearer any agreement.'

' Yes, I see that discussion is useless,' said the doctor, very gravely, 'but it was my duty to let you know that your doings were discovered. It is also my duty to tell you that Donovan is utterly destitute, and that if something is not——'

He was interrupted by a fresh voice.

'Who is speaking of Donovan?' exclaimed Adela Farrant, suddenly appearing at the open window. She was in her shady hat and gardening gloves, and in passing along the terrace she had caught the name which during the last year had passed into silence like that of little Dot.

'This gentleman has come to see me on business, Adela, I must beg that you do not interrupt us,' said Ellis, half forgetting his *rôle*. But Adela was not to be sent away like a child, and her brother's words only made her the more sure that the strange gentleman had brought news of Donovan.

'How is my cousin Donovan?' she asked, boldly turning to Dr. Tremain. ' I am sure I heard you speaking of him.'

'Yes, you are quite right,' replied Dr. Tremain, rising from his seat. 'I was telling Mr. Farrant that Donovan is now staying with me at Porthkerran, that he is without means of subsistence, and that he has had a hard struggle to live honestly; he would have got on well enough if his health had not given way. I have been urging Mr. Farrant to be just to him, but I fear with little success.'

'Wait a minute,' said Adela, with her usual prompt decision; 'wait just one minute.' She hurried across the room to the window, and called, clearly and unhesitatingly, 'Nora! Nora!'

'I do wish, Adela, you would be more careful,' exclaimed Ellis. 'It will agitate Nora dreadfully to hear about Donovan.'

'Let it,' said Adela, scornfully, 'she ought to be agitated.'

'I shall not attempt to resume our discussion,' said Dr. Tremain, coldly, when Adela went out on to the terrace to meet Mrs. Farrant. 'Only I hope you understand the grave responsibility which you incur.'

Ellis would have replied, but at that minute Adela returned with her sister-in-law.

Time had dealt kindly with Mrs. Farrant, she was still pretty, languid, gentle, and lady-like; but there was a shade of sadness in her face now which had never been seen in past days. Considering the unusual circumstances, her manner was marvellously composed, however, as she gave her hand to the doctor.

'Miss Farrant tells me you have news of my son,' she said, in her calm voice. 'I hope he is well?'

Dr. Tremain was so annoyed at the apparent want of feeling that he answered, almost sharply,

'No, madam, he is anything but well. Twice this year he has been at death's door. He came to me a week ago penniless and half starving.'

The next minute he almost regretted that he had spoken with such impetuosity, for he saw that after all she had something of a mother's heart hidden away in folds upon folds of self-love. Her eyes dilated.

'No, no!' she cried. 'You must be mistaken; it surely can't be my son! Donovan ill—Donovan starving! Oh! Ellis! you must have pity on him—you must help him!'

'My dear Nora, I have offered to help him before now, and he flung the money back in my face,' said Ellis.

'You must remember that in the last week his position towards you is changed,' said Dr. Tremain. 'That you can leave him in his present straits without help I simply will not believe.'

Mrs. Farrant began to question the doctor about her son's illness, allowing more and more of her real love to come to the surface, while Adela went over to her brother and began to remonstrate with him.

'Now, Ellis, do this boy justice, and make him a proper yearly allowance,' she urged. 'Give him his £300 a year, and perhaps in time I may come to respect you again. You can't say now that you sent him off in a sudden fit of passion, for here is a chance for you to set all right, and, if you don't take it, you'll be the most mean-spirited of mortals.'

Ellis smiled a grey smile. How little Adela knew what setting all right would involve! However, he would do something for his step-son, only not too much, for he had a selfish dread lest Donovan might possibly use the money against him, be tempted to go to law about this will, or in some way make life uncomfortable to him. So with pitiable meanness he scoffed at Adela's £300, and wrote instead an agreement by which he bound himself to pay to his step-son £50 half-yearly.

He gave the promise to Dr. Tremain with as condescending a manner as if he had been bestowing a princely favour, all the time knowing quite well that the very chair he sat on belonged to Donovan. Dr. Tremain took the paper without a word, and turned to Mrs. Farrant.

'I cannot say that this will convince Donovan that there is

such a thing as truth and justice in the world, but it will do him some good to know that he still has your love, Mrs. Farrant. You will send him some message, I hope.'

Her tears were flowing fast, but she made an effort to check them.

'Tell him I know I failed when we were together, that it was my fault. And oh! do be good to him, Dr. Tremain—make him understand that I do love him.'

'I think that message will help him on,' said the doctor, warmly. 'It is very good of you to entrust it to me. For the rest, I can only say that I will treat him like my own son.'

With that he rose to go, but he had scarcely left the house when he was called back. Mrs. Farrant hastened towards him.

'One moment, Dr. Tremain—will you take this to Donovan ?' She drew a ring from her finger. 'Ask him, if he still loves me, to wear it; tell him how I have longed to hear of him, how thankful I am of your visit to-day.'

'And as for me,' exclaimed Adela, coming forward and putting her hand in the arm of her sister-in-law. 'Please tell Donovan that I, being a free agent, shall write to him now that I know his whereabouts. I don't see why a freak of my brother's should come between us, and I shall expect him to answer me for the sake of old times.'

And so ended Dr. Tremain's visit. He left the Manor with mingled feelings; in one way he had received more than he expected, in another less. But the atmosphere of the place was unspeakably wretched, and the doctor was long in losing his keen impression of it. A loveless home, a treacherous scheming man for the head of the house, his languid wife, his rather flippant sister, among such influences as these Donovan had grown up. And yet in every one there was some good, entirely latent good in Ellis certainly, but in Mrs. Farrant there was a genuine touch of motherliness, in Adela a certain desire for justice and willingness to befriend the ill-used.

There was, too, one influence which Dr. Tremain had forgotten. He had learnt from his wife the story of little Dot; the sight of the church tower in the valley, with its giant yew-tree and clustering grave-stones, reminded him that there had been another member of the Manor household—that Donovan had had at least one ray of heaven's own sunlight in his life. He made his way to the little churchyard, and without much difficulty found Dot's grave; but as he looked down at the marble cross, with its inscription of 'I am the resurrection and the life,' his thoughts were more of the living Donovan than of the little child who 'after life's fitful fever' rested well. How that cross and motto must have mocked him in his hopeless grief!—how he must have dashed his heart against words to him so hollow and meaningless! The realization of what his sorrow must have been came to the doctor overpoweringly. For the first time he fully understood the ever-present look of pain in Donovan's eyes; it was there when he spoke of other things, when he was at ease, even when he was laughing—a look of hunger which could never be satisfied. If anything could have deepened the doctor's love for his guest, it would have been the sight of that hopeless grave. He turned away at last, feeling no longer the oppression of his visit to the Manor, for he was communing with that very Resurrection and Life who alone could lighten Donovan's heart.

It was not till the afternoon of the following day that he reached home. The house was quiet and deserted, but in the garden there were sounds of distant voices, following which the doctor was led to the orchard. There all the home party were gathered together, Mrs. Tremain working, Gladys reading aloud, Donovan lying on his wheeled couch under the shade of an old apple-tree, and in the background the two little ones at play. They looked so comfortable that he was loth to disturb them, but Jackie in climbing one of the trees caught sight of him, and in a minute, with shrieks of delight, had rushed forward announcing his advent.

Donovan's colour rose a little, but he waited patiently till all the greetings were over; then Gladys put down her book, and by a promised game of hide and seek drew the children away, so that her father might be able to talk uninterruptedly.

'I have not fared well,' he began, in answer to the mute inquiry in Donovan's face, 'but I have at least seen Mr. Farrant, which is something.'

Then he described the interview as well as he could, and Donovan listened without the slightest comment until the doctor spoke of Mrs. Farrant.

'You saw her!' he exclaimed. 'I am very glad of that. Tell me more. Was she looking well—happy?'

'Scarcely happy, but then she was naturally upset by hearing of your illness, and of the troubles you have been through.'

'You must be mistaken. She never really cared for me; she would never show more than a well-bred interest, and that only because she was listening to a stranger.'

'I think, Donovan, *you* are very much mistaken,' said the doctor, quietly. 'The mistake may be very natural, but I am

sure that if you had seen your mother you couldn't for one
moment have doubted her love. But stay, I have a message
for you.'

He repeated Mrs. Farrant's words just as they had been
spoken to him. Donovan was touched and surprised.

'Did she really say that!' he exclaimed. 'Don't think me
too unnatural and hard-hearted, but I can scarcely believe it.
You are sure those were her words.'

'Quite sure,' said the doctor, smiling. 'And I bring you
substantial proof. I had left the house when she called me back,
and begged me to take you this ring of hers, and to ask you, if
you still loved her, to wear it. The very last thing she said was,
"Tell Donovan how I have longed to hear from him, and how
thankful I am for your visit."'

'Poor mother! she must be very much changed,' said Donovan, taking the ring, and turning it slowly round in his thin
fingers. The stone was a white cornelian, and on it was engraved the Farrant motto. It was a ring which he remembered
to have seen on his mother's hand since his childhood.

The doctor watched him a little curiously, for there was some
hesitation in his manner as he twisted the ring from side to side.
At length, however, he put it on very deliberately, then looking
at the doctor he said, with a sigh,

'After all, I am half sorry she has done this. I am afraid
it is a sign that she is unhappy in the present, that Mr. Farrant
is making her miserable, as I always prophesied he would. I
would rather have been without her love, and believed her to be
happy, as she was at first after her marriage.'

'But supposing the old happiness were false, and that through
the disappointment she came to realize the truth?' suggested the
doctor.

'The truth—at least, if her love to me is true—can't do her
much good, can in fact only make her unhappy,' said Donovan.
'She will never see me, and of what earthly use is love if you
can't do something to prove it by service? That is why I half
doubted about wearing this ring; I shall never be able to do anything for my mother. I believe I do love her; but love without
service is the ghost of love, hardly worth the name.'

'You are right, I think, in all but one thing,' said the doctor.
'You can prove your love by this: you *wish* to help your mother,
but circumstances prevent you. If she were left alone in the
world you would be the first to go to her.'

'Yes,' said Donovan, with emphasis.

'And, besides,' continued the doctor, 'I don't agree that she does nothing for you. Does she not make the world a better place to you? Is it not something that you can say to yourself, "I am not cheated of this goodly birthright—I have a mother after all"? Is it not a great thing to know there is some one thinking of you, loving you—perhaps praying for you?'

'I can't do that for her,' he replied in a low voice.

'No, not yet,' said the doctor, quietly; and then there was a long silence.

At last Donovan spoke.

'You said that Mr. Farrant promised to make me some allowance. I suppose I'm not bound to accept it?'

'No, but I advise you to do so,' said the doctor, unable to help smiling at the very evident look of distaste which his words called up. 'You see, to begin with, £100 a year is better than nothing—that's the common-sense view; and, from a higher point, I don't think it will do you any harm to endure the discipline of those half-yearly cheques.'

Donovan laughed outright.

'I think I see myself writing the receipts every six months in the style of a Greyshot tradesman. "D. F., with best thanks, and soliciting Mr. Farrant's esteemed patronage for the future."'

The doctor was not a little relieved to hear such a hearty laugh, he laughed himself, but waited for Donovan to go on with the discussion. With amusement still flickering about his face he continued,

'Still, the great question is unsolved, what else am I to do besides eating these half-yearly slices of humble pie?'

'What have you a taste for?' asked Dr. Tremain.

'For nothing in the world except doctoring,' said Donovan, with decision. 'I suppose it's no good thinking of it though. The training is very long, isn't it?'

'Four years,' said Dr. Tremain. 'The longest of any of the professions. But if you've a real inclination for it, you should certainly follow your bent. In many ways I think you are well fitted for it.'

'Do you really?' exclaimed Donovan. 'I was afraid Nature had fitted me for nothing but the work of a mathematician, and I should be afraid to try that now.'

'Why?' asked the doctor, surprised at such an admission.

'Because I know I'm as hard as nails already, and don't want to get more so.'

'Proverbially, you know, the medical course hardens men, for a time at least, but every rule has its exceptions, and I half fancy you would make an exception to this.'

'How about the entrance fees at the hospital?'

'One hundred pounds, but you can pay by instalments. There are many other expenses, though, and you must live meanwhile. I don't quite see how you can do it. However, we will manage it somehow between us. A real inclination such as this ought not to be neglected.'

'You have given me enough discipline, though, already,' said Donovan. 'I can't become utterly dependent. Don't think me ungrateful, but unless I can scrape through on my hundred pounds a year I won't go up. But it must be possible—I'll do it somehow. I suppose there are scholarships, too, at most of the hospitals?'

Upon this ensued a long discussion as to the respective merits of St. Bartholomew's and St. Thomas's, and that evening it was arranged that Donovan should become a student at the latter hospital. His thoughts were successfully drawn from Ellis Farrant and the Oakdene property, by the prospect of going up in two months' time for his preliminary.

CHAPTER XXIV.

THE IDEAL WOMAN.

> But am I not the nobler through thy love?
> O three times less unworthy! likewise thou
> Art more thro' Love, and greater than thy years.
> The sun will run his orbit, and the moon
> Her circle. Wait, and Love himself will bring
> The drooping flower of knowledge changed to fruit
> Of wisdom. Wait: my faith is large in Time,
> And that which shapes it to some perfect end.
>
> TENNYSON.

'You look very hot and very much bored. Don't you think those great books are too dull for a summer morning?' exclaimed Gladys, coming into the breakfast-room, where Donovan was working one sunny day in August.

The table was dragged up to his couch, and, to all appearance, he was very busy with his examination work.

'It is not the *big* books that bore me,' he said in reply.

'But something has certainly happened to you since breakfast time,' said Gladys, laughing. 'Can Aunt Margaret have been here?'

There was such *naïveté* in her tone that Donovan could not help laughing.

'Yes,' he replied, 'Mrs. Causton has been here for the last hour. She is very—kind-hearted.'

Gladys smiled.

'Yes, very, but she worries people. Papa says it is because she thinks there is only one side. As if, you know, we were all made alike !'

'I told you it wasn't the big books that bored me,' said Donovan. 'What do you think of this?' He handed her a little brown volume, and turning to the title-page Gladys read—'An Inquiry into the Nature, Symptoms, and Effects of Religious Declension, with the Means of Recovery.'

The colour rose in her cheeks.

'Oh! I am so sorry !' she exclaimed. 'I hope—I hope you haven't minded it very much ?'

'I've no business to mind it, for she was very kind ; but there are some subjects which I had rather have touched reverently. Do you think that kind of spiritual hay-making does much good? that raking up of feelings, that tossing of texts ? It's the first time I've come across it.'

'Except when you met us in the train that day and Auntie gave you the tracts.'

Donovan laughed a little at the remembrance.

'Do you know though meeting you that day made me feel very much ashamed of myself; I never can think of those tracts without laughing. The first of mine was 'Are you a drunkard ?' and the second 'Are you a swearer?' We had a parrot at our rooms, a capital talker, but, like almost all parrots, it did swear most dreadfully ; some one fastened these tracts to its cage, and taught it to ask the questions—a very naughty thing, wasn't it ? but irresistibly comic.'

'Poor Aunt Margaret! what would she say !' exclaimed Gladys.

'It is not tracts that are wanted,' continued Donovan. 'Beautiful lives are the best arguments, the only ones which will ever influence me.'

'Lives like your little sister's,' said Gladys, gently.

'Yes,' he replied ; then, after a pause, 'Not that her life was what some people would have approved ; she never thought much of what is called the soul, she was a little Undine till she was nearly thirteen.'

'Was she thirteen when she died ? I had fancied her younger somehow.'

'So she was really in mind and ways,' he said, quietly. 'She was a thorough child. Your little Nesta reminds me of her, though I don't suppose you would see any likeness.'

He took the little miniature out and placed it in her hands. Gladys looked at it in silence ; it was a most beautiful child's face, with delicate features, clear, pale complexion, arched and pencilled eyebrows, and glorious hazel eyes—eyes which she thought very much like Donovan's, only they were quite without the sadness which lurked in his.

'Thank you so much for letting me see it,' she said, giving it back to him. 'She must have been far lovelier than little Nesta ; but I think I do see the likeness you mean. Was this taken long before she died ? '

'No, only a few months before,' replied Donovan. 'It was taken when we were staying at Codrington, and she was just beginning to puzzle herself over all the unanswerable questions. We talked one day about death, and of course I had no comforting things to tell her about it, I couldn't tell her what I believed to be untrue. Then for a time the thought of it haunted us both. There was an artist staying in the hotel, and I got him to do this miniature for me, knowing that the separation must come some day, but not dreaming that it would be so soon.'

'And did she ever learn that death is not an endless separation ? ' ask Gladys, the tears welling up into her eyes.

'Yes,' he answered, quietly ; 'she learnt all that could make her happy, how I don't know. Isn't it strange how easily belief comes to some ? I would give worlds to be able now to believe what you believe, to feel certain that I'd got hold of the real truth, but I cannot, it's an impossibility.'

'Oh, don't say that ! ' said Gladys, quickly, 'leave yourself at least a hope, or how will you ever have the heart to go on searching for the truth ? It may not always seem impossible to you.'

Her sweet, eager face, with its entire absence of self-consciousness, took Donovan's heart by storm ; hitherto she had influenced him, fascinated him, but now for the first time he knew that he loved her.

'Life is full of strange surprises,' he answered. ' You may be right, I'll unsay that " impossible." '

Then with a strange new sense of love in his heart, and the craving for her sympathy, he told her all about Dot's death, and Gladys' tears fell fast as she heard the details of that last night, and realized how terribly Donovan must have suffered.

From that time there was a great difference in their intercourse; they talked much more freely, gliding into a sort of brotherly and sisterly intimacy—at least, so it seemed. Donovan, though conscious of his love, was not in the frame of mind to think of the future, it was quite enough for him to live in the present, knowing and loving Gladys; and she, beginning with the wish to give him a little of the sister's love which he missed so much, drifted imperceptibly, unconsciously, into a love altogether different.

Very happy to both of them were those summer weeks. In the long mornings Donovan worked hard for his examinations, in the afternoon there were merry gatherings in the shady old orchard, games with the children, reading aloud, or attempts at sketching.

One afternoon, when they were all sitting in the shade of the great mulberry-tree, engrossed in their own various books, Gladys looked up laughing.

'Just listen to this! How would you have liked it? "He was constantly annoyed by being asked to write his likes and his dislikes in ladies' albums."'

'I know the horrid inventions,' said Donovan. 'A cousin of mine used to be always boring people to write in hers—their ideas of pleasure, pain, beauty, and so on.'

'Rather fun too, I think,' said Gladys. 'Only that one's ideas would be always changing.'

'I should have no difficulty in writing some of my ideas now,' said Donovan. 'The idea of happiness would certainly be "a sprained ankle at Trenant," and the idea of beauty, "the long grass and daisies in this orchard with the sunshine on them."' He added, in his thoughts, 'And Gladys sitting with her book among the daisies.'

Sometimes, in the cool of the evening, they used to drive out in the pony-chaise, along by the sea, or through the narrow lanes with their high, mossy banks, pausing now and then at some cottage to leave a message, or to visit some of Mrs. Tremain's innumerable friends among the poor. There was very little society round Porthkerran. In the winter Gladys sometimes went to one or two dances at some distant country house. In the summer there was an occasional picnic or garden-party, but the neighbourhood was thinly populated, and the distances were too great for very much visiting. So Porthkerran formed a little clan of its own; and as by good chance the squire and the rector were both fond of natural history, Dr. Tremain was able to gather round him a small scientific society. This, with the exception of the constant visits of Mrs. Causton, and of their nearest neighbour, a jocose old man, Admiral Smith, constituted the clan proper. But the Tremains knew almost everyone in the little fishing-town, and, though Gladys never undertook formal district-visiting, she was welcomed in any house, and there was scarcely a child in the place whom she did not know at least by name.

She was therefore never idle and never dull. There were always plenty of tragedies and comedies going on among her large circle of friends, in both of which she was interested. Or there were orphans to be sent to school, or blind people to be read to, or twin babies who must be worked for, or sick children to be amused. Donovan liked to watch her busy life; she evidently enjoyed it so much.

There was one event, too, which was constantly being talked of, namely, Dick's return from sea. He was expected in September, and Donovan used to listen half sadly to the daily hopes and wonders as to his progress. When the papers came, there was always a rush to find the latest 'Shipping Intelligence,' and delighted exclamations when H.M.S. *Cerberus* was mentioned as having left some port on her homeward journey. How strange it must be to be loved, and watched and waited for so eagerly!

By this time the first cheque from Ellis had been received and acknowledged, and immediately Donovan made use of the money to recover Dot's clock from the Liverpool pawnbroker's. He also sent a ten-pound note to the hospitable Devonshire man who had helped him out of the Foxtor mire. This last piece of gratitude was perhaps slightly rash, considering his very narrow means, but he could not rest till he had sent it.

His ankle was now quite recovered, and in September he was able to go up for his examination, but not before he had pro-mised to spend his last few days at Porthkerran. The doctor had proposed that he should share Stephen Causton's rooms in town. Stephen was still at St. Thomas's, and as his mother made no objection, and Donovan liked the thought of being with any connection of the Tremains, the arrangement was made. But unfortunately Stephen, who had been spending the vacation abroad, returned with his eyes in a very delicate state, and a bad attack of ophthalmia ensuing, obliged him to give up all thoughts of work for many months.

After his long stay at Trenant, Donovan felt rather at sea when he went up to town to begin his solitary life again. How-ever, he had no time to be dull, for he was very anxious about his examination. Besides, before many days he hoped to be with the Tremains again. He passed his preliminary successfully. The scholarship examination was not till after the beginning of term, so there was nothing to detain him longer, and another week at Gladys' home was not to be missed on any consideration. He went back to Porthkerran in excellent spirits. It was about half-past five on a bright September afternoon when he reached St. Kerrans, the nearest station. He had only just set out for the five-mile walk along the dusty road, when he was overtaken by a fellow-pedestrian, who, on seeing the direction he took, hurried after him.

'Are you going beyond Porthkerran?' he inquired.

'No, to Porthkerran itself,' replied Donovan, looking at the speaker with some curiosity. He was apparently about his own age, a lithe, active-looking fellow, with a very sunburnt but good-looking face, and merry, blue-grey eyes.

'Let me send your bag with my traps, then; the carrier leaves in an hour's time.'

There was a very evident 'Who are you?' in Donovan's eyes; but the stranger, nothing daunted, took the bag from him and ran back to the little inn; then, returning in a moment, he said, apologetically,

'You must excuse this "hail fellow well met" business, but I am Dick Tremain, and, if I am not very much mistaken, you are Mr. Farrant.'

They shook hands.

'You are a very clever guesser,' said Donovan. 'I ought to have known you, but I had no idea you were expected to-day.'

'I'm not, that's just the fun of it,' returned Dick, accommodating his seaman's gait to Donovan's long strides. 'They don't the least expect me. We got into Plymouth Sound this morning and I made up my mind to come straight on and surprise them. They're all right at home, I suppose?'

'Yes, when I left they were all very well.'

'And your ankle is mended again, to judge by the pace you're going at. I heard all about that cliff adventure.'

'It brought me the pleasantest two months of my life,' said Donovan. 'I'm coming down now to say good-bye before starting at St. Thomas's in October. I'm sorry, though, that I just chanced to come back on the same day you did.'

Dick laughed.

'I might take that as a bad compliment, and you know we have still four miles to walk. But in all seriousness you really must take back your words, for I have been particularly hoping to see you, and at Trenant it is always "the more the merrier." So you are going to St. Thomas's? Is Stephen Causton still there?'

'Yes; we were to have shared rooms, but his eyes had given out, so he won't go up this term.'

' Better luck for you, I should say. Perhaps you've seen him, though ? '

' No, he's only just home. What sort of a fellow is he ? '

' A regular sawney—good-humoured enough, but weak as water. He's never been allowed to shift for himself; he's a mother's son.'

This was a genus unknown to Donovan; he asked several questions about the Caustons, and, as Dick possessed the genial manner and the ready speech of his family, the five-mile walk was quite sufficient to make the two pretty well acquainted. At last they reached the turn in the road which brought them into sight of the little fishing-town.

Porthkerran was a very picturesque place; it stood at the head of a tidal inlet, which in olden times had been one of the most frequented harbours of the west. The building of the breakwater had, however, caused it to be superseded by Plymouth Sound, and Porthkerran was now obliged to content itself with seeing from afar the passing ships. It had been a noted resort of smugglers, and the irregularly-built streets, with their narrow twistings and windings, the innumerable passages and mysterious flights of steps, the houses with their second doors and secure hiding-places, all bore witness to the bygone times when the one interest, excitement, and object in life of the inhabitants had been to smuggle, and to escape from the coast-guardsmen. Many curious stories were still handed down in the village of great-grandmothers who had concealed fabulous numbers of silk dresses under their own ample skirts; of perilous escapes down dark alleys ; of kegs of brandy which some daring sexton had once concealed for several days in the church itself. The rising generation listened with interest to these tales of the evil deeds of their forefathers. Sometimes they even went so far as to wish that their own lot had been cast in those more venturesome days, that they might have enjoyed in peace a little of the excitement of smuggling.

The little place looked especially pretty in the sunset glow of the September evening ; the quaint, compact little town, with its curling columns of blue smoke, telling of the supper in preparation for the fishermen, the narrow strip of beach, dotted here and there with brown nets spread out to dry, the calm bay, with its orange-sailed boats, and aslant from the west a broad pathway of tawny gold, ever, as the sun sank lower, deepening to crimson.

And this was Gladys' home! Donovan's heart gave a great bound when he realized how near he was to her. It was a beautiful little place certainly, but he would have thought the Black Country beautiful if Gladys had lived there. How he had pictured it all to himself up in those dull London lodgings!—how he had paced in imagination that very road, had reached that ivy-covered house! Well, here he was in sober reality, and even as they drew near the door was thrown open, and Gladys' own fresh voice was ringing in his ears.

'Dick—oh! Dick! you dear, delightful boy to come so unexpectedly! How exactly like you to walk in so quietly! And Donovan, too! How clever of you to find each other out!'

Donovan felt the real welcome of her voice and hand; it was, moreover, the first time she had directly spoken to him by his Christian name, for, though he had long ceased to be 'Mr. Farrant' to any of them, these two had as yet kept instinctively to that most indefinite of all personal pronouns, 'you.'

In a minute all the household came flocking out into the hall to welcome the sailor after his long absence. Donovan watched the greetings with a strange mixture of pain and pleasure, his new nature sharing in the general happiness, his old nature viewing all with silent, deep-seated envy. His usual helper, however, came to his aid; a delighted cry of 'Dono! Dono!' made him look up, and there, slowly coming down the broad oak staircase, her right foot solemnly stumping in front, her left foot following with less dignity in its wake, was little Nesta.

'Dear Dono to tum back!' she cried, gleefully. 'Lift me over the ban'sters, Mr. Dono, up on to you shoulder.'

He lifted her across, received a half-strangling hug, and was not a little flattered that only from her perch on his shoulder would she be induced to kiss the strange brother.

After the seven o'clock dinner was over, Donovan made his escape from the rest of the family, strolled down the garden, and gave himself up to a rather sombre reverie. The last words he had heard spoken by Dick to Gladys ran painfully in his ears—'Oh, and don't you remember——' There was no one in all the world to whom *he* could now say, 'Don't you remember.' He had to an almost morbid extent, too, the dread of intruding himself where he was not wanted, and this evening he argued to himself logically enough that it was impossible they should not prefer his absence. And it certainly was true that for a time no one missed him, that the father and mother were engrossed in their boy, that even Gladys did not at first understand his non-appearance. But, delighted as she was at Dick's return, and

interested as she was in his stories, she was nevertheless conscious
of an undefined sense of trouble, which grew and grew, until at
length it flashed upon her suddenly that Donovan must be pur-
posely keeping aloof, afraid of spoiling the freedom of the family
talk. She remembered now that she had been talking to Dick
as they left the dining-room. How inconsiderate she had been!
how absorbed in her own happiness! It was just like Donovan
to take himself off alone. He must be found and taken to task.
She would not disturb her father or mother, but, putting down
her work, she slipped quietly out of the room, looked into the
study, but he was not there, into the dining-room, but it was
empty and deserted, finally snatching up an old wide-awake
of her father's as protection from the dew, she instituted a
search in the garden.

At last in the twilight she caught sight of a dark figure
pacing to and fro by the strawberry beds. He did not notice
her till she was almost close to him, then suddenly turning
round he found himself face to face with a white-robed apparition, and started a little.

'I'm not a ghost, though I have a white frock,' she exclaimed;
'and I'm not papa, though I have his hat. Why are you wandering up and down the very froggiest and toadiest path in the
garden?'

'Birds of a feather flock together,' he said, lightly. 'I've a
good deal in common with the frogs, a love of croaking and a
coldness of heart—or absence of heart altogether, is it?'

'I came to scold you,' said Gladys, 'not to laugh. Why have
you not been listening to Dick? You've no idea what adven-
tures he has had this voyage.'

'Why are *you* not with him?' returned Donovan. 'I hoped
—I thought you would all forget that I was here, and enjoy
him to yourselves.'

'Why to *ourselves?*'

'Is not that the only way really to enjoy him?'

'Not when you won't be one of the selves. I thought you
did really take this as a home.'

'So I do. Never doubt that, in whatever way I act.'

'Then why not act as a part of the home, taking it for granted
that we like you to be interested in all our interests. Can't you
understand that of course we do?

He did not answer for a moment, but even in the dim, shady
garden-walk Gladys could see how his face lighted up—what a
strange new look of rest dawned in his eyes!

'I have believed in neither God nor man,' he said at last,

U

but you have forced me to believe in human goodness. Ever since I came here you have been teaching me. If ever I doubt again, I shall only have to remember that there is such a place as Trenant in the world.'

'Then if that is so,' said Gladys, smiling, 'I shall thank my hat for blowing over the cliffs that day, even though it did give you so much trouble and pain. However, we've wandered from the point. You will come in, won't you? It was so stupid of me not to remember sooner that you would be sure to take yourself off.'

He laughed a little.

'You own, then, that it was natural?'

'Not at all; most people would never have dreamt of doing such a thing.'

'But you knew that I should,' said Donovan, triumphantly gaining the assurance that she understood his character.

'Well, yes,' she owned, 'I thought it would be very like you to feel in the way and not wanted.'

'Don't be too hard on me for that; you've no idea how I've been shut out of things all my life. No one has ever loved me but a few children and a dog or two.'

'Oh, you must not say that!' she exclaimed, in a voice so pained, so unlike itself that it even startled her. 'You know—you know that is not true!'

As the words passed her lips, she knew for the first time that her own love for Donovan was no sisterly love, no friendly liking. That brief sentence of his and her own impulsive reply revealed to her the wholly unsuspected depth of her feelings. Had she been aware of this sooner, it would have been impossible for her to run out into the garden to find him, as she had done only a few minutes before in perfect simplicity. It was twilight, that was one comfort; he could not see that her cheeks were glowing with maidenly shame, that she was trembling in every limb. Strange as it may seem, though he loved her, he did not notice her sudden change—that is, it did not convey to him the faintest idea that her own love caused that pained tone in her voice. They walked on for a minute or two in silence.

Donovan was the first to speak; she knew by his manner that she had not betrayed herself.

'I was wrong to speak bitterly; this evening's welcome to Porthkerran ought to have reminded me of the love I have found here. One of your father's hand-shakes is worth travelling three hundred miles for.'

Gladys turned in the direction of the house.

'And Nesta was so delighted to have you back again. You can't think how fond she is of you; we used to hear her telling Waif long stories about you while you were in London. Nesta's stories are such fun. I think she has a good deal of imagination.'

They reached the house as she finished speaking, and, finding the drawing-room window open, she went in that way and soon had the satisfaction of seeing Donovan really join the family group.

The mantle of his taciturnity seemed to have fallen instead upon her; before long she slipped out of the room and slowly and dreamily wandered away, she hardly knew whither. This strange new conviction, this consciousness of love, seemed to have transported her into a new world. Presently, finding herself by the night nursery door, she stole softly in, and sat down by Nesta's little bed. The curly brown head nestled down on the pillow, the rosy face half hidden seemed the very picture of peace. And Gladys too, though her face glowed and her eyes shone with the love which had just dawned in her heart, was not otherwise than peaceful. There was a great deal of the child about her still, not a thought of the future had crossed her mind.

'You love him too, little Nesta,' she whispered, bending over the sleeping child, 'but not as I do. Oh, Nesta darling, can you ever be so happy as I am to-night! Can there possibly be such another for you to love!'

CHAPTER XXV.

COBWEBS AND QUESTIONS.

Then fiercely we dig the fountain,
Oh ! whence do the waters rise ?
Then panting we climb the mountain,
Oh ! are there indeed blue skies ?
And we dig till the soul is weary,
Nor find the waters out !
And we climb till all is dreary,
And still the sky is a doubt.

Search not the roots of the fountain,
But drink the water bright ;
Gaze far above the mountain,
The sky may speak in light.
But if yet thou see no beauty—
If widowed thy heart yet cries—
With thy hands go and do thy duty,
And thy work will clear thine eyes.
                          Violin Songs. GEORGE MACDONALD.

THE church at Porthkerran stood at some little distance from the
village. It was one of those old square-towered granite churches
which abound in the West, and the picturesque grave-yard, with
its rather sombre-looking slate tomb-stones, commanded a wide
view over the bay of Porthkerran and the great blue expanse
beyond. The south wall of the church-yard was on the very
verge of the cliff, and here, one evening in the end of September,
Donovan and Waif established themselves. Service was going
on, but both dog and master felt that they had no part or lot in
such things, and, though not much given to 'meditations among
the tombs,' they had for some reason found their way up to the
church-yard. It was the evening of the Harvest Festival, Donovan had been too busy to feel bored by the details of the decora
tions with which in old times Adela used to rouse his ire, but he
could not help regretting that his last evening at Porthkerran
should be spent in enforced solitude.

The sense of isolation came to him for the first time since he
had been among the Tremains; Sunday after Sunday he had
stayed contentedly behind when they went to church, but this
evening a regret that he could not be with them was stirring in
his heart. A chance word of Nesta's had awakened it.

'Dono will stay with us till we do to bed,' she had announced
triumphantly to Dick as he was leaving the house. 'Dono is
much betterer than you, he doesn't do away and leave us.'

It was impossible to escape from the small elf, she was on his shoulder and her arms were clinging fast round his neck, but Donovan's face glowed at her next remark.

'Don't you want to see the flowers and the corn they've putted in the church, Dono? Won't you do when we're in bed?'

Dick came to the rescue.

'Mr. Dono will be much too busy with his skeleton, Nesta; don't you know that he loves the skeleton better than he loves you?'

'The steleton's a very ugly thing,' said Nesta, pouting, 'and he oughtn't to like it so much.'

Then ensued a noisy romp; the rest of the party started for church. Presently Jackie and Nesta were fetched by the nurse, and Donovan shut himself into the study alone. But somehow Nesta's rival the 'steleton' engrossed him less than usual; the fascinating study of bones did not still the feeling of unrest which the child's unconscious words had stirred.

Did he not really want to join with the others? Was it any pleasure to him to keep aloof? Had he not felt a pang of envy when he saw the real delight which the prospect of this thanksgiving service gave to the Tremains? Would it not be an infinite rest to be able to believe in anything so ennobling, so comforting as Christianity? For nearly three months he had been watching the life at Trenant. The Tremains were by no means a faultless family, but their lives were very different from any he had hitherto seen, and it had dawned on him as a possibility that their belief might have something to do with this difference. Christianity had hitherto shown itself to him as a thing of creeds, not as a living of the Christ life, and how to explain this new phenomenon he did not know. Were these people loveable in spite of their creed, or because of it? One thing was plain, however inexplicable it might be: they possessed something which he did not possess, something which—it had come to that now—he *longed* to possess. While he was restless and unsatisfied, they were at peace; while he was daily becoming more doubtful as to the truth of the views he held, they were absolutely convinced that their Master was not only true, but the Way to knowledge of all Truth. The more enviable this certainty, however, the more impossible it seemed to him to make the faith his own. Study and thought had indeed brought him from his more positive atheism to a sort of agnosticism, but, although this had at first seemed hopeful and restful in contrast with his former creed, it now forced upon him an even worse agony. He had accepted his dreary certainty with stoicism, but to waver in doubt, to know nothing, to feel that in knowledge only could there be rest, and yet to despair of ever gaining that knowledge, this was indeed a misery which he had never contemplated. He saw no way out of his difficulty. To believe because belief would be pleasant was (happily) quite as impossible to him now as it had been at Codrington, when the chorus of ' I *will* believe' had driven him into a bitter denunciation of 'cupboard' faith. The only prospect then which seemed before him was a constant craving after the unknown.

To be conscious of hunger does not always bring us bread at once, but it does prove our need of bread, and it does make us ready to receive it when given.

The half-stifled thoughts which had lurked in his mind during his stay at Trenant now forced themselves upon him. He grew too restless and unhappy to work, and at last, whistling to Waif to follow him, he left the house, and sauntered out in the cool evening. Instinctively he mounted the hill to the church, stretched himself on the wall already described, at no great distance from the cross which marked his father's grave, and listened to the singing which, through open door and window was borne to him clearly. There were special psalms that night. He found himself listening intently for Gladys' voice, and in so doing he caught the words of the grand old descriptive poem.

> They went astray in the wilderness out of the way.
> And found no city to dwell in.
> Hungry and thirsty,
> Their soul fainted in them.
> So they cried unto the Lord in their trouble;
> And He delivered them from their distress.
> He led them forth by the right way
> That they might go to the city where they dwelt.
>
> .   .   .   .
>
> For He satisfieth the empty soul;
> And filleth the hungry soul with goodness.

He heard no more. The recollection of the time when he *had* ' cried ' unto the great unknown in his trouble, the time when his atheism had brought him to the verge of madness, when his philosophy had failed, and helplessly and illogically he had prayed that Dot's agony might end, returned to him now. But that appeal had been an involuntary one. He could not calmly and deliberately address a Being in whom he did not believe; though he was hungering to find the Truth, he could not try to find it by any unreal means.

Thus much he had arrived at when his attention was drawn

away to a tragedy in insect life which was going on close
beside him. In an angle of the wall was a large spider's web;
caught in its meshes hung an unusual victim—a wasp, who, in
spite of his size and strength, found the clinging gossamer threads
too much for him. The spider drew nearer and nearer. Donovan speculated which would get the best of it, the spider with
his cunning, or the wasp with his sting. Buzz! whirr! buzz!
the web would not yield, the prisoner struggled in vain, on came
the stealthy spider, evidently the victory would be his. But a
sudden fellow-feeling for the imprisoned insect rose in Donovan's
heart, he sprang up, demolished the cobweb, and had the satisfaction of seeing the spider scuttle away as fast as his long legs
could carry him, while the wasp flew off in the still evening air.

'Free! you lucky beast!' he exclaimed.

'Who is the lucky beast?' said a voice behind him.

He looked round and saw Dr. Tremain.

'I've just been fetched out of church to see a patient. I hope
that wasn't intended for a congratulation!'

Donovan laughed.

'No, I was apostrophizing a wasp I've just rescued from a
cobweb. Are you going far? May I come with you?'

'By all means. It's a message from St. Kerrans. Come and
drive me, will you?'

They left the church-yard arm-in-arm, and before long Star
and Ajax were bearing them rapidly away in the pony-chaise.

'It's a glorious night for a drive,' said the doctor. 'And I
am glad not to have missed you on your last evening. We shall
be very dull when you are gone, Donovan, and as to Nesta, I think
she will break her heart. You have become a necessity to her.'

'Or she to me?' said Donovan, smiling. 'It's extraordinary
what a difference it makes to have children in a house.'

'Is it not Huxley who speaks of "the eminently sympathetic
mind of childhood"?' said Dr. Tremain. 'That has always
struck me very much—the readiness with which a child makes
itself one with all around it, the freedom with which it gives its
confidence, and the delight with which it helps others. That
readiness to serve and love always seems to me stronger proof
than anything that as

> Trailing clouds of glory do we come
> From God, who is our home.'

'Your Wordsworth is too spiritual and mystical for me,' said
Donovan, with some bitterness.

'Or too simple?' questioned the doctor.

'No, no; or simple only to the favoured few who had these

intimations of immortality. For my part, I am not aware that
heaven ever "lay about me in my infancy." I know that injustice
and tyranny in very visible forms were there, and only now do I
know what a grudge I owe them. If from your very babyhood
you have had to fight your own battles, and rely on yourself, it
isn't very possible at two-and-twenty to—to——' he hesitated.

'To become a child again,' said Dr. Tremain, quietly, 'and to
recognize that above the petty tyrannies and injustices of the
world is the Eternal Truth.'

'You have never spoken to me of these things before,' said
Donovan, trying to banish a certain constrained tone from his
voice.

'No,' replied the doctor. 'And I should not have spoken
now unless you had led me up to it. There are some things,
Donovan, for which it is well to "hope and quietly wait." I am
glad you have spoken. Of course such a change as you speak
of is infinitely hard, but if the lesson of life be thoroughly to
learn that truth of Father and child, we shall not grudge the
difficulty we find in learning it.'

'If it seemed the least probable that one ever could learn it,'
said Donovan, sadly. 'But I own that I don't see my way to
doing so. Never was there a time when I realized so well the
beauty of Christianity, or felt so anxious to prove my own creed
false, but yet never was there a time when the usual belief
seemed to me more glaringly illogical, more impossible to hold.
You don't know what it is to toss about in a sea of doubts. I had
rather have my old hard and fast security in the material present
than flounder in this cobweb like my wasp friend just now.'

'Not if the old belief was a mistake and delusion, which for
aught you know it is,' replied the doctor. 'Besides, to take your
wasp as a parable, its flounderings were of some avail, it proved
its need of a rescuer, and the rescuer came—one who could sympathise even with a vicious, stinging, six-legged ne'er-do-weel.'

'But all I have got is a mere desire.'

'Quite so, a desire to find the truth,—the right thing to start
with.'

'No, it seems to me only a half-selfish desire to prop up a
beautiful legend, a discontent with the truths of science.'

'I should call it a natural and by no means selfish desire, and
an inevitable discovery that Science, great, and noble, and
mighty as she is, cannot satisfy all a man's needs.'

'If you could give us scientific proof in religion, then belief
might be possible,' said Donovan, his voice losing all its constraint and changing to almost painful earnestness. 'But see

what a contrast there is—in science all is proved with exquisite clearness, in religion there is absolutely no proof. I am crazy with sorrow, and a man comes to me and says, "Be comforted, we are immortal," I ask for proof, and he tells me it is probable, and instances the case of the grub and the butterfly. Will that argument comfort a man in bereavement?'

'No, for it begins at the wrong end,' said the doctor. 'There *must* be faith before there can be belief. As to mathematical proof, of course it is impossible when you are not treating of mathematical subjects or dimensions, but the conviction of the existence of God will be as entirely independent of proof as my conviction that my wife is true to me.'

Donovan did not speak, he seemed rather staggered by the breadth of this assertion, not having as yet grasped the fact that the ' truth ' which he was struggling after was not so much concerned with intellectual difficulties to be overcome as with the awaking of a spirit which slept.

'There are thousands of things of the truth of which we are convinced, and which we nevertheless fail to prove like a mathematical problem,' continued the doctor. 'Take the case of the great heiress, Miss Carew, whom I am now going to visit. We will suppose that she falls in love with a penniless man ; her parents laugh at the affair, and bring forward the usual arguments, "My dear, he only wants your money, he is not in love with you." All the time the girl knows perfectly well that these arguments are false, and she asserts boldly, " He does love me, I know he loves me," but she can give no scientific proof of this love, though it is to her the most intense reality, a reality that alters all her world. It seems to me to hold true that all things connected with the highest instincts of our life—merely as natural beings, I mean, you know—are incapable of mathematical or even experimental proof. But now-a-days people are so apt to make the most sacred things mere blocks on which to chop logic, that a morbid and unreasonable desire rises to have everything explained to us in black and white.'

' But religious people are so dogmatic ; they assert " this is so, that is so, believe it or perish ! "' complained Donovan. ' I mean the ordinary run ; I don't call you a religious person.'

''Thank you,' said the doctor, laughing. ' But surely, Donovan, you used to be—I don't say you are now—quite as dogmatic as anyone, and asserted "there is no spirit because everything is matter, no supernatural because everything is natural."'

' Yes, I plead guilty to that, and could half wish now to fall back on the old convictions. There are too many inexplicable mysteries in religion; I shall never get further than this fog of agnosticism.'

'Are there no inexplicable mysteries to an atheist?' said the doctor, quietly. 'How do you explain the existence of that immaterial thing the will? Science can tell us nothing with regard to it, but you are the last person who would deny its existence; on the contrary, without any proof, you have a stronger belief in the power and functions of the will than anyone I know.'

'Because I know—I *feel* its existence.'

'Quite so, and just in the same way, though science can't demonstrate to me the existence of God, I know and feel His existence,' replied the doctor. 'Or to take another argument which is often used: some one asserts that there can be no Creator of the universe, because the idea of such a being is not mentally presentable; yet one of the greatest men of science of the present day is obliged to own that *consciousness* is not mentally presentable, although it exists.'

'I see you have faced all these questions,' said Donovan, his sense of union with his friend deepening. 'From what I saw before knowing you, I should have said that Christians accepted their belief on authority, and stopped as wrong or presumptuous all free thought and inquiry.'

'I believe we all have to "face" the questions, as you say, sooner or later,' said the doctor. 'My dear fellow, I have been through something of this fog which you are now in, and to a certain extent have felt what you are now feeling.'

'You!' exclaimed Donovan, in the greatest surprise.

'Yes, in spite of every possible help in the way of home and education. And speaking as one who has lived through this darkness, I would say to you, don't grudge the suffering or the waiting, but go on patiently.'

'Go on doubting?' questioned Donovan.

'Go on living—by which I mean doing your duty,' replied the doctor. 'Depend upon it, Donovan, that's the only thing to be clung to at such a time—the rightness of right is, at least, clear to you.'

'That much is clear, yes,' said Donovan, musingly; 'for the rest, I suppose the humiliation of uncertainty is good for one's pride, the ache of incompleteness wholesomely disagreeable.'

'The beginning of health,' said the doctor, half to himself; then looking at the unsatisfied face, he added, in his firm, manly voice, 'Be patient, my boy.'

'Patience implies hope,' said Donovan, in a low tone, which veiled very deep feeling. 'Now tell me honestly'—he fixed his

eyes steadily on Dr. Tremain's face to read its first expression,
—'do you think I shall ever get beyond this wretched uncertainty?'

The doctor's face seemed positively to shine, as he replied,

'I am certain you will; sooner or later, here or there, all will
be made plain to you. Do you suppose that when we give
thanks for the "redemption of the *world*" we leave you out?
Only be patient, and in the right time the "Truth shall make
you free." In the meanwhile you are not left without one unfailing comfort: you can work, you can act up to your conscience,
and to any man who desires to do His will knowledge of the
truth is promised. You make me think of the words I used just
now, there is a seeming contradiction when we are told "it is
good that a man should both hope and quietly wait for the salvation of the Lord." It seems impossible that waiting for *health*
can be "good," we wish to have done at once with all weakness,
all restrictions; it is not till later on when we come to look on all
things with other eyes that we see the good of the waiting, its
very necessity.'

There was silence after that for some minutes, one by one the
stars were beginning to shine out in the pale sky, the wind
ruffled the leaves in the high hedgerows. Star and Ajax trotted
on briskly. Everything that night left a lasting impression on
Donovan's brain; he could always see that glooming landscape,
with the faint starlight and the lingering streaks of gold in the
west, always feel the freshness of the evening air which seemed
invigorating as the new hope which was just dawning for him.
But he was too choked to speak when the doctor paused, too
much taken up with the thoughts suggested to him, to care to
put anything of himself into expression. Presently they came
to a gate; he sprang out to open it. Then, as they drove up to
the house, the doctor said,

'I shall be half-an-hour, I daresay, so, if you like, drive on
to the post-office.'

The postman did not come to Porthkerran on Sunday, and
Donovan, glad to be of any use, readily assented to the doctor's
plan, and drove on to the post-town—St. Kerrans. His mind
was still full of the subject they had just been discussing, and
half absently he drew up at the private door of the office and
asked for the Trenant letters; it was an understood thing that
the doctor called for them at any time he pleased. There were
two letters this evening. Donovan took them, hastily glancing
at the directions by the light of the street lamp—one was for
Dr. Tremain, the other was directed to 'D. Farrant, Esq.' A

certain pleasurable sensation stole over him, mingled with surprise, for the writing was Adela's. She would send him news of his mother, and though still only half allowing it to himself Donovan did care for his mother.

He paused to read the letter by one of the carriage lamps as soon as he had left the streets of St. Kerrans behind. Then, still more to his surprise, he found that Adela had only written a note, just explaining that the enclosed was from Mrs. Farrant.

The pretty but meaningless characters recalled him to his school-days, when the arrival of his mother's occasional letters had generally been the cause of more pain than pleasure. Things were different now. The letter was very different.

'MY DEAR DONOVAN,
        'Since Dr. Tremain's visit in the summer, I have felt very anxious about you; but it is some comfort that we know where you are, and Adela has promised that she will direct and post this to you. I am not, as you know, a free agent. I have been shocked to think of the straits you have been reduced to, and send you in this letter £20, which is all I could save from the personal allowance my husband makes me. I have been very poorly for some time. We are thinking of spending the winter abroad. Poor Fido died last week, and I am still feeling the shock. Docry has an attack of rheumatism, and her temper is very trying; but Phœbe, who is now my maid, is a great comfort to me. Forgive this short letter, I do not feel equal to writing any more to-day.
        'With love, believe me,
                'Your affectionate mother,
                        'HONORA FARRANT.'

The saving of that money was the first voluntary act of self-denial which Mrs. Farrant had ever made. Donovan knew how to appreciate such unusual thought; the letter, which might to some have seemed uninteresting and self-engrossed, meant a great deal to him, for was it not more than he had ever dreamed of receiving?

When Dr. Tremain re-joined him, he saw at once that something must have happened to raise his spirits in a most unusual degree.

'You found some letters?' he asked as they drove home.

'One from my mother,' said Donovan, without any comment, but in a voice which spoke volumes.

'I am very glad,' said the doctor, warmly.

'She has sent me some money,' resumed Donovan, 'for which, of course, I care less than for the letter; it will be a great help, though. £20 will get me some books, and then, if I can only get a scholarship, I shall manage well enough. If not, I shall take to the sixpence-a-day mode of life.'

'I'm afraid, even if you get a scholarship, you'll find very rigid economy necessary,' said the doctor, unable to suppress an angry thought of Ellis Farrant's calm enjoyment of his unjust gains, but too prudent to allude to a subject which his guest seemed to have willed to put altogether away.

'Oh, I know I shall only have enough for the necessaries of life,' said Donovan. 'But Waif and I can put up with the loss of a few comforts.'

'Bones and cigars, to wit?' said the doctor.

'Bones are cheap luxuries,' replied Donovan, laughing. 'As to cigars, I've given up smoking for the last three months, so that will be no new privation. Oh, we shall scrape through well enough.'

The doctor then fell back to reminiscences of his own hospital career, which, stimulated by Donovan's questions, lasted till they reached Trenant. The rest of the party had returned from church; they found themselves just in time for that most restful part of the Sunday, when no one was busy, when the unity of the household was most apparent, when the reality of the peace and love which reigned was most strongly borne in upon Donovan. To-night there was a tinge of regret over all, for was not this his last evening with them? He did not speak much to Gladys, but followed her everywhere with his eyes, and when Dick asked for music took his place by the piano, turning over a portfolio of songs while Gladys played the 'Pastoral Symphony.' When it was ended, he took up his favourite song, Blumenthal's 'Truth shall thee Deliver.'

'May we have this?' he asked, hoping that he had not overstepped those incomprehensible boundaries which marked off Sunday from week-day music.

But Gladys was well content to sing Chaucer's beautiful old song, since Mrs. Causton was not there to be shocked, and perhaps, in her low sweet voice, she gave Donovan the best counsel he could have had for his new start in life. The quaint words lingered long after in his memory.

Fly from the press, and dwell with soothfastness,
Suffice unto thy good, though it be small.

• • • • • • • • •

Rede well thyself that other folks canst rede,
And truth shall thee deliver, it is no drede.

That thee is sent receive in buxomness,
The wrestling of this world asketh a fall;
Here is no home, here is but wilderness;
Forth, pilgrim, forth! Best out of thy stall!
Look up on high and thank the God of all,
Waive thy lusts, and let thy ghost thee lead,
And truth shall thee deliver, it is no drede.

The following morning Star and Ajax were once more bearing Dr. Tremain and his guest to St. Kerrans; the ivy-grown house was left behind, and with Nesta's appealing 'Come back adain very soon!' ringing in his ears, and a last smile from Gladys to fortify him, Donovan began the next era of his life.

*

CHAPTER XXVI.

A CROWN OF FIRE.

You well might fear, if love's sole claim
Were to be happy: but true love
Takes joy as solace, not as aim,
And looks beyond, and looks above;
And sometimes through the bitterest strife first learns to live her highest
    life.

If then your future life should need
A strength my life can only gain
Through suffering, or my heart be freed
Only by sorrow from some stain,
Then you shall give, and I will take, this crown of fire for love's dear sake.
                                        A. A. PROCTER.

YORK ROAD, Lambeth, is not the most cheerful of thoroughfares; its chief enlivenment consists of the never-ending succession of cabs bound for Waterloo Station, and its sombre, narrow-windowed houses are eminently dull. Here, however, Donovan took up his abode, and with the advantages of all Stephen Causton's unused books spent the first year of his course. Here he worked early and late; here he practised plain living and high thinking; here he struggled, fought, and doubted.

In spite of many drawbacks, however, this first year of real work was one of the most contented years he had ever spent. He had great powers of application, in spite of his desultory education, and he worked now with a will—worked with no let or hindrance, for duty was plainly marked out for him, and he had comparatively few temptations or distractions. After the excitement of the successful competition for a scholarship was over, the days and weeks passed by in uneventful monotony, broken occasionally by an unaccountable craving for his old pastime, to be fought with and conquered, or by one of those darker times in his inner life, when the sense of incompleteness, the oppression of the impenetrable veil which shrouded him in ignorance, outweighed his hope, and left him a prey to blank despondency. From such interruptions he would free himself by an effort of will, and, resuming his work, became after each struggle more absorbed and interested in it.

Then, too, the thought of Gladys was never far from him ; her memory filled his solitude, and made it no longer solitary, her sunshiny face haunted his dull rooms, and made their unloveliness lovely. Had Donovan been at all given to self-scrutiny, had he ever analysed his feelings or followed out the dim glory of the present into a possible future, he would have realized at once the insuperable barrier which lay between him and his love. But he lived in the present—lived, and worked, and loved, and, lacking the dangerous habit of self-inspection, he drifted on, happily unconscious that he was nearing the rapids.

But that brief happiness, heralding as it did a sharp awaking and a terrible void, did a great deal for him ; it gave him a momentary insight into the ' Beauty and the blessedness of life,' and it made his ideal of womanhood a lofty ideal. The truest of truths is, that in nature there is no waste, and in regretting what seems like prodigality, we sometimes forget those hidden results which are none the less real and vital because they lie deep down beneath the surface.

> The old order changeth, yielding place to new,
> And God fulfils Himself in many ways.

At length, when the summer days were growing long, and London was becoming intolerably hot, when even congenial work became a species of drudgery, and ' much study a weariness of the flesh,' the hospital term ended, and Donovan, who had promised to spend the long vacation with the Tremains, set off for Porthkerran.

Very natural and home-like did the little Cornish village seem, and, after his long months of solitude, the bright, merry family life was delightful. Nesta had grown, but was still the household baby, and not yet able to say her g's ; the two school-boys were at home for the holidays, and made the house unusually noisy; the doctor had added photography to his many hobbies, and Mrs. Tremain, with the cares of half the village on her mind, seemed still as ready as ever to sympathise with everyone.

And Gladys?

Gladys was changed. Donovan felt that at once. Her eyes seemed to have deepened, she was less talkative, she was even a little shy with him. The last time he had returned to Porth-kerran she had greeted him with delighted warmth, had called him by his Christian name. This time she was very quiet and wholly undemonstrative, and when her face was in repose there lurked about it a shade of wistfulness—almost of sadness. She had not lost her characteristic sunshine of manner, but the sunshine was no longer constant, and often grave shadows of thought stole over her fair face. No one but a very close observer would have noticed the change in her, but Donovan, who was always very much alive to the traces of character revealed in manner and expression, felt at once that the Gladys he met at the beginning of that long vacation was not the Gladys he had left in October. Her mind had grown and expanded, but what had brought that shade of sadness to her face? Her life was apparently so cloudless, what unknown source of anxiety could there be to trouble her?

From the very first evening that question lay in his mind, but only as a wonder, not as an anxiety. It was all so peaceful and satisfying here at Porthkerran, he could not brood over anything as he might have done had he been alone. The happiness of being near Gladys blinded him for the time to everything else, the very doubts and questionings which beset him at every turn in his ordinary life seemed left behind; for one delicious month he was supremely happy. He drove out with the doctor, played lawn tennis, romped with the children, gave Gladys lessons in Euclid, read, walked, boated with her, for it always happened that, although they went out a large party, the boys and the younger children kept pretty much to themselves, leaving Donovan and Gladys to almost daily *tête-à-têtes*.

If Gladys had been an ordinary girl, Donovan would probably have seen far sooner all the dangers of their present intercourse; but she was so simple-minded and maidenly, so entirely void of all desire to draw attention to herself, that it seemed the most natural thing in the world to make her his confidante. Who was so quick to sympathise with him as his ideal? Was it not right that he should tell her of his difficulties, his interests, his schemes for the future? If their conversation had ever even bordered on sentiment he might have realized that he was putting her in a false position, but it never did. They talked on subjects grave and gay, discussed religion and politics, argued earnestly or merrily on every imaginable topic, each with a hardly confessed interest in the other's opinion. But Donovan was at times conscious of a certain reticence in Gladys which he had not before noticed; in their most interesting talks he was often checked by an unexpressed yet very real barrier—a 'hitherto thou shalt come, but no further'—which baffled him, and generally produced an unsatisfied silence, always broken by a somewhat irrelevant speech or suggestion from Gladys.

Mrs. Causton was away from home. Stephen, who, after months of suffering, had just recovered from his attack of ophthalmia, had gone for a voyage with his father, and would not return till the beginning of the October term; and his mother, being a good deal worn out with her constant attendance on him, had gone abroad with some friends for a thorough rest and change of scene. Donovan's stay at Trenant was therefore free from all interruptions, and there was, moreover, no worldly-wise or prudent on-looker who could hint to Dr. Tremain the exceeding likelihood that his little daughter might think too much of that 'dangerously handsome guest,' who, in former years, had been the terror of all the careful mothers in the neighbourhood of Oakdene.

Even in the absence of prudence and Mrs. Causton, however, the awakening from that summer dream came at length.

It seemed as if a glamour had been cast over the whole household in those sunny August days, never even at Trenant had there been such enjoyment of life; meals *al fresco*, music, moonlight walks by the sea, and boundless home mirth and good humour.

One sunny afternoon the whole family were gathered together in the orchard. There among the daisies, and buttercups, and the grass—the children's favourite playground—Dr. Tremain had planted his photographic apparatus, and, with a leafy background, was preparing to take a group. It was the first attempt he had made at anything of the kind. His victims had hitherto been single, but this afternoon he had induced the whole 'kit,' as he expressed it, to be immortalised, and with much fun and laughter they all tried to arrange themselves, an attempt fraught with the direst failure.

'Not an idea as to artistic grouping among you!' exclaimed the doctor, emerging from his black-velvet shroud. 'You must be much nearer together, too. You boys in the background. Ah!

x

now that is much better. Now you do look like living beings instead of mummies. Look, mother, if you can without disturbing yourself.'

Mrs. Tremain turned round to see the group behind her, who, in disarranging themselves, had fallen into natural attitudes. Donovan had taken Nesta on to his shoulder, Gladys was holding up a rose which the little girl had dropped, and for which she now stretched out one fat, dimpled hand, while Donovan, by sudden and unexpected movements, always prevented her from reaching it.

'There! that will do!' said the doctor. 'Stand exactly as you are. Keep still, and don't laugh, Nesta. Now then!'

Half-a-minute's breathless silence followed, Nesta relieving herself by holding on with desperate firmness to Donovan's hair, and nearly upsetting Gladys' gravity by the resolute way in which she pressed her lips together to prevent the laughter from escaping.

The moment they were released there was a chorus of inquiry —who had moved? who had kept still? who had smiled? while Donovan, Gladys, and Nesta relieved themselves by a hearty laugh over the difficulty and absurdity of their positions.

'If I come out with a right eyebrow drawn up like a Chinese, and an expression of Byronic gloom, you'll understand that it is all Nesta's fault,' said Donovan. 'Remember from henceforth, Nesta, that hair should be lightly handled.'

'And now I shall det my rose,' shouted Nesta, triumphantly, making a sudden raid downwards. She succeeded this time, captured the rose, and after much teasing on Donovan's part and baby coquetting on hers, ended by fastening it in his button-hole.

The doctor returned in a few minutes in a state of great excitement. The negative was excellent. He would not trouble them to sit again, but he wanted Donovan to help him in some of the mysterious processes in the little black den he had consecrated to his new hobby.

By the time this work was over, it was nearly four o'clock. The doctor was called out, and Donovan, finding there were visitors in the drawing-room, sauntered out again with a book under his arm. In the orchard, however, he unexpectedly found Gladys. She was sitting at the little rustic table under the old apple-tree, her sleeves tucked up, and her white hands busily occupied in stoning some peaches which were piled up on a great blue willow-pattern dish in front of her.

She made a very pretty picture sitting there in her cool, creamy-white dress, a stray sunbeam glancing every now and then through the flickering leaves above, and making gold of her brown hair.

'You should have been photographed with your dish of peaches,' said Donovan, drawing up a garden-chair to the other side of the table.

'Cook is in despair about the preserving, so I'm getting these ready for her,' explained Gladys. 'Have some, won't you?'

'No, thank you, I'm no fruit-eater; but let me help you.'

'Read to me, and then I shall work faster. Mother and I were reading George Eliot's "Spanish Gipsy;" do you know it? Oh! but you have a book, I see; read me that instead.'

· Donovan laughed.

'I'm afraid you would scarcely thank me for reading you Heath's "Minor Surgery." Let me have the "Spanish Gipsy." You are near the end, I see; just give me an idea about the characters. Who is Don Silva?'

'He is a Spanish nobleman in love with Fedalma, the daughter of a Moorish chief. Silva renounces Christianity, and promises to serve and obey the Moor, so that he may not be separated from Fedalma. This is the place——' she handed the book to him, and Donovan, taking it, began the scene in which Don Silva, tortured by seeing the martyrdom of Father Isidor, breaks his promise of fealty to the Moor.

He was not exactly a good reader; he was sometimes abrupt, sometimes hurried, but he had a beautiful voice, which went far towards making up for any other defects. As he read the wonderful parting scene between Silva and Fedalma, when in obedience to the will of the dead chief, and for the good of the Moorish people, they agree to part for ever, Gladys felt that his whole soul was being thrown into what he read. Involuntarily her hands ceased their mechanical work; though she could hardly have explained the reason even to herself, this reading was becoming a slow agony to her. Donovan's face was kindling with enthusiasm, there was an almost terrible ring in his voice as he read the closing scene; she knew that while her heart was crying out against the bitterness of such a renunciation he was feeling only its beauty and worth.

Neither of them spoke when the poem was finished; Donovan, as if engrossed with it still, and forgetful that he was not alone, turned the pages over again, reading half to himself passages which had struck him. Gladys, troubled by her own agitation, heard as in a dream, till a sudden deepening of tone recalled her fully to the present. Donovan was reading the parting words of Don Silva.

> ' Each deed
> That carried shame and wrong shall be the sting
> That drives me higher up the steep of honour
> In deeds of duteous service.'

He closed the book after that and sat musing. Then, looking up with the light of enthusiasm still in his face, he said,

' That is a wonderful scene!   It is like a bit of Sebastian Bach, a sort of mental tonic.'

Gladys' eyes were full of tears, but for that reason she was the more anxious to speak unconcernedly; she hurried out the first trite sentence which came into her head.

' It is so terribly sad.'

' Yes, sad but grand.'

Somehow, as he spoke, Gladys was constrained to look at him, and, as she met his grave, deep eyes, there rose in her an inexplicable longing to make him express at least pity for the suffering involved by this sacrifice he so much admired.

' But surely, surely it was a cruel thing to sacrifice their very lives to an only possible good ? ' she said pleadingly.

' I don't think you put it quite truly,' he replied. ' They renounced their own happiness for the general good of that generation certainly, probably of many generations.'

' You speak of happiness as if it were such a little thing to give up,' said Gladys. ' I suppose it is selfish to think of it, but—but—oh, I hope there are not many Fedalmas in the world ! '

She was quite unconscious of the pain which lurked in the tone of this almost passionate utterance, she scarcely knew that it was an aching dread in her own heart which prompted her words, she only felt constrained by some unknown power to plead with Donovan. But it was at that very moment, when she herself was least conscious in the present of her love to him, that he realized the truth.

He had hitherto loved her as an ideal, loved her with little thought of the future, never even framed to himself the idea that she could possibly love him. Now there surged over him a very flood of bliss—joy such as he had never imagined possible. In one instant countless visions of dazzling happiness rose before him. She, his ideal, his queen, loved him ! How he knew it he could not have explained, but he did know it ! Had his unspoken love drawn her heart to his? How came it that she loved him ? Oh ! unspeakable rapture ! one day she might be all his own !

But the moment that thought of the future came to him, it was as if an icy hand had suddenly clutched his heart.

The dazzling visions faded, and in their place was only a horror of great darkness, out of which, like a death-knell, his own conscience spoke.

'There is no possible union for you. You would bring her the worst of miseries, perhaps even drag her down to your own hopeless creed.'

He was too much stunned to think, but for some time now he had been clinging blindly to duty, had said to conscience, 'Call, and I follow,' and even in the confusion and anguish of that moment it was made clear to him what he ought to do.

With an effort of will he banished every trace of his real feelings from his face and tone, and answered as quietly as he could Gladys' last remark.

'I didn't mean to underrate happiness, though it certainly is not meant for everyone in the world, unless we find that sacrifice itself is the most real happiness; but I have not found that yet.' Then, pushing back his chair, he added, 'I think I shall go over to St. Kerrans. I want a good long walk. Can I do anything for you?'

'Nothing, thank you,' said Gladys, mechanically taking up and putting down one of the peaches.

Donovan whistled to Waif and walked away in the direction of the house. Gladys sat motionless till the sound of his footsteps died away into silence; then, pushing aside the willow-pattern dish and the fruit, she hid her face from the light and burst into tears.

Although he had spoken of walking to St. Kerrans, Donovan was too much stunned to know or care in what direction he went. He closed the front door behind him and strode rapidly through the village, up the steep hill, and along the road leading to the forge. Trevethan, the blacksmith, had become a great friend of his; to-day, however, he had not the slightest intention of going to see him, and, in fact, did not even know that he was passing the forge till the blacksmith's voice fell on his ear.

'Mr. Farrant, I was wanting to speak to ye, sir. Can ye step in a moment?'

'Yes,' said Donovan, though he had never felt less inclined to speak to any human being.

'Well, sir, you see it's this way,' began Trevethan, putting down his hammer, and folding his arms as if in preparation for a lengthy speech. 'I've told ye all about my son Jack as left home six years ago, and as I haven't heard from. Well, the

Lord be praised, I've heard from 'm now, he's wrote me a fine letter, and sent a Bank o' England note along with it. But, sir, he's not said where he is, except there being "London" marked on the front of the letter. Knowin' ye knew the place, I thought I'd ask ye how I could best find the lad. London's a big place, ain't it?—a sight bigger than Porthkerran?'

Donovan smiled a little.

'Yes, Trevethan, I'm afraid it'll be very hard to find him. I'll do my best to help you though; tell me what he is like.'

The blacksmith's powers of description were not great. He knew that Jack was 'fine and big,' but could not tell the colour of his eyes, or any single peculiarity in his manners or appearance.

'You mustn't be too hopeful,' said Donovan; 'but I'll keep my eyes and ears open, and do all I can for you; I'm afraid, though, the only chance of your finding him will be his own voluntary return.'

'Thank ye, sir, I'm obliged to ye for your help,' said the blacksmith. 'And as to hoping, as long as we're sure our hopes is runnin' the same way as the Lord's, I reckon we can't be too hopeful.'

Donovan did not speak. He had had many a talk with the old Cornishman, had sometimes laughed at the quaint phrases of his Methodism, but had always admired and reverenced the man's unswerving faith—faith which had stood fast through countless troubles and losses. He could not help shrewdly surmising that this hope as to finding his son would never be fulfilled, and yet, as he watched the blacksmith's contented face, he felt that his strong faith in the inevitable Right which ruled all things was a very enviable possession.

After a little further conversation as to the search for Jack, the smith took up his hammer again, and Donovan took leave of him, and set out once more on his solitary walk. The interruption had quieted him for the time, but, as the consciousness of his pain returned to him, the contrast between his own state of conflict and Trevethan's quiet trust forced itself on him. This unlettered, ignorant old man had the knowledge which he was hungering and thirsting for, the faith which he would have given the world to possess.

But then with a sudden sharp pang came the full recollection of all that had happened, and his mind became capable of only two ideas—Gladys and pain. He threw himself down on the grassy slope bordering the cliff, and for a time allowed those two presences to work their will on him. Gladys, with her appealing blue eyes, her wistful plea for happiness, and an agonizing consciousness that sorrow and separation must come. As he grew quieter, or, rather, as his thoughts became more clear, he saw as distinctly as he had done when speaking to her in the orchard that union between them was impossible. He remembered the sense of separation that had come to him when Dot had first drifted away into those regions of thought into which he could not follow her. She had not suffered much from their difference of thought, it was true, but then she had been a little child, and there had been only a very few months of that divided thought and interest. If she had been older, his atheism must have been both a sorrow and a perplexity to her. Should he bring such a sorrow into Gladys' life?—should he lay upon her pure heart such a burden as he had to bear? Never! All the man in him rose at such a thought. It should never be! He got up and began to pace rapidly to and fro, his hands locked tightly together. It was no use idly to wish that he had never seen her; he must go away now, at once—that much was clear. She must learn to forget him. 'Oh! I hope there are not many Fedalmas in the world!' her pleading tones rang in his ears, and his hands were clenched more tightly as he realized the pain he must in any case give her.

He must go, but it was hard—bitterly hard. His love was strong and true, no mere weak sentimentality; but it is a cruel tax on love to choose the very plan that will inflict pain on the loved one. The pain may be salutary, wise, necessary for future happiness, but the infliction is keenest suffering.

He knew that he should always love her, but his love must be kept in, restrained; a poor, cramped kind of love it would be, for he could never serve her. Deliberately, of his own accord, he must cut himself off from all but the pain of love. Unless, indeed, this bitter pain proved to be service. There might come a time when she would bless him for what he had done. Some day, when with a husband one with her in every way, and children of her own, learning from their father's lips the first lessons of the faith, might she not *then* bless him for the pain of the present? Might not this be his ' duteous service'? this the ' steep of honour'?

But Donovan was very human; the thought of his own suffering began to appeal to him. The thought of life without Gladys *would* come before him. It hung round him like a heavy pall, shutting out all brightness, all hope of future happiness, all hope—so he thought—of ennobling himself. For was not she the light he had looked to, the goal he had set before him? Now everything was shut out. Blank and black, dreary and hopeless, life stretched out before him.

As he paced up and down battling with himself, his attention was drawn to the little strip of beach at the foot of the cliff. Two children were there, laughing, shouting, waving their hands to a fisherman who was just nearing the shore in his boat. The keel grated on the pebbles, the man sprang out. He had not had good luck, his lobster-pots had been empty, but, in spite of it, his voice was hearty and cheerful as he hailed the little ones. Donovan saw them run to meet him, heard their cry of 'Father! father!' Another sore regret surged in upon him then. He could never have a child of his own, no child would ever call him 'father.' He might love and be beloved by other people's children, but the fatherhood which this honest fisherman could enjoy might never be his. And then the terribly tempting thought of what might be, the haunting happiness of the home, the wife that might be his, came again to him with double force.

It is not so hard to bear what the force of circumstance brings; the Christian, the Fatalist, the Agnostic, all from a variety of reasons learn the sort of endurance which life can hardly fail to teach, and endure joyfully, abjectly, or doggedly. But deliberately to choose the pain, that is not easy, not easy because it is God-like. Only by slow painful degrees can we fight our way upward and break loose from the clinging hold of self-love.

Donovan had now fully faced all sides of this great question of his life; again he came to the decision which must be made at once and for ever. And now for the second time out of the depths he sent up a cry to the Unknown. No 'sense of sin' had prompted either of those hardly conscious appeals. His first prayer had been that Dot might be taken from him into peace, his second that he might have strength of will to leave Gladys That will of his which had failed—he distrusted it now!

The battle ended at last. Slowly and firmly he pronounced the 'I will' which must banish him for ever from all that he loved.

The sun was just setting when he reached St. Kerrans; he had struck inland from the Porthkerran Cliff road, and had gone across country, Waif following him through stubble-fields and over hedges and West-country walls with untiring perseverance. The shops in the little town were still open, for it was market-day. Donovan went as usual to the post-office, and there to his surprise found a letter for himself—an exceedingly rare event. He opened it and read the contents with as much curiosity as he was capable of feeling about anything just then.

'S—— House, Freshwater, I. W., Au_gu_st 27.
'MY DEAR DONOVAN,

'You may very possibly have forgotten an old friend of yours, who, however, has often thought of you in the long interval which has passed since we met. I saw your cousin, Miss Adela Farrant, a few weeks ago, and she told me of your whereabouts. I am very glad you are thinking of entering the medical profession. Has your vacation begun yet? If so, will you not come and spend a week or two with me? Plenty of boating and fishing for you, and as much or as little as you like of an old man's society.

'Yours very truly,
'H. G. HAYES.

'P.S.—I am only here for three weeks, so come at once if you can.'

Here was a real help to his resolution, an invitation which would blind the Tremains to the strangeness of his abrupt departure. He looked at his watch; it only wanted two or three minutes to the time when the telegraph-office closed. Should he go back and send the message which would fix his fate? He wavered a minute, but finally returned to the office, snatched up pencil and paper, and, feeling much as if he were signing his own death-warrant, wrote the following words—' Your letter forwarded to me from London. Many thanks for invitation. I will come to-morrow evening.' The telegram dispatched, he set off at a sharp pace for Porthkerran, along the familiar road which had so many associations for him—the first meeting with Dick, his last return to Trenant only a month ago, and—most vivid recollection of all—that drive with the doctor one Sunday evening in September, when they had spoken of his doubts and difficulties, when Dr. Tremain had spoken so hopefully, so confidently of the light which would come to him. Poor Donovan! he did not feel any such confidence now. Black darkness seemed gathering round him. In renouncing Gladys, he felt that all which had hitherto been most helpful to him would be swept away, that he should be left alone to face ' the spectres of the mind.' Happily he saw the danger of dwelling on this thought, however, and, putting it from him, he strode rapidly along, wondering how he could best veil his feelings from Gladys, or arouse least suspicion in the minds of her parents.

At last, in the twilight evening, he reached Trenant. How little he had dreamed that the sight of the gabled house, with its mantling ivy and cheerful lighted windows, would ever give his heart such a stab of pain! Well, he must think as little as he could, and just *do*. It was rather a relief to him on entering the drawing-room to find old Admiral Smith there. The doctor had his microscope out, Mrs. Tremain was working, Gladys was playing chess with Bertie.

'Here you are at last!' was the general exclamation. 'Where have you been? And how tired you look!'

'It was very rude of me to cut dinner,' said Donovan, shaking hands with the admiral, 'but I felt inclined for a good long walk.'

'After your cramping position in the photograph, I suppose,' said the doctor, laughing. 'You are in great disgrace with Nesta though, for having gone without wishing her good-night.'

'You will have some supper now?' said Mrs. Tremain, with her hand on the bell.

'No, thank you,' said Donovan. 'I really want nothing. Let me have the rest of the evening with you all, for I'm afraid this will be my last.'

'Your last evening!' exclaimed the doctor, greatly astonished.

'Well, at St. Kerrans I found a letter from a very old friend of mine, Mr. Hayes, a neighbour of ours at Oakdene. He is staying in the Isle of Wight, and wrote to ask if I would come down and see him. His time is limited, so I was obliged to answer him at once, and promise to go.'

'How beastly!' exclaimed the two schoolboys.

'Must you really go to-morrow?' said Mrs. Tremain, regretfully. 'It is very hard for us to be robbed of so much of your visit, but I suppose we must not grudge you to an older friend.'

'Mr. Hayes was very kind to me in the old time. I think it is right that I should go to see him, though of course I——'

He broke off abruptly, unable to speak any trite commonplace regret.

He had carefully avoided looking at Gladys, but as the doctor and Mrs. Tremain were still discussing this sudden change of plan with him, Bertie's voice forced itself upon his notice.

'Well, Glad, you *are* a muff! You've let me take your queen, when you might have moved it as easily as possible.'

'I'm very sorry, Bertie. I wasn't thinking,' was the answer.

'It's very dismal indeed,' said the doctor. 'However, I suppose we must grin and bear it. You'll come down for the next long vacation anyhow. And we won't allow Mr. Hayes to cheat us a second time. You can go to him for Christmas Day. He is more accessible than we are for a short holiday.'

Gladys sat moving her chessmen mechanically, feeling as if

she were in some dreadful dream. What did it all mean? Why
was he going away? Had he guessed her secret? had she
betrayed herself? No, she thought not, for he looked so perfectly
natural, and even as she finished her game, he crossed the room
and took the vacant chair beside her, asking in the most ordinary
way,

'Did you finish stoning your peaches?'

And then he told her about his talk with Trevethan, and
made her describe Jack to him, so that in a very little while her
cheeks cooled, and her relief would have been almost happiness,
if there had not been the haunting consciousness that this was
the last talk she should have with Donovan for a year. Her
heart was very heavy. They made her sing, too, which seemed
hard, but Admiral Smith was fond of music, she could not refuse.
Donovan lit the candles for her, and opened the piano. She
turned over her portfolio, but every song seemed to bear some
reference to the subject that was filling her heart. However,
Admiral Smith decided the question for her.

'Now, Miss Gladys, let us have the "Flowers of the Forest."
That's the prettiest song ever written, to my mind.'

She got through it somehow, but there was more pathos than
she wished in the mournful refrain—

The flowers of the forest are a' wede away!

Donovan never heard that song in after-years without a *serre-
ment de cœur.* As he held the portfolio open for her to put it
away, her hand touched his for a minute, he felt that it was icy
cold, and a sudden longing to take it in his almost overmastered
him. The old admiral was disappearing with the doctor into the
adjoining room, the boys had gone to bed, Mrs. Tremain had just
gone into the dining-room to ring the first bell for prayers, these
two were quite alone. Why might he not take that poor little
cold hand into his and tell her the truth, tell her that he loved
her with his whole heart. After all, it was a mere shadow which
stood between them! why should he sacrifice his own happiness
and hers, because what to her was a conviction was to him a
vague uncertainty? He loved her so dearly, why must he be so
cruel? It was a moment of terrible temptation. But it was
only a moment. With lips firmly pressed together he bent down
over her music, turned over the pieces, and not in the least
knowing what he had taken up, said rather hurriedly,

'Will you not play something? There will be time for this,
I think.'

She sat down again at the piano, and he moved away to the

fireplace, waiting there with his head propped between his hands, and steeling himself to endure. Quite unknowingly he had given her a transcription of ' O rest in the Lord.' He scarcely heard it, but to her the beautiful air brought infinite comfort. When she had ended it she was quite herself again, and could speak naturally and composedly, and before many minutes the prayer-bell rang, and she went away, leaving Donovan alone.

That wretched evening ended at length, the last good nights were said, the house settled down into quiet. But lights burnt long in two of the rooms ; in one Donovan, with a rigid face, bent over his dryest medical book, in a vain endeavour to banish thought, in the other Gladys knelt and prayed.

CHAPTER XXVII.

GOOD-BYE.

She smiled : but he could see arise
Her soul from far adown her eyes,
Prepared as if for sacrifice.

She looked a queen who seemeth gay
From royal grace alone.

E. B. Browning.

When, after spending a winter in the sunny south, beneath clear blue skies and constant sunshine, the traveller returns to the capricious springtide of the north, the violent contrast is very often both dangerous and depressing. Rain and fog and lowering skies seem more noticeable, more unforgetable than before ; east winds, which in former years we had laughed at or ignored, are now an unpleasant reality, and every breath drawn tells only too plainly that, although the heart of the north may be ' dark and true and tender,' its winds are sharp and keen and bitter.

In that one night of suffering Gladys passed as it were from the sunny south to the northern springtide. She woke the next morning fully conscious of the change that had come, wearily, achingly conscious of it. Hitherto her life had been almost untroubled, her sunny temperament made her less susceptible than most are to the small trials and annoyances of life, and now for the very first time there came to her a longing for pause and rest. Every other morning of her life her first healthy waking thought had been a thanksgiving for the happiness of beginning

a fresh day, now with a great load on her heart she only longed
to shut out the light, to forget a little longer. If only the drama
of life would go on without her! If only she might give up her
part—her hard difficult part!

It was no use wishing, however. She got up and went
straight to the looking-glass to see what sort of face she could
bring to that day's work. Somehow her reflection made her
angry, the wide, wearied eyes, with their dark circles, the grave
lips, the unusual paleness of the whole face. 'I will certainly
not look like this,' she determined, and though as a rule she
thought scarcely at all of her appearance, this day she took great
pains with herself, put on a pink print dress, which made her
look much less ghostly, fastened a rose in her belt, and ran down
to breakfast with an air of assumed cheerfulness little in accordance with her heavy heart.

Donovan was already seated at the table, he was to start in
half-an-hour's time, and the doctor had arranged his rounds so as
to drive him first to St. Kerrans Station. There was nothing the
least unusual in his voice or manner, he talked on steadily about
the Isle of Wight, geological books, fossils, all the most ordinary
topics. No one could have guessed in the least that all the time
he was bearing the keenest pain, doing the hardest of deeds.

It was not easy to speak quite naturally to Gladys, but silence
between them would have been so marked that he was all the
more anxious to overcome the difficulty.

'I am afraid the Euclid will come to a standstill,' he said, as
they stood at the open door waiting for the carriage. 'You are
safely over the Pons Asinorum, though, which is some consolation.'

He had spoken lightly and with a smile, his tone jarred a
little on Gladys. What did it all mean? Did he really care for
her? If so, why did he speak like that?

Her father had answered the remark.

'She must wait till the next long vacation before she becomes
a thorough "blue-stocking." What will you attempt then?
Conic sections, I suppose.'

Donovan did not answer, but allowed himself to be mono-
polised by Jackie and Nesta, and Gladys stood leaning against
the doorway, feeling sick at heart as she watched their noisy
romp, while the sound of wheels drew nearer and nearer. Waif
came up to her with low whines of delight and wagging tail.
She bent down to pat him with a full-hearted reproach. 'What,
you too, Waif! Are you so glad to go?' Waif comforted her a
little, however, in spite of his eagerness to start, happy Waif, who

had saved his master's life, who would always be his friend and companion.

A few minutes more and the end had come. She felt her hand taken in a strong firm grasp, and, looking up, met Donovan's eyes; there was an almost hard look in them which puzzled her, but his voice was pleasant and natural.

'Good-bye,' he said. 'And if you are seeing Trevethan, please tell him that I'll do my best to find Jack.'

'I will,' said Gladys, softly. 'Good-bye.'

'Dood-bye, Mr. Dono, dood-bye,' shouted Nesta, as the carriage drove away. 'Please lift me up, sissy.'

Gladys took the little girl in her arms, and Nesta threw innumerable kisses after the departing guest; Donovan looked back, smiled and waived his hand, and a turn in the road soon hid the pony-carriage from sight.

'I am very sorry he has had to go like this,' said Mrs. Tremain, re-entering the house. 'I think, Gladys dear, you might give the children their lessons early; I shall be glad of your help at the clothing club this morning.'

'Very well, mother,' said Gladys, obediently, and she went at once with her two little pupils into the school-room, giving all her attention to 'Reading without tears.'

It was not till night that she had time fairly to face her trouble, and when the work of the day was over she was too weary to think; she shut herself into her little room and threw herself on the bed just as she was, only conscious of relief that at last she might let her face relax, that at last she might be miserable alone. It was bad enough that Donovan should be gone, that for a whole year she should not see him, but the real sting was that he had gone in such a strange way. Could it be that she had mistaken mere friendship for love? Had she given her whole heart to one who merely wanted a good listener, a pleasant companion? Well, it was done now, and there could be no undoing; she loved him, and clung to her love perhaps all the more closely because of the pain it was bringing her.

Never once did she realize as Donovan had done the impossibility of real union between them. He, knowing all the misery of such differences as had existed between himself and Dot, taking too the darkest view of his own future, had felt his agnosticism to be an insurmountable barrier. But Gladys could not feel this. She saw in Donovan a noble, self-sacrificing character, a resolute cleaving to right at whatever cost to himself, a tenderness to children, a great capability of endurance, an untiring search and desire for truth. Surely the light would come to him, surely already he was far on the road to that knowledge he craved!

And then too she could not help knowing that she had a great influence over him; he had almost told her so in words, and by his questions, his anxiety to learn her opinion, his eagerness to gain her approval, had certainly borne it out in actions. Yes, she loved him, was ready to give up everything for him, to leave home, and comfort, and prosperity, to share his poverty, to bear for his sake reproach and suspicion, to be doubted, to be evil spoken of, if only she might bring one ray of light into his gloom, if only by her love she could win him to believe in the everlastingness of love.

It might be a hard life, in some ways it must be lonely, but what was that to her? The mere possibility of bringing any real joy—joy worthy the name—into Donovan's life, outweighed to her all thought of the suffering involved. All *self* suffering, that is. If she had known that at that very minute she was giving him the keenest suffering possible, she could not have borne it. But of this naturally she knew nothing, thought in her ignorance that the present pain was almost entirely hers, that in that possible future too the ache of loneliness would be all for her to bear, and in her unselfishness rejoiced in the thought.

Her mind, however, was too healthy to busy herself unduly over the future, the present was to be lived in, she turned back resolutely to make

The best of 'now' and here,

by which she meant chiefly ceaseless prayers for Donovan, while the daily round of home life went on unaltered. Her bright face was still the sunshine of the house, for gradually the self-pity, the vain regrets, and the useless puzzling over Donovan's change of manner passed away; in the constant communion with the All-Father her love was being perfected.

With Donovan himself matters went more hardly. It could not be otherwise. The parting which had tried Gladys, had been to him a frightful effort, while the future, which to her was veiled in uncertainty and lightened by hope, was to him one long blank desert of pain.

It was evening by the time he stood on the deck of the little steamer which plied between Lymington and Yarmouth, a dismal evening too, well in accordance with his own feelings. A heavy sea-fog shut out the view, a fine chilling rain fell, the passengers grumbled, two tired children wailed piteously, nurses alternately

coaxed and scolded them.   At length in the dreary twilight they
reached the little port, Donovan rescued his portmanteau from
the chaos of luggage and slowly made his way up the long wooden
pier, to the old-fashioned coach, which with its patient horses
and good-tempered driver stood waiting outside a cheery little
inn.   The wailing babies were packed away inside, Donovan
mounted to the top, where he was presently joined by two or
three other men, and by a forlorn little girl who could find no
room inside; he held his umbrella over her, and talked to her a
little; she looked tired and sad, he had a kind of fellow-feeling
for her.   Presently all being ready the driver cracked his whip
and the horses started off at a brisk pace, they went swinging
along through narrow country lanes and under dripping trees,
till at length the lights of Freshwater shone out in the distance,
and gradually the passengers were set down at their various
destinations.   Before long Donovan's turn came.

'S—— House, sir.   Here you are,' said the coachman.

He tucked Waif under his arm, wished the little girl good
evening and clambered down.   The door of the villa was wide
open, a flood of light streamed out into the dusky garden, revealing old Mr. Hayes in the doorway.   Donovan had fancied himself
hopelessly, irrevocably miserable, but he was considerably cheered
by the old man's hearty welcome.   It was after all something to
have your hand grasped by an old friend, to be questioned
and fussed over, to be taken into a comfortable brightly-lighted
room, to sit down to a well-spread supper table, and to end the
evening with the long foregone luxury of a cigar.   Not so
romantic perhaps as to pine away in appetiteless melancholy, but
more rational and manly.

He made the most of his three weeks' visit, and though the
green downs of Freshwater always had for him associations of
pain and conflict, he yet managed to get some enjoyment and
much bodily and mental good from his stay there.

'And have you got your castle in the air, yet?' Mr. Hayes
would laughingly ask him.

His face would sadden a little, but he would always answer
laughingly that Sanitary Reform was his darling project, or that
his pet hobby was the Temperance Cause.

CHAPTER XXVIII.

A MAN AND A BROTHER.

Charity is greater than justice? Yes, it is greater, it is the summit of justice—it is the temple of which justice is the foundation. But you cannot have the top without the bottom; you cannot build upon charity. You must build upon justice, for this main reason, that you have not at first charity to build with. It is the last reward of good work. Do justice to your brother (you can do that whether you love him or not), and you will come to love him.

Wreath of Wild Olive. RUSKIN.

THE 30th of September was a cold, blowy day, the wind seemed to take a special pleasure in howling and whistling about the dismal lodgings where Donovan was working. It was evening, the table was covered with bulky volumes, with papers of notes and manuscript books; he had always had the faculty of doing with a will whatever he undertook, and he was so absorbed in his work that he scarcely noticed a violent peal at the door-bell. It was not till the howling wind was eddying through the passage and the infirm fastening of his sitting-room door had succumbed to the blast and burst open, that he became alive to the fact that Stephen Causton was to come up to town that evening, and that this gust of wind probably announced his advent.

It was a blustering arrival altogether, the landlady's welcome was almost lost in the general hubbub. Donovan heard a loud and rather rough voice replying.

'Well, Mrs. Green, how are you? Here, you boy, put down the portmanteau.'

Then came a slow counting out of coin.

'Please, sir, it were awful 'eavy,' pleaded a shrill voice, 'it were fit to break a chap's arm.'

'Nonsense,' came the loud voice again, 'it's not more than three hundred yards from——'

'Good-evening,' interrupted Donovan, suddenly emerging from the sitting-room, and finding himself in the presence of a light-haired, bushy-whiskered double of Mrs. Causton.

'Oh, good evening,' said Stephen, holding out his hand, and hastily glancing at his new companion. 'I've all sorts of messages for you from Porthkerran.'

Donovan's hands clenched and unclenched themselves. It was a little hard to hear messages from Porthkerran spoken of in such a careless tone.

Y

The little street boy who had carried the portmanteau began to plead again for 'another copper or two.'

'Nonsense, be off, you beggar!' was Stephen's lordly reply, and he passed into the sitting-room, giving a chagrined exclamation at finding no supper ready for him.

Donovan left the landlady to pacify him, and partly from dislike to the tone which his companion had used, partly from his horror of under-paying labour, made the little street boy happy with a sixpence. Then he pushed the front-door to with a vigorous slam, and slowly returned to the sitting-room.

Stephen, feeling that he had a somewhat taciturn companion, talked more than usual, and pleasantly enough. However much he resembled his mother in face, he was singularly unlike her in every other way, and Donovan was surprised that Mrs. Causton should tolerate such very free and easy manners, or that anyone strictly brought up should sprinkle his conversation so plentifully with slang and mild oaths. Was this Dick Tremain's specimen of a 'mother's son'? Surely he must have broken loose from his leading-strings!

The fact was that Stephen at Porthkerran and Stephen in London were two very different beings He did not at first intentionally deceive his mother, but inevitably he had struck out into a line of his own widely different from hers. Too weak to care to set up his principles in open defiance he lived a sort of double life, taking his fling when alone, and meekly deferring to his mother's opinion when at Porthkerran. The result of this falseness was most unhappy. Donovan scrutinized his companion's face keenly that first evening, but after all, in spite of the narrow forehead, and the eyes which rarely looked straight into other eyes, he took rather a liking to Stephen—was he not a friend of the Tremains? the one link which might still exist between them.

It was not for some days that he found out the truth about his new companion. He knew that his bringing up had been of the narrowest, and guessed from the very first that he had shaken off the old traditions, and was taking his own way, but it was not all at once that he realized what that way was.

One October evening when the day's lectures were over, and the two had just finished dinner, the conversation drifted somehow to Porthkerran. It was a very chilly night, Stephen had insisted on having a fire, and dragging up an arm-chair to the hearth, sat crouched up like any old man. Donovan, with his feet on the mantel-piece, American fashion, listened silently to the continuous flow of talk, not taking great note of it until the name of Tremain fell on his ear.

'Johnson's a good enough fellow,' Stephen was saying. 'Not, perhaps, what Dr. Tremain would approve of, but one can't be so strait-laced as he is.'

'The doctor strait-laced!' exclaimed Donovan. 'That's the last word you can apply to him. Strait-laced! why, he's the very soul of liberality.'

'In some ways,' replied Stephen, coolly, 'but not all round. I was a year in his surgery, and I can tell you he's not the easiest master to serve. I wouldn't have him know that Johnson and Curtis were my friends for—"a wilderness of monkeys," as old Shylock has it. Not that they're either of them bad fellows, but they're the sort that the doctor can't abide.'

Donovan only knew the two students by sight, but he was able to guess pretty well to what set they belonged, and he knew that they were probably the very worst friends for anyone so weak-minded as Stephen. The reference to the Tremains, however, brought too many painful thoughts to his mind to admit of his dwelling on his companion's words. He did not speak, and Stephen, thrusting his feet almost under the grate, continued,

'One can't be a slave to another man's opinion, but of course I do try to keep in the doctor's good books, not altogether to please him either. I suppose you saw a good deal of Gladys, didn't you?'

'A good deal,' replied Donovan, steadily; but as he spoke he swung down his feet from the mantel-piece, and pushing back his chair began to pace up and down the room.

'She's an awfully jolly little thing, isn't she?' continued Stephen. 'And she's grown uncommonly pretty too.'

Donovan longed to kick him; Stephen talked on in easy unconsciousness.

'Her colouring's rather too high, certainly, but she's a very fine girl. I lost my heart to her years ago, and though of course I've had half-a-dozen flames since, not one of them was fit to be compared with her. I'd a fortnight at Porthkerran before coming up here, you know, and jolly enough it was too. Between ourselves, my mother is quite ready to help me to see plenty of Gladys Tremain, nothing would please her so well as to have Gladys for a daughter-in-law, and, by Jove, she'd make a stunning good wife. I don't believe she dislikes me either, she was much more ready to be talked to than usual. We shouldn't be half badly matched. What do you think?'

'Discuss your love affairs with anyone you please, but not with me,' said Donovan, reining in his voice with difficulty. 'You ought to have found out before now that I am made of cast iron, and chosen your confidant better.'

'Well, all right, I won't bore you,' replied Stephen. 'Where are you off to? don't go.'

'I can't read yet, I'm going out.'

'Johnson said he'd look in this evening, we'll have a round of 'Nap,'' that'll be better than turning out on such a night as this.'

'You won't play while I'm in the house,' said Donovan, decidedly. 'Look here, Causton, just understand once for all that if you bring those fellows here we dissolve partnership at once. I can get rooms elsewhere, but get into that set I will not.'

'All right, my dear fellow, don't get into such a fume,' said Stephen, trying to yawn carelessly. 'They shan't come here if you feel so strongly about it, though after all you don't know that we shouldn't play for threepenny points.'

'I wasn't born yesterday,' said Donovan, shortly, and with that he went out, snatched up his hat, and, slamming the front door after him, hurried out into the street.

His brain was in a whirl of confusion, he strode on recklessly down the dingy street, out into the broad road, past the brilliant lights of Sanger's Circus, past the hospital to Westminster Bridge. Then he paused, and leaning on the southern parapet, in the very place where Noir Frewin had met him years ago, he let the wild confusion work itself out into distinct realities.

This fellow loved, or professed to love, Gladys; the thought was intolerable to him. He loved her, but spoke of her as Donovan would hardly have spoken of Waif, loved her, and, sanctioned by his mother, evidently meant to woo her! And—worst misery of all!—what was there to prevent it? he was absolutely helpless, he could only look on in dumb despair. Never more could he go to that Cornish home, never more see the face of the woman he loved, but he should hear of Stephen Causton's visits, *he* might go there with impunity, he might spend long hours with Gladys, might woo her, and win her! It was maddening! the thought of it roused all the stormiest passions in Donovan's heart. He hated Stephen, hated and despised him, dwelt with bitterest scorn on his weakness, his many failings. The fiend of jealousy rode rampant over every better feeling, quenched for the time all that was noble in him. But it was only for a time. Before long he was taxing himself—not Stephen—with cowardly weakness.

What right had he to be angry because another man ventured to admire Gladys? What concern was it of his? Had he not resolved on absolute sacrifice of self?—yet here was the wily self coming to the fore again, firing up indignantly because another man desired what he had renounced.

Enjoyment, happiness, was not for him; a line of plodding duty—of entire sacrifice—was the course marked out instead. The 'steep of honour' was before him, his reward must be in the 'deeds of duteous service' themselves.

It should be so. The fire of indignation died down, leaving him quiet, passive, depressed, but still resolutely determined to keep on in this dreary round of duty.

The cold night wind blowing up from the river helped to brace him for the struggle; air and wide open space had always a very strange influence over him, this evening he felt their influence more than ever. The river flowed darkly onward, the lights on its margin threw their yellow reflection in a second golden chain, to the left stood up the sombre towers of the Abbey, and the huge mass of the Houses of Parliament loomed grandly out of the darkness. Sounds of life and traffic rose, too, out of the night. Trains flashed like fiery serpents over Charing Cross Bridge, with shriek of whistle and snort of engine; carriages, horses, passengers of every description hurried on. After all it was a grand old world, no world of units. There was a national life to be lived as well as a private life, there were national grievances which would outweigh and eclipse all private griev-ances, there was—even to a sometime misanthrope—the enthu-siasm of humanity, a wonderful panacea for self-pain.

He was conscious of that widening influence, but more con-scious of a sudden contraction caused by the sound of a voice he knew. Glancing round he saw Stephen and two other men within a few yards of him.

'No, I've never played there,' Stephen was saying.

'Time you were initiated, then,' replied one of his companions. 'Smithson will be there by nine. He's better at billiards than anyone I know, a regular——'

The rest of the sentence died away in the distance, there was a general laugh, and then Donovan heard no more.

He watched the three as they crossed the bridge, and saw them turn to the right; he guessed well enough where they were going. It was evident that Stephen was getting completely under the influence of Johnson and the set to which he belonged. In an instant all the thoughts of brotherhood, freedom, and self-sacrifice were banished from Donovan's mind, and a very devilish idea took possession of him.

Stephen was deplorably weak-minded, he would get under Johnson's thumb, would very likely go to the bad altogether, and, if so, he would unfit himself for Gladys. In one moment there rose before him a picture of the future, Stephen the orthodox dragged down into disgrace and rejection ; himself, an agnostic indeed, but the model of virtue and morality, rewarded by success.

It was a fiendish imagination, lasting only for a minute ; he dashed it down, and stood shamefaced and full of self-loathing in the world of realities again.

The Westminster chimes rang out into the night. Big Ben boomed the hour—nine of those deep, reverberating strokes fell on Donovan's ear. Before the last echo had died into silence he had made up his mind what to do. With the natural instinct of a generous character, he, having wronged Stephen in thought, was anxious now to redress the wrong by some kind of service. Thoughts of the Tremains, too, came crowding into his mind. Stephen was their friend, the doctor's godson—if he went wrong the Tremains would be infinitely sorry. He must at any rate try to get him away from that set into which he had fallen, make some effort to dissuade him from a course which would so greatly shock his mother.

He hurried along with rapid strides, trying not to think how much he disliked the task before him, racking his brain for some excuse by which to draw Stephen away, at any rate for this evening. He had only a few minutes in which to form his plans ; before long he had passed under the dark railway bridge, and had turned up Villiers Street. He had not been in this particular place since the miserable New Year's Eve just before his illness, when his one longing had been to stifle his remorse, and to still those awful recollections of Dot's death-bed. An extraordinary change had passed over him since then, but he did not think of that himself, or contrast the present Donovan with the past, only as he went through the swing doors into the brightly-lighted saloon, a vague association of pain and misery came to him, a sort of ghost of the past seemed to hover about the place.

His quick eye had soon taken a survey of the tables, and had descried Causton cue in hand. The place was crowded ; he made his way towards him and stood for some time watching him in silence. Stephen was betting on his own play with despicable rashness, and he was playing exceedingly ill. Donovan had an insane desire to snatch the cue from him and play himself, it was most irritating to watch the game.

Presently he became conscious that some one's eyes were riveted upon him, he glanced round in involuntary reply to that strange magnetic influence. It was only the marker, a dark-haired man, with a face which somehow seemed familiar to him. As Donovan's eyes met his he turned away, however, apparently

that fixed scrutiny had been quite purposeless. Curious deep
blue eyes, a somewhat broad face, and black hair—why, the
fellow had a Cornish look! And then it suddenly flashed into
Donovan's mind that the likeness which had struck him was a
likeness to Trevethan the blacksmith. Surely this must be Jack
Trevethan for whom he had promised to search. He went round
to the marker's seat, there was no time for beating about the
bush, he just bent forward and said in a low voice,

'Is your name John Trevethan?'

The billiard-marker started violently, and his dark face
flushed. Donovan felt at once that his guess had been correct,
even though the man gave an angry denial.

'My name's Smith. What do you want with me?'

'Nothing. But I have a message for a man named Trevethan from his father,' said Donovan, carelessly. 'I see I was
mistaken, but you look like the description given me.'

He moved away then, and made his way to Stephen. A fresh
game had just begun, this time Stephen was only looking on;
he had lost a good deal, and was not in the best of tempers.

'What, you here, Farrant!' he exclaimed, with surprise, for
he had been too much engrossed to notice Donovan before he
actually spoke to him.

'You passed me just now on Westminster Bridge, I came in
here to try to get hold of you. Haven't you had enough of this?
Come with me and hear the "Cloches de Corneville," we've not
had so much as sixpennyworth of music since you came up.'

'I can't come now, I'm with these other fellows,' said Stephen,
irresolutely.

'Can't!' ejaculated Donovan, scornfully. 'You've not sold
yourself to them, I suppose. Come along, you've had your
game, and we shall just be in time for the half-price.'

Stephen was always easily led, a little more persuasion and
the stronger will triumphed, Donovan gained the day.

As they passed out of the saloon he glanced once more at
the billiard-marker; he was so convinced of his identity with
Trevethan's son that he could not make up his mind to go without one more effort. Hastily scrawling his name and address on
a card he once more crossed over to the Cornishman, and said,
with apparent carelessness,

'If you happen to know anything of this Trevethan, he will
be able to get news of his father at this address.'

The man did not speak, but he took the card, and as Donovan
turned away he neglected his duties to look after him as he
passed down the long saloon.

'The light one was young Causton, but who can he be?'
mused the billiard-marker. 'Farrant! there was no such name
at Porthkerran. He's a knowing hand, wanted to get the other
out of this, and hooked him neat enough, but I was up to him, I
wasn't going to be fooled out of my name.'

With which reflections he put Donovan's card into his waistcoat pocket, and with a sigh returned to his neglected duties.
But in spite of his satisfaction at not having been 'fooled' into a
confession, the thought of his old father at Porthkerran haunted
him uncomfortably.

Meantime Stephen was listening with great delight to the
music at the Opera Comique, Donovan fancied some resemblance
to Porthkerran in the little fishing town represented on the stage,
and therewith heard and saw little else, but in a sort of dream
lived again the months he had spent with the Tremains, returning
every now and then to the prosaic realization that he was in a hot
theatre with his rival beside him, this Stephen Causton to whom
he must before all things be perfectly just. The orchestra twanged
and scraped, the songs and choruses succeeded one another, the
audience applauded, and Donovan forced himself away from the
thoughts of the little Cornish village, and made himself face the
present and think out his plans with regard to Stephen.

The result of this was that as they walked home he told him
a little about his former life, and Stephen was for the time
impressed, liked Donovan better than he had ever liked him before,
and perhaps for the first time thoroughly respected him. But,
though he made many resolutions not to be led away by Johnson
and Curtis, daylight and some disagreeable chaffing from his
former companions about his capture by Donovan Farrant, undid
all the good that had been done.

Donovan saw that something was amiss when they met at
dinner-time. He had made up his mind to do all possible justice to
Stephen, to ignore his failings, and to be friendly with him, but
his patience was severely tried by the resolute sulkiness of his
companion's manner.

Hardly a word was spoken during the meal; as soon as might
be, Donovan turned his chair round to the fire and took up the
Daily News; Stephen too got up from the table, and stood with
his back against the mantel-piece. Presently he broke the
silence.

'I say, Farrant, just understand at once, please, that I won't
have you dogging me again to-night.'

'I thought you were due at the hospital,' said Donovan,
carelessly.

'So I am; but you know well enough what I mean. You know that you dogged me last night.'

'If by knowing where you were and following you, you mean dogging, I certainly did,' said Donovan, throwing aside his paper. 'I suppose Curtis and Co. have been chaffing you?'

'That's no concern of yours, and I'm not going to be interfered with, so just understand.'

'I've not the least wish to interfere,' said Donovan. 'I told you last night why I tried to get you away. I believed that you didn't know what that sort of thing leads to. Now you do know, and if you choose to run into danger with your eyes open, the more fool you.'

'You're the last fellow in the world who has a right to dictate to me,' said Stephen, with offended dignity.

'I don't dictate, I only warn you that you'll come to grief unless you break with that set.'

'And what concern is that of yours, pray?'

'More than you fancy,' said Donovan, quietly. 'You are a friend of the Tremains, and so am I.'

'But I'm not going to bow down to Dr. Tremain in everything, and I told you so before; he's a good enough old fellow, but——'

'Take care how you speak of him,' said Donovan, his eyes flashing.

'Don't look so furious; what did I say? You seem to consider the Tremains your special property. I've known them more years than you have months.'

'Then I wonder that you care to take up with fellows whom the doctor would disapprove of. And besides, Causton, if what you told me last night is true, if you really care for—for Miss Tremain, I should have thought you wouldn't have been able to go about with such cads.'

'Of course I care for Gladys; but what on earth has that to do with the chums I have here?'

'A great deal,' said Donovan, vehemently. 'Do you think you'll ever be worthy of her if you go on making such a fool of yourself? You know you're hardly fit to look at her now, and what do you think you'll be like if you let such fellows as Johnson and Curtis lead you by the nose? You'll be a weak-minded, despicable fool. I tell you, if you mean to dream of marrying Miss Tremain, you must fit yourself for her.'

'You're wonderfully exercised about it; I believe you want to have her for yourself,' said Stephen, tauntingly.

The hot blood rushed to Donovan's face, his eyes blazed with anger; in ungovernable fury he snatched up a boot-jack and hurled it at his companion's head.

The next instant, however, the threatened tragedy became utterly comic. Stephen, to save his head, warded off the blow with his arm, and the boot-jack hit him with considerable force on the elbow. Numb, and tingling to the very finger tips, he danced with pain. Waif's tail got trodden on, and he howled dismally; the fire-irons were knocked down, and went clattering into the fender, and Donovan, overcome by the absurdity of the scene, forgot his anger, and fell into a paroxysm of laughter. Stephen laughed too.

'You wretch! it was my funny-bone. By Jove! I believe you've broken it.'

'A medical riddle for you,' said Donovan, as soon as he could speak for laughing. 'Why is the funny-bone so named?'

Stephen gave it up, and, as the clock struck, remembered that it was time he went back to the hospital. He went off, laughing at the answer, 'Because it borders on the humerus,' and apparently the incident of the boot-jack had really dispelled his sulkiness. Donovan picked up the fire-irons, patted Waif, and then, taking an armful of books from the sideboard, settled down to his evening's work. The boot-jack was ever after a theme for laughter; but they neither of them alluded again to the conversation which had led to the quarrel, nor did Stephen ever think there was the smallest truth in his taunt. He could not imagine anyone so matter-of-fact as Donovan actually falling in love, and the stony silence with which all his remarks about Gladys were met only confirmed him in the opinion that his companion was indeed of the 'cast iron' philosopher type.

To Donovan that year was a hard struggle. The continual worry about Stephen, and the friction of his presence, were perhaps good for him, they certainly prevented him from becoming self-engrossed; but there were times when he felt unbearably jaded and harassed, as if he could not much longer keep up the weary fight. He grew curiously fond of Stephen, and Stephen returned the liking in his own odd way, vacillating between Donovan and his old companions, and proving his miserable weakness of will. But, though Donovan saved him from much, he could not prevent the steady downhill course into which he had fallen.

The approach of the long vacation brought another struggle, and another hardly-won victory. There was a very urgent invitatation to Porthkerran. Of course it must be refused, but Donovan had to go through the old battle once more before the letter was written. He made it a question of economy this time; his finances were low, and he had made up his mind to stay in town through the summer months, having obtained temporary employment in working up the book-keeping of some small tradesman. The Tremains were sorry, but could say nothing against such a plan, and Donovan saw Stephen go westward for his three months' holiday close to Gladys' home, and felt a bitter pang of envy.

He worked almost fiercely through those stifling summer months, and in every spare moment read hungrily on all sides of the great question which was gradually filling his mind more and more. There was temporary satisfaction in the actual reading, but he seemed to gain little from it. Arguments for, repulsed him; arguments against, pained him. He felt no nearer the knowledge of the truth.

October brought a return to his hospital work, and fresh difficulties with Stephen, who came back from Porthkerran inclined to break out into violent reaction after the subdued atmosphere of his mother's house.

Mrs. Causton herself had not been altogether satisfied with her son during the vacation. She wondered whether Donovan's influence could be bad for him, and after he had left she worried herself so much about him that she at length resolved to go up to town for a week, visit him in his rooms, and satisfy herself that the doctor's *protégé* was not corrupting him.

One morning when Donovan was sitting at breakfast, discussing a tough essay on 'Spontaneous Generation,' over weak coffee and leathery toast, there came a knock at the door, the landlady announced 'Mrs. Causton,' and, much surprised, he found himself face to face with Stephen's mother.

'I have taken you by surprise, Mr. Farrant,' she began, in her rather demure voice. 'I came up unexpectedly to town on business, and was anxious to find Stephen before his lectures began. I arrived too late last night to come and see him then, as I had intended doing. Stephen is not unwell, I hope? I see you are breakfasting alone.'

'He will be down directly,' said Donovan. 'Let me give you some coffee, Mrs. Causton, and then I'll go and call Stephen.'

'Yes, pray tell him I am here,' replied Mrs. Causton. 'No coffee, thank you. I breakfasted at my hotel. Pray call Stephen. I hope he is not often so late as this?'

Donovan judiciously ignored that question, and went to summon the hope of the Caustons, whom he found sleeping the sleep of the just, and in the meantime the anxious mother took a

rapid survey of the sitting-room. It was redolent of tobacco
but no doubt that was due to Donovan Farrant ; for the rest she
could see nothing to find fault with, unless indeed the evil lurked
in those books piled up on the sideboard. She crossed the room,
and put up her double gold-rimmed eye-glasses to read the titles.
There were several works on medicine and surgery, and some
bulky volumes of science, then came an untidy pile of a strangely
heterogeneous character. She read the titles with great dissatisfaction. Maurice, Renan, Haeckel, Kingsley, Strauss,
Erskine, and at the top an open volume, Draper's 'Conflict
between Religion and Science.' She turned to the fly-leaf. It
was a much worn, second-hand book, but under two half-erased
names was written 'D. Farrant.' Of course all these books
belonged to him, but how could she tell that Stephen did not
read them too ?

Her manner when Donovan came down again was decidedly
stiff. He felt it at once, and it hurt him a little, for the recollection
that she had left Porthkerran only the day before, had raised a
great hunger in his heart for news of Gladys.

'I hope they are all well at Trenant ?' he asked, hoping that
her answer might go a little into details. But he only extracted
a general reply that everyone was well, that Porthkerran was
very little altered, and that old Admiral Smith had been suffering
very much from rheumatic gout.

Before long Stephen appeared, having evidently performed a
very hasty toilette, and Donovan, thinking it well to leave the
mother and son alone, whistled to Waif and went out.

'How do you like Mr. Farrant ? is he a pleasant companion ?'
asked Mrs. Causton, as the front door closed.

'Oh, he's a very good sort of fellow,' said Stephen, ringing
the bell for his breakfast, 'he's very clever, and works like a
nigger.'

'Then I wonder he has time to waste on such a paper as this,'
said Mrs. Causton, laying her black-gloved hand on the *Sporting
News*.

The *Sporting News*, as it happened, was Stephen's paper, but
he could not allow his mother to know that; with a slight prick-
ing of conscience, he merely turned the conversation.

'Oh, of course even the hardest working fellows must have a
little relaxation. Farrant reads on every subject under the sun.'

'I hope you never open those dreadful books of his which I
see over there ?' asked Mrs. Causton, apprehensively.

'Oh, dear no,' replied Stephen, this time with perfect truth
'They're a great deal too stiff for me.'

Mrs. Causton gave a relieved sigh and the conversation drifted away from Donovan to the examination which Stephen was going in for that term. He had lost much valuable time when his eyes had been bad, but was nevertheless very sanguine.

'I must own,' said Mrs. Causton, as she walked back to her hotel with Stephen, 'that it will be rather a relief to me when your course is over. I don't altogether like this arrangement of sharing rooms with Mr. Farrant. I hope he never speaks to you about religious matters.'

'Never; he's a very taciturn fellow, and as to theology, we should never dream of discussing it, so you may be quite happy, mother.'

His manner re-assured Mrs. Causton, and he spared no pains to please her during her week's stay, escorting her to the National Gallery, and the British Museum, and one night even submitting to the very dullest of meetings at Exeter Hall.

'If that poor Donovan Farrant would have come with us,' sighed good Mrs. Causton, at the close of a speech which had roused her to enthusiasm.

'Not much in his line, I'm afraid,' said Stephen, heartily applauding the speaker with hands and feet in a way which delighted his mother.

'Dear Stephen was so much impressed by Mr. ——,' she told one of her friends afterwards. And the poor lady went back to Cornwall quite satisfied that her son was doing well, that even Dr. Tremain's suggestion that he should lodge with Donovan Farrant had not proved really dangerous. It was, she still thought, a somewhat rash experiment, but certainly dear Stephen was not the least contaminated.

CHAPTER XXIX.

A BRAVE SPRITE.

Wonder it is to see in diverse mindes
How diversely love doth his pageants play,
And shewes his powre in variable kindes :
The baser wit, whose ydle thoughts alway
Are wont to cleave unto the lowly clay,
It stirreth up to sensuall desire,
But in brave sprite it kindles goodly fire,
That to all high desert and honour doth aspire.
Ne suffereth it uncomely idlenesse
In his free thought to build her sluggish nest,
Ne suffereth it thought of ungentlenesse
Ever to creep into his noble breast ;
But to the highest and the worthiest,
Lifteth it up that els would lowly fall :
It lettes not fall, it lettes it not to rest ;
It lettes not scarse this Prince to breath at all,
But to his first poursuit him forward still doth call.
Faeric Queen. Spenser.

'Curtis sent you word that he was going by the 9.30 to-morrow,' said Donovan, coming into the sitting-room one autumn evening, and finding Stephen for once really hard at work.

'All right,' was the laconic answer.

'You're not going to the Z—— Races ?' asked Donovan, abruptly.

Stephen looked up with a smile.

'In the words of the old Quaker I must answer, " Friend, first thee tellest a lie, and then thee askest a question." '

'But with the examination so near and your preparation so frightfully behindhand,' urged Donovan.

'Am I not grinding like fifty niggers now to make up ?' said Stephen.

'But it's such nonsense your going,' continued Donovan, rather incautiously. 'Why, you hardly know a horse from a donkey ! you'll only get fleeced, and come home up to your neck in debt.'

'I wish you'd let me alone,' said Stephen ; 'I tell you I'm going, and you won't bother me out of it, so do shut up.'

'What do you imagine your mother would say to it, if she knew ?'

The question was an uncomfortable one, and, moreover,

Donovan had the power of forcing Stephen to listen to him ; he went on, gravely,

'However much you may kick at the word dishonourable, you can hardly say the way you are going on is anything else. Only a few weeks ago you were going to an Exeter Hall meeting with Mrs. Causton, and now you are going to the Z—— meeting, with a set of snobs who, as sure as fate, will get you into some scrape.'

Stephen was imperturbably good-humoured that evening; he did not take exception even at this very plain speaking, he only swung himself lazily back in his chair and yawned prodigiously. When Donovan had ended, he sat musing for a minute or two, then said, abruptly,

'I tell you what, Farrant, you won't persuade me out of going, but I don't care a rap about being with these fellows if you would go. Come, you can spare a day well enough, and we can have no end of a spree.'

Donovan could ill afford such an unnecessary expense, but he knew that his presence would probably keep Stephen straight, and, after some deliberation, he consented to go.

The day proved to be exceedingly fine, one of those still autumn days when scarcely a breath is stirring, when the limp yellow leaves float down slowly and noiselessly from the rapidly thinning trees, and the sun sends its softened beams through a golden misty haze. It was most delicious to get out of smoky London ; except for long walks every Sunday, Donovan had not actually been out of town for more than a year, and the change was thoroughly enjoyable. In spite of sundry recollections of old times which would intrude themselves upon him, the day really bid fair to be a pleasant one. Stephen was companionable enough, and everything was so fresh to him that Donovan found it easy work to keep him out of difficulties.

All went well till the races were over, then, as they were elbowing their way through the crowd surrounding the grand stand, Donovan suddenly felt a hand on his shoulder and a well-known voice ringing in his ear.

'Well, milord, who would have thought of seeing you here! How are you, my dear fellow ?'

He turned round to have his hand grasped by old Rouge Frewin. There he was, as unchanged as if for all this eventful time the world had been standing still with him, the same genial, cheery, red-faced old captain who had watched by his sick-bed at Monaco, and cried like a baby when they had parted at Paris. Donovan would have been both ungrateful and unnatural if his

first thought had not been one of real pleasure at meeting again
the kindly old man.

'Why, captain, this is an odd chance that has brought us
together! How natural it seems to see you again! What corner
of the moon have you dropped from?'

'Tacking between London and Paris ever since you left us,'
said Rouge, with a sigh. 'I've missed you, lad; it's a hard life
for an old man like me. I'm growing old, Donovan, growing old
fast, and Noir has been hard on me since you went.'

'Is Noir here to-day?'

'No, he was to come back from Paris to-night. I don't know
the ins-and-outs of it, but Noir is very uneasy just now, he
won't settle down in England comfortably, and it's a miserable
life this knocking about among foreigners; it's killing me by
inches, and poor old Sweepstakes too.'

'What, is Sweepstakes still in the land of the living?'

'Yes, he's at my rooms in town, not the old place in Drury
Lane, Noir wouldn't go there again. By-the-by, milord, what
are you doing with yourself now?'

The question first reminded Donovan that there were reasons
which made it advisable not to give his address to the Frewins.
He replied that he was at present a medical student, and then as
he spoke he recollected Stephen, and turned hastily round, but
Stephen was gone.

The races were over, he might possibly have gone back to the
station, but Donovan thought that he had probably caught sight
of some of his friends and had gone to speak to them; he was
a good deal vexed. It was impossible, however, to find him in
such a crowd, he was obliged to give it up, and, quitting the
race-course with the old captain, made his way as quickly as
might be to the train.

They had not gone far when a block in the long line of
carriages attracted their notice.

'Some accident,' said Rouge. 'Never was yet at any races
without seeing a spill of some sort.

Donovan pushed on quickly without speaking a word. He
felt almost certain that Stephen had somehow got into mischief.

By the time he had made his way through the throng of
people a dog-cart which had been overturned was being raised
from the ground, and Donovan at once caught sight of Stephen's
friend Curtis standing at the head of the terrified horse, whose
violent kicking and plunging had caused the accident. Many
people were offering their help, several were stooping over a
prostrate figure, he pushed them aside; it was indeed Stephen

Canston who lay there perfectly unconscious, the blood flowing slowly from his mouth.

Donovan's authoritative manner soon sent back the mere idlers, while the really efficient helpers came to the fore. Rouge offered his brandy-flask, and in a very short time an extemporized litter was brought up, and Stephen was borne away to the nearest hotel.

It was all done in such a business-like way that for a time it seemed to Donovan only like his hospital work; it was not till a doctor had arrived and his own responsibility was lessened, that he realized that it was Stephen Canston, the Tremains' friend, Stephen for whom he felt himself in a manner accountable, who was lying there in danger of his life. In a disjointed way he gathered from Curtis the facts of the accident. Stephen had caught sight of them, and had gone to speak to them, Curtis had offered him a seat in the dog-cart, and they had driven off, intending to dine together in the town; something had startled the horse, and the dog-cart had been overturned. The rest had escaped with bruises and a severe shaking, but Stephen had broken a rib, the bone had pierced the lung, and he was for some hours in a very precarious state.

The first moment that Donovan could be spared he ran down to dispatch a telegram to Dr. Tremain, and not till he had with some difficulty worded the message did one thought of himself come to trouble him.

'*D Farrant, Royal Hotel, Z——, to Dr. Tremain, Trenant, Porthkerran. Canston has met with a bad accident. Please tell his mother, and come at once if possible.*'

What a panic poor Mrs. Canston would be in, and how strange it would seem to them all that he—Donovan—should be with Stephen at Z——. Of course Dr. Tremain would know that the Z—— Races were on, and would naturally arrive at the conclusion that he had led Stephen there. It could not be supposed that the orderly mother's son, who attended Exeter Hall meetings, would have gone to such a place without great persuasion. In a moment there rose before Donovan the whole situation. The decision must lie with Stephen; if he chose to confess his long course of self-pleasing all would be well, but, if he chose to be silent, Donovan felt that he could not betray him, that even at the risk of being misunderstood, he must hold his tongue, an easy enough task surely—merely to keep silence—a task in which he was already well practised!

He went back to the sick-room and forgot all his presentiments in keeping anxious watch over Stephen. The hæmorrhage

z

had been checked, but all through the night the most alarming prostration continued, and it was far on in the next day before the immediate danger was over, and the patient fell into an exhausted sleep.

Donovan left him then for the first time, the landlord's daughter keeping guard over him, and went himself to get much-needed food and rest.

Gladys never forgot that autumn evening when the telegram arrived. For some days the household at Trenant had been disturbed and anxious, for Jackie and Nesta were both laid up with the measles, and Nesta, always a rather delicate little child, was seriously ill. The nurse had gone down for her supper, and Gladys had taken her place in the night nursery. As she sat beside the sleeping children she heard a sharp ring at the door-bell, a message for her father she supposed, and thought no more about it, little dreaming *what* message it was, and from whom. And yet, as she sat there in the dim light, her thoughts did drift away to Donovan. What was he doing in those dull London lodgings which he had described to them? His letters had been fewer and shorter lately, and he never spoke of any future visit to Porthkerran. Were their lives growing farther apart? Was it never to be anything but waiting and trusting? Should she never learn that he had found the truth? She covered her face and prayed silently, hardly in thought-out words, but only, as it were, breathing out her want of patience, her love for him, and her longing that he might think and do that which was right.

The nurse came back, and Gladys, released from her watch, went down to the drawing-room; she was strong to meet the news that awaited her, and she needed all her strength. Over and over again she read the words scrawled on that thin pink paper, hearing with painful acuteness all her father's surmises as to what could have taken Stephen and Donovan to those races. She hated herself for it, but it hurt her a great deal more to hear a shadow of blame attached to Donovan than to hear that Stephen was lying perhaps in mortal danger. The one caused her a sharp stab of pain, the other only a shocked awed feeling— a vague regret.

Her father went away in a few minutes to break the news as well as he could to poor Mrs. Causton. Mrs. Tremain was called away to little Nesta, and Gladys sat crouched up alone by the fire, feeling supremely wretched. It could not be that Donovan had led Stephen astray—and yet her father had evidently thought it must be so! Her tears flowed fast, but still not one was shed at the thought of Stephen's accident; it was a tall manly figure

that rose before her, excluding everything else, a strong face
with dark sad eyes and resolute mouth. It could not be that
Donovan had forgotten his high aims, had thrown aside his search
after truth, and sunk so low—it could not be! His face rose
before her in vivid memory; she felt certain that he had not
done this thing. She dashed away her tears, choked them back
angrily, resolutely.

'It can't be, it *isn't* so; I will never, never believe it!' she
cried, passionately. 'Though all the world accuse him, I will
never believe it! I will trust you, Donovan—always!

She was calm again now, invincible in her woman's stronghold
of absolute trust. The arrows of logic, the force of argument,
the stern array of steely facts spend their force in vain on that
stronghold.

Her father came back before long from his sad errand; she
went to meet him in the hall to ask after Mrs. Causton.

'Oh! there you are, dear,' he exclaimed. 'I came back to
fetch you. Aunt Margaret is terribly upset, and I promised that
you should go to her.'

Gladys trembled a little, but she could make no objection,
and ran up to fetch her things.

'You must try to induce her to go to bed,' said the doctor, as
he walked back with Gladys to Mrs. Causton's house. 'We
shall start quite early to-morrow morning, but she will be fit for
nothing if she does not sleep first.'

Mrs. Causton was exceedingly fond of Gladys, and, in spite of
the real want of sympathy between them, this evening she clung
to her more than ever, probably, in the depth of her misery, not
noticing that there was a little shadow of restraint in her manner.
For, though Gladys had the sweetest and most delicate tact and
sympathy, she often let herself become absorbed in sympathising
with one person. She was one of those characters who love the
few ardently, but are a little wanting in breadth, and now every
doubt or reproach cast on Donovan pushed her further away
from Mrs. Causton.

However, she did her best, listened in silence to Mrs. Causton's
sorrows, helped her to make all the necessary arrangements for
her journey, soothed her by mute caresses, and at last persuaded
her to go to bed. Then she lay down beside her, and tried to
sleep, but long after Mrs. Causton had forgotten her troubles in
restful unconsciousness, Gladys lay with wide-open eyes, keeping
rigidly still for fear of disturbing her companion, and in spirit
sharing Donovan's watch beside Stephen's sick-bed.

In the morning Mrs. Causton awoke little refreshed. She

was almost disabled by a terrible headache. Gladys had to do everything for her. As she brought her a cup of coffee, it seemed to dawn on the poor lady that very soon she should have to part with her.

'Oh! Gladys,' she said, pleadingly, 'could you not come with me? I don't know what I shall do without you.'

'I would willingly come,' said Gladys, trembling violently, 'only—I'm not sure whether mother could spare me——'

She broke off abruptly, as her father drove up in the pony carriage. The thought of meeting Donovan once more had set all her pulses throbbing painfully, but she could not make up her mind to ask her father whether she might go, she could not even repeat Mrs. Causton's words to him.

The idea had, however, taken a strong hold on Mrs. Causton. She greeted the doctor with an urgent entreaty that he would allow Gladys to go with them.

'I am so poorly, and she has been such a comfort to me. I don't know how I can do without her.'

'Very well, Gladys dear,' said Dr. Tremain, putting his hand on her shoulder. 'If you will come with us, and can do without any more preparation, it shall be so. Nesta is better to-day, and we will send a note back to explain to the mother.'

It was all settled in a few minutes. Gladys hurried away to put on her walking things. The maid hastily packed her little night-bag for her, and before long she was driving with her father and Mrs. Causton to St. Kerrans.

The journey seemed endless; though they had started very early, it was four o'clock in the afternoon by the time they reached Z——.

Gladys was very stiff and weary, but she had hardly time to think of herself, she was so taken up with the effort of sympathising with and helping Mrs. Causton, while, as they drove through the busy streets of Z——, the consciousness that every moment was bringing her nearer to Donovan made her heart beat quickly, and the bright colour rose in her cheeks.

At length they reached the Royal Hotel, learnt at once from one of the waiters that Stephen was doing well, and were ushered upstairs. Mrs. Causton leant on the doctor's arm, Gladys followed tremblingly, glad enough to cling to the banisters. They were shown into a private sitting-room. Already the afternoon light was failing, but a fire blazed in the grate, and by its ruddy glow Gladys saw Donovan. He was stretched at full length on the hearth-rug fast asleep. The waiter hesitated.

'Poor young gent! He was up all the night. Perhaps

you'll wake him, sir, if you see fit,' and then, with a curious
glance at the three visitors, the man withdrew, mentally ejaculat-
ing that he 'wasn't going to disturb the poor fellow, not if it
was to see the queen herself.' But as the door closed, Donovan
started up.

'Is he awake?' he cried, fancying that Stephen's nurse had
come ; then, catching sight of Dr. Tremain, he sprang to his feet.
'I am so glad you've come. He is really doing well now. The
immediate danger is over.'

As he spoke he shook hands with the doctor and Mrs. Causton,
then, for the first time catching sight of Gladys, he was all at
once speechless. For one moment their eyes met, that strange
meeting which seems like the blending of soul with soul. That
was their real greeting. The conventional handshake was nothing,
and in another moment Donovan had turned hastily away, and
plunged abruptly into details of Stephen's accident.

Mrs. Causton was painfully agitated, and was indignant when
Donovan insisted on the extreme rashness of going at once to see
the patient. To wake up and to find his mother unexpectedly
there would be the very worst thing for him, and though Dr.
Tremain quite agreed, and in fact took the law into his own
hands, Mrs. Causton regarded Donovan entirely in the light of
an enemy.

Dr. Tremain went himself to the sick-room, and it was
arranged that he should relieve guard, and, when Stephen awoke,
tell him of his mother's arrival. Donovan left him there, and
steeling himself for the encounter, went slowy back to the
sitting-room, where Mrs. Causton was lying in an easy-chair,
and Gladys was trying to persuade her to take a cup of tea.

'You will have some tea, too, will you not ?' she said, looking up at Donovan. 'They told us you had been up all night ;
you must be very tired.'

'Thank you, yes, I should like some,' said Donovan, allowing
himself to watch the little white hands as they lifted the big
plated tea-pot and poured out the tea. And as she handed him
his cup, he noticed, in that strange way in which the minutest
trifles are noticed when there seems least time to waste on them,
that the china was thick, white, with a pink rim, and bore the
stamp of the Royal Hotel.

He was startled when Mrs. Causton first spoke to him ; the
waiting seemed to embitter her, and she made him feel that his
presence was very distasteful.

'Have you any other particulars to tell me of my son's
accident ?' she asked, very coldly.

'I think you have heard all now,' he replied, 'all that I myself know, for I did not actually see the carriage upset.'

'Having brought Stephen to such a place, I should have thought the least you could have done was to stay with him,' said Mrs. Causton, with a quiver of indignation in her voice. 'It has been a miserable mistake from the very beginning. I hoped he might have had a good influence over you, but you have abused my trust cruelly. If I had ever dreamt that you would be the stronger of the two, he should never have shared your rooms.'

Donovan did not speak; but Gladys, glancing up at him, saw that he was passing through some great struggle. Her heart ached as she heard Mrs. Causton's unjust words. One effort she must make to check the conversation.

'Will you not come to your room and lie down, auntie?' she suggested. 'You will be fitter to go to Stephen when he wakes, if you rest first.'

'I shall rest quite as well here, thank you,' said Mrs. Causton. 'We need not trespass further on your time, Mr. Farrant. I am sure you can ill afford to waste two days in the middle of term.'

'I should be sorry to annoy you by staying,' said Donovan, quietly. 'Good-bye.'

He held out his hand gravely.

'I only hope you may take warning yourself by my poor Stephen's fate,' said Mrs. Causton, relapsing into tears. 'It is one of those mysterious dispensations so hard to resign oneself to, the innocent suffering and the guilty escaping. I am sure I hope and pray that you may repent while there is yet time.'

He wished Gladys good-bye and left the room.

For one moment Gladys sat quite still; then a sudden impulse seized her. She *could* not let him go like this, it was too cruel, too heartless! She opened the door and ran down the passage, catching sight of him far in front. Would he never stop! Would nothing make him look round! By the time she reached the head of the stairs he was half way down them; it seemed to her as if miles of grey and crimson carpeting stretched between them.

Half timidly, and yet with a ring of despair in her voice, she called to him.

'Donovan!'

For a moment his heart stood still; he caught at the rail, turned, and saw her standing far above him. He did not speak, but waited—waited till she came to him in complete silence. His lips were firmly pressed together, his face rigid. Was it hard of him—was it cruel to her to meet her thus?

The very sound of his own name from her lips had re-awakened the wildest longing for all that he knew must never be. He waited for her to speak, but her words only made the tumult within him wilder, the struggle more intolerable.

'Do not go like this,' she said, pleadingly; 'please wait and see papa. Aunt Margaret doesn't know what she is saying. I know you could explain it all to papa. Please, please wait!'

She had not the faintest idea that she was putting the most terrible temptation before Donovan, but she was almost frightened by the spasm of pain which passed over his face; his voice too was strange and hollow, as he answered, sadly,

'You are mistaken, I can't explain anything.'

His words caused such a sudden downfall of all her hopes that the tears rose to her eyes, fight against them as she would it was of no use, and nothing but a sort of despairing womanly pride kept them from overflowing.

Poor Donovan saw all, and turned away. That moment was as the bitterness of death to him. He was giving her pain, making her think badly of him—for what? Was it indeed for her good? It could not surely be—it was so unnatural—so hard—so merciless! He would speak to her, tell her of his love, tell her that he would do anything—everything—for her sake!

And yet was that really true, when he could not keep silence? Oh, weakness! here he was fighting the old battle which he had fought in the orchard at Trenant, on the Porthkerran cliffs, on Westminster Bridge! Each time he thought he had conquered, yet now this deadly temptation had risen again, as strong—far stronger—than ever. Should those bitter efforts be wasted? Should his longing for present relief—for happiness even for her —lead him to speak words which he had no right to speak? But this silence, this silence as to Stephen, it was anguish. He must right himself to her! Had not his own character some claim upon him? Had he not his own rights as well as Stephen's to bear in mind? That was the great question, it was clearly Self *versus* Stephen, a just claim for himself, certainly, yet a claim for self *only*. Yes, he would be truthful in his self-arguing, even though it brought keenest pain,—to right himself would not be to serve Gladys, would not even make her really happier, he had resolved long ago that she must learn not to care for him. He would be silent now for her sake as well as for Stephen's—the proof of his love should be his silence!

All this passed through his mind in a very few moments. He

turned back to Gladys, she was leaning against the banisters, her head drooped low, the light from a coloured lamp hanging over the stairs threw a golden glow over her sunny hair; her face was partly in shadow, but in the half-light her bright colouring looked all the more lovely.

He knew it was the last time he should see her, but he would not let his eyes soften, would not let one trace of his love show itself.

'It is better that I should go at once,' he said, taking her hand, 'believe me, it is much better. Good-bye.'

Gladys looked steadily up at him, her blue eyes were quite clear now, there was a sort of triumphant trust in her look.

'Good-bye,' she said, softly, not one other word.

She watched him as he went down the stairs, watched very quietly, but very intently, noticed his firm, almost sharp step, heard him call for his bill and ask the time of the London train, lastly heard the silence, the aching silence of the quiet hotel when he was really gone.

But in spite of her heartache there was the dawning of a rapturous joy for her even now. For when Donovan had turned to say good-bye to her, there had been that in his face which had raised her out of herself. He had looked utterly noble, the very light of Christ had shone in his face. She thought it was indeed probable that he did not care for her as he had once cared, but what did that matter? in the intensity of her joy for him she could not think of her own pain. For she loved Donovan with her whole heart and soul, and she felt, nay, she *knew*, that he was 'not far from the kingdom of Heaven.'

CHAPTER XXX.

OLD FRIENDS.

Wouldst thou the holy hill ascend,
And see the Father's face?
To all His children humbly bend,
And seek the lowest place.

. . . . . .

Thus humbly doing on the earth
What things the earthly scorn,
Thou shalt assert the lofty birth
Of all the lowly born.
Violin Songs. GEORGE MACDONALD.

LONDON was shrouded in the murkiest of November fogs: Donovan groped his way with some difficulty down York Road, opened the door of his lodgings with a latch-key, made his way into the cheerless sitting-room, lighted the gas, and threw himself back in a chair in hopeless dejection. The sharpness of the struggle was over, the bitterness of the pain past, his was now the

> Stifled, drowsy, unimpassioned **grief**
> Which finds no outlet or relief.

Perhaps the most real and unforgetable form of suffering.

He sat motionless, the light which had so cheered Gladys had died from his face now, it was clouded, haggard, with dark shadows under the eyes.

He was roused at last by hearing Waif's bark in the distance, then came sounds of opening a door down below, a rush and a patter of feet on the kitchen stairs, and a violent scratching and impatient whining at his own door. He dragged himself up, opened it, and received a frantic welcome from his dog, who had been shut into an empty cellar during his absence.

Waif was almost crazy with delight at seeing him back again; he dashed round and round him, bounded up in the air, whined and snorted, licked him all over, and finally tore across the room in a violent hurry to perform his usual act of loyal service, to drag out the boot-jack, and, one at a time, to deposit his master's slippers in the fender.

This evening there was no fire; Waif found that out, and seemed perplexed; he was not quite capable of striking a match, but he worried Donovan into doing it, and then sat contentedly watching the yellow blaze, thudding the floor with his tail in the intensity of his satisfaction. Donovan watched him thoughtfully.

'We must jog on together, Waif, my boy,' he said, patting the sagacious black and tan head.

Waif's eyes twinkled and shone, his tail beat a joyful tattoo on the floor.

The dog and his master understood each other, and Donovan would certainly have chosen to spend the rest of the evening with his dumb companion, to indulge his sad thoughts in silence, but it was not to be so. There was a knock at the front door before many minutes had passed, he heard a voice which seemed strangely familiar asking if he were in. Another moment, and Rouge and Noir were ushered into his room.

'Tracked you at last,' said Noir, his dark face lighting up with a gleam of satisfaction as he wrung Donovan's hand.

'And all owing to those lucky races and my quick eyes,' said the old captain. 'How's the chap that was pitched out of the dog-cart?'

'Badly hurt, but doing well now,' said Donovan. 'How did you find me out?'

'Through the light-haired fellow who was holding the horse, a fellow-student of yours. Why, Waif, old dog, you don't look a day older!'

Waif sniffed cautiously at the old captain's clothes, recognized him after a few moments, and was pleased to renew the friendship. Noir meanwhile was speaking in a lowered voice to Donovan.

'I came here on business—can I have a few words alone with you? Let us take a turn outside.'

'All right,' said Donovan. 'You'll stay and have some supper; we'll be back before long, captain, there's an evening paper for you, and as many medical books as you like.'

Rouge settled himself comfortably in an arm-chair, and Noir and Donovan went out into the foggy street.

'I am in a scrape,' said Noir, abruptly. 'I have come to ask if you will help me. Perhaps, though, you are so respectable and virtuous now that you have forgotten all about the old times.'

'My memory isn't ruled by will,' said Donovan, hoarsely. 'Go on.'

'Well, I don't blame you for wishing to forget that year—I wish to goodness I could, for, milord, I am decidedly up a tree. You remember Darky Legge? Well, he has been arrested, discovered at last, after carrying on his old game for years. After you left us, I was thrown a good deal with him—in fact, at Paris we acted together—and the wretch, who has no sense of honour, has betrayed me. Unless I can leave the country at once, I'm a lost man.'

'I can't offer you money,' said Donovan, 'for I can hardly scrape along myself.'

'It isn't that I want,' said Noir, quickly. 'It is this: I can't afford to take the old captain with me to America—I haven't the cash for one thing, and besides, he would be like a mill-stone round my neck. He can live on quietly here for very little, and I will send him what I can from time to time. But you know what he is with no one to look after him—he'd kill himself in a year. I want to know whether you'd mind keeping an eye on the poor old fellow.'

Donovan had at first felt the most intense shrinking from any renewal of their old friendship; the remembrance of those dark days was a sort of nightmare to him. He listened to Noir's story silently and painfully, wondering how he could ever have shared in such doings. What a wretched misanthrope he had been, half maddened by sorrow and injustice, hating everything in the world except his dog!

But he was touched by Noir's thought for his old father, the poor, weak, old man whom he still, in his rough way, loved and shielded. They walked a few paces in silence, then Donovan spoke.

'He had better put up at my place. Causton will never come back to those rooms, and though I'm out most of the day, I shall be able to see something of him, and will do my best to keep him straight.'

'You are a trump!' exclaimed Noir, heartily. 'But won't he be in your way? I know you're a cut above us.'

'You forget I am a Republican,' said Donovan, quietly. 'Let him come to-morrow, and do you make the best of your way to America.'

Noir was struck by the change in his sometime follower; he had always respected Donovan since their quarrel and final separation at Paris, but he felt now at an immense distance from him. After all, he mused, honesty did indeed seem the best policy. No words which Donovan could have used would have impressed him half as much as this visible change and growth, and more than all his readiness to help the old captain roused a feeling of gratitude which lasted as one of the few softening influences through the rest of Noir's life.

And so it was ordered that Donovan should not live alone, should not be free to indulge his misery in silence, but should again have his affections drawn out towards a very weak member of the human brotherhood, should bear again the burden of another's sin, and struggle perseveringly for his deliverance.

CHAPTER XXXI.

SILENCE.

As for me, I honour, in these loud babbling days, all the Silent rather. A grand Silence that of Romans;—nay the grandest of all, is it not that of the gods!

. . . .

Commend me to the silent English, to the silent Romans.

CARLYLE.

DR. TREMAIN was very much vexed when he found that Donovan had left without seeing him, nor could he gather any very distinct account of what had passed either from Mrs. Causton or Gladys. Mrs. Causton irritated him considerably by her tearful and highly-coloured descriptions of the evil which she imagined to have emanated entirely from her son's companion; Gladys was strangely silent and would volunteer nothing, but, in answer to a direct question, told her father that Donovan had refused to see him, and would not allow her to disturb him. All this tended only too effectually to confirm the doctor's fears. Donovan had fallen back grievously, there could be little doubt of that; if it had not been so, could he have rushed off at a moment's notice in this way, studiously avoiding him after a separation of more than a year?

Stephen was too ill to be thoroughly questioned on the subject, but the doctor could not refrain from one or two attempts to gain from him the favourable testimony to Donovan's character for which he hoped against hope.

Once in the night, when he woke refreshed after a long sleep and lay in listless quiet, Dr. Tremain hazarded a question.

'I don't wish you to talk much, Stephen, you are not fit for it; but just give me a simple yes and no to one or two questions. Has Donovan Farrant been influencing you in a way which your mother and I did not expect?'

'Yes,' replied Stephen, glad that the question was put in so ambiguous a way that he could reply in the affirmative. But the next question was more direct.

'I am to understand, then, that my finding you in his company at the Z—— Races is only one instance in many, that he has often been with you to places which Mrs. Causton—which I myself would have disapproved?'

Stephen's colour deepened; this question might still be answered by that deceptive 'yes,' but not without very uneasy stirrings of conscience. And yet how much that was disagreeable might be averted by that affirmative! He had been led astray, what could be more probable and pardonable? He should of course repent, turn over a new leaf, get into the doctor's good graces again, and in no way damage his prospects as Gladys' lover. But if, on the contrary, the ugly truth came out? Then there would be endless reproaches from his mother, unbearable humiliation; what harm could there be in giving a slight turn to the meaning of the word? In a minute, by that strange process of self-deception often noticed in very weak characters, he had almost persuaded himself that Donovan *had* led him into evil.

He turned a flushed face towards the doctor, and unable to

speak the downright lie in one word, softened it down in a
sentence.

'I got into the way of playing, and lost a lot at billiards. Farrant went with me. I hoped to have made it up here, but——'

'That will do,' said the doctor. 'You have spoken more
than you ought.'

There was such pain and disappointment in his tone that
Stephen's conscience tormented him to speak the truth boldly
even then, but it requires a certain amount of moral courage
not to stick to a lie when it has been told, and moral courage
was a virtue entirely wanting in Stephen. He lay silent in pal-
pitating misery, wishing that he had never seen Donovan, or
had never heard of the Z—— Races, wishing that many things
had been otherwise, but strangely forgetting to wish for the
much-needed increase of his own courage and honour.

In spite of this mental disturbance, however, he slept again,
and the next day he was so much better that Dr. Tremain felt
justified in leaving him for a few hours. He could not rest now
till he had seen Donovan, and entirely satisfied himself that there
was no shade of doubt as to the truth of his fears.

It was no use to question Stephen or Mrs. Causton any
further, but he made one more attempt on Gladys, who apparently
had been the last to speak to Donovan.

'Now tell me, dear, plainly what passed between you,' said
the doctor, far too deeply engrossed in other matters to notice
the painfully bright colour which rose in Gladys' cheeks.

'I will tell you, papa, exactly,' she said, quieting herself with
an effort. 'Aunt Margaret said that she was sure he couldn't
afford to waste two days in term time, and then Donovan, seeing
that she wished him to go, said good-bye at once. I went to
the head of the stairs to speak to him, for it seemed wrong to let
him go like that, but he would not let me call you away from
Stephen. And then—then——' her voice faltered.

'Well?' said her father, with some lurking hope that a fresh
light might be thrown on the matter.

'I begged him to stay and explain all to you, for I thought
he could. He didn't answer at first, and looked very, very
miserable, but after a minute he told me that he couldn't explain
anything, and that it was better that he should go at once.'

'Was that all?' said the doctor, grievously disappointed.

'That was all,' said Gladys, firmly. 'But, papa,' she added,
with a sort of proud enthusiasm in her voice, 'if you had seen his
face when he spoke, you could not have believed for a moment
that he has done this.'

For the first time it dawned on Dr. Tremain that his child might possibly have thought more of Donovan Farrant than was wise. Mrs. Causton's old advice flashed back into his mind; he had talked of open-armed Charity, and Prudence with tied hands, and was this the ending of it all? He sighed very heavily.

'Dear little Gladys,' he said, drawing her towards him, 'we must not trust too much to faces.'

He could not say more, but he looked very sorrowfully into Gladys' wistful eyes.

'You will go to see him, papa,' she said, quietly, 'and I think you will believe in him then.'

Her words almost inspired the doctor with a new hope; warm-hearted and impetuous, he set off at once for London, and early in the afternoon reached the York Road lodgings. It was Saturday, and, knowing there would be no lectures, he hoped to find Donovan.

The servant thought he was at home, but was not quite sure. She asked him to come in. Dr. Tremain, following her into the sitting-room, found himself in the presence of an apple-faced old man, whose scanty reddish-grey hair was covered by a scarlet smoking-cap, and who seemed to be dividing his attention between a long clay pipe and a tumbler of brandy-and-water.

'I must have made a mistake, sir,' said the doctor, apologising to the odd figure before him. 'These cannot be Mr. Farrant's rooms, I think?'

'Donovan Farrant? Oh! yes, these are his rooms. Stunning good fellow he is too. You know him?'

The doctor was puzzled and annoyed.

'Yes, sir, I do know him. Is he in?'

'Gone not ten minutes ago,' said the captain, surveying the doctor from head to foot with his little, good-humoured, watery eyes.

Dr. Tremain gave an exclamation of annoyance.

'Gone! how provoking. I specially wanted to see him. Where is he gone—do you know?'

Rouge was all at once seized with the conviction that this stranger was trying to track Noir and prevent his departure; so, mentally congratulating himself on his acuteness, he resolved on a course of diplomatic hindrance.

'Mr. Farrant will no doubt be home in half-an-hour or so,' he said, in his blandest tone. 'Allow me to offer you a chair.'

'You seem to be established here,' said the doctor, with a slight frown. 'Do you share Mr. Farrant's rooms?'

'I have that honour,' said the old captain. 'We are old friends—

very old friends, I may say—and now in trouble and destitution, he, like the good fellow he is, holds out——'

The captain suddenly remembered his line of diplomacy, and covered his confusion by a cough and a return to the brandy and water.

The silence was broken by a shrill voice from the window.

'While-there's-life-there's-hope. While-there's-life-there's hope. While-there's-life-there's-hope!' screamed Sweepstakes, in his harsh nasal voice, with maddening monotony.

The doctor, chafed and annoyed as he was, could not help laughing, Sweepstakes mimicking him in a senseless titter, and old Rouge himself joining heartily.

'Clever bird, isn't he? Brought him from West Africa years ago. Would stake my life he's the best talker in England.' Then, looking keenly at the doctor, he said, hesitatingly, 'You are not a detective, are you?'

The doctor laughed, and told him his name and profession.

'Oh! that's a comfort,' said Rouge, heaving a sigh of relief. 'Now we can talk freely. To tell you the truth, I thought you were tracking my son, who is just off to America. Boat sails this very day; in fact, Donovan's now gone to see him off. I doubt if he'll be home till evening.'

'Why, you told me half-an-hour just now,' said the doctor, impatiently.

'When I took you for a detective,' said Rouge, with a sly smile.

The doctor was so much vexed that he fairly lost his temper.

'I don't know who you may be!' he exclaimed, 'but I must say I am surprised to find Donovan Farrant living with people who are in terror of a detective's visit. Have the goodness to tell me at what time you *do* expect him to return.'

Poor Rouge was so much flustered by the doctor's hasty speech, that he was quite incapable of giving a plain and satis-factory answer.

'I wouldn't for the world bring discredit on the lad,' he faltered, the ever-ready tears slowly trickling down his wrinkled cheeks. 'I'm as fond of the lad as if he were my own son, and it's a son he'll be to me now that my own has left his native land.' Here he began to sob like a child, but still struggled to make himself heard. 'I'm not such a fool as I look—time was when I was captain of the *Metora*—I was driven to it'—he pointed to the brandy-bottle—'I was driven to it—and it's made me what I am!'

'Will you tell me when Mr. Farrant will be home?' said the exasperated doctor.

'Towards evening,' faltered the old captain, 'but I couldn't say for certain. Perhaps you'll leave a message?'

'I will come in again later on,' said the doctor, and he hastily took up his hat and left the room, quite out of patience with the tearful old captain.

It was a miserable afternoon, cold and foggy; a fine drizzling rain fell continuously. The doctor felt very wretched, he had hoped to gain some fresh light by a conversation with Donovan, but his interview with Rouge Frewin had only perplexed and disheartened him. How was it that Donovan had taken up again with his old companions? How could he endure to have such a maudlin old wretch as a fellow-lodger? Things certainly looked darker and darker!

Evening came, Dr. Tremain went back to York Road, still Donovan had not returned, and by this time the old captain had solaced his grief so frequently and effectively that he was by no means sober. A wretched hour of waiting followed. The doctor looked at his watch at least twenty times, the minutes were passing rapidly by, and at the end of the hour he knew he must leave the house to catch the last train to Z——.

Five minutes to eight! the doctor held his watch in his hand now. Three minutes! No sound but the heavy breathing of the old captain, who had fallen asleep. Two minutes! how fast the hands moved! the doctor's heart sank down like lead. One minute! with a heavy sigh he put back his watch, absently brushed his hat with his coat sleeve, and got up. At that very moment a key was turned in the latch, the front door was opened and sharply closed, a quick firm step which must be Donovan's was heard in the passage, the door was opened. Yes, there he was; the doctor stepped hastily forward.

'I had just given you up; I've been in town since two o'clock, hoping to see you!' he exclaimed, anxiously scanning every line of Donovan's face.

His last hope died as he did so, for an unmistakable expression of surprise, annoyance, and perplexity passed over it; his colour rose; he glanced from the doctor to the old captain before speaking, then, with no word of regret at having missed so much of his friend's visit, he hastily inquired after Stephen.

'Stephen is better, going on perfectly well,' replied the doctor, shortly. 'I must be off at once, though, or I shall not be able to get to Z—— to-night. Perhaps you'll walk with me to the station.'

Dr. Tremain was human and he had had a great deal to try him that day, his tone was almost bitter, Donovan winced under it. One comfort was that the ordeal must be short; a five minutes' walk—surely he could hold his tongue for five minutes, keep self down, strangle the words of self-justification which must expose so much of another's guilt! And yet never before had he felt so little confidence in himself, the struggle of the previous day seemed to have exhausted his strength, as he stepped out into the dark rainy November night he felt an almost unconquerable shrinking from the inevitable pain which was before him. If he could but win through with it! If he could but do the difficult Right! and there floated through his mind the definition of Right which both he and the doctor held—that which brings the greatest happiness to the greatest number of people for the greatest length of time. He honestly thought that his silence would be right, and clung desperately to the one strengthening thought of the gain to others which this five minutes might bring. It was the generous mistake of a utilitarian. The doctor's voice broke in upon his mental struggle. He set his face like a flint and listened.

'I wanted some explanation of all this, Donovan, and I had hoped for plenty of time with you, we are limited now to a very few minutes. I must say that all I have seen of your way of life both to-day and yesterday has surprised and grieved me. I come to your rooms and find a disreputable old man, in dread of a detective's visit, and not too sober; he tells me he is an old friend of yours. I thought you made up your mind to break with such friends as those?'

'There were special reasons why Captain Frewin should be an exception to that rule,' said Donovan, in a voice so well reined in from yielding to any sign of feeling that it sounded cold and indifferent.

'There are always special reasons, I suppose, for backsliding!' said the doctor, hastily.

There was a silence, then Dr. Tremain went on more quietly.

'That is, of course, your own concern; but, as to your relations with Stephen, I have some right to ask. His father is my oldest friend; he will hold me responsible for having allowed you to share his rooms. Stephen has himself told me that he fell into habits of gambling. I am not surprised—he is grievously weak. But he tells me that you were with him, and that explains everything far too easily. You are strong-willed enough to lead him as you please. Only I could not have believed it of you. I never would have believed it if I hadn't met you with him at Z——.'

Donovan breathed hard, but did not speak.

A A

'Have you nothing to say?' said the doctor, in the tone of one clinging to a forlorn hope. 'Can you not tell me that I am at least in part mistaken? Can you not explain anything to me?'

He looked steadily at him as he spoke, thinking perhaps of Gladys' words, 'You will believe in him when you see him.' But Donovan's face was dark and cold and hard-looking now. The doctor had never seen such a look on his face before; he misinterpreted it entirely. But his very grief made him speak gently and pleadingly.

'God forgive me, Donovan, if I have been harsh with you! but just let me know from your own lips that you cannot explain things—cannot free yourself from blame. Gladys told me what you said to her, but I couldn't rest till I had heard the truth from you yourself.'

'I have nothing more to say,' said Donovan, clenching his hands so fiercely that even then the feeling of bodily pain came as a relief to him. 'I can explain nothing. It would have been better if you had not come to see me.'

'Ay, better indeed!' said the doctor, with bitterness, 'for then I should at least have had some hope that I was mistaken. The only thing is that Stephen is in part excused if, as he says, you did go with him, did lead him wrong. One more question let me ask you; I don't wish to play the inquisitor, but just tell me whether this was the reason you would not come to us in the summer?'

For the first time the burning colour rose in Donovan's face. How could he answer that question? They had just entered the crowded station; there under the flaring gas-lamps, amid the noisy traffic, his reply must be made—somehow. What if he told the doctor his real reason, told him that he loved Gladys? He hated mysteries; it would be infinitely easier to be perfectly open. Besides, the confession would explain so much, would at once bring him into his old place with Dr. Tremain. And yet, taking all things into account, it would be better for everyone but himself if he just held his tongue. Better for Stephen, better that he should lose his place in the Tremain household, and be entirely forgotten, better—infinitely better—for Gladys. If his name ceased to be mentioned, if they all believed him to be what he now appeared, in time she too would come to share that belief. He honestly believed that to forget him would be her truest happiness, and the remembrance of their last interview, when she had been unable to hide her pain, strengthened him now. Anything to save her from a lifelong sorrow! 'Think

evil of me, dear love,' was now his inward cry, ' suffer, if it must
be, that short pain, but only learn to forget!'

And yet! Even now came a passionate sigh of longing,
human weakness alternating with the lofty self-renunciation.
If only there had been no obstacle! *Why* was he hemmed in by
thick darkness? *why* were his doubts insurmountable? And
then he shuddered to think that he was beginning to long for
knowledge of the truth, chiefly that he might be in a position to
win Gladys.

These thoughts had rushed tumultuously through his mind,
and meantime the doctor waited for his answer, and they had
walked up the platform. ' Was this the reason you would not
come to us?' He could not tell an untruth; the crimson flush
which had risen to his brow, the long pause, both told unfavour-
ably against him with Dr. Tremain. So did the iron voice in
which at length his unsatisfying answer was made.

' I invented an excuse last summer—my real reason for not
coming I entirely decline to tell you.'

' I am disappointed in you, Donovan,' said the doctor, and
his voice even more than the words carried a terrible pang with
it, and sent a momentary spasm of pain over Donovan's strong
face.

' Just forget me, that is all I ask of you,' he said, unable to
free his tone from all expression as he would have wished.

The doctor had taken his place; something in that last speech
of Donovan's touched him; he would have spoken in reply, but
one of those trivial interruptions which break in so rudely upon
the most anxious moments of life prevented him.

The shrill voice of a boy intervened.

' *Punch, Judy,* or *Fun, Evening Standard,* and *Echo.* Paper, sir?'

Some passenger wanted an *Evening Standard;* at that minute
the train began to move. By the time the newspaper boy had
sprung down from the step, Dr. Tremain was too far from Donovan to do more than wave a farewell. Once more Gladys' words
flashed back into his mind, ' You will believe in him when you
see him,' and this time, in spite of all that had passed, the doctor
did waver. For in that tall dark figure on the platform there
seemed to him a certain majesty—a majesty inseparable from
right or absolute conviction of being in the right. He could not
clearly see the face now, but the last look he had seen on it had
been a strange blending of pain and strength, the strength
predominating over the pain. Could he after all have been mistaken? Like the warm-hearted, impetuous man that he was, the
doctor at once tore a leaf from his pocket-book, and, with tears

in his eyes, wrote Donovan such a letter as the best of fathers might write to his son.

The ordeal was over, the victory had been complete, self had been kept under; but the victor was too entirely crushed to feel even a shadow of triumph. He stood perfectly still, watching the train as it steamed out of the station, with an odd sensation —more numbing than keenly painful—that it was dragging with it a great part of himself. Presently he must rouse himself to go on with life, to make the most of what was left. There are great rents and voids in most lives, at first we feel stunned and helpless, but after a time we become accustomed to the new order of things, and live on, 'learning perforce,' as some one has well expressed it, 'to take up with what is left.'

That the loss had come about by his own will did not at all soften matters to Donovan, but rather the reverse. He was past reasoning, almost past thought. When the red lamps on the last carriage had quite disappeared, he turned slowly away, aware that he had deliberately, with his own hand, turned the brightest page of his life's history. A new page must be begun; of that too he was dimly aware.

He left the station and walked slowly through the wet, muddy, cheerless streets. It did not actually rain, and the wind had risen, there was some comfort in that. With his usual craving for air and space he bent his steps to the river, walked along the Embankment, turned on to Blackfriars Bridge, and chose as his halting-place one of its recesses.

Not since the first days after Dot's death had such a crushing, deadening sense of loss oppressed him, and now, as then, he had to bear his pain alone. But he was stronger than in the old days, stronger because he was growingly conscious of his own weakness, and because his heart was infinitely wider in its sympathies. He was not in the mood to see anything, though the dark flowing river, and the reflected lights, and the great looming outline of the dome of St. Paul's would at any other time have pleased his eye. To-night he just leant on the parapet, getting a sort of relief from the fresh night wind, but almost unconscious of time and place.

He was roused at last by becoming aware that there was another occupant of the recess. A small elf, whether boy or girl he could not at first tell, was yawning and stretching itself, having just awakened from sound sleep. Presently a dismayed exclamation made Donovan draw a little nearer.

'By all the blissed saints! if they ain't wet through, all the three of 'em!'

Then came sounds of violent scraping. Donovan, stooping down a little, saw that his neighbour, a small ragged boy, was trying whether a light could possibly be kindled from a box of fusees which had been soaked through and through.

'Ye were a fool, Pat, me boy, to go to sleep in the rain!' exclaimed the elf, with a few superfluous oaths. Finding his efforts to strike a light ineffectual, he scrambled to his feet, and with great deliberation and muttered ejaculations about the 'blissed saints,' threw the three boxes of fusees one after another into the river.

'Why do you throw them away?' said Donovan, with some curiosity.

'They was wet through, yer honour,' said the small Irish boy, looking up at Donovan with a friendly grin. 'I chucked 'em into the river for fear the devil should get into 'em.'

'How?' asked Donovan, with an involuntary smile.

'Och! yer honour has had no dealings with the devil thin, or he'd niver ask such a thing. Why, says I to meself, "Pat, me lad, lave 'em to dry and ye'll sell 'em right enough;" but thin says I to meself again, "But, Pat, maybe the devil 'ud be in the coppers ye'd get for 'em." Yer honour don't know how terrible aisy it comes to chate a bit when there ain't nothing else to do.'

'Yes, I do know,' said Donovan, gravely.

'Do ye railly, now?' said Pat, with a broad grin. 'And did the devil get inside yer honour? Och, he's a terrible cratur to have dealings with! Last year, yer honour, I was half starved, and one day I prigged a loaf hot and frish from a baker's and ate it up like a shot for fear o' being cotched by the peeler, and if ye'll belave it, yer honour, the devil was in the loaf. Och! I could have danced with the pain of it, and after that says I to meself, "Pat, me lad, kape clear o' the devil, or maybe he'll gripe ye warse next time."'

'Do you see that fire at the other end of the bridge, Pat?' said Donovan, looking down gravely at the little, grubby-faced Irish boy.

'The petatie stall, yer honour?' said Pat, wistfully.

'Yes,' said Donovan, with a smile. 'Do you think the devil would be in the potatoes?'

Pat nodded emphatically.

'Bedad and I do, yer honour, if I was to stale 'em.'

'But if I were to give them you?'

'Why, thin, yer honour,' cried Pat, grinning from ear to ear, 'it wud be the blissed saints as wud reward ye!'

'Come along, then,' said Donovan, and the strangely con-

trûsted companions walked off together, the barefooted, super-
stitions, but honest little *gamin* and the grave, perplexed, but
honest agnostic.

'If yer honour wud but eat one!' exclaimed Pat, looking up
with shining eyes from the double enjoyment of the hot potatoes
and the charcoal fire.

So Donovan ate a potato—and began his new life.

CHAPTER XXXII.

TEMPTATION.

Thy face across his fancy comes
And gives the battle to his hands.
                            TENNYSON.

THE encounter with Pat served to turn Donovan's thoughts for a
short time from his trouble, it made him realize that there were
other beings in the world besides Tremains, men, women, and
children more or less poor, more or less suffering, more or less in
need of help.

By-and-by, however, being but human, his own sorrow overpowered him again, shutting out for the time all thought of
others. He was no novice in sorrow; one by one, everything
that was of most worth to him had been either taken away or
voluntarily renounced, but this last call, this greatest sacrifice,
seemed to have exhausted his strength. He went about his
work more like a machine than like a man, he lost all interest in
what, but a short time before, had absorbed him. Had he been
ordered never to go to the hospital again he would have acqui-
esced without a word; had he been warned of the most imminent
danger, his heart would not have beat more quickly. To rouse
his energy, to awaken his love, hate, interest of any sort, seemed
impossible.

Dr. Tremain's letter did indeed sharpen his pain; and in a
few days' time Mrs. Tremain wrote too—a long letter, cruelly
kind, cruelly trustful, urging in almost irresistible words that
Donovan would write to her and tell her all he could, that he
would be open with her, would remember what old friends they
were, and would not allow any formality, or even any mistake, to
raise a barrier between them.

' Be sure to write to me when you can,' the letter ended, ' for till I hear I shall not be happy about you, and you know your place in my heart is very near Dick's. You see I put my request on selfish grounds entirely! My husband seems to have seen so little of you the other day, and I can't help fancying that you misunderstood each other.

' Even if it was not so, please let me hear from you ; remember that you adopted Porthkerran as your home, and that even if things have gone wrong we should like to have a little home confidence.'

Perhaps Donovan had never before realized how much Mrs. Tremain was to him ; in actually leaving Trenant the year before, he had been too much absorbed with the pain of leaving Gladys to have a thought for anyone else, but now, as he read the motherly letter and recalled all Mrs. Tremain's goodness to him, he did realize the truth very bitterly. How wonderful her sympathy had been at the time of his illness, how comforting it had been to tell her about Dot! ' Remember that this is your home,' how cruelly tempting were the words! If he could but have written in answer to that letter, if he could but have given that ' home confidence ' for which she asked !

Well ! it was no use going over the old arguments again. He had to be silent,—merely to hold his tongue, merely to let all letters remain unanswered, an easy enough *rôle* surely—merely silence. Nothing to be learnt before that part can be played, no need for beauty of voice or grace of speech ; for the silent player nothing is required but self-restraint.

The end of it was that Mrs. Tremain's letter was quietly dropped into the hottest part of the fire ; when the sudden blaze died out, Donovan turned away, and with something added to the dead weight of depression which he had borne before, set out for his day's work.

For some weeks things went on in this way, the only change was that those black depths of dejection lost their horrible novelty ; it seemed as if for long ages he had fagged through weary uninteresting days, had borne this load at his heart. In time, however, he came to realize the truth that dejection is selfish· ness, and no more excusable on the ground of naturalness than selfishness is. It was natural certainly to be dejected after a great loss, it was also natural to put self first, but it was not for that reason right. He had been wrapped up in himself for weeks, in himself and in those bitter-sweet recollections of the past. When he was fully awake to the fact his strength came back again, dejection was not an easy foe to combat, but he went at it

tooth and nail, and the strange incentive to the work was none
other than the old captain.

Poor Rouge was a curious person perhaps to save a fellow-
being from spiritual death, but nevertheless his presence did save
Donovan. It was the sight of that feeble old man dragging
through his useless, aimless days, with his pipe and his brandy-
and-water, his weak fits of laughter and his maudlin tears, which
first roused him.

How he had neglected the poor old fellow! what a gloomy,
taciturn companion he had been! what single thing had he done
for Rouge beyond offering him the use of his sitting-room? He
must alter his conduct, or the old man might as well not have
come to him at all, and would really have some excuse for slowly
drinking himself to death. It was on a Saturday that Donovan
first became alive to these facts. It was raining heavily, a walk
was out of the question, the old captain was asleep on the sofa,
Waif slept on the hearthrug, the fire smouldered in the grate, the
only waking creature in the room besides himself was Sweepstakes. By way of a first step out of his self-absorption, Donovan
walked across to the window, and tried to get up a quarrel with
the parrot; it was desperately hard work.

There is an old legend which tells how two monks, finding the
tedious routine of their life intolerably dull, resolved that they
would try to quarrel by way of enlivenment. They agreed that
one should make an assertion and the other should contradict it,
this would make an opening for impassioned argument.

'Black is white,' asserted the younger monk.

'It is not,' replied the elder.

'Black is white,' repeated the first speaker.

'Oh, very well, brother,' rejoined the other, meekly, 'if you
say so.'

The habit of meek deference had grown so strong, that they
found it impossible to quarrel.

Neither Donovan nor Sweepstakes was meek, but nevertheless their quarrel was but a tame one. It required such an exertion to get up the requisite energy. However, after a time the
bird did call forth the good-natured teazing which he liked best,
and was stimulated into flapping his wings, screaming, chattering,
swearing; finally he made it up again, and accepted a Brazil nut
as a peace-offering.

When the parrot subsided into quiet, Donovan turned his
attention to the outside world, which for days he had seen without seeing. York Road looked very dreary it must be owned.
Exactly opposite his window was the establishment of Swimming

and Vapour Baths, then came grim, uninteresting houses; far down to the left was the entrance to a timber-yard, where he could see the tops of wooden planks swaying to and fro in the wind. And all the time the rain came down steadily, ceaselessly, with a dull, monotonous drip on the flags, the wheels on the road passed by with a dull, hollow roll, the foot-passengers on the pavement with dull, thudding footsteps, the wind in its gloomy strait of houses with dull, faint moanings. A grey world, but one which must be gone through with, and made the best of.

He felt that his absorption in his trouble had weakened him not a little. All this time his brain had seemed half dead, he had read to no purpose. Worst of all, the sense of his complete and final separation from Gladys had come to him for the first time in full force, proving only too clearly that, though he had willed more than a year before not to see her again, he had all the time nursed a faint hope of a possible re-union. He had really renounced her before, but the most honestly-intentioned being in the world cannot altogether shut out every ray of hope; he had hoped without knowing that he hoped, he only knew that it had been so by feeling aware that he had sunk now into a blacker depth. Clearly the only thing for the present was to will not to think of her, the hardest thing in the world. But the idea of putting every thought of her away from him was more tolerable than the idea of letting her memory chain him down in a selfishness which she would abhor.

Now for more days than he cared to remember Donovan had allowed himself the pleasing pain of continually looking at the photograph which the doctor had taken in the orchard on that summer afternoon which had ended so painfully. To study that family group, to note Gladys' sweet face turned up to his, to see little Nesta on his own shoulder, to recall that beautiful summer dream, was gratifying but very weakening torture. Looking out on the grey world this afternoon, the world which contrasted so strangely with the bright picture of the past, he made up his mind that he must waste no more—well, yes—*sentiment*, he was honest enough to use the true word, over the photograph. Without any more delay he fetched it from his room and burnt it. Also a certain sixpence, which he had worn with Dot's miniature since Gladys had put it into his hand one summer day at the door of Trevethan's forge, was deliberately removed, and found its way into his pocket with the ordinary unhallowed coins. Then, having done his best to clear out his heart, he set to work to fill up the vacuum with that strange substitute—the old captain.

Rouge at once perceived that, as he expressed it, the wind had changed, when he awoke that Saturday afternoon; his companion for the first time seemed approachable, he no longer felt uncomfortable in his presence, he felt as if he could venture to talk freely. After dinner they had a pipe together, and then Rouge launched out into one of his long 'yarns,' about which there was generally a sort of dry humour. To-night the old man, who was shrewd and curious, made his story turn on his first love, and Donovan listened with an imperturbable countenance, till the idea of old Rouge Frewin in love with a beautiful Venetian lady of high rank tickled his fancy and made him laugh. The name of the fair one, too, Ceccarella Bonaventura, when reduced by Rouge's pronunciation to 'Kickerella Bunnyventury,' was sufficiently ludicrous, and when it came to the description of the gorgeous palace on the grand canal, with eight masts at the door, when Rouge graphically sketched the beauties of Venice from the Bridge of Sighs to 'the beautiful cafés in the Piazza,' when he related how he had 'got into hot water' over his serenade, that is, had had a pailful poured on his head from a window by way of recompense, it was impossible to resist the keen sense of the ridiculous which was almost his only Irish characteristic.

'And did you really love this signorina?' asked Donovan.

'Love her!' exclaimed Rouge. 'I adored her, kissed the ground she trod on—there's not much ground though in Venice—ruined myself in gondolas that I might pass fifty times a day under her windows, wrote verses about her, raved about her, dreamed of her—and then——'

He paused, a merry twinkle lurking in his little grey eyes.

'Well?' asked Donovan.

'The good ship sailed down the Adriatic, and knowing of course that it must be so, I became resigned, and—forgot her again.'

The prosaic tone in which he said the last words had a very comical effect. Donovan smiled.

'We all do,' said Rouge, in a tone of one adding the moral to the story. 'It's the way with first loves, you know.'

'Indeed!' ejaculated Donovan, mentally. But guessing that the observant old captain had discovered the real cause of his depression, and had produced his moral tale on purpose, he gave an apparently careless turn to the conversation, for he would not for the world have had him come a degree nearer his secret trouble, that aching loss, of which it would have seemed sacrilege to speak to one like Rouge.

Not many days after this, however, the dull, tedious monotony of life was suddenly broken. Donovan had felt as if he could never again really care for anything in the world, but now a sudden and violent reaction set in.

'Do you ever go to Israel's now?' questioned Rouge one evening.

'Not since I went last with you,' returned Donovan.

But therewith arose a fearful craving for his old pastime. He had, during these years of self-denial, been occasionally seized with a great desire for play, and when Stephen had shared his rooms he had often had to bear the great irritation of seeing cards in the hands of other people. But never before had the desire been so irresistible, the temptation so terribly strong. He had resolved not to play, had willed that he would utterly renounce gaming, but he found himself now rebelling against the restraint, albeit it was a self-restraint. He had a horror of pledges as pledges. The consciousness of this self-made curb began to gall him unbearably. He questioned its wisdom. It might have been necessary once, but now might he not safely indulge in his favourite amusement—of course in moderation? Having schooled himself all this time, might he not relax a little, and satisfy this miserable craving? It was hard that by his own doing he should cut himself off from the one amusement that seemed left to him in the dull, grey world.

His strong nature would not quickly yield, however, to such arguments. The struggle went on with fearful intensity for days. Perhaps he would have stifled it sooner had he not been worn out with the trouble of the last few weeks; however it might be, the temptation proved the most severe of his whole life. It was as if the lower self were making one final and desperate effort to gain the mastery.

One day, in the thick of this inward struggle, he happened to be at work in the dissecting-room, and though, as a rule, he took very little note of the talk that went on there, it chanced that day that, being anxious to escape from his own thoughts, he made himself listen. There were plenty of Freethinkers among the students, and many were at the dogmatic stage of atheism which Donovan had just passed out of. Discussion on the points of discord between religion and science was very frequent, but Donovan rarely joined in it, partly because he was taciturn, partly because he was too much in the borderland of doubt to care to make any assertion, partly because of that strange and unaccountable sense of reverence which was pained by hearing the Unknown —the possibly non-Existent—spoken of slightingly. The discus-

sion to-day on the existence of the soul was neither edifying nor
interesting. Donovan, who was in the worst of tempers, was
chafed and irritated by the worthlessness of the arguments on
each side. 'Pack of idiots!' he exclaimed to himself, 'if they
must babble about what they don't understand, why can't they
put a little life into their talk?' He wandered back to his own
all too haunting thoughts, but was recalled by the peculiarly confident tone of his neighbour, a young fellow of about two-and-
twenty, who was eagerly attempting to prove the truth of the
theory admirably summed up once by old Mrs. Doory, that
' Death ends us all up.'

'Well,' remarked the student, as if he had got hold of a
clinching argument, 'I've been at work here for some time, but
I never yet found a soul in the dissecting-room.'

There was a general laugh, but it was checked by a quick
retort, uttered in a voice which was made powerful by a ring of
indignation and a slight touch of scorn.

'No one but a fool would look for one there.'

'Bravo!' cried Donovan, delighted with the ready reply,
though by no means convinced of the existence of the soul.

He glanced with some interest and a good deal of curiosity at
the speaker. He was a certain Brian Osmond, a clever, hard-
working, silent fellow, with the reputation of being stiff and very
'churchy,' the latter accusation having probably for its sole
foundation the fact that his father was a clergyman. Looking at
him to-day, Donovan for the first time felt drawn towards him; he
admired him and respected him, as much perhaps for his subsequent silence as for his sharp retort. Few know when they have
said enough. Apparently Brian Osmond did know, for he spoke
no more, but went on with his work with a slightly heightened
colour, as if the speaking had been something of an effort.

That night it so happened that Donovan and three other
students were told off for duty in the accident ward. There was
a patient who needed constant attendance; these four were to
take it in turns to be with him, two at a time. Not a little to
his satisfaction, Donovan found that Brian Osmond was to be
his companion—he really wanted to know him; they were now
of course on speaking terms, but, being both reserved men, they
would never have got nearer had not an opportunity such as this
been thrown in their way.

Now all the evening Donovan's fierce craving for play had
been growing more and more irresistible; when the other two
students relieved guard, and he and Brian Osmond went to rest in
an adjoining room, the first thing he saw on the table was a pack of

cards. He did not say anything, but Brian at once caught sight of them.

'Hullo! these fellows have been playing,' he remarked. 'they've done their game—let's have a turn at *écarté* to keep us awake.'

Donovan did not speak an assent, but he took up the pack; if his hands had been steel, and the cards so many magnets, the power which drew him towards them could not have been more irresistible; the struggle within him was ceasing, a delicious calm set in. The mere sight of the cards was to him what the sight of bread is to a hungry man—to feel them once more in his hands was bliss. Was the world, after all, so grey? With scarcely a word he shuffled and dealt. His hand was one to make the heart of a card-player leap within him, the old passion had him well in its grip, the old fierce, delicious excitement sent the blood coursing at double time through his veins; after years of plodding work, after weeks of blank depression, this was rapture.

'Stop a minute,' said Brian; 'we didn't settle points. I draw the line at sixpence—is that too mild for you?'

Donovan produced a handful of coins from his pocket; among them was the sixpence with the hole in it—Gladys' sixpence—he saw it at once, and that instant her face rose before him in its purity and guilelessness. Then the delicious calm gave place to deadly struggle, his better self pleading eagerly—'This play calls out all the bad in you, makes you the direct opposite of all that is pure and noble, all that is like Gladys.'

But the lower self was ready with bitter taunts—'What! a strong man letting himself be bound by a mere ideal of a girl—a girl whom he has renounced—who is nothing to him! Have your game, and don't be a fool.'

'You willed not to play, and it was the right you willed,' urged one voice.

'Nothing is so weak as to stick to a mistake,' urged the other; 'there's no such thing as actual right and wrong—you can't prove it.'

'There is right and wrong, there is purity of heart,' urged the higher counsellor—'think of Gladys.'

He did think, and it saved him.

Brian thought him slightly crazed, for he threw down the cards, got up from the table, and began to pace the room like a caged lion. Before very long, however, he quieted down, threw himself back in a chair, and in a matter-of-fact tone which belied his look of exhaustion, said,

'I beg your pardon, Osmond, but I can't play; the fact is, it makes a sort of demon of me.'

Brian was surprised, for Donovan looked much too stern and self-controlled for his idea of a gambler, but the struggle he had just witnessed proved the truth of the words.

'I suppose there is a tremendous fascination in cards, if you're anything of a player,' he said. 'I'm sorry I suggested a game.'

'You couldn't know whom you had to deal with,' returned Donovan, gathering up the cards—he was strong enough to touch them now. 'Who would have thought that in this trumpery pack there was such tremendous power? It's horribly humiliating when one comes to think of it.'

Feeling that he owed Brian a sort of apology for spoiling his game, he overcame his reserve, and continued,

'You wouldn't wonder that I daren't play, if you knew how low these magical things have dragged me. The last time I played, which is getting on for three years ago, I won a small fortune, which my adversary had in his turn won at Monte Carlo. On losing it he absconded, hinting to his wife that he should commit suicide. The horror of that was enough to make one renounce gambling, you would think. Lately, though, the craving after it has come back; but I see it won't do for me even in moderation. I suppose, having once thoroughly abused a thing, you're never fit to use it again.'

'That holds, I think, in some other cases,' said Brian.

'You're thinking of the drunkard and total abstinence,' said Donovan, laughing. 'Never mind, I don't object to being taken as a parallel case, for it's perfectly true—the two vices are very nearly akin. I daresay it's as hard to you to understand or sympathise with my temptation as it is to me to sympathise with the poor old fellow who shares my rooms, who is slowly drinking himself to death. No one can understand or make allowance for utterly unknown temptations.'

'I don't know that,' said Brian, slowly. 'One man at least I know who can sympathise with anyone; but then he is that rare being—a Christ-like man.'

'Rare indeed,' said Donovan, drily; 'not too much of that sort of thing in this nineteenth century. I see you think I speak bitterly; perhaps you are right. I speak as an unbeliever, and I can count on my fingers the Christians who have had so much as a kind word to give me.'

Brian began to feel very much drawn to his companion; in their next interval of rest he took up the thread of the conversation again.

'That is almost too horrible to be believed,' he said. 'I know people are intolerant, but that so few should have——' he paused for a word, and Donovan broke in.

'Mind, I don't say I laid myself out for their kindness. didn't cringe and fawn or disguise the views I then held; but to be conscious that people would receive you if you were judiciously hypocritical, does not raise your opinion either of them or of their religion.'

'No indeed,' said Brian.

'Besides,' resumed Donovan, 'if they are in earnest, as people who have made such a profession ought to be, surely they must see that isolating atheists as if they were lepers is the worst thing both for themselves and the atheists. I don't think it's in a man to feel kindly to those who treat him unjustly, and the good folks of our neighbourhood drove me as fast as they could into misanthropy. One man put a spoke in the wheel, but he was an atheist—the apostle of atheism.'

'What, Raeburn?'

Donovan nodded an assent.

'I don't know that I agree with his views now any more than I agree with Christianity, but I do believe that man gets hold of selfish fellows and makes them downright ashamed of their selfishness.'

'You have heard him lecture?'

'Only once, but I shall never forget it. The magnetism of the man is extraordinary; he means what he says, and has had to suffer for it—that, I expect, gives him his tremendous force. If you Christians only knew the harm you do your cause by injustice, you'd be more careful. St. Paul is not the only one who, for the sake of what he believed the truth, has borne imprisonment, stonings, watchings, fastings, perils of robbers, and perils of his own countrymen. I don't wonder at St. Paul making converts, and I don't wonder at Raeburn making converts, and as long as you persecute him, as long as you are uncharitable to him, you may be sure atheism will spread.'

'If you admired him so much, why did you not go to hear him again?'

'Because, when I could have heard him again, I had sunk too low. I had suffered a great injustice, and it had made me hate the whole race—for a time. Once I half-thought of going to see him, for I was in great need of work; but, do you know, I was ashamed to. Christians may scoff at the idea of being ashamed to go to see Raeburn, but anyone who is living in the vindictive misanthropy which I was living in may well be ashamed to go to one who leads a self-denying, hard-working life for others, whatever his creed.'

'But you do not go near him now, though you still admire him ?'

'No, for I've found the great blank in atheism; it can never satisfy a man's needs.'

'Have you ever given the other side a hearing ?' asked Brian.

'A reading, not a hearing; it is difficult to do that without either being a hypocrite or disturbing a congregation.'

Brian seemed about to speak, but he checked himself, and very soon they were called to go into the ward. They did not have much more conversation that night, but their friendship was begun. When Donovan gave confidence and liking at all, he gave them without stint, and Brian, in spite of his reputation for stiffness and punctilious observance, became more and more fond of him. In some points they were a little like each other, in some they were curiously different, but both had found— Brian as a High Churchman, Donovan as an agnostic—that the secret of life is loving self-sacrifice.

They were exactly fitted to rub off each other's angles.

CHAPTER XXXIII.

CHARLES OSMOND.

Thou art no Sabbath drawler of old saws,
Distill'd from some worm-canker'd homily ;
But spurr'd at heart to fiercest energy
To embattail and to wall about thy cause
With iron-worded proof, hating to hark
The humming of the drowsy pulpit-drone
Half God's good Sabbath, while the worn-out clerk
Brow-beats his desk below. Thou from a throne
Mounted in heaven wilt shoot into the dark
Arrows of lightnings. I will stand and mark.
TENNYSON.

THE deadly temptation of that night did not return, but, though Donovan was no longer torn by the fierce, inward struggle, what had happened made him think more seriously. He was disappointed and perplexed to find that, after these years of struggle and repression, the old passionate desire was still as strong as ever within him. With all his endeavours—and he knew that he had honestly tried with all his might—he had only been able to check the outward actions; he had cut off bravely enough the visible growth, he had, as it were, razed to the ground this evil passion, but its roots were still untouched. He smiled a little as he thought of it.

'Radical that I am, can I fail to root out the evil in myself? Professing to go straight to the root of all grievances, must I yet be unable to get rid of this?'

He was obliged to own that his power was absolutely limited to the suppression of evil in action; he had come to the very end of his strength, he might by great effort be pure in deed, but pure in heart he could never make himself. Yet actual purity was no dream. Gladys was pure, purity was written on every line of her face; he could not imagine her harbouring an impure thought or desire for an instant. Yet he knew that she was not in herself perfect; he was not at all the sort of man to fall blindly in love; he had noticed many trifling thoughts in Gladys, had heard her speak hastily, had discovered that she was a little too desirous of standing first with those she loved, was apt to exaggerate and to tell small incidents with pretty little imaginative touches of her own. She was not faultless, but, in spite of occasional and momentary falls, she was pervaded by a purity of thought and deed, of word and desire, which to Donovan was utterly incomprehensible. He was conscious, as he had latterly been with Dot, that she was breathing an altogether different atmosphere. He was like the shaded valley, little air and little light reaching him, she was like a beautiful snowy mountain peak in sunshine; a passing fault like a cloud might for a time dim the brightness, but only for a time—the sunshine would illumine all again. And then his own metaphor flashed a conviction on him—it must be a reflected brightness, a reflected loveliness that he saw in Gladys! ·

Unsatisfied as he had long been with agnosticism, he was now fully aware that he had reached the limit of what it could give him; he had tried with all his might to live a self-denying, pure life, and in some degree he had succeeded, but if he lived a hundred years he saw no chance of getting further. There would of course be constant opportunities for fresh self-denial, but he could not of himself ever attain to purity of heart. What then? There was a great want somewhere; he was incomplete, he reproached himself with being so, but yet had he not striven to the utmost? Might there not be a living Purity, a living Strength other than himself, to fill this void, to round off this incompleteness ? It was only a speculation, but speculations are helpful if they go hand-in-hand with honest work ; if they lead to nothing they at least teach us our own ignorance, and they may lead towards the unveiling of the hidden truth.

One Sunday, in January, it happened that Donovan was out alone, for though Rouge generally went with him on his long Sunday rambles, the afternoon had seemed so raw and cold and unpromising that he had preferred to stay indoors. It certainly was not a comfortable sort of day, but the weekly chance of a twenty-mile stretch was not to be lightly lost, and, rain or shine, Donovan generally spent the greater part of the Sunday in exercise. Even had he not been exceedingly fond of walking, there was Waif to be considered ; as it was, both dog and master looked forward to the day of rest, and used it to the best of their present abilities.

It was quite dark by the time they had reached the suburbs; walking on at a brisk pace, they made their way further into London. The bells had ceased ringing, and, becoming aware that he was exceedingly hungry, Donovan glanced at his watch, finding to his surprise that it was already a quarter to eight. They were passing through a very poor neighbourhood, and he had just turned from a crowded thoroughfare into a quiet side street, when a man, flushed, bare-headed, and breathless, dashed out of a building to the left, and in his haste almost knocked Donovan over.

' Beg pardon, sir,' he panted. ' A lady in a fit in the church, and heaven knows where I'm to find a doctor ! '

' Better have me, I'm half a doctor,' said Donovan. ' Be quick, anything's better than losing time.'

' A providence ! ' gasped the verger. ' This way, sir, this way.'

Now the church had been built on what an architect would have considered a very 'ineligible site,' for it was wedged in between the houses in a way which cruelly spoilt its beauty. The site, however, was in other respects exceedingly 'eligible,' that is to say, it was within a stone's throw of hundreds of the poor and ignorant. It was not, however, a convenient church for people afflicted with fits, for there was no separate entrance to the vestry, and the vestry was at the east end. The verger, followed by Donovan and Waif, walked straight up the church, to the distraction of the congregation ; some people were amused, some were scandalised, at the entrance of the fox-terrier. One of the churchwardens tried to drive him back ; but Waif's master had called him to heel, and to heel he would keep, though all the churchwardens in the world were to set upon him.

Donovan found his patient stretched on the floor in an epileptic fit, an old woman kneeling beside her, vainly trying to restrain her wild movements. The little room was used as a choir vestry, two unused surplices were hanging on the wall, he snatched one of them down, crushed the white folds remorselessly together, and put them between his patient's teeth. Presently she grew quieter. Donovan, seeing a half-open door, glanced in, and found a second room with a sofa and a larger window; with the verger's help he carried the girl in, and soon she became herself again. He decreed, however, that she should rest where she was till the service was over, when the verger could get her a cab.

Leaving her under her mother's care, he went back into the little outer vestry, but realizing that Waif might be considered *de trop* in a church he would not again go down the aisle; besides, it might be better that he should see his patient fairly out of her trouble. The waiting, however, was dull; to pass the time he noiselessly opened the vestry door and, through the narrowest of openings, took a glance at the congregation. They appeared to be listening very intently. He could not see the preacher, but he could hear him quite plainly, and instinctively he too began to listen. How many years was it since he had heard a sermon? Very nearly seven, and the last had been that never-to-be-forgotten sermon in the school chapel. Even now the recollection of it brought an angry glow to his face.

But the remembrance died away as soon as he began to listen to the clear tones of the present speaker, whose rather uncommon delivery attracted him not a little; it was manly, straightforward, quite free from the touch of patronage or the conventional sanctimonious drawl which goes far towards making many sermons unpalatable.

' I speak now more particularly to those who have some faith in God, but whose faith is weak, variable, largely mingled with distrust. I ask you to look at your everyday life and tell me this : Which suffers most, the father who disciplines, or the child who is disciplined? You who have had anything to do with little children will surely answer, " It is the one who disciplines who suffers most—the father bears his own pain and his child's as well."

' Look once more at your daily life and answer me one more question. Two friends are estranged, which suffers most, the one who doubts or the one who is unjustly doubted? You who can speak from experience will, I think, answer without hesitation, "the one who is doubted."

'Believe me, you who are in the twilight of a half faith, you who are in the darkness of scepticism, you who are hungering after you scarcely know what, hungering perhaps for an unknown goodness, a far distant holiness, your pain, cruel and gnawing and remorseless as it is, is a mere nothing compared with the pain which He whom you doubt suffers.

'Yes, look again at your own experience, realize as keenly as you can what is the pain of being unjustly doubted. Take it all ways, the sting of the injustice, the grievous disappointment in your friend, the dull ache of forsakenness, that is your own share, but you bear your friend's as well. There is his disappointment, his loneliness, his sense of betrayal, his indignation to be taken into account, the thought of it weighs on you more than your own personal pain. Oh! without question the pain of the one doubted is keener than the pain of the one who doubts, it is double pain. And in proportion to the strength of the love will be the sharpness of the suffering.

'To infinite, unthinkable love, therefore, we who doubt must bring infinite, unthinkable pain.

'It can hardly be, however, that in this congregation there have not been many dissentient thoughts during to-night's sermon. Even as I read my text I wondered how many will object to those words, "the Father of lights with whom is no variableness, neither shadow of turning."

'Father! How many shrink from using the word! Sometimes they are people who tell you they believe in "a God;" I notice that they always use the word "a," they do not say "we believe in *the* God." Sometimes they are people who accept the latter part of the text only, they believe in a "force" in which there is "no variableness." Sometimes they believe in an "impersonal God," which—allowing that by person you mean the "ego," the spirit—is about equal to speaking of an "unspiritual God." I do not wish to say one harsh word about those of you who hold such views, but before you urge again the old objections, "degrading ideas," "anthropomorphism," and such like, I should like you to ask yourselves, with perfect honesty, this question. "Did not my first objection to the word father rise from dislike to the necessary sequence that I was His child, rather than from real belief that the term was degrading to the Deity?"

'Spiritual life has its analogies with natural life; there does come a time when, with the consciousness of a certain strength, we long to be free agents, to shake off all authority, to go out in the world and fend for ourselves. And the real recognition of a father implies obedience, and obedience is hard to all men.

'But, on the other hand, I must defend my use of the word father from misconceptions. Not in the Mahomedan sense of a gigantic man do we call God our Father. The term given to us by Christ brings to our mind a conception of love and protection, it ought to rouse in us the child sense of reverence, obedience—in a word, "sonship." "Words!" you exclaim, "mere terms!" But remember that we must use finite terms in this life, even in speaking of infinity. You feel the terms to be a limitation? Perhaps that is well; to be conscious of limitation points to a larger, fuller, grander possibility dawning for us in the hereafter. Why should we for that reason be too proud to use the grand, simple Anglo-Saxon word "father"? You will not better it with all your laborious efforts, your many-worded and complicated substitutes.

'Using, then, this much abused term, let us turn back to our recollections of childhood. Some of us at least—I hope very many—have had fathers worthy of the name. We did not understand our father, but we revered and loved him, he was at once friend and counsellor, our standard in everything. What would have been his feeling if in later life we had doubted him, doubted his very love for us, cast off our family name, lived in independence and lovelessness? The really loving father would be grieved, cut to the heart, never vindictively wrathful.

'This father I would take as the shadow of the Divine reality. I cannot doubt that God has often been represented to you as a jealous potentate, an autocrat with human passions; but I would beg you to-night to put those thoughts from you, to turn instead to the revelation of Jesus Christ, the revelation, that is, of the "Father of lights," the Father in whom is no variableness or shadow of turning; who, in spite of our sin, our doubt, our unworthiness, will be our Father for ever and ever.

'My friends, my brothers, will you not think of the infinite pain which is caused by the doubt of one heart? Will you not struggle to free yourselves from it?

'"But," I think I hear some one say, "this man can know nothing about doubt or unbelief; if he did he would know the impossibility of willing to believe, willing to free yourself from doubt."

'Yes, that is true. To will belief is quite impossible. By struggling to free yourselves from doubt, I mean making a constant effort to live the Christ-life—the life of self-renunciation that God has consecrated and ordained as the high road to Himself. There may be some here who know nothing of God, some who know Him in part; but to all alike there is but that one road which can lead to knowledge of things divine—the road of the cross.

'"The law of the spirit of life in Christ Jesus," says St. Paul, "has made me free from the law of sin and death."

'The law, that is, of loving self-sacrifice, Christ's new law, is the law which sets us free from selfishness and ignorance of God.

'And that hard road of self-denial, so uncongenial to us all in itself, has proved, to everyone who has taken his way honestly along it, in very truth the way of light. For the Father of lights will Himself meet us as we walk that road, when we are "yet a great way off" He will appear to us from afar, saying— "Yea, I have loved thee with an everlasting love; therefore with lovingkindness have I drawn thee."

'Now unto Him that is able to do exceeding abundantly above all we can ask or think,' etc.

The congregation rose, Donovan pushed the door to.

'H'm, so that's what you think about it,' he muttered to himself, giving his mind a sort of matter-of-fact twist because he was conscious of a certain choking sensation in his throat. 'Yet could anyone imagine such a Being? It would take a strangely pure mind to form such a conception. If there were a God, He must be like that! the utter lovelessness of Doery's "offended autocrat" had been its own disproof. Could there be truth in that saying in the sermon on the mount, "The pure in heart shall see God"?'

From a confused train of thought like this he was roused by the sound of one of Dot's favourite hymns, Newman's 'Lead, kindly light, amid the encircling gloom.' Why it had been such a favourite of hers he had never found out, it was hardly a child's hymn, and Dot had been the simplest of little children. Perhaps the pure Saxon English had attracted her, as it usually does attract simple childlike souls. How many times could Donovan remember playing the tune for her! He seemed now almost to hear the soft child-voice singing with the congregation. With almost painful intentness he listened, the words of the last verse floating in to him with perfect distinctness.

> So long Thy power hath blessed me, sure it still
> Will lead me on
> O'er moor and fen, o'er crag and torrent, till
> The night is gone.
> And with the morn those angel faces smile,
> Which I have loved long since, and lost awhile.

He turned away with hot tears in his eyes. He had lost all his 'angel faces,' and did not yet believe that 'the morn' was coming, he could not believe in the hereafter, and he had given up all that was beautiful in the present. Life will feel black to such.

He began to poke the fire, he picked up the crumpled surplice from the floor, folded it methodically, and laid it on the table, then, finding such work too mechanical to answer his purpose, he retreated into the inner vestry, and began to talk to his patient's mother.

Before very long there was a hum of voices in the next room, then the door opened and the verger appeared, followed to Donovan's utter amazement by Brian Osmond.

'Hullo, who would have thought of seeing you here!' he exclaimed. 'Why didn't you hurry to the rescue?'

'I was the other side of the choir, and didn't see what was up,' said Brian; 'the first thing I did see was the entrance of you and Waif. How's your patient?'

'All right again,' said Donovan, 'we must get her a cab.'

'Brown will do that. You come with me now, I want you to see my father.'

'Your father?'

'This is his church, did you not know?'

Was it then Brian's father who had been preaching? Donovan did not ask, but followed him into the other vestry, where several rather shabby-looking little boys were just disappearing through the doorway, having left what Mrs. Docry would have called their 'whites' behind them. There was only one clergyman, he was standing by the fire talking to a churchwarden, and Donovan had a minute or two in which to take a survey of him.

Charles Osmond was a man of eight-and-forty; he was tall —nearly six feet—squarely made rather, muscularly very strong, but constitutionally delicate. His character was much like his body; he united in a very rare way the man's strength and the woman's tenderness. Looking at him superficially, he seemed older than his years, for he was nearly bald, and the fringe of hair that remained round what he called his 'tonsure' was quite grey, but his eyes were young, his voice was young, there was a sprightliness, almost a boyishness, in his manner at times.

'Clever and honest, and not too clerical,' was Donovan's comment, the last adjective being, from his lips, of the nature of a compliment, for he had a great dislike of the clergy as a class. He had received from individual members of the profession some injustice and no kindness, and he not unnaturally proceeded to judge them as a class, and to abuse them wholesale. A patient who has received mistaken treatment from a doctor, invariably scoffs at all doctors, and ever after terms them quacks. A client receiving an exorbitant bill from his solicitor, relieves his annoyance by proclaiming all lawyers to be grasping and avaricious. In this, as in other cases, a little fire kindles a great matter.

Charles Osmond turned in a minute or two, and Brian introduced Donovan.

'I saw you and your dog come in,' he observed, with laughter in his eyes. 'Now, if certain religious newspapers get hold of that incident, we shall have some beautiful paragraphs. "Strange new innovation," "Canine processions," etc. I hope your patient is better?'

By this time Donovan liked the man, instinctively liked and trusted him. Charles Osmond had a very strange fascination about him. He had an extraordinary power in his touch; to shake hands with him was to receive no conventional greeting, but to be taken closer to the man himself, to be assured of his hearty, honest sympathy. His eyes were to Donovan like Waif's eyes; all his soul seemed to look out of them. They were eyes which never looked in a hard way at people, never seemed to be forming an opinion about them, but, like the bright eager eyes of a dog, expressed almost as clearly as words, 'let us come as near each other as we can.'

He was a man who cared not a rush for what was said of people, a man who would have preferred dining with an excommunicated heretic to dining with the queen. He was no respecter of persons, and rather disliked official dignitaries as such, but he could admire worth whatever its surroundings, and he had a profound respect for man as man.

For a few minutes he was left alone with Donovan while Brian and the verger were helping the patient to a cab.

Before this there had been ordinary small talk, a sort of jumble of epileptic fits, fox-terriers, Barnard and Bishop stoves, etc., but as soon as they were alone, Donovan, obeying the plea of those dog-like eyes, did draw a little nearer, a little more out of his shell.

'I heard the end of your sermon to-night,' he said, rather abruptly. 'It is the first I have heard for several years. If it wouldn't be asking too much, would you let me have it to read?'

'With all my heart, if it were readable,' said Mr. Osmond, with a humorous twinkle in his eyes, as he handed half a sheet of paper to Donovan, with a few notes written on it.

'Oh! you preach extempore. I am sorry,' remarked Donovan.

'It is the only way for a church like mine,' said Mr. Osmond. 'But I can, if you like, give you plenty of sermons on that subject, and books too, much more to the point than anything you can have heard to-night.'

'Thank you,' said Donovan, 'but I am afraid I must ungraciously refuse that offer. I have read some dozens of theological books to very little purpose, and have just made a clean sweep of them, and bought a polariser for my microscope with the proceeds.'

'And find it of much more use, I daresay,' said Mr. Osmond, laughing. 'But if you cared enough for such matters to get and read theological books, why were you so many years without the far less tedious process of sermon hearing?'

'Because I am an agnostic,' said Donovan, 'and as there is no necessity, I do not care to stand, sit, and kneel through a meaningless form. I would not do it even to hear you again, and I own that I should like to hear you.'

'Then any Sunday that you care to look in here at a quarter to eight, you shall find the seat nearest the door empty,' said Mr. Osmond. 'Of course we extend the invitation to the dog as long as he'll sit quiet; I see you are inseparable. What an intelligent-looking mortal he is!'

'I could not quite tell you the number of times he has saved my life,' said Donovan. 'He won't defile your church; he's much more of a Christian than many church-goers I have known.'

'Did you ever hear the story of the eccentric men of Bruges?' said Mr. Osmond. 'He was passionately fond of his dogs; the curé remonstrated with him, and told him that if he went to heaven he must part with them. "I will go nowhere," exclaimed the good man, "where I cannot take my dogs."'

'Capital fellow!' said Donovan, laughing. 'I quite agree with him.'

By that time Brian had returned; the verger was beginning to turn out the gas.

'Come and have supper with us,' said Mr. Osmond, as they walked together down the empty church.

'Thank you,' replied Donovan, 'I am afraid I must go home; I have been out most of the day.'

'Microscope, or the old man of the sea?' questioned Brian.

'The latter,' said Donovan, with a laugh. 'Good-night.'

He whistled to Waif, and they disappeared in the dark street.

CHAPTER XXXIV.

WHAT IS FORGIVENESS?

Skilful alike with tongue and pen,
He preached to all men everywhere
The Gospel of the Golden Rule,
The new commandment given to men,
Thinking the deed, and not the creed,
Would help us in our utmost need.
With reverent feet the earth he trod,
Nor banished Nature from his plan,
But studied still with deep research
To build the Universal Church,
Lofty as is the love of God,
And ample as the wants of man.
Tales of a Wayside Inn. LONGFELLOW.

As he walked home, Donovan thought a good deal of the scene he had just left, and for the first time it struck him that the sermon had been rather an unusual one for such a congregation. Charles Osmond seemed to take it for granted that his people thought; the congregation was chiefly composed of working men and women and tradespeople, but he by no means preached down to what some would have considered their level. He entered into all the questions of the day freely and fearlessly, and took as much pains with his sermons as if they were to be preached before the most searching critics in the country.

How he came to be in such a place was another question which perplexed Donovan. Had he known the reason, he would have been doubly attracted to the man; but it was some time before he found out.

Charles Osmond's history was a strange one. He was exceedingly clever, an original sort of man, full of resources, intensely conscious of latent power which he might probably never have time or opportunity for bringing into exercise. But the strength of the man was in his extraordinary gift of insight; there was something almost uncanny about his power of reading people. He would have made a good diplomatist, a first-rate detective, had not his power of sympathy been quite as strong as his power of insight. He had that gift of 'magnetism' which Donovan had ascribed to Racburn; almost all who had anything to do with him were attracted, they scarcely knew why or how. He had a way of treating each individual as if for the time being his only desire was to get nearer to him, and although he was the most wide-minded of men, he could so concentrate his world-wide sympathy as to bring its full power to bear on one heart. His influence was marvellous! he was like a sort of sun; the coldest, most frozen, icebound natures melted in his genial presence. He could draw out the most reserved people in a way astonishing to themselves. He spoke little of 'souls' in the lump, never obtruded the conventionel red-tapeism of clerical life, but each individual was to him a wonderful and absorbing study. He rarely even in thought massed them together as 'his parish,' but took them as his inner circle of brothers and sisters, a tiny fragment of the one great family.

Of course he was almost worshipped by those who knew him, but with a certain class of character he could make no way. He had one great fault—a fault which repelled some people, generally the 'unco guid or rigidly righteous,' or those comfortable people who feel no need or desire for sympathy. His fault was this—he was too conscious of his influence; he knew that he had exceptional gifts, and all his life long he had been struggling with that deadliest of foes, conceit. He had the exquisite candour to call his fault by its true name, a very rare virtue ; and few things angered him more than to hear conceit confounded with self-respect or proper pride of independence. Conceit was conceit pure and simple; the word pride had lost its objectionable meaning. To tell a man that he was proud would make him feel almost gratified, would give him a sense of dignity, but to tell him he was conceited would be sure to give him a hard home-thrust. So he went on in his straightforward way, struggling with his deadly hindrance, daily—almost hourly—checking himself, pulling himself up, as he drifted into the all too natural habit of self-approval. He had not crushed his foe as yet, but he has risen immensely by the effort. It had helped greatly to increase the manliness, the honesty, the large-minded tolerance which characterized him. Fully conscious that he had not 'already attained, neither was already perfect,' he was a thousand times more helpful to those in need than many of his brethren who looked down on him, blandly content with their own progress in righteousness—at any rate, convinced that Charles Osmond's very apparent fault must unfit him for his work. Certainly it *did* prevent his ever assuming the conventional tone of priest to penitent ; he never felt himself on a higher platform than his congregation, but perhaps for that very reason he succeeded in attracting those whom no one else could attract.

The reason that he was still to be found toiling away in an

obscure parish in one of the poor parts of London was not without its pathos. Very few were aware of the real cause. Naturally
he was not without a good deal of ambition, and at a certain
time in his life his advances had been rapid. He had written a
series of articles which had brought him into notice, and almost
at the same time two offers were made to him. The one was the
offer of a living in London worth perhaps £300 a year, the other
was to a position of great responsibility, invariably made the
stepping-stone to high places. Charles Osmond was human; it
cost him a great deal to give up the prospect of rapid and
honourable preferment, and in refusing the offer he gave up
many other things which he much desired—the opportunity of
mixing with his equals, the chance of intellectual society, the
greater ease of speaking to a highly educated congregation. In
many respects he was, and knew that he was, admirably fitted
for such a position, but, weighing it all in his honest mind, he
came to the conclusion that he could not trust himself to accept
it. His power, his influence, his worldly position would be immensely raised; he did not feel himself sufficiently strong to
resist such increased temptations.

So the chance of promotion was honourably rejected, and
Charles Osmond settled down to terribly up-hill work in London.
Life never could be easy to such a man; he was too sensitive,
too wide-minded, too Christ-like to be ever without his share of
Christ's burden—the burden of the suffering, the sinning, the
doubting. He was, too, in a certain sense, an isolated man; all
through his life he had been greatly misunderstood. By one set
he was stigmatized as 'High Church,' by another as 'dangerously Broad,' by a third as 'almost a Dissenter.' Attacked thus
from all points, his life would have been almost intolerable had
it not been for the growing love and devotion of his own particular people. His church became a sort of Cave of Adullam—a
refuge for numbers of the distressed; and as years went by, the
work began to tell, and a real improvement could be noted. This
alone was almost enough to make up for the hostility which he
encountered in other quarters, though he was not the sort of man
to whom persecution could ever be otherwise than painful.
He had lately incurred great odium by urging in public that
Raeburn, the atheist, ought to be treated with as much justice,
and courtesy, and consideration as if he had been a Christian.
The narrow-minded were thereby much scandalized; the atheists
began to believe that it was *possible* for a clergyman to be honest
and unprejudiced.

The walk home after Sunday evening service was generally

the part of the day's work which Brian dreaded most for his
father.   He knew it was then that the burden pressed most
heavily on him, for the sin and evil were fearfully apparent in
those back streets, and Charles Osmond keenly alive to it all,
wearied with the exertions of the day, and aware of his inability
to cope with the immense wickedness around, often fell a prey
to the haunting consciousness of failure and to blank depression.

This evening, however, as they parted from Donovan at the
church door, he seemed quite unusually brisk and animated, and
though generally too tired to care to speak an unnecessary word,
he had not walked a hundred yards before he began to question
his son.

'So that is your new friend?'

'Yes,' returned Brian, 'what do you think of him?'

'I think he's a friend worth having.'

'I knew you would like him,' said Brian, triumphantly, 'if
it were only because he is one of your "sceps." Is there an
honest atheist in the world whom you don't like, I wonder!'

'I hope not,' said Charles Osmond, with a touch of quiet
humour in his tone.

'I wouldn't say much about Farrant before you had seen him,
for he's not the sort of fellow to be known at second hand, and I
was determined you should somehow meet him.   Odd that such
a chance as that girl's illness should have brought you together
after all.'

'Just as well,' said Charles Osmond.   'He is a fellow to be
led, not driven, or to be driven only by the One who knows when
to use the snaffle, when the curb.'

'Yes, one is afraid of pushing him the wrong way rather,'
said Brian, 'even, I mean, in chance talk without any intention
of pushing at all.'

'That we always must feel in speaking to those whom the
world has held at arm's length.   I should like to know what
helped to bring that fellow to atheism, have you any idea?'

'The un-Christlikeness of Christians, I fancy—and something
he said of injustice with which he had been treated, but he has
only once spoken of it at all, and then merely because he grew
hot at the mention of Raeburn.'

Charles Osmond sighed heavily, it was another instance added
to the hundreds he already knew of the harm caused by injustice
and want of charity.   He fell into a sorrowful reverie, but
roused himself after a time to ask what his son knew of Donovan's
history.

'I know very little,' said Brian, 'he seems to be alone in the

world, and he is very poor. We are of the same year; he came
up at October two years ago and got a scholarship at once.
He's by far the cleverest fellow we have, no one else has a chance
while he's there; any amount of brains you know, and works
furiously—as if it were the only thing he cared for.'

'I thought as much,' observed Charles Osmond. 'There's
the dog though—wonderful to see the devotion between those
two; no man in the world, as the old saying goes, who can't
find a dog and a woman to love him. Who is the "old man of
the sea" you spoke of?'

'The queerest old fellow you ever saw, who has come to live
with him, an old captain something, I forget the name. Quite
of another grade to Farrant, and trying to live with, I should
fancy, for he's a regular old tippler, but he's devoted to "Donovan," as he always calls him.'

'Oh! that's his name; is he connected with the Donovans of
Kilbeggan, I wonder? grannie has their family tree by heart.'

'There's nothing Irish about Farrant,' said Brian.

'I'm not so sure of that, I fancy there's a good deal of humour
in him, stifled by circumstances perhaps, and I'll stake my reputation as an observer that somewhere in his ancestry you'll find
an Italian!'

Brian laughed; his father was very fond of tracing the tokens
of differing nationalities, and had many theories on the subject;
sometimes his theories fell wide of the mark, however, and Brian
was inclined to think he had made a bad shot this time, for to
him Donovan seemed entirely—almost typically—English.

A few days after this Donovan was induced to dine with the
Osmonds, not without much persuasion from Brian, who was now
sufficiently his friend to be comfortably rude to him.

'You'll grow into a bear, a misanthrope, if you never go any-
where,' he urged, as Donovan pleaded his want of time. 'You'll
addle your brains, knock up before the exam, grow into the "dull
boy" of the proverb. I can see that this unmitigated grind is
beginning to tell on you already; you look as old again as you
did before the October term.'

Donovan flushed a little at this, said abruptly that he would
come, and gave a rapid turn to the conversation.

The Osmonds lived in Bloomsbury, in an old house which
had belonged to Charles Osmond's grandfather in the days when
Bloomsbury was a fashionable region. It was a comfortable, roomy
house, not too far from the parish to be inconvenient, and all the
better for being far removed from West End gaieties, as the
Osmonds were something of Bohemians, dined at an unpardon-

ably early hour, and rather set at naught the conventionalities of life.

Donovan was shown into a charming, old-fashioned drawing-room, not old-fashioned according to the recent high art revival of spindle-legged forms and Queen Anne uncomfortableness, but such a room as might have been found at the beginning of the century. Everything was massive and good of its kind. There were capacious arm-chairs and most restful sofas covered with the real old chintz worth any number of modern cretonnes, an old-fashioned Erard piano that had seen good service, beautifully inlaid tables, some good oil paintings, and a delightful array of books in long, low bookcases, bound in old yellow calf and that everlasting morocco which was somehow procurable in the good old times when bookbinding was an art, not a trade. A few modern knick-knacks here and there relieved the stiffness of the furniture, while a faint smell of dried roses was wafted from old china bowls and vases which would have awakened the envy of anyone suffering from the china mania.

Mrs. Osmond, Brian's grandmother, just completed the old-world picture. Donovan fell in love with her at once. She was indeed a very beautiful old lady, her silvery hair, her mild, blue eyes, her peculiarly sweet smile were all in their way perfect, but it was the exquisite courtesy, the delicate grace of the past day that attracted everyone so irresistibly, that beautiful old-fashioned sweetness of manner which has somehow perished in the heat and struggle—the 'hurrying life' of the nineteenth century. She made him a charming, gracious, little curtsey, then held out her hand, and Donovan, Republican though he was, did not shake it, but, acting as he occasionally did by impulse, bent low and kissed it.

The old lady seemed touched and gratified; she at once introduced the names of her old friends the Donovans of Kilbeggan, and there ensued an animated discussion as to the younger branches of the family, resulting in the oft-made discovery that the world is smaller than we think, and that Donovan's grandfather, General Donovan, had been Mrs. Osmond's old playfellow. The gong sounded, and the dear, old, stately lady went down to dinner on Donovan's arm, still talking of her young days in Ireland, then drifting on to the London life of long ago, dwelling in the loving, tender way of the old on the celebrities of her time, the Kembles, Jenny Lind, Grisi, Sontag, Miss Stephens, and Braham; then on to the Chartist rising of '48, when Charles Osmond took his turn and spoke of the 'Christian Socialism' scheme, from which they passed to the Radicalism of to-day, a subject which Donovan himself would not have ventured to introduce in a clergyman's house, but which he found discussed with perfect fairness. Indeed, though Charles Osmond rarely meddled with politics, his work lay so entirely among 'the people' that he was really able to see matters from their point of view, and in the main he was ready to agree with Donovan.

About the house, or rather the home, there was the same atmosphere as at Porthkerran, the same wideness of sympathy, the same loving regard for the work and interests of others, the same 'one and all' principle carried into beautiful practice. The parish was not made a bore to the other members of the family, Brian's work was not obtruded in a tiresome way, nor Mrs. Osmond's manifold feminine occupations; all was well balanced, well regulated, and Donovan realized how perfect a home can be in which are the three generations. Past, present, and future, when really united, do make the strongest threefold cord, and perhaps no house is quite complete without the quick perception of the young, the steady judgment of the middle-aged, the golden experience of the old.

Part of the evening Donovan spent alone with Charles Osmond in his study, a comfortable room, methodically arranged, and lined with books, theological, anti-theological, and scientific. Judged by his books, it might perhaps have been hard to say which of Charles Osmond's abusers were right; whether he was really High, Broad, or half a Dissenter; perhaps he was a little of all three, or perhaps he had reached above and beyond those earthly distinctions.

However this might be, as the two sat that evening over their coffee, Donovan fairly forgot he was speaking to that, to him, obnoxious being—a clergyman. Not even to Dr. Tremain had he ever talked with such perfect openness. Those dog-like eyes, with their constant appeal, 'let us come nearer,' were irresistible. He found himself almost thinking aloud, and as his thinking meant great questioning, the possibility of having a being outside himself capable of listening, sympathising, and answering was a rare delight. And because he was conscious of Charles Osmond's unasserted but very real superiority, he cared not what he said, felt no restriction, no fear of going too far, or of giving too much confidence. The really clever, really great, really good, inspire trust where the mediocre inspire dread.

As they talked, a little of Donovan's private history, which Charles Osmond had speculated about, was revealed. They had been speaking of Mill's notable admission that, on the whole, men could not do better than try to imitate the life of Christ.

'But,' urged Donovan, 'however much one may resolve to do so, I find endless difficulties when it comes to actual practice. Take this, for instance—I wish to find what is Christ's law of forgiveness, and am met with such contradictions as these: I am first told to offer the other cheek, to let my cloak follow my coat, not to resist evil. I am told another time to bring the matter before witnesses, before the church, and if it is all of no avail, to let my enemy be to me as a heathen man and a publican. How do you explain that?'

'I think the first referred to injuries received by a Christian from an unbeliever, the second to injuries received from a fellow-Christian,' said Charles Osmond.

'Then what is an atheist to do when injured by a Christian?' asked Donovan. 'I will tell you the actual case, and then you will see the difficulty. A certain cousin of mine has defrauded me of my property. I know, though unfortunately I can't go to law about it, that he destroyed my father's last will; he then married my mother, and when I came of age coolly turned me out of the house without a farthing. He now lives on my estate, spends my money, enjoys himself thoroughly, as far as I know, and kindly condescends to make me an allowance of £100 a year, though he knows that I know of his villany.'

'You can't bring an action against him?'

'Unfortunately not. It is too great a risk. It would just be a contest of character, and the expenses would be enormous. Now, what I want to know is, what you expect me to feel towards that man.'

'It is a hard case,' said Charles Osmond. 'I should like to know what you do feel.'

'All I have been able to do is to will to think of him as little as possible. When I do think of him, I confess that I often get red-hot with indignation. Happily, I've plenty of work and need not dwell on it, so that except twice a year, when his beggarly cheques come in, I nearly forget his existence. If this is letting him be to me a heathen and a publican, I have so far fulfilled the Christian law, but——'

'Ah! yes, I'm glad you put in a but,' said Charles Osmond. 'For though, after you have done all in your power to reconcile and win back your enemy, you are told to leave him and have no more to do with him, you must remember that that command pre-supposes that you are a Christian, and therefore one who loves all men, who recognizes the universal brotherhood, who tries to imitate the One who makes His sun to shine on the evil as well as on the good. The very first principles of Christianity show that you must love this man, though he is your enemy, and though it may be best for you to have no personal communication with him.'

'You mean I must love Ellis Farrant? It is impossible. You've no conception what a scoundrel he is. I could horsewhip him with the greatest pleasure.'

'Then of course you have not forgotten him ?'

'No, I have not,' said Donovan, emphatically. 'And I don't see how you can expect me to while every day the fellow is adding to his sin, while every day he's defrauding me of my own.'

'You must not think me hard on you,' said Charles Osmond. 'Your feeling is exceedingly natural, and I think perhaps you can't get much further than this until you believe in God. It was Christ who taught us what real forgiveness is. Now you tell me that although you do not believe in God, and regard Christ merely as a very good man, yet you consider the ideal God as a very beautiful ideal.'

'Yes,' said Donovan.

'Well, then, just listen to me while I put your words as though they were spoken by the ideal God. "This man is mine, I caused him to be, gave him all that he possesses, he owes me love and obedience, for years he has defrauded me of both, defrauded me of my due, and he has done it wilfully. I am full of indignation, and I will not to think of him any more. To love him is impossible, he is a perfect scoundrel, and every day he is adding to his sin." The God in whom I believe did not speak like this; you will allow that if He had thus spoken He would not have been an ideal God at all. Instead of thinking of the right of which He had been defrauded, He thought first of the child of His who was defrauding Him, how miserable his existence was in reality, how everything was distorted to his view so that he had even lost sight of their original relationship, and regarded his Father as an angry tyrant. Somehow the child must be made to understand that, although it had sinned, its Father, being its Father, was only longing to forgive it, to break down the barrier which had risen between them. He revealed His wonderful love in such a way that the simplest could not fail to see it, His forgiveness was there, waiting for all who would take it. It was not a forgiveness to be obtained after much pleading, it was there as a free gift for all who had the least real and honest wish to be reconciled. That is the forgiveness of God, and the example which you must follow.'

'It is impossible,' said Donovan, with sad emphasis

'Perhaps it may be until you have realized what God has forgiven you.'

'But how am I to love what is hateful?'

'I never asked you to do so.'

'The man is utterly hateful, a lying, deceitful, hypocritical knave.'

'No man is altogether evil, there is latent good in him that you cannot perceive. I don't ask you to love the evil in him, but to love him because he is a man. He is your brother whether you will or not, and if you want to imitate Christ you must love him.'

Donovan shook his head, and sighed.

'It's no good, I can hardly make myself even wish to love him; it's somehow against one's sense of justice.'

'"Though justice be thy plea, consider this, that in the course of justice none of us should see salvation,"' quoted Charles Osmond, smiling. 'But don't think I am speaking easily of the thing, forgiveness *is* hard, in a case like yours it is frightfully hard. I have merely told you what I consider ideal forgiveness, if you aim at the highest you will often and often fall short of the mark.'

'The worst of it is this struggling to copy the life of Christ is such frightfully discouraging work,' said Donovan. 'The more one tries the harder it gets, and one is always coming to some new demand which is almost impossible to meet.'

'Did you ever climb an Alp?' asked Charles Osmond. 'As you get higher you find it harder work, the air is more rarefied, the way more abrupt; but when you reach the summit, what do you care for all the labour? The work was weary, but the end was worth all! When the full vision breaks upon us——' he paused, and there was a minute's silence, but the light in his face was more eloquent than words.

'If there be a summit and a vision,' said Donovan, in a low voice.

'Though it tarry, wait for it,' was Charles Osmond's answer.

After that they passed to matters nearer the surface, and before long Brian came down, and the three drew in their chairs to the fire, and sat smoking and talking till late in the evening. Charles Osmond had, in spite of his harassing life, kept a wonderful reserve fund of high spirits, and just now in the relief of having to do with one so honest and high-minded as Donovan he forgot the hundred and one cares of his parish, and was the life of the party. His comical anecdotes, told in the raciest way imaginable, drew forth shouts of laughter from the listeners, and, feeling convinced that Donovan did not often exercise his lungs in that way, he kept up an almost ceaseless flow of the very wittiest talk. A great love of fun and a certain absence of conventional decorum proved the nationality of the Osmonds, but it was with something far beyond the sense of good fellowship that Donovan went home that night. He was cheered and amused certainly, but the home-like reception at the clergyman's house had already widened him and softened his clerical antipathies, while his growing admiration for Charles Osmond did him a world of good.

Who does not know the delight of intercourse with a greater mind, the enthusiasm which springs from the mere fact of looking up to another, the inspiriting sense of being bettered, raised, stimulated to fresh exertion?

Cut off by his act of self-sacrifice from the Tremain household, and with poor old Rouge Frewin for his sole companion, Donovan was in great need of friends whom he could revere as well as love; the Osmonds were exactly fitted to meet his need, and perhaps for that reason the friendship deepened and strengthened very rapidly.

After he had left that evening the father and son lingered over the fire, indulging a little in that general habit of discussing the departed guest.

'Wasn't it rare to hear him laugh?' said Brian. 'I'd no idea he'd such a lot of fun in him. His hatred of the clergy will die a natural death now that he has got to know you! It was the biggest joke to see the way in which every now and then he chanced to notice your tie, and received a sort of shock realizing that you were actually one of the hated class.'

'It is hardly to be wondered at,' said Charles Osmond. 'We clergy are terribly apt to forget that we must follow St. Paul, and try to be "all things to all men." I should like to know how many parsons have said as much as a kind word to that fellow, who must have been nominally under the charge of some one all his life. Our beautiful parochial system is fearfully apt to degenerate into a mere skeleton.'

'What do you think? will he come round? or will he always be an agnostic?'

'I can't tell,' said Charles Osmond, with a sigh, 'he seems to be living with all his might up to the light he has, but he is not the sort of man to change rapidly, and his private history is all against it. An atheist shamefully wronged by those who call themselves Christians cannot but feel that he has a strong case against Christianity.'

'But he will never rest satisfied with what he has got,' said Brian. 'His very face tells that he knows he is incomplete.'

'Yes, he knows that,' said Charles Osmond. 'In talking to him to-night I couldn't help thinking of Browning's description of the grand old ship dismasted and storm-battered, but still bearing on, with something in her infinite possibilities which raised her above the mere lifeboats,

> Make perfect your good ship as these,
> And what were her performances !'

'And yet you doubt whether he will be perfected ?' said Brian.

'Never !' exclaimed Charles Osmond, warmly. 'I never said so! That he will be the grand character he was meant to be I have not a doubt, but whether he will be anything but an agnostic in *this* world, God only knows.'

No more was said. Brian fell to thinking of all the contradictory statements about the Eternities, his father returned to the almost ceaseless intercession which was the under-current of his exceedingly practical life. Highly illogical according to Raeburn, and a great mistake according to others, as most of the intercessions were for those whom a righteously indignant Christian once denounced as '*past* praying for'! But to him it was a necessity of life ; one of the world's sin-bearers, he would long ago have sunk under the burden if he had tried to bear it alone. As it was, how *could* he be intolerant, how *could* he be uncharitable ? For were not the nineteenth-century 'publicans and sinners' among the strongest of his bonds of union with the Unseen ? He was one of those who cannot help caring more for the lost sheep than for the ninety and nine in the fold, and though he was by no means inclined weakly to condone sin, or to make light of it, no one had ever heard him denounce a sinner, or speak a harsh word of any whom society had condemned.

CHAPTER XXXV.

CONTRASTED LOVERS.

What we love perfectly, for its own sake
We love, and not our own, being ready thus
Whate'er self-sacrifice is ask'd to make;
That which is best for it is best for us.
SOUTHEY.

STEPHEN CAUSTON did not return to the hospital till March. Coming home one afternoon, Donovan found the sitting-room in some confusion, scraps of newspaper and dilapidated note-books scattered about here and there, and a yawning space in the book-shelves which Stephen's books had hitherto occupied.

'Hullo! has Causton been in?' he asked old Rouge, who, with a somewhat disturbed air, was sitting over the fire with his long clay pipe.

'I don't know if that's his name,' replied the old captain, in an offended tone, 'but a tallow-faced, bumptious lad has been here, making no end of dust and noise, carrying off your books, too, for aught I know.'

'No, no, they were his own,' said Donovan, smiling. 'But tell me about him, captain. Did he ask for me? did he leave no message?'

'Not he,' said Rouge, angrily. 'He walked in as coolly as if the place belonged to him, rowed the landlady for not having his things ready packed, and pitched the books into a carpet-bag as if they were so many pebbles. Then, facing round on me without so much as lifting his hat, he said, "I suppose you are a friend of Farrant's?" There was a sneer in his voice, and my blood got up as I said I had the honour to be your friend, and that it was an honour the best in the land might covet.'

Donovan laughed. Rouge continued,

'At that he sneered again, and said, "You needn't preach about his virtues; I know a little more about him than you do." "Indeed!" said I, hotly; "then I wonder the knowledge hasn't improved your manners." "I might return the compliment," he said. "But of course living with a knave like Farrant is enough to contaminate anyone." At that, milord, I sprang up and thundered at him. I wasn't going to sit still and hear you libelled, and, if you'll believe it, the coward turned as white as a sheet when I challenged him.'

'By Jove!' said Donovan. 'You don't mean you really did. His mother will never get over it.'

'He won't come poking his nose in here again in a hurry,' said Rouge, with satisfaction. 'He skulked off at the double quick time, muttering that duelling days were over.'

'Well, I agree with him there,' said Donovan, 'though it was good of you all the same, captain, to stand up for me as you did.'

'As if I could help it,' said old Rouge, with tears in his eyes. 'It's not likely I should let that scamp have his say out without putting in my word. I flatter myself he has heard more home truths to-day than in all his priggish young life before. How does he come to hate you so, milord?'

'He has done a shabby thing by me,' said Donovan, 'and that's the surest way in the world to make him hate me. But we won't rake it all up again; he can't do us any good, and he's already done me all the harm he can.'

But, though he would not speak any more of Stephen, the thought of him would not be banished. He had come straight from Porthkerran, might have told him something of Gladys, might possibly have brought him one of the unanswerable letters from Mrs. Tremain or the doctor, or at least a message. And then he could not help wondering at the extraordinary malice of his gratuitous insults. Had his weak and distorted mind really worked itself into the belief that *he* was the wronged one? What account would reach Porthkerran of his stormy interview with the old captain? Something tremendous might, without much difficulty, be twisted and squeezed out of the truth. Here was another case demanding Charles Osmond's ideal forgiveness. But he was nearer forgiving Stephen than Ellis, because he had a great deal of pity for him; besides, the consciousness that he might have cleared himself by exposing Stephen was in itself of a more softening nature than the terribly irritating sense that Ellis had been very unjustly in his power.

Brian Osmond did not fail to notice that Causton, who had been formerly Donovan's companion, now cut him entirely. When he had heard the true explanation, his righteous indignation was pleasant to see. He came constantly to York Road for the sake of reading with Donovan, and before long had become really fond of the poor old captain, while Waif and Sweepstakes, with their touching devotion to their respective masters, added a sort of picturesqueness to that curiously-assorted group. In the summer vacation Brian persuaded Donovan to take a real holiday. The two years of unbroken work added to his private troubles were beginning to tell on him; he looked worn and fagged, but brightened up at the suggestion of taking a walking-tour with his friend. They set off together in August, had a glorious tramp through Derbyshire and the West Riding of Yorkshire, roughing it to an enjoyable extent, and both coming back to town all the better for their outing, and as inseparable in their friendship as David and Jonathan.

It was not, however, until late in the autumn that Brian learnt even the existence of Gladys.

One November evening his well-known knock at the house in York Road roused old Rouge from his after-dinner nap. Donovan, who was stretched at full length on the hearthrug, was so absorbed in some of the abstruse speculations which now very often occupied him that he heard nothing, and did not stir till Brian was fairly in the room.

'Hullo! doing the *dolce far niente* for once,' he said, laughing. 'Who would have thought of catching you away from the books!'

'Comes from the effect of Yorkshire air,' said Donovan, getting up and stretching himself. But the real fact was that he was beginning now to dare to allow himself brief intervals of rest, his thoughts did not wander so hopelessly to Porthkerran, his work instinctively slackened a little, he worked as well—perhaps better—but less furiously, and without the sense that relaxation was, above all things, to be distrusted and avoided.

'I've got a spare ticket for Gale's lecture at St. James's Hall,' said Brian, 'will you come with me?'

'Who's Gale? I never heard of him.'

'What! you a teetotaler and never heard of Gale! why, he's the great champion of temperance, and a first-rate speaker!'

'Better take the captain,' said Donovan, half in earnest, as he glanced round at the sofa; but Rouge had already fallen asleep again. 'It would be no good, I'm afraid.'

'Poor old fellow,' said Brian, 'has he had another outbreak?'

'Yes,' replied Donovan, 'and his brain is too fuddled now to take in anything; it would be no use taking him, he'd only be asleep in two minutes. I somehow make an awful failure of keeping other folk in order.'

'Rather an unmanageable couple, yours,' said Brian; 'I wonder what Gale would say to a case like the captain's.'

'Incurable,' said Donovan. 'He means well, but his power of will has gone. I used to think he might conquer it, but the more I see of him the more I doubt it. I can do nothing for him except make his remorse keener each time, for he thinks his outbreaks are a personal injury to me; and then we have any amount of maudlin tears and good resolutions never to do it again—till the next time.'

He sighed.

'Poor old fellow,' said Brian, 'you were never meant to have such an old man of the sea tacked on to you. I like to fancy the different mortal you'll be by-and-by when you settle down with your ideal wife, home, and practice.'

'Ideal humbug!' exclaimed Donovan, with a short laugh, in which there lurked more pain than merriment. 'Come on, what time does the Gale begin?'

They walked off arm-in-arm, and were early enough to secure front seats in the balcony close to the platform. Donovan seemed in good spirits, he leant forward with his arms on the crimson velvet rail making comments on the audience below, classifying them into rabid teetotalers, sensible supporters of the cause, and merely fashionable adherents. A sudden exclamation of surprise from Brian put a stop, however, to his ease.

'Why, who would have thought it! there's Causton in one of the stalls. What can have brought him here? Don't you see him? To the left there, talking to that pretty girl.'

Donovan looked and saw only too plainly Stephen and Mrs. Causton, and between them Gladys.

Yes, she was there, not a hundred yards from him, her pure, fresh, child-like face not in the least altered! he remembered an old fancy of his that she was like a blush rose; she looked very flower-like now in that crowd of London faces. For a minute he watched her quite calmly, then, strong man as he was, a deathly pallor stole over his face, he drew back with an uncontrollable shudder.

'Look here, I must go,' he said to Brian, and without further explanation he made his way along the balcony. In another moment he felt sure his eyes must draw hers, there always had been a strange magnetism between them without any conscious willing on his part. It would never do for her to see him, he must leave at once.

Brian, not liking his looks, followed him out of the hall; he seemed as if he were walking in his sleep, never pausing for an instant, noting nothing, and yet passing all obstacles. At the head of the staircase Brian linked his arm within his, they went down silently into the street. There Donovan seemed to come to himself again, his rigid face relaxed, the strange glassy look left his eyes, and for the first time he realized that he was not alone.

'What, you here, old fellow!' he exclaimed. 'Don't let me lose you your lecture.'

'All right,' said Brian. 'I don't care about it. You're in some trouble, Donovan—don't pretend, now, that you're not. Was it that you saw Causton with that girl?'

'In a way, yes—I mean it was the seeing her at all,' said Donovan, incoherently. 'Come on quick, only let us get out into the open, away from these houses.'

'You don't imagine he's in love with her!' said Brian. 'Causton's an awfully cold-blooded creature; it's not at all in his line, I should think.'

'I don't know,' gasped Donovan; 'it—it won't make much difference to me.'

'Why?' asked Brian, boldly. They were both by nature reserved men, but their friendship was real and strong, and Brian knew intuitively that he had touched the secret spring of Donovan's trouble, and that, unless he could get him to speak of it now, a barrier would always be between them; so he spoke out boldly that monosyllable—'Why?'

'Because,' answered Donovan, in a quick, agitated way—'because, years ago, I made up my mind not to see her again. It's impossible—it can't be—I'm a fool to be so shaken just by the sight of her.'

'Has she refused you?'

He turned his strangely powerful eyes full on Brian's face at the question, and answered, with a sort of indignation,

'Do you think I am fit to ask Gladys Tremain to be my wife?'

There was something grand in his humility. Brian could only mentally ejaculate, 'You splendid fellow! you're fit to ask a queen among women.' But he was carried away by his enthusiasm, and he could not but own that there was truth in Donovan's next speech.

'It could never be—there could be no real union between us. It's all very well in the way of friendship; you and I can rub up against each other's differences without any hurt, but when it comes to anything nearer, it doesn't do. I've tried, and it's torture—torture that I'll *never* bring to her.'

'Is Causton her cousin?'

'No, but a two generations' friend.'

'I should dearly like to give him a piece of my mind,' said Brian. 'However, of course she'll have nothing to say to such a fellow.'

'There are times when I could wish she would,' said Donovan, hoarsely. 'Not now, though—not just now.'

'My dear fellow, that's rather too strong,' said Brian. 'Even I, a mere stranger, can see that she's miles above him.'

'Of course,' said Donovan ; 'but it might save her from worse pain.'

'Well, if Miss Tremain knows you, and has any idea that you care for her, her face must belie her strangely if she could turn to a fellow like Causton.'

'She does not know I love her—at least, I hope not.'

'You old brick of a Roman ! I can quite fancy how you would hide it all.'

There was a silence after that. They had reached the Embankment, and Donovan seemed to lose the sense of oppression, and to breathe freely again. Presently he turned to Brian, speaking quite in his natural voice.

'Well, I'm sorry to have lost you your lecture, but I'm not sorry that you know about this, which is more than I could say to anyone else in the world. I must get to work quickly, or the blue devils will get the better of me. Come back, too, won't you, and we'll have a grind at Niemeyer.'

So they went back to the York Road lodgings together. The old captain was too stupid to notice them, but Waif was unusually demonstrative, and, even as he read, Brian noticed that Donovan kept his arm round the dog, while Waif tried to put all his devotion into the soft warm tongue with which he licked his master's hand. Trouble had an odd way of drawing those two together.

Brian went home that night with much questioning going on in his mind. He honoured Donovan for his conduct, and yet regretted very much that he should thus be cut off from one who must have had so much influence over him. He could not help seeing the matter from his friend's side, whereas Donovan thought only how it would affect Gladys.

Little indeed did Gladys think, as she sat in the crowded hall, that she was so near Donovan. Though she was actually thinking of him, it never occurred to her that he might be there. Instead, she was recollecting some of their discussions at Porthkerran on this temperance question, and recalling his stories of the old captain who had nursed him in his illness, and had with great devotedness managed to keep really sober at Monaco, in case 'the Frenchman' should poison his patient !

She was not very happy just now, poor child. They had fancied that she needed change of air, and Mrs. Causton had been charmed to have her at Richmond for a few weeks, in the same little villa which they had rented four years ago. But the change did her more harm than good, for the Causton atmosphere was oppressive, and the consciousness that Stephen was in the way of seeing Donovan every day, added to the impossibility of hearing anything about him, was almost more than she could endure. She found herself losing self-control, and drifting into more constant thoughts of Donovan than she considered right ; nor were her feminine occupations so helpful in the difficult mental battle as his mind-engrossing studies.

As they went home that night from John Gale's lecture, it chanced that for the first time since her arrival Donovan's name was mentioned.

'What a pity you could not have done good for evil,' sighed Mrs. Causton, 'and induced that poor drunkard who challenged you in the spring to come to this lecture. I fear there is no chance that Donovan Farrant would take him to hear such a man.'

'I should rather think not,' said Stephen, unpleasantly.

'Oh ! but he is a great temperance advocate,' said Gladys, thankful that in the darkness her burning cheeks could not be noticed.

'He *was*, my dear,' said Mrs. Causton, markedly, 'but you must remember he is greatly changed since you knew him, and he is living with a most disreputable companion.'

Her heart beat so indignantly at this that she felt almost choked, but seeing that she was losing her opportunity she quieted herself with an effort, and asked gravely, but quite naturally,

'Donovan is still at the hospital, I suppose? Do you see anything of him now ? '

'I see him,' said Stephen, ' but of course we're not on speaking terms.'

'It is much better that you should have nothing more to do with him,' said Mrs. Causton, solemnly, and she added a text which seemed to her appropriate, but which drove Gladys into a white-hot passion—dumb perforce.

All this time she was far too much absorbed to notice an impending danger. The days dragged on slowly, she cared for the visits, picture-galleries, and concerts only in so far as they brought her into closer proximity with St. Thomas's. However angry she might be with herself at night for having allowed her thoughts too much liberty, the following day always found her with the same unexpressed but unquenchable longing. Nothing but the heart-sickness brought by that long-deferred hope could have blinded her to the fact that Stephen's half-boyish admiration was re-awaking, that his attentions were disagreeable and obtrusive,

that he was as much in love with her as it was possible for such
a man to be. But, as it was, she noticed nothing, she only wearied
intensely of the long evenings, when Stephen tried to enliven
them, and of the long mornings when she was alone with Mrs.
Canston; of the two she disliked the evenings least, but merely
because there was a chance of hearing the one name she cared
to hear.

It came upon her like a thunderclap at last. One Saturday
morning she was sitting in the little drawing-room, writing to
her mother, when Stephen, who had no lectures that day, sauntered
into the room. He began an aimless conversation, she was a
little cross, for it seemed as if he might go on for ever, and she
wanted to write. After enduring half-an-hour of it she grew
impatient.

'Let me finish this, Stephen, or it will be too late for the post,'
she said. 'We are to go out after lunch, you know.'

'You grudge me the one free morning I have,' said Stephen,
reproachfully, 'but listen to me a minute longer, Gladys; for days
I have been waiting to find an opportunity of speaking to you.
I think you must have seen that I love you, that all I care for is
to please you; will you say that you will try to love me?—won't
you try, dear?'

In spite of Gladys' surprise and dismay she had hard work to
suppress a smile, a wicked sprite seemed to chant in her ear the
refrain of the song in 'Alice in Wonderland,'

Will you, won't you, will you, won't you, will you join the dance?

She found herself going on with the parody in a sort of dream,
instead of giving Stephen his answer.

He was far on in a second and more vehement statement of
his case before she fully recovered her senses; then at once the
true womanly unselfish Gladys hastened to check him.

'Hush, Stephen,' she said, quietly, but with a touch of dignity
in her tone. 'Please do not say any more of this. I am very,
very sorry if you have misunderstood me in any way, we are such
old friends, you see; but indeed it could never be as you wish—
never.'

'You don't know what you are saying,' he cried. 'You are
ruining all my life, all my happiness. Surely you won't be so
utterly cruel? I will wait any length of time, if only you will
think it over—if only you will try to love me.'

'If I waited fifty years, it would make no difference,' said
Gladys. 'I can never love you, never, *never*. Don't think me

unkind to speak so plainly. It is better to be true than to let you have false hopes.'

'Then you love some one else,' said Stephen, in a voice in which despair and malice were strangely mingled, 'that is what makes you so positive, so merciless.'

Gladys' eyes flashed.

'I might well be angry with you, Stephen, for daring to say that, but since you wish it I will tell you quite plainly why I cannot love you in the way you wish. The man I love must be true and strong, faithful to his friends and merciful to his enemies, he must be so noble and self-denying that I shall be able to look up to him as my head—my lord—as naturally in the lesser degree as I look to Christ in the greater.'

'If you set up an ideal character like that, of course I've no chance,' said Stephen, with a very crestfallen air.

'It is not I who set it up,' said Gladys, a little impatiently. 'Have you forgotten what St. Paul said? Oh! Stephen, I don't want to vex you more than I need, but indeed, indeed you must not speak of this again.'

'It is all very well to talk about not vexing me, but you are taking away every hope I have,' said Stephen, petulantly. 'You girls will never learn how much you have in your power. With you to help me, I might perhaps grow better, become the paragon of perfection you wish, but if you turn away from me——'

He paused. It did not strike Gladys just at that minute what a strange manner of making love it was, but her clear common-sense showed her that to yield to such an argument—even had it been possible—would have been exceedingly foolish.

'You may be right, Stephen,' she answered. 'Perhaps we have more in our power than we know, but I don't think it ever can be right for a woman to marry one whom she cannot look up to. You and I have been friends—old playfellows—for years, but, though of course I wish still to be your friend, I can't say that I very much respect you. Don't think I want you to be a paragon of perfection, but after last autumn I don't think you can——'

He interrupted her.

'It is cruel to bring up past mistakes against me.'

'I don't wish to do so, but I am afraid, till you can think of them as something deeper than mistakes, you will yourself often remind us of them. How can you really forsake them till you are really sorry?'

'You are very hard on me,' said Stephen. 'You forget what excuse I had; you forget that I was left alone with Donovan Farrant, that he led me into temptation.'

He hardly knew what he was saying, for he was very desperate in his intense selfishness, but he had just enough shame left to flush a little as the untruth passed his lips.

Gladys' eyes seemed to search him through and through. There was a moment's silence. Then, with a little quiver of indignation in her voice, she said, gravely,

'You are telling a lie, Stephen, and you know it.'

He did not attempt to exculpate himself, he was too thoroughly abashed. When he looked up again in a minute or two he found that she had left the room.

Mrs. Causton was too genuinely good a woman to resent Gladys' refusal of her son, but at the same time it was such a bitter disappointment to her that it was impossible she should be quite just and kind to her visitor.

'You see, my dear,' she kept urging, as she sat beside the sofa in Gladys' bed-room, 'though you may be quite right to refuse dear Stephen, yet, humanly speaking, you did seem so exactly fitted to make the real helpmeet for him.'

Gladys was by no means selfish, but she did not think it either right or necessary to sacrifice herself so entirely on the altar of the well-being of Mrs. Causton's son, she could only repeat that she was very sorry, but it was quite impossible, and entreat Mrs. Causton to let her go home at once. However, it was too late to think of going down to Cornwall that day, and the next day was Sunday, so she had time enough to be exceedingly miserable, and to long unspeakably for her mother before the happy moment of her departure arrived. She was so much relieved to be away from the Caustons that she could have sung from mere lightness of heart when her train had actually started, but Mrs. Causton had put her in charge of an elderly lady, so she had to discuss the weather and make herself agreeable instead.

That night in her mother's room she forgot all her trouble, however, in the delicious peacefulness which seemed always to come in those evening talks. And as they sat hand in hand in their own particular nook on the old-fashioned sofa, Mrs. Tremain gradually won from Gladys not only the history of her visit to the Caustons, but much that had never passed her lips before. Her mother had long ago guessed what was the secret of her trouble ; she had said nothing because she thought silence the best cure ; but now—*being* her mother—she knew that the time for speaking had come, and very wisely and tenderly she met Gladys' shy confidence half way. Then, when all was told, she sat thinking for a minute or two in silence, while Gladys nestled more closely to her, too tired to think at all, but tracing in an aimless sort of way the ivy-pattern chintz of the well-known sofa cover.

'I think, little girl, that the truth of it is this,' said Mrs. Tremain at last, 'I think you had a good deal of influence with Donovan, you were almost the first woman he had known well, and you were a good deal thrown together. For the present he has passed away out of our lives, you know how sorry I am for it, it is quite his own doing; but whether the separation is for ever or not, I think you may have this comfort, that whatever in your love was true and unselfish will not be wasted, but will always last. I do not think it very likely that he will come here again, and even if he did you will perhaps find it all quite different, and have a cold waking from your dream.'

'Then ought I not to think of him?'

'I think you should not allow yourself to believe that he is in love with you. No woman has a right to think that till a man has actually asked her to be his wife. Put away the selfish side of the question altogether, but don't make yourself miserable by trying to kill the spiritual part of it. However much you have been mistaken, there was most likely a bit of the real truth in your love; don't be afraid of keeping that, no one need be ashamed of the pure, spiritual, endless side of love, and I should be sorry to think that Donovan should be defrauded of it. You may do more for him even now, Gladys, than you think.'

'If we could find out the truth,' sighed Gladys. 'I am sure Stephen has somehow misled us.'

'I would not worry about that,' replied Mrs. Tremain. 'You can't sift that matter to the bottom, and I don't think it is very good for you to dwell upon it. Only be quite sure of this, that the more pure and unselfish and trustful you try to become, the better you will be able to help him, even if you never see him again. The side of love you must cultivate does not depend upon sight, or time, or place. Have I been too hard on you, little one? Does it seem very difficult?'

'It is always hard to be good,' said Gladys, with the child-like look in her face which had first awakened Donovan's love; 'but I will try, and you will help me, mother. I'm so glad you know.'

In another hour she was sleeping as peacefully as little Nesta; but her mother had a very wakeful night, thinking over the future of her child, and grieving over Donovan's defection.

CHAPTER XXXVI.

'LAME DOGS OVER STILES.'

We cannot kindle when we will
The fire which in the heart resides;
The spirit bloweth and is still,
In mystery our soul abides.
    But tasks in hours of insight will'd
    Can be through hours of gloom fulfill'd

With aching hands and bleeding feet
We dig and heap, lay stone on stone;
We bear the burden and the heat
Of the long day, and wish 't were done.
    Not till the hours of light return,
    All we have built do we discern.
              MATTHEW ARNOLD.

'THERE's been a scrap of a child here asking for you,' said the old captain to Donovan, as they returned to their rooms one evening after dining at a restaurant. 'I couldn't make out what she wanted, but she's been here twice to see if you weren't come home.'

'What sort of child?'

'Oh! a shabby-looking little lass. She wouldn't tell me what she wanted with you, only she must see Mr. Farrant, and when would he be in.'

'She'll turn up again, I suppose,' said Donovan. 'I'm pretty free this evening; shall we do those slides?'

Old 'Rouge had lately developed a most satisfactory love for the microscope, and whenever it was possible Donovan asked his help over it, or awakened his interest in some new specimen to be seen. There were now actually three things in the world besides himself and his toddy which the old captain cared for—Donovan, Sweepstakes, and the microscope. He loved them all exceedingly in his odd way, and, on the whole, the year which he had spent in York Road was almost the happiest year of his life.

They were hard at work with their slides, specimens, and Canada balsam when the door-bell rang and the mysterious 'child' was announced.

'Show her in here,' said Donovan to the landlady.

'Indeed, sir, she ain't fit,' returned the woman. 'It's a-pouring with rain, and she be that wet and dirty.'

Donovan frowned the frown of a Republican, deposited his section of the brain of a gorilla in a safe place, and went out into

D D

tho passage. The smallest little white-faced child imaginable stood on the mat; the rain had soaked her, the water dripped down from her dark hair, from her ragged shawl, from her indescribably-draggled skirt; she looked the picture of misery.

'Come in and dry yourself by the fire,' said Donovan, and the small elf, too frightened to refuse, followed him into the sitting-room. The old captain bowed to her as gallantly as if she had been a princess, Waif sniffed at her wet frock and yielded up his place in front of the fender, Donovan drew a stool for her on to the hearthrug, and the elf sat down and instinctively spread out her frozen fingers to the blaze.

'You wanted to see me?' asked Donovan. 'What was it about?'

'Please it was father, sir.'

'What is your father's name?'

'Smith, sir, and please he's very ill with something in his inside, and he wants to see you.'

'But I'm not a doctor; he must get the parish doctor.'

'Oh! please, it isn't for his inside he wants you,' said the elf, looking frightened.

'What does he want?'

'Please I don't know, but he said I was to ask Mr. Farrant to come.'

'But I don't know your father; he's not been at St. Thomas's, has he?'

'No, sir, but please do come, for he'll be dreadful vexed if you don't,' and her eyes filled with tears.

'Don't cry,' said Donovan, 'I'll come with you. Is it far? You must show me the way.'

They set off together, Donovan taking the elf under his umbrella to her unspeakable pride and delight, and Waif soberly trotting at their heels.

'And how did your father know where I lived, do you think?' he asked, as they crossed Westminster Bridge.

'Please he had it all wrote down on a card, and he can read very well indeed, father can.'

Big Ben struck nine, and therewith a recollection awoke in Donovan's mind, a fierce struggle which he had once had just on that spot, a sight of Stephen passing by, a hurried pursuit to a well-known billiard-saloon, and a strange recognition of a Cornish face. He had written his address on a card, of course! He remembered it well now. This must be a message from Trevethan's son.

The elf did not speak again, but led him down Horseferry

Road into one of the most horrible of the Westminster slums. He took the precaution of picking up Waif and carrying him under his arm; he was his only valuable. They were unmolested, however, and the child, turning into a forlorn-looking house, led the way up a steep and dirty staircase, and turning a door-handle showed Donovan into a perfectly dark room redolent of tobacco.

'Here's the gentleman, father; give us a light,' she said, groping her way in.

A match was struck, and Donovan could see by the fitful light a comfortless-looking room, and in the corner a man propped up in bed with a short pipe in his hand. The elf produced a tallow-candle, Donovan drew near to the bed, and at once recognized the billiard-marker.

'I thought the message was from you; I'm glad you've sent for me at last,' he said.

'I thought it was too late,' said the man, 'and then, when the child found you out, I thought it was that you wouldn't come. Sit down;' he pointed to a chair, then went on speaking in the most free and easy tone. 'I'm dying, or next door to it, so I thought I'd like to hear of the old man down at Porthkerran. He asked you to look out for me, did he?'

'It was his greatest wish to find you,' said Donovan. 'And after you sent him that five-pound note he told me about you, said he thought you must be in London, and, having very little idea of the sort of place London is, he asked me to look for you. You are like him; I recognized you at once that night.'

'No flattery to the poor old man to say I'm like him,' said Trevethan, with a laugh. 'This one is like him, though. Come here, little one, are you wet? it rains, don't it?'

He drew the child towards him, touching her ragged dress with his thin white hands.

'The gentleman made me dry it by the fire, and he held his umbrella over me as we comed back,' said the elf.

'Thank you, sir,' said Trevethan, a softened expression playing about his cynical mouth. 'She's a bit of the real Cornish in her, though London smoke has nearly spoilt it. There, run away and get your supper, Gladys.'

Donovan started and coloured.

'Yes, 'tis a queer name for the likes of her,' observed Trevethan, scanning Donovan's face curiously with his keen blue eyes. 'But I made up my mind the little one should have at least one good honest name, though may be Miss Gladys wouldn't be best pleased to have her name given to such a poor little brat.'

'Oh, yes, she would be very glad to see that you remembered

Porthkerran and still cared for it,' said Donovan. 'But it's a pity to let the poor child grow up here when your father would be only too glad to have her.'

'That's what I wanted you for,' said Trevethan. 'Would he be kind to her? is he too strait-laced to take in my poor little lass? Some of those religionists are hard as nails, and I want my little lass to be happy.'

'He would be very good to her,' said Donovan, without hesitation. 'Your father is one of the best men I know.'

'Odd that he should have such a son, isn't it?' said Trevethan, trying to laugh.

'Happily, the least deserving of us do often have good fathers,' said Donovan, rather huskily.

Then he listened to the history of the blacksmith's son, a very sad history, which need not be written here. The man was now evidently very ill, not at all fit to be left alone with no better nurse than his child, but he had fought against the idea of being moved to a hospital because he could not endure the thought of leaving little Gladys alone, or of having her sent to the workhouse. Donovan offered to pay her expenses down to Porthkerran, but even that seemed intolerable to the poor man; as long as he lived he could not make up his mind to part with her. Nor would he let Donovan write to his father.

'Not now. Don't write now,' he urged, 'it would only make the old man miserable, wait till I'm either dead or better. Do you think there's a chance of my getting better? I should like to make a fresh start.'

'There would be a very good chance for you if you would go to a hospital; you cannot be properly nursed here. Think over it, and I will see whether I can't find some one in London who would look after your child.'

'If she could come to see me,' said Trevethan, wistfully.

So Donovan left, promising to look in again the next evening and talk things over.

There was evidently no time to be lost, he thought the matter over as he walked home, and suddenly arriving at a possible solution of the difficulty, he turned into the station instead of going on to York Road, took a ticket to Gower Street, and was soon making his way to the Osmonds.

Charles Osmond was at church, but Brian and Mrs. Osmond were at home, and were quite ready to hear the story of the sick man.

'Another *protégé* for you,' said Brian, laughing, 'and of course a ne'er-do-weel.'

'Birds of a feather flock together,' said Donovan, smiling. 'We've a natural affinity, you see. The great difficulty is about the child, I don't know what's to be done with her.'

'We might get her into some home,' said Mrs. Osmond. 'I know one or two where she would be happy.'

'But she wouldn't be allowed to go and see her father,' said Donovan. 'And it would never do to separate them, the child is the great hope for him.'

'What child is the great hope, and for whom?' said Charles Osmond, coming into the room with his peculiarly soft slow step. 'Do I actually hear you, Donovan, discussing such things as men and children? I thought you were up to the eyes in work for the exam?'

Donovan told his story.

'You see,' he added at the close. 'From any school or home she would never be allowed to come out and go to the hospital.'

'What's the child's name?'

'Gladys.' Then as Brian looked greatly surprised and Charles Osmond made an exclamation, he continued—'Trevethan comes from Porthkerran, and Miss Tremain is worshipped down there; she is the tutelary saint of the place—and he called his child after her.'

'Well, I think Gladys had better come to this home,' said Charles Osmond. 'What do you say, mother—will Mrs. Maloney make the kitchen too hot to hold her?'

'Oh, no, she is much too good-natured.'

'But you don't realize, I'm afraid,' said Donovan. 'She's the most neglected-looking little thing, altogether dirty and unkempt, and too young to be of any use to you.'

'She must be an odd child if we don't find her of use,' said Charles Osmond, with a strange smile in his eyes. 'Why I thought, Donovan, you were one who believed in the influence of children.'

'For those who want it, yes,' said Donovan. 'But——'

'But we *don't* want it, and are to be left to ourselves—is that it?'

'She's scarcely fit to come here,' said Donovan; 'she's ragged and dirty to a degree.'

'Oh, you soul of cleanliness,' said Charles Osmond, laughing. 'Is there not water in the land of Bloomsbury?—can we not scrub this blackamoor white? And as to raggedness, it will be odd if with four women in the house—all of them longing to be Dorcases—we can't clothe one poor little elf. Can you get your man admitted to St. Thomas's?'

'I think so.'

'Very well, then, as soon as he is moved we will be ready to have the little girl.'

Donovan went home with the words ringing in his ears, 'A stranger and ye took Me in.' And instinctively his thoughts travelled back to a certain summer day years ago, when, with muddy travel-stained clothes, he too had been taken into a home, ill and penniless and utterly ignorant of that strange love which had been revealed to him. He feared it was against the rules of political economy, and quite against all worldly wisdom; but, however that might be, such living Christianity had a strange power of touching his heart.

It seemed to touch Trevethan's heart too; evidently kindness to the child was the way to get hold of him. For attention to himself he was not particularly grateful, grumbled at the prospect of losing his pipe at the hospital, swore fearfully if, in helping him to move, Donovan caused him any pain, and was so surly and off-hand in manner that, had his attendant been a believer in class and caste, he could hardly have borne it patiently.

Every evening for the next week he went to that dismal room in Westminster; it was thankless work, and yet Trevethan was very fond of him, and would hardly have dragged through the wretched days without the hope of those nightly visits. He was far too sullen and miserable and ashamed to let this appear, however, and made it seem rather a favour to admit his visitor. At the end of the week he was able to be moved to St. Thomas's, and on the afternoon of the same day Donovan took little Gladys to the Osmonds.

When he got back to his rooms he found, to his great surprise, that, instead of old Rouge's well-known figure sitting over the fire, there was a lady in the arm-chair, well-dressed, quite at her ease, apparently engrossed in a newspaper. He made a sort of inarticulate exclamation, upon which she turned hastily round.

It was Adela.

'My dear Augustus Cæsar, how delightful to see you again!' she exclaimed, holding out both her hands. 'Were you very much astonished to see an unknown female in possession of your fireside?'

'How good of you to come and look me up!' said Donovan, really pleased to see her, for she was the first of his family whom he had met for years.

'Good!' exclaimed Adela, in her old bantering tone—'why, I've been longing to come ever since I knew your whereabouts— ever since that good Cornishman came and enlightened me at

Oakdene. But there's been a conspiracy among the fates against me! if you'll believe it, I've hardly been in town since that time. I've been half over the world since I saw you last—Italy, Austria, Greece, Switzerland—in fact, the grand tour; but as to getting a day in town unmolested by friends or dressmakers, in which to visit you, I assure you it's been as unattainable as the moon.'

Donovan, a good deal amused by this characteristic speech, brought a footstool for his cousin, poked the fire, rang the bell for tea, and finally settled himself on the opposite side of the fire-place.

'We will be comfortable, and you shall talk just as you did in the old times,' he said. 'I declare it makes me feel quite in-clined to turn misanthropical again for the sake of one of the old arguments.'

'There, I was right then. You have actually renounced it all and become a philanthropist! To tell you the truth, the im-mediate cause of my visit was this: I happened to be in the Underground this afternoon, and imagine my feelings when, on the platform at Gower Street, I caught sight of my misanthropical cousin pioneering a little City Arab through the crowd. My curiosity was so intense that I was really obliged to come and solve the problem at once. Besides, it was tantalizing to see you so near, and to have my frantic signals disregarded. You are immensely altered, Donovan; I almost wonder now that I knew you.'

She looked at him attentively for a minute, as if trying to find out in what the great change consisted.

'It is a long time since we met,' said Donovan; 'I should think it rather odd if I were not changed.'

'You have had a hard life, I'm afraid,' said Adela. 'You know, of course, how vexed I am about Ellis's conduct; he ought to have made you a proper allowance. I said all I could to him, but that brother of mine is terribly like a mule; when once he has made up his mind to dislike a person, nothing will change his opinion.'

'We won't discuss him,' said Donovan, afraid that inadver-tently he might reveal to Adela the real depth of her brother's treachery. 'Tell me instead about my mother, it is more than a year since I had any news of her.'

'She is well, I think,' said Adela, in a doubtful voice; 'but, to tell you the truth, I have been very little at Oakdene. Whether Ellis has any idea that I act as a medium between you and your mother, I don't know, but he makes it unbearably un-comfortable for me. I oughtn't to say it to you, I suppose, but

I must confess that that marriage seems to me to have been a fearful mistake. Ellis is not half as jolly as in his poor bachelor days; he has all that heart can wish or money buy, and yet every time I go to stay with them he seems to me more depressed and irritable and dissatisfied with things.'

'Does he manage the estate well?'

'Oh, he leaves it all to the bailiff; he knows nothing whatever about it, moons about all day with his cigar, scolding anyone who dares to interrupt him.'

'Are they coming up for the season?'

'No, he has let the Connaught Square house till July, but they think of spending next winter either there or abroad, for your mother fancies the Manor damp, and she has certainly had a good deal of rheumatism lately. That is absolutely all I know about them. Now let us talk of something more cheerful; haven't you got some nice, wicked, medical student stories for me? You are a dreadful lot, are you not? Now amuse me a little, there's a good boy, for, to tell you the truth, I'm dying of *ennui* in this most prosaic of worlds.'

'We are very prosaic here,' said Donovan, smiling, 'nothing, I fear, to re-vivify you except ponderous works on anatomy and medicine. Come, you shall be my first patient; in less than a year you will perhaps see the family name on a brass plate, not a useless brass in a church, but a most utilitarian plate on a surgery door.'

'You dreadful boy, what made you take up such a trade?'

'Take care how you speak of my profession,' said Donovan, laughing. 'I'll prescribe the most horrible remedies for your *ennui* if you are not respectful. I chose it because it's to my mind the only really satisfactory profession.'

'If you had any interest in the medical world, and were likely to get a good West-End practice; but otherwise, just think of the sort of people it will throw you among! You'll have to go among poverty and dirt and everything that's disagreeable. Besides, you will lose caste.'

'You forget that I don't believe I have any to lose,' said Donovan, smiling. 'You should turn Republican, it saves so many small annoyances.'

'What were you doing this afternoon with that beggar-child?'

'Taking her to some friends of mine who have promised to house her while her father is in the hospital.'

Adela lifted up her hands in horror.

'Taking that child to a gentleman's house, my dear boy—

what an odd set you must have got into! That sort of thing sounds very nice, but it's dreadfully extravagant and romantic.'

'It has a way of seeming very practical to the one who is taken in,' said Donovan, in a voice which revealed a good deal to Adela.

'You are thinking of your good Cornishman,' she exclaimed. 'But you were a more eligible subject than that little beggar-girl, more fit to be in a gentleman's house.'

'Much you know about it!' said Donovan, with a sad smile, and again Adela realized that the five years which had passed so uneventfully with her had brought to her cousin a knowledge both of evil and good quite beyond her understanding.

'I tried my misanthropical creed for some time,' he continued, after a minute's pause, 'and found it a dead failure. And then I had the good fortune to come across some people who lived exactly on the opposite system.'

'From extreme to extreme, of course,' said Adela, 'that is always the way. I suppose you've become a Wesleyan or a Methodist.'

He could not help smiling a little at her tone, and at her fashionable horror of Dissent, but his grave answer brought back to her the remembrance that even in the old days he never could endure to have matters of religious belief or unbelief lightly touched upon.

'I do not see my way to Christianity at all as yet.'

'And you don't go to church?' said Adela, regretfully. It had always been the one great thing she had urged upon him.

'Not quite in the way you would approve of,' replied Donovan, smiling, 'but I do go in for the sermon now and then at my friend's church. I am afraid you would think his teaching of the "extravagant and romantic" order, he has a habit of bringing Christianity to bear on every-day life in rather a difficult and inconvenient way.'

Adela looked thoughtful.

'He is right, of course,' she said, sadly; 'but I don't think people know how hard it is when one is a great deal in society. I can't adopt beggar children or teach in Sunday schools, it's not in my line.'

She spoke so much more seriously than usual that Donovan's heart went out to her.

'I sometimes think,' he said, 'that in its way Dot's life was about the most perfect one can fancy. It seemed such a matter of course that she should be the patient, loving little thing she was, that at the time it didn't strike one. But just think of it

now; with everything to make her selfish she was always the first
to think of other people, with scarcely a day of her life free from
pain she was always the one bit of sunshine in the house. And
yet she was as unconscious of it as if she had been a baby.
Depend upon it it's not the teaching in Sunday schools or the
adopting of children that makes the difference, the spirit of love
can be brought into any kind of life. What had Dot to do with
philanthropy and good works? Yet if it had not been for that
little child's life I should have been a downright fiend long ago.
I don't believe you women know how much you can do for us,
not by your district-visitings and conventionalities, but by just
being the pure beings you were meant to be.'

Adela was silent. She knew she had talked a great deal of
nonsense in her life, had flirted with innumerable men, had
flattered dozens of foolish young fellows whom in her heart
she had all the time despised. She felt truly enough that her
influence must have all gone into the wrong scale, and that,
while meaning harmlessly to amuse herself, she had all the time
been lowering that standard of womanhood of which Donovan
seemed to think so much.

'And yet you know,' she said piteously, 'if you subtracted the
vein of fun and banter and chaff from me there would be nothing
left but a dull old spinster beginning to turn grey, whom you
would all wish to get rid of. I'm like poor little Miss Moucher,
volatile I was born, and volatile I shall die.'

'We can ill afford to lose any of the real fun in the world,'
said Donovan. 'I hope you won't turn puritanical. I don't
think I could like a person who had no sense of humour, so
please don't talk of subtracting yours.'

'I suppose the real fun, as you call it, is good,' said Adela.
'And the artificial nonsense is bad. At the same time it is hard
to get up anything but forced fun when life is a long bit of *ennui*.'

'But you have the secret for making life something very
different,' said Donovan.

I believe you envy me!' said Adela; 'but, oh, my dear
Donovan, it is quite possible to have prescriptions, and medicines,
and a doctor within reach, and yet to be very ill and miserable.'

'It seems then that we are both in a bad way,' said Donovan,
smiling. 'You know the remedies, but have not will enough to
use them. I have the will to use them, but have not the remedies.'

'Well, what is to help us?' said Adela.

'Go to some one better fitted to tell you,' replied Donovan.
'This is a good sort of working motto, though.'

He opened Kingsley's life, which was lying on the table, and pointed to the following lines :

> Do the work that's nearest,
> Though it's dull at whiles,
> Helping when you meet them,
> Lame dogs over stiles.

'I'll be your "lame dog" for this afternoon, and you shall grace this bachelor room and pour out tea for us. By-the-by, talking of bachelors, how is old Mr. Hayes? it is an age since I heard of him.'

They drifted off into talk about Oakdene and Greyshot neighbours, feeling that they had touched upon deeper matters than they cared to discuss.

CHAPTER XXXVII.

OF EVOLUTION, AND A NINETEENTH CENTURY FOE.

> Say not the struggle nought availeth,
>   The labour and the wounds are vain,
> The enemy faints not, nor faileth,
>   And as things have been they remain.
>
> .   .   .   .
>
> For while the tired waves, vainly breaking,
>   Seem here no painful inch to gain,
> Far back, through creeks and inlets making,
>   Comes silent, flooding in, the main.
>
> And not by eastern windows only,
>   When daylight comes, comes in the light,
> In front the sun climbs slow, how slowly,
>   But westward look, the land is light.
>   A. H. CLOUGH.

LATE in the afternoon of a sunny August day two pedestrians might have been seen skirting the shore of one of the beautiful little lakes which lie cradled in the arms of the grand old monarch of Welsh mountains. The elder, grey-bearded and somewhat bent, had yet an air of alertness, a certain elasticity of step which bespoke a buoyant temperament; the younger, lacking entirely this touch of triumph, walked firmly and sharply, following in his companion's wake, and himself closely followed by a fox-terrier. Very still was the mountain side, for miles round not another living creature was in sight. Above them to the

right towered the most abrupt side of Snowdon, rugged and wild
and grim-looking, its chaos of grey rocks relieved here and there
by tufts of coarse mountain grass or clumps of fern. To the
left, in striking contrast, lay the little lake, small and insignificant
enough to be scarcely known by its name, and yet in the beauty
of its situation and in its majesty of calmness attracting the eye
almost as much as its stately bearer.

'There's a stiffish climb before us,' said Charles Osmond,
pausing as he looked up the mountain path. 'What do you say
to an hour's rest here? we couldn't have a lovelier place.'

'Very well, and Waif shall have a swim,' replied Donovan,
'I'll just give him a stone or two. We have plenty of time if we're
to see the sunset from the top.'

Whistling to the dog, he ran down the slope to the lake,
while Waif, in a tremor of delighted excitement, plunged into the
cool water after the sticks and stones which his master threw.
Charles Osmond, stretched out on the grass with one of the grey
boulders by way of a pillow, watched the two thoughtfully, the
spirited swimming of the fox-terrier, the fine strongly-made figure
of the man hurling the stones into the lake with a vigour and
directness and force which—albeit there was no mark—bespoke
him a good marksman. After a time he made his way again up
the slope, and threw himself down at full length beside his companion with a sigh of comfortable content.

'You old Italian!' said Charles Osmond, with a laugh, 'what
a way you have of throwing yourself in an instant into exactly
the most comfortable position! now a true-born Britisher fidgets,
and wriggles, and grumbles, and in the end does not look as if
he'd found the right place.'

'One of the bequests of my great-great-grandmother,' said
Donovan, 'by nature I do go straight out on the hearthrug when
other fellows would crouch up in an arm-chair.'

'Oh! it is four generations back, is it! I staked my reputation as an observer that you had a bit of the Italian in you the
very first time we met, though Brian scouted the idea.'

'It comes out in that and in the way I owned to you before,'
said Donovan, 'the endlessness of the feud when once begun.
We've some bloodthirsty proverbs as to enemies in Italy.'

'I shouldn't have thought you revengeful by nature.'

'It smoulders, and does not often show itself in flame,' said
Donovan. 'I'm afraid there have often been times when I could
have done something desperate to Ellis Farrant if I'd had a
chance. Even now, professing to go by very different rules, I
believe if I saw him fall into that lake, the fiend of revenge in

me would try hard to hold me still on the shore. Good folk may
shudder, but that's the plain unvarnished truth. I have shocked
even you, though, by the confession.'

'No,' said Charles Osmond, slowly, 'you've only surprised me
a little. Having come to such blanks in yourself and your
system, I wonder rather that the fitness of Christianity to fill
those blanks does not seem more striking. The lesson of forgiveness, for instance, could only have been taught by Christ—by
the great Forgiver. I wonder that your need does not throw more
light on Christianity.'

'Proof,' sighed Donovan. 'It is that we want.'

He thought of his talks with Dr. Tremain as the words
passed his lips, but, though the doctor's argument was still fresh
in his mind, he had by no means come yet to think that logical
proof could be willingly renounced.

'But the sense of need *is* an indirect proof,' said Charles Osmond.

'I cannot see it in that way,' said Donovan. 'That a man in
a desert is dying of thirst is no proof that there is water in the
place.'

'No; but it *is* a proof that the natural place for man is not
the said desert, and that the water he longs for does exist, that
it is his natural means of life, and that without it he will certainly die.'

'It is not much good to talk by metaphors,' said Donovan,
'and, since we have broken the ice, I should very much like to
ask you one or two questions in plainest English. It is all very
well to speak of need and thirst and the rest of it, but there are
gigantic difficulties in the way. I should very much like to know,
for instance, how you get over the evolution theory.'

'You speak as if it were a wall,' said Charles Osmond, laughing a little. 'I never thought of "getting over it." To my
mind, it is one of the most beautiful of the "ladders set up to
Heaven from earth," and if folks hadn't been scared by the con-
glomeration of narrow-minded fearfulness and atheistical cock-
crowings, the probabilities are that more would have seen the
real beauty and grandeur of the idea.'

'I noticed Haeckel's "Creation" and "Evolution of Man" in
your book-shelves the very first night I came to you,' said Donovan; 'and I've always wondered how you did get over it.'

'There you are again, making my ladder a wall,' said Charles
Osmond, with a little twinkle in his deep, bright eyes.

'Well, it *is* a wall to me,' said Donovan. 'Having all come
into existence so exceedingly well without a God——'

'And,' interrupted Charles Osmond, 'finding it so hard to live without Him, being so conscious of a grave deficiency in our nature which yet nature does not give us the means to supply. In honesty, you must remember that you've previously admitted that.'

'Yes, but surely you see the difficulty,' said Donovan, with a touch of impatience in his tone.

'I do,' said Charles Osmond, gravely, 'that is, I think I see where your difficulty is. For myself, as I told you, the theory of evolution seems to be in absolute harmony with all that I know or can conceive of God. I accept it fully as His plan for the world, or rather, perhaps I should say, as an imperfect glimpse of the beauty of His plan, the best and clearest that present science can give us. In another hundred years we may know much more.'

'But you cannot make Haeckel square with the Bible.'

'I certainly do not accept all Haeckel's conclusions, for they are often drawn from premisses which are utterly illogical; nor do I accept all his assumptions, for he often practically claims omniscience. At the same time, he has done us a great service, and the false deductions of a teacher cannot spoil or alter the truth of his system. If it were so, it would be a bad look out for Christianity, with its two hundred and odd sects. Do you consider that spontaneous generation is already proved?'

'No,' said Donovan, 'but quite sufficiently for working purposes, and in time I daresay it will be completely proved. What will then become of the Author of the Universe, to adopt the current phrase?'

'If it should be proved, as I fully expect it will be,' replied Charles Osmond, 'it will merely carry us one step further back in our appreciation of the original Will-power. We shall still recognize the one Mind impressing one final and all embracing law upon what we call matter and force, and then leaving force and matter to elaborate the performance of that law.'

'You assume a good deal there,' said Donovan. 'Why should we imagine that law—still less, a personal Will—existed before the existence of primordial cells?'

'You must either assume that there existed only one primordial cell, or else that there was a law of order impressed upon the infinite number of primordial cells,' said Charles Osmond.

Donovan left off twisting the grasses which grew beside him, and knitted his brows in thought. This idea was a new one to him. He was silent for a minute or two, then, keeping his judgment entirely suspended, he said, slowly,

'And what then? I should like to hear that borne out a little.'

'The question is, how has the absolute uniformity of action been attained? If matter be self-existent, there must have been at the very first outset an infinite number of cells, and also an infinite possibility of variation. Say, just for illustration, a million cells, each capable of varying in a million ways. Now just calculate the mathematical chances that ultimate order *could* result from this disorder, and, if so, what length of time, approximately, it would occupy, allowing each cell an hour of existence, and then to give birth to another cell, probably *differing* from itself!'

Donovan laughed a little, and mused, and presently Charles Osmond continued.

'No, it seems to me that orderly transmission of hereditary form or habit is only possible on the supposition either of the one self-existent cell, to which there are many objections, or on the supposition of a law of order, which must have been antecedent to the cells, or it could not have impressed them.'

'I daresay many would willingly concede as much as that,' said Donovan. 'It is only when you go on to assert that the law came from a law-giver that we cry out.'

'Well, where did it come from?' said Charles Osmond.

'I suppose it was a fortuitous concourse of atoms,' said Donovan, doubtfully.

'That is a thoroughly unscientific hypothesis,' returned Charles Osmond. 'Mind, I don't assert that my theory is *proved*, but I claim this, that both physical and mathematical science demonstrate the probability of some law existing before primordial cells existed, and that this probability is at least as reasonable as a working hypothesis, as is that of evolution in explaining the *method* in which that primordial law has operated.'

'But what will my old "soul-preserving" friends say to you?' observed Donovan, smiling. 'You agree to the disenthronement of that all-important being—man.'

'Do I?' said Charles Osmond.

'Well, you accept as your oldest ancestor something more insignificant than an amoeba.'

'Yes, but I thought the longer the pedigree the better,' said Charles Osmond, with laughter in his eyes.

'But, seriously, where do you make your spirit-world begin?'

'I think,' said Charles Osmond, 'there was once a wise man, but who he was I haven't an idea, and this was his wise utterance, "The spirit sleeps in the stone, dreams in the animal, and wakes in man." The revelation, or, if you will, the awakening, appeared to be sudden, it came as it were in a flash; but it was the result of long processes, it followed the universal rule—a gradual advance, then a sudden unfolding. And in this way, I take it, *all* revelation comes.'

Donovan looked full into his companion's face for a moment, a question, and a very eager one, was trembling on his lips, his whole face was a question, *the* question which Charles Osmond would fain have answered if he could. But a reserved man does not easily talk of that which affects him most nearly, and in this case certainly out of the abundance of the heart the mouth did not speak. The firm yet sensitive lips were closed again, but perhaps the silence revealed more to Charles Osmond than any spoken words could have done, and by a hundred other slight indications he knew perfectly well that Donovan's heart was full of the spirit hunger.

'Let me just for a minute fall back on the Mosaic account, he said, after a little time had passed. 'You think that account incompatible with the evolution theory, to my mind it expresses in a simple, clear way, such as a wise teacher might use with young children, the very truths that recent researches have wonderfully enlarged upon. If you will notice it carefully the very order given to the creation in the first of Genesis is exactly borne out by modern science. Then we are told in the grand old simple words which only were fit for such a purpose—that God breathed into him, and man became a living soul. To man evolved probably from the simplest of organisms, to gradually perfected man the revelation is made : God breathes into him the breath of life, that is, the knowledge of Himself, life according to Christ's definition *being* knowledge of God. Man was now fully alive, fully awake, the spirit had slept, had dreamed, but the revelation was made, and his dormant spirit sprang into life.'

'But I am not conscious of this spirit,' said Donovan, 'I am aware of nothing that cannot be explained as a function of the brain, thought, mind, will.'

'Yet you are conscious of being incomplete,' said Charles Osmond. 'It seems to me that for a time we get on very well as body and soul men, or body and mind, if you like it better, but sooner or later comes the craving for something higher, which something, I take it, is the spirit life. And one thing more, if you will let me say it, you tell me you are conscious of nothing but body and mind, but I can't help thinking that your love for that little sister whom you mentioned to me was the purest spiritual love, to which no scientific theory will apply.'

For many minutes Donovan did not speak, not because he was actually thinking of his companion's words, but because a vision of the past was with him; little Dot in her purity, her child-like trust, her clinging devotion, rose once more before him. How had she learnt the truths which to him were so unattainable? Brought up for years in a way which could not possibly bias her mind, how was it that she had, apparently without the least difficulty, taken hold of such an abstraction, such a mysterious, incomprehensible idea? She had not believed on 'authority,' for naturally the nurse-maid's authority would have weighed less with her than his own, yet in some way the Unseen, the Unknown, the to him Unknowable, had become to her the most intense reality. She had very rarely spoken to him on that subject because she knew it grieved him; he could only remember one instance in which she had definitely expressed the reality of her faith. He had been remonstrating with her a little, and she had answered in a half-timid way which somehow angered him because it was so unusual with her.

'You see, Dono, I can't help knowing that God is, because He is nearer to me even than you.'

He could almost feel the little face nestling closer to him as the shy words were ended, and clearly could he recall the terrible pang which that faltering childish sentence had caused him. He had then believed that she was under a great delusion, now he inclined to think that her pure soul had grasped a great truth which still remained to him unknowable. This was almost all that he had actually heard her say, except the last half unconscious prayer, the speech of a little child to its father, containing no pompous title, no ascriptions of praise, but only the most absolute trust. She had never fallen into conventional religious phraseology; but perhaps nothing could have so exactly met Donovan's wants that summer afternoon as her last perfectly peaceful words, 'He is so very good, you know—you will know.' No argument, however subtle, no sermon, however eloquent, had the hope-giving power which lay in the little child's words— words which had lain dormant in his heart for years, apparently with no effect whatever.

Charles Osmond saw that his reference had awakened a long train of thought; he would not look at the changes on the face of his companion, for just now in its naturalness it was exceedingly like a book, and a book which he felt it hardly fair to read. Instead, he gazed across the quiet little lake to the sunny landscape beyond, battled with a conceited thought which had arisen within him, and was ready with his beautiful, honest mind and

E E

hearty sympathy to come back to Donovan's standpoint as soon as he seemed to wish it.

Waif, having studied the group from a distance for some minutes, and having given himself a series of severe shakings to wring the water from his coat, seemed to consider himself dry enough for society. He came back to his master, sniffed at his clothes, and, finding that his remonstrating whines received no notice, began to lick his face. Then Donovan came back to the world of realities, and perhaps because of the softening influence of the past vision, perhaps merely out of gratitude to the dumb friend who understood his moods so well and filled so great a blank for him, he threw his arms round the dog, wet as he was, hugged him, patted him, praised and petted him in a way which put the fox-terrier into his seventh heaven of happiness.

Charles Osmond was touched and amused by the manner in which the silence was ended. Presently Donovan turned towards him again with a much brightened face.

'There is one thing which you Christians will have to face before long,' he began, 'or rather I should think must face now, with the theory of evolution so nearly established.'

'Well,' said Charles Osmond.

'I mean this,' continued Donovan: 'Our original ancestors and their living representatives can hardly be left out of your scheme of immortality. It seems to me a very half-and-half scheme if it only includes mankind. You know,' he added, laughing a little, 'even the idea of heaven you gave us in your sermon the other night—about the least material and the most beautiful I ever heard—would scarcely be perfect to me without Waif.'

'I quite agree with you,' said Charles Osmond. 'Nor can I understand why people object so much to the idea. Luther, you know, fully admitted his belief that animals might share in the hereafter, and to appeal to a still higher authority it seems to me that, unless we deliberately narrow the meaning of the words, St. Paul clearly asserts the deliverance of the *whole creation* from the bondage of corruption into the deliverance of the glory of the children of God. I believe in One who fills all things, by whom all things consist, therefore I certainly do believe in the immortality of animals.'

'Well, seeing how infinitely more loving my dog is than most men, I own that it seems to me unfair to shut him out of your scheme. The old Norsemen walked with their dogs in the "Happy Hunting Fields," and, however material that old legend, there is a touch of beauty in it which is somehow wanting—at any rate, to dog-lovers—in the ordinary, and I must say equally material, descriptions of the gorgeous halls of Zion.'

'You two are very fond of each other,' said Charles Osmond, looking at the dog and his master.

'We have been through a good deal together, and I believe, to begin with, the mere fact of his wanting me when no one else did, of his following me so persistently in the Strand just at the time when everyone had hard words to throw at me, drew me towards him. I've watched him nearly dying with distemper, and somehow dragged him through. He has watched me nearly dying in a bog, and, by his sense and persistency, got me rescued. Besides that, at least three times he has saved me from a worse death, just by being what he is, the most loving little brute in England.'

'Brave little Waif! I shall never forget my first sight of him,' said Charles Osmond, smiling. 'It was a wonder you two didn't put me out that night, the fit was distracting enough; but when I saw you and the fox-terrier walking up the aisle, head No. 1 nearly went into space, though I could have told the people every one of your characteristic features, and should have known Waif among a thousand dogs!'

'But to go back once more to our old subject,' said Donovan; 'does not your theory bring you to something very like Pantheism?'

'I think it *is* the Higher Pantheism,' said Charles Osmond. 'While we've been lying here, Tennyson's lines have been haunting me. You know them, I suppose?'

Donovan only knew one poem in the world, however, and he asked to hear this one. Charles Osmond repeated it, and, because he loved it, rendered it very well.

'You see,' he said, after a pause, 'it is this Higher Pantheism which leads us up to the greatest heights.

> Speak to Him thou, for He hears and Spirit with Spirit can meet,
> Closer is He than breathing, and nearer than hands and feet.

It leads us to no vague impersonal Force, but to the Spirit by whom and in whom we live and move and have our being.'

Donovan did not speak, and before long they began to climb their mountain; but though he said no word to his companion, he moved to a sort of soundless tune which set itself to a verse of the poem,

> Dark is the world to thee: thyself art the reason why;
> For is He not all but thou, that hast power to feel 'I am I'?

The climb was rather a stiff one, and by the time they reached the summit they were glad enough of the fresh breeze which was there to greet them as they made their way up to the little cairn. The sun was within a quarter-of-an-hour of setting, its red beams were bathing the landscape in a flood of glory; around the mountains stood in solemn grandeur, as if doing homage to the parting king, the red beams lighted up one or two, but more were in solemn shade, varying from pearly grey to the softest purple. There was something perfectly indescribable in the sense of breadth and height and beauty combined; in their different ways the two pedestrians revelled in it. The creases seemed to smooth themselves out of Charles Osmond's brow, he lost the weight of care which the long year's work brought, not always to be shaken off in the summer holiday. But here it was impossible to be earth-bound; his whole being was echoing the words

Are not these, oh! soul, the vision of Him who reigns?

And Donovan, exulting in that sense of space which was so dear to him, realized as he had never realized before that it is the Infinite only which can satisfy the Infinite.

The lofty is often closely followed by the prosaic, and in the neighbourhood of great heights there lurk the dangers of the precipice. Donovan had reached the high ground, but in a minute came the most violent reaction, the most humiliating fall.

They were not the only tourists who had made the ascent that afternoon. A very different party sat drinking and smoking on the other side of one of the huts; their laughter was borne across every now and then to the westward side of the cairn, but both Charles Osmond and Donovan were too much absorbed in their own thoughts to be at all disturbed by it. The rudeness of the shock was therefore quite unbroken. From high but unfortunately fruitless aspirations, Donovan was recalled to the hardest of facts by a sudden shadow arising between him and the sun. A dark and rather good-looking man stood on the very edge of the rock looking at the sky, very possibly not seeing it much, but looking at it just for want of something better to do. Charles Osmond glanced at him, then, as if struck by some curious resemblance, he turned towards his companion, and at once knew that the stranger could be none other than Ellis Farrant, for Donovan's face bore a look of such fearful struggle as in his life of half-a-century the clergyman had never before seen.

Before long Ellis turned, and, finding himself face to face with the man he had so shamefully wronged, had the grace to flush deeply. But in a minute he recovered himself, and assumed the *rôle* of the easy-mannered gentleman, which he knew so well how to play.

'Why, Donovan!' he exclaimed. 'Who would have thought of meeting you up here? Pity your mother's not with me, but I'm only here for a week's fishing with Mackinnon.'

The struggle had apparently ceased, Donovan had set his face like a flint, but his eyes flashed fire, and as he drew himself up and folded his arms, at the same time making a backward movement in order to be as far from Ellis as the narrow platform would admit, he was certainly a formidable-looking foe. There was no doubt whatever as to his sentiments; he might have stood for a model of one of the old Romans righteously hating his enemy. Ellis shrank beneath his glance, but it somehow made him malicious.

'You must remember Mackinnon,' he continued, in his bland voice. 'He was with us, if you recollect, on the night of that unfortunate dance, when poor little——'

He broke off, for Donovan, with the look of a man goaded beyond bearing, bent forward, and, with the extraordinary vehemence which contrasted so strangely with his usually repressed manner, thundered rather than spoke the words,

'Be silent.'

Being a cowardly man, Ellis did not feel disposed to stay in the neighbourhood of his foe; he not only obeyed the injunction, but disappeared from the scene as quickly as possible.

Donovan once more leant back against the cairn with folded arms, and for many minutes did not stir. Charles Osmond did not venture to speak to him; in perfect silence the two stood watching the setting sun, which was now like a golden-red globe on the horizon line. Many hundreds of times had the sun gone down on Donovan's wrath, and this evening proved no exception to the rule. By the time the last red rim had disappeared, however, all traces of agitation had passed from him, and he turned to his companion a quiet cold face, observing, in the most matter-of-fact tone,

'We must be making our way home, I suppose.'

'Certainly, if we're to eat the captain's trout for supper,' said Charles Osmond.

And without further remark they began the descent, Donovan showing traces of latent irritation in the headlong way in which he plunged down the steep path. Charles Osmond, following much more slowly, found him beside the little lake where they had rested in the afternoon; perhaps the place or some recollection of their talk had softened him, at any rate, he was quite himself again. Charles Osmond put his arm within his, and they walked on steadily down the less abrupt part of the mountain to Pen-y-pass, and along the Capel Currig road to Bettws-y-Coed.

Presently Donovan broke the silence.

'Well, you have seen Ellis Farrant at last. Odd that he should have turned up just after we had been talking of him. I hope you were satisfied with my Christian forbearance.'

Charles Osmond was silent, not quite liking his tone.

'I have offended you,' said Donovan. 'I will take away the adjective.'

'I daresay your forbearance was very great,' said Charles Osmond, 'and your provocation far greater than I can understand, but you must forgive me for saying that I saw nothing Christian in it.'

'What did you see?' asked Donovan, a little amused.

'I saw a perfect example of the way in which a nineteenth-century gentleman hates his enemy, the hatred of the ancients kept in check by the power of modern civilization.'

'And how would you have had me meet him?' cried Donovan. 'Did you expect a stage reconciliation, while he is still defrauding me? Did you wish me to embrace him and wish him good speed?'

'I wished you to act as I think Christ would have acted,' said Charles Osmond, quietly.

'Oh! once more I tell you this idealism is impossible!' exclaimed Donovan, impatiently. 'I am but a mortal man, and cannot help hating this fellow.'

'You see, in copying Him whom I consider to be *more* than mortal man, we do realize our own shortcomings,' said Charles Osmond.

'Well, what do you imagine Christ would have done in such a case?'

'I think you can answer that question for yourself,' said Charles Osmond. 'But to put it on what to me is a lower footing, consider how the best man you ever knew would have acted, and then carry his conduct still further. Your father, for instance—how would he have treated an enemy?'

Unconsciously Charles Osmond had touched on Donovan's tenderest part. He fell into a reverie, and they walked a mile before he spoke again.

'I believe you are right,' he said at last; and there was something of pathos in the words coming from one so strong and so exceedingly slow to own himself conquered. 'I'm afraid up there on the mountain I've fallen when I might have risen.'

'I daresay you will have another opportunity given you,' said Charles Osmond, by way of consolation.

'Don't be in too great a hurry,' said Donovan, smiling. 'I'm afraid I can't honestly wish for it yet.'

Then they fell to talking of every-day matters, and late in the evening they reached the cottage where they were spending a few weeks—a somewhat curious quartette—the Osmonds, father and son, old Rouge Frewin, and Donovan. The captain was supremely happy, went out fishing every day, and partly from his love to Donovan and his desire to do him credit, partly from his awe of a 'parson out of the pulpit,' really managed to keep sober through the whole of their stay in Wales. But perhaps no one got quite so much from the Welsh holiday as Donovan himself. He went back to work with both body and mind invigorated, having learnt more in that month's intercourse with Charles Osmond than he would have learnt in years of solitary life.

There now remained only a few months of his medical course. Then 'the world was all before him.' He had not as yet formed any plans, but as the autumn advanced public events pointed the way for him, and he found his vocation.

CHAPTER XXXVIII.

DUTY'S CALL.

Faith shares the future's promise ; love's
   Self-offering is a triumph won ;
And each good thought or action moves
   The dark world nearer to the sun.

Then faint not, falter not, nor plead
   Thy weakness ; truth itself is strong ;
The lion's strength, the eagle's speed,
   Are not alone vouchsafed to wrong.

Thy nature, which through fire and flood,
   To place or gain finds out its way,
Has power to seek the highest good,
   And duty's holiest call obey !
               WHITTIER.

ENGLAND was just at this time engaged in a contest of which Donovan very strongly disapproved, but perhaps his political views only increased the desire which had arisen within him to go out as assistant surgeon to the seat of war. The belief that many hundreds of Englishmen were being sacrificed in an unjust cause could not fail to rouse such a lover of justice, and he lost no time in making arrangements with an ambulance society which was sending out help, and was in want of assistants. Charles Osmond, on the whole, approved of his choice, though regretting very much that he should for some time lose sight of him; but he felt that the life of action would be quite in Donovan's line, and that the entire change of scene would be good for him. Brian would have been only too glad to join him, but his work was already cut out for him in London, where he was to take the place of junior partner to an uncle of his who had a large practice in the Bloomsbury district.

It so chanced that Stephen Causton, who had been hindered both by illness and idleness, went in for his final examination at the same time. All three passed successfully. The autumn had been a very busy one, but Donovan was well and in good spirits, eager to begin his fresh life, and too much engrossed with the present and future to let the past weigh upon him. Still, as one January day he went in to St. Thomas's to take leave of Trevethan, not even his strong will could prevent a few very sad thoughts arising as he spoke of Porthkerran and the Tremains. Trevethan's recovery had been very slow, but he was now really well, and it had been arranged that he should go down to Porthkerran with his little girl the following week. His illness, and the kindness he had met, had softened him very much, and, though his manner was still brusque in the extreme, no one who really knew the man could have doubted his gratitude. In his odd fashion he half worshipped Donovan, and it was really from the desire to please him that he had overcome his shame and reluctance, and written to ask his father to receive him again. The blacksmith's intense happiness was so evident from the ill-spelt but warmly expressed reply, that Trevethan the younger began to feel drawn to him, and to look forward to his return with less apprehension and more eagerness.

Having left him directions as to fetching little Gladys from the Osmonds, Donovan took leave of him and went home to make his final preparations, a trifle saddened by the conversation. But after all, he reasoned with himself, he had more cause for rejoicing, for he had certainly been of use to one of the Porthkerran villagers, and Gladys would be heartily pleased to hear old Trevethan's good news. To have helped even indirectly to please her was something to be thankful for; besides, had he not renounced the thought of personal happiness as such? had he not chosen the way of sacrifice and willed to find his happiness in serving his fellow-men? And then once more he returned with all his former eagerness to the anticipation of his coming work, work which bid fair to call out all his faculties, and which made his pulses beat quicker even to think of, for perhaps no one but an awakened misanthropist can feel with such keenness the delights of the enthusiasm of humanity.

His key was in the latch when the sound of a carriage stopping at the door made him glance round; to his utter astonishment he saw his mother. He hurried forward, surprise and not unnatural emotion in his look and manner.

'Why, mother! this is very good of you,' he exclaimed, helping her to alight.

'My dear Donovan!' she said, in a hurried nervous voice, 'let me come into your rooms for a minute, I am in dreadful trouble.'

He brought her into the little sitting-room and made her sit down by the fire, perplexed by her agitation. It was many years since they had met, and time had altered Mrs. Farrant, she looked worn and faded; there was something piteous in the alteration. Donovan bent down and kissed the once beautiful face with a sort of reverence which he had never felt before.

'How did you get leave to come to me?' he asked.

Then Mrs. Farrant's tears began to flow.

'Oh! the most terrible thing has happened,' she said, vainly trying to check her sobs. 'Ellis, your cousin, has been unwell for some days, and this morning the doctor declares that he has small-pox, and, if you will believe it, I have actually been in his room the whole time! they said I had better leave for Oakdene, but I am so unnerved, so shaken, I thought you would take me to the station and arrange things. I thought I should like to see you and tell you. Oh, Donovan! do you think I shall take it? do you think it is infectious at the beginning?'

It was the same selfish nature, the same incapability of thinking of the well-being of others, which had caused Donovan so much pain all through his life. His mother was, after all, only altered externally. The hard look of his childhood came back into his face.

'Then you mean to go to Oakdene and leave your husband?' he asked, with a severity in his voice which he could not disguise.

'Don't be hard on me,' she sobbed, 'I have such a horror of this; if it were fever I would have stayed, but small-pox! No, no, it is impossible, I must go, I must indeed. Besides, I am not strong enough to nurse him. The doctor will send a trained nurse. Indeed, you must not urge me to go back, Donovan, it would kill me.'

Her agony of distress made him reproach himself for having spoken so strongly; he paced the room in silence. It was unnatural of her to leave her husband, but yet there was truth in her words, she would be useless as a nurse, and her nervous terror would very likely render her liable to infection. Besides, what right had he to judge her? He could not trust himself to discuss the right and wrong of the question, he felt that he must leave it to her own conscience, and when he spoke it was merely to ask details of Ellis's state, and the doctor's opinion of it.

'You had better rest here for a little time,' he said, when she had answered his questions in her unsatisfactory way. 'It must have been a great shock to you!' He spoke in a very different tone now, and Mrs. Farrant, feeling all the comfort of having a stronger will to repose upon, allowed herself to be made comfortable on the sofa, and lay silently watching her son's movements with a sort of interested curiosity, like a placid patient watching the preparations of a dentist, or a sleepy child following with its eyes the nurse as she sets the room in order for the night. Her son was very much altered; he still set about everything in the same quiet methodical way, but his angles had been rounded off, and the bitter cynicism which had always alarmed and repulsed her seemed quite gone. He had taken paper and ink and was writing hurriedly; presently he pushed his chair back from the table, and, folding the written sheet, came towards her.

'I am just going to the hospital, and then to the telegraph-office with this,' he said. 'I have ordered Mrs. Docry to have everything ready for you. Presently I think you must let me vaccinate you. It is something new to have a doctor in the family, isn't it?'

'I'm only so shocked that you should have been driven to it,' sighed Mrs. Farrant. 'You should have gone into the army. You have grown so like your father, Donovan.'

He bent down once more and kissed her. Then, promising she should not be disturbed, he hurried away with the telegram.

'So like your father!' The words rang in his ears, but never had he felt further from any likeness to the noble, calm, self-governed man whose image stood out so clearly in his memory, the three days' intercourse with the pure mind having left a deeper impress than months and years of intercourse with those of lower type. But just now his mind was in a seething chaos, his whole world shaken, whether by conflicting duties or conflicting passions he hardly knew, only he feared it was the latter.

Rapidly walking along the crowded streets he tried to fight the battle out, mechanically taking off his hat to an acquaintance, mechanically going through his business as people must do even when the deadliest mental conflict is raging, even when —perhaps unknown to them—the decision for good or evil, for life or death, is hanging in the balance. Previous arrangement and strong inclination drew him almost irresistibly towards the fulfilment of his engagement to the ambulance. Of course other men would willingly take his place at a day's notice, but his whole mind was set on going out to the war, the thought of foregoing it was almost unendurable. And yet a perverse voice within him kept urging on him that others might go out to the war, but that he was the only man called to take charge of a poor neglected wretch in a certain West-End Square.

Yet did not the fellow deserve his fate? Donovan would have suddenly changed natures if the justice of the thing had not struck him. Was it not perfectly satisfactory? Here was Nemesis at last—his foe would be justly punished! And then, being exceedingly human, he drew one of those fascinating little mind pictures which, if delineated by men, are certainly engraved by the devil. In this picture self, the hero, went out to the war, won unheard-of honours, received honourable wounds, and then was greeted with the news that his enemy had perished miserably in a luxurious house which he had no right to be in. 'So like your father!' with the sharpest satire the words again rang in his ears.

God be thanked that the devil's alluring pictures cannot stand side by side with the image of a true, noble, whole-hearted man! God be thanked that the ideal man has lightened the world's darkness!

Donovan's struggle was by no means over by the time he returned to his mother; it raged all the time that he was attending to her, all the time that he talked quiet commonplaces, brought her tea and toast and all that the house would afford, soothed her nervous terrors as to infection, and quoted small-pox statistics.

'Could you not come down with me to Oakdene?' said Mrs. Farrant, suddenly. 'You say your course is over, why not come with me now?

He knew then that the supreme moment had come.

'I will see you safely into the train,' he said, 'but I can't come to Oakdene.'

'Why not?' urged Mrs. Farrant.

There was a minute's silence, then, as quietly as if he had been speaking of an afternoon stroll, Donovan replied,

'Because I'm going round to Connaught Square presently.'

Mrs. Farrant stared at him. Perhaps he hardly felt inclined just then for inquiry or argument; muttering some excuse, he left the room, drew a long breath, and walked slowly upstairs.

In his bed-room were all the preparations for the coming journey—travelling gear, books, instruments. He felt a sharp pang as he realized that all his plans were changed—perhaps there was even a slight fear lest his resolution should be shaken, for he began to toss some clothes into a portmanteau in a hurried and unmethodical way quite unnatural to him. But he quieted down as he took Dot's miniature from its place. For a minute he looked at it intently, and afterwards there was no more haste in his manner.

Mrs. Farrant could not resist questioning him when he came downstairs again.

'Do you really think you are wise to go?' she urged. 'Why put yourself to such a risk?'

'You forget I am a doctor,' he said, smiling a little.

Mrs. Farrant of course knew nothing of her husband's real treachery, but she knew that he and Donovan were sworn foes, and could not understand her son's resolution.

'But he has a trained nurse,' she continued, 'and I should have thought that, disliking each other as you do, it would be unlikely that you could do much for him; he may not like to have you there.'

'Possibly,' said Donovan, 'but I must go and see.'

'And then you will have been in the way of infection for nothing,' urged his mother. 'Come, change your mind. Why must you go?'

'Because it is right,' said Donovan; and there was something in his tone which kept Mrs. Farrant from further objections.

She looked uneasy and troubled; perhaps for the first time it struck her that there could be an absolute right and wrong in such a question—perhaps she was a little doubtful about her own conduct. It was at any rate with a feeling of relief that she parted with Donovan at the Paddington Station, for people whose consciences are just enough awake to know that they are half asleep never feel comfortable with those who have and obey an imperative conscience.

When the Greyshot train had started, Donovan hurried off to make arrangements with the ambulance, to hunt up a substitute, to find the old captain and tell him his change of plans, to write notes, give orders, and make Waif understand the parting.

How much he disliked it all, how intensely he shrank from the work before him, he hardly allowed himself time to think.

Late that evening, as Charles Osmond was sitting in his study hard at work over the parish accounts, Brian hurried in, an open letter in his hand.

'Just look here!' he exclaimed, too full of the subject to notice that he interrupted his father half-way up a column. 'Would you have believed the fellow could have thrown it all up?'

Charles Osmond held out his hand for the note, and read as follows :—

'DEAR BRIAN,
 'After all, I'm not going south. Smithson was only too thankful to step into my shoes, and will sail on Saturday. If you can, get him to trade for some of my goodly Babylonish garments, as I can't well sport them in England. I only saw him for five minutes this afternoon, when we'd other matters to talk over. Ellis Farrant is down with small-pox, and I'm going to see after him. Look in now and then on Waif and the captain, if you can ; they are in the depths.
       'Ever yours,
           'D. F.'

'My grand old Roman!' exclaimed Charles Osmond, half aloud. 'You've grown a good deal since the day we climbed Snowdon.'

'But it's such folly to throw up this just at the last moment, said Brian. 'Besides, he's fagged with the exam, and now, instead of having the voyage to set him up, he goes straight into this plague-house all for the sake of one wretched man.'

'You may be quite sure that Donovan was very certain of the right before he took such a step,' said Charles Osmond; 'he's not the sort of fellow to change his mind or his plans lightly, whereas you——' He laughed and shrugged his shoulders.

Brian smiled too, for it was the family proverb that he was the most impetuous and impulsive of mortals.

CHAPTER XXXIX.

VIA LUCIS.

O Beauty, old yet ever new !
Eternal Voice and Inward Word,
The Logos of the Greek and Jew,
The old sphere music which the Samian heard.
Truth which the sage and prophet saw,
Long sought without, but found within,
The Law of Love beyond all law,
The life o'erflooding mortal death and sin !

Shine on us with the light which glowed
Upon the trance-bound shepherd's way,
Who saw the Darkness overflowed,
And drowned by tides of everlasting Day.
Shine, light of God !—make broad thy scope
To all who sin and suffer ; more
And better than we dare to hope
With Heaven's compassion make our longings poor !

WHITTIER.

IT was evening by the time that Donovan's preparations were ended. About seven o'clock he was set down at the Marble Arch, and hastily made his way to Connaught Square. As he stood on the steps waiting till the door was opened, the newly-risen moon looked full down on him through the trees in the garden ; the quiet silvery light was not quite in keeping with his state of mind, for the whole afternoon he had, as it were, been rowing against tide, and quietly as he had made his resolution, and steadily as he had gone through with all which it involved, there was no denying that it was sorely against his inclination.

It was certainly a curious position. Here he was, after years of absence, ringing at the door of his own house, not with a view to taking possession, but merely to see and help the unlawful occupant. He could not even to himself explain or understand the line of conduct he was taking, he did not think it particularly just, or at all politic, and there was no doubt that it was exceedingly painful. He was no saint at present, only an honest man walking in the twilight.

He rang at least three times, and was beginning to feel impatient, when at length the door was opened about an inch, and some one within asked what he wanted.

'I want to come in, Phœbe,' he replied, recognizing the voice.

The maid opened the door wider, astonishment and some perplexity in her look.

'Oh, Mr. Donovan, sir!' she exclaimed. 'How little I thought to see you again! But don't come in, sir, please don't, for we've small-pox in the house.'

'I know it,' said Donovan, 'and I'm glad to see that you've not deserted your master, Phœbe. I might have known that you at least would be staunch. We must keep you out of the way of infection, though. Have you been with Mr. Farrant at all?'

'I helped to move him, sir, this morning,' said Phœbe.

'Oh! he's up at the top, is he? That's well. Don't you come further than the second floor then, I will fetch everything from there.'

'You mean to stay, sir?' said Phœbe, surprised, but evidently relieved.

'I have come to nurse him,' said Donovan. 'You can make me up a bed in'—with an effort—'Miss Dot's room.'

In a few minutes more he was striding upstairs two steps at a time, perhaps moving the quicker because even now a voice within him was urging him to turn back, calling him a fool for his pains.

Since their meeting in Wales he had often wondered whether he should again see Ellis Farrant, and if so how they would meet and where. He had rehearsed possible meetings in which he might combine perfect coldness with the forgiveness which Charles Osmond had spoken of. Cold Christliness—a curious idea, certainly!

But when it came to the point he somehow lost sight of himself and his wrongs altogether. A dim yellow light pervaded the room, the sick nurse came to meet him as he opened the door, he gave her a low-toned explanation, then turned to the bed where Ellis Farrant lay.

After all, he was a man—a man tossing to and fro in weary misery, racked with pain, scorched with fever, fearfully ill, and fearfully alone, left at least with only paid attendants. He was delirious, but he at once noticed Donovan's entrance, mistaking him, however, for his father. He started up with outstretched hands.

'Ralph! dear old fellow, I knew you'd come,' he cried. 'Save me from that old hag, it's old Molly the matron; don't you remember her! Stay with me, Ralph, promise! She's a hag, I tell you, a cursed old hag! She's been trying to poison me. Don't leave me with her—don't leave me!'

'I have come to stay with you,' said Donovan, touched by the reference to the past, to the school-days when his father and Ellis had been the greatest of friends. 'I shall stay and nurse you through this; no one shall hurt you.'

After the promise had been repeated again and again Ellis grew more quiet.

'There's one other thing,' he began, incoherently. 'I owe a sovereign to one of the sixth; you'll pay it for me if I die—promise me—the honour of the family, you know—the Farrant honour. His name is—what *is* his name? I can't remember it! Plague on the fellow! *Donovan!* That's it. Pay Donovan a sovereign, will you? And there was something else—a paper; what did I do with it? Tell me, for heaven's sake! There were six bits; I could join them. Give them to me, give them, I say! Don't burn them, *don't!*' his voice rose to a scream. 'Fire! fire! the bits are flying around me. Save me, Ralph! It's that dreadful Donovan, he's pelting me!'

'I'll settle him,' said Donovan, quietly. 'Don't be afraid.'

'But you can't get the paper—it's the paper he wants, and it's burnt. Oh God! what shall I do? There he is again! he won't speak—his dreadful eyes are looking at me!'

'No, no, you've made a mistake,' said Donovan, re-assuringly; 'he doesn't want the paper, he wants you to go to sleep. Come, now, you must try to settle off.'

With that he laid his hand on Ellis's burning forehead, and before long had really quieted him; he fell into a sort of doze.

Then Donovan turned to make his peace with the much-maligned nurse, a good-natured old creature in a gorgeous dressing-gown rather painfully suggestive of defunct patients. She was not at all unwilling to share the burden of nursing with the young doctor, and it ended not unnaturally in his taking by far the greatest part. For Ellis remained for several days under the same delusion, and would accept no services from anyone but the supposed cousin and school-fellow.

His ravings were painful enough to listen to, and Donovan saw plainly that his guilt weighed heavily on him. The fatal 'paper,' with its six fluttering bits, sometimes red-hot, sometimes black and charred, sometimes only freshly torn, recurred constantly in his delirium. The last meeting on Snowdon haunted him too, and Donovan would have given much to be able to blot out the strong impression which his silent wrath had made.

By the time the fever subsided, and the second stage of the illness set in, he had grown so absorbed in the progress of his patient that all sense of the strangeness of his own position had

died away. He had scarcely time to realize that he was in his
own house; when in his brief intervals of rest he was set free
from the sick-room, and could emerge from the carbolic steeped
barrier which separated the upper part of the house from the
lower, he had no leisure to think of possessions or rights. There
were orders to be given, telegrams to be sent; every now and
then in the early morning, or after dusk when few passengers
were stirring, there was the chance of a breath of air in the park.

But to the sick man the discovery was a great surprise and a
very sudden shock. The fever left him, the delirium faded away,
and he found that the attendant from whom he hoped everything,
the only person he could bear to touch him, and the one in whom
he had put the blindest faith, was not his old friend and school-
fellow at all, but his enemy—Donovan. He tried in vain to
think that this too was a delusion. A hundred horrible fears
rushed through his mind. Had he come to take his revenge?
He dared not say a word, but accepted everything sullenly and
silently. At length, after many days, Donovan's persevering
care and tenderness began to touch his heart. When the
secondary fever set in, his ravings were less of the burning
paper, and more of 'coals of fire,'—coals which, nevertheless, he
could ill have dispensed with.

It was the strangest, saddest, most pitiful sick-bed, and in
many ways it was more of a strain to Donovan than the stiffest
campaign could have been.

Charles Osmond, coming one evening to inquire after the
patient, met Donovan on the doorstep.

'You are not afraid of me?' he inquired. 'I've just changed.'

'Not a bit,' said the clergyman, taking his arm. 'Let us
have a turn together. Do you think I've been a parson all these
years without coming nearer small-pox than this? How is your
cousin getting on?'

'Exceedingly well up till this morning,' replied Donovan;
'the disease has about run its course, but I'm afraid a serious.
complication has just arisen. There's to be a consultation to-
morrow.'

'You look rather done up; are you taking care of yourself?'

'Oh! I shall do very well; but between ourselves it has
been'—he hesitated for words—'about the saddest business I
ever saw from the very first.'

'Do you mean his remorse?'

'Yes, the sort of abject misery of it, and his agony of fear.
I wish he had some one else with him, some one who was at
least sure in his own mind one way or the other. If the poor

F F

fellow asks me anything, I can but tell him that I do not know
—that all is unknown and unknowable.'

'I will gladly come to see him,' said Charles Osmond, 'if you
think he would not object; but'—looking attentively at the
singularly pure and noble face of his companion—'I fancy,
Donovan, you are helping him better than anyone else could;
service from you must be to him what no other service could be.'

'"Coals of fire," according to his own account,' said Donovan,
with a little humorous smile playing about his grave lips. 'But
he does seem to like it nevertheless.'

Their conversation was cut short by a warning clock which
reminded Donovan that he must return. Charles Osmond
watched him as he walked rapidly up the square, and disappeared
into the darkened house, the house in which such a strange bit
of life was being lived. *How* those two cog-wheels would work
together the clergyman did not feel sure, but he was sure they
would in some way work the good. Ay, and that without his
interference! He was human enough to long to have his share
in helping this soul, honest enough to recognize that another had
been called to the work—that other being an agnostic. As he
walked down into the main road a verse from one of his favourite
poems rang in his head.

> And nerve his arm, and cheer his heart;
> Then *stand aside*, and say 'God speed!'

'Standing aside!' the hardest of tasks to a warm-hearted
man, very conscious of his own power! To a surface observer it
would surely have seemed right that Charles Osmond and Donovan should change places.

The sick man not being a surface observer, however, but an
actor in this life drama, would strongly have objected to such a
change. Very slowly and gradually his sullenness had disappeared, and in his heart a strange, helpless, dependent love was
growing up—almost the first love he had ever known. He was
quite himself now, and could think clearly; he had already
formed his plan, his poor, wretched bit of restitution, and how to
carry it out.

When Donovan returned that evening from his walk with
Charles Osmond, and took his usual place in the peculiarly
oppressive sick-room, he found Ellis much exhausted, his hoarse
voice sounded hoarser than usual, his inflamed eyelids were
suggestive of voluntary tears, he seemed rather to shrink from
Donovan's gaze.

For in his thin, wasted hand he held tightly the paper which

contained his brief confession. With infinite difficulty he kept
it out of Donovan's sight, with almost childish impatience he
waited for the morning, when, before the two doctors, he intended to make his declaration. He was too eager to gain the
relief to care very much what they thought of him. Perhaps he
half hoped, too, that he could make a sort of compact with
Heaven, and by the act of restitution secure a few more years in
the world; or perhaps, having lived guilty, he desired to die
innocent, or as nearly innocent as might be. Undoubtedly there
was a certain amount of selfishness in the action, but there was,
too, a very genuine sorrow, and that strange glimmer of love for
the man whom he had injured, the enemy who had come to him
in his need.

Donovan could not understand why he was so anxious to get
rid of him the next day; he humoured him, however, and was
not present when the two doctors arrived. After the consultation was over he was too much troubled to think of anything but
their verdict. He had known that Ellis's recovery was doubtful,
but he was startled and shocked to hear that he could not
live more than two or three days. To him, too, was left the task
of breaking the news to the patient. Never had he felt more
unfitted for his work, never had he so keenly felt his own incompleteness. To make matters worse, Ellis seemed suddenly to
have taken the greatest dislike to him.

'I know quite well what you have to say,' he interrupted,
when Donovan tried to lead up to the doctors' opinion. 'I know
that I'm dying, and that you'll soon be well rid of me. I tell you
I won't have you in the room, get out and leave me to the nurse.
Isn't it enough that I had you all last night?'

Till now it had been difficult to be absent even for a few hours
from the room, for Ellis had always begged not to be left to
the nurse, whom he greatly disliked. This sudden change was
perplexing and disappointing. Donovan went away discouraged
and wretched, and tried in vain to sleep. Late in the evening he
again went to relieve guard. Ellis did not actually object this
time to his presence, but he was alternately sullen and irritable,
in great pain, and, in spite of his confession signed and witnessed,
in terrible mental distress.

Donovan never forgot that night. It seemed endless! There
was not very much to be done; to quiet Ellis was impossible, to
reason with him was useless; he could only listen to his irritable
remarks, and make answer as guardedly as he could.

'What are you here for?' grumbled Ellis. 'What made you
come? Why do you stay? You know you hate me!'

'Nonsense,' replied Donovan. 'Should I stay here if I did?

'You have some evil purpose,' cried Ellis. 'You have come for your revenge. Why *did* you come?'

'Because it was right,' said Donovan, shortly.

'Right! Do you think I shall believe that? All very fine when you knew quite well I'd ruined you. Didn't you know, I say? Didn't you know well enough?'

'Of course,' said Donovan. 'But you were ill and alone.'

'Oh! yes, it's all very fine; but you won't get me to believe it. It's a very likely story, isn't it? I tell you,' he added, in a querulous voice, 'you're a fool to try to gull me like that—it's against all reason—you can't prove to me that you don't hate me—you can't prove to me that you didn't mean to poison me!'

'No, I can't prove it in words,' said Donovan; 'I can only flatly deny. But we have been so long together, surely you can believe in me now?'

He still murmured that it was impossible—against reason; but, perhaps exhausted by his own vehemence, fell at length into a sort of restless sleep.

Donovan too dozed for a few minutes in his chair, only, however, to carry on the argument. He woke with the words— 'Quite against reason' in his mind, and his own answer—'Surely you can believe in me now!'

He got up, went to the bed, and looked at Ellis; he was still sleeping, an expression of great distress on his worn face. Donovan sighed, and crossed the room to the window. The night was wearing on; he drew up the blind and saw that the first faint grey of dawn was stealing over the horizon. Everything looked inexpressibly dreary; the room was at the back of the house; he could see the bare trees waving in the wind, and the grim, white tombstones in the burial-ground stood out forlornly in the dim light. Death was certain, all too certain, but the beyond was dark and unknown. Yet here in the very room with him was one who must soon pass through those gloomy portals—to what? Was there a hereafter to complete this fearfully barren existence? Would that wretched life have a chance of growth and change? Or was it just ended here? Had this man, with all his gifts and talents, just wasted his life? was there no future for him? He had done no good works to live after him, he had left no memory to be revered, he had done no good to his generation, had left nothing for posterity. Was all ended?

When Dot had died, Donovan had dreamed of no possible hereafter, but now all seemed different. His creed was no longer a positive one, and besides, the idea of the wasted life dying out

for ever was less tolerable than the idea of the little child passing
from terrible pain to the 'peace of nothingness.'

What *was* the Truth? Did this awfully mysterious life end
with what was called Death?

And still a voice repeated his own words—'Surely you can
believe in me now!'

Then again he looked at the sleeping man, and again a
miserable sense of failure weighed down his heart. He had tried
hard to show no trace of remembrance of the past, never in look
or word to remind Ellis of the wrong he had done him, yet his
forgiveness had been rejected, insolently, contemptuously rejected.
He might just as well have gone out to the war and left Ellis to
his fate, for he evidently would not even believe that his motive
had not been one of self-interest. 'Against all reason,' a 'likely
story!' Evidently he could not bring himself to believe, and
how was it possible to give him proof! The most wounding sense
of rejection and disappointment filled his heart.

And still the voice repeated, 'Surely you can believe in me
now!'

Then for the first time in his life Donovan became conscious
of a Presence mightier than anything he had ever conceived possible. He realized that his pain about Ellis was but the shadow
of the pain which he himself had given to 'One better than the
best conceivable.' He saw that for want of logical proof he too
had rejected Him whose ways are above and beyond proof. The
veil was lifted, and in the place of the dim Unknown stood One
who had loved him with everlasting love, who had drawn him
with loving-kindness.

CHAPTER XL.

APPREHENSION.

Life has two ecstatic moments, one when the spirit catches sight of
Truth, the other when it recognizes a kindred spirit. . . . . Perhaps it is
only in the land of Truth that spirits can discern each other; as it is when
they are helping each other on, that they may best hope to arrive there.
Guesses at Truth.

IF rapture means the being carried away, snatched out of self to
something higher—if ecstasy means the state in which corporeal
consciousness is made to stand aside, to give place to a higher
and perfectly satisfying consciousness—then Donovan knew for
the first time both rapture and ecstasy. But real spiritual rapture

is the quietest thing in the world.   It is only when the senses are
appealed to that superstition and fanaticism win devotees and
evoke noisy and excited zeal.   The man who, after long search
and hard labour, is at length rewarded by some grand discovery,
will be very calm *because* of his rapture, very still, because his
feelings are true and deep.

It was characteristic of him that he stood upright.   After a
time the beauty of the scene without made itself felt.   The sun
had just risen—the window looked westward—all the land was
bathed in the rosy glow of sunrise.   The wind had gone down,
the bare trees no longer waved dismally to and fro, the white
graves in the burial-ground were softened and mellowed in the
glorious flood of light.   It was not unlike the change in his own
life—the darkness past, the sun changing all the scene.   For
was not the mystery of life solved?   had not even the grave 'its
sunny side'?   It was when the prophet realized the everlastingness of God that the conviction came to him—'we shall not die.'

And Dot's confident 'you *will* know' came to pass, and she
was, as it were, given back to him once more.

The sick man stirred.   Donovan went to the bedside.   There
too he was conscious of change.   The realization of immortality
brings relief, but it brings too a strange sense of awe.

The sleep had refreshed Ellis.   He was a little better, and not
quite so irritable, his assumed dislike too was put aside.   Once
more his only anxiety was to keep Donovan beside him.   As the
day advanced he grew weaker, however.   He was not in great
pain, but very restless and weary, and in an agony of fear.   At
last, to relieve himself, he began to talk to Donovan.

'Do you remember what you said when you left the Manor?'
he began, hurriedly, 'about hoping I'd remember to my dying
day?   This is my dying day, and you've got your wish.'

'I have unwished it,' said Donovan, quietly.

'I believe you have,' said Ellis, looking at him steadily for
a minute.   'But how can I forget?   The sin is the same whether
you forgive or not.   And I've not even enjoyed it—do you hear?
I've not been able to enjoy it!'

'No?   Then God has been very good to you,' said Donovan.

'Good!   What do you mean?' groaned Ellis.

'That the greatest curse you can have is enjoyment of wrong,'
replied Donovan.   'I know only too bitterly what it means.'

Ellis seemed to muse over the words, then he continued—
'I've done what I could.   I've got it signed and witnessed.
See!' and he drew a folded paper from beneath the pillow
'But it's no good, it's not a bit of good.   It's made me feel no better.

Donovan glanced at the confession and put it aside.

'Don't let it be lost, don't leave it about,' cried Ellis, nervously. 'Without it you won't get your rights, and, if not, I couldn't rest in my grave.'

Just at that moment Donovan felt supremely indifferent as to the property, but to please Ellis he put the paper in a safe place.

'It was all that wretched will that ruined me!' cried the miserable man. 'If it hadn't been so small, if I hadn't been alone, there'd have been no temptation. I wasn't such a bad fellow before then. And now I'm ruined, lost! Do you hear what I say? I've lost my soul! How can you sit there so quietly when in a few hours I shall be dead? Don't you believe in hell?'

'Yes,' said Donovan, slowly. 'And I think that you and I have already spent most of our lives there.'

'That wasn't what they used to teach; I believe you're half a sceptic still,' groaned Ellis. 'I'm sure there was a way of getting it all set right at the last, if only I could remember.'

'Would you like to see a clergyman?' asked Donovan.

'No, no, no,' cried Ellis, vehemently; 'I've been a hypocrite all my life before them, I can at least speak the truth to you—you who know just what I am.'

'Then,' said Donovan, very diffidently, urged to speak only by the extremity of the case, 'if you want one who knows all, you can go straight to God, who is nearer you than anyone else can be.'

'That's nothing new!' exclaimed Ellis, petulantly. 'I've known that all my life.'

'*How* did you know it,' asked Donovan.

'I don't know how; they told me—my mother, and at church and school.'

Conventional acceptance was a thing which Donovan could not understand.

'I think we must learn differently from that,' he said slowly, as if feeling his way on new ground. 'Before you can really *know*, must you not be conscious of God's presence?'

'I've had that,' groaned Ellis, 'it's dogged me through everything—a dreadful text that was up in the old nursery, it used to make me shiver then—great black letters—"Thou God seest me;" I can see it now, and the horrid feeling after one had told a lie. Do you think there's no way out of it? They used to say something—I forget what, it never seemed to me very real. Do you think one *must* be punished?'

'Yes, I do,' said Donovan.

'Oh! is there no way of getting off?' groaned Ellis.

'I don't think you'll wish to "get off,"' replied Donovan.

'Not wish! How little you know! What would you do if you were lying as I am, with only a few hours more to live?—would you not wish to get off?'

'I think I should wish—I do wish—to be saved from selfishness,' said Donovan, slowly, 'and to give myself unreservedly into God's keeping.'

Death has a strange way of breaking down the strongest barriers of reserve; afterwards it seemed almost incredible to Donovan that he and Ellis, of all people in the world, should have spoken with such perfect openness to each other. It was a little hard on him perhaps to be called so soon to speak of the truths he had so lately grasped, but the very freshness of his conviction gave his words a peculiar power, the very slowness and diffidence of his humility touched Ellis when glib, conventional utterances would have passed by him unheeded. And yet the sick man did not gather from his words one grain of selfish comfort. Donovan evidently did not believe in any charm for converting the death-bed of a wrong doer into that of a saint; he seemed quite convinced that punishment *did* await him, purifying punishment. And Ellis, who had all his life hoped to set things right at the last, was much more terrified at the idea of certain punishment, even with his ultimate good in view, than of everlasting punishment, which, by some theological charm, he might hope altogether to escape. The inevitable loss of even some small possession is much more keenly felt than the possible loss of all, which we hope to avert, and the very idea of which we can hardly take into our minds.

The one only comfort of that terrible day was in the realization of Donovan's forgiveness. By degrees this began to work in the poor man's mind, almost imperceptibly to alter his grim notions of the stern, inexorable Judge in whom he believed, and before whom he trembled.

It was night again, the room was dim and quiet, but beside the bed the dying man could see the face of his late enemy, the strong, pure, strangely powerful face, which, in his helplessness, he had learnt to love.

'Do you think God's as forgiving as you are?' he faltered. 'Do you think He's better than they say?'

Donovan was dismayed. Did the poor fellow know what he was saying? could he have such a terribly low ideal? He would not allow his surprise to show itself, however. He drew nearer.

'See,' he said, at the same time raising his cousin's head so that it rested on his shoulder in the way which gave the sick man most relief. ' I know very little of what they say, and am at the beginning of everything, but I am sure that whatever love I have for you is but the tiniest ray of His love ; and if you persist in shutting out all but one ray when the whole sun is ready to light you, you will find it, as I have found it, very dark.'

And then in the silence that followed Donovan fell into a reverie. Why was it that this man found it so hard to believe ? He had evidently no such difficulties as he himself had had—no intellectual perplexities. Had he believed in some terrific phantom ? or had the long selfishness of years brought him to a state in which he could not reach the idea of love ? Yet he could reach the idea of *human* love and pity ; he clung now almost like a child to Donovan.

' Who would have thought that you would be the only one with me at the last ? ' he murmured. ' But I shall have to leave even you ; I must go alone to face God, to stand before the Judge. I wish I'd never been born, I tell you ! '

Donovan felt almost choked ; he would have given worlds to have had Charles Osmond there at that moment. But there was no chance of getting a better man to speak to Ellis then, nor, had the greatest saints upon earth been present, would they have had as much influence with him as the man whom he had wronged.

The clock struck three. There was a long silence. Donovan seemed to have gained what he wanted in the waiting, for his face was strangely bright when he turned once more to Ellis.

' I am going to tell you something about my father,' he began. And then, much in the way in which he used to soothe Dot's restless nights with stories, Donovan told faithfully and graphically the whole story of his school disgrace. How he had cared not a rush for all the blame, how he had braved opinion, how the treatment he received had hardened and embittered him ; then of his return to the house, of the way in which his father had received him, of the forgiveness which had first made him repentant, of the fatherly grief which had made him just for his father's sake care for the punishment.

His voice got a little husky towards the end. Ellis, too, was evidently much moved.

' Do you think God is at all like your father ? ' he faltered.

It hurt Donovan a little, this bald anthropomorphism, but, recognizing that Ellis was really feeling after the underlying truth, he answered,

' I think my father was, as it were, a shadow of God—a

shadow of the great Fatherhood—and the shadow can't be without the reality.'

Ellis seemed satisfied. After that he slept at intervals, murmuring indistinctly every now and then fragments of the story he had just heard, or wandering back to recollections of his childhood.

Just as the dawn was breaking, he came to himself once more, speaking quite clearly.

'I should like you to say the Lord's Prayer,' he said.

So together Donovan and the dying man said the 'Our Father,' and sealed their reconciliation.

Then, tremblingly and fearfully, Ellis entered the valley of the shadow of death. Truly there are last which shall be first, and first last! The conventionally religious man, the man whose orthodoxy had always been considered beyond dispute, would have died in black darkness had not one ray of love been kindled in his cold heart by the forgiveness he so little deserved, had not a gleam of truth been given to him by one who but yesterday had been an agnostic.

At sunrise he passed away into the Unseen.

For thirty-six hours Donovan had been in constant attendance on his cousin. When all was over he could no longer resist the craving for air which had for some time made the sick-room almost intolerable to him. In the stillness of that early winter morning he left the house and made his way into the park. The ground was white with frost, the sky intensely blue, the air sharp and exhilarating. The outer world suited his state of mind exactly. He was awed and quieted by the death-bed he had just quitted, but above the stillness and above the awe there was that marvellous sense of the Eternal which had so lately dawned for him, a consciousness which widened the whole universe, which gave new beauty to all around. He walked on rapidly into the bleakest, most open part of the park, a peculiar elasticity in his step, a light in his eyes.

It took him back to a day in his childhood, when his tutor had first given him some idea of the most recent solar discoveries. He could clearly remember the sort of exultant glow of wonder and awe which had taken possession of him; how the whole world had seemed full of grand possibilities; how he had rushed out alone on to the downs near the Manor, and in every blade of grass, in every tiny flower, in every wayside stone had seen new wonders, strange invisible workings which no one could fathom or grasp. The very wind blowing on his heated brow had been laden with the marvellous; nothing could be common, or small, or ordinary to him again.

That had been his feeling when he first realized the physical unseen; his first realization of the spiritual unseen was a little like it, only deeper and more lasting, and that while the child's delight had had an element of wildness in it, the man's rapture was all calmness.

The park seemed deserted. The sole creature he met was an organ-grinder setting out on his daily rounds. Involuntarily they exchanged a *buon giorno*. His very dreams of 'liberty, equality, fraternity' took a wider and deeper meaning in the breadth and light of that morning.

There are more resurrection days than the world dreams of— Easters which are not less real because the church bells do not ring—which, though chanted of by no earthly choir, cause joy in the presence of the angels of God.

CHAPTER XLI.

TREVETHAN SPEAKS.

But Thou wilt sin and grief destroy;
That so the broken bones may joy,
And tune together in a well-set song,
   Full of His praises,
   Who dead men raises.
Fractures well cured make us more strong.
              GEORGE HERBERT.

THE years had wrought very little visible change in Gladys. Outwardly her life had been very quiet and uneventful since her last meeting with Donovan, and whatever anxiety or inward trouble she had had was not registered on her fair, open brow, or in her clear, quiet, blue-grey eyes. That time was passing quickly, and that years had elapsed since Donovan had been at Porthkerran, was shown much more clearly by the change in Nesta, who, from a remarkably small child, had shot up into a slim little girl of eight years. The two sisters were walking together along the Porthkerran cliffs one winter afternoon, Nesta telling an endless fairy tale for the joint benefit of her doll and her sister, Gladys listening every now and then for a few minutes, but a good deal engrossed with her own thoughts.

The Caustons were spending a few days with them, and Stephen's presence was rather tiresome and embarrassing. She had really come out chiefly to escape his company, for the afternoon was not at all tempting. A strong west wind was blowing, the sky was dull and leaden, the sea grey, and restless, and stormy. Gladys was not easily affected by weather, but to-day the dulness seemed to tell on her. There was something depressing in the great, grey expanse of sea heaving and tossing restlessly, in the long white fringe of foam along the coast line, in the heavy gloomy sky. Only one boat was in sight, a little pilot-boat which had just left Porthkerran Bay. It was tossing fearfully; every now and then a great gust of wind threatened to blow it quite over. She watched it bending and swaying beneath the blast, but still making way, until at length it disappeared in the grey mist which shrouded the distance.

Gladys sighed as it passed away out of sight. It reminded her—why she scarcely knew—of a life which for a little while had touched her life very nearly, of a strong, determined, resolute man struggling hard with adverse circumstances under a leaden sky of doubt. He, too, had passed away into a grey mist. For years she had heard nothing of him; their lives were quite severed. Was he still under the leaden sky? she wondered. Was all still so fearfully against him? Was he still toiling on against wind and tide? A rift in the clouds made way for a gleam of sunlight, and it so happened that the gleam fell on the horizon-line in one golden little spot of brightness. Right in the centre of it she could clearly make out the dark sail of the pilot-boat. It brought to her mind a line of George Herbert—

> The sun still shineth there or here.

And she walked on more hopefully, strangely inspirited by that momentary glimpse of sunlight. What right had she to doubt that the sun would shine for him sooner or later? Might not he, too, have even now reached the brightness? lived out his bit of grey?

'We will go and see Trevethan,' she said to little Nesta. 'It is quite a long time since we heard anything about him.'

They passed the place where Donovan had climbed down after the lost hat, and before many minutes reached the forge, where Trevethan was hammering away at his anvil, the sparks springing up from the red-hot metal like fire-flies. Standing beside the blazing fire was a little pale-faced girl.

'Good day, miss,' said the blacksmith, glancing round and laying aside his hammer. 'I'm right glad to see ye, miss. I was a-coming up to the house this very night to tell ye our good news.'

'News of your son?' asked Gladys, feeling certain that nothing less could have called out such radiant satisfaction in Trevethan's face.

'Not news of him, Miss Gladys, but himself; he's come, he's here now, and this is his little one, miss, called after you. Jack was determined she should have a good Cornish name. He be out now, more's the pity, but we be both a-coming to-night to see the doctor, to tell him of Mr. Farrant, and how it's all his doing.'

'Mr. Farrant?' questioned Gladys, her colour deepening.

'Yes, miss, Mr. Donovan as was here three years gone by. He promised to look out for Jack, and you'd never think, miss, what he's been to my poor lad, a-nursing of him his own self, and a-persuading of him to come home when Jack was frightened whether I'd give him a welcome or not.'

'Was your son at St. Thomas's?' asked Gladys.

'Yes, miss, but Mr. Farrant he found him out in his own place. You tell, little one, how you fetched him to see father.'

So little Gladys told shyly, yet graphically, too, how she had gone one rainy evening to fetch Donovan, how he had made her sit by his fire, how he had held his umbrella over her on the way back, and had done all he could to help them. The tears would come into Gladys' eyes for very happiness. Had she not known that the truth would come out at last! Had she not been right to believe in him without the slightest proof!

'Will Mr. Dono come to stay with us again?' asked Nesta, as they walked home.

'I don't know, darling,' she replied. 'Some day perhaps.'

But her heart was dancing with happiness, that 'perhaps' had a good deal of assurance in it.

The two Trevethans had a long interview with the doctor that evening. Such an unexpected opportunity of hearing about Donovan was not to be neglected, and Dr. Tremain made the most minute inquiries. Jack Trevethan was a very shrewd fellow; from the most trifling indications he had long ago guessed all the facts of the case. He had seen Donovan flush quickly at the mention of Miss Tremain, had found that he was no longer on speaking terms with Stephen Causton, had put two and two together in the quick way common to observant people, especially when they are watching life in a circle above them. He was devoted to Donovan, and very eager to do him service. Very carefully and minutely he told Dr. Tremain of their first meeting in the billiard saloon. Then for the first time Donovan's true relation to Stephen transpired. The doctor could hardly believe that he heard rightly. It was such an entire reversing of all that he had feared, all that he had unwillingly believed. Could it indeed be that Donovan had only tried to keep Stephen out of evil? Could he possibly have gone with him to the Z—— Races merely to prevent his going with the set which Trevethan very graphically described? The ex-billiard marker disclosed several very damaging facts; Stephen had often visited the saloon with the same set of students, but Donovan had never again entered the place.

Gladys could not understand why her father looked so worried and perplexed when he came back to the drawing-room that evening. Did he not believe the good news? Must he not be infinitely relieved? A sudden light was thrown on her perplexity, however, when her father spoke.

'I want a word with you, Stephen, will you come into the study?'

Of course whatever proved Donovan's innocence must at the same time convict Stephen! She had not thought of that!

Stephen had a sort of presentiment that his time was come. He followed the doctor into the next room.

'I have nothing pleasant to tell you,' began Dr. Tremain, speaking rather quickly, and in a tone of one who fears he may lose his temper. 'I have just had an interview with a man who was present at a certain billiard saloon in Villiers Street at the time you were in the habit of frequenting it. The man was one of the markers; he has described to me the *one* evening when Donovan met you there and persuaded you to leave. Is that what you call being led into temptation by him?'

Stephen turned pale.

'It is exceedingly hard that you take the word of a mere stranger before mine,' he said. 'This man, whoever he may be, has no doubt been instigated by Farrant! Why should you believe him?'

'Because he has truth written on his face,' said Dr. Tremain, 'and you have not. Stephen, I do not wish to be hard on you. I will try not to prejudge you, but I implore you to tell me the whole truth.'

To tell the whole truth was unfortunately not at all in Stephen's line; he began to excuse himself.

'Farrant is as hard as nails, he judges everyone by himself; because he had once been a regular gambler was no reason that I should follow his example. He'd no business to spy on me.'

'Take care,' said the doctor, quickly, 'your own words are condemning you.'

'It is you who force me to condemn myself,' said Stephen, sullenly. Then after a pause he all at once broke down and buried his face in his hands. 'If Gladys could have loved me,' he sobbed, 'it would all have been different; it's been my love for her that has undone me, made me want to seem better than I was.'

The doctor, at once sorrowful and angry, paced the room in silence, but there was something so selfish in Stephen's confessions that, in spite of himself, the anger would predominate.

'You call by the name of love what was nothing more than mere selfish desire,' he said, sternly. 'How could you dare to ask any woman to be your wife when to gain her you had acted one continual lie! Do you realize that all these years an innocent man has been suffering for your guilt? Do you realize that one word from Donovan, the word he was too generous to speak, would have brought all your falseness to the light? What do you expect him to think of Christianity if that is the way you behave? You have brought shame to your religion! You have disgraced your name! And not only that, but you have utterly misled me, caused me to misjudge the man of all others I would have treated with greatest delicacy—greatest justice. How could you tell me such lies? Had you no generosity—no sense of gratitude?'

Stephen cowered under the storm, but kept silence.

Presently, in the saddening consciousness of his own grievous mistake, the doctor's anger died away.

'I will say no more, it is scarcely fair to reproach you with my own hastiness of judgment, my own want of insight,' he said, in a voice full of sorrow, which reproached Stephen far more than his anger. 'But when I think of what Donovan has borne in silence, from the very people too who should have been his best friends, it is almost more than I can endure.'

Stephen's better nature began to show itself at last, his heart smote him as he realized all the pain his deceit had caused. He left off excusing himself, and somewhat falteringly told the story from the very beginning, revealing the sort of double life he had led for so many years, wild and self-indulgent when alone, falsely religious and proper when with his mother. The doctor was very good to him, promised to help him as far as he could by speaking to Mrs. Causton, and perhaps for the first time thoroughly awakened Stephen's love and respect. Before they parted that night they had discussed the future as well as the past, and Stephen had made up his mind to go abroad, to try with all his might to redeem his name.

Trevethan had after all been detained at St. Thomas's later than Donovan had expected. He had learnt at the hospital that his friend had not gone out to the war, that instead he was nursing some relation. This was all he could tell Dr. Tremain, but of course the impulsive doctor, even with such slight information, prepared to go up to London at once. Letters had failed so signally before that he would no longer trust them; he must see Donovan to explain matters fully, to apologise as he wished.

Some cruel fate seemed to have ordained that he should always have to endure a most irksome time of waiting in the York Road lodging-house. Donovan was of course not at home; the old captain was out, but was expected in an hour's time, he was the only person who knew Mr. Farrant's address. The landlady invited the doctor to come in and wait. The room seemed very dull and quiet, the only trace of Donovan which it bore was in a sheet of writing-paper pinned up in a conspicuous place over the mantel-piece, whereon was inscribed a high-flown but affectionate declaration that John Frewin, late captain of the *Metora*, bound himself hereby to touch no alcoholic drink until the return of his friend Donovan Farrant.

Apparently the old man had kept his pledge, for he came in before long looking exceedingly respectable and sober. Dr. Tremain had to listen to the whole account of the drawing up of the paper, the surprise it was to be to the captain's 'dear friend and benefactor,' and the dreariness of the place without him, before he could elicit Donovan's address from the talkative old gentleman. Even then Rouge tried to scare him with terrific accounts of the small-pox.

At length, however, he was really on his way to Connaught Square; by this time it was evening, and when he reached the house it seemed dark and deserted. He rang, and, after a long delay, was admitted. Phœbe eyed him with some suspicion, but, hearing that he was a doctor, she let him come in and showed him into the dining-room, lighting the gas for his benefit. Then for the first time they discovered that Donovan was stretched on the sofa fast asleep.

'Don't wake him,' said the doctor, 'I'm in no hurry and will wait. I suppose he has had very hard work. Is Mr. Farrant any better?'

'You have not heard, sir? He died early this morning,' replied Phœbe, gravely. 'Mr. Donovan should have rested before, but we couldn't persuade him; there has been many things to see to to-day, for they say the funeral must be to-morrow.'

Neither the lights nor the voices roused the sleeper; by-and-by Phœbe went away, and the doctor waited with eagerness not unmixed with anxiety for the awaking, remembering with a pang their last parting at the station, recalling painfully the last words which even then had touched him, 'All I ask is that you will just forget me.'

At last a noise in the square roused Donovan, he started up, rubbed his eyes, caught sight of Dr. Tremain, and sprang to his feet.

'You here!' he exclaimed, in astonishment, and then a sudden shade passed over his face, and the same peculiar expression of doubt, almost of annoyance, showed itself, which had so grievously hurt the doctor at their last meeting. He understood it well enough now, however.

'Yes, I am here at last,' he said, grasping Donovan's hand. 'Here to ask your forgiveness, to tell you that we all know now how much we have been misled.'

Donovan's eyes lighted up, but he waited in questioning silence, careful still not to compromise Stephen in the slightest degree.

'I learnt all from Trevethan's son,' continued the doctor. 'And then a very few questions brought out the whole truth from Stephen. Can you forgive us, Donovan, for misjudging you so abominably?'

'It was my own fault—my own doing, at any rate,' said Donovan, smiling. 'You were very slow to judge me at all, and it seemed best all round that you should believe me to be in the wrong.'

'It shielded Stephen, of course,' said the doctor, 'but he did not deserve shielding, and it gave the rest of us a great deal of pain. It was very generous of you, but surely mistaken.'

'I asked you to forget me,' said Donovan. 'I hoped and believed you would do so. It was not only or chiefly for Stephen's sake. I believed that it would be better in every way.'

'You said so when we last saw each other,' said the doctor, 'but even now I cannot see why it was necessary. And why did you refuse to come to us that summer, and then tell me you invented an excuse? Was that in any way connected with Stephen? Can you not tell me now why you could not come?'

'Yes,' replied Donovan, with a strange thrill in his voice, 'I can tell you even that now. I could not come because I loved your daughter. I was not sure that I could help showing it; I thought—it may have been presumptuous to think so—that she might possibly care for me. It was right, I think, to go away, and I hoped that she—that you all—would forget me.'

'And little Gladys was the one who told me from the very first that I must be mistaken, that I had judged you wrongly,' said the doctor, rather huskily. 'We have all been very poor hands at forgetting you, Donovan; do you want us to go on with the dreary farce any longer? Will you not come back to us?'

'You must yourself give me the power of saying "Yes" to that question,' said Donovan, his colour rising a little. 'A few days ago I must still have refused; but if you could trust Gladys to me, if she can possibly love one who has lived the life I have lived—who has but seen, as it were, one ray of light in which she has lived all her life—then I will come to you.'

The two men wrung each other's hands.

'Gladys must speak for herself,' said the doctor. 'For my part, I would trust my little girl to you unreservedly. I will not thank you for the way in which you have acted, but'—he struggled with his emotion—'it has made you very dear to me, Donovan. No man in the world would I so gladly call my son.'

Then, being Englishmen, and not caring to trust themselves to talk more on a subject which moved them so much, they plunged rather abruptly into other topics, discussed Ellis Farrant's illness, the legality of his duly-witnessed confession, the great increase of small-pox in London.

It was not until after the funeral, late in the following day, that Donovan had time to go to the Osmonds, and then it was only to take a hurried farewell, for Dr. Tremain had made light of all fear of infection, and had insisted on his returning with him to Trenant.

'So you see,' he added, after briefly alluding to all that had passed since the night he and Charles Osmond had last met, 'life is beginning to open out for me in all sorts of unexpected ways. I can hardly realize yet—I have hardly tried to think—that Oakdene is really mine. How am I ever to turn myself into the respectable country gentleman?'

Charles Osmond laughed.

'I am not much afraid for you,' he replied, quietly. 'It will be a more difficult life than the hard working surgeon-life you had planned for yourself; but I fancy you can make a great deal of it.'

'It would be hard to face,' said Donovan, 'if I had not a hope that the truest of helpers, the sweetest and best woman in the world, may possibly begin the new life at Oakdene with me.

It is nothing but a hope—to-morrow I shall know; but I could not help telling you of it—you who have helped me through these black years.'

'I wish you good speed,' said Charles Osmand, conveying somehow in tone and look and touch a great deal more than the mere words.

Then the two parted.

CHAPTER XLII.

'MY HOPES AND THINE ARE ONE.'

O we will walk this world,
Yoked in all exercise of noble end,
And so through those dark gates across the wild
That no man knows. Indeed I love thee; come,
Yield thyself up! My hopes and thine are one:
Accomplish thou my manhood and thyself;
Lay thy sweet hands in mine and trust to me.
The Princess.

In spite of the inevitable excitement and anxiety, Donovan slept almost the whole way from London to St. Kerrans; he had large arrears of sleep to make up, and the doctor was glad enough to see him settle himself in a corner seat and take the rest he so much needed. By the time they reached St. Kerrans he was quite himself again, quiet rather, and not much inclined to talk, but with an unusual light in his dark eyes. Star and Ajax were waiting for them at the station; they drove through the little Cornish town, with its grey houses, and out into the narrow winding lanes, which Donovan remembered so well. It seemed almost a lifetime since the Sunday evening when he had first spoken unreservedly with Dr. Tremain—long years ago since their last drive to St. Kerrans, when he thought he had parted with Gladys for ever. His heart beat high with hope; every step was bringing him nearer the woman he loved! the very trees and hedgerows seemed to welcome him as he passed, even the cross-grained old man at the turnpike had a friendly greeting for him.

It was dark by the time they reached Porthkerran; the stars were shining brightly through the frosty air, the ponies' feet rang sharply on the hard road, in all the quaint, irregular houses

shone friendly lights; he could see them climbing far up the hill,
old Admiral Smith's house forming the apex. She was here in
this home-like little fishing village! in a few minutes he should
see her again! every pulse in him beat at double-quick time at the
thought of it. They drove on through the quaint market-place,
with its stone fountain, surrounded now with rows of boats drawn
up from the beach into winter quarters. A blaze of light came
from the little inn where he had stayed with his father, where he
had first met Dr. Tremain; lights shone, too, from the windows
of the school-house, and children's voices rang out clearly into
the street—they were singing Dot's favourite old carol—the
refrain reached him distinctly:

> O tidings of comfort and joy,
> Comfort and joy,
> O tidings of comfort and joy!

The doctor made the ponies draw up.

'Gladys must be at her choir practice,' he said. 'We will
see if she is ready to come home.'

He gave the reins to the groom, and Donovan followed him
into the school-room.

There was Gladys surrounded with little blue-eyed Cornish
children, sitting queen-like in a sort of bower of holly, and ivy,
and laurel branches, for the next day was to be the children's
winter school-treat. It had been postponed once or twice, but,
though somewhat late in the season, they were to celebrate it
in Christmas fashion, and would not dispense with either carols
or greenery.

She was not the least altered; it was just the same sweet,
pure, sunshiny face, the remembrance of which had so often kept
him from evil. They greeted each other in the most ordinary
way. Then she turned to speak to her father, but Donovan was
quite content, scarcely wished for more than the sight of her just
then.

'Shall we drive you home?' said the doctor. 'Is your
practice over?'

'It is just finished, but I wanted rather to see old Mrs. Carne
—she seems worse again.'

'I will take back Jackie and Nesta then,' said the doctor.
'Donovan will see you safely home, I've no doubt.'

Donovan, inwardly blessing the doctor, carried off Nesta to
the pony-carriage, impatient to have them all out of the way.
Was not each minute wasted which did not bring that perfect
mutual understanding which he so longed for! She might not

care for him, still they would understand each other, make an
end of the miserable silence and doubt of these long years.

The pony-carriage drove off, the last carol was sung; with
..es and salutes the small singers ran noisily out of the school.
Donovan, whose 'duteous service' had so long consisted in
silence and absence, now made the most of his opportunity;
raked out the fire, tidied the school, turned out the lamps, then
with, in spite of himself, a certain sweet sense of possession—
possession if only for these few minutes—he turned to Gladys,
who for once seemed a little shy and silent.

They went out into the market-square, closely followed by
Waif.

'It is a house down on the shore I want to go to,' said Gladys,
wishing her heart would not beat so uncomfortably. But somehow, when Donovan next spoke, there was that in his manner
which calmed her.

'I am so glad to have this walk with you,' he said. 'It was
good of your father to give me this time with you at once. I
want, Gladys, to know how I am to come back to Porthkerran
this time. The first time I came to you it was as a penniless
outcast; the second as a friend; the next as one who loved you,
but dared not speak. I have come this time ready to speak to
you, if you will hear me; to ask if you can give me more than
friendship—whether you care to take a love which has always
been yours. May I go on? Will you hear me?'

She seemed to speak an assent, but her voice trembled, he
took her hand in his, made her lean on his arm, still holding the
little hand in his strong grasp.

'You see,' he continued, 'ever since I was a mere boy you
have been my ideal. In a very strange way I had three passing
glimpses of you, the first just after my father died, when I was
miserable and disgraced, then again those two meetings when I
was wronged and revengeful. Oh, Gladys! you little know what
you did for me, what depths you saved me from. I think I am
glad you saw me at my worst, without it I should hardly have
dared to speak to you like this. You know all that I was, you
were my friend when others shrank from me as an atheist, you
have taught me what love is, and now that I am beginning to
learn something of the everlastingness of love, I want your help
more and more. Gladys, will you be my wife?'

'I think I have always loved you,' she answered, quite simply
and quietly. 'And I was always sure the Light would come to
you.'

'Yes,' said Donovan, holding her hand more closely, 'you

could look at things from another point of view, you believed in
a higher power; I, you see, only knew myself, and how could I
dare to think of you as my wife? My darling, even now I half
tremble at the thought. Can you trust yourself to one who is
at the beginning of everything? I have spent my life in learning
what you have always known. Can you put up with such incompleteness? Can you trust me?'

'After trusting in the darkness it is easy to trust in the light,'
said Gladys, softly.

'You did believe in me then, though I tried so hard that you
should not,' said Donovan, half smiling.

'You are not a good deceiver or concealer,' replied Gladys.
'That day at Z—— on the staircase when you said you could
explain nothing, I could see by your face that you had never led
Stephen into harm. I couldn't help believing you.'

'I should have thought I was flinty enough,' said Donovan,
smiling now, though the remembrance of that parting still
brought a cold chill to his heart.

'Yes,' said Gladys, 'in one way. I mean,' she added, shyly,
'that I thought you did not care for me.'

'That was because I did love you. Will you take that
silence now, darling, as a proof of the love I cannot speak even
when I may? I thought it would only make you wretched then.
I knew so bitterly what a difference of faith means between those
who are very dear to each other.'

Gladys looked up at him, a beautiful light in her face. How
much he had thought of her! how true and unselfish his love
was! she could not help contrasting it with Stephen's blindly
selfish love and strangely different proposal.

'Directly you came into the school just now,' she said, 'I
thought how like you had grown to the picture of little Dot—
it is your eyes that have changed so. Oh, Donovan! how glad
she will be!'

He pressed her hand, but did not speak. They walked along
the shore in silence; presently reaching the little cottage where
the sick woman lived, Gladys went in, and Donovan waited for
her outside, not sorry for a minute's pause in which to realize his
happiness.

In a little while she joined him again, and for a minute they
stood still looking out seawards. A faint streak of yellow
lingered in the west, but above the stars were shining brightly,
while across the dark rolling sea there gleamed from the light-
house two long tracks of light athwart each other. The same
thought came to each of them, the sweet old saying—'Via crucis,

via lucis.' Neither of them spoke, but to each came the longing
that their love might always be that self-sacrificing love which
alone can lead into the light. It seemed to Gladys like a sort of
sacrament when Donovan stooped down and with a grave reverence pressed his lips to hers.

'You will teach me,' he said, after a time as they walked
along the beach.

She felt like a baby beside him as he spoke; in his humility,
in his grand self-denying nobleness, he seemed to tower above
her.

'Teach you!' she said, smiling. 'I should as soon think of
teaching papa! And yet papa always says the little ones _do_
teach him. Perhaps in that way, Donovan—can you be content
with that sort of child-wife who cannot understand half the
great things you think of?'

'My darling, how can you use such a word?' he exclaimed.
'Content! And have you not been teaching me all these years?
How little the world knows its true teachers! How little the
pure-hearted ones think of the lessons they teach!'

'We will learn together,' said Gladys, softly.

'There is one thing I should like to tell you now,' said Donovan. 'I had arranged, you know, to go out to the war, and I
find there is still a vacancy in one of the ambulances. You
will not mind my going out, darling? I feel in a measure bound
to go, and I should like, at any rate, a few months of good stiff
work. Some time must pass before the legal matters are settled
and the Manor really becomes my own, and I should like to be
doing something in the waiting-time. You will not mind my
going?'

Gladys did of course shrink from the thought, but she knew
that, in marrying such a man as Donovan, she must make up her
mind to much sacrifice. The delight of even now being able to
share his work helped to lessen the pain.

'I think,' she replied, 'you would not have been Donovan if
you had not wanted to go.'

'And then with you,' said Donovan, 'I shall be strong to
begin what I feel fearfully unequal to—the life as master of
Oakdene. There is plenty of work for us at Greyshot, and you
must help me to love the neighbours, who perhaps may not hate
me now so much as they did. I almost fancy even Mrs. Ward
may be civil now that I have found a woman brave enough to be
my wife! Are you ready, darling, to be the wife of a radical!—
to be looked down on perhaps as the wife of a sometime
atheist?'

'To be *your* wife,' said Gladys, gently.

They had made their way up the steep winding street and were in sight of Trenant, the dear old gabled house with its ivy-covered walls and welcoming lights.

'This is the place where I first saw you,' said Donovan, glancing in at the drawing-room window. On the very spot on which he now stood with Gladys, he had once stood lonely and despairing, watching with bitterness a glimpse of home life. Some thought of the infinite possibilities of the future, of the limited view of the present, came to him.

'How glorious life is!' he exclaimed. 'How different from what one used to think it! Oh, Gladys, if we can but do half we long to do! What a grand old working-place the world is!'

'You will be a grand worker,' thought Gladys, but she did not reply in direct words.

They had reached the porch, some one had heard their steps, and, as they drew near, the door was thrown open. Donovan saw in a blaze of friendly light a sweeter home drama than the one he remembered long ago. There they all were—a welcoming group. Nesta, Jackie, Dick just home from sea, the father with indescribable content written on his face, and before all the mother—the truest mother Donovan had ever known—her soft grey eyes shining into his with loving welcome and understanding.

'Home at last!' she said, smiling; and then, seeing all, she gave a mother's greeting to both 'children.'

THE END.

PRINTED BY BALLANTYNE, HANSON AND CO.
LONDON AND EDINBURGH